ANGELA

South of the Lights

Nowhere Girl

Wanting

Also by Angela Huth

FICTION

Virginia Fly is Drowning
Sun Child
Monday Lunch in Fairyland and other stories
Such Visitors and other stories
Invitation to the Married Life
Land Girls
Another Kind of Cinderella and other stories
Wives of the Fisherman
Easy Silence
Of Love and Slaughter
The Collected Stories of Angela Huth
Another Kind of Cinderella/Easy Silence Omnibus
Land Girls/Wives of the Fisherman Omnibus

NON-FICTION

The English Woman's Wardrobe

FOR CHILDREN

Eugenie in Cloud Cuckoo Land
Island of the Children (ed)
Casting a Spell (ed)

PLAYS

The Understanding
The Trouble with Old Lovers

ANGELA HUTH OMNIBUS

South of the Lights
Nowhere Girl
Wanting

ANGELA HUTH

An *Abacus* Book

This omnibus edition first published in Great Britain by
Abacus Books in 2003

Previously published separately:
South of the Lights first published in Great Britain in 1977 by Collins
Published by Abacus in 1994
Reprinted 1994, 1995, 1996, 1998, 1999

Nowhere Girl first published in Great Britain in 1970 by Collins
Published by Abacus in 1995
Reprinted 1995 (five times), 1999 (twice)

Wanting first published in Great Britain in 1994 by Harvill Press
Published by Abacus in 2000

A CIP catalogue record for this book is available from the British Library.

ISBN 0 349 11667 9

Printed and bound in Great Britain by
Clays Ltd, St Ives plc

Abacus
An imprint of
Time Warner Books UK
Brettenham House
Lancaster Place
London WC2E 7EN

www.TimeWarnerBooks.co.uk

South of the Lights

'I did not know
That heydays fade and go,
But deemed that what was would be always so.'

Thomas Hardy

PART I

Chickens, thought Evans. Bloody chickens. Their pernickety clucking had become a background to his life. Sometimes, good days, he could tolerate them. They reminded him of the years ahead, the house he and Brenda would have, the strip of garden at the back, the hen-house and run he would make for them. They would be free-range birds, of course, and lay brown eggs which Brenda would gather in a basket. Other times, in the dim smelly shed where he and Brenda seemed to spend so much of their time, he felt like putting a bomb to the place. He felt like blasting for ever their mouldy feathers and indignant red eyes and peevish chatter. Oh, he was sorry for them all right. But God, he hated them too. Today, he'd make sure to stay outside the shed. Today they'd get on his nerves.

Evans walked through the farmyard, May sun hot through his shirt. It hadn't rained for two weeks. His feet made small clouds of dust rise from the dry dirt track. He sniffed the rank smell of animals and manure. Brenda would like an hour off for lunch, he thought. Or perhaps she wouldn't. She was unpredictable like that. But just in case, he had bought two pork pies and cans of beer. It would be nice to sit in the field behind the sheds and eat in the sun. There, the farmyard smells were less strong.

He turned the corner. A hundred yards ahead stood the familiar hulk of tarred sheds where Wilberforce's chickens lived, laid and died. Brenda's territory. She leaned against the door, one knee bent, heel lodged behind it on some rough piece of wood. Her head was tilted towards the sun, eyes closed. A lighted cigarette drooped between her fingers. She raised her hand slowly to her mouth and inhaled, without opening her eyes.

Evans felt a swarm of love for her, giddying his head. He moved faster. She would not hear his step in the soft earth.

He would surprise her. She might be pleased. A few feet away from her he stopped to anticipate her pleasure, and to enjoy the sight of her before she became aware of his presence. She was wearing his favourite shirt: cream cotton covered with a pattern of chicks breaking out of their shells. Beneath the crowd of chicks her breasts rose and fell with her slow, even breathing. Last night they had overflowed from Evans's hands. She had shouted to him to be careful: the straw was scratching her something awful, she had said, and he had silenced her shouts with his mouth. Evans swallowed. No matter how good the night had been, he always felt uncertain how to approach her in the morning.

'Brenda,' he said.

She opened her eyes, turned her head slowly towards him, leaving it tipped towards the sun so that her chin was a defiant point.

'Oh, it's you.' No surprise in her voice. She puffed at her cigarette again. Evans allowed himself to be dazzled for a moment by the sparkling ring on her fourth finger, a small pink stone which, on less bright days, faded disappointingly.

'You smoking again,' he said. 'You'll cop it if Wilberforce catches you.'

'Wilberforce can't tell me what to do. I've got the sense to be careful, haven't I? Not likely I'm going to set his bloody ricks on fire.'

'But he said you'd get the push next time.'

'What would I care about that?'

'You'd miss the hens.'

Brenda flung her cigarette stub on to the ground. It landed beside Evans. He squashed it with his foot, buried it with the dusty earth.

'There are plenty of other hens.'

Evans felt an explosion of gunshot beneath his ribs. Its reverberations quickened the pace of his heart. He stepped towards her, roughly pulled down her chin between his thumb and finger, and kissed her.

'Don't be daft,' he said, the words smudged by her lips. She smelt of corn. Sometimes, evenings, when they went to the cinema, she would dab herself with lavender water or essence of bluebell, which her mother sent from Birmingham every Christmas. But the scent always wore off very quickly and gave way to the essential corn smell of her skin which, as Evans often said, made him feel drunker than a dozen double whiskies.

'Leave off,' said Brenda, pushing him away. 'It's too hot.'

'Just feel my heart.'

Brenda put her hand to his heart.

'You and your heart. You might as well give up if your heart didn't beat faster sometimes.'

Evans smiled, causing his drooping left eyelid to sag until it almost covered his eyeball. Moonlight nights in the barn, Brenda said it was his funny eye that made her feel sexy. In bright sun, he noticed, she often looked away from him, or concentrated on his mouth or other eye. So by day he had learnt to restrict his smiles.

'I brought us a bite to eat,' he said, flourishing the paper bag. 'I thought we might need it after . . .'

'After what?' Brenda was in a teasing mood.

'After all that. I'm shagged, myself.'

'Are you? I'm fine. Quite hungry.'

'We could go and sit in the field.'

'I like it just standing here.'

'We can't eat just standing here.'

'Don't see why not, pork pies.'

'How d'you know I've brought pork pies?'

'You always do, don't you?'

Evans's voice dropped.

'Sometimes I bring the steak and kidney, don't I? They were out of them today.' He handed her the bag. She took one of the pies. Its greasy pastry had a whitish sheen. They ate standing up.

'How's the post office, then?'

Every day, Evans dreaded the question. Manager of the

village's sub post office had not, in three years, turned out to be the job he had once expected. It was devoid of both interest and excitement. Promotion had not come his way and indeed, now Brenda was his life, in some ways he would not relish it: to be transferred to the local town would add to complications. Privately, Evans went so far as to pray for a hold-up. If such a thing took place he would act with commendable cool and bravery. He had rehearsed it many times in his mind, and he longed for it with a force that surprised him. For nothing less than a masked gunman would flame Brenda's interest in his job. Nothing less than near death would transform Evans into her hero.

'Quite a few parcels for the time of year.'

'Perhaps they're posting early for Christmas.' She said it in a lifeless tone. Only twelve hours ago, Evans found himself thinking, her voice had been husky, musical with desire. The remembrance brought a chill to his brow.

'Perhaps they are,' he said. 'But I wish there was more exciting news for you. I just seem to sit behind the grille, day after day, waiting for the next centenary stamp to brighten my life.'

Brenda shrugged, smiling. Sometimes, when he didn't try, the most unexpected things would make her smile.

'Elizabeth's not laying,' she said. 'Would you like to take a look at her? She looks right down.'

'No, I wouldn't, really. Not if you don't mind.'

'I told Wilberforce last week she was seedy, but he said don't be so stupid, he could tell a mile off when a bird was seedy. So now this afternoon I'll have to tell him she's not laying and he'll say: so what? The bird's not laying. Floribunda's going to be the next one. But I shan't say anything. He can find out for himself if he knows so much.'

'Wilberforce got a birthday coming up soon?'

'Not that I know of. Why?'

'Mrs Wilberforce was in this morning. Took twenty minutes choosing a card. Landed up with a picture of a bowl of hyacinths, a bit of real satin ribbon round the bowl and

Happy Birthday Dearest Love inside. Been in the place six months. Thought I'd never get rid of it.'

'Now that *is* news.' Brenda shifted her position. 'That wouldn't be for Wilberforce. That would be for the man she's seeing in Luton. Sees him every week, says she's visiting her cousin.'

'You know everything,' said Evans.

'I just hear without meaning to. Doesn't mean anything to me.' Brenda sighed, put her hands in the pockets of her jeans, stood with legs astride. Evans found the stance irresistibly provocative. He looked away.

'Come on,' Brenda sighed. 'Let's have the beer then I can get back to grading the eggs.' She had a curious way, on occasions, of sounding dismissive. Evans opened a can. The froth spurted out, spilling on to the ground, splattering the dark earth with deeper spots. He handed it to her, the liquid running over his wrists, his hand shaking.

'Wilberforce not bothering you any more, is he?'

'Wouldn't be worth his while, again, would it? I keep out of his way. He makes me sick.'

'I'd kill him if he laid a hand on you,' said Evans.

'No you wouldn't. You wouldn't kill a worm.'

'He's a bastard.'

'He's not worth bothering yourself about. He knows he doesn't stand a chance with me.'

'He better not try.'

'Oh, he *won't*, Evans. Do stop going on about Wilberforce.'

Evans watched the beer running down Brenda's chin. She had never learnt to drink properly from a can. He passed her his handkerchief.

'What would you like to do tonight?'

'Tonight?'

'You could come over to my place.'

'Not if it's your Dad's night in. I couldn't face your Dad, not tonight I couldn't. Besides, I want to wash my hair. Lark said she'd do it for me.' She put her hand behind her back and opened the door to the shed. At once the clatter of hens, which until now had been a subdued murmur, swelled to irritate Evans's ears.

'It's all very unsatisfactory,' he said, 'this not having anywhere to go.'

'Well, we're saving, aren't we?'

'We've been saving two bloody years, and we don't seem much nearer. If we had somewhere of our own, it'd be easier.'

'I'm not complaining.'

'Sometimes you sound as if you don't care.'

'No point in being impatient, is there?'

She pushed the shed door further open. Through the mottled light inside Evans could just discern the stacked coops, the pathetic heads and claw-like beaks that jerked from each one of them. If he stayed one moment longer Brenda would persuade him in to see Elizabeth.

'I'll pick you up this evening, then,' he said.

'I told you I was washing my hair, didn't I?'

'I'll pick you up and run you home in the car.'

Brenda took a packet of Woodbines from the pocket of her jeans. 'And shut up your nagging, Evans, will you?'

'I didn't say a thing.' His hands tightly clenched, one on each empty beer can.

'You get at me with your looks as bad as words. You'd better get back to sorting your parcels.' She turned and went into the shed. Her body at once shed its skin of light, became submerged in shadow, speckled and untenable as a trout under water. Evans walked back up the dirt track, uneasy in the heat. Three and a half stifling hours behind the post office grille before he could return to her, and, in the brief drive to her flat, try to find out what he had done wrong.

Rosie Evans pushed her wheel basket of groceries up the mild hill to the cottage in which she and Henry had lived all their married life, thirty-eight years. It was one of a row of thatched and beamed cottages adjacent to the church, the last remaining part of the original village. Since Rosie's childhood some fifty similar dwellings had fallen into a state of irreparable decay and been pulled down. They were replaced by a growth of ill-conceived contemporary houses which architects wrongly imagine are desirable: sour red brick, identical bubble-glass front doors and cement front paths. The kind of houses Rosie supposed might be all very well in a New Town, but were quite out of place in what once had been a small and pretty village. Even the old vicarage had been demolished. (No one could claim it was the best of Victorian architecture, but it had had thick Virginia creeper, and a lovely front porch, as Rosie and Henry knew from experience, for courting.) It had been replaced by a flat-roofed brick box, whose windows, which flowed from roof to ground, seemed to have been designed to expose the vicar's entire private life. His wife, although supporting her husband in the theory that a shepherd should always be available to his sheep, felt that this kind of availability was going too far. Her first week at the new vicarage was spent sewing old surplices together to form some measure of protection. These, she explained, would be no ordinary curtains: more, a kind of religious mist clinging permanently to the windows. The vicar saw light. They would add a mystical air to his movements, he thought, and he was able to rejoice.

Rosie, whose eyes could never be intent upon so ugly a building as the vicarage, glanced instead up at the three tall elms which grew in a triangle where the lane to the church and cottages petered out. They were still healthy. One day, no doubt, they would be stricken by the fatal disease, and have to be pulled down. Rosie hoped they would last her lifetime. She knew them well, in all seasons, and loved them. Every new demolition in the village had saddened her. Had it been ruined twenty years ago, she and Henry might have considered moving away. But its final devastation had only taken place within the last few years, and now they were too old to move. Besides, from the rooms of the cottage their small views had not changed: at the back, the graveyard, at the front the elms and the mossy green fence that surrounded the grounds of Wroughton House. So they were lucky, really. Lucky compared with Evans and Brenda, who would be forced to the wicked expense of buying a new place. Still, according to Brenda – and Rosie could understand – young people preferred bland walls with no beams, and all the conveniences of a modern building. She and Henry would leave the cottage to Evans, of course, but he wouldn't want it. He would sell it and spend the money improving his own house – if by then he had managed to buy one. She hoped he would be happy.

Rosie, whose sympathies were universally available, spent a considerable part of her life wishing for other people's happiness. She herself was embalmed in a contentment she had woven for herself, and made inextricable. Her own pleasures were simple, added to almost daily, while the pleasures of people around her, and people on television, added to the web of satisfaction. But she was not complacent. Aware that happiness is inevitably a precipice at the edge of an abyss, she regarded the good fortune of her life as something to be banked, and called upon to fortify if and when the fall came. She had a recurring nightmare that Henry, whose only skittishness became apparent in his fourteen-year-old Morris Minor, would one day be mangled in a car crash. She had been prepared for the tragedy for years. When it came she would be able to cope. She would recall that she had had thirty-eight loving years with Henry, more than the fair share of most human beings, and surely the grateful knowledge of that would help ameliorate the loss.

Meantime, the act of loving her husband had its positive rewards, even if they were not always in abundance. He had never been the easiest of men, but in him Rosie recognized a challenge to which she rose with most persistent enjoyment. She had learnt two very good tips from her own mother on how to provide a husband's pleasure: always have something warm in the oven, and never cease to welcome him. Lately, since the stability of Henry's teeth had been causing some concern, his unexpected appetites for a hot pie at odd times of the day had declined. Now, he was happier to suck gently at a ginger biscuit and, accordingly, Rosie had cut down on her baking. But in relinquishing one of her stable methods of assuring love, Rosie found herself doubling her efforts when it came to the other. In this, their peaceful retirement, her welcomes to Henry flourished. Even now, as she paused to enjoy the great yellow-green spread of the elms' branches, Rosie chided herself. She had been dawdling. Henry, sitting by the small coal fire, would have finished the *Daily Mirror*. He would be wondering where she was, missing her. She pushed at the handle of her wicker basket, impatient with herself. In the few yards left to the front door she pondered upon today's greeting, a fresh way to assure Henry that all was well, that here she was, back again.

Henry Evans was exhausted by his wife's welcomes. He sat in his armchair by the fire bracing himself for Rosie's return, relishing the last few moments of peace. Any moment these would be shattered by her kind smiles and eager questions and hopes for his well-being. Over the years he had learnt that to respond to her benevolence merely led to further, wearying counter-response. In self-defence he had become a taciturn man, only speaking if it became necessary to further the plot of his life. Which was not, as he had been reflecting this afternoon behind the *Daily Mirror*, a very exciting life. Nor had it ever been. In sixty-five years nothing surprising had happened: except for one wild storm in the Bay of Biscay, in his Navy days, he had known neither drama nor fear. He could have done with a few more storms. The murderous waves had raced his blood, somehow, giving him energy and adrenalin which had lasted for a year or so, then faded, leaving him dull to himself again. It was in his year of exuberance that he had married Rosie, a pretty young thing then, in spite of her hands. In those days he had been equal to her energy. But as the benefits of the storm receded, he found himself no match for her. She had been a tiringly good wife for thirty-eight years, and wasn't likely to change her loving ways now. In retirement, her cocoon of benevolence was particularly claustrophobic. There were so few chances, or reasons, to get out. Saturdays and Tuesdays he went to the pub, alone, because Rosie was of the opinion beer and darts were men's things, and she'd want no one to accuse her of pushing herself into a man's world, making a nuisance of herself where she might not be wanted. Mondays and Fridays he went to the local ironmonger for a couple of hours to look through the books. He'd always been good with figures, and he liked the small, stuffy back office where he was put to work with a mug of strong tea. He liked the smell of nails and potash and rubber plugs, and the half-dozen inevitable interruptions from Mr Daly, his boss, who had a lively line in complaints about what the Government was doing to his shop. In spring, Henry would sometimes try to escape for a walk in the bluebell woods, up on the hill, where he would listen to the thrushes and smoke his pipe. But however unadventurous he tried to make his proposed walk sound, Rosie would not be taken in. Undaunted by his warnings of wasps, stinging nettles and all manner of unexpected hazards, she would often insist on coming too. She would enjoy the walk with an energy that made Henry's heart retract into an impenetrable shell, and he would make no word of response to her reminiscences of times past when in their youth they had picnicked – and more – beneath these very trees.

'Do you remember, Henry, love? You in your uniform and I said take off your cap before you do anything like that to me.'

Her incessant jabbering drowned the birdsong – she drained the woods of all their peace. Lately, Henry had given up. He went for no more walks. He had grown fatter, slower, with resignation. He anticipated no excitements or changes before his death, and accepted the realisation as quite bearable. It was therefore with some surprise that he had found himself enjoying this afternoon more than he had enjoyed an afternoon for many a year. It was with even more surprise that he had discovered precisely what had caused the pleasure.

As it was a Tuesday he had gone to the Star for his usual pint at lunchtime. He had taken his drink to his accustomed table and was looking about him, in his quiet way, thinking they'd have to invest in a new carpet soon, judging by the fraying at his feet, when a woman came into the pub. This was not an unusual event: women in the pub caused no comment in spite of Rosie's beliefs – but this was a strange woman, one Henry had not seen before. She was not an old woman, nor a young one, and yet the term middle-aged, with all its implications, seemed most unsuited to her. She wore a fur coat, extravagantly dotted with leopard spots, and gripped round her small waist by a broad leather belt. Her short hair was blonde and curly and she had a freshness about her, a confident gaiety that caught the attention of everyone in the room. At her entrance the clink of glasses, the small sounds of low talk and shifting feet, seemed to diminish. Everyone could hear her order. A double Dubonnet with a twist of lemon, please, she said. Bill, the landlord, apologised, but he had run out of lemons. In response she turned away from him. Her eye fell upon Henry and she smiled an uncontainable smile, as if something within her could be withheld no longer.

'No lemon? How about that?' she said.

Henry, feeling her direct address to him must have been a mistake, hurriedly covered his face with his beer mug and drank too fast, making himself hiccough loudly. The woman turned back to the bar, drank her lemon-less Dubonnet, and paid for it all in a moment. Then she left in a hurry, smiling round the room as she went. Henry, his confusion still upon him, glanced at his fellow drinkers. He perceived that each one of them, behind his gesture of apparent indifference, was likewise a little shaken. Although an intangible thing, impossible to discuss, the strange lady's brief visitation seemed in some way to have ungrounded the secure, unexciting structure of an ordinary Tuesday. Henry could tell by the flush on the landlord's cheeks, and the way that old Jo let his moustache become confused with the froth of his beer – a thing that would never normally happen. For his own part, Henry felt unusual weakness in his knees. He walked home carefully, wondering. He tried to place the feeling: something long past, almost forgotten. Then, at the elm trees, very bright in the sun, it came to him. The storm. All those years ago, landing in Spain when the waves had subsided, realising he was both alive and safe, the combined sensations of exhilaration and weakness had struck him: and here they were again. Henry paused, letting his eyes wander up through the great blur of leaves, and he sighed with great contentment. Incredulous, he felt. Almost forty unfluttering years, and here was some new irrational flame, some pretty hope. He might never re-encounter the nymph in the leopard coat who had caused it, but that was no matter. He would feed upon what she had left behind for his own private pleasure: he would eke out the goodness, and when the bloom wilted at the end of some season, he would remember with gladness.

'Henry! You're back early. That's lovely. I'll be dishing up in just a moment!' Rosie was calling to him from the front door. Rosie was always bloody calling to him in her cheerful voice, but he was doubly protected from her beneficence now.

On his own, in the afternoon, Henry put aside his *Daily Mirror* as soon as his wife had gone. Legs stretched out before him, the warmth of the fire gentle upon his shins, he let the smile of the strange lady return to him. It was very bright in his mind. In fact, he could almost imagine her sitting there opposite him, smiling away, the afternoon light through the small window making her hair greenish, like a plant. Of course, in real life she'd be most uncomfortable, in her smart coat, on the old leather chair. Her polished shoes would skitter about on the tiled floor, and perhaps she would smoke, and need an ashtray, and there were no ashtrays in the room. On the other hand, she might just be the sort to curl up, knees under her, and listen.

If she would care to listen then Henry would like to tell her things, he thought. He would like to tell her how cumbersome he found his retirement, and with what nostalgia he looked back upon his working days. He had been a loader at the brick fields. In thirty years some hundreds of thousands – perhaps even millions – of bricks had passed through his hands. He knew the feel of them as well as he knew the feel of any part of his own body: the weight, the texture, the even dip of their spines, their raw reddish colour that looked quite sore on bright days, but mellowed under cloud. Henry could load up a lorry of bricks quicker than anyone: over the years he became known for his agility, his precision in stacking, his strength and tirelessness. What he never displayed was the pleasure a well-loaded lorry gave him. The satisfaction of the neatly piled structure – to last merely for the journey, then to be demolished by less loving hands – never decreased. He was offered many other jobs in the works, and he tried some of them, but always returned to loading. Indeed, as an unsurpassable loader he became something of a legend. (For all his modesty he was prepared to admit this.) The day of his retirement he had a friendly talk with Mr Dingley, the young manager, in the small office awash with all the paperwork of the business. Mr Dingley said Henry was the kind of man England needed to get industry back on its feet, and he would be sorry to see him go. Then he gave him an inscribed watch. Rosie had said it would be a gold, after thirty years. In fact it was silver, with a soft stretchy strap that felt comfortable on Henry's wrist. His mates had bought him more beers than he could drink that night, and slapped him on the back and said they hoped he'd come back to see them often – make sure they were doing things right. Henry said of course he would. But he never returned: he meant to, one day, but so far he had not been able to bring himself to do so. Besides the watch, he also took home a single brick. (He did not ask Mr Dingley's permission but felt that, in the circumstances, it would not be considered stealing.) The brick sat on the window sill in the kitchen. Gathering dust, Rosie said. But Henry refused to move it. Sometimes, alone, he would hold it in his hands, feeling its familiar weight, reminding himself.

If the lady with the gay smile was here now and asked him about the brick, and she cared to listen, he would tell her the truth. He would tell her that most people in these parts resented the brick fields, scooped as they were out of the countryside, ugly, clustered with rail-tracks for the trucks, and the humped buildings where the bricks were baked. But Henry liked them. He liked the vast chimneys that speared the sky like masts, the sour sulphury smell their smoke sent into the murky clouds. Henry supposed he must have known hundreds of sunny times at the brickworks, but in retrospect the days he pictured were the ones he liked best: yellowish skies dappled with cloud. It may have been his imagination, but small clouds often seemed to gather round the chimneys in a busy, protective way. Sometimes there was a whole cluster of them over the brick fields, while not far away the sky was quite clear.

Winter was the time Henry liked best of all. Fraw, sullen, the bricks themselves the only bright things, gusts of warmth from the baking ovens as you walked past, the sulphur smell very keen on a frosty morning, stirred by an east wind. One year Henry had volunteered to guard the works on Christmas Day. He told Rosie and the Boy it was his turn: they had believed him, and sympathised. He arrived at the watchman's small office at five in the morning to relieve the man on night-duty. He stoked up the fire, boiled the black kettle and made himself a cup of tea. He walked round the works once or twice, checking all was well; but most of the day he sat in that small office drinking tea, listening to music on the radio, studying the picture of the Queen on the wall calendar, very demure in all her jewels. And when he listened to her speech in the afternoon he felt it as if it was to him alone she spoke, from the dingy wall. Impressed, he stood up and saluted her. Then he ate his cold mince pies, looked out at the high chimneys and their everlasting puffs of dun smoke, and felt glad not to be round the Christmas tree with Rosie's relations. It grew cold in spite of the fire, and was quite dark at four. He left much later, bicycling slowly through the night frost, past lighted trees in small windows, and was happy to be outside it all. At home, Rosie welcomed him with hot cherry brandy and much sympathy and concern. But he had needed no one's sympathy: it had been the best Christmas Day he could remember, though he could not tell them that. Pity: because he would have liked to have explained about it to just one person before he died, and the lady with the curly hair, he had a strange feeling, might have been a little interested. Something in the lively way she had said, 'A double Dubonnet with a twist of *lemon*, please.' Silly of Bill to have run out of lemon.

'Henry? Here I am back again. Sorry to have been so long.' The clatter of Rosie coming through the front door. 'Hope you haven't been missing me, love . . . Now, what can I get you for your tea?'

She might have learnt by now Henry never answered such questions. Tea, more than ever this afternoon, held no interest for him. He gathered up his paper.

Brenda sat on an upturned box in the chicken house smoking the last of her Woodbines. She had fed the hens and there was nothing further for her to do. It was the time of day she liked best: evening sun coming quite sharply through the high cobwebby skylights – which it never managed to do earlier in the day – the smell of chickens, sweet and fusty. When she came in at eight-thirty in the morning, after a night of messing, the smell was more pungent, almost stifling. By midday she had grown accustomed to it and by evening, as now, it filled all her senses with well-being.

Brenda was worried about Elizabeth. Elizabeth's eyes had settled into an unbroken stare during the afternoon and the lashless yellow lids, shaped like small petals but rough with pimples, drooped almost to closing. Elizabeth was queen of the shed – Brenda had made her so – and she was going to die. This time tomorrow she might well be dead. Brenda wondered who should succeed her: Clarissa, by rights. Clarissa was an old bird who laid more and bigger eggs than any of the others. She emitted terrible squawks of triumph each time she did so and the other birds, judging by their clucking protests, resented her boastfulness. Besides, she was not glamorous. Roberta had pecked great lumps out of the left-hand side of her neck, and no new feathers seemed likely to sprout over the patch of raw pink skin. She was a bird of strength, but no dignity, not ideally suited to be queen. Marilyn (after Monroe) would perhaps be better. Marilyn, had fate made her a free-range bird, would have been sex-mad, taxing the most virile cock with her demands. As it was, from the confines of her cooped-up life, she brooded with particular frustration. Brenda could tell from the sad, coquettish way she bent her head against the bars, murmuring to herself in a husky voice. Perhaps, though, she was more of a sex queen than a real queen and Daisy, a duller, more upright bird, would be a better leader. Daisy's comb was certainly the brightest in the shed: upstanding, a fiery red, a real crown. Daisy it would have to be, though the appointment would cause terrible jealousy in Floribunda's heart. But Floribunda, for all her fine show of feathers, was ailing. One of her legs seemed to be paralysed. She would probably die soon, too, and Brenda wished to be practical. No point in changing queens every few weeks.

Her cigarette finished, Brenda began to fold and unfold the piece of foil paper from out of the carton. She dreaded Elizabeth's death. Well, she wouldn't be there. Wilberforce could deal with the whole thing. She'd go out. Where? Anywhere. Walk about, walk about fast in the fields trying not to think of Wilberforce's hands round Elizabeth's neck. She knew what a man's hands looked like on a chicken's neck, twisting. That time Uncle Jim had killed Hen – she would never forget that. She wasn't supposed to be around, but she had peeped out of her bedroom window and seen the whole thing. It was the afternoon she had bought her new green shoes, the ones with high heels and bows on the front. Uncle Sam had given her the money for them on condition she promised not to mention to Uncle Jim he'd been visiting her mother. Of course she wouldn't have mentioned any of the uncles to any of the other uncles. For a start there were so many of them she got them confused. Uncle Sam must have been daft to think she'd tell on him. She took the money gladly. She didn't care what any of them did so long as they didn't bother her. The only one who bothered her up till now was Uncle Ernest, whose whisky breath smelt right down the street. He beat up her Mum once so she had a black eye for weeks. And then Mum got the sack from the café as the stinking old manager said he couldn't have a waitress looking as if she'd been through a mangle, it was bad for business. She and Mum had eaten bread and cheese and tinned soup for a week. She didn't mind for herself: food didn't matter to her. But Mum got a thin greenish look around her mouth, and her headaches came on so bad she hadn't got the energy to go and look for another job. It was then that Uncle Jim, who had been around for a few weeks, suggested he kill Hen, and make her into a nice chicken casserole. Brenda had cried: broken down right there, banging her head against the kitchen table, till her own sobs and screams became a cloudy dome about her head from which she could see no escape. Then she heard Mum shouting to her to stop making such a bloody racket. She stopped at once, a sudden silence: and in the quiet she saw Mum's own eyes were skinned with tears.

'No use being sentimental,' Uncle Jim had said, cramming sliced cheese into his mouth. He was always eating sliced cheese, letting tongues of it hang out of his mouth, waiting for the inner bits to melt before sucking up the rest. At least he bought his own, but it was one of his habits that Mum said drove her mad. She said she doubted she could live with a man who had such a thing about sliced cheese, although Uncle Jim seemed pretty well installed already.

'It's no use being sentimental,' said Uncle Jim again, who believed repetition made for greater truth, 'the fucking bird hasn't laid for a year, and she doesn't have much of a fucking life in the backyard, does she?'

Brenda didn't answer. It was true, Hen hadn't laid for a year and some of her old vitality – her very thorough pecking for scraps in the concrete strip of backyard – seemed to have dwindled. But Uncle Jim hadn't seen her as a chick mewling in a cardboard box in the kitchen. Uncle Jim hadn't eaten dozens of her speckled eggs and been lulled by the sound of her clucking, lonely evenings, while Brenda sat in the kitchen waiting for her mother to come home.

'Uncle Jim's right, of course,' Mum said, who was afraid of the man. Brenda saw a look pass between them and she knew the hours were closing in on Hen.

'I hate you, that's all,' she said quietly to Uncle Jim, and ran out of the house. It was down the road she met Uncle Sam who had given her the money for her shoes, and tweaked the skin of her arm under the elbow. She ran straight on down to the shop, not caring about the mess she looked, dried tears blotching her face, and bought the shoes right away. They had been in the window for weeks. They fitted perfectly. She looked in the mirror a long time, incredulous. They were hers. Her first pair of grown-up shoes. The bows made her ankles look skinnier than ever, but they were so pretty. Her friend Lindy Badger, who had tons of money for shoes, would be right jealous. She ran home wearing them, ran straight up to her room to have another look in her own mirror. Then she heard the squawking, the bird screams of fear. She rushed to the window. Uncle Jim's hands were round Hen's neck. They gave a small sharp twist. Hen's head flopped over his wrist, beak opened mid-cry. He turned to the kitchen, walked towards it, swinging her limp body.

'That's finished the fucker,' Brenda heard him shout to Mum. Brenda expected to cry again, but she felt no tears. She sat down, took off the green shoes, put them in their box and shoved it under the bed. She would never wear them, now.

Brenda did not discover whether or not Mum made a casserole of Hen. If she did, then she and Uncle Jim must have eaten it at dinner-time, while she was still at school, and hidden the bones. A few days later Mum got a job cleaning up at the local cinema, and they ate better again, though every time there was frozen chicken Brenda refused it. She thought she could probably never eat chicken again.

A year later Uncle Jim was still living with them, though sometimes, when he was on night shift, other Uncles would come round for a while, and without being asked Brenda would go up to her room. On those occasions Mum would dab behind her ears with a bit of Essence of Gardenia (which Uncle Fred brought from Manchester) that she kept hidden behind the tinned food in the kitchen cupboard. She would brush her hair and take off her apron and undo two buttons of her dress, and look quite pretty, for all the mottled tiredness of her face. On those occasions Brenda would think that if only Mum had had the chance she could have made something of her life, and they could have had a nice house in the country, perhaps, instead of years in bloody Birmingham. But Mum hadn't had the chance, and she hadn't the strength to make one. Everything had gone against her, in spite of her generosity. Men, she said, were all shits with magic wands, and once they'd shoved their wands up you all the magic went, and off they'd go to try their tricks elsewhere. She said this quite often; she'd been saying it for as long as Brenda could remember – long before she knew what it meant, and she could see that Mum believed it. But one day, Mum said, you might find a man who wanted to keep all his magic for you, if you were lucky. But that was a chance in a million and meantime, well, you had to keep believing, trying out new magic, just in case. When Mum said things like that she looked so sad Brenda felt an ache go all through her own body, and she didn't know what to do or say. But Mum was very brave: that was the wonderful thing about her. The next moment she'd be laughing – some silly thing she'd seen on one of the films up at the cinema – and telling Brenda to snap out of it and get on with her homework.

One day Mum was promoted to part-time usherette. She was very pleased about this, although it meant working late hours, leaving Brenda at home by herself a good part of the evening. Brenda did not mind. She was just sixteen and, on evenings she didn't go out with friends, unafraid of being alone. She'd sit looking at telly all evening, or read a magazine and smoke her Woodbines, quite happy. Sometimes she'd even try her hand at making something for Mum to eat when she came home, warming up a pie and boiling frozen vegetables. But usually she forgot and simply made herself cups of Nescafé into which she poured an extravagant amount of condensed milk.

One evening she was curled up on the sofa, watching a thriller on television, when Uncle Jim came in. His night shift had been changed, he said, and he hadn't gone down for a drink as he wanted to watch the football. Without asking Brenda's permission, he switched channels to the game, and flopped down on to the sofa beside her. He smelt of cheese and tobacco and sweat. He rarely washed. Brenda wrinkled her nose and watched the game. After a while she said:

'I was enjoying that thriller.'

'Poor little Brenda. Uncle Jim goes and spoils it all for her, doesn't he?' He put his hand on her knee. Brenda looked from the television screen to his hand. It was large and calloused, the nails black arcs, the knuckles chipped like dry wood. Heavy. She watched it slide up her thigh, over the flat plain of her stomach, and come to rest again on her breast.

'One day our little Brenda's going to have the prettiest boobs in Birmingham,' he said. 'Give them a year and they'll be hanging out.'

'Leave off,' said Brenda. The hand was a comfortable cage round her breast, but it made her angry.

'Just a feel. A feel doesn't do nobody any harm, does it?' He squeezed her.

'I said take your filthy hands off me, Jim Roach.'

'They're bigger than your mother's already.'

Brenda slapped his face. He drew back, surprised.

'No need to get nasty, now, is there? Just a cuddle. Your age, I'd been screwing all over the city. They called me Jim the –'

'– I don't care what they called you! You lay a finger on me ever again and I'll tell Mum and you'll be out.'

'They knew they'd get it big and good,' he sneered.

'Mum'll put you straight out on the street.' Brenda stood up, shaking.

'She wouldn't dare. I give it to her too good.'

'Shut up! You pig!' Brenda turned to the door. At that moment her mother came in, scarf over her head, face shining with rain.

'What's all the shouting?' she asked.

'We was just having a little ding-dong.' Jim stood with his hands on his hips, thick legs apart, flushed. 'Brenda's getting temperamental now she's getting a big girl.'

Brenda ran from the room, not wanting Mum to see her distress.

The incident seemed to have spurred some kind of desire in Uncle Jim: Brenda grew to dread being in the house alone with him. He said he wasn't going to do night shifts any more, and came back to the house early most evenings. He did not try to touch her again, but lay slumped back in a chair, one hand rubbing his pelvis, the other stuffing his mouth with sliced cheese. His eyes crawled over Brenda, his cheeks a solid crimson. He said just to watch her made him feel good. He said if only she wasn't her Mum's daughter he knew what he'd like to do to her. He'd pinch her tits, all nice, so's she'd cry to him not to stop. Brenda, hot, weak and frightened, would go to her room and lock the door. Sometimes she would cry. She couldn't tell Mum, because Mum would be wild and want Jim to go: though in her heart she would want

Jim to stay. In a way he was good to her: gave her several pounds a week and took her out for a drink Saturdays. No: it would be unfair to Mum to say anything. Brenda kept silence for several weeks.

Then one Sunday morning she was drying her hair in the kitchen. As it straggled wetly over her back she had pulled down the neck of her tee-shirt, and undone several buttons. She sat in a shaft of sun rubbing at her head with a towel, thinking of the afternoon she was going to spend with Robert, with the beautiful face, who seemed to be her boyfriend now. All the girls wanted Robert and she'd been out with him three times. Last time he'd kissed her. He'd kiss her again this afternoon, for sure. At the thought Brenda rubbed her hair harder, full of energy and excitement.

Uncle Jim came in. He'd been down to the pub for an early beer. There was white foam at the corners of his mouth. He was full of menace, sweaty. Brenda looked up from her towel, afraid. Instinctively she did up the buttons of her shirt. Uncle Jim laughed, and tugged at the belt of his trousers, began to unbutton his flies. Then he started saying filthy things, very fast, the words stumbling over one another. Brenda flung her towel at him with a scream, got up and ran. She ran to her friend Lindy's house and told her all about it. Lindy was barely sympathetic. So what? she said. At least it was Brenda's *uncle*. In her house it was their Dad who was always begging them to have a look every time their Mum's back was turned. For some reason this made Brenda laugh. It gave her strength, to think she wasn't the only one being pursued by filthy middle-aged men. It also gave her resolve. She dried her hair and went to the cinema with Robert. He kissed her again, very gently, and she felt a wild elation that was quite new to her. She told Robert she was going to run away. He said that was a good idea, and if she sent him her address he'd come and visit her.

That evening Brenda told her mother she was leaving. She wanted to see the world, she said. She'd be all right, easy enough to get a job somewhere. Perhaps in the country, she was sick of cities. Her mother gave her a funny look, didn't ask any questions. Instead she went to her savings – a tin of canned peaches which didn't look as if it had been opened – and took out all the money: £20.

'I been saving it for emergencies,' she said. 'Here, you take it. It's probably time you left home. But let me know you're all right, and come back sometimes.'

Brenda took the money and briefly touched her mother's scratchy hair, not quite knowing what sort of gesture she should make in the circumstances. Uncle Jim didn't come home that night. She and Mum opened a tin of rock salmon which they spread thickly with salad dressing and made it into great oozy sandwiches. They drank whisky from the small bottle that was kept for other kind of emergencies and, in front of the small fire, both admitted to feeling a bit spinny. Brenda promised she'd keep in touch, and Mum said don't get pregnant if you can help it.

Brenda left Birmingham next day. She travelled south of the lights in a meat lorry which she hitched in the suburbs. The driver told her he was going to London. Brenda thought she might as well go too, unless she saw somewhere that caught her fancy on the way. Two hours down the motorway she saw the chimneys of the brick works looming in the sky. It was still early morning. Brenda liked the way they made a tall, precise pattern against the saffron clouds. They seemed to be protecting the country behind them.

'I fancy it here rather than going to London,' she said. The driver obligingly pulled up on to the hard shoulder. He said the local town wasn't much, full of Italians, but there was a nice bit of country roundabout.

Brenda thanked him and jumped down from the high seat. From then on, as she wrote and told Mum, she fell on her feet in the funniest way. She hitched another lift to the local town and, hungry, went straight to a coffee shop. She hadn't been there five minutes when a thin, sad-looking girl sat down opposite her, and asked if she knew anyone who'd like to share a flat. Brenda said yes straight away. The girl was called Lark, a typist for a firm of engineers. She said there was plenty of work in the town, especially in shops. Brenda shouldn't worry. Brenda didn't worry. She was so excited by her good fortune her breath came in uneven gusts. She and Lark went directly to the flat: two small rooms, a stove in a cupboard, and a bathroom on a landing upstairs. It overlooked a jumble of dark buildings, beyond which rose the high walls of the prison. Brenda cried out with delight. The peeling wallpaper and gloomy paint meant nothing to her. It was her own flat – well, hers and Lark's. She was to sleep in the living-room: by day the bed was covered with an Indian cotton cover, excitingly patterned. Lark had made everything very clean and neat. A smell of polish came from somewhere, though Brenda could see nothing that was actually in need of polish.

'It's *lovely*,' said Brenda. 'Are you sure I can come?'

'I've been looking for the right person for two weeks,' said Lark. 'I'm sure you're her.'

'What makes you sure?'

'I'm just sure. And don't worry about the money for a week or two till you get a job. I can tide us over easily and you can pay me back. I've nothing but rent to spend my money on.'

'I got plenty, all me Mum's savings.' Brenda tapped her bag.

'You get settled in, then, and I'll be back this evening. There's plenty to eat, nothing to worry about.' Lark wore a grey jersey stretched down over her flat chest. She had yellow-green eyes, cat-shaped, the saddest Brenda had ever seen.

Alone, Brenda unpacked her small case. On the shelf above the gas fire she propped up an old Polyfoto of Mum, and an even more faded print of the man Mum had always claimed was her Dad. He was a Polish sailor with a long blond beard and wonderful eyes: even through the dimness of the photograph you could tell they must have shone more brightly than other men's. He had come into the café where Mum was working in the war in Solihull, and they had taken an immediate fancy to each other. He had taken her out dancing when the café closed – there had been no time for Mum to change, she had gone in her working clothes. Zeus, as he was called, said he didn't care. He gave her two pairs of nylon stockings, a great luxury in those days, and spent the night with her. Then he had to be on his way, but said he would come back. Mum, pregnant, waited. Although she hardly knew him, she felt he would have been pleased about the baby – she was positive it was his. He'd had the deepest kindest voice she'd ever heard. Yes, he'd be pleased all right and give her more stockings, perhaps. But the months passed and he never came. The night Brenda was born Mum prayed especially hard, through all the pains, that Zeus would come: all she had of him was the one photograph (the stockings were long since worn out). He had taken it from his wallet and told her to keep it till he returned: he had said it as if he meant it. Brenda knew the story off by heart. Every time Mum told it, even now, her voice went all low and a small pulse in her neck began to tick, and she'd be forced to sip at the emergency whisky. Brenda liked the idea of having a Dad called Zeus who was a brave Polish sailor. (She had no doubts as to his bravery.) She supposed he was probably an admiral by now, clanking with gold on his uniform and very important. She took particular interest in pictures in the newspapers that were anything to do with the Navy. One day she might spot him. She was proud of her unknown father.

When Lark came back she took great interest in the photographs, and asked many questions. Brenda told her a lot about Mum, and gave the merest hints about her father. Within an hour she liked Lark more than she had ever liked Lindy or Sybil or any of her Birmingham friends. Lark was marvellous, all drawn into herself, somehow, and yet seemingly full of interest in outside things. They ate egg and chips, then took a bus to the local village. Lark said there was a nice pub there called the Star, and on the way they'd see a bit of the countryside. They saw fields of kale. Brenda said they were a lovely green, and Lark said what got her was the red of geraniums.

They met a friend of Lark's in the bar, a fat man who bred pigs. He was talking to a tall young man with a droopy eyelid, introduced as plain Evans. Lark started talking most earnestly to her friend about pigs: Brenda was left to Evans. He didn't seem to have much to say. She asked him about jobs, and at once he perked up. When he was able to be helpful, she discovered later, he became his most vivacious. Yes, he knew of a job, if it was the sort of thing she might consider. Wilberforce, the poultry farmer, needed someone to look after his chickens. Not bad wages, though of course Brenda would have to come out on the bus every day if she was living in the town. Brenda was warm from the two whiskies Evans had bought her. She thought back, first time for two years, to Hen. Silly tears came to her eyes. Evans said he'd arrange an interview with Wilberforce.

He drove Lark and Brenda back to their flat in his white Mini with the posh red seats, and promised to be in touch next day. By now Brenda was tired, but too excited to sleep. When Lark had gone to her room, she sat at the small table and wrote a letter to Mum. Then, taking more time, she wrote to Robert. He could come at once, she said. Everything had happened smashing. There was plenty of room for him, Lark wouldn't mind. She must leave off now but she loved him, she really loved him, and she hoped he loved her. In the weeks to come she wrote again and again to Robert, but no reply. Now, she could scarcely remember the colour of his hair.

Now, three years later, people said Brenda had changed out of all recognition. She was both buxom and lithe, long legs topped with a high small bottom, luminous skin, shining hair the colour of conkers. She was quite aware of the fact that men fancied her no end. They made all sorts of suggestions and sometimes she was tempted to let them try out their skills, without going too far. For basically she felt quite an affection for Evans, and trying to remain faithful to him was something of a masochistic pleasure. He was no Gary Cooper, as her Mum had said on their first visit to Birmingham: but he was a good man, kind and loyal, solid, and willing to please. Brenda appreciated these things; for the time being they were good substitutes to the unreliable excitements that Robert had wrought in her. She could rely on Evans. If she wanted, she could have him just where she wanted for the rest of her life. The very realisation of this filled her with guilty unease. For the most part she put such thoughts from her mind.

Brenda rubbed her pink ring on the knee of her jeans. She reflected that it seemed to grow smaller every day, but it was pretty in the sunlight. People remarked upon it – at least they used to. In two years the wonder of it had somewhat decreased. In two years the excitement of the whole engagement had dimmed alarmingly: not even on the day Evans had given her the ring, here in this very shed with all the birds looking on, had Brenda felt the kind of ecstasy she had assumed might grip her. No wonder, really. It was with reluctance she had agreed to the arrangement at all. Engagement didn't mean much to her: both Lindy and Sybil had written from Birmingham to say they were having babies and might get married later. They had no rings, but they lived with their boyfriends. Here, Mr and Mrs Evans and, surprisingly, even Lark, would have been upset by that sort of thing. So after Brenda had been going out with Evans for a year – yacketing on about marriage and security for most of the time, he was – Brenda finally gave in. She said yes to please him and shut him up. She did please him but he didn't shut up. Every day he'd come up with some new idea about the prospective kitchen or fireplace or life assurance, till she thought he'd drive her bloody mad. Sometimes she shouted at him, sometimes she didn't listen. Either way he didn't stop producing his plans, but inflation swiped at his savings and meant their fruition was still a long way off. Privately (something Brenda wouldn't even tell Lark) the distance of the marriage gave Brenda a feeling of curious, pleasurable safety.

Evans was in the doorway, evening sun behind him. He'd put on a clean shirt, rolled up the sleeves in the way Brenda said she liked. Only he should have rolled them up a bit further. He had no natural style, though he did try. He was big-boned, clumsy, awkward about his funny eye. He began to walk down the passage between the cages, pushing through the sunbeams as if they didn't exist. The chickens flicked their heads at him with no pretence at interest: nothing could stir the apathy of their lives. Evans reached Brenda, looked down at her. She covered her cigarette stub with her shoe. Evans flushed. The blood surged right across his chest, clashing with the lemon of his shirt. Irritation pricked Brenda's skin. She'd wanted a quiet time with Elizabeth.

'All afternoon I've been thinking,' said Evans. The chickens continued their purring with no respect for his coming thoughts. He had on his quiet voice, the one he used at more appropriate times, when Brenda was past minding what he said. Now, she sighed. Tried for patience. 'All afternoon I've been thinking that it's the tilt of your eyes makes you seem nearer to smiling than other girls, even when you aren't feeling like smiling at all.'

Brenda glanced up at his red face. She wanted to laugh, but saw his seriousness.

'Quite the poet, aren't we? What's that supposed to mean?' She stood up. Evans kissed her, roughly squashing her breasts against his crisp shirt. She could feel the heat of his chest.

'It's not supposed to mean anything. You just get to thinking, sitting in a post office all afternoon.'

'I told you, Lark's doing my hair tonight.'

Evans stepped back. His arms drooped, weighted by sad hands.

'I told you I was coming to give you a lift home.'

'You didn't need to change your shirt for a lift.'

'You could always change your mind, I thought.'

'No. I'm not changing my mind.'

'When we're married, we'll be together every evening.'

'Well, we're not married yet, are we?'

The flush which had cleared from Evans's face returned. The crooning of the chickens seemed to swell a little as if in renewed and united indignation.

'How's Elizabeth?' Evans asked quietly.

'She's very bad. She's got worse all afternoon. She'll be dead by this time tomorrow.'

'Wilberforce can cope with that, can't he?'

'He can cope, but he'll despise me for it. He'll say if you take on a job looking after chickens, you should kill them like a man.'

'Bastard,' said Evans. 'Tell you what. I'll have a word with him if you like. After dropping you home. Save you having to be insulted. I'll tell him to . . . finish her.'

Brenda was grateful.

'Tell him top row, third from the end. He doesn't even accept they have names. They're just egg machines to him.'

'All right.'

'I don't fancy her empty cage tomorrow morning.'

'It'll soon be filled.'

'It won't be Elizabeth.'

'Come on. Let's go.'

'I'll have to make Daisy queen.'

'I'm sure she'll be a good queen.' One side of Evans's mouth curled slightly.

'Don't laugh at me.'

'I'm not laughing at you.'

Brenda followed Evans down the aisle of the shed. He had a narrow back, sloping shoulders. He dodged very slightly from side to side (hoping that Brenda wouldn't notice) to make sure the heads that darted from the cages would not touch him. Brenda did notice.

'They wouldn't bother to peck *you*.' She stopped at Elizabeth's cage. 'Look at her.' Evans turned, noted the dying eyes. 'You better say goodbye to her.' Brenda waited, staring at him. 'Go on. Say goodbye. Or can't you bring yourself to that?'

For the third time Evans blushed.

'Goodbye, Elizabeth,' he said. His voice was foolish.

'Goodbye *Queen* Elizabeth,' Brenda repeated. 'Though goodness knows you're not much of a queen now.' She tapped the bird's beak with her nail. The head swung a little to one side, too weak to return to its former position.

Outside the light was blindingly gold after the shadows of the shed. There was a distant smell of fresh manure, a slight breeze.

'You're insensitive to death, plainly,' said Brenda.

'I'm not insensitive to death.'

'It doesn't matter to you if an animal you love dies.'

'Of course it does.'

'You think I'm just sentimental, feeling like this about Elizabeth.'

'I don't. You know I've always been impressed, such affection for hens.' Brenda glanced at him, moving a little way from him in case he should take her arm. He walked looking at the ground, frowning. 'Anyhow, when we're . . . when we've got our own place and you have all the hens you want, we'll see to it they have a good life. We'll see to it they live a long time.'

Brenda shrugged. So often, in his well meaning way, Evans was nothing but irritating. He could not see that the thought of future hens was no consolation for Elizabeth's death. He could not understand the ache of an empty cage. By day, it seemed, Evans could understand practically nothing. Only at night, in the dark, in the hay, he instinctively knew what she wanted. Then, they didn't have to talk, and that was best. One day she would have to sit down and think, really think, whether she could continue her life with Evans for the sake of the nights. Lark would advise. Lark was good with advice. For the moment, all that mattered was that the next time she walked down this path, early tomorrow morning, the dry smell of pig feed in the air,

Elizabeth would be dead. She said nothing. To Evans, there was nothing further to say.

Brenda hurried straight into Lark's room without knocking. Lark was lying on her bed, newly painted geranium nails pointing to the ceiling. The wallpaper was dense trellis-work through which trailed scarlet and pink flowers, mostly geraniums. The window ledge was crowded with pots of the real thing. On the small table by Lark's bed stood a dozen small, spiteful cacti. 'My protection,' she called them. Summer evenings, warm with western sun, the room felt like an indoor garden, though it smelt of nail polish.

'The queen's dying,' said Brenda.

Lark sat up at once.

'Oh, Lord. Don't look so tragic. Wilberforce'll see to it, like he did to the others, won't he?'

'But he doesn't even *know* she's queen.'

Lark shrugged.

'Some people are that callous. Well, we must do something to take your mind off it.' Lark was practical about happiness. 'We'll have a nice supper of poached eggs on sweet corn, your favourite, and gin. There's half a bottle, so we won't need to stint ourselves. Then we'll get on with the patchwork.' They were making a patchwork tablecloth, all red materials, for Lark's widowed mother who lived with her arthritis in Westgate-on-Sea. 'There's Mahler on Radio 3, so we can listen to that and put brandy in our cocoa.'

Brenda had never heard of Mahler and was unskilled at sewing: Lark completed three hexagonals to her one. But the positive suggestions calmed her. She only had to knock at the door of Lark's small red world to be let in, comforted, eased.

'Come on,' said Lark, going to the door. 'First things first. Gin.' There was a ladder in her tights, a hole in the elbow of her grey jersey, her greasy hair fell into partitions. She bounced. If Brenda could have thought of a good way to put it she would have liked to have told her, to have paid her a compliment: Lark, you're strong, she would have liked to have said.

Rosie divided the bacon and egg pie in her mind. She calculated that if she took a smallish piece herself – and she never liked to appear a greedy eater in public, though one of her secret foibles was to pick at things in the larder – then they would just manage. It was really most difficult of Evans, being so vague about his evening plans. If only he had said yes quite definitely, then Rosie could have made a stew: but if he was going to be out, then it would be silly, all that meat and potatoes just for Henry and her. Rosie didn't like waste, but she also didn't like to inflict such worries upon her family. Therefore she struggled by herself, measuring out the pie with a knife, the inspiration of a tin of new potatoes in the back of her mind in case Evans *did* return. Would he, wouldn't he? The question rattled at her. He had come in and put on a clean shirt – she had only pressed it that morning, was worried whether it might not still be damp – and hurried out saying he might be back and he might not. The trouble was, and Rosie would admit this to no one in the world, Brenda had a terrible hold on Evans. He ran round her in circles, doing everything she required and more. He wouldn't hear a word against her: she was his life. Rosie had thought that once they were engaged, officially, things might have been different. But they weren't. Brenda continued to have the upper hand, anyone could see that. What's more, she had no sense of romance. Conversations about their new home seemed to bore her. Everything seemed to bore her except her blooming chickens, and they were a funny hobby for a girl, weren't they? In her heart, Rosie worried for her son. Even now, as she took the risk and opened the tin of potatoes, she felt a twist of anxiety in her stomach. Don't be a fool, Rosie Evans, she said to herself at once. Many's the time you've seen them go out together in the Mini, all smiling, off for a picnic somewhere, taking the rug and the basket of sandwiches in the back seat. Maybe alone they were all right. They must be, or Evans wouldn't stick around so long, would he? Not her Evans. He'd have more sense.

Rosie took a bunch of knives and forks to the table. She smoothed the white damask cloth just for the pleasure of feeling the silky knots of delphiniums, embroidered by her mother fifty years ago, beneath her hands. In the summer evening light that made their kitchen a smaller, huskier room, Rosie noticed her hands didn't look so bad, vulnerable though they were on the whiteness of the cloth. Nothing could take away from their shape – huge boxes, they were, Henry had once said, daft at the end of small arms like hers – but the warmth of the day had muted their colour. They were still a reddish mauve – nothing on earth would pale their skin to the white of the rest of the body – but at least the ugly mottles, so sharp in winter that the skin resembled tortoiseshell, had subsided for a few months. Rosie would have liked to call Henry's attention to the fact they were better today: funny how he only commented on them when they were at their worst. But Henry was deep in his paper again. Henry was a very thorough reader of papers, though usually he didn't spend quite so many hours over the *Daily Mirror* as today. Rosie thought it must be the heat playing havoc with his concentration. She herself had to read more slowly in the heat, so she understood. She kept her silence, and moved the egg cup, holding its one iris, a fraction of an inch nearer the centre of the table. Odd how one bloom could give so much pleasure. Evans often criticised her for being so mean with flowers, in the friendliest possible way, of course, just teasing. What she couldn't make him understand was the lesson she herself had learnt from a calendar of Japanese flower arrangements: how beautiful are just one or two blooms rather than a whole lot bunched together. Admittedly, she didn't have the right kind of vases, the kind in the colour photographs. And there were no exotic lilies in these parts, not even in the local florist's, to work with. So Rosie adapted in her own way: a single iris, a bunch of fuschia and two buttercups, a strand of ivy or honeysuckle bending wispily from a milk bottle.

Strange, really, how her arrangements had never achieved so much as a highly commended in the local flower show. But she understood why it was. Even in the world of flowers, the British were so insular: they would never look to arrangements beyond their own shores. Still, now we were in the Common Market, there was some hope. Now we had accepted Europe we might be persuaded to open our eyes further east and glance upon, and one day even seize upon, the Japanese way with apple blossom. That would be the day. For the moment, Rosie's arrangements were too far ahead of their time for the village. But, with faith in her theory, she was prepared to wait, quite patiently. She touched the blue petals with a gentle finger, and smiled to herself.

Evans came in. Henry turned a page of his paper.

They sat at the table, eating. As Rosie always helped the men to their food she had managed to divide the pie fairly between them, and disguise her own narrow wedge with a margin of potatoes. Henry held his knife like a hammer. Rosie could never feel quite happy about this particular habit of his, but in weighing it up over the years she had decided it was one of those things not worth mentioning. Even after three decades of love there are areas which must be left untouched, protected by silence. Evans ate with more refinement than his father, but drank his tea fast and noisily, treating it like beer. Rosie wondered how he managed not to burn his mouth, and what had happened between him and Brenda to cause his return. He had obviously been to see her down at the sheds, judging by the faint smell of chickens.

'Busy day?' she asked.

'Fairly. A lot of parcels.'

'People must be posting early for Christmas, thinking it's going up again.'

'That's what Brenda said.'

'Brenda all right?'

'Fine.'

'I thought she looked very nice, Sunday, that skirt.'
'Yes.'
'Perhaps you'd both like to bring Lark with you to tea this Sunday? I always think she has such a quiet life, Lark.'
'She's happy enough. I'll ask her. She's washing Brenda's hair tonight.'
Any news of Brenda's innocence in Evans's absence filled Rosie with a sense of private relief. Relief that made her almost skittish.
'Henry, love, you funny old thing, you've left all your nice pie,' she observed.
'Not hungry.' Henry was scratching his neck, all around the inside of his collar. In an ideal world, the sort of gesture that Rosie would have preferred him to carry out in the privacy of the bathroom rather than at table.
'But you always have an appetite for your tea.'
Henry stood up.
'I'm off down to the Star for an hour.'
'But it isn't your night for –' Rosie stopped herself. She would never wish to be accused of criticism. She watched him go, decided not to shout out to him he'd forgotten his jacket.
'The heat doesn't suit your father,' she said to Evans when Henry had slammed the door.
'Dad's never liked the heat.'
Evans helped Rosie clear away the plates. Then he, too, more gently, said he was going out. Once again Rosie controlled herself not to ask questions. The odd departures of the men in your family, with no explanations, was part of the lot a wife and mother should bear without apparent worry. She managed a smile.
'Have a nice time.'
But she did wish Evans wasn't so weak where Brenda was concerned. He should leave her alone, hair-washing nights. Not always be after her, always there. A small dose of doubt would do a girl like her a power of good. If she didn't have it all quite so easy she might be inclined to come running. That

would be much better than things as they were now – Evans, in his kindness, always the one chasing after her.

After a small battle with himself Evans came to a decision: he would not go to Brenda. The firmness of his purpose made him free to leave the house. He was in no mood tonight to be left alone with his mother's subtle sympathy. He wanted merely to walk, he needed air. Space, he required, in which to think. Quietness, to quell the turmoil in his blood.

He looked up at the elms, a deeper evening green now, and then towards the ugly shape of the vicarage. Behind their surplice curtains Evans could make out the shapes of the vicar and his wife at supper. Then the church bells began to ring: choir practice night. With a reverent little jump the vicar rose from the table, mistily as the Holy Ghost. In a moment he would be at the front door, hurrying with shining face to the church. Evans had no wish to meet him. Rather than turn back into the kitchen, he quickly crossed the small patch of common land between the cottages and vicarage and went through the front gates of Wroughton House. There, he hid behind the fence.

From his protected position he watched the vicar make his eager way to the graveyard. An encounter had been missed by seconds. Evans's heart beat fast with unholy gratitude. He leaned against the trunk of one of the elms – they grew both sides of the fence – feeling the deep ridges of its bark cutting into his back. The four desolate bells repeated over and over again their monotonous descending scale. He was vaguely aware that technically he was trespassing, that he was on private property, but he didn't care.

Moments went by. Evans edged round the trunk of the tree, looked up the drive towards the house. Elms grew each side of the drive. They protected the church on the right, fields on the left. In the distance Evans could see a small part of the façade of the house.

There was no one about. He began to walk, stopping only when he came to the large pond at the end of the front lawn.

It was a man-made pond, perfectly round and lined with cement, crowded with water-lilies and bulrushes. Behind it, dividing the lawn from the fields, grew a vast willow tree whose meandering boughs dipped and swayed almost continuously. Some of its lower fronds ruffled the brown pond water. Suddenly aware of his exposed position in the drive, Evans went to hide again, behind the willow tree. There, hands in pockets, legs set apart in a comfortable position, he contemplated the house once more. His heart had resumed its normal beating, the church bells had stopped ringing. They left a profound silence in their wake. A silence which dissolved his guilt at trespassing. Hidden as he was, he felt at peace in the garden.

In all his life in the village Evans had never really looked at Wroughton House before. It was protected from the rest of the community by its fences and tall trees, an impenetrable oasis among the new houses surrounding it. The only previous times he had walked up the drive had been to accompany Rosie to the annual summer fete on the lawn. Those occasions Evans remembered with little pleasure. Rosie insisted he toured the rose garden with her, and he could never think of any compliments to pay flowers, especially with the British Legion silver band blasting in his ears. He could never understand Rosie's awe of the place; but then he supposed it was to do with the fact that her mother had been a housemaid there after the First World War, and had married the under gardener. It was his own grandfather who had planted most of the bloody roses – a fact which left Evans quite unmoved, year after year, as Rosie repeated the story. She herself had never worked permanently in the house, though up until last year she was often called upon to help out at weekends. These invitations caused her a dither of excitement and pleasure. She would come back with stories of parties which held so little interest for Evans he scarcely listened and, now he tried to remember, he could recall no details. But he was aware that things had changed: that Mrs Browne, the owner, lived by herself now because Mr Browne had left. There were no more parties. Evans overheard gossip in the pub, but did not take it in. He had only seen Mrs Browne on a few occasions, darting about in a silver car. Smallish, not his sort of woman. For one who had lived all his life so near the house and its inhabitants, he was curiously uninformed.

Evans, who would never call himself a keen observer of fine buildings, continued to stare at the house. He supposed it was what people who knew about architecture would call beautiful – built in the time of William and Mary, he remembered his mother saying. It was very grand by his standards, the grandest house he had ever seen. But not intimidating. He would not be afraid to knock at the front door. He liked the way its tall windows reflected the pale flecks of late evening sky; the way its roots were settled in a wave of bushy lavender. He liked the colour of its walls – an irregular ochre, something like a winter beach he had once visited, buffetted to varying shades by the wind. A strange excitement came upon him. He was aware he was experiencing one of those moments that make an ordinary day a memorable one. He would have liked to wander round the rest of the garden and take a look at the sides and the back of the building. But the church bells started up again, reminding him he should not be there at all, jarring his conscience. Reluctant to move, he cast his eyes to the pond, where the water image of the façade hung absolutely still. A light went on in one reflected window. Glancing back at the house, Evans saw a woman standing there. She pulled down a blind. It was then he remembered: the house was for sale. His mother had been talking about it only yesterday. Mrs Browne was staying on alone until it was sold. The woman at the window must have been Mrs Browne.

Evans left his place behind the willow tree. It was almost dark. He walked without caution back down the drive. His excitement had crystallised into an idea, an idea that needed much attention. He would slip upstairs, avoiding his parents, and go to his room. There he would think it all out, calmly as he was able, and make up his mind before the night was through.

Gin, Lark always said, silvered the mind. By eleven at night both she and Brenda had achieved the silvery state they desired, and were happy. Lark was drying Brenda's hair with a hand dryer, its engine buzzing like a swarm of summer flies. Mahler had been turned down to a background hum to make talking possible. There was brandy in their cocoa.

'What's the betting he comes up here wanting his oats?' Lark asked.

'Don't think he will tonight. I said I wanted some sleep.'

'D'you think he's crying his heart out for you?'

'Expect so.'

'Perhaps you should try being nicer to him. Or he should try being nastier to you.'

'Let him try.' Brenda giggled. 'I'd be off. I'd be all right, wouldn't I?'

'You'd be all right.'

'Lark, how come you're all right, without any men? Without anyone, really?'

Lark pulled at a strand of coppery hair, tugging Brenda's head back, and pushed the hot nozzle of the dryer into the gaping scalp. Brenda grimaced in silence.

'Haven't the time,' said Lark.

'Haven't the time? You've got tons of time. You're in this flat night after night painting your nails and listening to your music. Think of all the other things you could be doing.'

'You've got to have your pride as a typist, even if it's only keeping your nails nice.'

'Haven't time! You're barmy, Lark. If you washed your own hair more often, and bought some decent clothes, you'd have them all after you.'

'What for?'

'Don't be so daft: what for? For a bit of fun, of course. Better than sitting in your room humming to yourself.'

'Singing. If I could find a choir near here I'd join it, then you wouldn't worry so.'

Brenda shrugged.

'Oh, I don't really worry. Don't think that. Did you really want to be a singer, thrilling away on a platform all by yourself?'

'All those bunches of flowers they throw up to you at the end. I could imagine it.'

'Hey, don't leave my hair.'

'It's finished.'

'Why didn't you go on with it?'

'They said I wasn't up to the training. My lungs.'

Brenda stood up. She turned round to see Lark, holding the hair dryer away from her like a conductor's baton. Her face seemed to have parted a little to match her hair.

'Why don't you try it?' asked Brenda.

'I tell you, I tried to persuade them to let me –'

'I don't mean singing.'

A pink flush seeped up through the grey skin of Lark's face. She snapped off the dryer. The Mahler was distinct.

'Don't go on, Bren. I tell you, I haven't the time.'

Through the silver of her mood Brenda recognised this to be one of Lark's mysterious remarks, but with the gin spreading like mercury through her veins the effort to ask Lark what she meant eluded her.

'Well, Evans isn't coming,' she said. 'I was right. I'm going to bed.'

'Sweet dreams and God bless.'

'You're not going through your whole blinking rosary *tonight*, are you?'

' 'Course I am. God forgive me for the gin, I'll say.'

'Crikey,' said Brenda. She pulled at her cotton bedspread. Its patterns seemed to have run into one another with bright confusion.

Rosie lay in bed looking at the dark shape of her husband's shoulders beside her. He was deeply asleep, she could tell by the way he kept quite still. Under the sheets her hands were clasped in a large knot on her chest. She moved them gently, so as not to disturb Henry, and rubbed the tops of her arms. In their fine lawn mittens they felt wonderfully smooth. She had started wearing night mittens seventeen years ago when Henry had said her knuckles scratched his chest. After the announcement he had gone straight to sleep, easy as if it hadn't been an accusation, as if he'd meant it as a friendly remark. Rosie had lain awake listening to rain against their window. It was a warm night but she felt cold. She wondered what to do, if there was a doctor she could consult about the terrible ailment of her hands. She would pay any money to improve them, but probably a doctor would merely laugh. By dawn she had had the idea about the mittens. The next day she had set about making them, and had worn them every night since. In seventeen years she had been through eleven pairs. After the first few nights of shyness – Henry had made no remarks – she had dared to stroke his shoulder with a covered finger. Then his back, his neck. But Henry remained silent. 'Don't they feel better, love?' she had eventually asked. Henry stiffened – she could just feel the muscles trying to disguise their contraction, and did not answer. Nor did he turn over, pulling the bed-clothes from under the mattress, which always seemed to happen when he felt desirous. He went quickly to sleep. Since then, on special occasions, New Year's Eve and birthdays, Rosie still stroked his shoulder blades tentatively with her muslin fingers, but he did not respond. She had given up, really. She realised that when that side of married life dies you cannot bring it back, and must make the best of other, more important things. Still, she had her regrets: one of the most profound was that she had ever started wearing the mittens. It had occurred to her some time ago that *they* were what had dampened Henry's urges. They were the culprits. In trying to disguise the burden of her hands she had inadvertently emphasised them. And on nights like these Rosie was haunted with new resolve: when she dared, she would throw away the wretched things. There were still a few years left in which they would make up for lost opportunities, she and Henry. 'Oh, there are, my love,' she said to herself.

Henry lay wide awake looking at the moon perched on the elms like an owl. The Leopard, as she had become in his mind, had not been in the pub. He had drunk three beers and two double whiskies, something he was quite unused to at night. Still, the alcohol had inspired him. On his walk home he had had a brainwave. Tomorrow he would go and see his old friend Mackay. Mackay ran a small market garden a mile out of the village. He was known for his prize vegetables, in particular his cauliflowers. Henry didn't know why, but he had a strange strong feeling that the Leopard, sophisticated creature though she was, would appreciate good things straight from the earth. She was the kind of woman, he felt, who would go out of her way to attend a Harvest Festival Service. Now, if he could talk Mackay into it, he would persuade him to have one or two of his best cauliflowers constantly at the ready. He would have to be careful how he put this, of course, or Mackay, a sly old dog, would know something was up. But that was no real problem. The next part of the plan was less clear, he would have to work upon it. Roughly, it was this: the next time he saw the Leopard in the pub he would slip quickly out, muttering some excuse if anyone was interfering enough to draw attention to his departure. He would hurry along to Mackay – which would probably mean coming home to fetch the car, so an explanation to Rosie would have to be thought up – buy a couple of cauliflowers, and hurry back to the Star. There, he would hang about outside. He might even light his pipe, to look more casual. When the Leopard emerged he would wish her the time of day and fall into casual conversation, bringing the talk, of course, round to the magnificent cauliflower he was holding, which she would be bound to remark upon. Then he would say, 'Well, a beautiful cauliflower for a beautiful lady,' or something like that.

The precise words he would think out more carefully to-morrow. He might even write them down, trying out different things. The main thing was to hand her the cauliflowers with a small, old-fashioned bow. It would be such a surprising gesture, so much more subtle than flowers, she could hardly refuse them. After that, it would be easy enough to ask if she would care to have a drink with him one day, next time she was passing through the village. After *that* . . . well, anything could happen.

The idea of playing with such fire burnt into Henry with a thrill that made him want to roar out loud like a forest animal, and clap his hands, and kick his feet in the air. As it was, he lay clenched into stillness, grateful for the self-control taught him by the Navy. Now all he had to get to grips with was patience. *Patience, patience, Henry old fellow.* The whisky was a sour pain in his chest. He would have liked to have moved his position. But it was never worth moving before Rosie was asleep. The smallest heave to greater comfort and she would start up with her confounded tickling. Henry shut his eyes.

Augusta Browne clung to her house. It was inevitable that it should be sold, now Hugh had gone, but she was doing her best to delay the sale. She had had her latest success this morning. A furrier and his wife from Hampstead had arrived in their Rolls and Persian lamb collars. She had let them carry on with their insults for quite some time (strange how rude are prospective buyers in front of owners, as if selling was a complete protection from hurt), smiling at their suggestions. 'We'd have to change the dining-room, of course,' said the woman. 'Terra cotta hurts my eyes. We could do it in a nice brocade paper and put beading on the shelves, like at home.' The man ran a fat hand down the walls which had undulated gently for 300 years. 'We'd have to smooth out these,' he said. 'It's all very well emulsioning walls like this, but you'd never get a decent paper to stick.'

Augusta waited until they reached her bedroom. The time

had come for her triumph. The small couple stood at one of the soaring windows looking out at the lime-coloured lawn, the ponds, the vast elm, polluting the view with their gaze. The man screwed up his nasty eyes into the distance.

'Are those the chimneys we saw from the motorway?'

'Yes. The brickworks.'

'Do they give you any trouble?'

Augusta paused.

'As a matter of fact they do.' She watched the woman, sniffing, judge the Williamsburg cotton of the blind between her fingers. 'When there's an east wind the smell is pretty bad.'

'What kind of smell?' The man was almost prurient.

'Rotten eggs. To be honest, it stinks.'

The man pursed his bulbous lips.

'Well, we'd be in Town a good deal, you see. I dare say the smell wouldn't worry us too much, once or twice a year. We could be away those days.'

'Well, on average, there's an east wind at least three times a week,' said Augusta.

They didn't bother to see the rest of the house after that, but hurried back to Hampstead muttering about a wasted journey. As soon as they had gone Augusta went to her study. It overlooked the walled garden – the wall was built of soft mellow stone. Augusta leant back in her comfortable, high-backed chair, lay her arms along its arms, conscious of their support. She watched a couple of blue-tits pecking at the bricks. Over the years they had chipped out several caves in the wall where they sometimes huddled, as if in a nest. This morning the birds were bright, elated. Augusta telephoned Hugh.

'Those people the agents said were very keen – they've just gone. They weren't at all interested.'

'Oh.'

In the silence Augusta sensed her husband was in a hurry.

'Hugh, if I came up next week, could we have lunch? We could talk about things.'

'No.'

Another pause. Augusta's voice trembled.

'If you won't have lunch with me, I'll never marry you again.' She slammed down the receiver before she could become any more ridiculous.

Now, the evening of that day, it rained for the first time in two weeks. The rain glittered down over the garden making sparks on the emerald of the May grass. The pond water, paled by the sky's reflected clouds, was pocked with rain-drops, suddenly alive beneath the weight of its water-lilies. Augusta stretched up her arms among the branches of the lilac bush, struggling for the purple cones. It was the nature of the best lilac blooms always to be out of reach. She stood on tip-toe, rain from the leaves pouring down her arms. Her light shoes were soaked in the long grass, she could hear the squeak of her toes as she moved them. She reached the branches, snapped them off, buried her head in the tight buds, aware for a moment only of their intense scent, of their wetness against the wetness of her face. She moved away, then. Walked across the wide lawn that sloped from the side of the house down to another, natural pond. There at its banks grew cow parsley shoulder-high, heads white as summer clouds. Augusta pushed her way through the frail jungle, listening to the quiet clatter of the shower. She picked the odd stalk, then bent to gather a bunch of cowslips. The rain had intensified their yellowness, their honey smell.

The ritual of the flower-gathering over, Augusta walked slowly back to the house. Her long cotton skirt clung about her ankles, she was suddenly cold. A fire, she decided. When she had put the flowers in water she would light the fire in the hall. And then . . . what would she do for the long evening? Oh, there was plenty of time to think. She would get warm first. Have a bath. Finish that half-bottle of Hugh's Sancerre. Some idea would come to her.

Evans, who had been cogitating upon his plan all day in the Post Office, was disturbed by the wet evening. He had not reckoned with rain. Now Rosie's fussing about his mackintosh would have to come into his calculations – easy enough to deal with, but a possible risk to his firmness of purpose. As it turned out, he need not have worried. Soon as she had cleared the tea, Rosie hurried off under her umbrella to a Mothers' Union meeting. At her exit Henry emerged from behind his paper, stood up and scratched at his ribs luxuriously.

'Well, Boy, don't know about you but I'm slipping down for a quick one.'

'Second night this week, Dad. Becoming quite the alcoholic.'

Henry, through lack of practice, was as diffident as his son about smiling. But Evans observed a tilt of humour flare at the corners of his father's tight mouth.

'A man's got to have some vices in his old age, Boy.' Then, in silent recognition of the other's private intentions, they put on their mackintoshes and parted at the front door.

Evans waited until Henry was out of sight before he crossed the strip of common grass and slipped through the gates of the house. He walked up the middle of the drive, hands in pockets, rain sloping pleasantly against him. He liked the gravel crunch under his feet, the swiftness of the clouds above him. The nervousness of the day had gone. Chances were his plan would fail, but he was no longer afraid to try.

He paused when he reached the part of the drive that unfurled into a broad sweep directly before the house. He moved his head from side to side, taking in the two rows of tall windows, feeling the rain running down his neck. He went to the porch, rang the door bell. Two minutes' wait. No answer. He rang again. Still nothing. He peered through the glass panes of the door: another glass door. Beyond it, murkily, the impression of a large hall and the flames of a huge fire. Eventually Evans opened the doors and went in.

As soon as he had done so he realised his mistake. This was

quite the wrong night to have come. The place was set for a party.

The hall was filled with music. The tunes seemed vaguely familiar to Evans, the sort of thing that accompanied old thirties films he watched on television. There was lilac everywhere: a pyramid set upon an oak chest, another one on the round centre table. The smell of the wet blooms, combined with the winter smell of the fire, almost stifled Evans. He put a hand over his nose, confused for a moment by the sweet power of the scents. *I must go*, he thought. *Quickly, before anyone knows I've been.* Reluctance was embedded in the thought. He made no move, but remained where he was, conscious that raindrops from his mackintosh fell on to the stone-flagged floor, encircling him in a grey ring of water. He looked about. Like church, and the gym at his old school, the place gave him a comfortable feeling of being a normal size. Here no one could accuse him of being clumsy, too big.

There were archways each side of the fireplace. Beyond one of them rose a pine staircase, shining with polish. As its half-landing was a magnificent arched window, an echo of the inside shapes, its panes blurred with rain. Evans, still motionless, was wondering about the practical problems of window-cleaners, when a woman he supposed to be Mrs Browne appeared on the stairs. From where he stood he had not seen her coming down the upper flight. She appeared as if from nowhere, startling. Evans saw her before she saw him. He had a few seconds in which to observe her unseen. She seemed to glide down the staircase, in time to the music, head high, one hand just brushing the wood banister. It was as if she supposed a hundred people to be gathered in the hall below, and was making a grand entrance, expecting their appraisal. She wore a long, soft skirt, same colour as the pine, so that half her body merged in with the backdrop; and a pinkish cardigan, cobwebby stuff, its sleeves pushed up her arms.

Halfway down the lower flight of the stairs she noticed Evans, and paused. She was dwarfed by the high window behind her. Its light made a subdued halo of her hair.

'Hello,' she said.

Then she descended the rest of the stairs very fast, not looking at her feet, one hand holding up her skirt. Evans felt a brief sensation that this was all theatre: that in some mysterious way he was inextricably involved in the action on a stage. A waking dream.

She stood before him, surprisingly small now she was on the ground.

'Who are you?'

'Evans. Er, Evans Evans.' The absurdity of his own name, when he was forced to give it, still caused Evans embarrassment. He clutched at the pockets of his raincoat. A small shower of water ran over his hands and added to the dark ring on the floor. 'You know my mother, Rosie.'

'Of course I know Rosie. She's always talking about you. How can I help you?'

'Well, as a matter of fact . . .'

'The cricket match, the Boy Scouts or some sort of raffle? Let me guess.'

She moved over to the fire, smiling. Stood with her back to the flames, arms folded under her small breasts, clutching to herself a small shiver.

'None of those things.' Evans had to speak loudly against the music.

'Then for goodness sake get rid of that soaking mackintosh and we'll go next door and have a drink.'

'Are you sure?' Evans was already struggling out of the mackintosh. 'I mean, it looks as if you're expecting company. I'm sorry, I didn't . . . a party?'

'A party?' Mrs Browne smiled again. Wistful this time. 'Oh, no. I just like to keep things going. Come on.'

She went to a door at the corner of the hallway. Evans followed her. The room they entered at once infused him with an unfamiliar sense of warmth, of caring. He had no eye for detail, was only aware of impressions: high windows in two of the coral walls: round the fire a gathering of sofas and chairs that seemed to have been built for large people; ancestral portraits and spring flowers. The music was quieter in here.

'Now, what will you have? Whisky? Let's both have whisky, all this rain . . .' She was moving about against the windows, swaying to the frail voice of the olden-days singer. *Love me or leave me* . . . Made bold by his part in the play, Evans sat down by the fire without asking. The well-stuffed back of the sofa eased him as no sofa had ever done before. He crossed his legs and stared at the oblong chunk of his thigh. In this radiant world of make-believe he felt curiously at home.

Mrs Browne handed him a drink. She sat opposite him, huddled into the corner of an armchair that was much too big for her, legs drawn up beneath her. Again the light from the windows behind her made her turbulent hair an almost colourless mass. Evans judged her to be about ten years older than Brenda. For her age, she wasn't at all bad. Come to think of it, he remembered his mother having said just that on several occasions. He sipped the whisky. It was strong.

'You've a very nice place, here,' he said. Mrs Browne looked down into her drink. Pale eyelids. In a lull in the singing they could hear the splatter of rain on the windows. 'I understand it's all going to be sold,' went on Evans. 'That seems a pity.'

'It's on the market, but it will take a long time. Not many people want a house of this size these days.' Something about the flatness of her voice made Evans realise the selling of the house was not a subject she wished to continue. 'What is it that I can do for you?'

'I had this funny plan. It came to me, sudden like, last night.' Evans wondered if Mrs Browne was aware of the fact that she was making the unfolding of his plan surprisingly easy. Her very position among the cushions seemed sympathetic. 'You see, it's like this. I've got this girl, Brenda. Mum may have told you we're engaged.'

'Yes.'

'Well, Brenda and me have been together two years now. We're saving up for one of those houses on the new estate so that we can start our marriage in a decent place, as it were. Well, we've still got some time to go before we can manage the down payment. And as you can imagine, waiting, like, a long time, has its problems.' Evans took another sip of the whisky, shifted his look from Mrs Browne to the rain beyond the windows. The warm room, with its outdoor smell of flowers, was protective in a way he had never previously experienced. Perhaps Mrs Browne had conjured this protection for herself, and was innocent of the effect it had upon her visitors. 'The thing is, we've never had anywhere to go. To be alone, I mean. Brenda shares this flat with a friend called Lark. She's a nice enough girl, but not a one for going out. She's always there. She stays in her own room, very tactful, but it's not the same as being alone, is it? Then of course at home – well, the house being that small, it's always crowded with Mum and Dad.'

'I see. So where do you go?'

'Fields, barns. It gets on your nerves.' Evans put his hand over his right eye, pretending to scratch his forehead. Then he allowed himself a slight smile. 'It's not what you'd call most comfortable, either.'

'Quite.' Mrs Browne smiled in return.

'So this is what I was wondering. You here in this big house all alone, I thought. Maybe, I thought, you'd have a room, somewhere in the attics, we could rent . . . until the place was sold.'

Mrs Browne nodded immediately.

'Of course,' she said, quietly. 'Of course. What a good idea.'

Evans noticed that the flames were growing brighter then, and his hand shook a little round his icy glass.

'I could pay you a month's rent in advance. We'd take good care of it, I can assure you that. We wouldn't disturb you.'

Mrs Browne swung her legs to the ground with a quick, determined gesture. She was suddenly vivacious.

'Of course you can have a room, but only on one condition: no money is involved.'

'But, in that case, we couldn't . . .'

'You could. Don't you see? No, I don't see why you should.' She stood up. 'The thing is, I'd *like* to feel someone was in the house, upstairs, having . . . nice times again.'

Evans stood too. There was something about Mrs Browne that made him realise it was pointless to argue further now. He was determined to bring the subject up again, later; but at this moment of the charade it all seemed irrelevant.

'Let's go up there right now,' said Mrs Browne. 'I can show you what there is.'

Evans followed her upstairs to the attic floor. She led him along a dusky passage.

'We ran out of money before we could do much up here,' she was saying. 'But at least it's warm. You could have any of the rooms, but I think this one is best.' She opened a door.

The room, by the standards of the Evans house, was large. It had a sloping ceiling and two casement windows. There was an ink-stained rug on the wooden floor, a brass double bed, and the shapes of other furniture under dust sheets.

'There's masses of stuff up here,' said Mrs Browne. 'You can have what you like.'

'No, really, we could –'

'Please. It would do the things good to be used again.' She went to one of the casement windows. This time the rainy light caught her face, threw a violet shadow from her chin on to her neck. Again she hunched her shoulders and folded her arms beneath her breasts, a gesture that seemed to be a habit with her. The position of her small body, as she stood like that, indicated a melancholy that was not betrayed by her voice.

'The garden is perfect for parties,' she said. For a moment Evans was confused, wondering whether she assumed he and Brenda were the kind of people to throw garden parties. 'We always planned to have one on this lawn. I'd had it all arranged to the last detail. We were going to have a merry-go-round down there, look – and gondolas on the pond by the field, and fireworks over the round pond, and a marquee covering the rose garden at the back. But it didn't ever happen, of course. We hadn't the money. And now it never will.'

Evans was aware of the stuffiness of the room. It was evident that the windows had not been opened for some time. Mrs Browne had the same thought: she struggled with the catch.

'Here, let me.' Evans was beside her. He opened the window with a strong push and a small flight of rain instantly blew in on them. Mrs Browne laughed.

'That's lovely! We'll leave it open for a few days to air the place. It smells of dust.'

They remained by the window looking out at the dappled garden, the blossom on the bushes of May very white, the distant trees blousy with rain, the brickworks' chimneys half-hidden in a tangle of cloud and smoke. Evans sensed that the end of the charade was near. He felt suddenly compelled to be inquisitive, even if his question might jeopardise the arrangements that had already been made.

'Did you spend your life here giving parties, then?'

Mrs Browne disguised a sigh.

'Oh, no. Nothing like that. I must be giving a very flippant impression. Most of the time both of us were working very hard. But we did like having lots of people here: they seemed to enjoy it. We had wonderful nights, dancing, singing, playing silly games – I expect Rosie may have told you. But that was only a small part of our lives, until the money ran out. Then it had to stop.' She wiped a streak of rain from her cheek. 'But I do *remember* the parties, I have to admit. I remember them, perhaps better than anything else, partly because of the peace when they were over. We loved it when the house was full of people and music and things. But then we loved it even better when it went back to being quiet, like this.'

She put her hand on the window ledge, wiped dust from it

with her finger. They listened to rain on the roof. Near as he stood to her, Evans felt Mrs Browne was very remote. Not in a week in this room, imprisoned with her, could he touch her: she inspired in him no desire. He saw that some people might find her beautiful, but for him she was too self-contained. Everything about her suggested she needed nothing more than her house. She was friendly enough, generous, kind, but something of an enigma. And Evans had no time for enigmas. He preferred the instant, animal appeal of Brenda with her great warm body and wicked eyes. At the thought of Brenda, here in this room in that bed, the spell of Mrs Browne was broken for Evans. But as he followed her back downstairs to the drawing-room, he realised that in some curious way, as strangers sometimes are, he had been very close to her for a short while. The visit to her house, her private world in which ordinary things seemed to have been infused with some of her spirit, left him feeling that the indefinable magic he sometimes imagined could exist, *did* exist. It was a possibility. Mrs Browne had proved it.

Back in their seats by the fire she made practical suggestions.

'You can have a key to the back door, and if you use the back stairs I'll never know when you're coming and going, which I'm sure you'd like best. You must let me know if there's anything you want. In the meantime come up any time you want and get it all arranged. I'm here all the time.'

Evans had finished his whisky. Judging by the darkening windows it was getting late. He felt he ought to go.

'Don't you mind living in this huge house all by yourself?' he asked.

'Never for one moment. I like aloneness and it's never lonely. Besides, I have to keep it going in case . . . Well, no, I suppose Hugh will never change his mind about selling it, or coming back. But I like to keep it as it was . . . until it finally goes.'

'I'd go out of my mind,' said Evans, 'all alone in a place like this. I couldn't take the silence.' The unusually strong drink had speeded his words. 'I wouldn't know what to do with myself. It'd be quite spooky, I'd think, especially when those bloody church bells get going. If you don't mind me asking, Mrs Browne, what do you do with yourself all day?'

'Keep guard.' She smiled.

'I've never met a woman like you before. I mean, not even a *type* of woman.'

'Would you like another drink?'

'Don't know whether I should. I ought to be getting back, oughtn't I?'

Mrs Browne was a little hazy before him now, flitting about with glasses and ice. The room seemed full of shadows too hazardous to cross on his weak legs. He had never had a strong head when it came to drink.

'Not unless there's something special you have to do. And anyway, I'd like to hear a bit about Brenda.'

In the next two hours Mrs Browne listened almost without interruption to the frustrations of Evans's life, his hopes, his ambitions, his love for Brenda. When he left, much confused by the act of putting on his damp mackintosh, he heard her urging him to return soon, too. As he walked unsteadily back down the drive he reflected, in a confused way, that his plan had gone better than he could ever have anticipated. A room at last, and a smashing room at that. It was nothing less than a triumph. Evans gave a celebratory leap over a shallow puddle which quivered with moonlight. Unnerved, he almost fell. Recovering himself, he set about thinking how and when to break the news to Brenda. First he needed sleep, time to recover his calm. Then, in the morning, if he woke to find it had not been a dream, he would make more plans. Probably it would be best to keep it from her until the room was quite ready. Then he would take her there – she'd never believe him till she saw it – and they would celebrate in the way they both liked best.

There were times, not more than twice a year, that Rosie and Henry had a row. In retrospect Rosie could never be certain of the superficial reason for these rows. For all the love, it seemed that some friction which they could never discuss cumulated over the months and burst out in a guise that was little to do with the real cause. The guise, in fact, was nearly always the same: the name of their son. This was a subject that had meant anguish from the time he had been conceived, and they had had their ritual fights about it ever since. These fights had never shifted their own particular convictions that the other one was wrong. When over, each went their own way, nurturing his own inarticulate hurt. For her part, Rosie would clutch at the physical pain in her ribs with her clumsy hands, shed a few quiet tears under the sheets, and begin the next day as if nothing had happened. This was not entirely due to stoicism. She believed that rows were something everyone had to go through, once in a while, and, like childbirth, when they were over their pain was impossible to recall. They did nothing to clear the air because the air, she believed, in the case of she and Henry, was devoid of tension, full of love, *daily* love. The occasional outbursts were no more serious than a rare storm, Rosie told herself, natural to the rhythm of things. They were of so little consequence that she divulged them to no one, did not muse upon them herself. She simply made sure they never took place when Evans was there.

But for all their unimportance, the unease of an impending row twisted into Rosie's gut in a way that made her hands tremble and her mouth stiffen. She often thought that if it wasn't for the rigidity of her mouth she could smile at Henry and thereby dissolve the situation before it really began: but the paralysis made this impossible. Impeded as she was, there was no alternative but to endure the fray, trying to remember it was not the real Henry and Rosie taking part, but devils within them temporarily escaped.

Back from her meeting, as soon as she opened the front door, Rosie knew what was going to happen. Henry's mackintosh, hanging in its usual place, was wet. He had been out. It wasn't his night for going to the Star, but she would make no issue of that. It was, however, a climax to the oppressive silence that he had lately inflicted upon them. As Rosie went into the kitchen a spasm drilled within her, and she saw her hands quiver with their own angry life.

'Evans not back?' she said. Henry put down his paper. He had guessed from her footsteps – they became staccato with an approaching storm – what was in store. Her tight face proved him right. In no mood for words tonight, the Leopard prancing in his mind, he made an effort to be flat.

'It's not late,' he said. Then he made his mistake. 'The Boy can come in when he likes, can't he?'

Rosie slammed a string bag full of papers on to the table. '*Evans!*' she shouted. 'His name is Evans! For twenty-seven years – do I have to keep on telling you? I registered him as Evans. He *is* Evans. It's registered as Evans, do you understand?' Henry saw the metallic sky through the window behind her. He heard the rain against the small panes, a gentle backing to her voice. 'All his life you've referred to him as the Boy. He's had to put up with it. I've had to put up with it. What sort of father are you, Henry Evans?'

'I wanted my son to be Sinbad. I told you I wanted that, I told you at the time.'

'Sinbad! Pah! You and your fancy notions about sailors, the Navy, the sea. What did you ever do at sea to make us proud?'

Rosie knew how best to goad her husband. Chide him about his naval career, and there was no hope of his remaining calm. He threw his paper to the ground, stood up.

'Shut up, woman, will you? I want none of this tonight. What do you know about the Navy? What do you know about anything but keeping your petty little house?' Rosie sat down, flayed. Henry had gone too far, attacking her house. 'You're the one who's done the damage, take it from me. Lumbering the Boy with a name like that, making his life a bloody nightmare of embarrassment. How's that for motherly love?'

He was shouting so loud the people next door would hear.

On the white tablecloth Rosie's great boxy hands lay flushed and swollen.

'If he'd hated it so much, he could have asked us to call him something else.'

'I suppose you've forgotten he did ask you, many times, when he was a kid? I suppose you've forgotten what a scene you made? I suppose you've forgotten that. I suppose you've forgotten the days he'd come home from school upset by the teasing? I suppose –'

'Oh, stop repeating yourself, Henry Evans. I haven't forgotten.' In truth, she had, almost. In these ritual shouting matches Henry always reminded her. But the times in between the facts dissolved in her mind. 'Please don't shout any more.'

Tonight, more quickly than usual, her anger withered. She felt merely drained, limp. These fights would get them nowhere. Nothing now would ever change the only thing that came between them: the name of their son. Looking up at her husband, his great craggy face looming oddly from such a narrow head of grey hair, she saw that he, too, had exhausted his anger sooner than was customary.

'I'll go back out, get a breath of wind on me,' he said.

'Very well. I'll put the kettle on for when you come back.'

When he had gone Rosie continued to sit at the table without moving. She felt about her the profound silence that Henry had left behind: a silence polluted with dissatisfaction that was almost tangible. Her mind, as it always did after such upheavals, went back twenty-seven years ago, when it had all begun. For most of her pregnancy she and Henry had argued about whether or not the child should be called Sinbad. Rosie had always been adamantly against the idea, but could not think of an alternative name that appealed to Henry. Then, that wintry afternoon, when the baby was three days old, milk-smelling, sucking at her breast, it had come to her: Evans Evans. In her mind's eye she could see the words in gold paint on the side of a smart navy blue lorry. *Evans Evans*: it would be a most distinguished name for a contracting firm, an engineering firm – almost any sort of firm. With a name like that her son would start off with an advantage. He would go far. She would see to it he would go far. When Henry came back from work he cradled the baby in his big arms and she had told him her idea. He would be pleased at last, she had thought. He would see the point.

'Never,' he had said, quietly.

Rosie had not thought it worth arguing. Normally, throughout their married life, she wanted whatever Henry wanted. This time, her own desire was all that mattered. She did not contemplate changing her mind. She registered the child's name and told Henry later. He said nothing at the time, just refused ever to call the child anything but Boy. The contention between them became part of their lives. They scarcely acknowledged its existence and continued in their pattern of apparent happiness. Only infrequently, like tonight, did they give vent to their resentment. Such rare occasions, they hardly counted, thought Rosie, and chided herself for having been overcome by the silly rage that had spurred her when she walked through the door. She sighed, got up to put on the kettle. When Henry came back she would apologise: that was part of the ritual pattern. She would say sorry, love, and mean it; hand him his tea and rub briefly at his shoulder with the back of her cupped hand. In anticipation of peace, the horror of the past scene vanished as quickly as it had come. The nasty silence evaporated, too. Rain on windows, hum of steaming kettle, normality returned. Rosie's smile came back; she tried it out on herself in the small mirror above the fire. She would smile at Henry when he came back, welcome him: and all would be well again for months to come.

A pale night, the moon a scavenger among shifting clouds. Warm. Evans made his way along the edge of a wheat field to the barn. There was a smell of wet earth and hedgerows, a profoundly English smell that suffuses summer nights after rain. He felt good. All day he had been savouring the thought of the attic room, tempted to tell Brenda but determined not to. Brenda waited for him in the barn. Its dark shape was solid and comfortable against the rags of sky and trees. Evans smiled to himself, trying to remember when it was he had first called the barn the Hilton, and Brenda had laughed.

She was standing at the door. She held a rug, a Thermos, and a packet of Woodbines. Her shirt was undone almost to the waist, revealing the melon shapes of her breasts. Evans was surprised. Usually, she hid. He had to find her. It was one of their nocturnal games. By the time he had chased her voice in the dark, pretending to miss her whereabouts several times, and then fell upon her, poorly hidden between bales of straw, he could wait no longer. He would take her quickly, that first time. Later, they would make the rug comfortable and start all over again, more slowly.

'Why aren't you hiding?'

'Don't know.' Her mouth drooped. Evans remembered.

'Did Wilberforce –?' He had not thought about Wilberforce, or Elizabeth, all day. Lucky he remembered now.

'Yes.'

'Good.'

'He must have done it before I got there this morning. Lark gave me a medicine bottle of gin for my elevenses to get over it.'

'You mustn't think of Elizabeth any more.'

'I don't.'

'Let's lay out the rug.' They moved into the barn, climbed three steep steps made by bales of straw to the first flat floor. 'Shall we stay here, or go on up to the penthouse?'

'Stay here.'

They spread the rug and lay down. Evans put a hand on Brenda's denim thigh. His fingers kneaded a seam.

'Your hair smells nice.'

'So it ought.'

'Good thing the rain's come.'

'Lark's herb shampoo.'

'Shall I call for room service?'

Brenda tapped the Thermos.

'After.' Pause. 'What are you waiting for?'

'Just taking my time. I like looking up into the roof, don't you? Reckon I know those rafters better than any rafters in the whole bloody world.'

'Evans . . . get on with it.'

Denim thighs spread like a water diviner's stick. Free hand rumbling under the shirt, ripping buttons. Breasts warm round swirls of flesh. Nipples hard as corks.

'Go on,' she said, 'touch me.'

'Patience.'

'No.'

'Patience, I say.'

'Go on, Evans. Hurry.'

'Where?'

'You know where.'

'All right?'

'Um. Quick. Oh, that bloody light.'

'Like it. Can see you now.'

Silver moon prying through the great doorway. Dew glisten of flesh. Clothes flung away, limp corpses, aping stillness before this desire. Corn smell, hair smell, dust smell.

'Evans, do everything to me Evans. Anything you like.' She squelched beneath him. He sucked her. Mouth, throat, nipple, stomach. 'Go on.' Decent cloud, suddenly, to frustrate the moon's prurience. Only the feel, the taste, in darkness. Mutual churning world, making ready. Then the taking. Quiet groans, squeak of straw, arms slippery with sweat, biscuit-smelling rug.

'Oh, Evans.'

'Bren.'

'Don't move.'

'Christ, I like fucking you, Bren. Christ, I love you.'

'Shut up.'

Mood already sliding out of reach. Compliance gone. She'd be wanting a cigarette any minute. Or maybe she wouldn't. She went back to being unpredictable, after. After a night without it, he'd like her again at once.

'Ready?'

'Course.'

They moved.

Eventually they lay quite still, listened to the small sounds of mice, the shuffle of a bird in the rafters. They watched the clouds skirmish across the doorway, heard the church clock strike two.

'Lark should try it,' said Brenda. 'I keep telling her.'

'She'd be crushed to death, her little bones.' They both laughed.

'It's lovely at the Hilton nights like this, isn't it?' In mourning for a dead chicken Brenda was always at her most gentle. Evans loved her best after a hen had died.

'Lovely.'

'I wouldn't mind, really, if we never managed to find a real bed. We could go on staying at the Hilton all our lives.'

She pushed herself up on to one elbow, stretched a hand into the folds of the rug for cigarettes. Evans thought of the attic room, curtains from somewhere at the windows, a bowl of Mrs Browne's lilac by the bed. He kept his silence.

'Don't be daft.'

'I mean it.'

'One day you're going to set this place on fire, then we'll be done for.'

'Promise I won't.' Her hip bone was a small sharp hill against the sky. She blew a puff of white smoke that filtered up into the darkness of the rafters. Then lay back close to Evans.

'What do you like best about me, Bren?' These sort of times, he often dared ask her silly things.

'What you've just done to me, 'course.'

'Don't you like me for my good looks, my money, my car, my bloody faithfulness?'

Brenda giggled.

'You're a silly sod.'

'You're not so bad yourself. Here.'

'Hey, wait. I haven't finished it.'

'Well, there's one way to stop you.' He took the cigarette from her, stubbed it out on the Thermos.

'Waste of money. Want some tea?'

'Tea can wait.'

'You're a rare one, you are.'

'Kiss me. Go on. I'm going to lie here.' He pushed her coppery head on to his chest, continued to push it. Here in the barn there was no doubt who was master. Here she'd do anything he wanted, beg for more, be the one to ask. Here she was his, completely.

His girl. Brenda. Brenda Evans one day. His girl. There was her mouth at last. Funny how she could make the moon writhe like that, the clouds jumble about his eyes, private summer snow falling from the sky . . .

His girl Brenda.

The next prospective buyer to see Wroughton House was disturbingly keen. His enthusiasm for every detail filled Augusta with dread. He would change nothing, he said. He liked it all just as it was and would be willing to buy the furniture and pictures as well. The smell of the chimneys would not offend him – seeing his seriousness, Augusta made more of this than usual – because he had lost his sense of smell when he was blown up in the war. In desperation, Augusta was driven to decrying the garden: it was much too big for one man to cope with and no one else in the village was available to come even part-time; it was an endless expense and a perpetual worry. The elms were strangled with disease, he'd have to cut them all down, Augusta said. But the buyer was still undaunted. He waved his hand and mentioned contract gardeners: didn't matter how far they had to come. It wasn't till they reached the stable block Augusta discovered his Achilles heel. The old building, of historic interest, was in truth in the last stages of decay, its beams and bricks crumbling, its garage roof unsafe. To renovate it would cost many thousand pounds.

'At the moment,' said Augusta, 'the local pop group rehearse every evening in one of the loose boxes. But I told them they can only use it at their own risk. The roof may fall on top of them *at any moment.*' She avoided showing the man that particular loose box, whose roof was in fine order, and was rewarded to see the blood drain from his face. It seemed he was not interested in the bother of any kind of renovation. He liked to move into a place that needed no changes whatsoever. Responsibility for the stables would cause him more worry than he was prepared to take on. A pity, for he had so liked the house. He apologised for having taken so much of Augusta's time and left – as do all disappointed house hunters – very quickly.

The danger temporarily over once again, a little more time in hand, Augusta wondered where to glut her pleasure. She decided to go up to Evans's room in the attic, which she was preparing with much energy. To do something positive again, for someone else, had filled the last few days with great delight. She had found curtains, more rugs for the floor, a table and two armchairs. She had polished, dusted and swept, given a coat of white paint to the small fireplace and window sills. Evans had returned on a couple of occasions. He had stood about awkwardly, wondering what he could do to help, and had seemed relieved to find Augusta organising it all with such efficiency. She had made up the bed yesterday, and promised it would all be finished by the weekend. Now she fetched a pile of things she had collected from all parts of the house with which to finally bring the room alive: books, pictures, ashtrays, mugs and candles, bowls of cowslips. She busied about trying out the things in different places, and at last there was nothing further left to do. She sat in one of the armchairs, creaky but comfortable and looked about her.

Hugh would have been pleased, could he see the room now. He had always regretted they had not been able to finish the attics, and rarely visited them. She had told him about the transformation on the telephone. He had tried not to sound interested, and had asked if all the effort wasn't a bit silly for so short a time? Augusta had assured him it was most sensible, quite apart from being nice for Evans, and Hugh had said, 'Well, you'll do whatever you want, as usual.' 'I *can't* be as foolish as you say I am,' she had replied, and put down the telephone. Their conversations always seemed to end on a fatuous level, these days. It was no good on the telephone. If only Hugh would come down, just for one day. They could talk properly, then. But he refused. He said there was no more talking to be done.

Perhaps he was right. Going round in circles was merely destructive. There was nothing new to add. She had repeated so many times that she knew it to be almost entirely her fault, this catastrophe, and asked to be forgiven and to be granted one more chance. He had equally repeated that he forgave her: of course he forgave her, but she had killed something within him (and it was not the first time she had killed the thing she loved, remember) that could never be resuscitated. A substitute arrangement would be no good. He would rather go. And so he had gone.

Oh, Hugh, thought Augusta. What have I done?

This was their house. Other people haunted it, slightly, but she could scarcely remember them. In this very room, one chilly afternoon, she had spent an hour with a lover, for whom she cared nothing, uncomfortable on the bare prickly mattress. Hugh had never found out, but it had been a mistake. When it was over she was glad the man had gone quickly, leaving the house alone for her and Hugh again. A sentimental old film on television, that particular evening, she remembered; she had cried at the end, using it as a front to her terrible deception, the thing that in truth was the cause of her crying.

Now there was no possibility of more years together. She had destroyed all that and had to accept the consequences. While despising self-pity, and indeed never allowing herself to indulge in it, Augusta accepted the fact that regret was something she would have to live for the rest of her life. She reflected that regret is an indestructible weed that can exist among fine emotions; not a killer, just a strangler that can exhaust its victim.

She looked at her watch: four o'clock. Always the worst time of day, for her. Since Hugh had gone, Augusta was tempted to sleep much more in the daytime. She half-relished this easy way to traverse the hours, but at the same time cursed herself for losing precious time in the house. Now, faced with the long evening, she was suddenly depressed by the thought of the ashes in the fire downstairs. Conscious of her guilt, she went to the bed she had caringly prepared for Evans and Brenda. She lay down on the quilted cover, and slept there till next morning.

Henry Evans stood at his front door, looked at the sky above the elms, and made his judgement. It wasn't going to rain. He pulled the door shut behind him, buttoned up his jacket, and started off down the road.

Rows always released in him a new silence, and after the little upheaval last night, though all of course was calm now, he did not see fit to tell Rosie where he was going. He walked fast, just in case she should shout after him, striding widely over the puddles rather than skirting them, to help release the stiffness in his legs that had come from a morning of sitting in his chair. He enjoyed the sound of his own footsteps on the wet road, the wind against his face, the bright green of the hedgerows. Mackay lived a mile outside the village, in a pre-war bungalow. He and Evans had been to school together. A wiry little sandy-haired thing he was, then: not up to much as far as books went, but a good fighter. Henry could remember being flayed by Mackay's inky fists in the playground one day, thoroughly beaten. The cause for the row he could not recall, but in the end Mackay had passed his handkerchief for Henry to wipe his bloody lip, and they had become friends. Mackay had been a pilot in the war, but returned to the village; one of the few from their school-days to do so. Unmarried, he kept to himself, making annual appearances at local horticultural shows, where he consistently won all the big prizes for vegetables. He and Henry had little in common these days, and never intruded upon their sparse relationship by making plans to meet. But Henry counted Mackay among his friends. On rare occasions when they ran into each other in the Star, where Mackay celebrated his victories, they exchanged the odd word, shorthand acknowledgement of days past spent blowing robins' eggs and poaching pheasants in the bluebell woods.

Henry pictured Mackay's surprise. He would not, he knew, be asked into the house. Mackay was not an inhospitable man – it simply never occurred to him anyone would care to pass through his front door. As on the only other two occasions Henry had come to visit him, they would doubtless stand one each side of the wrought iron gate at the end of the front path.

Mackay's bungalow stood close to the road. Behind it rose an impressive amount of greenhouses. In front, the small patch of ground that divided it from the road, which most proud gardeners would have crammed with flowers, was completely cemented over. Not a blade of grass, not a ruffle of aubretia to soften the back-yard appearance. Only a miniature windmill, broken arms whirling in the wind, and a single stone gnome hunched over his fishing line, were rooted in the hard ground. Henry always wondered why Mackay, whose pleasure in life was to care for prize vegetables in the soft earth at the back of his house, should create such bleakness in the front. He could only conclude that the contrast was the thing that appealed to Mackay. Dead ground in one place, young shoots in another – perhaps Mackay had intended a constant surprise for himself.

His face was at the window. Henry stopped at the road side of the gate, not presuming to enter the cement territory. Mackay hurried out lest his friend should do so. His boots made an urban clatter in his garden. He was bent, old-looking, soil engrained in his hands, black nails.

'There, Evans, I was just giving myself a cup of tea.'

'Hope I'm not at an inconvenient time?'

'Not at all, not at all. I'm my own master, master of my own hours.' They looked at each other. Henry had imagined the encounter taking place on a sunny day. This greyness, all his rehearsed words seemed to have fled.

'Vegetables coming on all right, are they?'

'Lovely, just as ever.'

'Ah.'

'You keeping all right? And the wife?'

'Very nicely, thanks.' Henry put a hand on the curly top of the iron gate. Mackay backed away a pace, fear of entry by his friend clear on his face.

'Ah, Evans, you were just passing by, then?'

'Just passing. I'll be on my way. Though I was wondering . . .' The sky seemed darker, the wind pecked about his trousers. But it was Mackay who noticed the rain first. Alert of hearing, he heard a drop fall behind him.

'There, I knew we'd have another shower.'

'We could do with a drop. Do you ever sell your stuff, Mackay? Privately, I mean.'

'Take a load to the market couple of times a week.'

'Privately, though? Cauliflowers in particular, I mean. I was referring to cauliflowers in particular.'

'Cauliflowers in particular?' Mackay scratched the back of his neck. Rain was splattering down on the cement quite fast by now. 'Can't say I've ever really thought about it.'

Henry removed his hand from the gate. The gesture caused Mackay some relief: he folded his arms to think, unaware of the increasing damp of his shirt. Henry was grateful for Mackay's apparent oblivion to so heavy a shower. If he hurried away now there would be no chance to settle the matter.

'It's like this, Mackay.' He heard a note of confidence in his own voice. 'Some time soon, in the near future, like, there might be an emergency situation. Not to trouble you with details, I might find myself in a position when I should like to drive here, no notice, and buy a couple of cauliflowers off of you. How would that strike you?'

Mackay shrugged.

'Easy. Why not? You'll always find me out the back.'

'But prize cauliflowers, Mackay. I'd want a couple of the prize jobs. You know, make a person sit up when they saw them.'

Sudden comprehension swarmed over Mackay's wet face. He narrowed his eyes, making rain fall faster down his cheeks. He licked some of it away with his tongue.

'Would I be right in thinking you'd want them for someone in hospital?'

Henry paused only an instant.

'That sort of thing. For someone in hospital, in a manner of speaking, yes.'

'I took tons of green stuff up to my mother when she was dying in the Royal, you know. She said take away your blooming gladioli, Jack, she said: you can keep your blooming flowers. What I want is nice spring greens.'

'That's why I want the cauliflowers.'

'I never took her caulis, come to think of it.'

Henry felt the rain pouring down his neck.

'Would that be all right, then, Mackay – Jack? If I just came sudden like and got a couple of cauliflowers?'

'Dare say. Though I couldn't promise you the real prize stuff, could I? The second best would have to do you. Don't suppose many people could tell it was second best. Lovely heads.'

'Wonderful, how many prizes you get, you know, Jack.' His mission happily accomplished, Henry felt it easy to be complimentary. Mackay shrugged again.

'Got a few in my time.'

'Well, I'd best be getting back. The rain. You'll be expecting me when you see me, then?'

Mackay nodded.

'Mind, you'll have to twist their arms up at the hospital kitchens,' he said. 'They're devils about cooking brought-in greens.'

Henry turned his face into the slant of the shower, head held high. The rain soaked his feet and splashed his trousers, but he had no care. If the sparkling hedges had been covered in diamonds he could not have felt more excitement: never had he imagined his little transaction could have been so easy. He felt a warmth of gratitude to Mackay and all such uncurious men in the world, men with an instinct for making things easy. Now all he had to do was wait. Soon, the time would come. There he'd be, the two heads of cauliflowers in his hands, their pale crumbly flowers bursting from their leaves, huge, huge. The Leopard would be amazed.

The Leopard. His dear Leopard. There were tears among the rain in his eyes.

Henry's blood pumped fast with the joy of having achieved something that was linked with the woman who consumed his thoughts. The fact that she was unaware not only of his existence, but also of the surprise he was preparing for her, made no difference to his elation. He would feed off the pleasure for weeks, if necessary, trying to be patient, keeping a constant watch on the Star. He would be protected from the irritations of every-day life by his private anticipation. In such high spirits, even Rosie's concern about his wet condition, her chivvying about with hot drinks and dry clothes, could not touch him. The success of his cauliflower plan had brought the Leopard wonderfully close. No one would guess, from looking at him, he was alone with her in his heart.

It was still raining at nine that night when Evans drove along the same road towards Brenda's flat. The room in Wroughton House had been ready for a week now. For some reason which he could not decipher, even to himself, he had preserved the news all this time. Tonight, irritated by his father's sniffing by the fire, Evans had on impulse decided to get out of the house, and tell Brenda. It was not one of their regular nights. She would not be expecting him – she would be washing her hair, probably, having one of her gossipy evenings with Lark. Still, armed as he was with good news,

Evans imagined he would be welcome.

Lark answered the door. Surprise clouded her small face. Brenda was out, she said. Just gone down to the Air Base for a drink. Some party, she thought it was; why didn't he come in and wait? Brenda was bound not to be late.

Evans followed Lark into the sitting-room. The remains of a solitary supper lay on the table: half a piece of burnt toast, a jar of salmon fish paste, a bottle of tomato ketchup. Lark switched on the gas fire. The room was always dank.

'So who's she gone with?' Evans managed to sit himself quite jovially in the chair by the fire.

'That I don't know exactly,' said Lark, carefully. 'Some bloke she met somewhere, I think. Quite harmless.' She glanced at Evans's face. 'Like a gin?'

'Thanks.'

'I've eaten, but I could get you something.'

'No thanks, just a drink. She never mentioned this bloke to me.'

'No, well, she probably didn't think it important. Some men aren't important, are they, after all? Not worth mentioning, really.' Lark gave a small laugh, handed Evans a glass half full of neat gin.

'You've given me a whopper, Lark.'

'Go on. Drink it slowly.'

Evans took a gulp of the drink.

'We are engaged, you know,' he said, 'Brenda and me.'

'Well, that's very old news.' Lark smiled kindly.

'And would you consider, seeing as we're engaged – would you consider, in the circumstances, it's right that my fiancée should go gallivanting off to some party at the Air Base with another bloke, without so much as a word to me?'

'Well,' said Lark, 'depends.'

'Depends on what?'

Lark searched her mind for a word Evans had recently used.

'Circumstances,' she said.

'Ah, circumstances.' The gas fire's blue flames were

rubbing heat into Evans's shins. For a moment he experienced the dream-like feeling of running fast and yet not moving from the same spot: help from Lark seemed a long way off. 'In which circumstances would all this be correct?' he asked.

'Well,' said Lark, pouring herself a large measure of gin to give herself time, 'I think if you've been engaged to someone for a long time, like you and Brenda, and you trust each other, like you two do – well, then, there's no harm in it, is there? I mean going to a dance with someone else will only make her *appreciate* you much more. Don't you think?'

Evans looked at her. There was no doubt in her eyes. 'I don't know,' he said. 'Perhaps I'm being ungenerous.'

'I think perhaps you are. A bit, anyway.'

'I wouldn't have minded if she had told me. I would have understood, wouldn't I?'

'Oh, Evans, stop worrying. It's nothing to worry about, honestly. She'll explain all right. She'll be back soon. You just wait here by the fire. But if you don't mind –' she went to the door ' – I'll get back to my room. I was just in the middle of doing my nails.' She held up a hand. Three nails were scarlet, two were still unpainted.

'Who are you tarting yourself up for, then?' Lark liked to be teased.

'Just keeping my hands nice. You never know what to expect round the next corner, do you?'

'You're a funny girl, Lark.'

'You keep helping yourself to gin. It silvers the mind, you know.' She shut the door behind her.

Evans drank the first glass slowly. It was not a taste he liked, but it did indeed silver the mind. He listened happily enough to the small wheeze of the gas fire, and let his eyes curl about the twisted flames. He thought of silver birches, for some reason, their leaves up-brushed by the wind. He thought of his collection of sixpences: as a child, he had dropped them in the snow. They had made small glinting holes, like the beginnings of a thaw. Picking them up, the cold had bitten into his fingers, making them clumsy as he tried to stuff them back into the jar. Perhaps Lark was right, he thought, and there was no need to worry. In all this time Brenda had not betrayed him. Why should she now? Probably, as Lark said, she was just enjoying the dancing. There'd be nothing funny, no funny business. Brenda would never allow that, would she? But then why had she said nothing? Why hadn't she said there's this bloke, Evans, who wants to take me dancing?

He finished the last of his drink. No one ever wanted just to take a girl dancing these days, did they? Especially a girl like Brenda.

The realisation broke savagely within Evans. He stood, poured more gin from the bottle on the table, conscious that his head, chest and shoulders were all hurting, a physical pain. Away from the fire, the heat of his legs began to fade: a chill, as if he'd been caught in a sudden wind, lashed over his body. The small, ordinary things in the room, the plain furniture and thin curtains, trembled as if they too were affected by the wind. Evans picked up the piece of burnt toast, ate it. It was bitter on his tongue, but food would steady him, he thought. He would ask Lark if he could help himself to a piece of bread and butter.

Carrying his drink he left the room, hesitated on the dark landing, then knocked at her door. She called to him to come in. He opened the door, quickly shut it behind him lest the stuffy warmth, which flowed up to him like the corner of a summer afternoon, should escape.

'All this gin,' he said, 'could you let me have some bread and butter, Lark?'

Lark was lying back on her bed in her dressing-gown. Barefoot, her scarlet toe nails plucked at the candlewick bedspread, making it writhe between them. She held her hands above her head, the nails flashing at Evans like a procession of ladybirds.

'Oh, dear, of course,' she said. 'Give us a minute and I'll get it for you.'

'Thanks.'

Lark smiled at him.

'I can see you're not a gin drinker,' she said.

'No.'

'I like it. It makes me feel happy.' She sat up, swinging her legs on to the wool rug beside the bed. There was a long silence between them. Then Evans said:

'One thing I've always meant to ask you, Lark: I've never understood about your name. I suppose your Mum said to you one day, when you were a kid, "you sing like a lark". And it stuck.'

Lark laughed.

'Yes, she did, as a matter of fact.'

'Funny how names stick.'

'Funny, yes.' She put her hands to her waist to tighten the cord of her dressing-gown.

An absurd pleasure at having made Lark laugh, at having guessed correctly the reason for her name, caused Evans to sway a little on his feet. Then the vision of Brenda, obliterated briefly by the gin, came back to him. She was dancing close to some man. Close to him and wanting him.

'Take that thing off,' Evans said. He was surprised, considering the fuzzy condition of his head, at the harshness of his own voice. With an economic gesture that conveyed a life of response to duty, Lark undid the dressing-gown. She threw it to the bottom of her bed. Then she lay back, eyes wide but showing no surprise.

Evans looked at her. The small fierce light that hung from the ceiling glared on to the flat white surfaces of her body, reminding him of snow. Her nipples were black chips, hard as charcoal: her limbs, scattered in awkward shapes, thin as winter branches. From her breastbone to her naval ran a jagged scar, its ruckled join a shining silver membrane. Each side of the scar, pink dots dimpled the flat white skin. Evans licked at the corners of his mouth, tasting the gin.

'You know what I'm going to do to you?' he said.

Lark lowered her eyes to look at him. She put one hand on the scar, feeling down its ridge with a scarlet fingernail.

'Yes.'

'What do you think about that?'

'Oh, get on with it, Evans.' Her voice was weary, impatient, without care.

Evans struggled to undo his belt, his trousers, his shirt. His hands were clumsy. Lark's eyes, very bleak, remained upon him. In his impatience, he shuffled himself awkwardly to the bed, trousers round his ankles. He crashed down upon her, felt her small bones writhe beneath him, the helpless flutter of a dying bird. He smelt nail polish – her fingers were clattering about his ears – and the sickly smell of hairspray as his nose dug about the brittle, frosty mesh of her hair. He felt himself to be lying on cold flat earth, enraged by the lack of undulations beneath him, but too desirous of release to get up.

It was over in a moment. Evans cried out, Lark remained silent. She pushed at his shoulders, eager for him to be gone. He sat up, swung his legs on to the floor, pulled his trousers up over his knees.

'Do you often do that?' he asked.

'Time to time. Not here. I wouldn't like men in my room, except you.'

'Brenda and me have often wondered if you had a boyfriend. Where do you do it, then?'

Lark, eyes shut, shrugged her bony shoulders.

'There are people at the office. Randy men. Lunchtime. Here, give me that.' Evans threw the dressing-gown over her. 'There's a room where they keep the files. Airless in summer, freezing cold in winter.'

Evans stood up, pulling his clothes together. Lark was a childlike mound on the bed. Impossible to imagine her, grey jersey and skirt pulled up, giving pleasure to some randy clerk who had backed her up against the files.

'Can't be much fun, like that,' he said.

'It isn't.'

'Well, it can be good.'

'Brenda says it's good with you.'

'Did you think so?'

Lark opened her eyes, cast upon him her usual consideration.

'Well, you didn't try with me, did you? I could hardly expect that, these conditions. Still, it was better with you than with the others. Don't worry though – I won't remember it.' She sat up, patting at her dead hair which, in the skirmish, had lost its temporary boost and had fallen back into its old partings. 'Now I'd like you to go, please, Evans. You can go back to the other room, help yourself to bread and butter, sit by the fire. You can wait there. Brenda shouldn't be long. I want to go to sleep.'

Evans took the remains of his drink from amongst the cacti on the bedside table. He felt in need of more alcohol. Deflated. His body still ached with an unfamiliar pain.

'You might tell me now, then, who she's with.'

'I won't, and I can't. I don't know his name and if I did I wouldn't tell you because she's my friend, Brenda.'

Evans laughed.

'Your friend? And you've just –'

'Go on, Evans, get out.'

'If I were you, I wouldn't tell her, for all she's your friend!'

'I wouldn't say too much about it either, if I were you.'

'You can trust me. But if she buggers off, some other bloke, I've every right to –'

'Go on, Evans. Please. I'm tired.' Lark stood up. In the moment before she succeeded in securing her dressing-gown Evans caught sight of red marks on her flat breasts, the beginnings of a bruise beneath a sharp hip bone. Perhaps he had hurt her. He could not remember how it had been. But her eyes were limp, in deep shadow despite the blaze of the overhead light. She seemed to be exhausted, very old.

'I'm going,' he said. 'You all right?' Lark nodded. 'I didn't intend, you know . . .'

'No need to explain.'

'Night, then, Lark.'

Back in the sitting-room he closed the door and sat at the

table. It was two-thirty by the clock on the fireplace. The bottle of gin was empty. The gas fire hissed and spluttered: there was a faint smell of gas. Evans felt both sick and hungry. He opened the jar of fish paste, scraped inside it with a knife. It had a sour, smooth taste, nothing to do with salmon, difficult to swallow. He heard Lark open her window and switch off her light. In a few moments, he hoped, poor battered scrap of a thing, she would be asleep. Perhaps by morning she would not remember much of tonight. Perhaps she would be able to cocoon herself back into the small scarlet world of her room unharmed, unresentful. She was a good friend, Lark. He would not want to hurt her.

Evans lay his head on his folded arms. He had no wish to think about it any more. He slept.

Two hours later he was woken by Brenda opening the door. In the stone-coloured dawn, increasing in the window, he saw that she wore a shawl over her shoulders – a shawl he had not seen before. Her hair was glossy as usual, but then it was the kind of hair that never tousled, no matter how energetic had been their love-making. Her face? How was her face? Through his aching eyes Evans found it hard to tell. Soft, somehow. The lines of defence, so familiar to him in daylight, evaporated. Sulky.

'What the hell are you doing here?'

She leant up against the door, head back, one knee bent, the pose she so often used against the chicken shed when she knew Evans was approaching. 'It wasn't your night for coming round. Spying on me?'

Evans picked up the empty fish paste jar, rolled it in his hands, feeling the ridged glass. Confused by sleep, head full of searing pains, he had to be careful. He had to take things slowly: not do or say anything reckless, or she'd go. She was in a mood, Brenda was, he could see. If he was too hard on her, she'd go for ever.

'It's half-past four,' he said, looking at the clock.

'So?'

'That's late to be out with another bloke when you're

engaged to be married to me.'

Brenda slouched towards the sofa, her bed, and slumped down upon it. She crossed her legs, pulled the shawl round her breasts, leaned against the wall. An uncomfortable, uncaring position.

'I haven't done nothing wrong,' she said.

'I don't know what you've done, do I?'

'I'm telling you.'

'Who was he? Why didn't you tell me?'

'He gave me a lift last week.'

'I've told you, Bren, you shouldn't go getting hitches any more, not looking like you do. You're asking for trouble.' In his effort to be calm, reasonable, Evans spoke very slowly.

'He was nice enough, works up at the Air Base. Said there was going to be this party, would I like to go? You know how you don't like parties. I didn't think there would be any harm.'

'Is this the first time you've done anything like this?'

'Like what? I haven't done nothing wrong.'

'Gone out with someone else, not telling me. I wouldn't have minded if you'd told me.'

'You would. Bet you would. You'd have got yourself so screwed up I wouldn't have been able to go.'

Evans sighed.

'Where'd you get that shawl?'

'Bought it.'

'What, for the party? Specially for the party?'

Brenda shrugged. She ran a finger round the outline of her lips, to test if they hurt, a thing she often did after Evans had kissed her fiercely.

'I needed a shawl.'

Evans felt his heart quicken. He rolled the jar faster in his hands. Brenda, defiant, was beautiful on the bed. Out to provoke him.

'We're engaged to be married, you know,' he said.

He had intended to say something quite different. Something witty and light, to make her laugh and ask forgiveness.

Then, in spite of the cruel headache, he would kiss her and take her, make her cry out she was sorry –

'So why did you come round? Spying?'

'I came round to give you some news.'

'Oh, yes.'

'Honestly.'

'Postage going up again, is it?'

'Bitch.'

Brenda laughed.

'You look quite furious, sitting there. Quite the furious fiancé. Here, come and sit down.' For a moment, patting the bed with a hand that slipped from out of the shawl, she was almost coquettish. Without giving himself time to think whether he did the right thing, Evans went to her. He too leant his head uncomfortably against the wall, stuffed his hands in his trouser pockets. They made ugly lumps, material growths, upon his solid thighs. Through the window he could see a strand of lemony light on the prison walls.

'I'm not yours, you know,' said Brenda. 'I'm not yours to possess, absolutely. Not now, or when we're married, or ever.'

'But we're engaged.' Frustrated to hear himself repeating this feeble protestation, Evans tried to scour the thumping mess of his head to find a more lucid reason for his distress. 'And when people are engaged, there are usually rules. Duties to each other.'

'So there may be,' said Brenda. 'But people make their own rules. So if yours are different from mine, well then, you have to live by yours and I have to live by mine.'

'That attitude takes no account of love.'

'Ah, love.' She pouted. 'If you really loved me you wouldn't be making this silly scene. You'd be letting me get to bed.'

With sudden relief, Evans took this as a hint. He leant towards her, fumbling at the shawl, aiming his mouth at hers. Brenda pulled back, grimacing.

'You smell horrible! You smell of gin. Take your hand *off*, Evans. You're hurting.'

Evans tightened his grip on her shoulder. The sudden energy of anger flowed through him, giving strength to his drained body, numbing the pain in his head. Incredulous, he kneaded her flesh. Brenda was rejecting him. Back from the Air Base with another man, she was rejecting him, her rightful fiancé.

'What did he do to you?'

'Leave . . . me . . . *alone*.' Brenda struggled. 'He didn't do anything.'

'Is that the truth?'

'That's the truth – you wouldn't know the truth.' She closed her eyes. Her mouth squirmed open in pain. Evans felt a smile spread across the stiff skin of his own mouth.

'I'd kill him if he touched you.'

'Bragger!' In spite of her discomfort Brenda managed to spit out the word. 'You wouldn't hurt a mouse.'

'That's what you think. Did he touch you?'

'No! You're hurting me, Evans! Let go.' She kicked uselessly at his shin. In her struggle to get away from him she slid to a lying position on the bed. Evans glared down at her, his breath fast.

'Did he touch you? Did he touch you?'

'No! Stop shouting. You'll wake – all right, in the car! In the car, if you must know, he put his hand on the back of my neck and I told him, I told him, Evans, *not to go on*!'

She was crying now. Evans gave her just one slap on the face. It stung his hand.

He stood up, examined his own palm and huge fingers in the light that was now pale and clear. Then he looked at Brenda, head in her shawl, whimpering. The sound bubbled in strange harmony with the hiss of the gas fire. One of her shoes had fallen off. Her bare foot, moving slightly, was blackish between the toes.

'I'll not be seeing you for a week or so, then,' Evans said. 'I'll have to be thinking things over.'

Outside, he was struck by the chill of dawn. He had

arrived, so long ago, without a coat. Now, in the car, he shivered.

Evans drove home but could not tolerate the idea of spending the two hours till breakfast in his room. Instead, he decided, he would go to the room awaiting him in Wroughton House. He had the key to the back door. He would not wake Mrs Browne.

He walked slowly up the front drive, no longer aware of the cold. Ground mists were rising from the lawns and distant fields. They frothed, too, about the base of the house, confusing the more solid lines of lavender. Evans felt stiffness in his legs. He moved from the drive, whose scrunch broke the silence, to the grass. He took long strides across to the natural pond, dew soaking his shoes. The air was soft with promise of a fine day, but no mere panacea of early morning could quell the feelings insurgent within him. When madness settles upon men's minds, the madness of lust or rage or jealousy, the path to reason is quite lost: the desire to find it, even, obliterated. Thus it was that Evans strode almost blindly about the gardens, the bright trees, the white of hawthorn flower and brown glint of water hurting, rather than healing, his eyes. One thing only was clear to him: Brenda, always so elusive, was now quite lost to him. Knowing little of her Birmingham childhood, Evans judged her to be a girl unused to violence: they had had rows before, but never like this. She would have every right to leave him, now. His reckless behaviour had not 'accounted for love'. The irony of his own words, chiding words of just an hour or so ago, tightened the band of terrible pressure about his head.

He passed the kitchen window for the third time. A figure waved at him from within. The church clock struck six. He went inside.

Mrs Browne had made the kitchen warm. Coffee puckered on the stove. Evans sat down at the white table, chosen in the days when efficient cooking was required to fill the needs of constant guests. Mrs Browne, small as Lark, it occurred to Evans, was in a dressing-gown – pretty quilted cotton stuff, nothing like Lark's, *that*: he might have had the energy to admire it on a more ordinary occasion. There were shadows under her eyes: deep as evening shadows upon tired faces, strange so early in the morning. Taking a seat opposite Evans she poured two cups of coffee, pushed a bowl of sugar and jug of milk towards him.

'I was up early. I saw you wandering about,' she said.

'I've had a night.'

'Aren't you cold?'

'Warmer now, thanks.'

They sat in silence for a while, two people so deeply submerged in that state of preoccupation with their own thoughts that neither could summon the energy to enquire about the other. Eventually Evans said:

'I went to tell her the news about the room. I thought she'd be pleased, and I hit her.'

'She'd been out with someone else?' Evans nodded. One of several good things about Mrs Browne was that she understood things before there was need to explain.

'So I didn't tell her in the end. About the room, I mean. No use now, really. I mean, I suppose it's all over between us.'

Curiously, considering the seriousness of the situation, Mrs Browne smiled.

'Of course it's not! I should go and tell her tonight, if I were you. Bring her here.'

'I told her I wasn't going to see her again for a week or so. I told her I had to think things over.'

'Oh, I shouldn't do that.' Mrs Browne was almost gay. 'There's no point in thinking things over if you know what you ultimately want. Besides, leaving her for a week will give *her* time to think up all sorts of things against you. Stupid.'

'But I hit her.'

'Women can survive a few bashes.'

'Never imagined I could do such a thing, not in all my life.'

'I expect she provoked you.'

'She did. She provoked me all right.' He paused. 'The thing about Brenda, it's always been the same, I never know where I am with her. She's my fiancée. She's mine, isn't she? Yet I can't seem to . . . get a real hold of her. I can't seem to be sure of her, ever. I'm always scared she's just out of my reach.' He poured himself more coffee, warm now. The heaviness of his head was lifting. 'I don't know how to set about it, I've tried all different ways. I do everything I can for her, show her I love her. I'm always there when she needs me. She knows she can rely on me. We're marvellous in – well,' he managed to smile, 'in the barn. It's just this unsureness. It unnerves me. I don't know if you can understand.'

'Perhaps it makes you too anxious, too clinging, too demanding. Perhaps it irritates her, your constantly wanting her reassurance and presence.' Mrs Browne looked at him. 'Perhaps you're claustrophobic.'

Evans looked back at her. Her eyes were humorous.

'Never thought of that,' he said. 'I thought women liked all the reassurance bit. Thought I was doing the right thing.'

'Some women do, same as some men. Others, only to a certain extent. But to a few people, I think, the confines of absolute security are inhibiting, imprisoning. To be escaped from. The clever thing, once you've judged your partner, is then to judge just how strong you should make your net of security. It must have some – ' she searched for the word ' – *slack*. It must have some slack which can be taken up. Cast it too tight and the natural reaction, to some people, will be to escape.'

They remained in further silence, Evans thinking about her words. He was not entirely clear what she meant, but he had caught her gist. Her understanding, anyhow, was a comfort: she had renewed in him an almost inevitable hope that perhaps after all the ghastly night was not the end with Brenda.

'That shows your education,' he said at last.

'Oh, I haven't much education. I don't know much.

Nothing of any consequence when it comes to . . .' Evans's problems seem to have faded from her.

'Why were you up so early?' he asked.

'There are more people coming today to see the house. There haven't been any for ages, but they're coming today. People who want it for an office.'

'Don't worry, it's no good as an office, is it?' Their roles suddenly reversed, strength gathered within Evans.

'Well, it might be. A *prestige* office they say they want, whatever that is.'

'You can go on to them about the chimneys, can't you? The smoke, the bloody awful smell.'

'Oh, I shall. I shall tell them the whole place is falling down.' She spoke like a defiant child.

'But you can't go on staying here for ever, can you? I mean, one day, someone's going to buy it whether you like it or not.'

'Of course I can't stay here for ever. That's quite impossible. Anyhow it would be ridiculous, wouldn't it? Just me all alone in a house like this, no money left? Oh, I quite see how ridiculous it would be. But I shan't go before the autumn. I can't go before the mulberries . . . I want another Christmas here. I must be here another Christmas.'

'What, alone?'

'I don't mind being alone.'

'Well, I don't suppose the office people will want it. It would be quite wrong for an office, wouldn't it? Lovely place like this.'

Evans got up. Mrs Browne remained where she was.

'Tell Brenda tonight,' she said. 'Bring her here.'

'Might,' said Evans. 'I'll think about it. I must go now. Thanks very much for the coffee.'

Outside the sun was high, the dew melted. He walked back down the drive elated by the rise of new optimism. Events of the night, unlike happy events which harden into reality in retrospect, had become insubstantial in the daylight. Their consequences no longer threatened.

Evans looked forward to a breakfast of eggs and bacon. He would relish, this morning, his father's taciturnity and his mother's cooking. Rosie met him as he opened the door.

'Good Lord, Evans,' she cried, 'and where have you been all night? Your father's ill. I've been up hours with him, and you not here. The doctor's on his way. I've not known what to think.'

Five miles away Brenda and Lark were also much preoccupied with their own thoughts. It was their custom to speak little in the morning, a habit which, properly observed between close friends, saves all the inaccuracy of recounting nocturnal events too soon. Later, an evening alone together, her opinions finally set, Brenda would reveal what had happened. (Lark, naturally, would be called upon to do no such thing: *her* night, as Brenda would suppose, as usual having been spent in dull solitary fashion.) For now, Lark kept to their arrangement of asking no question that strayed beyond politeness. As usual she had got up before Brenda and made breakfast. Baked beans, this morning: knowing them to be Brenda's favourite, she chose them, perhaps a silent apology.

'Marvellous,' said Brenda, sitting at the table. 'I'm ravenous.'

'Evans finished the gin and finished the fish paste waiting for you,' said Lark, 'so there's nothing to go on our toast.'

'He was in a right mood when I got back, I can tell you.'

'Thought he might be. Have a good time?'

'Not bad.' Brenda's mouth was full. 'You're a bloody marvellous cook.'

'Oh, I don't know.' Lark was naturally modest about her talents. 'Anyhow I've had this good idea. In the night – it came to me in the night.'

'What's that?'

'I've decided that I shall put it about that I'd be quite willing to sing for charity.'

'How do you mean, sing for charity?'

'Well, you know, if there's a do somewhere in aid of something, and they want a singer, I'd be quite prepared to do it for nothing. For just a drink and something to eat. For the experience.'

'Good idea,' said Brenda. Another morning she would have been more receptive to a new idea to further Lark's career. As it was, wiping up the last of her beans with a piece of toast, she lacked concentration.

'So that's what I'm going to do,' said Lark, 'let it be known I'm available – in that way.' She smiled at her own joke. 'And if you want to do me a great favour, you'd put it about a bit, too.'

'Put what about, Lark?' Brenda was blowing her tea.

'What I've just been saying. Weren't you *listening*?'

'Oh, that. The singing. Yes. All right. 'Course. I'll put it about a bit too.'

'Thanks very much.' Lark was gathering up the plates. 'Sometimes you don't know what a friend you are. I'll be sure to get you free tickets and seats in the front row.'

'That'd be wonderful, Lark. I'll look forward to that, really I will. Honestly,' said Brenda.

Henry Evans was not very ill, but the plight of his mind had exacerbated the condition of his body. A soaking in the rain, the excitement of anticipation – the combination had been too much for his normally stable equilibrium. His temperature soared. He had a feverish chill, Rosie said, and, spelt out like that, the courage Henry had shown among the waves gave way to alarm.

Soon as Evans had gone out (after Brenda, no doubt, foolish Boy, though now Henry felt a new sympathy) he had allowed himself to be put to bed. Rosie, naturally, put a good face on the whole matter: her stalwart smile, slightly askew with real concern, would have touched the heart of anyone who had not lived with her for thirty-eight years, and who knew how delighted she was at last to have found a good reason to exercise her love and caring to the full. She stuffed the pillows into new cases – the old ones had only been on two nights – took clean pyjamas from the airing cupboard, and filled three hot-water bottles. She put aspirin, water, and a single iris in a milk bottle by the bed, cluttering up the small table in a way that left Henry speechless with irritation. She brought him the *Daily Mirror*, newly folded, knowing he had already read it thoroughly, but wondering if he might like to go through it again. On the matter of whether or not the window should be open she was undecided for some time: but after a series of tests, darting her head in and out, licking a finger to find a breeze, she came to the conclusion that it should be shut now, while Henry warmed up, open for a while to air the room later, and finally shut when they put out the light. A moment later, having made this final decision, she snatched at the privilege of changing her mind: perhaps her plan was unwise after all. That way, she said cheerfully, Henry was bound to catch his death. No: the door should be left open, the window firmly shut. That was the solution. She herself, of course, was unable to sleep in a room without plenty of fresh air: but that was no matter because she would be quite comfortable downstairs in the armchair. Henry wasn't to worry about her at all. With a silent nod he agreed he would do no such thing, and at last she left the room.

Protected as he was from Rosie by the visions of his Leopard, the steely needle of real alarm, that punctured even this protective skin, concerned death: what if he should die, now, unable to see the Leopard again? That he should go to his grave without ever speaking of his love, without enriching her life with the knowledge of its existence, seemed to him a tragedy beyond contemplation. It also seemed quite likely. He felt very close to dying, at this moment: sweat seeping over his body, head thumping, eyes pricking, hands weak, three hot-water bottles scalding his shins. It would not be a dramatic death, a courageous death, his: it would be a mere death. There would be no reason for the Leopard to hear of his passing, unless she happened to be in the Star on the day of his funeral and someone mentioned it. There would be no possibility of her extending so much as a sigh of regret. In the circumstances, Henry reflected, perhaps it would be better to start wresting himself back from the gaping jaws – pull himself together, face the horizon, breast the waves: for where there was life, in his case, there was at least constant new hope of seeing the Leopard again.

The thought invigorated him. Almost at once he felt better. Unused to illness – not a day in bed for twenty years – Henry remembered it was a question of mind over body: think yourself well and the battle is half over.

During the night he braced himself to put his theory into practice and, in some measure, it worked. The fact that the swirling, sweaty sheets clung to him like tendrils, his damp pyjamas chafed, his head ached and his throat was a hollow cinder mattered to him not at all: such bodily discomforts were quite bearable. What he could not endure was the torment of his mind: mind over mind – there was the weakness. That was the part that did not work.

For no sooner had Henry re-established himself firmly upon the banks of life (a not ignoble feat which one day he would confide to the Leopard) he was at once beset by one of its tribulations: worry. Searing worry that increased its grip with every moment – the worry that the Leopard would return to the Star and here, in his prison bed, Henry would miss her. At the thought of such irony, having surreptitiously managed to visit the pub every day since her appearance, Henry groaned out loud. Rosie, wonderfully alert to any such signs of distress, came hurrying from her armchair downstairs.

'Oh, my poor love, what's the matter now?' she asked, in a voice appropriately low for a sick room. 'What can I do for you?'

As there was nothing Rosie could do to alleviate Henry's real suffering, but as he felt too weak to say so, he remained silent. Rosie took this to be serious. With great diligence she repeated all her useless ministrations – pumping pillows, straightening sheets, even blowing her warm tea-and-biscuits breath on to the burning skin of his forehead. Henry nodded ungratefully and finally, imagining that the information would put him at least partly at his ease, she said again how comfortable she had managed to make herself downstairs, considering.

Henry's night then bloomed with cauliflowers. Over and over again he imagined himself, the magnificent frothy white heads in his hands, placed auspiciously in the car park as the Leopard swung out of the pub door in her inimitable style. Over and over again he imagined his beautifully timed approach, the look of amazement and wonder in her blue (blue? blue-green, more) eyes, the grateful way with which she took the cauliflowers and clutched them to her breasts – a moment which inspired Henry with the new idea of how delightful it would have been to be born a vegetable, tendered by Jack Mackay. But once she had the cauliflowers firmly in her pretty hands, what happened next was a little confused in Henry's vision. He knew quite definitely they were suddenly in her Jaguar, speeding down a car-less motorway, the cauliflowers back on his lap as her hands were on the steering wheel. But when he went to return them to her she was mysteriously coming out of the pub again. They went through the whole process of the meeting once more, and the journey in the Jaguar. All this happened twenty, thirty times maybe, the non-fruition of the car drive, as each time it made a mysterious U-turn back to the pub, driving Henry to greater realms of frustration.

Wracked by such sudorific thoughts, he tossed noisily about, maddened, aching. As the church clock struck four, Rosie paid another of her regular visits, this time to say there was no need to worry, no need at all, but she thought he ought to know Evans was not home yet. Whatever could have happened? Whatever had happened, Henry brought himself to say, it was neither their business nor concern. The Boy was grown up now, and the sooner she got that into her head the happier her life would be. He spoke so sharply that Rosie hurried away, having only dabbed at a crumpled pillow, full of understanding about how in sickness people say things they do not really mean.

In the peace that followed her departure an idea then came to Henry that was to boost his low spirits for the rest of the night. The Boy: that was it, surely. Could not he be Henry's salvation? It could all be done so delicately, why, the Boy might never need to know just what act of goodness he was undertaking. Fired by his inspiration, the next part of the plan came easily to Henry's troubled head. He heard the conversation, loud voices in his ears, as it would be next morning.

Henry: You going down to the pub, Boy, lunchtime?

Boy: Yes, Dad. Why?

Henry: You keep your ears open for any news, there's a good lad. Don't like to miss anything, stuck up here.

Boy: 'Course, Dad. But not that much happens down at the Star.

Henry: Well, you never know. Old Joe might have a heart attack, a flightly Luton woman might do a striptease – wouldn't want to miss anything like that.

Boy: (laughs) I'll keep an eye out, Dad, don't worry.

It was so easy. Why had he not thought of it before? That sense of tranquil pleasure, peculiar to times of sought-after solution, brought calm to Henry's fiery limbs and eventually, much to Rosie's disappointment, he slept. She would not, now, in truth, be able to say he had been awake *all* night. Nonetheless, they had been worrying hours which had caused a not unwelcome stir in the ordinary fabric of her life.

When Evans had gone Augusta Browne gathered herself together once more to protect her house. She wandered about from room to room, each one quiet and husky with early sunlight. She despised herself for these nostalgic pilgrimages, reminding her as they did of the bright times that were over: but she indulged in them all the same, ashamed of her weakness. Restless, afraid, she touched the pale wood of the panelled walls, she paced the stone flags of the hall, confining to memory for ever the places where they dipped unevenly. From her study she saw that the first roses were in bloom. Later, she would pick them. But not now: she must detract, somehow, not add, to the pleasures of the house, till the predators had gone. Mounting the stairs, dazzled by sunbeams, she prayed for vile skies, torrential rain and an east wind to inquinate the place with a sulphur smell unbearable to the noses of all prestigious office men.

In the upstairs room at home Evans felt particularly large. He stood at the end of his parents' bed, head bowed to avoid the ceiling. His father was propped up among an extravagance of pillows, uncomfortable, flushed. A crochet pattern of sun and shadow, made by the elm leaves outside, played upon the bed cover.

'You not so good, then, Dad?'

'Had a rough night, Boy.'

'Ah. I'm sorry. Mum says Doctor Kennet is on his way.'

'There was no need to fuss the doctor.'

'Well, anything I can do for you? Anything I can get?'

Henry swivelled his eyes towards the window. Their whites were strung with brown veins.

'Going down the pub, lunchtime, Boy, are you?'

'Yes, Dad. Why?'

There was a long silence. Henry continued to look out of the window.

'Well, you never know,' he said at last. He flung out his hand towards the bedside table, an indeterminate gesture, his mind fixed on the casual way he should say the next words. He knocked over the milk bottle that held the single iris. Water poured down the side of the bed. The iris head and small stump of stem lay on the table like some obscene purple organ, smile full of stamen dust, mocking.

'Dratted flower,' said Henry, 'throw the thing away, Boy.'

Evans was at the bedside, clumsily wringing part of the wet sheet.

'I'll get Mum. She'll soon clear this up.'

'Yes.' Henry picked up the iris, scrunched it up in his hand. He watched the slimy purple juices run into the lines of his palm.

'I must get to work, Dad. Sure there's nothing I can do for you?'

'No, Boy. Thank you.'

Evans waited a moment.

'Take care, then,' he said, and left.

With a clenched fist Henry wiped a trickle of saliva from his chin. There was a horrible sweet taste of tea in his mouth, but the thought of having to take out his teeth, put them in a glass of water and give them to Rosie to scrub, in order to get rid of it, was intolerable. She should not be allowed the pleasure of such intimacies, not Rosie. He would endure the tea-taste. Endure, somehow, the stifling day ahead. Already, at eight-thirty, Henry was beginning to realise he had taken the wrong decision: perhaps, after all, he should not have made so fine an effort to fight the lure of gentle death which had beckoned him last night.

By mid-afternoon Rosie was exhausted, what with all the running up and down stairs, changing the sheets, hurrying to the shop for instant coffee (Henry had suddenly taken against tea) filling hot-water bottles, making two lots of junket (the first hadn't set), emptying the chamber pot, opening and shutting the window – quite apart from all the usual housework. Doctor Kennet had pronounced the illness to be a slight chill, and even given that the doctor was a man of exaggerated understatement, Rosie could see Henry's condition could cause no alarm. But the way he was carrying on, just like a man, you'd think he was dying. Still, to be fair, it was the first time he had been ill in twenty years: he had every right to make the worst of it – and this gave Rosie a good opportunity to make the best of it, which she felt secretly she was doing, and was not displeased.

Now she sat in her small neat kitchen, slippered feet on a stool in front of the fire – an unaccustomed position, for her, mid-afternoon. The chair and stool were Henry's property, but in his absence she felt the rest was deserved. Besides, as he was too weak to come downstairs, he would never know of her laziness, and that was important because one of the things he loved her for was her energy. (Or so he once said, some thirty years ago.) He would also never know that at lunchtime, while he had been sipping at his junket upstairs, complaining it hurt his throat, she had stood in the larder, eating small slices of cold canary pudding. Solid and clammy, just as she liked it, it had stood in its plate of congealed treacle, wonderfully tempting. She had happily given way to temptation, running her finger through the treacle, slicing the sponge with a small knife. Picking, Henry would have called it: a habit he deplored – a habit, unable to relinquish, Rosie continued at subtly chosen times of day in the privacy of her larder. Oh, you've been playing truant today, Rosie Evans, she said to herself.

There was no need, of course, this time of year, to have a fire: it was a warm June afternoon. But Rosie liked a fire all year round. One of her little luxuries, she called it. An empty grate gave her the spooks, a strange feeling of hollowness in her stomach. And so she watched the small flames and the shifting sun patterns on the floor, and turned her mind to Evans. The look on his face when he had opened the door this morning had given her quite a turn. She would not like to think what he had been up to and tried to remember, in her anxiety, if she had plied him with the sort of questions a son prefers his mother not to ask. He had been very offhand and gruff, she thought, leaping upstairs to see his father without any kind of satisfactory explanation. Rosie had not wanted to know any details, naturally: but surely it was up to a son to put his mother's mind at rest after a whole night out?

Ah, the young. They were hard to understand, sometimes. Their lack of thought, their funny ideas about right and wrong. Not that she could complain in general. No, on the whole Evans was a good and kind son, a bit quiet, like his father, but diligent and appreciative, good-natured. It was only since Brenda had come into his life that Rosie had begun to worry about him. The merry dance she led him was quite a strain, sometimes, judging by the pallor of Evans's face. But still, there was a long time to go until the actual wedding day. Anything could happen before then. In fact in her most secret heart, as Rosie once confided to the vicar, she wouldn't be that surprised if anything *did* . . .

She looked at the lumps of her hands lying on her lap, their imperfections diminished in the speckled light, and smiled to herself. Part of her present contentment was due to the fact that she had decided, this afternoon, to put the first part of her plan into action. This afternoon she would burn her mittens. This afternoon would mark the passing of a seventeen-year phase which had, perhaps, been a mistake. Still, better late than never, and she was sure it was not *too* late.

When Henry was better, she had decided, and longing for exercise again, she would let him go off on a walk alone. She would then, taking a different route, hurry to the woods herself. It was lovely up there, this time of year, the place he would be bound to visit. He would come upon her in one of the glades, sitting in the long green grass, wearing her straw hat (she would get a new ribbon) and nice new seersucker blouse. Amazed, he would ask her what she was doing. She would be very careful what she said. Not talk too much. Just smile at him and say something like was that a missel-thrush or a song-thrush, Henry? I was wondering which it was. He would be delighted to tell her. He knew a lot about birds and warmed to people who shared his interest. Well, though she couldn't tell a hedge-sparrow from a female chaffinch herself, and didn't privately much care, from now on she would be interested. Henry, surprised and filled with pleasure, might then suggest she join him for a drink in the Star. Not that she liked pubs *in themselves*, but she liked to be in a public place with Henry. She liked to be beside him up at the bar, to hear him say, 'A shandy for the wife, please.'

If all this happened, as in her bones Rosie felt it might, she would further please him with steak-and-kidney pudding for supper, gentle on his teeth, and roly-poly pudding. She herself couldn't abide suet for two courses, but Henry could live on the stuff. If the plan was to work, of course, much sacrifice was required on her part, and she was prepared for that. Because in the end she would be rewarded. In the end, her unmittened hand on his shoulder, surprising him, moon in the window, window ajar as he liked it – he would turn to her.

At the thought of it, the heave of the bed as Henry rolled over, Rosie's heart gave a small flutter. She pulled the pair of white lawn mittens from the pocket of her apron and threw them on the fire. The flames quickly consumed them, leaving a small dust of ashes on a lump of coal.

'A good thing that's done, then, Rosie my girl,' she whispered out loud, 'it was about time.'

Leopard spots among the elm leaves in the window: damn leaves and their confounded bloody moving, never still for a moment, never possible to catch clear sight of her face, shifting sun and leopard spots always hiding it. My dearest Leopard keep still one moment dearest Leopard for me to see you. Smile upon me and I shall come to you and we shall go to a place which is quiet and still, no elm leaves, and you will take off your coat take off your Leopard spots and then be warm against me. Dearest Leopard what are you doing now? How cruel it is that you might be at the Star while I lie helpless here . . .

Towards evening Henry's temperature rose again. The one comforting thought was that the Boy would be bound to come and see him, soon as he got home, and mention he'd been at the Star. It shouldn't be too difficult to ask if there had been any new life down there, anything going on.

Oh, yes, that was certain: Henry could rely on the Boy to come back and tell him. Not long now. He tossed in the hot sheets. An hour or so. Impatiently, he waited.

Even without Augusta Browne's encouragement Evans would have found himself walking towards Wilberforce's farm when work was over. There was no possibility of his not seeing Brenda for a week, no matter what she had done. As the emerald rage diminished during the day his desire to be with her again had increased.

They met at the door of the chicken shed: Brenda was locking up for the night. She turned to him, head high, but docile eyes.

'I wasn't expecting you.'

'Thought I'd better come.'

'To apologise?'

'I'm sorry I hit you.'

'Well, I suppose I should have told you I was going out.'

'That's all right.'

'Where are we going?'

'I have a surprise for you.'

She walked with him quietly to Wroughton House, asking no questions, though she seemed surprised when they turned into the back drive. She was further amazed when Evans took a key from his pocket and unlocked the back door.

'Are we going to pay a social visit on Mrs Browne or do a burglary?' she giggled.

'Wait and see,' said Evans.

The house was quite silent. No sign of Augusta Browne. Evans led Brenda up the stairs to the attics, flung open the door of the furnished room. She stepped inside, looked about at the comfortable arrangement of things, the evening light on flowered curtains and patterned rug.

'Ours,' said Evans.

'Are you mad?'

'Ours till she sells the house.'

'I don't know what you mean, I really don't.'

Brenda sat on the double brass bed, testing the mattress. Evans would have liked to have sat next to her, but thought better of it. Instead, he paced up and down, hands in pockets, explaining how the whole idea had come about. Brenda seemed bemused.

'No more nights at the Hilton, then?' she said at last.

'Not unless we want them. Are you pleased?'

'I suppose I am. Here – let's look in the cupboard.'

She began to explore the room, opening drawers, counting hangers. 'There's everything here, isn't there? She's thought of everything. Quite luxurious, I must say.'

Evans attempted to contain his pleasure.

'Not too bad. Tide us over till we've got our own place.'

Brenda joined him standing at the casement window. They looked down on to the wide lawn. Four men wandered about. One of them made solemn gestures, casting his arms in various directions. Augusta stood a little apart from the men, arms folded under her breasts.

'Who are they?'

'She said people were coming to see the house today. Thought it might do as an office.'

'Never! Not a place like this. It'd be wicked.'

'Terrible. I don't suppose they'll want it.' Evans turned to her, remembering the time he had recently stood here next to Mrs Browne, her pale face all violet shadows. He had not had the slightest desire to touch *her*. It was only with a great strength of will he managed to keep his hands off Brenda. This close, he could smell strongly her peculiar scent of corn and lavender water, and the irresistible warmth of her skin seemed to roll off her, almost a tangible thing. They listened to the church clock strike six.

'What about your Dad, Evans? Is he any better?'

'He's all right. Just a bit of a chill.'

'Hadn't you better go and see him?'

'He won't want to see me. Reckon he likes being left alone, when he's ill.'

'What are we going to do, then?'

Evans thought for a while.

'Perhaps we should drive out for a bit of food somewhere, then come back here for a while.' He smiled. 'Try the place out.'

Brenda nodded, repentant eyes. Strange, thought Evans, how the terrible events of the night had made her to act just as she did when a chicken died: soft and malleable, looking to him for a lead, making him feel master. Long may it last, he said to himself. Gently he took the part of her arm he had hurt last night, in the fight that now seemed like a bad trick of the imagination.

They left the room.

When the office men had gone Augusta remained in the garden. They had said very little, but made copious notes in black note-books, each one stamped identically with a silver eagle. She had said a great deal: all her usual *spiel* about the enormous disadvantages of the place. But they had taken little notice of her, merely shrugged, and said things could be overcome. What most unnerved Augusta was the fact that they asked no questions. They seemed ominously uncurious, although they made their own small private investigations, digging their heels into the lawn and glancing at the turf as if they were experts in such matters; tapping with their hairy knuckles at the wood panelling in the hall. Augusta, trying to conceal her hostility as their hideous eyes travelled without appreciation over Hugh's pictures, felt a strength of hatred that chilled her skin in the warm air, and she clutched at herself to stop trembling.

In the rose garden, now, she fingered the first blooms, yellow petals that deepened imperceptibly into pink, and tried to wipe the memory of the last two hours from her mind. Unless she quickly engaged herself in some practical activity – she would pick and cook a bunch of asparagus, perhaps – there was danger on such an evening of falling into a state of inextricable melancholy. Turning towards the kitchen garden, clattering along the small paths between low box-hedges much in need of a trim, the wild thought then came to Augusta that she should telephone Hugh. Surely he would have some sympathy about the office men? After all, she was not alone in loving the house. Had things been different he would have wanted to keep it, too. Perhaps – she could make a sauce mousseline – he would drive down for dinner. Even stay.

But by the time she reached the asparagus Augusta admitted to the foolishness of her idea. He would never come. He would never change his mind, now. She started to pick the thin green spears, enough for one.

Later, awake in her bedroom, Augusta heard footsteps in the room above. Then the churning of the old bed. She was pleased to think someone was enjoying her house again: to guard its pleasures to herself, as she had been doing with reluctance for the last three months, was a terrible waste.

Rosie was sitting in Henry's chair in front of the fire when Evans got home soon after midnight. The disturbances of the past night had inflated the pouches of brownish skin beneath her eyes, but she was stoic, calm. She had determined, during the evening, to curb her curiosity and ask Evans no questions. He would no doubt tell her what was up all in good time.

'Your Dad was asking for you,' she said. 'He kept saying you'd be back for sure at six.'

'Oh, dear. I thought of coming but I reckoned he'd rather be left alone. How is he?'

'He seemed very restless. I expect it's the fever. Burning itself out, you know. I gave him a couple of pills. He's asleep now.'

'You're not going to spend another night down here, are you, Mum?'

'No. I'll come on up now. With those pills I'll not disturb him tonight.' She gave a small smile. 'I was just waiting up for you, see if you wanted anything.'

'You shouldn't have done that.' Evans bent down and

lightly kissed his mother's grey hair. 'You spend far too much time thinking of other people.' She smelt of oatmeal soap and knitting – grey wool, he recalled it had always seemed to be, as a child: she would put down her yards of grey knitting and clutch him to her oatmealy bosom, always pleased to see him, full of interest in the small events of his day.

'Nonsense. There's milk by your bed – you look as if you could do with a good night's sleep yourself.' The remonstrance, in Rosie's version of a brusque voice, was twofold: it spanned both his night out and the compliment he had paid her. Praise confused Rosie. Twisting her hands, she remembered she was about to spend her first mittenless night for seventeen years. It was a relief to think that Henry, knocked out by the pills, would not know. She would appreciate, just at first, getting used to the strange new feeling on her own.

A week later, better but thinner, his normal strength not wholly returned, Henry Evans went to the Star for his Tuesday drink. During the long boring days of his convalescence, body slumped in his chair, mind constantly beside the Leopard, the cauliflower plan had inexplicably turned sour on him. Cauliflowers, he had decided after all, were rarely associated with romance (though he did recall, one shore leave in Marseilles, having a very good French cauliflower cheese with a generous girl called Hélène). However magnificent a specimen, there was something a little absurd about a cauliflower: the originality of his plan, Henry saw in a moment of lucky revelation, might not be appreciated by one of the Leopard's sophistication. His next inspiration was a canary in a cage – a green canary in a pretty cage made of filigree stuff, like one he had once seen in a junk shop. But the practicalities of carrying out this plan soon killed that idea. Even if he bought the canary, supposedly for the pleasure of the Evans household (and Rosie hated birds) he could think of no way of explaining his snatching it up one day and hurrying it off to the Star. Finally, the perfect solution came to him: strawberries.

There were few women on earth who could not be won over by a punnet of hand-picked strawberries. For Henry, of course, would pick them himself. Only a mile from the village lay acres of strawberry fields. He would go there, as he had done so many summers, and collect the finest berries: hands rummaging expertly among the warm evening straw, parting the ferny green leaves, sucking at one or two to test their sweetness. The clear sky would be corded with smoke from the distant chimneys (Henry's post-fever mind automatically included references to happy days at work, along with his new romance) and he would feel strong with the satisfaction that this back-aching task was all for the possible love of his Leopard. Yes: that was it. Settled. Two or three times a week, strawberry season, off he would go. Only disadvantage would be Rosie's jangling delight at the harvest in the larder. But if he supplied enough strawberries it should be easy enough to steal a single punnet, come the time, without her ever knowing.

Henry arrived at the pub calmly pessimistic. The Leopard would not be there, of course; but if she was, it would be a surprise beyond all imagining. Henry pushed his way through the door. At once he stopped short, clutching at the back of a nearby chair. There, sitting up at the bar, back to him, alone, *was* the Leopard: spotted coat, beautiful haze of curly golden hair.

With incredible speed – Bill behind the bar scarcely had time to notice him – Henry stepped back outside, again. His heart thrashed so fast he felt close to fainting. He leant against the wall, dizzy and sweating.

In his preoccupation with the strawberry plan, Henry had not fully prepared himself for the shock of surprise: he had girded himself only for disappointment. This amazing turn of events, combined with his physical weakness, stunned him into helplessness.

In a timeless moment all the old ideas, scorched deeply into his brain during the last week, flashed in strobe lights before his eyes. Canaries? There were no canaries for miles

. . . Strawberries? Oh God, they were not ripe. Cauliflowers? The possibility of returning to his original plan brought Henry's first calm breath. But someone was speaking to him. It was the Boy. What was the Boy doing here?

'Coming in for a pint, Dad? Look as if you could do with one.'

'No, Boy, thanks. No, I – '

'You all right? You look pretty shagged.'

'I'm all right, just getting back on my feet. Takes a few days. First time out and all that.'

'Well, I'm just going to stand myself a quick one. See you later.' Evans went into the pub.

Henry continued to lean against the wall. His breathing was very fast and noisy. He looked wildly about. Precious moments were speeding past. If he didn't make a decision within seconds, his chance would be lost. But he was in no condition – weak, hollow legs – to hurry home and get the car. His eyes fell upon an old-fashioned bicycle propped up against the pavement, the property of old Joe. Henry made a lightning calculation. If he rode very fast to Mackay, snatched up the vegetables with the promise of payment tomorrow, he could be back here in a quarter of an hour at the most. Old Joe always spent two hours, midday, at his drink. He would never know his bicycle had been borrowed.

In a trembling rush Henry grabbed at the handle bars, huge hard rubber things – kicked the pedal away from the pavement. It was a heavy, ill-balanced machine, snatching at Henry's arms as he tried to guide. But the madness of love gave him energy to fight. He swung his leg over the seat, unsurprised at the easy way it soared. He raised his head, and pushed down upon the pedals with crazy strength. Suddenly, he was off.

Evans always felt a sense of well-being in the lounge of the Star. He liked the smell of hot sausage rolls and cool rubber flooring. He liked the thunk of darts on the cork board – there always seemed to be players – and the small open fire.

The beer was good, too: without asking, Bill pulled his pint at lunchtime, gave him a single whisky in the evening. He felt the privilege of being a regular: he knew everybody, everybody knew him.

Today, a rare thing, there was a stranger in the lounge – a blonde woman in a leopard skin coat, sitting up at the bar. Evans was instantly aware of the slight change of atmosphere her presence caused: voices were fractionally lower, silences between the sips of beer a little longer. It was as if the regulars, usually relaxed, were mutually alert to the possibility of something happening.

Evans took an empty stool beside her at the bar. Bill passed him his mug of beer. They exchanged a few comments, cricket scores and the miners' strike. Evans noticed the woman's drink was a small glass of Dubonnet with a twist of lemon peel. She smoked, holding her cigarette in a long ebony holder between her third and fourth finger. Both the way she drank – frequent tiny sips, and the way she smoked, pecking at the holder so that it clacked against her teeth, indicated she was in a state of some unrest. At one moment she twittered her fingers on the wood of the bar, making a mouse sound with her silver nails. Then she pushed back her fur cuff to glance at a gold watch.

'Do you suppose he's not coming?' she asked Bill.

'Couldn't tell you, madam. Couldn't tell you what he's up to.'

It was the first time Evans had ever heard Bill call anyone madam. He winked. Bill winked back. The woman missed the signal: her spikey black lashes were fluttering down at her drink. Evans realised that both he and Bill were struck by a powerful smell coming from the woman: nervous sweat undisguised by the sickly scent of some hot-house flower. Tuberoses, Evans thought. Bill sniffed.

'Well, I don't know,' said the woman, apparently to herself. 'Really.'

Evans asked Bill to give him a sausage roll. The woman shifted her position, leant a little further over the bar.

'Give me one of those, too, will you? And one more Dubonnet.' She pushed her glass forward and turned to Evans. Her eyes were matching starfish, the lashes of each one divided into not more than four or five jet points. 'Do you recommend them?'

'They're very good.'

The woman smiled. One of her middle teeth was chipped at the corner, the colour of a bruise. The skin round her mouth, heavily powdered, puckered into a network of small lines. Friendly.

'I'm famished,' she said. Then they ate sausage rolls in silence.

Evans had a further pint. The woman looked at her watch again and turned to him.

'Well, I might as well give up. I'm not waiting any longer. Could you tell me the bus situation in this place? I've got to get back to the station to catch the 3.30.'

Evans rubbed his chin. He was unacquainted with the local bus timetable, but the possibility of being helpful always spurred his adrenalin.

'Don't believe there's anything till four o'clock,' he said. The woman looked alarmed. 'Bill, when's the next bus?'

'Four-fifteen.' Bill was dusting the bottle of Dubonnet. It hadn't been called upon since the blonde lady's last visit.

'Oh, Lord. That's marvellous, that is,' she said. 'What the heck am I going to do?'

Evans had been brought up by Rosie to believe that practical help was often of more value than the sympathy of words. He replied by instinct.

'Well, I've got my car out the back. I could run you to the station.'

'You couldn't?' The starfish eyes dazzled with relief.

'No trouble. It's not far. I don't have to be anywhere till two-thirty.'

'That would be absolutely *marvellous*!' She was already slithering down from the stool, pointing her sandalled feet – thin straps round smashing ankles – towards the floor.

'Think nothing of it. Always pleased to help a lady in distress.'

The woman led the way to the door, head high, scarlet lips parted. Following her, Evans was aware that every eye in the place relished the scene. Christ, he'd be in for no end of a wigging tonight. His blush was uncontrollable.

In the car the smell of sweat and tuberoses was almost overpowering. Evans opened the window. She wouldn't think it rude, he thought, considering the warmth of the summer's day. Starting the engine, he wondered if she was aware of her own smell.

' If you don't mind my asking,' he said, 'why do you wear a great thick fur coat on a day like this?'

The woman pushed at the collar so that it stood up round her neck.

'I always feel the cold,' she said, 'all year round. Think I must have thin blood.' She gave a slight shiver and smiled her nice smile. Evans, with particular care, turned into the road.

In retrospect Henry could remember little of the journey to Mackay. The bicycle seemed to have a will of its own, shying at things in the hedgerows, jolting at the slightest touch of the brakes – on several occasions he was nearly thrown. But, half-blinded by the sweat in his eyes, scared by the loud wheezing noise in his throat, Henry kept up his manic speed. Although the road seemed interminable, he must have reached Mackay's house within seven or eight minutes.

Stopping with a jerk at the gate – almost falling once again – he flung the bicycle on to the verge and ran up the front path. The ring of his feet on the cement enhanced his own sense of urgency. He rang the bell, waited a few seconds, rang again. He heard its silly chimes echo within. No reply. He banged the door. Still nothing. God in heaven . .

Henry then noticed the blinds in both front windows were drawn. That meant Mackay must be out at the back: he was the sort of man who would draw the blinds if he was not actually in the room. Henry ran again, slamming his way through a series of small gates, a bursting feeling in his chest. But the market garden, its cloches and greenhouses and neat strips of vegetables, was plainly deserted. Henry called Mackay's name out loud several times, but there was a deadness about the place, a feeling of absolute desertion, and he knew there would be no answer. Tears mixed with the sweat round his eyes. He cursed Mackay out loud, spewing forth a jumble of obscenities unused since his days at sea.

Once again, he had to think quickly. There was no alternative but to hurry back to the Star, wipe the damp from his face, and join the Boy for a pint after all. From then on he would be in the hands of Fate. But surely, so near to the Leopard, it would not be untoward to offer her a drink?

He began the return journey, clumsy in his hurry. His previous energy was ebbing away. He tried to pedal fast, but his legs were useless. The ride was a nightmare of slowness.

Then, as the Star at last came into sight, Henry sighted a further setback to his plans: the Boy's white Mini was nosing out of the car park. Damn him! He must be stopped. He must return to the lounge *with* Henry to ease any possible awkwardness. Recklessly he let go of one handle and waved. The whole bicycle lurched as the front wheel swung from side to side, and Henry fought to regain his balance. The car was almost level with him now: in a split second he saw the Boy's face, smiling, his hand raised in a wave. He saw also, a one-dimensional vision behind the glare of sun on the windscreen, the blonde hair and smiling face of the Leopard, a small ridge of spotted fur round her neck. Then they were gone.

With the dazed movements of people who have been in an accident or earthquake, Henry dismounted the bicycle. He propped it up against the pavement, just as it had been before. Then he went to the slatted wooden table, with its two matching chairs, left on the pavement in summer in case anyone should feel like sitting outside.

Henry crashed down upon one of the chairs, instantly

conscious of pain as the slatted wood cut into his thighs. He felt his mouth fall open, sweat thick as rain running down his face. After a time the noise of his own groans subsided, and he listened to the silence of the afternoon which roared about him in great waves.

At first Evans hadn't recognised the old man, white hair blown stiffly out over his ears, wobbling about on the bicycle. When he saw it was Henry, he laughed.

'Good heavens, that's my old man! Whatever can he be doing?' In fact Evans did not stop to think what his father *was* doing. Uncurious by nature, the most unlikely sights held little wonder for him. If he had met his father in a Soho brothel he would have been neither surprised nor interested: their relationship had always thrived on their apparent mutual indifference.

'He looks pretty unsafe,' said the woman, and they both waved.

At the station, Evans got out and held open the car door for her. She was very grateful.

'That was really kind of you, dear. Honestly, if it hadn't been for you, I'd have been in terrible hot water, I can tell you. Well, so long, and perhaps we'll run into each other again one day in the Star. Nice knowing you.'

She smiled again, her chipped tooth blacker in the bright light and her hair a less delicate gold than it had seemed in the pub, dark at the roots. Back in the car Evans opened the other window: her smell was still thick and sickening in the air. He better get rid of it, he thought with a smile, before picking up Brenda tonight.

The show of mastery by Evans on the night of Brenda's excursion had induced in her a flutter of new respect. He had not hurt her physically, and the blow had been no surprise. She had often guessed, particularly on wild nights in the barn, violence rumbled within him. One day, provoked far enough, Brenda imagined Evans might lose control: she had speculated with interest on just how wild he would be when the time came. The events of that night had also made her feel unusually grateful to Evans. After his initial burst of jealousy he had chided her no further – indeed, he had made no further mention of the matter. This, Brenda considered privately, generous behaviour. For all her protestations to him about having done nothing wrong, she knew his reactions to her own behaviour were not unreasonable, and his outrage had caused a stimulating ripple in their uneventful days.

Also, the room at Wroughton House had done much to increase Brenda's inclination towards Evans in the past week. His idea, and its realisation, boosted her respect for his imagination (an element she previously felt he lacked). They had already spent many hours in the room: the barn and its discomforts were a thing of the past. Never lacking in concupiscence, Evans seemed to have been spurred by Brenda's night out to even further desire. She was temporarily sated. Her flesh felt mousse-like. Too dazed by love-making to think sharply, the feelings of dissatisfaction that so often haunted her daily life had temporarily vanished.

Benevolent inspirations come most easily to contented minds, and in her present sated state Brenda found herself thinking that it would be a good idea to reward Evans for his charity: she would, she decided with pleasure, turn up at the post office a few minutes before he was due to open it for the afternoon. He would be amazed and pleased: she had never made any such gesture before. It was always he who came to her, and was often barely welcomed. But this afternoon, in the warm still air, it would be no trouble to flatter him: to observe how nice and orderly his post office was, and to take an interest in his neat files. She would ask him to buy her an ice-cream on a stick – the sight of her licking an ice-cream always aroused him, and he would kiss her, the ice melting between their mouths, pressed up against the counter.

Full of such happy intentions Brenda locked the chicken shed behind her and walked up the dust path to Wilberforce's farmhouse. On her way to the post office she had to call in and ask him about a late delivery of grit. She had not spoken to Wilberforce for some time – since the death of Elizabeth – but the urgency of dwindling stocks forced her now to break her silence. She knocked at the back door, went in.

Wilberforce was sitting at the kitchen table. Unshaven, he held a half-eaten pork pie in one hand while he filled in his football coupons with the other. Steam rose from a mug of tea beside him and the table was littered with a mass of papers and unopened letters, unwashed dishes and unemptied ash-trays. The windows were shut. Brenda gasped as two smells, cramming the room, surrounded her: Wilberforce's sweat, and pigs' trotters boiling on the stove.

She closed the door behind her but remained standing close to it, hands behind her fingering the cracked paint. Wilberforce looked up at her briefly: his eyes flicked down to her breasts. In the greenish light of the room his skin had the glow of discoloured lard while his hair, smarmed down with grease, gave him the look of a third-rate gangster. He wiped his nose on the back of his hand.

'I know what you've come about, girlie, don't I?' he said. He spoke with his mouth full so that Brenda could see the mush of pork on his tongue. He reminded her of Uncle Jim.

'We're down to three more feeds. Four at the most.'

'Bugger. The order was in weeks ago.' He sniffed again. 'Care for a cup of tea, would you?' Brenda shook her head. 'I'm in a hurry, right now. But I'll phone them again this afternoon, put a bomb under them.'

He gave no appearance of a man in a hurry, chewing slowly on his pie, pushing at the litter around him to make more space for the pools coupon.

'Thanks.'

'Birds all right, are they?'

'Fine.'

'Laying good, I see.' He stood up, holding his belt with both hands. The position was menacing. From his side of the table he now looked down on Brenda.

'Boyfriend all right?'

'Evans is fine.'

'He's a lucky man.' Wilberforce licked a speck of pork jelly from the corner of his mouth. Brenda was unlatching the door.

'Well, I must be going,' she said. In the back of her mind she wondered, should she stay another moment or so, what might happen. Wilberforce took the slightest pause for encouragement, as she had learnt in the past.

'Honoured by the visit, believe me.' He smiled and came round to the door. Unnecessarily he held it open for her. So close, the stench of his sweat was foul. 'Sometimes, you know, I get the distinct impression you try to avoid me.'

'Do you really?' Brenda intended to sound hostile, but had a feeling she was friendly instead.

Wilberforce ran a hand round his scrubby jowl.

'Tell me this, anyhow,' he said, 'give us a piece of advice for old time's sake. Just supposing I was off to meet one of the opposite sex, as they say, man to woman. Just supposing that was the case . . .' Brenda, sun on her shoulders out here, the gate to the road only ten yards away, felt safe. 'Then would you say I needed a shave?'

He snatched at Brenda's hand, ran it over his prickling skin. Seeing that this was all he meant to do – safe as she was out here – Brenda did not try to pull it back.

'Yes,' she said. 'Definitely. You filthy old thing, you.'

Wilberforce pressed two of her fingers to the wet squelch of his mouth, dabbed at them with his tongue.

'Then that's what I'll have to be doing, my lovely girl,' he said, and let go of her hand. Brenda, not meaning to, smiled. Pathetic, Wilberforce was, really: always trying to make you think he was going off with a lorry-load of chorus girls, bragging he could have every girl in the village if he felt that way inclined. She ran from him, thinking she must be strangely content if even so revolting a man had no power to annoy her.

She walked the short distance down the road to the post

office, enjoying the sun. There was no one about except, in the far distance, an old man on a bicycle. He approached so slowly he seemed hardly to be moving. Brenda wondered if her own progress on a cumbersome bicycle in fifty years' time would be similar. But she had not much patience with visions of the future – herself as a sexless old woman was quite unimaginable, for a start – and quickened her pace at the thought of an ice-cream with Evans. She'd like him to lock the place, keep the customers waiting a while, let them bang on the door . . . She wondered if she could persuade him.

She turned right, hurried across the disused car park to the prefabricated post office building that had been 'temporary accommodation' for nine years now. It was still shut, the plastic blinds drawn. No sign of Evans. Brenda was annoyed. She disliked postponement of her plans: it was now or never, this particular kind of visit. What was Evans up to? He was never late.

She turned back to the road to see the white Mini passing, Evans driving, a woman beside him. In that fraction of a second Brenda was quite sure it was a woman. She ran to the pavement, looked up the road. The car was turning the corner, almost out of sight. But there were quite distinctly two heads. Incredulous, Brenda stood with legs apart. Then she heard a cry, a dreadful groan. She spun round the other way to see, on the opposite side of the road outside the Star, that the old man on the bicycle, trying to get off, had only just managed to stop himself falling. He staggered to the wooden chair, slumped down behind the table and beat his temples with his fists, just as Brenda had seen people acting in films. She was about to cross the road and go to him when she saw it was Henry Evans. She stopped herself. Henry Evans! She hadn't known he had a bicycle – surprising. But this was no time to wonder about *him*. Oh, no. It was his son who was going to have to answer the questions this afternoon. It was Evans Evans himself, the man so outraged by her little waltz down to the Air Base, who was going to have to face the music this time. Christ, he was.

She would wait for him. Hours and hours, if necessary – bugger the hens, this was an emergency. (They would understand.) Oh, she'd wait any amount of time, work out in her mind how best to begin. When Evans returned he'd be amazed to find her there. What you doing? he'd ask. She'd smile up at him, all innocence, watching his confusion. Waiting for you, course, she'd say. Where've you been, Evans?

Where've you been, Evans? she'd ask again.

Who was that blonde bit in your car, Evans?

Ah. He'd have some explaining to do. Brenda, by the post office wall, leant back her head, shutting her eyes. The sun dazzled behind the lids, two blots of shooting light. The concrete wall behind her was warm against her back. She began her wait.

Rosie happened to look out of the window just as Henry, on his way home, was a hundred yards from the door. It occurred to her – though perhaps this was her imagination playing her up – that since his illness his hair was whiter. Definitely whiter. Surely, only a fortnight ago, the back of his head was a deep steely grey, as it once had been all over? Now, there seemed to be nothing dark left. Also, he stooped. His gait was normally so upright and firm: today his manner of walking was that of an old man. Poor dear Henry, thought Rosie: shows that at our age a chill can take its toll. Still, a few weeks' convalescence, quiet days and early nights, plenty of good food, and he'd be back to his old self.

Rosie felt glad there was a cold rice pudding in the larder. Henry's favourite, she had cooked it for lunch but he had not come home. His first day back at the Star after a week's absence, she supposed, had meant a little celebrating. A few more drinks than usual with the boys. He had probably eaten a couple of their greasy sausage rolls (Rosie wouldn't touch them herself) and forgotten the time. That was unlike him, he was a punctual man – but, well, it was understandable. The way to keep a happy marriage going was to be understanding, even if it meant food was sometimes burnt or wasted and the person left at home was subjected to a deal of worry. She had always done her best to be understanding, Rosie, and she doubted if anyone could accuse her of failure on that score. So, today, she determined to put a cheerful face on the whole incident, to make no mention of the worry she had suffered when he still hadn't appeared at half-past one, and suggest he might like the rice pudding with a cup of tea.

Henry came through the door, leaving it open behind him so that he stood waist-deep in a ray of sun. The lower part of his body, dazzling, made his head and shoulders seem strangely shadowed and Rosie, looking hard at his face, was shocked. He appeared haggard and ill. Grey, drawn, vacant.

'Henry, love, it's gone three. Whatever –?'

'I'm all right. Sorry I'm late.' He went to his chair and sat down. The sunbeam, now a pure shaft, slanted through the door, making a yellow pool on the tiles at its base. Henry kicked at it. The toe of his shoe caught in the light and glinted.

'Let me get you – I was just thinking what you'd like was a cup of tea and a nice bit of rice pudding. It's all ready – '

'Don't want any rice pudding.'

'But Henry, it's your favourite – '

'Don't want any rice pudding at this time of the afternoon. Or any tea. Or anything. Least of all suggestions.' He gazed at the floor. Rosie, alarmed by his ferocity, kept her silence. At last she said,

'Well, I can't think how to help you.'

'You can't help me.'

In face of his dejection Rosie instinctively became more cheerful. If she could only make him realise that he had done too much too soon, that the reason for his present fatigue was nothing more than that – why, the simple facts would raise his spirits.

'You've been overdoing it, you know, love. First day out

you shouldn't have stayed so long. In bed all that time, quite low, you should have taken things more easily at first.'

Henry looked up at her: the lifting of his eyes seemed a great effort.

'I'm going out,' he said. 'It's too bloody hot in here. I'm going up the woods for a breath of fresh air.' He stood and went quickly – movements more like his old self – to the door.

'But Henry! That's very silly, overdoing it, love. Please – '

But Henry was gone. Rosie would not shout to him from the door, of course, and have all the neighbours thinking something was amiss. She stepped back into the kitchen, mind spinning, and went to the larder. There, spooning up small helpings of the rice pudding, things became instantly calm and clear. She had not had much warning, but here was her chance. The chance she had been waiting for, planning. Sucking the sweet, creamy grains of rice from her teeth she went upstairs to the bedroom. Quickly she took off her old cotton dress and replaced it with a navy gaberdine skirt, the one she wore summer Sundays, and her new seersucker blouse. That she had never worn. She had sent for it by mail order, having been attracted to its pin-tucked bodice in a newspaper. It wasn't, in reality, quite the elegant shirt the drawing had conveyed, but it was neat and handsome, suitable to Rosie's age, and a good clear blue. Then she put on her straw boater – a hat which years ago Henry once said he liked because it made nice shadows on her face. (They had been walking back from evensong at the time: he had said the shadows were full of holes and needed darning. She had laughed and he had said keep your laugh down, woman, we're still in the graveyard. At the same time he had taken her arm so she knew he wasn't really criticising her.) The straw had gone a bit droopy, and the striped ribbon was quite faded. Still, there was no time to change that now. Chances were Henry would never notice a ribbon: Rosie rammed the hat on the back of her head. Grey hair spurted out beneath it, making a fuzzy frame to her face. She looked in the mirror. There was not much light in the room through the small window – the elms so thick with leaves across the way – but, their shadows dancing about her cheeks, veiling the ruddy colour of her skin, it occurred to Rosie she didn't look too bad. She dabbed a puff of yellowish powder on her nose: a sudden small breeze spun a shower of molecules on to the walnut wood of the dressing-table, and on to her navy skirt. She wiped at the material, impatiently, making a pale smear: but decided there was no time to start messing about with damp cloths. Besides, her hands were trembling. You're all of a dither, Rosie my girl, she said to herself. Fancy that. Now, where was that rose water? She found it in its place in the drawer, quickly uncorked the pretty bottle. Evans had given it to her a couple of years ago for Christmas. He had said its scent was so subtle it was suitable only for her. In two years the subtlety seemed to have vanished altogether, but then Rosie had never had a sharp nose where commercial things were concerned, though she could tell you any flower by its smell in the dark.

She stabbed the neck of the bottle on to her own neck: the transparent liquid flowed down the gulleys of her throat and made damp patches on the collar of the seersucker blouse. Never mind, they would dry in a minute in the sun. The same thing had happened, once, when Henry had been courting. In the excitement of getting ready, she had spilled lavender water all over the bodice of her dress and hadn't known how to hide the damp patch from her mother, who considered perfume a vulgar habit of the upper classes, not to be copied by those of the lower orders. But Henry had loved it, nuzzling his nose into the fabric stretched across her chest until she had had to cry out to him to go no further . . . *Stop, Henry, love*, she had cried out, very feeble, and, because he was one of nature's gentlemen, Henry had stopped.

Rosie smiled at the thought of the incident, so long ago, and pulled herself back to reality. There was no time to lose. She hurried downstairs, pulled the door behind her. With a quick look at the neighbouring cottages, to see no one was about, she patted her hat more firmly on to her head and set off up the road towards the woods.

For the second time that afternoon Brenda's plans were foiled, this time by Wilberforce. He came striding across the waste ground towards the post office, a look of annoyance twisting his face. Brenda opened her eyes, angry at the disturbance.

'You're going to be late back, aren't you? What, waiting for the lover boy?' Brenda said nothing, kept her eyes on his newly shaven cheeks. He had cut himself twice. Two sparks of dark blood, not quite congealed, were forming into drops ready to start falling. He wore a clean checked shirt: sickly after-shave mingled with the old smell of sweat.

'He's not in the Star,' said Wilberforce, 'I just been there.'

'I know,' said Brenda.

'Something the matter?'

'No.' She shrugged.

'Daresay he's gone home for a bite.'

'Daresay he has.'

'Come on, or I'll be docking your wages, won't I? Extended dinner hours. I'll ring about the chicken food, tell you what they say.'

There was nothing Brenda could do. In silence she walked beside him back to the farmhouse. If she had insisted on staying at the post office for another five minutes he'd most likely have given her the sack then and there. She knew his moods: something had happened to annoy him and, in that state, he acted without thinking. On many occasions she had seen him lose his temper and sack employees with no explanation. It was lucky she had managed to last out so long, and she had no wish to lose her job. It suited her, the solitude, and she loved the chickens. She had a private and rewarding kind of communication with them, each one individually. In spite of what she had told Evans recently, about not caring if Wilberforce gave her the push, she knew in truth she would miss them if she had to go.

They returned to the kitchen. Wilberforce shut the door, pushed a few things from the table on to the floor to make himself enough space to sit, and lifted the dirty telephone on his lap. Brenda went over to the stove, sniffed at the pigs' trotters, turned out the flame beneath them.

'If I don't turn it off the water'll boil away,' she said.

Her initiative seemed to please Wilberforce. He smiled.

'Anyhow where's Mrs Wilberforce – Eileen?' went on Brenda. 'Haven't seen her for days.'

Wilberforce picked something from between his teeth.

'She cleared out last week. Gone to London, I believe. I told her to go, mind, bloody trollop, carrying on like she was. Here – ' he inclined his head – 'come and listen to what they say while I give them a piece of my mind.'

Brenda went and stood by him. She leaned her head close to his, the telephone receiver at his ear between them. The various smells made her feel sick again, and the heat was something terrible. Evans was in his car with a blonde, first time he'd ever been unfaithful to her, she could swear, and Wilberforce was breathing noisily. When he put his free hand on her stomach, and ran it gently down to her thigh, Brenda felt an extraordinary sense of helplessness. Revenge was not precisely in her mind. But she had no more energy, no desire to move.

It was a particularly dull afternoon in the post office for Evans – scarcely a customer, two flies buzzing and flicking against the window panes. He busied himself with a sheaf of pink papers, but could not concentrate on the small print. He was trying to define for himself the line of demarcation between sexual attraction and sexual vulgarity. What imperceptible thread of gold divided one from the other? How was it that Brenda, for all her warm and vibrant sluttishness, could never be called vulgar? – While the fur-coated woman, she was quite a different matter. Neat, in a way: expensive clothes, shoes and hair. But coarse. Calculated. Hard. A lot of men, thought Evans, would find her sexy, couldn't wait to make her. But not him. He wrinkled his nose, remembering her smell. Not in a whole year, on a desert island, would he lay a finger on her. It was a dreadful thought, all that powder and lipstick. No. She was definitely the kind of woman, no matter what the circumstances, he would make a special effort to avoid.

The land surrounding the village was flattish, the fields unlush. They provided scant grazing for sheep and cattle or, when ploughed, dull earth. It was an unlovely part of the Midland countryside, scarred by the quarries and brick-works, untempting to the builders of suburban houses. Even the beauty of the elms would soon be a thing of the past: fast ravaged by the disease, they were being slaughtered by the hundred. Except from the lawns of Wroughton House, there were no pleasing views – and even from there, the detached observer might say, there was nothing much to fulfil the visual senses. At the foot of the great sweep of lawn to the west side of the house lay the natural pond: beyond it, fields inclined gently towards a minor peak. In these parts such a rise was considered a hill: a hill crested by the woods which had become Henry's refuge over the years.

They were owned by a local farmer who cared little for such an unproductive gathering of trees. His lack of attention had resulted in thick undergrowth and the general tangle of unpruned boughs. But still there remained a few paths through the rubble of foliage, worn down by generations of people from the village in search of privacy and shade. At bluebell time the ground was an almost solid, steamy haze of blue and later, in September, the place was rich with blackberries. Henry knew and loved every part of the woods: the sharp snapping sounds in winter, the softer summer noises, the spring birdsong. He liked, from one side of the trees, the distant view of Wroughton House, classic façade aloof above its bed of lavender. He liked even better, in the other direction, the sight of the tall, smoking chimneys, five times the height of trees, against changing skies.

But fond though he was of the woods, Henry doubted whether they could provide him with much solace this afternoon. The happenings of the last few hours, at the risk of being dramatic, formed the greatest catastrophe of his life. He was still stunned by incredulity, and yet he knew them to be true. He had had to believe his own eyes. The Boy and the Leopard driving off together – his son and the only woman he had ever loved, mightily, causing his blood to churn and his mind to writhe night and day – the two of them had disappeared before him. It was his own fault, what's more. Why had he been such a bloody fool as to make his decision with rash speed, dashing off to get the bloody cauliflowers? It wasn't as if she would have *wanted* the things, even had he been successful. What woman in her senses could be wooed with vegetables? He must have been out of his mind.

He must have been out of his mind, too, not to have accepted the Boy's invitation. Had he only said yes, and gone with him to the bar for a pint instead of darting away like a scared rabbit, it might be *him*, Henry, the Leopard was passing her afternoon with now, instead of with the Boy. At this very moment they might be gliding through the lanes in the Morris Minor (taking the corners at quite a speed, to impress) looking for a good field, or a small café, in which to have their first conversation. Whoever it was up there guiding our destinies – and surely God as Henry believed in Him could not be so unfair – had made a right balls-up. What, now, was to be done? Cursing himself, over and over again, whiplashes in his mind, Henry could see no solution.

But there was one thing he was quite positive could *not* be done: he could not question the Boy. They had always preserved between them a lack of interference and that, at all costs, should not be broken. The Boy was reserved about his own affairs, so it was unlikely he would drop any hints, even in jest. He might, of course, mention – when Rosie wasn't there – having seen his father on a bicycle: but even if he did, it would not be up to Henry to enquire who was with him in the car at the time, or why. That would be breaking the rules. No: the only thing he could do, without any intention of spying, was to watch the Boy carefully, and to spend every possible moment in the Star.

Henry tramped heavily up and down the same path: he had no energy to turn corners and find himself in a denser part of the wood. He sucked on his pipe and listened without pleasure to the thrushes. A horrible restlessness fluttered with him, sour as indigestion. His own son so near the Leopard, in a car with the Leopard, *touching* (most likely) the Leopard – regoaded by these thoughts, he stopped sharply. He leant against the trunk of a larch tree, needing physical support in his despair. Oh God, he thought, I am no match for the Boy. Really, I should be glad: this turn of events might take his mind off Brenda. And yet, I am not glad. I am twisted and ugly with regret. I want what he has. I love the Leopard. I want her for the rest of my life. I want someone to live for: she has inspired in me that need. I must have her, or I must die.

Henry blinked. Through a small space in the branches he could see two distant chimneys. In his vulnerable state, they increased his desolation. He thought, as he had on the day he first saw the Leopard, of his happy years among the bricks: of his good mates, and of the satisfaction of getting through the work. To Rosie, it had been no more than his job, not worth talking about. The Leopard, if and when he could explain, would understand it was more than that: the point of his existence. But it was no use thinking of such a luxury: the Leopard would never be his, now. He could never tell her the multitude of things piled up in his heart, and the burden of them was too great. Moving again, this time towards a small grassy clearing he often visited, furnished only with an old tree stump that made a comfortable seat, Henry made his decision to die.

But even in his raging gloom practicalities came bubbling to his mind. Out here, he was equipped with neither a gun nor pills. And as the woods were the only place he could find the courage to do it, there was but one alternative. Henry took a box of matches from his pocket. There were three left. Even if he lit three different parts of his clothing at once it would be a horrible death. Once on fire, it would be unlikely he could put out the flames should the agony of it force him to change his mind. However, he doubted he would do any such thing. Physical suffering would be trivial in comparison with his present feelings: it would be worth enduring the vilest death rather than continue to live a life without the Leopard, knowing his son was enjoying her. 'The only antidote to mental suffering is physical pain.' The words came back to Henry for the first time in thirty years: a friend in the Navy had tried to make him read Marx. It had not made much sense to him, except for that one message. An encouragement, now, he'd have Marx on his side. Shaking the matches, Henry reflected briefly on how he would be mourned: Rosie, knowing her, would have a search party out by evening and they, poor things, would experience the nasty shock of finding his charred body. Rosie would be hysterical, need tranquillising shots from the doctor. The Boy, well, he might be quite upset. They'd arrange a decent funeral, pile up the coffin with Rosie's favourite flowers, no doubt, and his friends at the Star would bend their heads in respect at the graveside. There might be a small paragraph about him in the local paper, if they were short of news this week, and he would be remembered as a loyal, happy husband and devoted father.

Henry reached the clearing. He stood looking at the tree stump, trying to choose his spot. There was an old straw boater on top of the stump. For a moment Henry presumed somebody had left the hat behind. Then he saw it move. His heart surged. One more twist in the bad dream of the afternoon, perhaps? Had the Leopard somehow arrived here?

Even as he contemplated such a thing Henry realised his own foolishness. The hat was a cruel trick. Someone from the village was here to usurp his privacy. He would have to go elsewhere, to the far end of the woods.

Quietly, not wanting to disturb whoever it was, Henry edged his way round the clearing, protected from sight by the trees. Then he saw that the hat belonged to Rosie. There she sat, dressed up in her Sunday clothes, looking about her in some kind of trance as if a choir of angels up in the trees, invisible to anyone else, sang her lullabys. She had thrown off her shoes and her stockinged toes wiggled in the grass. Every now and then she touched her hair, or patted the absurd hat, with one of her huge red hands. Henry, hardly breathing, stared.

His instant reaction was that she had gone mad and he would have to hurry off for help. She had been acting strangely, of late, since he had been ill: smiling constantly, filling the larder with small dishes of pudding, and brandishing her hands in the strangest manner at bedtime, as if she expected him to remark upon them. But now, here, there was no madness in her eyes – rather, a kind of waxy calm. Unfortunately, Henry coughed. Rosie instantly spun round, standing up. She spied him at once in the tangle of branches.

'Henry! Oh, Henry.'

She had trapped him. If he turned and ran away now she would come screeching after him. All he could do was to get rid of her as soon as possible.

'What the hell are you doing here?' he asked. His gruff voice in no way damaged her expression of beatitude. She merely smiled, an aged nymph daft as a button in her gaberdine skirt.

'I thought, like you, it would be nice up here,' she said. 'And of course it was – it is. I've been listening to the birds. They make quite a noise, don't they, when you're just sitting, listening, alone?'

'Not this time of the afternoon, they don't,' said Henry, but Rosie was still not snubbed.

'Anyhow, I've been enjoying myself and I hoped I might run into you so that we could walk back together for tea.'

'Not much chance of missing another person in woods of this size,' said Henry gloomily. 'Why don't you go off home and put on the kettle? Cut me a slice of rice pudding' (anything to get rid of her) 'and I'll be along later.'

'Henry! That's very unfriendly.' She moved towards him, stood very close so that he could count the bubbles of seersucker on her blouse – a dreadful blue. He looked at her eyes, remembering them as they had been forty years ago: clear and bright, not a line on the skin around them. She had had a fine pair of eyes when she was young, he had to admit. Now they were quite dim, trapped in a mesh of pouchy lines, small blood vessels wiggling across the whites like a continuation of the marks on the skin. At this very moment they were full of pleading. Henry's stomach heaved. The bravery of spurned women was only slightly less bad than their tears.

He sucked on his pipe and spat out a bitter piece of tobacco, a thing that always taxed Rosie's tolerance to its hilt. But she said nothing. Henry lit one of the matches, held it to the dying tobacco, then let it fall to the ground. With only two matches left, his problem increased.

'Do go on home, Rosie,' he said. 'Can't you understand a man likes a few moments' peace on his own sometimes?'

But on such occasions, when Rosie's will surged strongly within her, understanding evaporated. She took Henry's arm, laughed. She slid her feet into her shoes, and patted her hat.

'Oh, come *on*, you silly old thing. You've been quite ill, you know, and you need someone to take care of you. What's a wife for if it isn't to support a man when he's down?' She was horribly flirtatious, flapping her great hands perilously near to Henry's face. He kept his pipe firmly in his mouth to protect himself from her actual touch. And all the time he felt the strength of resolve draining from him. 'You spent far too long out at lunchtime – you looked quite done in when you came home. And I shouldn't wonder you've had nothing to eat since breakfast. There's a fruit cake in the tin, and a new pot of honey. So come on, my love, for I shan't go without you.'

In a reluctant daze Henry felt himself move forward, close

to her. They retraced his old steps down the path, Rosie keeping up her blinking chatter all the while. Henry remained silent. At least, he thought, the search party would be spared a gruesome time: that was the only good thing about Rosie's unwanted appearance. God, she was a nuisance, the woman. It was all he could do not to hit her. And yet, in the depths of his sad and empty stomach, he felt a pang of hunger. If she forced him, he wouldn't say no to a bit of fruit cake. It would give him the strength to work out what to do next.

They reached the edge of the woods, started down the gentle hill. The late afternoon sky was cloudless, the soft grass bent about their ankles. They moved slowly, locked into that uncomfortable position when one person clutches and the other leans. Augusta Browne, standing by the pond at the bottom of her lawn, looked up and saw them. She thought what a loving old couple they made, and reflected that her own chance of ever becoming one of such a partnership was now quite over.

Augusta, too, had had a disturbing afternoon. The agency had rung to say the office men were keen for the house, and would shortly return with their architect to discuss its possibilities. Its possibilities: Augusta tried to put from her mind all the ways in which such people could destroy the house. In great anguish she attempted to keep herself busy: picking flowers, dusting, sorting out a cupboard – all unnecessary things which did nothing to alleviate her gloom. She tried to think, as she had so many times in the past months, about her future. For there was no escaping the reality of the situation: eventually the house would be sold. And what then? A small flat in London? A country cottage? She would never mind the solitude: that would not perturb her. But she doubted she could find the strength ever to care about a house again, once Wroughton House had gone. She would have to work, of course. She would not expect Hugh to support her. In any case, she would enjoy working again.

But she could not, at this moment, contemplate looking for the kind of job she wanted any more than she could consider looking for somewhere new to live. The future was a murky space she had no energy to inspect. Only the present was vital: the savouring of each moment as time ran out. Lowered by such reflections, Augusta felt a sudden and rare longing for company. She hoped that Evans and Brenda would be coming to the room tonight. She would like to waylay them and invite them to supper. She would like to hear about *their* lives – and so put aside for a while the melancholies of her own.

That same day Lark, at work, felt ill. She had a sharp pain in her lungs – a familiar pain, it had often struck her in the past few years. She knew it to last a couple of days, then to vanish as fast as it came. Its cause she could not discover, hard though she tried to work out whether it was to do with something she had eaten or drunk. She had given up cheese at night and had cut down her smoking: but still the pain returned from time to time. The doctor – whom she hadn't thought worth consulting for a couple of years – said it was surely indigestion, and prescribed tablets. They did her no good. She was forced to the conclusion the mysterious pain was something she would have to put up with every now and then.

Today the pain had been stronger than she could remember: typing at her desk, she bent forward a little, hoping to release it, but hoping also that her boss would not notice there was anything wrong. She hated sympathy and she hated days off. With the help of aspirin and cups of tea she would make an effort to disguise the discomfort: the idea of a day in bed filled her with apprehension.

But by the time she got home Lark was bent almost double in her attempts to quell the pain. She filled a hot-water bottle and, falling back on to the bed, rested it against her aching ribs. She had discovered that on some occasions if she fixed her mind on pleasurable things, happy memories and small hopes, the pain subsided. But this evening there were few good things she could recall: in fact, in the last week she had had more than her share of problems for one who tried to maintain a quiet grey life.

For a start there had been no lucky break in her singing career: this puzzled her because she was, after all, offering her services for nothing. She had imagined that people would grab at anything for nothing. She had imagined that people would grab at anything free. This was not so in the case of her prospective performance. She had written out a dozen small cards claiming she would be willing to entertain any kind of gathering with a few songs – 'a vast repertoire' – she had called it, in return only for but expenses. These cards were prominently stuck in the windows of local shops. To add to the allure she had called herself, simply, Lark: by eliminating the plebeian Jackson she felt she increased her chances. But only one person had shown any kind of interest, and that turned out to be the wrong kind. A gentleman had telephoned explaining he'd like a private cabaret – if she liked to throw in a few songs, well, he wasn't fussy. The lack of response depressed Lark, but she knew the way to success was a long, hard, soul-destroying one, and there was nothing for it but to be patient.

Then there was the problem of Evans. She had broken her word to him – not that he was aware of this, or ever would be. But the private knowledge troubled Lark. She had told him she wouldn't remember their love-making – if you could call it that. And she *had* remembered it, too clearly. Far from being able to forget it, the memory clung to her all hours of the day. Not an unpleasant memory either – in truth, confusingly, an exciting one. She had never before been taken by a man so large and handsome as Evans. She had assumed such men were reserved for the likes of Brenda, but had always had a secret fancy for Evans, knowing him to be right out of her reach, and knowing he felt not the slightest desire for her. His seduction – and Lark was quite aware that in his anger about Brenda he had used her simply as accommodation

– was the surprise of her life. She hoped she had acted with appropriate cool: cool was not what she had felt.

They had not met since. Indeed, since the availability of the room in Wroughton House, Brenda had not been here much either. Lark missed her. She missed Evans: his heavy feet on the stairs, his friendly teasing, the evenings he came to fetch Brenda. They used to take her with them, sometimes, to Sunday lunch at the Evanses' cottage, or the occasional cinema. There had been no such outings for a long time. Not that they would be so enjoyable now, were they ever to happen again: Lark would be closely observing Evans's attentions to Brenda while longing for such attentions herself. Oh, Lordy, what a muddle. So much easier not to fancy anyone, ever, and avoid such confusions. She'd been pretty good at that to date. Perhaps it was now her turn for an era of amorous discomfort.

Lark shifted her position. The pain seemed no less bad in spite of the heat of the bottle. She wished very much Brenda was here, but supposed it was much nicer for her to be in Wroughton House. Still, when she did return, no matter how late, Lark would call her in. Brenda would be kind and worried – she was always at her best when worried. She would probably, as she had on other such occasions, suggest sending Evans along to cheer Lark up. 'He'll come and tell you a bit of post office news, get you laughing no end,' Brenda would be bound to say. 'You can trust Evans to take your mind off the pain.' In which case, Lark decided, she'd do well to stay right here where she was, in bed, tomorrow. Much though she disliked a day off from work, she would sacrifice anything if there was a chance of seeing Evans again, alone, for a few moments. The strength of these new feelings puzzled her a little, but the pain continued to grind too hard into her bones to concentrate upon them. Instead, she put her mind to anticipation. Evans would most likely come at lunchtime. The pain wouldn't be bad enough to stop anything – that is, if he wanted . . . With an effort she raised herself on one elbow and searched among the bedside cacti for a bottle of geranium nail polish. Can't let him catch me looking a real wreck, she thought. Nails first, this evening, then a nice glass of neat gin.

Brenda let Wilberforce kiss her once. As his sour tongue moved over her teeth she remained placid, hating his mouth. When his hands began to scrabble at her breasts she removed them firmly.

'Fucking teaser,' he said, 'you deserve a spanking. If you wasn't so good with the birds you'd be out on your arse.'

Brenda decided the best thing was to humour him.

'Oh, come on, now, Mr Wilberforce. Don't be like that. I give an inch and you want a yard. That's not right, with my boss, is it? You're lucky to have got anything at all.' She smiled at him, pushing out her bottom lip. 'And don't forget, I'm engaged. Other people's property. Evans would break my neck if he knew about this – and yours. First.' She smiled again, apologetically.

The threat of Evans quickly douched Wilberforce's present desire. He backed away from Brenda, resigned.

'Creates something terrible in a man's mind, having a girl like you around and not being able to touch her,' he said, quite amiably. 'You'd better be off for now. But bear in mind I'll not give up trying.'

'You'll never get me.' Brenda went to the door.

'Want a bet on it? Bit of persistence and they all give in in the end.'

'Not me, Mr Wilberforce. I'll be on my way.'

Brenda went to the chicken shed and the incident quickly left her mind. She had more important things to think about than sods like Wilberforce this afternoon: she had to think about what to do next. Maybe it was the time to make a major decision about her life. That she should go, for instance. Leave this whole crummy joint and go to London, and take a job as a model – so many people had told her she would be a smashing model, hadn't they? Live it up a bit. And yet, that idea held no great appeal. If luck wasn't with you, you could come an awful cropper in London, get into drugs and crime and even prison. She'd seen enough of Mum struggling to know that she wanted no kind of struggle herself – ever. Here, at least, was security. Evans might not be the most exciting man in the world, but he was solid and kind. Boring though he was about their future, it was the kind of future Brenda aspired to, (in some moods) so long as she was *someone* in the community. That was important to her. And which of course she was, and would be, as a couple, with Evans. Every girl in the village fancied him and he never gave them so much as a glance. Every man fancied her and she, well . . . She never quite said yes, put it like that. Certainly, as a couple in the village there would be nothing to touch them. They'd have chickens and children and a quiet life, envied for their looks, perhaps: no great ambitions and no great worries. She wouldn't be a bad wife, either, if she tried: cooking and dusting, and that. And should she suffer from a little human weakness over the years, not always able to manage to resist, she'd never in a million years spoil Evans's trust by telling him. That would be barmy. Sure way to upset the applecart.

Brenda walked up and down between the chickens. She let their clucking trickle over her, a strange sound, half restless, half content, rather like water jerking at irregular speeds over a pile of loose stones. (She must remember to put that in her book of Thoughts when she got home: a book she kept instead of a diary. It was full of the kind of silly thoughts that come to a person's mind during a day alone, far too stupid to tell anyone. For months now she had been trying to work out exactly what chicken clucking was like – how you could explain it, accurately, to anyone who had never heard it so they would get the sound in their ears. She had had several goes, none of which was any good. This water over loose stones idea was the best yet. Just the sort of thing that would have made Robert, had she told him, laugh at her and pinch her and tell her to shut up while he kissed her.) Robert! She hadn't thought of him for some months. She lit a Woodbine. His face was dim. How had it been, exactly? She had heard it said that faces you know really well never go from you. But they do. In the end they fade. Well, that was good to know, to have proved, anyway. Bugger Robert like bugger Evans. Everything Mum had said about men was true: even the faithful type like Evans. In the end they let you down.

Brenda stopped by Daisy, newly queen. She was a sulky bird, Brenda had concluded of late. Her honourable appointment had made no difference to her general apathy. She barely clucked, in the shadow of Brenda's attention: just lowered her gritty yellow eyelids and looked fed-up. Floribunda, next to her, was much livelier. Floribunda was sprucing herself up as if for a date, murmuring in useless anticipation. Floribunda would have sympathy, were she able to understand.

'Bloody mess,' Brenda said to her, out loud. 'This is one hell of a bloody mess, Florrie, isn't it? All because I go down to the Air Base for a bit of innocent fun, didn't I? Didn't do nothing wrong, did I? Well, not so's you'd notice. Not so anyone'd notice. Just a bit of a snog, nothing much, was it?' She blew a bulb of smoke through her nostrils. 'Sorry my love. Get in your eyes, did it? Well, I mean: I mean it's not my fault if a man gets a hard-on dancing, is it? Nothing I can do about it, don't you think, Florrie? And what's the price I have to pay? My faithful old fiancé whips round and gets himself a blonde not five hundred yards from here. Cheekiest thing I ever heard of.' She paused. The sympathetic chicken seemed to have lost interest, continuing to pluck at her own frayed breast. 'What am I to do, Florrie? I don't want him going off, really. Not in the end, I don't, all things being equal.'

Brenda let herself cry for a while. There seemed no point in making the effort to stop. The tears released her sadness, but stimulated her anger. She put out the cigarette and blew her nose. One thing for certain – she wasn't going to have Evans thinking she cared. Oh, no, the last thing she'd ever do was allow him the luxury of thinking she cared. He could go to hell, as far as she was concerned: if he wanted to play it that way, then so would she. There was another do down at the Air Base this evening. Well, she'd tell him. She'd tell him she was going. She'd have her good time while he was out with his fancy lady. That was only fair – if that was how it was going to be, they might as well start as soon as possible.

And so, determined upon war, Brenda left the chicken shed and crossed the yard to the small building which she liked to call her office. In fact it had been built as a place in which to sort, grade and stack the eggs before they were collected to be sold. Brenda had persuaded Wilberforce to let her install an old table and chair under the window. This, her 'desk', she kept tidily furnished with a few biros, the book in which she recorded the daily number of eggs, and an old jam jar filled with whatever flowering weeds were in season in the farmyard.

Brenda guarded her office jealously. If she was in it when Evans came for her she would join him outside, never invite him in. Wilberforce had never set foot in the place: Brenda would take the book to him once a fortnight in the kitchen, where he made a perfunctory show of interest. When the van came to collect the eggs she handed the boxes to the driver from within. Mean sanctuary though it was, Brenda liked to feel it was a room uncontaminated by any other humans. While in the chicken shed itself she felt a sense of companionship, alone in the office among the eggs-scapes she revelled in a protective shell that she would not wish to be broken.

In winter the office was unbearably cold but, in her mittens and scarves, Brenda declined to ask Wilberforce for the luxury of an electric fire. In summer, as now, it was stuffy, airless. It smelt of grey cardboard egg boxes, and the groggy light meshed by cobwebs in the window gave no indication of the sunniest day outside. But Brenda liked the gloom. Having hurried through the brightness of the yard, she shut the door behind her, panting hard as if she had run a long way. When her eyes had grown accustomed to the dim light she raised her chin to the small piece of mirror fixed to the one free space on the wall – her only concession, in this place, to vanity. Her eyes and nose glistened with that scaly pinkness that comes after tears, her lips were dry. She licked them, and tossed her head. She'd get Lark to wash her hair tonight, before going down to the Air Base, and she'd try a little experiment with make-up. Give herself bright cheeks and emerald eyelids, perhaps – give them all something to think about. She'd wear her new white cotton shirt and leave most of the buttons undone, and swill the last of her bluebell essence everywhere, not just behind her ears . . . Brenda narrowed her eyes at herself. In a few hours' time she would look and feel smashing.

For the moment, there was nothing useful she could think of doing in the office. The eggs were all collected, washed, graded and stacked in their boxes for today. They filled the shelves, waiting for collection next morning.

Brenda sat down at the desk. The splintery edge of the chair, as usual, caught the back of her knees. Now would be the chance to sandpaper the wood, but she felt disinclined to do so. Instead, she opened the egg book and turned to a clean page at the back. She took up a wettish biro, chewed it for a moment, then began to write.

Dear Evans – I want you to know I'm going down to the Air Base this evening to another dance because its all over between us and there isnt any reason why I shouldnt do what I like now. Theres no use you thinking you can get away with it so easy going out with blondes because you cant. I saw you with her so theres no use denying it is there? Sorry in a way because it would have been nice being married to you tho I expect I would have made a bad wife and you with your fancy for blondes would have been a bad husband so we can spare ourselves a lot of rows this way. Sorry about this messy pen, I will return the ring if you like.   Bren.

She read it through. It lacked the note of firmness she had intended – but still, it would have to do. She had never been much of a one for letters. Tearing the page from the book Brenda looked around for a drawing-pin. She knew there was no such thing, here, but she meant to stick the note to the door and leave just before five-thirty, sure to miss Evans. The lack of a drawing-pin frustrated her unreasonably: what should she do? Helpless, suddenly, she felt near to tears again.

Increasingly, Evans found himself much affected by the boredom of his post office job. In the beginning, taking over from the previous postmaster, who had let the business decline into a dreadful muddle over the years, he had found it a challenge. With great energy (and inspired by some vague idea of being required for an interview on *Panorama* in ten years' time) he got the place on its feet again – sorted out the files, threw a mass of obsolete stuff away and, best idea of all, installed the deep-freeze full of ice-cream and lollipops. He also took pains with the choosing of the Christmas and birthday cards, and replaced the old-teeth colour of the walls with a wash of pale blue. He knew all his customers by name and made a point of being consistently cheerful, willing and friendly. As a result of his efforts, trade picked up – a little. Except in the few weeks before Christmas the place could never be called lively, and since the catastrophic rise in postal rates Evans had noticed a distinct decline in the sending of letters and parcels. Consequently the hours at work felt long and dull.

The afternoon Evans had given the Leopard a lift to the station had been particularly oppressive. Maybe this was in contrast to the small flutter of excitement he had felt in driving a strange woman, however undesirable to him, in his car. He couldn't wait to tell Brenda about the whole incident: they'd have a good laugh . . . As a matter of fact it would be no bad thing for her to realise that strange women in beautiful coats weren't averse to his offering them a lift . . . Sometimes, he thought, Brenda made out she had Evans exactly where she wanted him. This might give her a beneficial jolt. Teach her to go gallivanting off to the Air Base . . . Annoyed with himself, Evans put that thought from his mind.

He had forgiven her long ago, and disliked the nagging feeling of unquiet that rose within him every time he recalled the incident.

At five past five, having changed the blotting paper in the two blotters, and dampened the rubber sponges, Evans decided that, at the risk of being sacked, he would leave. He could no longer stand the buzzing flies and the warm stuffy smell of ink and linoleum. Soft evening air was what he longed for: a walk with Brenda round Mrs Browne's garden (she had given him permission to go where he liked, but so far he had not taken up her offer). They might go to the rose garden. Brenda, like Rosie, was a sucker for flowers. Then they would take a couple of cans of beer and a packet of crisps up to their room, open the window, lie on the bed, and see how things went from there. Evans, locking up, was pretty sure he knew how they'd go: since the famous night she'd been almost insatiable.

He swung his jacket over his shoulders and walked swiftly to Wilberforce's farm. Down through the yard, warm familiar manure smell all about him, Evans looked towards the shed for Brenda. No sign of her. Strange. Evenings like this, she usually stood about in the sun, smoking away at her bloody Woodbines in defiance of Wilberforce's threats. Evans poked his head round the chicken shed door: filthy stench, cluck cluck bloody cluck, but no Brenda. He couldn't think how she could stand the hens, day after day, let alone feel affection for them. He crossed the yard to her office, cautiously knocked on the door. No answer. He pushed the door ajar, looked in.

She was sitting at her table, shoulders hunched, back to him. She gave no sign of having heard him.

'It's me,' he said.

Brenda turned her head. Even in the etiolated light Evans could see there was a kind of silvery sheen over her face, perhaps sweat. It was so hot in here. Then he noticed two curling rims of what looked like fine sand at the corner of one of her eyes: the salt of dried tears.

'You can't come in here,' she said. 'You know you can't come in here.'

But Evans remembered the lesson he had learned that terrible night. Brenda responded best to mastery.

'I'm in here,' said Evans, half shutting the door behind him. 'Is anything the matter?' He could not be sure – this dimness was confusing after the bright sun outside, but he thought Brenda was regarding him with antagonism. He found it difficult to breathe in the close, grey cardboard air, and Brenda's silence was troubling. 'Anything the matter, Bren?' he said again, and let his eyes wander from her face over the small mountain ranges of eggs. Trays and trays of eggs, piled almost to the ceiling – brown ones, speckled ones, white ones, he wondered how many –?

'Get out,' said Brenda. 'Go on, get out.'

Evans stepped back, pushing the door completely shut behind him.

'Come on, Bren, don't be silly,' he said. 'Look, I got off early – risk the sack for that, you know. But I thought it was such a nice evening we could go up to the house and take a turn round the garden, take a sniff at the roses, you've been on about the roses, Bren, haven't you –?' Under her gaze he found himself running on, anything to break the silence, to appease her. In one movement she rose from the chair and sat on the table. This way she did not have to look so far up at him: her head was at his shoulder level. She folded her arms under her breasts, heaving them up, forcing a cleavage to show in the undone neck of her shirt. She swung one foot backwards and forwards, gently hitting the chair each time.

'I'm not coming up the house or anywhere else with you, Evans Evans, thank you very much. I'm going back down the Air Base. There's another dance on tonight.'

'What?' Evans could hear his own heart, its sudden booming thump.

'I'm going to a dance.'

Calm, Evans, calm, he said to himself. I'm not understanding right. There must be some mistake.

'I don't understand,' he said.

'Perhaps you'd understand if I told you I know all about you and your blonde.' Brenda gave her breasts an almost enjoyable heave.

'My blonde?' For a moment Evans could not think what she meant. His mind broke into a blinding white star of guilt, and yet he could not think why he was guilty. 'My blonde?' he said again, and he knew his mouth had fallen open and his bad eye was beginning to twitch.

'Oh, come off it, really! Don't waste my time with your pretended innocence. You know quite well what I'm talking about.' Her voice was nasty beyond recognition.

'I don't, Bren. I really don't know what you mean.' But even as he said it, he did. Even as he uttered the feeble denunciation, he knew what must have happened. She must have seen him, wondered, brooded all afternoon . . . Oh, really, it was laughable. His slow smile reflected the pace of his clearing thoughts. Brenda jumped down from the table. She faced him eye to eye. Christ, what a stupid drama all for nothing . . .

Evans stumbled back as Brenda hit him on the cheek. She was shrieking something about it being no laughing matter. What did he think he was? The shit, the swine, the deceiving bastard, getting at her like that the other night when she'd done nothing wrong, when all the time he'd been having it away with some filthy blonde tart – the words shot out, ricocheting off the darkness of Evans's comprehension. There was cuckoo spit at the corners of her mouth. Her hair was swinging about in heavy chunks, cider coloured, conker coloured, changing as she moved. As her hand rose to swipe him again Evans caught hold of her wrist.

But she twirled around, snakily escaping his grip, shouting all the while.

'Deny it, deny it, deny it!'

She's gone mad, thought Evans. Off her bloody head. He snatched her wrist again, missing it.

'And keep your fucking hands off me. Just you try denying

you were in a car with her this afternoon.' Brenda paused for a moment, backed up against the table, breasts quickly rising and falling as she panted.

'That's quite true,' said Evans, 'but keep calm a moment while I explain.'

'I knew it!' Brenda screamed, and suddenly her arms seemed to be flailing everywhere, filling the whole small mottled space. Vaguely, as he backed himself against the door, shielded his eyes with an arm, Evans saw her clutching at a tray of eggs. He saw the jolting of their neat mountain ranges as Brenda raised it above her head – he smelt a new whiff of cardboard. It bashed down upon him, a mad cloudburst. He heard the prickling sound of three dozen cracking shells, small explosions beneath the wild soprano screech of her voice.

Then he felt the mess. Slime among his fingers, threads of yolk, less rubbery, skulking through his hair, falling in a fringe over his bad eye. He saw an abstract pattern of yellow on the wall, a glinting pool of transparent slime on the floor. And Brenda's wide mouth, screaming screaming screaming unjust abuse.

He hit her. He left a mess of yolk on her face. She swung about, reaching for another tray of eggs, but slipped. Quickly Evans snatched the tray and saved it from falling: as Brenda tried to right herself, tried to stand, Evans crashed it down upon her head. It covered her hair with a web of yolks, whites and broken shells. He felt her fists in his stomach, his balls. He lashed back, enraged by the pain. They both reached for single eggs, clumsily hurled their ammunition at each other, screaming obscenities all the while. In the moments of timeless insanity Evans saw the raw eggs as injured eyes, the foul yellow of their pupils split and running into the liquid shapeless globs of their eyeballs. Christ, the bitch the bitch the bitch, he'd kill her.

Then Evans felt a searing pain in his own eyeball, the bad one. Cowering against the shelves he shouted to Brenda to stop, he had eggshell in his eye. He heard his own moan from a long way off, and felt a warm jet of tears stream from the eye.

Brenda stopped, sat back on the desk. Through his good eye, Evans focused on the absurd sight of her – hair, face, arms, breasts, legs, everything enskeined in dripping yellow, chips of shell, translucent slime.

'Help me,' he said.

Brenda came over to him. He dropped his hands, which he had made into a mask over his eye. Brenda gently lifted up the lid with trembling fingers that smelt of egg.

'I see it,' she said. Tears from the smarting eye ran among her fingers, ran over the egg whites like oil over water. 'Here, wait. My hanky.'

She pulled a handkerchief from the sleeve of her shirt. Part of its hem was stained yellow. She screwed up a corner and pulled Evans nearer to the dun light of the window. With her spear of white cotton she skimmed about his eyeball. Evans clenched his teeth and ground his fingers into his palms to stop himself screaming. It was as if she was nicking at him with a razor: he tried not to think what happens to a sliced eyeball.

'There.' Her head was bent over a tiny chip of shell on the handkerchief. 'It's out. Sorry if I hurt.'

Evans put out a hand to Brenda's shoulder. His eye still overflowed with water and he could not see her clearly. Her shoulder was covered in mess, gritty with broken shells. He felt the movement of a noiseless sob.

She moved away from him, sat back in her old position on the table.

'Glory be to God, Evans, I don't know what got into me.'

Evans ran a hand through his gluey hair, and round the back of his neck. He could feel trickles of liquid slobbering down his back.

'She wasn't my blonde,' he said quietly. 'You got it all wrong. She was a woman I never saw in my life before. And, good God, I never want to see her again. She was waiting for some fellow in the Star who didn't show up. She had no way of getting back to the station. I took her out of the goodness of my heart, otherwise she would have missed her train.'

'Oh,' said Brenda. She looked up. Her eyelashes were stuck together, yellow spikes blurred by fresh tears. Evans managed a smile.

'Don't think I've ever seen such a sight as you in all my life,' he said.

'You should take a look at yourself,' said Brenda. 'What are you going to do about all this?' She looked around.

'We'll think about that later.' Evans pulled her towards him. 'Here.' They kissed, tasting the raw egg splayed round each other's mouths.

'God, we're revolting,' said Brenda.

'I love you, girl,' said Evans. 'I love you, you silly jealous bitch. I wouldn't go out with a blonde. You know I wouldn't go out with a blonde, don't you?'

'Don't suppose you would, as a matter of fact.' With the useless handkerchief Brenda was trying to rub off some of the egg from her shirt.

'Lucky I got the car at the top of the yard,' said Evans. 'I daresay we can get there with no one seeing us, and slip in through the back of the house. Mrs Browne never seems to be around.'

'Just a minute. We'll go in a minute.' Brenda let the slimed handkerchief drop to the floor. She seemed quite exhausted, but her tears had stopped. They remained in silence for a while, looking round at the ludicrous mess left by their violence. 'What was all this about, Evans? What was all this about?' She reached behind her and picked up the folded note she had written two hours before. 'I wrote you this letter saying I was going because I saw you in the car with that woman.'

'You always act so hasty, Bren. Without thinking.'

'So do you. Who beat me up for going down to the Air Base?' She scrunched up the piece of paper and threw it on the floor.

'Let's talk about it later. Let's go. Come on. It stinks in

here. We'll come back later and clear up.'

Out in the yard, dazzling with evening sun, they laughed at the sight of each other. The egg whites were beginning to congeal, streaking their skin with silvery trails: splatterings of yellow yolk clung to them everywhere. They held sticky hands.

'I just saw red,' said Brenda.

'You drove me mad,' said Evans. 'So unreasonable.'

'A person has every right to be unreasonable sometimes.'

'Never knew you had it in you, jealousy.'

''Course I wasn't jealous, silly. I was just angry at being deceived. That's quite different.'

'Ah,' said Evans, 'but you weren't being deceived.'

'Thought I was, so it comes to the same thing.'

'Bloody women,' said Evans.

They managed to get unseen in the car to the back drive of Wroughton House. They slipped through the back door and along the passage to the narrow flight of stairs that led directly to the attic. But halfway up they heard Mrs Browne below them, calling. It was almost as if she had been waiting for them. They stopped. They turned to her, noticing small blotches of egg yolk in their wake. For a moment Mrs Browne's eyes trembled with enquiry, then she smiled.

'You both look as if you could do with a bath,' she said. 'There are masses of spare bathrooms.' She sounded apologetic. 'Come on, I'll show you.'

She led Brenda to her own bathroom, Evans to one that overlooked the walled garden. She provided towels and soap and shampoo. She asked no questions and they volunteered no explanations. Later, she helped Brenda rub dry her hair. Brenda would only talk about the size of the bathroom, which impressed her.

'Twice as big as our living-room at home,' she said. 'If I had a place like this I'd lie in the bath hours and hours just looking at the view and thinking nice thoughts.'

'I do.' Augusta was being efficient, folding towels. 'As a matter of fact,' she said, 'I seem to have made myself far too much kedgeree, and there's lots of cheese and salad. Would you and Evans like to stay for supper?'

'That would be smashing.' Brenda, sitting on the mahogany lavatory seat, bare-breasted, was dabbing at her hair with a comb. 'Smashing, if it's not too much trouble.'

'Lovely. I'll go and get some wine. Help yourself to anything you want. There's make-up and stuff in the bedroom.'

She left the bathroom very quickly. Brenda, in a kind of day-dream, continued ineffectually to comb her hair, staring all the while out of the window at violaceous shadows fluttering over the lawn. She did not question the unreality of her present position just as, earlier, she had not questioned the unreality of the extraordinary fight. Sometimes, things just surged up, grasped you so tight you couldn't breathe or reason, swallowed you up, spat you out and left you sitting there, chewed, torn, exhausted. Then you recovered and went back to normal. Only when you looked back on the event could you see what it had all been about. Well, that's how she saw it, anyway. Meantime, this particular process of recovery, with a nice supper cooked by someone else in a posh kitchen to look forward to, was far from disagreeable.

Brenda and Evans changed into clothes they kept in their attic room, and joined Augusta Browne in the rose garden. She flitted from bush to bush, gently touching puffy blooms, bending her head sometimes to smell them, contradicting herself about her favourite – carrying on just like his mother, thought Evans. His eye still smarted and continued to spurt odd tears, blurring the rose colours in which he politely tried to show some interest. Brenda really did enjoy them: there was Mrs Browne telling her she should take as many as she liked, whenever she liked – it was a pity for them to be wasted. Women were a right soppy lot when it came to flowers: but still, it was pleasant out here, warm evening air and all that, and great slack feelings of release after all the tension and daft fighting.

Later, they ate in the kitchen. Mrs Browne had put a bowl of yellowish roses on the table, of course, and when Brenda had said they were the colour of egg yolks they had all laughed. There were a couple of lighted candles and three bottles of wine. Brenda, by candlelight, not quite dark sky in the window behind her, looked bloody marvellous, Evans thought. He had a good idea they would stay in the attic all night, tonight. So thinking, he scarcely concentrated on Mrs Browne's funny stories. She was making Brenda laugh a lot: oh yes, she seemed to be very gay, Mrs Browne, tonight. Her gaiety, it seemed to him after four glasses of iced dry white wine – went down easy as anything – was almost visible, spinning about the candle flame like a moth or something, rubbing up against them, affecting them – him and Brenda – too. Hell, he couldn't half be fanciful when he was a little drunk.

'Yes, just another glass, thanks.' He shouldn't have said yes, by rights, he'd have an awful head in the morning. But tonight, everything considered, seemed to be rather a special night: fight over, Brenda's flesh to look forward to – Christ, he'd show her how he loved her. Christ, he would. He picked up his glass.

A combination of gin and sleeping pills eventually eased Lark's pain. Weak with relief at its going, she struggled to keep awake, but hopelessly. The last real thing she remembered was ash coloured sky in her window. The last picture against her closed eyelids was of Evans bearing down upon her. She imagined his weight. She put a drowsy hand on her ribs, where he would lie. Painless, now. Pain gone. She remembered she would be fine in the morning. Have to go to work, after all.

For Rosie Evans it was another wakeful night in the bed beside Henry. She had much to reflect upon, much to sort out in her mind.

Already, eyes blinking at the summer stars twinkling through the elm leaves, she had been over the whole afternoon a hundred times. For all the rush, her plan had, surprisingly enough, gone almost perfectly. Henry had found her, and hadn't seemed to notice her slight limp caused by pins and needles sitting all that time on the tree stump. Judging by the look in his eyes he was nicely surprised by her appearance – hadn't gone so far to *comment* upon her romantic choice of clothes – but, then, he'd never been one for observations, and his very lack of comment was a compliment in itself. True, he had spoken a little gruffly, asked her to go away: but that was a natural reaction by anyone taken by surprise when they think they're on their own. And in the end, she'd won him over, of course. He came with her very meekly, biting on his pipe happily enough, listening to her reflections of the warmth of the evening and the blueness of the sky. At home, he'd settled down in his armchair and eaten three slices of newly baked bread spread thickly with honey, three chocolate biscuits and two lumps of fruit cake. Rosie hadn't seen him eat so much for weeks. The sight had overjoyed her. She had busied about, full of encouragement, trying to convince him he'd be quite better in no time if he kept eating like that. He'd refused the rice pudding, it had to be admitted, but that was quite understandable, considering the amount he had eaten before. When he'd finished, he got up and put on his coat, said he was going back down to the Star.

For a moment Rosie thought he meant her to go with him, like on Christmas Eve and her birthday, though he didn't go so far as to say that. 'Won't be long,' was all he said, and swung out of the door, wanting to be alone written all over his back.

Rosie was stung. Disappointment jabbed all through her, making her sniff and blow her nose loudly, as she would never have done in front of Henry or Evans. She was bemused. Her plan had gone so well till then. Why now had it failed?

Still, husbands were puzzling things and it was a wife's duty not to be got down by them. She tidied everything she could think of tidying, chose a tin of tomato soup to warm up when he came home, and sat down to read the paper. But she was restless. An uncomfortable feeling of nervousness jangled through her, stopping her concentration. She realised, suddenly, she was still wearing her boater. Well! In the excitement of Henry's large tea she must have forgotten to take it off. What a silly old thing she was. She must have looked ridiculous, serving him his tea in her hat. Why hadn't he said anything? Unlike Henry not to point out a mistake like that. She puffed up her hair and found herself making for the larder. It would be foolish to waste the end of the rice pudding, and it didn't look as if Evans was coming home. She scraped it up slowly with a small spoon, leaving the bits of gold skin till last, enjoying its sweetness. Then she went back to pace the kitchen.

Henry returned at eleven. He hadn't stayed out so late for years. Rosie quickly controlled the worry on her face, gave him a welcoming smile and suggested the tomato soup. But he wanted none of it. He seemed not to notice her, he seemed quite preoccupied. And then she understood. He had been drinking. Not just his normal two or three pints, mind. But real drinking. Whisky. She could smell it on his breath, see it in the liquid red-brown of his eyes. She did not manage quite to conceal a gasp, and then she saw, mounting the stairs, he was very unsteady. She had given him an arm, said there, there, you're all right, my love, Rosie's here – and helped him to bed.

He'd been asleep a couple of hours now. Snoring. Rosie sighed. Her plan had so nearly been entirely satisfactory. A pity . . . But still, you couldn't hope for everything. Not all at once. There was plenty of time.

Under the sheets Rosie rubbed her hands together, feeling the skin still greasy with tonight's helping of hand lotion. Oh, he would be amazed, Henry, when the time came.

He would not believe it, would he? She didn't mind waiting, really, of course. She was so sure all would be well at last. At the feel of her soft bare hand on his shoulder he would turn over, wouldn't he? Aroused, wanting . . . And all the old passion – no more than a memory for so long – would be upon them both again. Rosie Evans, she said to herself, squeezing her greasy fingers, you should have thrown away those mittens years ago. So much wasted time to be made up for: we must begin tomorrow night.

She heard the church clock strike three.

PART II

Summer expanded: hot, dry. Last year, Augusta remembered, was altogether more temperate. There had been a spate of light showers, sudden from a clear sky, catching them unawares. On several occasions they had had to run from tea in the garden – in those days Augusta still occupied herself with cucumber sandwiches of brown bread, honeycombs, and iced coffee swirling with whipped cream – anything, anything to delight Hugh, to deter his thoughts of leaving. With their guests they had had to pick up plates and glasses, run across the warm grass, the warm gravel, and into the sudden dimness of the hall whose flagstones, too, were warm beneath bare feet. Augusta recalled, in the present silence, the laughter of their friends: the released movements of people cooled by shadow when they have come in from the sun, cobwebs of rain on their hair, the high, irresponsible feeling they all shared of there being nothing to do but to please themselves till dinner. In fact the frail showers were a kind of bonus, making the view of lawn and trees a temporarily new place, a landscape of spun glass: then the sun would return to melt the sparkling, and on the barely dampened grass they would take up croquet mallets and continue their game. It was the laziest summer ever Augusta could remember, but, beneath the idleness, chimed reverberations of implacable fear.

To protect themselves from each other Augusta and Hugh surrounded themselves almost constantly with friends. Every weekend the house was full and it was not difficult to put discord aside. Hugh was wonderfully benign, proud of his house and exhilarated by the delight it gave other people. Augusta shared his feelings and, together among their friends, they were at their best. Funny, gay, they sparked off in each other ever more absurd plans which would never materialise, but the thought of them was nonetheless enjoyable. There was no time for dispute. In the pleasure of those armoured days there was no occasion for the deadening discussions of their own problems. High spirits would be the order of the weekend: not till Sunday afternoon did Augusta begin to feel the chill of an ebbing tide. It was the time of week she most dreaded: that peculiar sadness of an English Sunday afternoon, that long chilly slope that begins with the apple tart and cream and dwindles into the bleakness of cold meat for Sunday supper when everyone has left. This abhorrence, Augusta supposed, was inherited from her days at boarding school: the sickening feeling of imminent return to real life which no amount of jollity can disguise.

In happier days at Wroughton, Sunday afternoons had been less bad: while teasing her for neurosis Hugh had at the same time skilfully worked upon releasing her from it. Augusta, in retrospect, was unable to analyse just how he had done this: she simply recalled that, for several years, weeks of Sundays would go by with only an occasional lapse into familiar melancholy. But, their last summer, Hugh's magic worked no longer. The disintegration of Sunday symbolised the disintegration of their lives: the lamentable bells of evensong were a horrible cry. They would wander about their warm garden, soothed by the smell of tobacco plants quivering with their own scent, reluctant to face real issues and yet unable to avoid them. The problem of money increased daily, but they were united in their madness of overspending. Monday morning there would be more bills: Sunday evenings, discussions about how to pay them had an air of hopelessness. While butterflies flurried about the lavender, the reality of a vast overdraft seemed not quite to touch them with its deepest implications. But for all its moments of dread and fear, Augusta remembered last summer as gravid with idyllic days. It was a time not wasted, not regretted: for all its blemishes, it shone with that particular light that distinguishes a few seasons in a lifetime, and it would remain thus for ever in her mind.

This year it was harsher, starker. Lack of rain caused the

leaves to dry prematurely. Their crisp shapes, against blaring near-white skies, made eyes to ache with their brilliant green. Shade was anaemic: patches of lawn were burned yellow, birds were too parched to sing.

But the office men, impervious to heat, gleaming necks in nylon collars, returned with increasing frequency to survey the house and grounds. They became cockily familiar with the place, pouncing over and over again upon the same cracks, shouting possessively about the 'grand views' from the windows. Augusta came to recognise them as individuals: the strutting chairman; the managing director with his weird smile which looked as if his mouth, in reality very small, was permanently distorted by magnification; the fat spinster secretary whose plastic stilletos caused her to stumble uneasily across the lawns. She was unused to such spaces of grass, as she kept informing everyone in her Wimbledon voice, and was given to much panting when the chairman made her take notes while he traversed the garden in his puffed-up manner.

The seriousness of their intent was in no doubt, and they began to take dreadful liberties. One day they brought cans of beer and executive sandwiches – inappropriate Gentlemen's Relish – to eat in the shade of the elm tree for lunch: they did not bother to ask Augusta's permission until halfway through, and seemed insensitive to her disapproval. They merely tightened the laces of their suede shoes, as city office men find it necessary to do after a few hours in the country, and stubbed out their mini cigars among the daisies. They spoke of the possibility of the back drive becoming a car park, and enquired if domestic and secretarial help was readily available – they actually used the phrase readily available – in the village. Augusta assured them no one was in search of a job.

But she knew surrender would soon be forced upon her the day they brought the architect. A pale Mr Droby, of suburban inclinations, was the architect – a friend of the estate agent through whom the Brownes had originally found the house. Having accomplished his minor function of linking drains to new bathrooms, he had boldly suggested to Augusta and Hugh that he should then go on to improve the general architecture of the William and Mary building. His idea had been to embellish the place with archways, and alcoves of shelves lit with concealed bulbs. In his view it was advisable to flatten out the undulating walls, double glaze the windows and hide the beautiful pine stairs under a thick protection of Wilton carpet. Furthermore, he suggested, his wife could be very helpful when it came to interior design, as he grandly called it, should Augusta find herself with no ideas. He brought along snippets of man-made silk in 'various shades' to 'tone in' with unsubtle paints straight from a chart. He was sent away rebuffed, and disapproving of Augusta's plans. But he waited. Time would come for his revenge, and with the arrival of the office men, it did.

He was called upon for his valuable opinions and most vociferously he gave them. Augusta, in the background, overheard his frightful suggestions with increasing horror. She understood that Droby realised here was a renewed chance to ruin something on a grand scale, and this time he was not going to let that chance elude him. With a sense of complete helplessness Augusta listened to him describing the mock Georgian porch with which he would 'make a feature of' the façade: in his hands, she realised, there would be no end to the ruination of the house. It was imperative the office men should be deterred. But, by now, nothing could stop them. A week after Droby's visit, inspired by his optimistic views of how the place could be much improved under his guidance, they made an offer. The price was disappointing, but it was the only offer in six months. The money was guaranteed: Hugh, with surprising sadness on the telephone to Augusta, explained they could not refuse it. 'Because once the house has gone, we can't really mind what happens to it,' he said. 'Oh, but we can, we will,' retorted August. 'We must save it.' 'No good being sentimental,' said Hugh, 'I've agreed they shall take possession in January.'

January. Four months.

The positive news blasted Augusta with what turned out to be a new series of acute sensations. The nature of uncertainty, in which she had been living for the last year, is some protection. Stripped of that, and faced with an inescapable ending, it is a strong mind and body that can survive intact. Augusta knew that she must be calm: frenzy would waste the days. All she could do was to make the most of the last weeks, living each day, in the biblical sense, as if it was her last: praying for slowness of the hours. Self-pity she had always abhorred and never indulged in: her new problem was how to deal with the physical symptoms of incredulity. As they crushed her, that first evening she heard the news, she found herself little equipped to resist them. With no heart to go into the garden, she stood in the brown light of her study, head resting against the warm glass of the window pane, and allowed herself to weep outrageously. Tears were a strange sensation, she was unused to crying. Their release did nothing to ameliorate the anguish, but the sound of her own moaning in the silence provoked a detached curiosity about herself. She was spurred by self impatience. What was the good, what was the good? Glutting sorrow upon roses, Keats's facile suggestion, was no help outside poetry. No: she must return to the normal habits of an evening, continue as naturally as possible. But what were those habits? Since Hugh's departure the rhythm of things had been upset. Most days she floundered, restless, unable to concentrate, only intent on constantly re-establishing by actual touch the existence of her territory. It occurred to her – she smiled to herself – that if anyone in the past few months had observed her pacing about touching flowers, walls, pictures, they would have thought her quite mad. She must pull herself together.

Augusta blew her nose, thinking how ugly she must look. She had a long, cool bath, watching the elms dissolve into cumbersome shapes as the sky faded. And, later, she did in fact achieve some kind of exhausted calm, although a strange pain began to drill her jaw. She was determined there should be no more private outbursts: they did nothing but enfeeble. The uselessness of tears was disillusioning. She did not cry again.

Rosie Evans was inclined to see omens in small things that might escape the notice of less observant people. The afternoon the Red Admiral flew through the kitchen door – trying to escape the ruddy heat, poor thing – she knew at once her luck had changed. Although almost two months had gone by since she had burned her mittens, she had not yet approached Henry. Why, she could not exactly explain to herself, but some instinct warned her to remain patient for a little while longer. The fact that Henry had made no comment on her hands, naked now every night, seemed to her a good sign. They cannot have repulsed him, or he would have broken his silence. Maybe he thought they had improved, and when the night to touch him finally came he might not be surprised. He might even be pleased.

But the Red Admiral signalled the end of all such hopes. Rosie watched it fluttering against the window pane, seeking escape. She put up her hands to catch it and return it to the door. It was then she noticed, in the fierce midday light, their sorry state. Overnight, it seemed, the soft greasiness of her skin, achieved by two months of rubbing in hand lotion, had vanished. Her fingers were wintry again, dark and swollen, scored with rough cracks. She uttered a low moan. Tears came to her eyes. It could only be some confounded allergy – but to what? The doctors had no idea: she had been asking them for years. Dear God, it was unfair. She had no spirit to sew herself more mittens and tonight, if he noticed her hands, Henry would turn away his head, barely hiding his disgust. He would heave himself away from her to the far corners of the bed.

Rosie caught the butterfly. She felt its wings flickering in the black cage of her palms, vile palms rough as sawdust, which Henry could never forgive. She kept it trapped for a moment longer than was necessary, its fear a wicked comfort. Then she let it go, dropping her hands heavily to her sides. It flew up towards the elms, dazzling as illusion, and disappeared. Rosie licked the corners of her mouth. She tasted salt. She looked at the dry earth, the dusty lane, the unbroken blue of the sky, and struggled to control a sob. The luxury of weakness, she contemplated, would suit her now. She would like to slip into the cemetry, unobserved, go to her mother's grave in its shady place under the hedge, lean her head against the rough stone cross and roar out loud against the unfairness of her inherited hands, till all her grief was exorcised. As it was, she saw Henry in the road. Even from this distance she could tell he was unsteady on his feet. Rosie returned to the kitchen: in all the upset she was late laying the table for his dinner. But would he eat it? For several weeks, now, he had done no more than pick at his food, complaining of the heat. Every afternoon he had slept in his chair, no pretence of looking at his paper, waking just in time to return to the Star when it opened at six. Through the tangle of her own preoccupations Rosie was aware that all was not well with Henry. She put it down to the sun – every blinking day, there hadn't been a cloud in the sky for two weeks – and the monotony of retirement. He wasn't a man to take to rest easily, not after a life of vigorous work. Rosie worried about him. Perhaps, she thought, they didn't go out enough. The Morris Minor sat under its plastic cover, untouched, for months on end. Silly waste, really. Rosie herself had no taste for pottering along lanes in a stuffy car, whose brakes she could not credit, but she knew it gave Henry pleasure. Perhaps she should suggest . . . a cinema, one evening. They hadn't seen a film in years. That would make a break, surely. Something to talk about for a week or so – something to take Henry's mind off his wretched bricks.

Rosie brightened at her idea. Going out, evening, there would be nothing unnatural about wearing her nice lace gloves, which would give her confidence. She needn't always be hiding her hands. Perhaps, if she was feeling very bold, she might even try *brushing Henry's knee*, in the safety of the dark, as she reached to get a toffee from the bag she would insist he bought on the way in. Ah, hope! There was remedy for all things in hope, Rosie knew, and she wasn't one to be dashed by a spell of bad luck. Besides, there was so much to be thankful for. A happy home, a faithful husband who needed her at this time. She began to slice the luncheon meat, and to arrange her smile of welcome.

'Henry, my love,' she said, hearing him outside. She looked up. He stood swaying in the door, averting his eyes from her face. With a great effort of will, Rosie continued to smile.

'And this,' said Evans, with a sweep of his arm, 'will be the lounge.'

He stood on one of its walls, three bricks high, surveying the foundations of their future house: his and Brenda's. Heat and pleasure had caused damp patches under the arms of his shirt, and he imagined the bathroom, where next summer he would wash every day. He fancied tiles, some pale colour chosen by Brenda, and a mirror high enough for him to shave into without having to stoop. He also had in mind an especial front door, one that would be a cut above the other front doors on the estate, with a brass knocker in the shape of a cockerel's head. He hadn't managed to find such a thing as yet, but if the worst came to the worst he would have one made. A silly extravagance, his mother would say, but it would please Brenda no end, and when it came to the house she would take a bit of pleasing.

He knew that in her heart she longed for it to be ready as much as he did: to be married, settled, chicken-breeding, decorating – to be safely cocooned by the gentle monotony of their own lives. But something perverse in Brenda – and after all it was her spirit he loved her for – caused her to complain. Not only to complain, but to be downright insulting about the whole place, the whole idea. Her lack of enthusiasm might have daunted a feebler man. To Evans, it merely spurred his determination to enchant her with visions of their future.

'And that, there, where you're standing, Lark, will be the front path. A nice fine gravel I'll get from a mate up the road.'

'Bet the regulations won't let us,' said Brenda.

'Bugger the regulations.' Evans jumped down from the lounge wall. At the back of his mind lurked something far more worrying than the regulations – the money. The house would be finished by Christmas. Evans had persuaded his friend in the agency selling the houses, for the price of a few drinks, to secure this particular house – the best site, on a corner, a patch of trees not far away. But for the moment he was still short of £200 on the deposit money. How he would find it in time was a problem that kept him awake at nights, Brenda asleep in his arms, exhausted by his love-making. (Worry, he'd noticed lately, was a strange aphrodisiac.) She never asked him about money – such things as deposits and mortgages were beyond her understanding and interest. Evans considered it wise to keep the problem to himself, disguising it with cheerful optimism. He tilted his head to the sky.

'Our bedroom,' he said. 'Picture window, according to the brochure, overlooking the garden here.'

'Don't know how you can imagine it all,' said Brenda. 'Walls and everything, conjuring them up in your mind.' She was pouting, face gleaming with sweat, bored.

'Lucky one of us can.' Evans turned to Lark. She squatted on the wall that was to divide the lounge from the kitchen. They had brought her along because she had looked depressed, nothing to do with her evening except drink gin while she painted her nails. 'What do you think of it, Lark? What's your professional opinion?'

'Marvellous.' Lark grinned. She liked to be flattered by Evans. She'd let him have her opinion by the hour, given half the chance. 'Bloody marvellous, you lucky sods.'

Her glance followed Evans's to the sky. She could see it all: the bedroom, a simple square. White paint, patchwork quilt on the bed, the one she was making them for their wedding present: hexagonals all different reds. (She'd had the devil of a job finding enough different shades to make it dramatic.) A white dressing-table, kidney-shaped like she'd seen in a old Ginger Rogers film, its drawers hidden by frilled curtains: red roses would be nice, with curtains to match. One of those soft white carpets, of course, that tickle between your toes when you're bare-foot. Matching tables each side of the bed, piles of magazines. Pictures of flowers on the wall. Evans's clothes on a chair . . . Evans slumping down on to the bed, on top of the quilt, not bothering to draw it back. Work over, but no time to wash: the smell of ink and rubber stamps on his fingers, lunchtime pork pie still on his breath. Evans wanting her before supper.

And then the lazy straightening of things. Sated. The slow descending of the steep stairs, dressing-gown half undone, not bothering: the slumberous feeling of walking breast-high against a gentle current, limbs weak, eyes blurred as if with rain water. Here, where she was sitting, the kitchen neat and sparkling. A small roast in the oven, frozen sprouts in the freezer, toasted sliced bread and Cheddar cheese. Later, the television, there where Evans stood now in the lounge. His arm round her shoulder. His presence every day, every night. His weight on the sofa, his hand on her knee, wanting her again.

He was beside her on the low wall, thigh touching hers, clumsy fingers kneading the top of her spine.

'Glad you like it,' he said.

'Leave off, tickling,' she said. He removed his hand. Brenda was looking down at them.

'Can't keep his hands off anything in skirts, can he?'

'Piss off, woman.' He stood up, smiling good-naturedly, rubbed at one of Brenda's nipples. 'If you had as much imagination about what it's going to be like as you do about what I do with other women – you'd be better off.'

Placated, because she was never really alarmed by his flirting with Lark – he did it to be kind – Brenda gestured towards the invisible bedroom.

'Faces north,' she said. 'That's no good.'

'West, excuse me.' Evans was playing with the lobe of her ear, pressing it between thumb and finger. 'Sun in the evening.'

'Who wants sun in the evening?'

'Shut up being so difficult.' Evans leant over her to kiss her on the cheek, but Brenda, whole body stiffening, thrust her tongue into his mouth. From where Lark sat they looked tall as giants. She felt a sudden spasm of nausea and buried her head into the darkness of her arms folded on her knees. The familiar pain in her chest began to tick, rhythmically as a clock. Scarlet petals of a destroyed geranium swooped dizzily in her mind. She tried to shut out the voices from above her.

'First time you have me, it's got to be before we move in, right?'

'All right by me. November, some time.'

'On the bare floor.'

'Bloody hard, bloody cold.'

'I fancy that.'

'Bloody sex maniac, you are. Here, come on.'

When Lark opened her eyes they had parted. Evans looked down at her, gave her a hand, helped her to her feet.

'You all right? You're white as a sheet.'

'Fine.' Lark smiled. Even open-eyed the red petals still swam in her vision, but the sickness had gone.

'Look to me as if you could do with a drink. Coming?'

They left the outline of the future house, crossing a strip of bare earth that within months would be lawn. Evans walked between the two girls, an arm round each of their shoulders.

'You'll have to come and babysit, Lark,' said Brenda. Lark nodded. Her head was pushed forward by the weight of Evans's arm on the back of her neck. She relished her few moments of discomfort.

In the Star they found Henry sitting by himself, a double whisky on the table in front of him. At the sight of them he made some attempt to stir himself from his reverie: he invited them to sit down, and gave Evans a pound to buy a round of drinks. From his half-smile it might be guessed he listened to what they said, idle chat about the house: but a glance at his vacant eyes indicated his mind was on other things. Lark noticed that each time the door opened he shifted a little, as if expecting someone. His breath smelt quite strongly of whisky, and his hand shook when he raised his glass to his lips. Had there been a chance, Lark would have asked Evans if there was anything the matter with Henry: perhaps he had not fully recovered from his chill a couple of months back. But in front of Brenda she didn't like to appear inquisitive: Henry's well-being was none of her business, and Brenda never liked to discuss her future parents-in-law. She had little interest in them.

So Lark kept her queries to herself. At closing time, Brenda and Evans gave her a lift back to the flat, though she would have been quite happy to walk the two miles. They themselves were to spend the night at Wroughton House – it had become their habit. They were there most nights, now.

Evans saw Lark to the door. He kissed her on the cheek, as he sometimes did after a late evening, and said he was glad she liked the house, such as it was. She must come there often, he said. He and Brenda would like that. They'd be expecting her there most evenings, he and Brenda would, or there'd be trouble.

Henry resisted Rosie's dreadful idea for two weeks. Finally worn out by her enthusiasm he agreed to go.

The elusiveness of the Leopard was taking its toll and he no longer much cared what he did, where he went. The only thing he looked forward to was opening time at the Star. He sat there at a corner table for hours each day, refusing to be drawn into any kind of conversation, waiting. Each time the door opened a small pain of hope flickered within him, only to swell into a more universal ache as the new arrival turned out not to be the Leopard. Pain, ache: pain, ache: he was growing accustomed to the rhythm, and when it became too bad he ordered whiskies more quickly. Far from a complete remedy, at least they helped to blunt reality. And reality, this summer, was confusingly blank. No news, that was the worst of it. In all the hours he had sat in the Star listening for the smallest scrap of information about the glamorous stranger, Henry had heard no word of her. It was as if she had never existed, never sat at the bar asking for a Dubonnet with a twist of lemon, never cast her spell upon the place. The Boy had not mentioned her: that was the only minor consolation. Henry had observed him carefully over the last few weeks, and concluded that the Boy was as much infatuated by Brenda as ever, and that no other woman existed in his life. He must have been giving the Leopard a lift somewhere, to the bus, perhaps, out of kindness. If on that occasion Henry had gone ahead with his plans of suicide, he reflected, then his death would have been untimely. Not that he had saved himself for any rewards: his present life was an ordeal he doubted he could endure much longer.

The evening of the outing he fortified himself with three drinks before going home. He walked back from the pub slowly, reluctantly, the warm evening air irritating his eyes, making them water. He thought, as he always thought, that if the Leopard was here beside him, on his arm, that would be strong. Upright, firm. A man to be proud of, a man she could rely upon. As it was, lethargy dulled his limbs, making the act of moving at all difficult: the only release was to move his lips as silently he mouthed to himself her private name: *Leopard, my Leopard.*

On reaching home, Henry directed himself to his parked car. With great effort he took off its plastic cover. Folding this up seemed to take a very long time, longer than he ever remembered. It took his breath away, he needed to rest. He opened the driving door and sat in the small green seat: that, at least, was familiar, comfortable. He liked the smell of warm plastic and clean carpet: he noticed with pleasure the shining paint of the snub-nosed bonnet: he gripped the steering wheel with confidence. Then he let his hand pat the empty seat beside him. How many times, in his imagination, had it been filled by the Leopard! In his heart he was convinced she was a Jaguar lady, but she was no snob, his Leopard, and she would appreciate the feel of his car. She would wind down the windows and cry out for joy as they spun down the lanes, white with May, off to somewhere . . . somewhere far away where they could drink a Thermos of tea in the shade and she would invite him to hold her hand.

Henry looked up to see a different hand waving at him through the windscreen: Rosie, anxious. He must come at once and wash, or they would be late. Rosie was wearing the absurd straw hat again, God knows why. It would only irritate people behind her in the cinema. But Henry could not find the energy to tell her so. He could feel a pulse thumping in his temples, and getting out of the car was a less simple matter than he might have supposed.

Twenty minutes later he was back in the driving seat, hair greased flat, Rosie beside him. She could never embark on an expedition with the kind of calm that Henry respected, and the thing that troubled her now was the question of the window on her side.

'How do you open it, Henry?'

'Turn it to the right.'

'There.'

Henry started the engine. They moved a yard or so. Rosie let out a little shriek.

'Oh, my! I'll have to close it again. My hat will blow off, won't it?'

'There's not a breath of wind.' Henry's mind was so far from the problem in hand his patience could not be ruffled.

'There will be once we get going. You know how you drive.'

'Well then, close it.'

After several attempts at turning the handle the wrong way, Rosie closed it. She folded her hands, gloved in nylon lace, on her lap. From the corner of his eye Henry saw her turn the colour of a beetroot. Such maroon flesh, he thought, was particularly nasty against the electric blue of her blouse.

'Oh, Henry love,' she said, 'I do believe I can't breathe, now, this dreadful heat.'

Henry wound down his own window a couple of inches. He wondered if he had the energy to request her not to speak again: it interrupted his concentration. Besides, her voice, sharp with its various worries, exacerbated the throbbing pain behind his eyes.

He guided the small car down the lane, swinging it a little from side to side as if to pay his respects to both pavements. He had not the slightest inclination to show his mastery of the car: it would all be wasted on Rosie. All he required from her was continuing silence, right up till the time they had to decide on the price of the seats. As a precaution, to keep her quiet, he drove at a shameful twenty-five miles an hour, a speed at which he hoped he would meet no one from the Star who had in the past heard tell of his acemanship at the wheel.

He might have known it, though: his cornering troubled Rosie, for all his care.

'Brakes, Henry love,' she screeched. 'Did you get them seen to?'

'No need.'

'Oh, I don't know about that. You can never trust brakes.'

'I can trust these brakes.'

'*Henry!*' She fell against him as they swerved round a bend: his judgement had not been as accurate as he calculated. '*Brake!* You'll have us in the ditch.'

'If you could keep your voice down, I could put my mind to concentrating more.' He glanced at her hideous fat fingers, gripping each other. He despised himself for ever having said he'd come. It would be the last time, positively the last. He'd sell the car, take the Leopard on holiday with the money and not tell Rosie where he was going. Probably he'd never come back, for that matter – not to all Rosie's pestering to spend good money on a film neither of them wanted to see: not to all this shouting. Full of such resolves Henry crushed his foot down on the accelerator, goading the old car into a burst of speed accompanied by much triumphant snorting of the engine.

It took Rosie quite some time, settled in her cinema seat, to recover from the journey. Not for worlds would she mention it to Henry, but her heart was thumping alarmingly fast. To add to her discomfort, her blouse was damp from nervous sweat, and her feet had swollen uncomfortably in her shoes. Henry had always been a terror in a car and this evening, Rosie couldn't help thinking, it was almost as if he had driven dangerously to provoke her: well, he had not succeeded. After her first few shouts, too spontaneous to control, she had sat quietly, gripping at the door handle for support as they lurched about, praying for God's mercy. And He had granted it, for miraculously they had arrived at the cinema car park intact. Once out of the car, of course, Henry reverted to his usual mild self. He had bought two expensive seats without quibbling, and also a bag of toffees, now wedged between his knees, when Rosie had made the suggestion. It was true he had snapped at the usherette when she made off too fast down the steps with her torch beam, leaving them in darkness: but now he seemed quite settled, content, staring with expressionless eyes at *Tom and Jerry*. In spite of the inauspicious beginning, Rosie's spirits recovered. She felt that after all they might achieve an enjoyable evening, if the Lord continued to watch over them on the journey back: and, who knows, things might even develop unexpectedly.

If they had come last week, or the week before, as Rosie had suggested, they would have been able to benefit from films of a romantic nature. As it was, by the time Henry had agreed, the Odeon had switched its programme to an adventurous film of bloodshed and violence, the kind of thing which held little appeal for Rosie. But she had said nothing, taken her chance while it was there: Henry might not let himself be persuaded another time. Besides, there had been a picture of a battleship on a stormy sea in the advertisement, and, as Rosie had pointed out, it would do him the world of good to get a look at the sea again. And what mattered most, this evening, was Henry's pleasure.

Rosie sensed that this was unfortunately short-lived. The director had used the sea merely for a series of dramatic pictures before the titles, then had swung his attention to shots of mountains and jungles, and Rosie felt Henry slump beside her. She herself tried to concentrate, but within moments violence prevailed, corpses spewing blood all over the screen, which made her feel quite queasy even though she'd heard tell it was only tomato ketchup. The last film Rosie had seen was *Spring in Park Lane*. She let forth a sigh of nostalgia for Michael Wilding's gentle manners, so much more satisfactory than all this decapitation. What's more, it was hardly the stuff of romance, hardly the kind of thing that would encourage Henry to slip his arm round her shoulders and remember his youth. To take her mind off the general disappointemnt, Rosie reached for the bag of toffees. Henry, she saw, was asleep. Snoring, slightly. She hoped he wouldn't disturb the people nearby. She slipped a toffee into her mouth. Its familiar sweetness was a wonderful comfort. In no time she had finished the bag. Then, in spite of all the groaning activity in front of her eyes, drowsiness came upon her. She felt her eyelids droop, and a lovely confusion of food came to her mind. Perhaps they could go out for a meal when the film was over. It would make a change to eat in a restaurant again: she could not remember how long it was since they had last been out. Years. She'd like to try that new place – French, she thought it was, with gingham curtains in the window. By candlelight, she could look quite girlish, and surely there'd be some things on the menu that wouldn't turn her stomach: a nice fresh vegetable stew, perhaps, and French rice pudding.

Rosie woke with a start to find people all round her

standing up. For a moment she was confused: the music certainly wasn't *God Save the Queen*. Then she saw the gold curtains falling over the screen and realised it was all over. She arranged her hat, which seemed to have slipped over one eye, and nudged Henry. She saw that on waking he, too, was confused, and a little guiltily found herself taking advantage of his befuddled state. Determinedly she guided him out through the crowds, across the street and through the doors of the small restaurant she had observed when she came in to do her weekly shopping.

At once Rosie realised the place was not all it might be when it came to hygiene. For a start, there was a strong smell of garlic in the air, and burnt cheese. The tablecloths were paper, splattered with grease from candles stuck in bottles. High fire risk, she thought. Funny people. No sense of order. Didn't look as if business was doing too well, either. There was only one customer, at a single table in a corner, dressed in a blue and white fisherman's jersey. He got up, wiping his mouth.

'Did you book?' he asked, in a heavy foreign accent.

'No,' said Rosie.

'Did you want a table?'

Insolent type: what else would they be here for?

'I don't know we do, we could get a bite at home if you like,' Henry said to the waiter, blinking his eyes fast, focusing. But Rosie was already sitting herself down at a table near the window. She could make herself quite clear when her mind was made up.

'You could sit there,' said the waiter, indicating the table Rosie already occupied.

'Ah,' said Henry, inner protest too strong for further words, and sat himself opposite his wife.

Rosie now had a view of him that sometimes she had dreamed of: a candle flame within inches of his nose, making his white hair sparkle, and deepening the lines on his dear handsome face. How she loved him, still. She could feel the love within her, bubbles racing through her veins so that suddenly her breath came quite fast and she found herself panting. Surely, tonight, reinvigorated by his long sleep in the cinema, Henry's fancy might turn to things that had been dormant between them for so long. Even now he was raising his hand towards her . . . But it stopped at the candle. He snuffed out the flame between thumb and finger. A brown thread of smoke twisted up into the air between them, and she could hardly see his face.

'Oh, Henry!'

'Bloody thing. What are we doing here, anyway?'

'I thought it would be nice to have a meal out, to round off the evening.'

'Better off at home.'

'Well, we can't judge till we see what they have to offer.' Rosie was determined to be cheerful. Henry swung round in his chair and beckoned the waiter.

'La menu,' he shouted, and Rosie beamed with pride.

'I didn't know you could speak French,' she said. 'Perhaps we could go for a holiday abroad one year.' The Eiffel Tower and fancy cakes spun before her eyes. With Henry's command of the language they could order anything they needed and they would be quite safe so long as they took their own lavatory paper and insisted their water was boiled . . . In truth, Rosie did know Henry had picked up a few words in Marseilles, but tonight was a good time to flatter him, and a less talented man might have forgotten things he learned in the war.

When the menu came Henry said, 'bon, bon,' several times, and 'tray bien'. Then he fell silent. He handed the grubby bit of paper to Rosie.

'Can't make this out,' he said. 'Think it must be bloody Italian.'

He was right, of course. In the smudged writing Rosie recognised the word 'spaghetti' several times. Neither of them had any great partiality for spaghetti, but Rosie was determined this should not spoil the final lap of the evening. Now was the time for her to come to Henry's rescue, to ease him from the awkward task of decision making. She took a wild shot in the dark, praying to God the Italians were acquainted with ordinary decent food.

'We'll have two lamb chops with a portion of peas and some plain spaghetti with tomato sauce, if you please,' she said to the waiter, adding the spaghetti purely out of politeness. For a fraction of a second his pencil hovered doubtfully above his pad. Rosie's heart thumped. She smiled authoritatively, won the waiter's respect.

'And drinks?' he asked.

One last hurdle. With some relief Rosie saw the words *Unlicensed to sell alcohol* at the bottom of the menu. She scanned the list of soft beverages.

'Two orangeades,' she said.

'Bloody hell. I want a proper drink.' Henry was scowling.

'I'm sorry, we have no licence. You could go down the road to the pub and buy a bottle of wine,' the waiter said.

'Catch me buying wine.' Henry turned in his chair again. 'What's that you're drinking, stuff in the glass on your table?'

The waiter paused.

'Scotch whisky,' he said at last. 'I own this place, you see. It's my private bottle.'

'You wouldn't, for a consideration . . .?' Henry smiled up at the proprietor, causing a snip of jealousy in Rosie's heart: she had not seen Henry so soft since their courting days when he had wanted, that first time in the bluebell woods, to undo the buttons of her blouse.

The waiter shrugged, scratched at his greasy hair.

'See what I can do, if you like,' he said, and went away.

'Very obliging fellow,' said Henry. 'They're all right, these foreigners, if you know how to deal with them.'

But Rosie felt no gratitude to the waiter. Rather, she was filled with dread. It would require all her tact to prevent the demon whisky coming between them. The night was now in danger.

*

In the dim light Henry was not able to see too clearly the horrible mess of Rosie's chin. It shone with a mixture of grease and tomato sauce, which she kept dabbing with her paper serviette. To make matters worse she seemed to think the whole procedure of eating the filthy stuff was funny. Laughing as she spooned the spaghetti into her mouth, half of it would spew out again and hang like worms over her bottom lip. These she would attempt to gather up with her fat grey tongue, thereby splattering her blouse with tomato sauce, and asking for the aid of Henry's handkerchief, which he refused. From time to time she lifted her glass of orangeade to her lips, bunching up her fingers still in their hideous lace gloves, and closed her eyes in some kind of private ecstasy. She was a disgusting sight and Henry hated her with his whole being.

With every drink – the proprietor had most kindly sold him all that remained in the whisky bottle – Henry's feelings of loathing increased. They became strangely tangible, insects crawling on the table between them. He wondered why Rosie could not see them. How could she live with someone so many years and not recognise hate that sprouted from him like a skin disease? How could she be so impervious to his suffering, to the daily torment of his mind?

'How about a sweet?' she was saying, and ignoring any opinion he might have had on the matter, given a chance, asked the waiter for a strawberry ice with chocolate sauce.

Henry decided to kill her.

It occurred to him that he was not by nature a violent man, but if murder was the only way to freedom, then murder it must be. The best way would be to take her up to the woods, mid-week, when no one was about. One bonk on the head and she'd be down on the ground like a jelly. Then it would be easy to strangle her, or suffocate her, whichever took his fancy that particular day. He'd dig a grave and bury her right there, and have all the pleasure of listening to the thrushes singing in celebration as he trod down the earth. He could smoke his pipe in peace, and go home to make his own tea: no more bloody welcomes. They'd come for him in the end of course, and lock him away. But nothing on earth would bring Rosie back to life, and that triumph would remain with him until his own death.

He swilled the last of the whisky round his mouth, trying to clear the taste of fried onions and tinned peas. His decision made, he felt curiously at peace. Once Rosie was dead, he could pursue the Leopard more openly. Put advertisements in papers. Make enquiries at the Star. In the end, if only for a short time before he went to prison, they would come together: spend a week in Blackpool, perhaps, seeing the shows and walking the pier arm in arm. They'd stay in a nice boarding house, sea views from the window of their room: huge double bed. And late every night, a few drinks inside them, they would make use of that bed: bloody hell they would. Henry would do things to the Leopard she would never have imagined. Things he'd done to that girl in Marseilles, which made her cry sometimes, but beg him for more.

He paid the bill, scattering pound notes clumsily. Outside, the street lights seemed to be swaying gently, giant fireflies. And the dark buildings were tumbling towards him, crashing down like card houses.

'Steady,' Rosie was saying. He felt her appalling hand on his arm. Glancing down, he saw she was afraid. Stupid bloody woman. All her fault for making him come out on this daft expedition in the first place.

Somehow he managed to start the car. They lurched out of the gates of the car park. Rosie screamed, hurting his ears. Henry slammed on the brakes. They missed a passing lorry by a few inches. Swearing, Henry turned to Rosie, shouting it was all her fault. But Rosie merely smiled up at him, eyes full of fear, mouth askew in a courageous smile.

'That was the best evening I've had in years, love,' was all she said, and patted him on the arm.

Henry could have coped with anything but forgiveness. He felt the swift nausea of guilt, the stab of contrition. Only moments before he had been planning to kill her, now here she was declaring her pathetic pleasure in the evening. Well, he would make it up to her in his private way: he supposed she deserved that. He would drive as carefully as he was able, and buy her a drink in the Star on the way home. Thus killing two stones . . .

The view before him had disintegrated into separate scraps, flakes of solid snow. But he tried. He gripped the steering wheel with rigid hands, barely touched the accelerator. Rosie was humming. *The Last Rose of Summer*, Henry thought it was.

He managed to negotiate the journey without mishap, but was in no condition to survive the weakness of anticipation that struck him as he entered the saloon bar. He felt his legs unsteady beneath him, and was grateful for Rosie's arm. Bill, alert to his condition, at once handed him a double whisky, and a shandy for Rosie. Henry swallowed it in two gulps, and felt an unnerving mixture of dizziness and strength.

He managed to keep his eyes quite steadily on the door. It swung open and shut many times, but the Leopard did not come. On the few occasions that he glanced at her, Henry noticed Rosie looked unhappy. Her face had the same kind of puffed up indignation as when, once long ago, they had gone down to the beach and misjudged the tide. She had scowled at the approaching water, powerless as King Canute to insist on its retreat. The whisky was making his memory wonderfully clear, Henry realised, and smiled to himself, knowing any indication of enjoyment in a pub would annoy.

They stayed till closing time. The tricky business of negotiating their way to the door was not helped by Henry having to bend himself almost double to ease the burn of disappointment in his chest. Rosie took his arm again, and outside the warm night air struck him savagely, renewing his weakness.

'Shall we walk, love?'

Rosie's voice echoed through a tunnel. Henry shook his head. He could never make it, walking.

Somehow he managed to get into the car. And there, the steering wheel between his hands, a wonderful sense of peace, or rescue, came upon him. This was no Morris Minor, but a ship of war, a destroyer. The kind of vehicle he was used to. If they went with the waves, kept to the swell, they would make it to port without mishap. Through the windscreen the full moon spun like a coin: heads, and he would win the Leopard. Tails, and they would drown. He started the engine.

But forces of gravity pulled against his ship in a way that was quite surprising. And this particular sea was cluttered with strange hazards he was not prepared for: mighty trees and solid shapes, like houses. He wrenched the steering wheel from left to right, so hard he could feel the pull of muscles in his shoulders. But instead of the sough of well navigated waves, horrible moans came from his left, Rosie's voice contorted with silly fear. There was a fleeting sensation of having come to rest, of poising on the edge of a wave before it sent them spinning. Henry wondered if they were home. He heard Rosie whimper. Then silence. Something warm gushed out of his ear, tickled his neck. He opened his mouth to apologise to the Leopard, but no words came. A bloody great wave crashed over him, submerging him in its blackness.

When Henry came round he was instantly aware of the familiar bustle of his wife beside him. She was struggling to open the door. The whole weight of her seemed to have covered his knees, and was uncomfortable. They were in a strange position. Slipped sideways, he thought. Must have been a dreadful storm.

Rosie turned to him. In the tremulous moonlight Henry could see blood on her cheek and an absurd smile of welcome.

'You all right, love?' she asked. 'I think you went out for a moment. We're in a ditch.'

Closing his eyes, no will to answer, Henry felt this to be an unnecessary statement of fact. There was nothing wrong with a ditch. The liquid on his neck was warm, and he was quite comfortable if he didn't move his shoulder. The noise of Rosie banging at the door to open it – stupid woman, she'd never had the knack – was rhythmic and comforting.

'Good thing we're insured,' she was saying, 'there's bound to be a bit of damage. Blood everywhere.'

Some time later Henry answered, 'Don't worry, it's all tomato ketchup.' But by then he was talking to himself. Rosie had managed to scramble out of the car, and was stumbling towards the nearest house for help.

It came very quickly, or it may have been a long time. Henry neither knew nor cared. All he wished was that people would stop interrupting his thoughts. He heard the whispers of rescuers, and saw faces cracked like mosaics by the moonlight. He felt himself being carried, he felt a searing pain in his shoulder. Then he recognised the steadiness of his own bed beneath him. Safely at anchor at last, he thought. Time now to dream, to tell the Leopard how he had braved the storm, brought them all back to land. She would be quite proud of him, he had no doubt of that.

'My Leopard,' he muttered out loud. And in the last seconds before sleep he saw not the Leopard's eyes, but Rosie's – wide, troubled. Uncomprehending, as always, the silly cow.

Brenda had had a rough night. It had begun well enough by she and Evans taking their supper on to the lawn of Wroughton House. Mrs Browne had said she would join them, but then she declared she had a headache and was going to bed early. She had given them a bottle of white wine, very cold and tasting of grapes. They drank it in paper cups. Evans said Mrs Browne looked white as a sheet, didn't she? He wondered if anything was the matter. His note of concern annoyed Brenda: but she kept her silence, not wanting an argument on an evening like this.

She lay on her back on the grass, smoking Woodbines. She liked the smell of the dry lawn, the boughs of the trees above them moving lazily in the sky, as if some invisible puppet man had little energy left to pull their strings. She liked pushing her hard-boiled egg into a mound of pepper, and sneezing at its sharpness; she liked the warmth in her limbs caused by the wine.

Evans lay close to her. The church clock struck nine, the sky deepened into shadow colours. Brenda found her thoughts wandering in their usual direction.

'Shall we?' she asked. Evans's fingers massaged through her hair, soothing, arousing.

'Not here,' he said. 'Not tonight.'

'Why ever not?'

'If Mrs Browne looked out of the window, she'd see us.'

'So?'

'I wouldn't like that.'

Brenda drew deeply on her cigarette. She quite liked the idea of Mrs Browne seeing them at it, herself.

'Prude,' she said. 'It wouldn't exactly surprise her.'

'Nor it would. But it would be unnecessary.'

Brenda could see he was trying to be patient, not to cross her. He suggested they went in. It was getting cool.

But in the bedroom the mood of excitement between them, frustrated by Evans's refusal to make love outside, vanished. Brenda was left full of resentment: she hated her romantic ideas to be quashed. Instead of undressing she sat in the only armchair and began to chide Evans for the inadequacies of their own house. The subject, she knew, was a red rag to a bull.

'It's going to have poky rooms, no room to swing a cat. No feeling of country, either, looking outside just to see a lot of other identical houses. No privacy. Prying neighbours, complaining about our hens. And there's no space on the plan for a washing machine. Where will we put the washing machine? If you think I'm going to spend my life doing all your bloody shirts by hand . . .' She went on and on, her voice harsh. Evans, at the window, back to her, said nothing.

Suddenly – she did not notice any precise moment when it

happened – the room was dark. She paused. Evans turned to her.

'If you don't like it,' he said quietly, 'if it's going to be as bloody awful as you make out, you can go.'

Brenda registered the menace in his voice. She stood up. Perhaps she *had* gone a bit far, all that wine.

'Oh, come on,' she said, 'you don't want to take me too seriously.' She touched his arm, tried to drag him towards the bed. But he would not move.

'I do, you know,' he said.

'Come *on*!' She was being endearing now. She gave him one of her desirous looks: that always won him over.

'No!' he shouted, and shook off her arm. Brenda recognised his anger, and was annoyed. She could bait him too easily.

'Shut up! You'll wake Mrs Browne.'

'Maybe.'

In the dim light from the window Brenda could see him smile, and the smile made her stiffen with misgivings.

'Take me, Evans,' she said, unbuttoning her shirt.

'I don't want you, not tonight.'

'You do.'

'I tell you, you bitch, I don't.'

Brenda buttoned up her shirt again. He was stubborn as they come, sometimes.

'I do believe it's Mrs Browne you fancy,' she said, mocking. 'You seem all concern for her, these days. Don't know why I didn't think of it before.'

'That's an idea,' said Evans, 'the beautiful Mrs Browne.' His calm was maddening.

'She's got no tits,' said Brenda. 'She's not your type.'

'Look, would you mind going now? I'd like a peaceful night's sleep.' He turned his back again, leaning his elbows on the high window ledge.

'And how am I supposed to get home, may I ask?'

'Walk.'

'While you screw Mrs Browne?'

'While I screw Mrs Browne, if that's what you like to think.'

'Christ, I despise you, Evans Evans. Fucking sod.'

She stumbled to the bedside table, picked up a vase of roses and threw it at him. Inaccurate with rage, her aim was wild. It hit a wall, broke on the bare boards round the edge of the carpet. In a shaft of moonlight Brenda could see three yellow blooms in a pool of water. Still Evans did not move.

'Get out before you smash the whole place up,' he said, and Brenda went to the door. She slammed it behind her.

Outside, shaking, she was grateful for the coolness of the night air. By the light of the full moon it was easy enough to see her way. She began to walk down the lane. Just outside the village she saw the shape of a car lying on its side in a ditch. As she came close to it she saw it was a Morris Minor, pale green, the same as Henry Evans's. She wondered if it could be his: he hardly ever went out in it, she knew, but perhaps he had taken it somewhere this evening and had had an accident. It was said in the village Henry was drinking a lot these days, though Evans had never mentioned it. At the sight of the car Brenda felt all her anger spent. Weariness, suddenly. What had it all been about? Should she turn back, climb into the double bed, ask to be forgiven? Should she tell Evans his parents' car was in a ditch?

Brenda hesitated. To go back and find the room empty would be unbearable, and judging by Evans's coldness tonight she had no doubt there was a good chance he would try his luck with Mrs Browne . . . who could not, of course, refuse him. No one in their right minds could refuse Evans, the irresistible sod. Oh God, in all her confusion, in all her regret at having behaved so stupidly, she wanted him. It took uncommon strength to keep walking in the direction of the flat.

Augusta Browne went to bed at eight o'clock. She drew the blinds, but the evening sky seeped through the lilac cotton making the room an aquarium of mauve shadowed light. She stretched a leg into the cool empty area of linen where Hugh should have been. The sheets hurt her skin. She shut her eyes and probed at the flesh of her cheeks with her fingers. Pain rankled far beneath, gnawing through the bone. The doctor had said she was suffering from migraineous neuralgia, and there was little he could do to help. Against the pain she was conscious of the smell of lavender and roses by her bed. After a while she slept, deeply.

Two hours later Augusta woke to exploding pains in the bones under her eyes, and in her jaw. The room was still not quite dark. She reached for two more pills and a glass of water. Above her she heard angry footsteps, then the slam of a door. She switched on her light and picked up her book, *Swann's Way*. She had intended this to be her Proustian summer, but reading increasingly hurt her eyes, and progress was slow. Now, the print blurred. Her eyes were filled with neuralgic tears – a common symptom, the doctor said – and she knew if she looked at them they would be hideously bloodshot. She closed the book and lay quite still, for any movement made the sheets prickle like thistles.

More footsteps. Evans was coming down the stairs from the attic. Augusta wondered if he was going after Brenda. They led a hopelessly dramatic life, as far as she could tell. Perhaps it stimulated them. It would exhaust her: all *she* required was interesting peace. The footsteps crossed the landing outside her bedroom, came right up to the door, then stopped. Silence. Augusta raised herself upon one elbow. There was a soft knock.

'Evans? Is that you? Come in.' Through the hammering of pain in her face she found it difficult to muster her voice.

The door opened. Evans came in. He stood just inside the huge room, sleeves rolled up, a V of reddish skin in the open collar of his shirt. His face was pale and hard. Augusta realised he could see her breasts. He was looking at them without shame. She switched off the light.

'Sorry,' she said, 'my head. It makes everything dazzle.'

'That's all right,' Evans replied, and in that moment August understood why Brenda loved him. His voice was infinitely caring. 'I saw your light and wondered how you were.'

'Not too bad.' There was no point in trying to explain the peculiar condition of the sheets.

'Nothing I can get you?'

'No, really, thank you.' Pause. 'Brenda's gone?'

'She went off in some kind of state.'

'It'll be better when everything's settled, perhaps. When you're in the house.' Augusta was aware of the futility of her observation.

'Daresay it will.' Evans rubbed at his eyes with a large hand. 'Well then, I'll leave you if you're sure there's nothing I can get you.' His voice was quiet, his shirt almost luminous, his kindness a distant balm. Augusta recognised it beyond the pain.

'Thank you, Evans,' she said.

'Goodnight, Mrs Browne.'

'Goodnight.'

He left the room, closing the door gently behind him. His formality in the dark made her feel quite stupid with gratitude. She closed her eyes and tried to sleep again.

It had been a sleepless night, bright with visions of Evans and Augusta Browne. Now, at seven-thirty in the morning, Brenda was light-headed and restless. She dressed and made a pot of tea, wondering how best to patch things up with Evans. There was a small fear within her, not consciously felt before, that one day soon she would provoke him too far. He would feel there was no safety in their future, and cast her out for good. Someone else would be mistress of the house, someone else might even breed chickens in the garden. The thought was intolerable. Brenda dug a spoon into a tea bag, watching its brown liquid spiral into the water.

Lark came into the room, waving a letter. Face like a ghost, she had: thumping dark shadows under her eyes.

Brenda could never understand Lark's perpetual tiredness. She went to bed early most nights, and slept long hours, and yet every morning she looked like death. Today she smiled an uncontainable smile. Brenda scowled back. She was in no mood for anyone else's good spirits. Whatever joy Lark wished to share she should not count on Brenda to be responsive, not this morning.

'It's come,' Lark said, rather breathlessly, sitting at the table. 'It's come at last! My first proposal!' She flapped the letter in Brenda's face.

Brenda reacted slowly. As far as she knew Lark had not been going out with anyone, and it seemed a funny way to propose, by letter.

'When's the happy day?' she asked.

'December the thirteenth. How about that?' Lark was reading the letter again, incredulous.

'Who's the lucky man?' Any other time Brenda might have cared. The flatness of her voice indicated that, this morning, she could not. Lark looked up.

'The what?'

'The man. You said a proposal.'

Lark laughed. 'That's all you ever think of, Bren. Not a *man*, idiot. Not that kind of proposal. Something much more exciting – the real thing. My first concert. They've asked me to sing.' She flushed a little, her voice unsteady.

'December the thirteenth? That's a long way ahead.'

Lark giggled. She seemed to be quite weak with pleasure.

'Perhaps,' she said, 'they thought I might be booked up if they left it any later.'

Brenda couldn't help smiling.

'Where is it? Albert Hall?'

'Not exactly.'

'They paying you a huge fee?'

Lark hesitated.

'They're not really paying me anything, in cash, like. But they're giving me supper, and as many drinks as I like. And they're paying me expenses. You know, a taxi.'

'A *taxi*? To London and back? Or Luton, or wherever?' Lark said nothing. 'I think that's bloody mean,' went on Brenda. 'Ridiculous. A person's got to earn their living. I should say no.'

'I've already written to say yes. It would be stupid to turn down my first chance, wouldn't it? I don't care about the money. Really I don't.'

Brenda sighed impatiently.

'Who are these people you're to sing for?' she asked.

'I'm not telling you. Please don't make me tell you. I want it to be a surprise. I'll send you complimentary tickets, of course. I'll see to it you and Evans get complimentary tickets.'

'Thanks,' said Brenda. 'And we'll throw flowers on to the stage and shout for an encore. Why don't we celebrate with bacon and eggs? I'm ravenous.'

'Couldn't eat a thing, myself, the excitement,' said Lark, 'but I'll get you some.' She went to the stove and broke two eggs into a frying pan.

Brenda's interest in Lark's concert expired. Her head was now aching: she needed comfort. She stirred her tea.

'Lark,' she said, 'what would you say were Evans's chances with Augusta Browne?'

Lark looked up from her cooking, puzzled.

'I should say absolutely none. Why?'

'Supposing Evans and I had had a bit of a ding-dong. Would he go off screwing her to spite me?'

''Course he wouldn't, silly. He's the faithful type.' She sounded quite certain, Brenda thought. But then Lark couldn't really know. She wasn't the type Evans would be attracted to, ever. 'Well, I mean,' Lark went on, 'I don't know Mrs Browne, do I? I've only seen her once or twice. But she doesn't look the sort to me who spreads it about.'

'You can never tell,' said Brenda. Lark put a plate of eggs and bacon down in front of her. 'Thanks. I'll never be able to do breakfasts like this for Evans. You'll have to come round every morning, once we're in the house.'

'Delighted, except after late night singing engagements.' Lark's merriment this morning was almost more than Brenda could take, but she supposed it would be mean to make a sarcastic remark. Instead she asked,

'If he succeeded, if he had her, do you think he'd tell me?'

''Course he wouldn't, idiot. What a daft idea. Men don't tell about the odd screw if it's going to get them into trouble.' She sounded quite definite again.

'Well, then, do you suppose I'd *know*? By instinct?' Brenda wiped her plate with a piece of bread and sucked up the runny egg yolk, in imitation of her Birmingham friends in roadside cafés. It was a habit which had always annoyed Evans but she made no effort to give up.

''Course you wouldn't. People are good at disguising things.'

'Then I shall make it my business to find out.'

'Come on, Bren. What's *up*?' Lark was a bit impatient.

'We had a row last night. All my fault, I suppose. He turned me out. He hinted he was going downstairs for a bit of comfort.'

'Nonsense!'

'So I think the thing to do is to go and see Mrs Browne today. Find out the truth from her. I'll take her some eggs, six large brown. If it turns out I'm wrong I won't say a word to Evans, and I don't imagine she will either.'

'I'm all for leaving the truth alone, myself, cases like that,' said Lark, 'but if you've got to go nosing about, that sounds like quite a good plan.'

'You've got to get at the truth if things are going to work for ever,' said Brenda. 'There's not many things I believe, but that's one of them.' She noticed there was sun on the red rooftops outside. Breakfast had calmed her. Lark filled both their cups with tea. Poor old Lark, she was good in a crisis. You could depend on her for support. She deserved a nice man to look after her, one day. She deserved someone who would make her understand the disadvantages of independence.

'Where do you think I should go for a dress?' Lark was saying.

'For a dress?'

'For the concert.'

'Oh, for the concert.'

'I was thinking of a pale grey, almost a white.'

'Tea-time, I think I'll go.'

'Go where?'

'Up to the house with the eggs.'

'You could ask her, perhaps, if she'd be interested in coming.'

'What to?'

'The concert, of course. I'm sure I could get her a complimentary ticket, too. I mean, seeing as they're not paying me.'

'I'll take her six of the big speckled ones,' said Brenda. 'Hope Wilberforce won't catch me.'

Lark got up and began to clear the table. For all their tiredness, her eyes were sparkling in the light of the September morning.

'Perhaps I'll go for a silver,' she said. 'Christmas time, that would be appropriate, I think.'

By dawn the worst of the pain had receded, leaving Augusta's face merely a dull ache, and a pulse beating in her temple. She got up and dressed, went outside, and breathed deeply. The lawns shimmered with dew. Spider webs spun like Catherine wheels among leaves, and the bulrushes by the pond were parted from their roots by a ground mist.

Augusta went to the walled garden at the back of the house. The mulberry tree, a wizened old thing when stripped of its foliage in winter, was now rich with geometric leaves. Among them clustered dark red berries, more than ever this year. Augusta picked one and ate it. Sour, still, and quite hard. The juice ran from the corner of her mouth. She dabbed at it, and it came off on her finger like blood. The colour of their mulberry mousses – how many had they eaten in four summers? – had been altogether paler. A creamy pink. Swaying, fragile things, surprisingly sharp. Hugh was very fond of mulberry mousse. (He considered the mulberry far superior to the strawberry.) This year, there had been no mousses. *Oh God, I'm in mourning for the best puddings of my life* . . . Augusta leant against the striated bark of the tree's trunk. Its leaves made a low canopy all about her, variegated greens. The private acts of solitary behaviour were beginning to interest her. A year ago, had anyone suggested she would one day rise at dawn and stand in melancholy fashion under the mulberry tree meditating upon puddings – why, she would have laughed them to scorn. Now, it seemed quite natural. Now, it was no longer shocking to contemplate burning down the house. She had thought about it several times during the past few days. She would set light to it, then go up to the woods and look back at the flames. There would be no saving it. Its old panelling would be devoured in a moment, but it would never know the indignity of being altered by the office men. That, at least, it would be spared.

Christ, though Augusta, am I now deranged? (The last owner of the house, soon after she left, was sent to an asylum.) But there is a talent in endings. Some people have it: she felt she was not one of them. Some people can love, and leave without regret. Some people can achieve flights into the void: others fear swift grounding. If parting is a smaller death, there are few adequately equipped for that kind of dying. Augusta knew herself to be unprepared, and feared her own weakness. For a start, she could not persuade herself to accept the facts. The steady progress towards the precipice remained unbelievable, a nightmare from which she expected to wake every morning. And yet it *was* true. The contract was signed. Hugh had telephoned to break the news yesterday.

Augusta slipped to the ground, sat on the soft earth, supporting her back against the tree's trunk. She was weak from lack of food, yet eating nauseated her. She was drained by the storms of neuralgia which, on occasions, made her groan out loud: and as one unused to pain or illness of any kind, she was angered by their force, and by her inability to cast them out. Now, even as she sat beneath the mulberry tree listening to the church clock strike seven, Augusta felt the absurdity of her own position. But she was powerless to change it. To remain where she was, undisturbed, the tree's prisoner, was her only inclination. She would be quite happy to die there . . .

And mourn not me
Beneath the yellowing tree
For I shall mind not, slumbering peacefully.

As it was, she remained there all day. Sometimes she dozed. Sometimes, quite awake, she rubbed at the grass with her hand, and made small holes in the earth with her finger. At midday she felt the heat beneath the leaf canopy grow denser, and needles of sunlight penetrated here and there, making speckled shadows on her legs. By late afternoon it was quite cool. Augusta got up at last. Stiffly, she returned to the house. Swallows were gathering on the telephone wires and pigeons, their iridescent breasts puffed up in competition with the pinkish sky, preened themselves on the roof. She marvelled at the benevolence of God, or whoever, providing such an evening at the end of a lost day. Now, all she required was someone to talk to for an hour or so – someone to exorcise, temporarily, the useless ravings of her mind. She settled on a window seat in the bathroom. Outside, the distant chimneys of the brickworks sent spires of white smoke into the sky. The lawn was the lavender colour that grass becomes to indicate autumn. Augusta concentrated on willing someone to arrive. Anyone would do.

Brenda had no trouble in making off with the six largest, brownest eggs she could find. Wilberforce was not about. She had seen him little of late. In fact, his interest in his farm seemed to have declined. Weeds grew in profusion in the yard. Buildings rotted, hinges grew stiff with rust. There were several holes in the roof of the chicken house – Brenda's only concern. She would have to persuade Wilberforce to mend them before winter, but felt disinclined to approach him. She had decided to put off the tiresome day until the weather changed.

Brenda walked up the back drive of Wroughton House, carrying her carton of eggs, pleased to think that no one she knew had seen her on the way. She wanted this meeting with Mrs Browne to be private: above all it was essential Evans never discovered her plan.

She noticed the sickly smell of roses – hundreds of them tumbled over the wall that divided the drive from the kitchen garden – and the buzz of swallows on the telephone wires. Both things annoyed her. Irritation prickled along her spine. She was on edge: had been all day. The mental pictures of Evans having it off with Mrs Browne last night, just because of a bit of a disagreement, were enough to get anyone down. Not that she was of a jealous nature. Jealousy was not a thing she would succumb to, it made everyone so ugly. Though, to be truthful, when it came to Evans, a weird anger sometimes overcame her at the thought of his fancying anyone else.

Inside the house it was wonderfully cool. Brenda shouted to Mrs Browne. No answer. Silence. She went through the door that led to the front hall, clogs clicking on the flagstone floor. There, from the drawing-room, she could hear the melancholy whine of old dance music. Awful thirties stuff. Almost gave her the spooks, music like that playing in an empty house.

There was no one in the drawing-room. It looked as if it had been deserted all day. The other downstairs rooms were empty, too: each one smelling of roses. In Mrs Browne's study the windows were open and an ostrich-feather quill pen on the desk fluttered in a small breeze. Creepy as anything, thought Brenda, shutting the door quickly behind her. She was glad she would never be able to afford such a house herself. Thank heavens for the inventors of the ordinary estate.

She went upstairs, saw the bathroom door open, and crossed the landing. Mrs Browne was huddled up on the window seat, a silhouette against the huge window. Brenda knocked at the open door and went in. She held out the carton, aware that she trespassed upon some kind of private reflection.

'I've brought a few eggs,' she said. 'Large brown.'

Augusta turned towards her, her face conveying complete amazement. In spite of its suntanned skin, Brenda observed it was horribly pale. Unhealthy. Remindful of Lark.

'How kind, Brenda . . . I'm quite out of eggs, too, and somehow I didn't manage to go shopping today.' She smiled.

Now she was here Brenda wondered how best to get round to the subject that had brought her. The words she had been rehearsing all day to herself in the chicken house seemed to have fled her mind. There was a long silence while Mrs Browne opened the carton and looked at the eggs.

'Thank you so much,' she said. 'I shall boil two for supper.'

There were built-in cupboards all along one wall of the bathroom, and one of the doors was open. Brenda could see a mass of dresses squashed together: pale colours, mostly. Summer cottons and winter velvets, all muddled. She sighed. Some people had all the luck.

'Are you feeling better?' she asked at last. 'I mean, your headache, last night . . .? It must have been bad to go to bed so early.'

'Oh, yes, thank you. It's much better today.'

'You look a bit tired.'

'Do I?'

Brenda wondered why she didn't get up – normally she was so full of energy – and suggest they go downstairs.

'Evans and I had a lovely picnic supper on your lawn,' she said, 'but then we ended up rowing.' Augusta looked surprised. 'It's often like that,' Brenda went on. 'I don't know what gets into us, really. Anyhow, I hope it didn't wake you.

I made rather a noise, leaving.'

'I heard something, I think,' said Augusta. 'But I was awake anyway. Evans saw my light on, actually, and came and asked me if there was anything he could do, which was kind of him. Then the second lot of pills knocked me out.'

Her resounding truthfulness left Brenda weak and foolish. Well! All that daft worry for nothing. She might have known it, had she thought less hastily. Evans, for all his silly threats, was too decent a man to lay a finger on someone else. And Mrs Browne, of course, was not the type to entertain passes from those outside her own world, even if Evans had been so unwise as to approach her. She felt herself blushing.

A breeze came through the open window, stirring Mrs Browne's long hair and making the skirts of some of the dresses in the cupboard to dance a little.

'Lordy,' said Brenda, to change the subject and disguise her confusion, 'you've got enough in there for a film star, haven't you?'

Mrs Browne got up, then. She went to the cupboard and opened the door wider. Several of the lighter materials fluttered quite hard.

'Far too many,' said Augusta. 'I never throw anything away. They go back years . . . Goodness knows what I shall do with them when we leave. Give them away, I suppose.' She took a dress down from the rail and held it out – a chiffon gathering of indeterminate greys: a lot of pretty rags, it looked like, to Brenda. Augusta was swishing it about like a feather duster. '*A Midsummer Night's Dream* sort of dress, I think, don't you? It might have been worn by Peaseblossom or Cobweb or Moth . . . better than by me.'

'Oh, no,' said Brenda, 'it would look lovely on you, I can imagine.' She wondered if after all this time alone Mrs Browne had gone a bit funny in the head. Her eyes seemed very large, distant, as if she was addressing William bloody Shakespeare himself instead of her, Brenda.

'It was Hugh's favourite of them all,' Augusta was saying, holding it up, unmoving now, in front of her. 'Where on earth would I ever wear it again?'

At that moment inspiration struck Brenda blindingly.

'My friend Lark,' she said, 'you know about Lark? Well, she's my friend.' The impact of her own idea confused her. 'She's a singer, a marvellous singer. She's going to do her first concert in December, some huge hall somewhere, and she's looking for a silvery dress. I wonder if I could buy it for her? She's just your size.'

'Give it to her,' said Augusta, at once.

'No really . . .'

'Go on, please.' Quite firm, she handed the dress to Brenda.

'That's terribly kind of you. You can't imagine how pleased Lark will be. She'll get you tickets, of course, for the concert.'

'I should like that,' said Augusta. 'December . . . I leave in January.'

Brenda followed her out of the room and downstairs. Enfeebled for a moment by relief at the news about Evans, she was now exhilarated by her gesture towards Lark. Also, she felt that her short encounter with Mrs Browne in the bathroom had established an especial bond between them Evans could never achieve. Boldness overcame her.

'If you don't mind me asking, I don't like to be nosey, but all those parties you used to have . . . all those people here. Why don't you have them down any more? It would be more cheerful, like. This big house.'

'Ah,' said Augusta. She stood quite still in the hall, listening to the music from the drawing room. 'I suppose it's because I'd like them to remember it as it was.'

'There's something in that,' said Brenda, privately thinking the idea was barmy, 'though how you stick this place all alone I don't know. I'd go potty.'

Augusta smiled, and opened the front door. Beside her Brenda was conscious of feeling very large, big breasted, clumsy, too healthy. She understood there was no point in trying to prolong the visit, much though she would have liked to carry on chatting: she'd never met anyone so peculiar as Mrs Browne in all her life. But she looked very tired, and clearly wanted to be alone again with her boiled eggs. They said goodbye and Brenda left. Her plan was to return to the flat and lay the dress on Lark's bed. She would then go out somewhere for a while, and return later to find Evans waiting for her, a bit anxious, perhaps. It would be no bad thing to make him suffer a little. Then they would have a nice evening to make up for last night. They would take Lark with them – she'd be all of an excited dither about the dress – for a drink in the Star. Later, Evans might be persuaded to go back to the Hilton. They hadn't been there for weeks, and soon it would be too cold. And tonight she particularly fancied the barn, more than their bed in the attic. She felt randy as a cat. She'd give Evans his money's worth tonight, if she could keep her hands off him till closing time.

The bus arrived with lucky timing. Brenda sat on a warm seat whose stuff scratched the back of her thighs, the filmy dress flung over her knees. She lit a Woodbine, blew the smoke slowly out of her nostrils. She felt upon her the admiring gaze of other passengers – warming, to be honest, as she anticipated the pleasures of the evening ahead.

Lark had not felt so well for weeks. All morning she had hummed at her typewriter, counting the minutes till the lunch hour. Then she had made a dash round the shops in a preliminary search. It was disappointing, as she had told herself it would be. Not the right time of year for silver dresses, they all said. Come back nearer Christmas. But Lark knew she could not wait that long. She decided to go to Luton on her next Saturday off. Or, if that failed, to London.

She walked back to the flat, singing all the way, the only pain in her stomach caused by hunger. There had been no time to eat anything since breakfast. She planned her evening: a toasted Marmite sandwich and a glass of gin while watching *Coronation Street*. Then the Elgar concert on Radio 3 while she did her nails and thought more about the dress. She would also make a new list of songs to sing – she had already made three and discarded them. Oh, there was much to do. With a real concert ahead, the tempo of the hours was marvellously changed.

After the glare of the sun outside it took Lark some moments to accustom her eyes to the dimness of her room. Its shadows were split by the Venetian blinds. Only the massed geraniums shone scarlet as ever. On the bed lay a scant little dress, limp, bedraggled, reminding Lark of a dead bird left out in the rain.

She paused, blinked – it was still there, no hallucination. She picked it up, not understanding. Wisps of chiffon fluttered about, different tones of silvery grey. Without thinking, as if in a dream, Lark ripped off her skirt and shirt, and pulled it over her head. There was a faint smell of expensive scent, the cool swish of the silk lining on her bare breasts. She went to the mirror: face, neck and arms all horribly white and thin, she thought, but the dress fitted perfectly. She stroked its skirt gently with both hands, to check its existence, expecting it to expire like a puff of smoke. But still it remained. Incredulous, she stood without moving for a long time.

Then, footsteps outside. Brenda! Of course, Brenda. Who else could have done such a thing? Brenda was the dearest sweetest girl alive. She had always known it from the moment she had met her in that café two years ago. For all her funny gruff ways, her forgetfulness and dreadful untidiness, she was the kindest girl in the world

'Oh, *Brenda*!' she cried, and flung open the door. Evans stood there, worried face.

There was no time for Lark to rechannel her delight, to reach for calm. She threw herself upon Evans, clinging to his neck like a small monkey. She kissed his cheeks, his mouth, uttering incomprehensible explanations. For a second she felt him catch his breath, harden. Then, roughly, he pushed her from him.

'What's up?' he said. 'What are you all dressed up like a dog's dinner for, then?' His eyes went all over her, puzzled.

He followed her into the bedroom and shut the door behind him.

'Brenda gave it to me,' she said. 'It must have been Brenda, it can't have been anyone else. For my concert. They've asked me to sing, you see.' She blushed under his look.

'It's beautiful, Lark,' he said, eventually. 'You look smashing, really. Never seen you look like that before.'

Then Lark was sitting on the bed crying. The surprising tears had come too quickly to check: they dripped on to the dress spotting it like rain. Brenda's kindness, Evans's approval – it was all too much. Evans sat on the bed beside her, put an arm round her shoulder.

'Now leave off that noise,' he said, 'for heaven's sake. You'll spoil your looks.'

Lark managed a smile, felt her tears wetting Evans's shirt. *I love you, I love you, I love you. Oh, Evans, I don't half love you.*

'Can you get a couple of glasses?' was all she sobbed, 'and we'll have some celebration gin.'

Evans gave her his handkerchief and went off to the other room. Lark stayed in her dress, and they sat watching television, drinking their gin neat in respect of the occasion. Brenda arrived back some time later and admitted to being fairy godmother, but would not say where she had found the dress. She was surprised Lark did not guess, though her delight was so abundant all rational thought was impossible. Lark agreed to come with them for a drink at the Star. It was only with great difficulty they persuaded her to change back into her old clothes. She would try the dress on for an hour or two every night until the concert, she said, to keep proving its existence. Reluctantly she slipped out of it, head beautifully silvered by gin, now: the best evening for years.

Much later Evans and Brenda lay at the top of the Hilton. The harvest long over, the barn was almost full of bales of straw. They had had to climb high to find a suitable platform: the rafters of the roof were only a few feet above them.

Cobwebs, they could see by the light of the moon, dangled close. The occasional scuffle of mice was the only noise.

Brenda had been at her most insatiable. Evans had often thought it was not worth letting her have a night off: it resulted in such demands when they met again. But he was proud always to be able to quell her desires in the end. She lay quietly now in his arms, naked, coppery head on his chest, smelling of chicken feed and essence of bluebell, the two scents most dear to him in the world. He hoped she would not draw away just yet and reach for her cigarettes. There were things to tell her.

'Good news and bad news,' he said.

'Oh?'

'Mum and Dad had an accident last night. Dad put the car in the ditch.'

'I thought it might have been theirs I saw,' said Brenda. 'Are they all right? Why didn't you tell me before?'

'Didn't want to. You weren't in the mood, and Lark full of beans and that. They're not too bad. Dad bruised, and a cracked rib. He'll have to be in bed a few days. Mum's a bit shaken, but that's all.'

'How did it happen?'

Evans paused.

'I didn't like to ask. Dad's been a bit under the weather just lately.' So disloyal a confession he would confide to no one but Brenda.

'I heard.'

'What did you hear?'

'That . . . like you said. He's been a bit under the weather.'

'Don't let anyone tell you anything else.'

'No.'

'Promise, Bren?'

'Promise.'

Evans drew her closer to him and kissed her hair.

'Funny thing,' he said. 'I was in with them a while, this evening, before coming over to fetch you. I was standing by Dad's bed, Mum was downstairs. He didn't say much. Well, he never does. Then he takes this fob-watch from the table, a bloody great gold fob-watch, been in the family years, and he says he wants me to have it. He says it's no use to him any more. It goes all right, right as rain. But he doesn't want it any more. So I pick it up, listen to its tick, admire it, say that's very kind, Dad. He looks at me in a funny way, almost as if he can't see me. Then – you might not like this bit – I don't want you to leave it to Brenda, he says, or to your son if you have one. I want you to leave it to someone else. A very remarkable woman. You'll know who I mean if you think about it hard.'

'Who did he mean?'

'Don't ask me. Couldn't think for the life of me. Still can't.'

'Why didn't you ask him?'

'I did. But he didn't seem to hear. He seemed to fall asleep. Maybe he was asleep all the time, talking in his sleep. Suffering from shock, perhaps.'

'You know what I think? I think he means your Mum.'

Evans laughed. Suddenly the mystery cleared.

''Course he does! That's what he means. Don't know why I didn't get it at once. He finds it so difficult saying things straight, Dad. He's sometimes very puzzling. Anyhow . . .' He paused to kiss Brenda again. 'Know what I'm going to do with it?'

'No. What? Go on. Stop . . . all that and tell me.'

'I'm going to sell it.'

'Never!' Brenda stiffened with shock.

'I'm going to sell it, I tell you. What does my mother want with a man's watch? What do I want with it? I could get £300 for that watch tomorrow. With £300 . . . Get my meaning?'

'The deposit?'

'The deposit and a bit to spare. What do you think?'

The very idea was an aphrodisiac to Brenda. She ran a hand over Evans's cold buttocks, and along his thigh.

'Marvellous. No more worry.'

'So we can be in by January if they keep to schedule.'

'In January . . . That's lovely. But stop talking about the house just now.' Brenda sighed.

Evans raised himself upon one elbow and looked down at her. He picked up a single piece of straw from her stomach and threw it away. She had the largest darkest eyes he'd ever seen, a beautiful shining mouth that teased even in repose. He put a hand over one of her breasts, flicked at the nipple in the way she liked. He had no thoughts now but his love for her, no sensations other than an exuberant calm, knowing he could now provide for her. He would not let her down. She could do what she liked: rant at him, throw things, slam doors, quibble. But she would not shake him off. Never.

'Sorry about last night,' she was saying, voice husky as when in mourning for a dead chicken.

'Oh, that,' he said. 'That was last night, wasn't it?'

They quickened simultaneously, as was their way. Their flesh had cooled in the night air. Summer was over.

'I love you, you minx,' said Evans.

'So you bloody should,' said Brenda. 'Now shut up talking, will you, and get on with it.'

Henry stayed in bed for two days, then, against the doctor's orders, got up. He ached all over. His ribs were strapped with bandages, one eye was badly bruised, and there were cuts on his hands. It hurt to move. But Henry saw no chance of recovery in the claustrophobic atmosphere of his bedroom, Rosie fussing in every few minutes to rearrange things that were perfectly all right as they were, and being a general nuisance. Besides, the last of the whisky had gone, and Rosie refused to buy more. And what Henry needed, he knew, to get himself back on the road, was a good stiff drink.

He left the house when Rosie was out shopping. It was painful to walk, and his progress was slow, but he was glad to be out again. It was early October by now: leaves turning, sun still bright in the hard air. Good time, October. Best time of year, autumn. Going to the brickworks, early mornings on his bicycle, Henry remembered enjoying the sharpness of the countryside for a few weeks before the clamminess of November set in. He used to note with some satisfaction the progress in the fields he passed on his journey: Long Corner, a broad sweep of stubble that led up to its barn stuffed with hay, held particular memories that sometimes came dancing back on an October morning. The barn had been built when he was a lad, and had housed many a secret exploration between his friends and their pubescent girls. He himself had lain in the hay with one Lily, a girl of blubbery flesh and breath that smelt of acid drops. She had shrivelled into a mangey spinster, Lily: Henry saw her collecting her pension sometimes. But she kept their secret well, it had to be said. Her watery eyes gave no indication that she remembered those Sunday afternoons when they were both fourteen: but then perhaps she didn't.

Lily had given pleasure to half a dozen boys before Henry came along: for him it was the first time, too quick, but unforgettable. With Rosie, of course, it had been quite different. He had always fancied Rosie for her gentle mind rather than her polite body. He had scarcely touched her before they married for fear of ruffling her religious beliefs. She used to whimper, slightly, lying on the ground in the bluebell woods, but if Henry made to reward her desire she would smack at his hand as if it was an insect, chiding at him for being too fresh in their engaged state. He would lie back and think wistfully of the way Lily used to squirm in the barn, and of the passionate girl in Marseilles. Sometimes, home from the brickworks, he would report to Rosie the state of the fields: Long Corner was under plough, he would say, or they'd planted wheat in Bray's Field. But she never seemed interested: earth, sea, bricks, held no pleasure for her, as Henry learnt over the years, and so had given up encouraging her to understand them.

As it was too early for the Star to be open, Henry went to Mr Daly's office behind the ironmonger's shop. It was a private place, the office. Crammed with old papers and bits and pieces, a terrible mess, quite unlike home. Above the desk hung a 1954 calendar, a picture of ducks on the Cam. Cambridge, Henry had thought lately, would be a good place to take the Leopard – probably she would prefer it to Blackpool. There was a train timetable somewhere . . . he might look up a train. The Morris Minor was in no condition to make the journey to Cambridge, or indeed anywhere else.

Henry shuffled among the papers, pushing aside a bottle of dried ink, an assortment of pens with rusty nibs, a bag of screws and some lengths of fine chain. It pleased him to be back. No one could worry him here, he could do things in his own time. Daly would be in with a mug of tea, shortly, then he would go through the books before opening time. Regretfully – for he liked to do things that had some small connection with the Leopard, even though she was unaware of his existence – Henry gave up his search for the railway timetable, and turned to the first of the accounts books. In his absence Mr Daly had been filling them in each night. They were, Henry noticed at once, quite illegible. The writing was blurred, as if it had been left out in the rain. Henry rubbed his eyes. There was no improvement. The figures remained unclear to him. He remembered, then, he had had difficulty reading the paper yesterday. Come to think of it, ever since the accident his eyes had been giving him trouble. At this rate he'd have to arrange a private visit to an optician: one thing he couldn't tolerate would be Rosie's concern.

The door opened. Daly stood there, two mugs of tea in his hands. Their steam had misted his glasses.

'Back on the road, then? Better, are you? I reckoned you'd be away a week or so.'

'Mending nicely,' said Henry. Daly put one of the mugs on the desk, scattering a clump of drawing-pins. 'Thanks. Things all right here?'

'So so. Can't hope for too much seeing as the country's in the hands of the Unions.'

'No,' said Henry. The tea scalded his aching ribs, but

there was comfort in the beginnings of their ritual conversation.

'Small shopholder's bloody strangled.'

'He is, too,' agreed Henry.

'This rate, I'll be putting up the shutters within the next year or so.'

Henry looked up, surprised. It had always been Daly's habit to declare he would not be beaten by the system.

'As a matter of a fact,' Daly went on, 'while on that subject, there's something I shall have to speak of . . . to you, personally,' he added. He took off his glasses and polished the steam from them with a handkerchief streaked with grease. Henry sensed his awkwardness.

'Oh, yes?'

'It's the books, Henry.'

'The books?'

'There've been mistakes. A lot of mistakes.'

'Mistakes?'

'Errors. Call them what you will.' There was a silence between the two men. They sipped their tea, then, simultaneously breaking it. 'You've always been so accurate, you see. I was surprised. But these last weeks, there's no doubt, there've been bad mistakes.'

'It's been my eyes,' said Henry, at last. 'They've been giving trouble.'

'Ah,' said Daly. 'You should get them seen to.'

Henry ran a finger round his collar. The tea was unusually bitter. The smell of paraffin in the room almost stifled him. The words on the piles of papers all about him were a jumble. But clear in his mind was the picture of someone else checking his books. Someone else sneaking in, after hours, double-checking his calculations at Daly's request. Some nosey-parker accountant disputing his sums, criticising the impeccable neatness of the figures he had taken much pride in for the last few years.

'Why didn't you say something about this before?' he asked, at last. 'Why didn't you come to me, direct like, instead of checking up behind my back?'

'It wasn't a matter of checking up behind your back . . .'

'It bloody was.'

'Now look here, Henry. No need to take offence. We've had a good working partnership these last years, and I wouldn't like us to fall out. I'd be very sad about that, very sad indeed. I mean, we've always understood each other. But lately, common knowledge, you've been under the weather. Not your former self –'

'Common knowledge?' Henry felt weakness splinter his ribs.

'Well, people have been saying this and that.'

'What manner of things have they been saying?'

'Nothing offensive, mark my word. Nothing offensive. You're a well respected member of the community, take it from me. But it's been noted you've been spending a lot more time than usual at the Star. And on some occasions . . .'

'Ah, I understand,' said Henry.

'Well, any of us, some occasions, human weakness . . . I know how it is. Used to drink a bit too much myself, years ago.'

'Did you.' Henry's answer was too flat to be called a question. Daly gripped his mug with both hands, as if to brace himself.

'And the long and the short of it is this, Henry,' he said, 'I am terminating your job.'

Terminating. Terminal. A word from the world of trains and fatal illness. A chilly word. A word that pushed you outside, gave you the sack, said you'd lost your chance. Meant the end. No more peaceful mornings in the unruly office, – walls the colour of dead skin, as they sometimes seemed to Henry – crouched happily over the lined paper, ballpoint pressing into the spongey texture, adding up out loud, tongue slipping over dry lips between each column . . .

'I understand,' said Henry. When the end of something came, there was no point in hanging about. When he'd left the girl in Marseilles, he remembered, she'd stood on the jetty, waving her handkerchief, wiping her eyes: but he had turned away quickly, gone below decks. No use prolonging such moments. He stood up, put out a hand to Daly. They shook, quite friendly.

'Goes without saying, I'm very sorry about this,' said Daly.

'Quite,' said Henry.

'And I shall of course be sending you a suitable cheque – a small golden handshake, you might call it. A token of my appreciation.' He smiled slightly: teeth all shades of brown and black. 'Expect, anyway, you'll have no difficulty, man of your qualifications, finding another little job. Must be awkward, retirement, for someone like you.'

Henry attempted a return smile, but it turned out to be a grimace against the pain in his ribs.

'I shall do very nicely, I've no doubt,' he said, and glanced finally at the ducks on the Cam. 'Might even find time to visit Cambridge. A thing I've always had in mind.'

'Ah, Cambridge, now,' said Daly, and opened the door for Henry to pass through into the shop.

Outside, the air was invigorating, the sky still blue. He'd been worried for some time, of course, that calculating hadn't come so easily to him, that on certain days VAT confused his head considerably. But he had hoped Daly would not notice, would not catch him out. He had hoped he could have hung on, struggling through the figures, somehow, until the day of the Leopard, when everything in the world would be clear again. Well, luck had turned against him. It was a blow, but what was one more blow? Only problem was what to tell Rosie. The last thing he wanted was her sympathy. He'd have to make sure to avoid that. Think up some story over a drink.

Henry looked at his watch. Opening time. A double Scotch, he needed, to dull the bloody ache in his ribs, and to clear the water in his eyes. Slowly, he set off in the direction of the Star.

That afternoon it was Rosie's turn to do the church flowers.

This was a duty shared by three ladies of the village, and Rosie, allowing herself the small vanity, had always felt herself to be the superior arranger. Today she had picked a bunch of shaggy-headed chrysanthemums from her own garden, bronze and claret, and a few yellows, as bright as sunflowers. There was in fact a small supply of petty cash available to buy the altar flowers, but Rosie felt it a matter of pride never to use it. When there were no flowers in her own garden she made do with hedgerow things and, at rose time, she took advantage of Mr Browne's kind offer, when he moved to the house some years ago, to help herself from the garden of Wroughton House.

She stretched up now, patting the flowers into place, balancing their stems in the tall vases of golden china bequeathed to the church by a former vicar's wife. A shaft of late sun came through the stained glass window, fretting her bare hands and arms with blues and reds and greens. It was a peaceful place, and she liked to be there alone. She liked to run her hands along the altar cloth, feel the softness of its satin, and the sudden hard ridges of embroidery; arum lilies beautifully depicted in gold thread some hundred years ago. It had been just such an afternoon, she recalled, that she and Henry had stood looking up at the lighted candles on the altar, promising they would stick to each other for better or for worse, and Rosie had had no doubts in her heart that any event could change their resolution. Oh, it had been a happy day. Friends and relations squashed into the house for sherry and beer and sausages and wedding cake: the taste of her mother's powdery tears as they had kissed each other goodbye. And all the village, it seemed, had turned out to wave goodbye.

They had been driven away in an old upright taxi, its windscreen so thick with confetti the driver had had to use the wipers to clear his view, to a small village not far from Wroughton. They spent the weekend in a simple hotel run by a distant aunt: it stood on the banks of a river, and there seemed to be the permanent noise of river birds outside their window. What a night that had been! Rosie on her knees at the altar, sweeping up fallen leaves, felt herself blush. Such memories were out of place in church, she told herself, but, and may the Lord forgive her, Henry had done such wonderful things. She paused in her sweeping, newly aware of the hideous shapes of the hands that held the dust-pan and brush. What had she done to be so cursed? Had it not been for *them*, there might have been years of wonderful nights. As it was, once she had become pregnant, Henry's interest in any kind of night-time activity began to wane. Rosie had never liked to ask him what was the matter, of course, and tried to believe him when he pleaded tiredness at the end of a long day in the brickworks. But sometimes she caught him looking at her hands, as she sat by the fire sewing or knitting. He never said anything, but Rosie knew. She could tell by his look he regretted having married a woman with such ugly hands, however much, in those early years, he claimed he loved her (which, in truth, was not very often).

Rosie walked down the altar steps and closed the wooden gate behind her. Now, there was little hope. She might persevere – indeed, nothing would stop her determined perseverance – but there was no real hope. And faith without hope was of little value. This afternoon, forcing herself to face the reality of the situation, Rosie felt a heaviness of step. Her feet were clumsy, unusually noisy in the quiet of the aisle. There seemed to be a weight in her stomach. Neither the thought of God's great love, nor of the jam sponge she had made for tea, could lighten her darkness. She contemplated kneeling for a moment and praying for strength. But there was a danger that Mrs Jackson would come in to neaten the prayer books, as she bossily took it upon herself to do most afternoons, and catch Rosie at it. Well, to Rosie's mind prayer was a private matter, except when you were part of a congregation, and she didn't wish Mrs Jackson or even the vicar himself to see her down on her knees: knowing their minds, they'd instantly suspect she was in some kind of trouble and, God forgive her, she'd do anything to avoid *that.*

She returned the dust-pan and brush to the cupboard in the vestry, and threw away the bunch of dead flowers which Bridget Goff, bless her heart, had made a real mess of last week. Then she walked home to get the tea.

She found Henry asleep in his chair, mouth open, spittle running down his chin. Rosie uttered a small cry of relief: at least he was safely home. When she had returned from shopping this morning and found him gone, and then he had not appeared for lunch, she had guessed where he could be found and had steeled herself not to go in search of him. But it had been a worrying time because he was still in a shocked condition. The doctor said he should have had a week in bed before trying to resume normal life. And there he was, obstinate old thing, plain defying the doctor's orders. Though of course it was his spirit Rosie loved him for. All she could wish . . . and, apart from that, that he would let her know his movements, sometimes, to save her so much worry.

Rosie knelt on the floor beside him and gently dabbed at his chin with her handkerchief. He stirred abruptly, then swiped at her with his arm, pushing her roughly away. 'Bloody woman!' she heard him mutter. He moaned, as if the gesture had hurt his ribs.

Rosie gasped. She stood up, backing away from him. He opened his eyes. They were bloodshot, watering. His mouth moved, but whatever he said was incomprehensible. A terrible word came to Rosie, then: a word which had been trying to press its way through to her consciousness for weeks, and which she had kept rejecting. But now it screamed through her mind, wild, frightening: *drunk.*

Henry was absolutely drunk.

The heaviness Rosie had felt in church fled from her. Scarcely knowing what she did, she ran from the kitchen, coatless, slamming the door behind her. She hurried back to the churchyard, made her way to the dark corner where her mother was buried between two yew trees. Rosie flung herself down upon the tombstone. The chill of its marble flared through her thin skirt and blouse, and stung her forehead. She wept for a while, not knowing whether to call upon God or her dead mother: feeling neither would understand her horror. Henry seemed to be set upon a course from which there was no turning back. She doubted all the love she could give him could save him now. She should have faced the truth sooner, months ago: consulted the doctor, tried to talk to Henry. What had led him to this? It was as if there was some canker within him, consuming him, taking him further and further from the one who loved him with her whole being . . .

After some time Rosie dragged herself into a sitting position, and rested her head and hands upon the headstone. It was a bulky cross made of rough granite, and hurt her skin. Feeling the pain, Rosie dragged her hands along its arms till the pain increased. Then she turned her hands and scraped their backs along the cross, drawing blood. They looked as if they had been dragged through brambles, the blood a pattern of small dots. Rosie gazed unbelieving at what she had done. Then she stood up, noticing a ladder in her stocking. It was quite cold by now. The sun was setting behind the church. She shivered, wondering at her own behaviour. The strain, she thought, these weeks, had been too much: she must take a hold on herself. Never again would she give in to such a display of hysteria. Disgraceful, Rosie, her mother would have said. Quite disgraceful. She'd be turning in her grave.

Rosie walked back along the church path, calmed by her own shame. She would wash the blood from her hands and get Henry's tea as if nothing had happened: the weak moment would be banished from her mind. And this evening, when Henry returned to the Star, she would cut herself a new pair of mittens. Now, she was quite resigned.

By November the office men were taking further dreadful liberties. They sent men to measure up the rose garden, where they planned to build a prefabricated extension to house the typists. They sent men to judge the state of the elms, and the brick walls round the kitchen garden, and the ailing fig tree. They would stand in the sweep of drive by the front door, scratching at their nylon collars, envisaging the neo-Georgian porch with which the architect planned to improve it. Augusta, from an upstairs window, would watch them. They took no notice of her.

She would watch them and remember the day of the move to the house: it was May, very warm, white butterflies hovering like occasional snowflakes about the lavender, the village grocer bringing loaves, assuming they would need bread. In and out of the house she and Hugh went, directing where the furniture should be placed, always seeming to agree.

By evening the rooms were furnished though there were no curtains and many of the walls were still shabby with old paint. Among the piles of unsorted stuff in the hall Augusta found vases, and instantly arranged bunches of lilac: so that her earliest memory of the house included the smell of flowers. Hugh, she observed that night, already wore the face of a squire: he had laughed, said what nonsense, she was the grand one. They had wandered about till it was quite dark, carrying candles into unlighted rooms, making their endless plans; it had taken a long search to find this house, and buying it, they both knew, was probably financially irresponsible. But they were full of mutual optimism. Something would happen. Money would come from somewhere. They would do things slowly. After all, there were unlimited years.

But Augusta was of an impatient nature and organised the decorating, as economically as she was able, quickly. Within months, all but the attics were ready for living. And then came the friends, for weekends, for parties: so much pleasure. But, at quieter times, the problems: the rotting stables, leaking roof, new machinery needed by the gardener . . . Demands that seemed endless, but for a while, surmountable.

And now that Hugh was gone, and the house was almost gone, the weakness of nostalgia left her without defence. Despising her own frailty, she tried to fight the invious sorrow from hour to hour. But the empty house, the empty rooms, the empty garden crowded with happy recollections, made mockery of her battle.

She stood in the hall listening to the crackle of the fire behind her, smelling the smoke of apple boughs. Her problem this morning was whether or not to buy a Christmas tree. Every other year they had had one which reached the ceiling, frosted with firefly lights and glinting with glass balls. This year, she told herself, to decorate a tree would be absurd, a further mockery. And yet she was tempted. With only a few weeks to go, she might as well keep up the old standards, if only for her own benefit. But her thoughts were interrupted by the sight of an old woman walking up the drive, head swathed in a long scarf to protect her from strands of melting fog. Augusta opened the front door. The dank air slapped against her, at once causing the now familiar neuralgic pain to start up in her jaw.

It was Lily Beal. She had speckled skin and a distinct beard. She lived by herself in an old cottage by the post office, and was the village expert at laying out the dead. This was a task she willingly undertook in return for a cup of mournful tea. Until her eyes had become too bad she had earned her living making lace. Last winter her coal store had been raided and she had nearly died of hypothermia.

The warmth of the hall made Miss Beal shiver with relief. She clutched at her arms with bony hands. Augusta drew two chairs up to the fire. Miss Beal seemed nervous.

'Terrible out,' she said. 'Fog gets into your lungs. They say Harry Andrews has only got a few more days. So I expect they'll be calling me up in the middle of the night. They always seem to die at night, men. Women, now, are more considerate.' She gave a little sniff, and unwrapped her scarf. The face was still heart-shaped, the dim eyes set wide apart. Augusta saw that once she must have been pretty.

'Ah, yes,' she went on, 'I knew Harry Andrews as a young man. Fine young man, he was, then, too. You'd never have supposed . . . to look at him now. Well, that's how it goes, Mrs Browne. One day there's your man all strong. The next you're laying him out.' She gazed into the flames, apparently seeing the dying Mr Andrews as she had known him all those years ago. 'Anyhow, what I've come for, not to waste your time, is a request on behalf of the Darby and Joan Club.' She paused, took courage. 'Seeing as your husband is away, we were wondering if you might be so kind as to represent him at our Chrismas party this year?'

'I don't go out much, these days,' said Augusta. A mass of irrelevant thoughts came to mind: what if her face hurt as it did now? How could she bear to come back to the house, late, by herself?

'It would just be of an evening,' went on Miss Beal. 'We're laying on an entertainment, and everybody would be most obliged if you could come.'

Augusta smiled. It was impossible to refuse. Lily Beal stood up, triumphant. She promised Augusta it would be a good evening, and returned to the front to depart efficiently now that her mission was over.

'I see the swans are still with you,' she said, looking towards the pond. 'They've nested there every year since I was a child. We used to sneak into the garden and climb the willow tree to watch them. Those were the days I liked.'

When she had gone Augusta felt a small surge of energy. The Darby and Joan Club's Christmas party was a single date to look forward to in the decreasing days. Determined to take her chance, to make use of the energy while it lasted, she went to her study. She would begin the job she had been putting off for days: sorting out, throwing away, putting into boxes, dividing. That would be the worst part – the division of things.

She sat at her desk and opened the first drawer. It was filled with old letters from Hugh. She began to re-read them, knowing her own foolishness. But in moments of despair, when the essence of the past is distorted by present doubts, evidence of the truth brings some comfort. The irony of such evidence may mean renewed regret: but just to be reminded is an indulgence few can resist. Augusta, that November morning, gave way to temptation, and was able to postpone for another day the ordeal of packing up.

It was both cold and stuffy in the chicken house. Brenda sat on an upturned box smoking a Woodbine. She listened to the banging on the roof – Wilberforce was mending the leak at last. The noise disturbed the chickens. They shuffled from claw to claw, irritated: the noise of their clucking increased. For the last week, in fact, they had seemed generally unhappy. Perhaps it was the cold: they liked neither the intense heat of summer, nor this dankness of November. Spring and autumn was their best time. Well, it was hers, too, thought Brenda. Next spring would be a good one. Settled in the new house by then, maybe her own chickens at the bottom of the garden. Maybe pregnant. Of late, surprising herself, she hadn't half fancied having a baby. But doubtless the mood would wear off.

Brenda stood up, stamped to warm her feet, moved off down the rows of chickens. Some of them worried her. Some of them seemed really under the weather, and no one to care a damn about them except her. She couldn't tell what exactly it was to worry about. But she was aware of a general feeling of discontent, hostility. When she came into the shed, early mornings, they no longer set up their cluck of welcome. It was as if they'd ceased to care, as if they were exhausted by all the eggs they had laid and waited, apathetic about their fate, to die. Clarissa, for instance – Clarissa who laid the biggest eggs of all. She hardly laid at all now, and when she did the eggs were mean specimens, not much larger than a bantam's eggs. She no longer squawked boastfully as she laid, either, but kept her silence, ashamed, as she watched her tiny product slip through the grille for Brenda to collect. Roberta, most jealous bird in the shed, no longer considered it worth pecking at Clarissa: but still the patch of raw skin on her neck remained, implumed, a raw and shining pink. Brenda had a nasty feeling Clarissa would be next to die. She doubted if she could last the winter. She pushed her finger through the wire and stroked the bird's head. In the old days, Clarissa would have been proud of such a privilege, reacted with a murmurous purr. Now, she merely half-opened her pithy eyelids for a moment, dim acknowledgement of Brenda's concern, and let them fall again.

Marilyn, sex queen of all the birds, was brooding too. Spring was far off, and perhaps she knew it would bring no rewards of the kind she desired. She sat in her coop mourning her frustrated past, a streak of blonde feathers curling down one side of her head. Brenda had a plan for Marilyn: when her own chickens were established at the bottom of her garden, she would ask Wilberforce to sell her. Brenda would turn her into a free-range bird, give her a chance to strut the earth with puffed-up breast, and cast her coquettish eye towards the cockerel . . . But even as she reflected, Brenda knew that the plan was no more than a dream. After so long in her battery, Marilyn would be in no condition to withstand the rigours of an ordinary chicken run. She would be cast out by the other birds, the last of her sexuality demolished by their scorn. She would choke upon a cabbage stalk and die. It would be kindest to leave her where she was, an old flirt with no one to flirt for, rather than to know the bitterness of disillusion.

Brenda moved on to Floribunda, most faithfully affectionate of all the birds. Floribunda had acted with great dignity when Brenda had not made her queen. She had understood you could not have a queen of the shed with a paralysed leg. Quietly, she had clucked about the matter to herself, but otherwise gave every appearance of welcoming Brenda's decision. Each time Brenda passed her coop, Floribunda stirred herself on her good leg and murmured appreciation. Flattered, Brenda paid Floribunda more attention than the other birds in return. In fact, since the death of Elizabeth, Floribunda had become her favourite. She tried to fight against her feelings because she knew that for Floribunda, too, the days were numbered, and she did not look forward to all the distress of another bird's death. As for Daisy, next door to Floribunda, she hadn't turned out to be a very prepossessing queen. She was a dull bird, reliable in the matter of eggs, but with little charm. Responsibilities of her position had taken their toll, it seemed, too: her comb, once brightest in the shed, now drooped, an undistinguished red, symbolising a slipping crown.

'Poor old Queen Daisy,' whispered Brenda, 'you weren't really cut out for the job, were you?'

Lack of spirits in the chicken shed this morning had affected Brenda. She relied on her birds for understanding all her moods, and when they did not give it she felt at a loss. The dank air was particularly depressing, the stench of bird muck sour, and Wilberforce's perpetual banging jangled Brenda's nerves. She would have liked to have left the shed for the office, but a feeling of protection towards the hens kept her where she was. Should Wilberforce's confounded banging cause too much alarm, she wished to be there to comfort. Cold fingers shaking, she lit another Woodbine.

The door suddenly opened. Wilberforce stood there, massive, wisps of fog clinging to his hair and legs. He came in, swinging a hammer, pulled the door shut behind him.

'That's done,' he said.

'Good,' said Brenda.

'Thought I told you not to smoke in the sheds.'

'So you did.'

Brenda saw him loom towards her, unshaven face dark in the poor light. He snatched the cigarette from her mouth, threw it on the ground, crushed it with his foot. Brenda did not move.

'Bloody cheek,' he said, 'you deserve the sack. Anyone else, I'd tell them to go within the hour.'

'Sack me if you like,' said Brenda. Wilberforce looked at her in silence, eyes sneering all over her, prying through the thick wool of her jersey.

'No,' he said.

Brenda shrugged.

'It's up to you,' she said, 'I don't care one way or the other.'

Wilberforce leant up against the coops, blocking Clarissa's view. She gave a cluck of protest.

'That's what's the matter with women. They don't care a damn, one way or another. Treat you like dirt. They're all the same.'

Brenda smiled slightly.

'You having trouble?' she asked.

'You could put it that way. City women lead you a merry dance, judging by my experience.'

'Bad luck,' said Brenda.

'You don't sound very sorry.'

'I'm not, very. I daresay you give them as good as you get.'

'Unfeeling bitch, you are. I'd like to get my hands on you, one day. Teach you a thing or two.'

Brenda looked at him with defiance. She opened and shut her eyes very slowly.

'You'll never succeed there,' she said.

'We'll see about that,' said Wilberforce. He ran his hammer backwards and forwards across the wire of Clarissa's coop. She moved nervously. 'How's it you got such bloody long eyelashes?'

When it came to compliments, Brenda knew herself to be weak. She felt a shimmer of reluctant pleasure. To disguise it, she tried to look scornful.

'Don't do that, if you don't mind. You'll frighten Clarissa.'

Wilberforce laughed.

'That her name, is it? Pretty name for an ugly old bird, I'd say. What, you spend all your time thinking up names for the chickens, do you?' He bent down, peering into Clarissa's coop. 'Doesn't look to me as if she's much longer for this world, anyhow.'

'She's past her prime,' said Brenda. Wilberforce's callousness suddenly alarmed her.

'Better put my hands round her neck, perhaps. Replace her with a new one.'

'No!'

'What's the matter?' Wilberforce straightened up again, moved nearer to Brenda. He looked her in the eye, mocking. 'Got to be business-like, you know, in chicken farming, haven't we?'

'Clarissa's all right,' Brenda shouted, 'I'll let you know when she needs to be . . .'

Wilberforce held up his hand. He ground his fingers into his palm, twisted his wrist, in imitation of strangling an imaginary bird. The hand was huge and cruel as Uncle Jim's. It all came back in a flash, then, that loathesome day, the killing of Hen. Brenda screamed. Then the hand was upon her, its weight over her mouth, smelling of tar.

'Shut up, you bitch.' Wilberforce was shouting, too. The hens began an outraged cackling. Brenda struggled. She felt herself pushed against the coops. Wilberforce's hand slid away from her mouth, gripped her shoulder. His other hand caged her breast. His lips were on hers, tongue deep in her mouth. She could taste onions, and salt.

Brenda had no idea how long it was before she felt her body slacken. Opening her eyes, she saw Wilberforce's eyes were shut. She saw a great chunk of greasy hair had fallen over his forehead. She saw a net of cobwebs across the grey skylight. The officious chatter of the birds filled her ears, familiar music. One of Wilberforce's hands had left her breast, was sliding down her stomach, causing a spiral of vile desire for this man who repulsed her, leaving her weak.

Suddenly Wilberforce pushed her away. She almost lost her balance, grabbed at the wire of Clarissa's coop to stop herself falling. Perhaps Wilberforce had been aware of her reaction, and to spurn her now was his punishment for her rejections in the past.

He stood looking down at her, licking his lips, smiling, horrible.

'I'm giving you the sack,' he said. 'Do you want it?'

Brenda was panting. She tried to control herself. Anger, fear, frustration, tears – they all fought within her.

'Who would mind the birds?' she asked, eventually. She had intended her voice to be strong, but it came out feebly.

'No trouble in getting someone,' said Wilberforce, 'don't you worry.'

'You shit,' said Brenda.

'There's a word for you, too,' said Wilberforce. He banged at Clarissa's coop with a clenched fist. 'You won't go, then?'

'I didn't say that. I haven't had a rise in eighteen months . . .'

'I could give you another couple of pounds a week, daresay. That'd be fair enough.' The voice, for Wilberforce, was gentle.

'I could tell Evans about all this,' Brenda replied, 'and he'd knock the living daylights out of you.'

'I could tell him a thing or two as well. The way you carried on.'

'He wouldn't believe you.'

'Daresay he wouldn't. But it'd liven up his mind with a few suspicions, make him think twice about making you Mrs Evans, perhaps. Well, are you going or staying?'

'I'll think about it,' said Brenda. She knew she ought to go, right now, run from the shed, through the farmyard, and never speak to the bastard Wilberforce again. But then he would wring Clarissa's neck before she was due to die. He wouldn't care a bugger about any of the hens, just treat them as egg-laying machines. No, she couldn't leave them, not just yet. 'I'll let you know this afternoon,' she said.

'No word by two o'clock, then, and I'll assume you're staying.'

'Assume what you like,' said Brenda, 'but for Christ's sake fuck off out of here now . . . before I spit.'

Wilberforce smiled again.

'That's not the prettiest language I ever heard from the mouth of a beautiful girl,' he said, and left the shed.

When he had gone Brenda allowed herself to cry for a while. They were tears of anger. It was ridiculous that anyone despicable as Wilberforce could so affect her, but he was a cruel man and his cruelty frightened her. She shivered: revulsion. It occurred to her that the feeling she most dreaded, and she had suffered it many times in her life, was animal desire for a man who repelled her. Such perversity was beyond her understanding. On the occasions it happened it left her full of confusion, self-hatred and shame. That night at the Air Base it had been just the same . . . But she had no desire to start recalling all the occasions. She would leave the shed, walk to the house and see how it was getting on. Maybe she could concentrate on nice domestic things, like what colour they should paint the kitchen. Such problems would at least take her mind off Wilberforce, and the fate of his wretched hens.

That same morning Lark suffered such bad indigestion she had to leave the office. At home she took a clutch of pills and lay down for a while, but the pain was relentless. She decided that movement would be better. Walking, she was forced to bend almost double. But the concentration required to move at all, she felt, might alleviate the agony. She wrapped a long mohair scarf round her neck and went out.

On the bus to the village, perhaps dulled by the mass of pills or dislodged by the movement of the vehicle, the pain began to subside. The relief brought transitory happiness. Lark felt herself smiling at the fog out of the windows, at the occasional lighted window, and the bear shapes of the people on the pavements. She was a little amazed to find herself on this journey. There had been no conscious thought of going to Evans's and Brenda's house, but now she found herself making her way there the idea of wandering through the empty rooms, imagining them as she would make them, was exciting.

She arrived at the estate – walking in more upright fashion now the pain had almost gone – as the church clock struck eleven-thirty. Builders, fuzzy shaped in the fog, were working on several other half-finished houses: in the dank air chipping noises of hammer on stone sounded like tuneless bells. There was no one in the Evans house. Lark walked through the front entrance which still lacked a door. She saw at once there had been much progress since her last visit. The floors had been laid with concrete. The windows were in, the smooth plaster walls almost dry.

Lark went to the kitchen. There, the sink unit had been fixed under the window. She leant against it, feeling the hard ridge dig into the skin of her ribs where, much deeper, a different kind of pain had so lately seared her guts. She looked through the small square window, half-veiled with condensation. The garden was a narrow stretch of bald earth. At the end was the indefinite shape of a tree. Brenda would get to know this view so well she would no longer notice it. For years and years she would stand here, hands among the plates in soapy water seeing the tree in a haze of young green, or autumn gold, or with its bare winter arms: while behind her she would listen to the sound of Evans eating at the Formica table, and to the chatter of her children. Lark sighed. She knew it was not her fate ever to be part of so desirable a scene. This did not make for bitterness, but for a resigned sadness. For it was impossible not to think that if it had been *her* Evans had loved, instead of merely wanting to crush in a fit of lust, she would have made him so much more suitable a wife. She would have seen to his daily needs in a way that would never interest Brenda. Even now, Brenda couldn't fry a decent egg, let alone iron a shirt. It was unlikely she would ever master Queen of Puddings, Evans's favourite, and yet Brenda was the one he had chosen to stand at his kitchen window for all the years to come . . .

Lark looked up to see Evans standing in the doorway. From his stance she judged he might have been contemplating her silently for some moments. She was confused.

'Oh, Evans, I'm sorry,' she said. 'I hope you don't mind. I hadn't been over for a week or so, was wondering how progress –?'

'You look white as a ghost,' he interrupted. 'Anything the matter?'

'No.' Lark thrust back a long end of scarf over her shoulder.

'Then how come you're not at work?'

'One of my attacks of indigestion. They let me home but I thought it would be better to move about than to lie down and think about it.'

'I see.' Evans moved into the bare room. Lark thought he looked concerned. She had no wish for him to worry about her. She wanted simply to please him by showing the kind of enthusiasm for his new house that did not come automatically to Brenda. Evans stroked one of the smooth walls.

'We'll be in by New Year,' he said.

'It'll be lovely. I can just imagine it all.'

Evans smiled.

'Can you really? That's a talent, you know, being able to stand in a bare room and see it all furnished. I can't do that, nor can Bren. Tell me then, how d'you see it?'

Lark gave a wave of her hand. She described a pine dresser and table, a cork floor, gingham curtains, yellow walls, baskets of brown eggs.

'Really cosy, like a farmhouse kitchen,' she added.

Evans scratched his chin.

'But this isn't a farmhouse. This is a bloody housing estate!'

''Course it is, you nit, but that doesn't mean you have to make it look like a housing estate inside.' Seeing his smile of agreement, she felt quite bold. 'Besides, you'll have the chickens at the bottom of the garden.'

'Ah, yes, the chickens.' Evans ran a finger round the sink unit. 'First house, first sink,' he said. 'That must prove something, doesn't it?'

'It means you've come a long way, Evans Evans. Postmaster, after all. There's not many as can claim to be the good postmaster you are – everyone says.' She herself felt warm with the praise she dispensed with the intention of warming him. Evans smiled at her, tweaked her scarf, sighed.

'That's as maybe,' he said, 'but it's all a long way off, isn't it, to Postmaster-General?'

'Is that what you really want to be?'

'Postmaster-General no less. I'll tell you a secret, Lark. I've always fancied myself on *Panorama*. I've always had this conviction that given the chance I could make sense to the people. I speak their language, don't I?'

Lark, shaken by having been taken into his confidence, honoured with his greatest secret, could think of no immediately wise answer.

'Oh, yes,' she said eventually, 'you *do*, Evans. I think you do. But are you quite sure you're going about it the right way, the job of Postmaster-General, I mean, stuck out here?'

Evans frowned.

'Now, that's something I've often wondered, I have to admit. It's the right thing, of course, to start on the shop floor and work your way up. But take this morning. Practically no business, in spite of the time of year. People complaining they can't send Christmas cards any more. I ask you, will there ever be any Christmas trade again? Anyhow, there I sit, bored out of my mind, everything in order, everything done, staring at the bloody fog, hoping for a break. But when and how's my break going to come, I ask myself? When are the powers that be going to wake up one morning and say to themselves, bugger it, Evans Evans is due for promotion? I ask you, Lark, when is anything going to *happen* to the master of a sub post office?'

Lark could not resist laughing at his expression. She felt the warmth come back to her body, colour return to her face. She felt herself reeling a little on the concrete floor, giddily, happily.

'I don't know,' she said. 'I know you're being serious, very serious – it's all a serious matter. But oh your face! Worse than a funeral.' She stopped to take in his smile, far nearer to him than that time he had mashed her bones. She leant up against the sink unit again, where Evans too was standing.

'How would you like to live in a place like this?' he asked.

Lark made herself sound full of gaiety.

'Terrible,' she said. 'Wouldn't suit me at all. No, when I find the man of my dreams we'll live in a city attic and listen to the rain and the cats clattering on the roof. And breathe the permanent smell of cabbage from the communal hall.'

'Sometimes, Lark, I never know whether to take you seriously.'

'You must never take too seriously anyone who's searching.'

'Bet you'd fill the place up with bloody geraniums.'

'You bet I would.'

'All the same, it's a good place, here, for Bren and me.'

'It's a lovely place you've got, even though it wouldn't suit me.'

Evans looked at his watch.

'I might suggest the yellow walls,' he said, 'only I'd have to be careful. Bren would know I'd never have an idea like that myself.' He gave Lark a conspiratorial smile. 'Well, like a drink to warm you up? I was on my way to the Star.'

As Lark turned to Evans to accept, a sudden gust of weakness blew through her, rocking her on her feet again. She gripped his arm for support. Behind him the pink of the plaster walls divided into shapes like interlocking snakes.

'Lark, you all right?' Evans clutched both her shoulders with his hands. She nodded.

'The pills take away the pain and leave me a bit funny, that's all.' She leant against him, head on his chest, feeling the damp shiny stuff of his anorak. Shutting her eyes she craved to be a small animal who could cling to him for a while, undisturbed, letting him rub her head, as he did now, for a long time.

Then suddenly he was pushing her away from him,

talking to someone over her head.

'Hello, Bren! Surprise, surprise! I just found Lark up here.'

Lark turned to face Brenda, wondering at the insubstantial quality of the walls behind her. Through her own confusion she heard the mocking of Brenda's voice.

'Surprise, surprise indeed! Never thought I'd see the day when I'd catch you two at it!'

'Now look here, Bren, Lark's ill.' Evans's voice was wonderfully authoritative. He pushed Lark back to the sink unit so that she could lean there again. 'Take a look at her face! White as a sheet, in terrible pain. Indigestion. They let her off work and she thought a walk would make it settle.' He reached out a hand and rubbed at her hair again. Lark could feel his fingers shaking. 'Don't worry, love,' he said, 'Bren's only joking, aren't you Bren?'

There was silence. They all listened to the chip-chip of hammers on stone somewhere beyond the doorway. Lark's eyes met Brenda's. Things were no longer out of focus. Brenda's eyes were fierce as a tiger's, tawny in the flat light. Her thick black lashes were stuck together in clumps caused by the damp. Then quite suddenly they were no longer angry or suspicious, but worried.

'You all right, Lark?' she asked. 'You look awful.'

'I'm all right, blinking attacks. I'm off now, leave you two to a bit of deciding. A quick gin at the Star and I'll be as right as rain. Really.' She moved towards the door. They stretched out hands towards her. 'No, leave me.'

'We'll join you for a drink in half an hour,' said Evans.

'Wait for us, mind,' said Brenda.

Lark, nodding, buried her chin deeper in her scarf and set off down the road whose curbs were still merely indicated by lines of string.

When she had gone Brenda and Evans stood at opposite sides of the kitchen looking at each other.

'She looks ghastly,' said Brenda. 'I've never heard of such indigestion.'

'Still, if she hadn't looked so ghastly you might not have thought I was just supporting her.'

'You lay a finger on Lark?' Brenda laughed with confidence. 'Never. Not if she was the last girl on earth. She'd kill you if you tried – she's that loyal to me.'

'I believe she is, too,' said Evans.

Brenda fluttered her damp eyelashes.

'Come on,' she said. 'Something I've always promised myself. There's time.'

'What for?'

'Oh, come *on*, Evans Evans. You're a slow one, sometimes. Let's take a look at the view from the bedroom.'

She led the way upstairs. The small square room, pink plaster walls as downstairs, was floored with pale boards. It was both cold and airless. The high window was meshed with fog.

'It's bloody freezing,' said Evans. 'It'll be bloody uncomfortable.'

But Brenda was easing him out of his anorak, throwing it on to the floor. Then she grasped his belt, the neck of his shirt. All the while she panted, as if suppressing some far greater kind of groaning, and fluttered her eyes. Evans, despite dullness inflicted upon him by the tedium of the morning, despite his sharp hunger for something to eat, and despite the dreadful cold, felt himself quicken. Decades to come passed before him in a flash – years of love in some soft bed in this room, painted and carpeted. But perhaps this would be the only chance of the particular excitement of the room as it was now, stark.

Now Brenda, on a mattress of anorak and trousers on the floor, was ripping off her clothes. With one eye Evans saw a pattern of small bubbles swoop like half a necklace across the window: with the other he saw Brenda's breasts quiver beneath the cold as she thrust her arms above her head and called to him.

He lowered himself cautiously on to his knees, alert to splinters. The boards beneath his elbows were hard as stone.

Then the whole floor, proving it cheap as it looked, began to shake and squeak.

'Bloody lived-in, at last,' murmured Brenda.

After three measures of neat gin Lark regained her strength. She guessed that Evans and Brenda might be detained, and decided not to wait for them. She could go for a walk, and when she was far from any habitation she would sing out loud to practise for the concert. It was only two weeks away now.

She made her way to the bluebell woods. There would be no one there at this time of year: she could feel quite free to try out her repertoire.

Patches of fog moved in an indeterminate way, bustled about by a thin cold wind. Vapours trailed from branches and trunks of trees, and hid the skeleton shapes of dead teazles, tall as Lark, until she was almost upon them, so that she shrank back as they brushed by her, for a moment scared by their anorexic appearance. Dead branches and twigs were soggy underfoot. There were none of the crackling noises of a dry winter's day. No birds sang. The sky above the trees was flat as still water. It was impossible to imagine that spring would ever confuse ground and branches with a multitude of greens again. Or, summer, needles of sun would pick out lovers on the mossy ground. For now it was a place for ghosts, or for the old, to whom winter was an enemy and to whom, when they limped up winter Sunday afternoons to try to remember, the naked trees made mockery of a lifetime of remembered summer foliage. For to the solitary, like Lark, the sepulchral feeling of the woods was remindful of the state of complete aloneness which in winter can bring chill to the bones. She was not afraid, but devoid of any false hopes, such as can trick a single person beneath a blue sky. She knew without question that there was to be some important interruption in her life in the near future, and she waited for it with patience. She could not decipher what shape it would take, but assumed it must be some man, second best to Evans, who would love her enough to take her away from the typist's job and her geranium room. She looked forward to the prospect with no excitement. The only thing that warmed her in this wet air was the thought of the concert.

Lark came to rest by a silver birch tree. She lifted a hand to its trunk to support herself, for the shrouded undergrowth confused her vision – the pills were playing terrible tricks on her again. She determined to take no more. Her white hand, bones like small taut strings, lay against the silver brown bark. Her scarlet nails were arranged in a fan pattern, lady-birds stripped of their spots, horribly bright in all the gloom. Lark thought that if she could be granted a wish, she would request the silver birch to be transported to the concert hall. There, on the platform, in her wispy grey dress, she would lean against it for support, as she did now, and it would give her strength. She would sing better. As it was, she would have to stand alone on the stage, arms by her sides. Arms by her sides? What did singers do with their hands? The questions, which had not occurred to her before, suddenly worried her.

She began to sing, quietly at first, then pushing out her chest so that it rubbed against the scratchy wool of her jersey, and the sound poured clear and hollow through the mists. Lark was exhilarated by the contained power of her own voice. It had the quality of an echo. It haunted. She felt herself trembling, red nails clutching harder at the silver birch. She wondered that so pure a note could come from her own frail chest, and as she took a new breath of foggy air into her lungs she felt an icy sweat on her back, and sweat, or tears, scratch at her eyes.

Since the difficult afternoon when Henry had broken the news to Rosie that he had been sacked, he had felt more than ever debilitated by her welcomes, and went to great lengths to avoid them. On that particular afternoon she had not said much, but sat by the fire, sniffing, cutting out some fine white stuff with a pair of small scissors. Although he looked at her unflinchingly all the while he explained what had happened, she had not raised her eyes and met his. He had had the impression she was in an unusually untidy state: stockings wrinkled round the ankle, a smear of mud on her arm, revolting hands grazed as if by brambles. But he had lacked the energy to enquire whether any mishap had befallen her when she had run screaming from the house earlier, and, as she made no mention of the matter, he let it rest. She had not chided him for losing the job, of course: but she had not abused Mr Daly for his untoward action, either, which Henry felt would have been the loyal thing to do. No: she simply continued daily life with her usual calm, though it sometimes occurred to Henry from the pitch of her voice that cheerfulness caused her more effort than usual. She had doubled her efforts to welcome him on every homecoming, even on the occasions (and they were most occasions) she was forced to turn her head to avoid the smell of whisky on his breath, and to give an arm to support him to his chair. She constantly provided him with the kind of surprises he could not abide, and Henry knew himself to be surly in his lack of appreciation. Once he had found a lump of tissue paper on his chair. It contained a tie made of porridgy tweed, Woven by Countryfolk, it said on the label, which Henry would not have cast upon his worst enemy. She had bought it from the Boy who, in his misguided fashion, had started a small line in ties in the post office, supposing this might bring a little excitement to trade, and act as a small step in the direction of Postmaster-General. Henry had made no pretence at politeness or false gratitude, and had fallen asleep with the dreadful thing slung across his knees.

So lately it had become his habit to walk about for an hour or so after the Star closed, trying to summon the strength and the steadiness to face Rosie's welcoming tea. Most afternoons he went to the woods, knowing quite surely there would be no one else there: Rosie, he was convinced, would never visit them again. They were his protection from her and he needed their solace as much as he needed the increasing amounts of whisky he consumed every day.

It had become his custom to sit on the uprooted tree, the damp bark soft against his thighs, and let the silence lap about him while he contemplated the winter sky. On the bitterest days he would take off his tie and undo the top buttons of his shirt, and relish the cold against his chest. This way, he felt, he would be sure to die of pneumonia quite soon, which wouldn't be a bad death. But although he had continued this ritual for several weeks, so far he had not been assaulted by the mildest sniffle. Today's fog, therefore, filled Henry with hope. Surely the wet vapours would scorch his innards with some wicked disease, and he would pass away in the night. He breathed in deeply, mouth open, making a sucking noise, then spewed the air out again. He watched the small grey bulbs expand from his mouth and merge into the greater grey, which now, in the mid-afternoon light, was turning dun: and he felt the cold swipe through his lungs, stinging like smoke. His legs were no less confused by the fog than his eyes. At moments, stumbling over the soggy ground, Henry was near to falling. He decided to pause for a while, to try to consolidate the spinning greyness both within his head and all around him. He held on to the trunk of a larch tree, unsure where he was. He knew every inch of the woods but was unnerved to find his sense of direction had suddenly gone. Was he south or west? Screwing up his eyes, he peered through the trees attempting to see the brickwork chimneys on the horizon. But all was obscured. The fog seemed to be thickening. Perhaps he should not have come, but he liked to clear his head in the afternoon air. Even rainy days he enjoyed his pipe under the dripping trees, chewing at its stem, and hawking in a manner that was not permissible at home. On many an afternoon here, lately, he had found some kind of comfort among the trees: he had known the freedom to shout his sourest thoughts out loud, and to listen to them smash against the impervious silence, undisputed.

With his free hand Henry felt in his pocket for his pipe and matches. The simple job of lighting up seemed particularly confusing, but at last he had the stem between his teeth, could taste the tobacco on his tongue. He cocked his head on one side, straining for the sound of birds. Silence swirled round him for a while. It was broken by a thin piping of a clear voice, some tune Henry thought he recognised: more like a human than a bloody thrush. He moved a few paces, trying to decipher where the voice came from. Very puzzling. Who besides himself would want to be here on a day like this? The song took him back to some long forgotten childhood evening, haymaking in a Welsh valley one summer, years before the family had moved here: his mother used to sing that song as she lifted the bales, easily as a man with her strong arms.

Then the answer came to him. It resounded through his head with the force of a shot, clearing all inebriation, inspiring the kind of courage that spurned the confusions of mere fog. Fate, acting in its devious way, had sent her. For some reasons Henry did not bother to work out, the Leopard, on one of her visits to the village, had been drawn to the woods on the hill, and alone on her walk was singing to herself with uninhibited joy. So near at last, all he had to do was to find her.

In frantic anticipation Henry began to move between the trees, too fast to make a way for himself between the branches, so that they scratched wildly at the skin of his face and hands. The voice eluded him in a tantalising way. One moment he felt he was almost upon it, then it seemed to shift direction and he plunged again into maddening obscurity. After stumbling about for a long time, Henry stood still, heart racing: there, in what he dimly saw to be the familiar clearing, he saw the indistinct shape of a small figure. It seemed to be wearing something yellowish, though in the poor light no identifying spots were visible.

'Oh, my God, my Leopard,' he said out loud, and found himself running.

Within a few yards he realised his mistake. This was not the Leopard, or anyone at all like her. It was Lark, Brenda's friend, muffled in a yellow scarf, one hand at her throat, the other swiping vaguely at the fog in a helpless manner. As soon as she saw Henry she stopped singing. He realised he must have frightened her. He could see her hair was quite damp, as if she had been out in the rain, and her eyes were startled smudges in a white face.

'Sorry if I interrupted you,' he said. 'I couldn't think who it could be, up here in this weather.' He gave a small bow, remembering that once, years ago, some girl had told him he could be quite gallant if he put his mind to it. Somehow he managed to charm Lark.

'That's all right, Mr Evans. I was just practising for the concert – you know, they've asked me to sing.' She smiled. 'It's quite ghostly up here, isn't it? I was beginning to think I'd never find my way back, and it's coming down thicker, I think.'

Henry looked around. The spongey greyness of the air seemed to be closing about them. He wanted very much to spit, but Lark's presence inhibited him. Instead he cleared his throat, and rubbed at his chest, where a gash of disappointment lacerated his skin.

'It does indeed,' he said, 'but I know these parts pretty well. I can guide you back, if you like. You must be cold.'

Lark shivered.

'I suppose I am,' she said, 'and I could eat a horse.'

'You follow me, then, and come back to our place for tea. My wife would love to see you, you haven't been over in a long while.' Something about returning home with this waifish creature appealed to Henry: her presence would protect him from Rosie's enquiring looks. He told her to follow him, and turned back into the trees.

In some incomprehensible way Henry's instinct now acted like a laser beam through the fog: the path seemed clear to him as if it was a bright day, and in a short while they reached the gate that led to the field. From then on there were no problems. They descended the mild slope towards the garden of Wroughton House, which loomed in the mist, one lighted window upstairs, bleached to the colour of moonlight through the fog.

'You sing very prettily,' Henry said eventually. He had never thought of himself as a conversational man, but to pay a compliment was no bad thing, and it would give him a little practice for the day of the Leopard. 'Just like a choirboy I once heard. You must be happy to sing like that.'

'Oh, I am. Very.'

A few yards later Henry found himself overcome with indiscretion.

'I'm going to Cambridge, as a matter of fact,' he said. 'In the spring. To see the Cam.'

'That should be lovely. The daffodils.'

Something about her understanding increased his recklessness.

'With a companion,' he added. And the relief of having confided to one other human being in the world left him light-hearted as he had not been for weeks.

'Well, that's quite right,' said Lark. 'I mean, it would be a pity for anyone to have Cambridge in the spring all to themselves, wouldn't it?'

Henry agreed with her most emphatically, but in his temporarily cheerful state he was too overcome to say so. Instead he took Lark's arm and helped her climb the fence into the garden of Wroughton House where, in the new thickness of the fog, the one lighted window hung suspended, unsupported by walls, and casting an etiolated reflection into the waters of the pond.

As the church clock struck four-thirty Rosie opened the door to look out for Henry. She had resisted doing this for some time, but worry had finally overcome her. To her relief she saw him coming up the road, very hazy in the fog, but apparently quite steady on his feet. By his side was the small shape of a girl, muffled in a scarf, features impossible to recognise.

Rosie clapped her hand to her mouth to stifle a scream. Of

course! That was it. In a flash she blamed herself for not having understood before. It was another woman who had been causing all this trouble, and here he was, coming to explain at last. Coming to have it out. Well, at least the truth you know . . .

Fighting tears, Rosie realised there was no time to work out what her reaction should be. The two of them were almost upon her. A lifetime of self-control came to her rescue. She stood up very straight, braced herself with understanding, quickly calculated that they should drink tea from the best china. She would not have Henry accuse her of indignity or lack of hospitality, even in such a crisis. Automatically she arranged her smile. She was determined their first view of her should be a brave and smiling one, full of the kind of welcome that Henry would expect of her in any circumstances.

Much later that night Rosie was rewarded for her stoicism. Bustling about with plates of dumpling stew, having enjoyed entertaining Lark to a huge tea, she felt bold enough to admit to Henry the foolishness of her earlier supposition.

'You know for one minute, silly old me, I really thought you were bringing in a fancy lady,' she said. 'I said to myself, why, after all these years, Henry Evans has found himself a girl, and has come to tell me.'

For the first time in more weeks than Rosie could remember, Henry laughed.

'You women, daft notions you do have,' he said, before falling back into his customary silence. But the lightness of his tone was enough for Rosie. She went happily to the larder, unable to resist a spoonful of the cold baked custard she had made for lunch, sweet in its congealed sauce of golden caramel.

The house was on fire. Flames sprouted from the roof and every window, lighting the night sky. Their flickering was doubled in the water of the pond. Augusta, trapped in the branches of the weeping willow, struggled to get near the house. Her help was essential. Buckets of water. Alone she would put out the flames because there was no one else there. But the branches of the tree held her back. The more wildly she struggled, the more firmly they entangled her.

She screamed, waking herself. The house burning down had become a recurring nightmare. She was sweating, as she always was when she woke, very cold. Through the blinds she could see the beginnings of light.

Augusta got out of bed and went to the window. She raised one of the blinds. Mists of a winter dawn disguised the shapes of the garden, but the intensity of yesterday's fog had gone. The willow was a faint imprint, grey tracing against paler grey. Augusta looked to see herself fighting against its branches, but they were quite still. The pair of swans stood on the bank of the pond, heads tucked into puffed-up breasts. After a while, with one accord, they lifted their heads, stretched their long necks. Luminous white in the mist, they raised their wings, testing sleepy feathers. Then, grotesque ballet dancers, they launched themselves into the air. In a moment they were high above the garden, moving in the direction of the brickworks. Augusta, listening to the creak of their wings, watched them flying side by side till they vanished in the distance. Then she remembered that in a few hours' time a lorry would be arriving full of packing cases, and it was her job to start to fill them.

On the evening of the old people's party it began to snow. Not thickly, but enough to crust the ground with translucent white. Augusta prepared for her solitary return. She put four mince pies in a low oven and piled logs on the hall fire. She also lit the Christmas tree, which she had decorated that afternoon. Its firefly lights cast starry shadows on the ceiling and flagstone floor, and made tiny flames in the multi-coloured glass balls. Augusta left it with reluctance. Her feet crunched over the cobbles of the back drive, and the cold made her clutch her arms under her breasts. It was a pale night for December, clear stars.

In the village hall all was merriment and light. Augusta slipped in unnoticed. She stood looking around at the bustle of elderly people, listening.

'There were five or six of them up here all day, doing it.'

'They've made the crackers nice.'

'And Ellen had a stroke this morning. Did you hear? I popped round. Doubt if she'll get over it.'

'She was looking forward to it so much, too. She'd had her hair done, and all.'

There had been so much effort. A flurry of cottonwool snowflakes on every window, much thicker than the real stuff outside. Crackers stuck at sword angles on the walls. Streamers and balloons. Long trestle tables set with white cloths and primrose china, a funny hat at each place. Poinsettias on the stage.

She was welcomed by Lily Beal and Mr Roper, the chairman of the club, golden wedding a few days behind him. They were apologetic when they realised she must have been standing there awhile unnoticed. They led her to the place of honour at the top table beneath the stage. She sat between Mr Roper on her right, and a fat lady in a beige jersey dress and jacket, intricate piping on collar and cuffs. Augusta, judging by her expensive handbag, guessed she must be someone with benevolent interest in the village, who would no doubt replace Hugh as President when the Brownes finally left.

There was a sit-down hot meal for 75p a head. This had been provided by an up-and-coming caterer who chafed at the back of the hall, casting a bossy eye on his team of waiters. His moustache was the same shape as his bow-tie, wide at the edges, thin in the middle, and he smiled without rest. Mr Roper informed Augusta he was new to the area and at this, his debut, he naturally wanted to make a good impression. There was no doubt the members of the Darby and Joan Club were much delighted by his efforts: tomato soup, turkey, package-fresh balls of stuffing, peas, potatoes boiled and roast, tinned fruit salad with a puff of cream, cheese and coffee, candelabras and paper napkins thrown in. Augusta did her best to eat, but had little appetite. She noticed the ratio of women to men was ten to one, and wondered when it came to the aloneness of old age which it was least desirable to be, man or woman. The old ladies had paid a lot of attention to their party clothes and hair. There was a preponderance of pink diamanté brooches, sometimes a whole collection on one bosom, and crystal beads clustered in withered dewlaps. There was much laughter and the few old gentlemen, scattered with great fairness among the tables, were subjected to an abundance of nudges from their lucky companions. It seemed to be going, as Mr Roper pointed out, with quite a swing.

Supper finished, he tried to stand up. But his chair was too near the stage. It cut into the backs of his knees, causing him to topple over the table. Regaining his balance, with infirm voice he drew attention to the small brown envelopes by each place. He asked that everyone should give a big hand to the kind lady who had provided them – 25 pence in each one. Perhaps she might like to say a few words?

The good lady in matching beige tried to rise, a little flushed now her gesture had been exposed. She, too, had trouble with her chair and the stage, but she had learnt from Mr Roper. She gripped the chair's back rail with one hand, so that it should not butt her from behind, and clutched the table, screwing up the cloth, with the other.

'I'd just like to say thank you all very much,' she said, 'and as for the little envelopes – well, they come from the heart.' She sat down again, to applause. 'I've never spoken in public before,' she whispered to Augusta. She was shaking.

Augusta's own speech was brief. She read a telegram from Hugh, and said how sorry they were to be leaving the village. They would miss everybody, and remember all the good times. But soon she would come back and visit them. That was the only lie. By the time she felt capable of returning to the village, most of them would be dead.

As the hall was cleared the old ladies scraped back their

chairs and pulled their cardigans more tightly over their party dresses. One old man, knees apart, pulled a bowler hat down over his ears. He got a big, pent-up laugh. Encouraged by his success, he waved a walking stick in the air and sang the first line of *My Bonnie Lies Over the Ocean*. Several of the old people talked round Augusta, and reassured themselves.

'You like our new stage curtains? We got them from the WI for £5.'

'That was a lovely meal.'

'They say a professional compere's coming.'

'And professional dancers.'

'And professional singers.'

'My.'

'Anyone know if the milk for the tea is in the gents?'

Dancers first. The fluorescent bars of light went out and a blue spotlight shone on to the stage. A composed twelve-year-old fluttered out from behind the bargain curtains, her pubescent breasts flattened by a tight satin bodice. Scraped-back hair made her face very old. She danced to the thud of an upright piano played by the local music teacher. Sometimes her rhythm and the child's movements were not synchronised, but their concern to please was quite in harmony. Then came two eight-year-olds in huge ears, long tails and pink noses, pulling behind them a large cardboard box. Their teacher, a pink flower pinned like a beacon to her vast bosom, followed them.

'In case you didn't realise,' she said, 'these are two mice with a piece of cheese.'

There were a number of acts throughout the evening, smoothed on their way by the professional compere, who was also a policeman. There were Italian teenage twins with long wavy Drene hair, like 1940 stars, who sang *Puppet on a String*, and a semi-retired conjurer who moved away from the exposure of the spotlight to pull tangerines unconvincingly out of thin air. Augusta, looking round at the audience, saw their bodies had become slack with appreciation: knees slung apart, hands resting upon them with palms turned upwards.

Mouths hung open, some eyelids drooped a little. At the back of the hall, Augusta saw with surprise, stood Brenda and Evans, coats still on, collars turned up. She wondered why they had come. They had the air of people who don't intend to stay a long time.

'And now,' said the compere, clashing his knuckles like cymbals, 'and now, ladies and gentlemen, it is time for our star. And our star tonight is a little lady whose name may not be very familiar to your ears. But, believe me, ladies and gentlemen, she's a very big singer with a very big future.' He paused, pleased by his own sense of timing. 'Her name? Well, her name is very simple. As she sings like a bird it is, appropriately enough, just Lark. *Lark*, ladies and gentlemen. I ask you to give her a big hand.'

They clapped quite hard as Lark came on to the stage. The compere went away, having squeezed her shoulders and banged his big hands right under her nose. She placed herself in the middle of the circle of blue light, let her hands fall to her sides. She wore Augusta's Peaseblossom dress, its silvery folds limp against her bones, its jagged hem making shadows on her stick legs and silver shoes. She had painted her eyelids leaf green, to match her eyes: they shone with a strange light from out of the huge shadows beneath them, and the skin under her cheek bones was drawn back into angular hollows. Her hair had been washed and ruffled, and pinned with a Christmas-tree star. Lark swallowed and, just once, fluttered the scarlet nails of both hands on her skirt.

There was absolute silence in the hall. A sense of surprising awe. Lark's aloneness reminded them. In that moment of quiet there was almost fear, Augusta thought: in revealing the solitary nature of her own being, Lark might expose theirs, too. Then she smiled, to reassure them, and breathing could be heard again.

The pianist scratched a lump of suspender that was troubling her thigh, and began to play. She was an incompetent musician, but had the sense to remain *pianissimo*.

'I'm just going to sing a few songs I've always liked,' said

Lark. 'Nothing to do with Christmas, especially, but I hope you like them, too.'

She started with *Linden Lea.* One or two of the elderly people stifled gasps of admiration, as they might at beautiful music in church. For Lark's voice was so pure, so sweet, so sad, as to clear the most confused mind with the beauty of truth. No larger than a child, unmoving, the notes that soared from her pierced to those dormant areas of regret, or love, or distant pleasure that are from time to time rekindled by the workings of art. She sang a Welsh folk song, *Yesterday*, and *Silent Night.* Finally the theme tune from *The Threepenny Opera*, most melancholy of all. There was no one who did not recognise her quality. They applauded as hard as they were able, but it was the applause of those who have been ungrounded, rather than the riotous clapping accorded to lesser talents. In between songs Lark bowed her head and barely smiled. When it was all over she came to the front of the stage, but looked beyond the audience, overwhelmed, not seeing them. She could not be more than six stone, Augusta thought. Her shoulder bones pierced sharply through her skin, her arms were skeletal. She gave three small bows, bringing the dress briefly to life, making it flutter in imitation of its vivacious days, when Augusta had danced in it all night for Hugh.

Lark said thank you and left the stage. The applause continued, although not everybody could join in.

'I can't clap,' whispered an old man near Augusta, 'in case I break my hands.' They lay clasped together on his lap, rigid blue.

After Lark there were to be games and dancing to cover the anti-climax. Evans and Brenda, Augusta saw, had already slipped away. She thought that she, too, might leave. She said her farewells to Mr Roper and the others, and suggested she might drive Lark home. This was a welcome idea, for it would spare the club the price of a taxi.

Outside the snow was falling more thickly, sticking to the windows of the hall. The cottonwool flakes inside became caricature reflections. Lark was huddled into a coat of shaggy fur, her bony hands clutching at the collar, and at a Cellophane parcel of chrysanthemums. Her face was quite exhausted, but she smiled, incredulous. Augusta suggested that first they should go back to the house and get warm by the fire. She agreed eagerly. Simultaneously they turned for a last look through the snowy windows and saw the old people dancing with much abandon, skirts held above their knees, paper hats all crooked on their heads.

'Do you think they liked it all right?' asked Lark. 'I couldn't see any of them smiling.'

'I think they were too amazed,' said Augusta. 'You sang too well for any of us to smile.'

Lark had never been to the house before. Through the glass panes of the front door they could see the coloured lights smudged among the boughs of the Christmas tree, and the flames still burning brightly in the fire. Inside, Lark stood quietly in the hall, still clinging to her coat.

'What a tree,' she said at last. 'Is that all for you? Or are you having a party?'

'I leave in three weeks,' said Augusta. 'No party. But I thought I might as well . . . have a tree. We have one every year. Now, take off your coat and sit yourself by the fire. I've got some warm mince pies. Let's have them, shall we? And champagne. We must have champagne. Singers always do, you know, after successful first nights like that.'

'Do they, do they really? Oh Lordy, what a night.' Lark was laughing, throwing her fur coat on the golden flagstones in front of the fire, making it into a rug. She sat down, drew up her knees to her arms, so that the dress fell about in tatters, Cinderella's rags. 'I've never been to a place like this before,' she said. 'Champagne and Christmas trees and ceilings high as the sky. It must be funny, all alone. Brenda and Evans told me all about it. They love it here, you know.'

They sat for a long time in front of the fire, eating the mince pies and drinking the champagne. Augusta was anxious to convince Lark how remarkable her performance had been – how it had shaken them all. But she felt inadequate.

'You're a really marvellous singer, you know,' she said. 'I mean it. I don't understand why you never trained.'

Lark shrugged.

'Well, I wanted to. But it never worked out like that. I had to earn my living, didn't I? I had to help out my mother once my father died. Besides, I had these weak lungs. They said I'd never have the strength.' The firelight and the champagne had brought a flush to her face. 'Still, I enjoyed tonight. I might do more, if anyone would have me.'

'Maybe I could help,' said Augusta. 'I know people who might be able to help you.'

'That would be kind, though I don't expect you'd have much time with all this moving. Here,' she added, picking at a chiffon wisp on the skirt of the dress, 'I know where this came from, you know. Soon as Brenda brought it home for me I knew it couldn't have come from a shop round here. I knew it came from you – the quality.' They both laughed. 'It's the most beautiful dress I've ever seen. Did you wear it a lot?'

'Sometimes,' said Augusta. 'Hugh liked it.'

'He's gone, has he?' Augusta nodded. 'Swines, men are, aren't they? Always going. Still, I suppose that's the risk you take if you marry. Can't say I'd mind taking the risk, though. 'I'm always looking out for my chance. There's a man at my office, a drip always on the end of his nose and smelly breath. He says he fancies me, the silly sod, and he'd give me security if that's what I'd like. I say that's not what I want. Not just security. I wouldn't mind a bit of love thrown in, I say, and he says, poo, that comes. But you can see so often it wouldn't, ever, can't you?' Augusta nodded again. 'So you go on dreaming about Robert Redford and having the odd screw behind the filing cabinets. But what they don't realise, those sods who get your knickers down, is how little they're getting. They like to think you're all swoony about them. Grateful. Huh! One day I shall say what's really filling my mind. The dreadful price of tea, or something, just as they're huffing and puffing. Lordy, this champagne isn't half going to my head. I am going on, aren't I?'

She looked up at the lighted tree, twirled her glass in her hand so that the flames from the fire spun among the bubbles.

'I can imagine the parties you must have had in this house,' she said. 'I can imagine the rooms all full of people.'

'They used to come,' said Augusta.

'Still, it's nice, the quiet. Though it must be sad selling it. What are you going to do?'

'I don't know really. Go to London. Live in a flat. Try to forget about this.'

'Impossible, that,' said Lark. 'I'm telling you. How could you ever get a place like this out of your blood? Here, you know what? Whoever comes next, you'll haunt them. They'll see your ghost coming down the stairs, opening the door for them to go away. They'll feel the draught on their legs, the bastards. They'll be so shit-scared they'll leave and you can come back. Don't you think?'

Augusta laughed and raised her glass to meet Lark's.

'Here's to your ghost,' Lark said. 'Now, I must be going. But Evans told me you had a lovely piano. Before I go, would you let me see it? Don't know what it is, but I love pianos, the great big ones. I've always fancied myself leaning in that curved bit of a grand piano, you know, singing at the Albert Hall. Daft as a brush I am, aren't I?'

Augusta led the way to the drawing-room. She left the door open but did not turn on the lights because she did not want Lark to remark upon the packing cases. So the room was quite dark, the shadows scarcely broken by the glow from the Christmas tree. Lark went at once to the piano and ran her hand along its mahogany lid.

'Do you play?' she asked.

'Well, I used to. Not now.'

'Go on, try. I can't play a note.'

'I'm completely out of practice.'

'Doesn't matter. Just something. Please. Here I am,

aren't I? Leaning up against a grand piano after all this time. My mother'll die when I write to her about tonight. She won't believe it.'

Augusta sat down on the fat velvet stool. The champagne had mellowed her, and Lark made her want to laugh, or cry, she wasn't sure which. She felt for the notes, sounding them gently, chords coming back to her. She began a carol.

'I know that,' said Lark. 'I sang that when I was a child. I sang in the choir, solo, when I was ten. My Dad, he nearly bust himself with pride.'

She nestled into the crook of the piano and stretched one arm right across its lid. She hummed for a moment or two, then remembered the words.

Three kings from Persian lands afar
To Jordan follow the shining star . . .

She broke off to sip at her champagne.

'Lordy, I'm drunk as anything, aren't I? Gin never does this to me. Still, it's nearly Christmas, isn't it? Who said you couldn't play? Now, hang on a tick, it's coming back . . .'

And this the quest of the travellers three
Where the new born king of the Jews may be,
Full royal gifts they bear for the King,
Gold, incense, myrrh are their offering.

Her voice was remindful of a flute played by a hillside shepherd. Accustomed to the semi-darkness by now, Augusta could see that for all her claims to intoxication, Lark's eyes shone quite soberly. She had confused drunkenness with the happiness of singing by a grand piano. Perhaps they were almost the same. She ran both hands through her hair, dislodging the Christmas tree star, and laughing. Against the moon panes of the huge windows snow lodged in swooping curves. The church clock struck two. With the confidence of old partners by now, Augusta and Lark began the second verse.

Augusta refused all invitations to go out on Christmas Day. She stayed quietly in her study packing letters into boxes. It took her a long time because she read each one before putting it away. She hoped Hugh might ring, but the telephone remained silent: he had said he would be abroad with friends. In the old days he would ring from all parts of the world. She ate two kippers and two mince pies for lunch, and watched the snow fall in the garden, and swallowed several pills with a glass of Hugh's best port to kill the pain in her jaw. She went to bed at half-past four in the afternoon, made drowsy by the pills. Drawing the blinds of her windows, she saw a pattern of coloured lights on the snow in the drive: she had forgotten to turn off the Christmas tree. But she had no further energy to go downstairs again, and besides, she liked the idea of their colouring the snow all night.

If it had not been for the worry at the back of Rosie's mind about the extent of Henry's Christmas celebrations, she would have enjoyed the day very much. As it was, she had to steer the delicate course between remaining on her guard, and at the same time appearing to be full of the Christmas spirit. After church she was overwhelmingly congratulated on the state of the altar, which had taken many days to deck with holly sprayed with gold. She had refused all offers of help, knowing only too well the downfalls caused by inferior artistic effort: and in spite of all the work she had had to do herself, she had managed to find time to advise Mrs Tuffin about how best to decorate the tree, and the vicar's wife on how to gird the pillars with ivy. Warm with success she returned home to find the turkey cooked to perfection, and Henry sitting in his chair by the fire. He had been to the Star, he said, and treated himself to a couple of cherry brandies, seeing it was Christmas, and had come home early to open the sherry. Rosie swelled with relief. Henry had not remembered to give her a present, but this gesture more than compensated for the omission. To have him sober on Christmas Day was something she had not dared to hope for. In high spirits she set about laying the table, most of which was taken up by a landscape of cottonwool snow and mirror lakes, dotted with small plastic deer and nylon Christmas trees – a little surprise she had been planning for weeks.

Evans and Brenda and Lark came to lunch. Lark had knitted everybody long scarlet scarves. Brenda, of less imagination, had brought different-coloured tablets of soap from Boots. It occurred to Rosie, as she made her polite thanks, how happy she would have been if Evans had fallen in love with Lark instead of Brenda . . . But it was a disloyal thought and she quickly put it from her mind. She had to admit that when it came to looks there was not much competition between the girls. Lark was a mere scrap of a thing, painfully thin these days, while Brenda was a big strapping girl, well made. And Evans seemed happy enough, full of talk about the new house. She could only hope the marriage would be a happy one: for her part, she would do all she could to help and advise them.

In the afternoon Evans and Brenda went off for a walk. She overheard Brenda saying something to Evans about always having wanted to have a bash in the snow, and the remark caused Rosie to blush so hard she had to slip away into the larder and pick at the cold Christmas pudding while she awaited the return of her normal colour. Lark stayed with them by the fire, talking to Rosie, because Henry soon fell asleep. Rosie was able to pass on the news that the whole village had been talking about her performance at the old people's club, and it was certain she would now get many more professional offers. Lark seemed pleased. She ate a lot of Rosie's cake, the top decorated with a miniature ski-resort fashioned in icing, but declined to stay for supper. She left at six, saying how much she had enjoyed her day, but now felt a little tired and would go home for an early night. Rosie privately thought one of her attacks of indigestion was coming on, and suggested some tablets. But Lark shook her head, declining. She left to walk home, well wrapped up in her yellow scarf, saying it wouldn't take her long and she could do with the air.

Henry's good resolutions did not last quite the whole day.

At opening time in the Star he woke up and said he was going for a quick one. He then remembered that by some daft tradition he always invited Rosie to come with him on Christmas Day. He issued the invitation with little grace, and Rosie declined. She could not face watching him downing drink after drink, as on the evening of the car crash, and then having to help him home. No, she said, she would stay at home and prepare a cold supper and watch the Spectacular on television. Brenda and Evans were going to a party, but she would be quite happy by herself until he came back.

He returned earlier than she expected, a little unsteady, but not half as bad as he had been on so many occasions in the last few weeks. For the second time that day Rosie was elated by relief. She hummed to herself as she fried slices of Christmas pudding – which would sober him up completely – and couldn't resist observing, many times, what a nice family day it had been. To show her appreciation further, she went so far as to suggest they have a glass of sherry before they went to bed. This Henry refused, and took a swig of whisky from the bottle instead – a reaction to her offer which Rosie had failed to anticipate. Her own glass of sherry had the happy effect of making the day in retrospect even brighter than it might have been in reality. And then, in bed, it was her turn to remember a Christmas tradition.

Due to Henry's behaviour in the last few months Rosie had decided to postpone making any overture to him in bed, with or without her mittens. Tonight, although the sherry had made her a little carefree, and she would have done anything to rip the wretched mittens off and curl into his back, naked hands wandering his shoulders, she managed to remember resistance would be the wise thing. She prayed to God for strength, having thanked Him for such a nice day, and kept her hands to herself. But after an hour of wakefulness, sensing from Henry's slight shifting that he was awake too, Rosie gave in to the weakness of the flesh. Overpowered by the thought that Henry should be rewarded for having made today easy, and wanting to indicate a small part of the great love for him that welled chokingly inside her, she stretched out a mittened hand and laid it on his shoulder.

The only way that Henry had been able to get through Christmas Day with some semblance of civility was to remind himself every hour that it would, at least, be the last ever such day. He knew this without any doubt. He could not be sure precisely when it had come to him, but some time during the last few weeks a conviction had grown that the New Year was going to bring a change in his fate. This was fortunate, because once the Boy was married, the house without him would be intolerable. Whatever happened Henry would be forced to leave home. But the strength of his new instinct protected him from any qualms on this matter. He was sure Fate would plunge in with nice timing and produce the Leopard – who would, of course, go with him.

Henry had resisted going to the Star for more than two short visits not as a goodwill gesture towards Rosie, but because he guessed that on Christmas Day, drat it, it was unlikely the Leopard would be visiting a pub some distance from where she lived. Exactly what she *was* doing he didn't like to imagine. When pictures of her by a tree with children, a possible husband in the background, came to his mind, he fought against them. By evening he had managed to replace them with images of her, still in leopard coat, swopping presents by some vague fire with her parents.

But it wasn't till the clatter of the whole dreadful day was over, and he was in bed, could Henry finally indulge in his fantasies undisturbed. These were of next Christmas. Very clear, they were, too. He and the Leopard would be on a cruise – an inspiration that had come to him from an ad on the telly. Sunny days and balmy nights. Walking the decks under a tropical moon. Palm trees and white beaches, coconuts, deck chairs – did they have deck chairs in the tropics, Henry wondered? And the Leopard would be the toast of the ship, of course. All the men would want to flirt with her and buy her rum punches. But he'd take good care of her, not let her too far out of his sight. If a respectable gentleman asked her to dance (small orchestra in dinner jackets playing *The Nearness of You* over the Sargasso Sea) – well, he'd probably give his permission. Provided the fellow didn't look as if he'd be up to any hanky panky, and promised to keep a respectable distance in his waltzing. They'd have a top deck outside cabin, of course: and considering Henry's naval past he had no doubt he'd be able to pull a few strings when it came to who should sit at the Captain's table. Ah, it would be the hell of a good time. Something he'd been waiting for all his life, it occurred to him now, though in the past he had imagined no clear details, just a general hankering for something different. They would be drunk on love, he and the Leopard. Age was no barrier to passion. Time would stand still. Though if and when it did start up again, and Southampton appeared on the horizon – why, then would be the moment to go to Cambridge. In fact, if he calculated it all with naval precision, they would time their return for the daffodils by the Cam.

Henry gave no thought to the money necessary to finance his tropical future. He was of the opinion that if dreams were strong enough to become true, then Fate would play its hand again, and provide. Anything could happen on the Pools in the next few weeks, or – another thought – the Leopard herself might be the daughter of a millionaire. Judging by the coat, this was very likely. *Oh, my dearest Leopard, I hope you've had a better Christmas Day than me. What wouldn't I give to have you here with me now, your arms about me, your hands gentle on my skin . . .*

Henry shifted violently. For one delirious moment he imagined his wish had been granted. There was a scratching at his shoulder, soft as he required from the Leopard. Then the terrible unfairness of life twisted him into a position of physical agony. He groaned out loud and his pillow fell to the floor. Rosie's repellant foot, icy cold and scaly skinned, rubbed at his leg. She whimpered, pressing her vile hand deeper into the flesh of his shoulder.

'What's the matter, love?' she cried.

'Bugger off, woman,' he shouted back. 'And don't ever lay your hands on me again.'

He rolled as far as he could to his side of the bed, pulling the sheet and blankets with him. When Rosie began to sob he blocked his ears with a pillow, and decided to send off for travel brochures tomorrow. Soon as he got details of tropical cruises he'd set about making his arrangements.

My Leopard, we're nearly there. Leave it to me.

He fell asleep and dreamed that he went with a works outing from the brickworks on a cruise to the Caribbean. Just one condition had to be adhered to: all men should bring the ladies of their dreams, and leave their wives at home.

With some peculiar deference to Christmas, Evans decided to go back to his parents' house when the party was over. He dropped Brenda back at the flat first. She made no objection. A mixture of ginger wine and whisky had made her sleepy.

Brenda would have liked to have gone into Lark's room and told her about the party, as she used to in the old days before the room at Wroughton House, but there was no light under Lark's door and Brenda imagined she was asleep. She herself got into bed quickly, and slept at once.

She was woken by the sound of moaning from Lark's room. Hurrying there, icy floor beneath her feet, she found Lark on top of the bedclothes, doubled up, both arms clutched round her ribs. Her face was blanched, and shone with sweat. When Brenda, alarmed, asked if this was a bad attack of indigestion, Lark could only groan in reply.

It didn't look like indigestion to Brenda. She ran to the coin box on the landing and dialled the ambulance. Then she pulled on some clothes and returned to Lark's room. She sat on her bed dabbing at her forehead with a wet sponge. Lark's groaning was horrible. She kept opening her mouth so wide Brenda could see all her back teeth, black with fillings. Through the curtains loomed a foggy dawn.

The ambulance men took one look at Lark and returned

for their stretcher. With great skill and speed they carried her downstairs. In her terror, Brenda felt their efficiency to be the only thing she could count upon as reality. She had never witnessed a real crisis before, and found to her shame she trembled.

'I'm coming too,' she said, when they had put Lark into the ambulance.

'You a relation?'

'No, but she's my friend.'

She and one of the men sat on the bunk opposite Lark, who groaned more loudly when the vehicle moved. Her body made a small ripple under the scarlet blanket, no larger than a child's. Pity she can't see the colour of the blanket, thought Brenda. She would have liked that. Then the ambulance siren gave a great scream, making her own heart jump. It wailed continually as they drove fast down the roads. Brenda longed to ask the man what was the matter with Lark, but he was holding Lark's hand, letting her clutch it with her bony fingers, and Brenda's voice failed her. She reached into her pocket for a packet of Woodbines, but when she brough them out the man shook his head and she put them back again.

At the hospital Lark was rushed on a trolley along green passages rank with disinfectant and lit by strips of neon. She was pushed into a cubicle. There, someone pulled a curtain, barring Brenda's entrance. She stood for a moment, helpless, listening to Lark's noise through the curtain. The material was covered with sunflowers, larger than life, a hideous yellow in the neon lighting. Brenda had never seen such ugly flowers. She sat on an upright plastic chair, one of a small row against a wall, and wondered how many people had sat on that very chair waiting for verdicts from behind the sunflowers. She was aware of the smell of her own nervous sweat.

Two nurses appeared. They took no notice of her. Their faces were brightly made up, as if they were going to a party. The wall clock said five to four. Who were their made-up faces for? Night-time casualties, or the puny doctor who followed them into the cubicle? Brenda listened to their voices but could decipher nothing against the torrent of Lark's groans. Then, suddenly, silence. The small starched noises of hands against aprons, the dull tap of shoes on muted linoleum. The doctor's voice, quite clear.

'Riddled with it, if you ask me,' he said. 'Tests in the morning.'

The words meant nothing to Brenda, though she felt her heart turn wild with instinctive fear. The foul sunflowers were snapped back, shrinking their petals into ugly folds. The white-coated doctor held a clipboard. Brenda stood up. She could see Lark lying on her side, apparently asleep.

'I'm her friend,' she said. 'Is she all right?'

The doctor was suspicious.

'No relation?'

'Just her friend.' Friends, in a crisis, were apparently of little use. The doctor licked his pencil. Ominously, Brenda thought. 'We share a flat. I rang for the ambulance.'

'Can you tell me her name?'

'Lark.'

'What was that?'

'Lark.' She spelt it. The doctor looked impatient. His pencil hovered, incredulous, above the clipboard.

'I mean her real name.'

'That is her real name.'

'Funny sort of name.' It had never occurred to Brenda before that Lark was a funny sort of name. The idea seeped across her mind now, sluggish as oil. She felt the weakness of disloyalty. Behind the doctor the two nurses stood like a small chorus each side of Lark's bed, their party faces smeared with patience. 'Lark what?'

Brenda paused.

'Jackson,' she said eventually.

'And her nearest relative? Where can her nearest relative be contacted?'

As Lark rang her mother in Westgate-on-Sea twice a week Brenda knew the number by heart. She answered the rest of the doctor's questions, sensing the hostility between them. Then, he wanted to get rid of her. But Brenda stood her ground.

'What's the matter with her?' she asked. 'Will she be all right?'

The doctor chewed the pink worm of his bottom lip, denting it. Tact was a reflex action.

'We've given her something to make her comfortable,' he said. 'If you like to come back later on in the day we should have more news. We'll be doing tests in the morning.' He hurried away, clipboard under his arm, no kind words about not worrying.

Brenda returned along the green corridors without looking back at Lark. She had wanted to touch her, the small mound of a foot under the blanket, but had not liked to in front of the nurses. She walked through the swing doors into an opal dawn. The hospital grounds were divided by tarmac drives. A suspicion of disinfectant in the smell of wet earth from the mean flower beds. Dead plants, mournful laurels. Two bicycles propped up against a pavement with that ludicrous, urgent look that waiting bicycles have, as if charging themselves for a race. A long time ago Lark had suggested they might follow the Tour de France for their holiday. Brenda had been very scathing and Lark had not mentioned it again.

Infirm of purpose, Brenda found herself walking through the town towards Wroughton. She had no clear idea what best to do, or how to pass the hours until she could return to Lark. She walked the three miles fast, hot and sweating, uncooled by the dankness of the air. She reached the farm, went to the chicken shed. Unlocked the padlock on the door. It seemed natural to her the birds should be the first to know.

They were surprised by her early arrival, started a speculative clucking. They were not due to be fed until tomorrow but Brenda decided on a premature meal: it would give her something to do and her hands, running through the mash, would be forced to stop trembling.

It was almost dark in the shed but Brenda had no heart to turn on the light. She emptied a bag of mash into a mixing trough, then added three scoops of maize. She mixed the stuff with her hands, slowly, even in her fear liking the familiar sensation of fine grain scurrying through her fingers. Some time ago Wilberforce had come to her with a fancy idea about adding a new-fangled chemical to the mash, which deepened the colour of the egg yolks. But she had been adamant. No, Wilberforce, she had said: we're just a small farm here. Only three hundred hens. For God's sake, let's stick to the maize and paler yolks. The birds have a bloody enough life as it is. Don't take away what might be their only pleasure. Wilberforce had agreed, not really interested.

Brenda fed the birds. In the half-light their eyes were indignant at the shift in their routine. They conveyed no sympathy, only irritation. Hard-hearted buggers. 'Lark's ill,' Brenda suddenly shouted out loud, startling them: but immediately they continued their impervious chatter. For the first time, this morning, she hated them. She noticed that Priscilla, a bossy bird, had something wrong with her comb: it hung to one side, pale and swollen, the obscene shape of the hand of a foetus. Brenda didn't care. It reminded her that all the birds were fifteen months old. Six weeks, two months perhaps, and they'd be killed, their use over. Within hours they'd be replaced by the birds now in the rearing pens. But Brenda knew quite clearly she could not face a new generation, all the bother of finding a new queen, and new names. No. When this lot went – sold off cheaply as boiling fowls – she would go too. Her notice, this time, would be final.

Through the skylight the paling light indicated real morning. At seven Brenda would go to the Evanses' house and break the news. Meantime she began to collect the eggs: not in her usual manner, walking down the rows putting them in a basket, but one at a time. She picked up a single egg, weighed it in her hand and walked with it slowly to the box at the end of the shed where it would lie prior to sorting. Thus she strung out the job to last a long time, forcing herself to concentrate wholly on the shape of each egg, perfect in her hand, so that there should be no room in her mind for the vision of Lark twisted and screaming under the scarlet blanket.

Within a few days Lark was quite absumed by her illness. She lay back on the pillows, too weak to sit up, geranium nails spread out on the white sheet, unmoving. They had given her many pills and injections, and the pain now was a faraway thing like the shuffle of a distant train. She could see it rather than feel it, sense its approach. When its rattle became noisier she would tell a passing nurse and they would bring her more pills. She was allowed her gin: Brenda had made sure of that. A bottle of Gordon's and a glass stood on a tray at her bedside. Sometimes she swallowed the pills with the gin and for a few moments felt quite energetic as if, given the chance, she could stand up and sing.

The ward was a cheerful place: walls and high ceilings the colour of sand dunes, all strung about with streamers and balloons. For stretches of time Lark observed the other inmates clearly – mostly old people with moussy arms hanging from bright nightdresses: early daffodils and Get Better Soon cards by their bed. Sometimes they forgot to put their teeth in before they smiled, and clapped their hands over their gums in shame. They slept a lot, their skin less yellow in sleep. There was one younger one, long red hair, who thrashed about and moaned one night, and whose sunflower curtains were quickly drawn round her bed. She was no longer there next morning. Then there was a night when a few of the patients, great burly visitors round their beds, had struck up a chorus of *Auld Lang Syne*. New Year's Eve, they said it was, and the dreadful singing made Lark sad. All out of tune. She wanted to lead them: the notes were clear in her head waiting to be struck, but when she opened her mouth the strangest whimper emerged, far from the sound she aimed for. She felt tears on her cheeks and reached for her glass of gin. A nurse, hurrying by, said there, there, dear, don't upset yourself: everyone cries on New Year's Eve.

At other times a mist seemed to separate Lark from reality. Whether it was a mist of sleep, or some kind of actual vapour, she could never be sure: but it confused time, bringing cocoa and darkness when she had expected morning, or visitors when she thought it to be night. The Christmas decorations seemed to hang unsupported. Lark would move her eyes to see where they were fixed, but could see no place on the walls. There was a feeling of underwater living, dreamlike, never still. Everything was insubstantial. Solid forms melted. Faces became misshapen, voices obscure. Then the mist would clear, and the line of a window or the iron end of her bed would freeze into such sharpness that it hurt her eyes.

One thing Lark was clearly aware of: her illness had, curiously, brought good luck to her friends. A strange irony that she could not fathom, but a positive fact. They had all come to her with good news, and while they spoke their pleasure caused tangible happiness to seep through her veins, giving strength.

Mrs Browne, for instance, who brought mince pies, seemed no longer sad at leaving Wroughton House. With amazing cheerfulness she spoke of her new life in London: how she was looking forward to it, how she intended to start work again. She also said, when Lark was better, she would arrange for her to record a tape of her songs, and she then would take it to a friend in the music world. With a voice like hers, there was no reason Lark could not become famous overnight. Lark felt infinite faith in Mrs Browne's influence. She imagined a picture of herself, in the fluttery grey dress, on the sleeve of a record. She tried to smile. But her mouth was without saliva, and her lips tight as an elastic band across her teeth. Later, she dreamed the record had reached the charts.

Rosie Evans, who took off her meringue-like hat but kept

on her woolly gloves, had news that the damaged Morris Minor had been sold. She and Henry had decided – after a long discussion, she said – they no longer needed a car and could do with the money instead. Only yesterday they had received £75 in cash, which Rosie had hidden under a tin of apricots in the larder.

'I wouldn't tell that to anyone else, Lark dear, but you,' she said, and Lark, who was aware of the distant hum of the train, felt a small sense of honour. 'You're a person anyone can trust, so I'll tell you another thing. I'm saving up that money for a holiday. France. The French. Just Henry and me, first time for years. We went to a French restaurant, the other night, you know, and that's what gave me the inspiration. Only you mustn't say anything to Henry because I don't want him to know till it's all arranged. So you won't say a word, will you?' Lark shook her head. 'Well, I must be off. Don't want to tire you with all my silly plans, do I? Silly old romantic me, you know. Always have been. Anyhow, dear, you've got a lovely colour in your cheeks today. Much better. You'll be up and about in no time, and I'll feed you up with some of my puddings.'

She replaced her summery hat, patted Lark's knee and walked back down the ward, sniffing slightly at every bed as if each patient was some kind of food.

Her visit tired Lark. She slept awhile, and woke to find Henry Evans by her side. There seemed to be no visiting hours in this ward: people came and went as they pleased, even in the middle of the night, sometimes. Lark felt herself lucky to be in such a hospital.

Henry Evans looked awkward, ill-placed on the upright chair. His face was drawn, the skin of his nose and cheeks purple with broken veins. Lark had not remembered his hair to be so white, or his hands so shaky.

'Just on my way back from the Star,' he said. 'Thought I might as well pop in. The others told me you were better.' Lark tried to smile at him and he quickly looked away from her face. 'Anyhow, there's one bit of good news, that I will say.

You remember I told you, that time we were coming down from the woods, I was planning this visit to Cambridge? Well, it's all fixed up. Spring. Definite. Down to the last detail.' He moved his lips in a way that indicated the beginnings of a smile. But realising the rashness of this, he quickly dropped them back into their customary downward curve. 'There are also indications,' he went on, so low Lark could scarcely hear, 'the Cambridge trip might be preceded by a visit of a more adventurous nature – namely, to tropical places. I have in mind a cruise. The South Seas.' He paused, then added: 'With a companion, of course. Don't know why, but I thought you might like to know that.'

Lark moved her head on the pillow. She had never heard Henry Evans speak so many words at one time. They had exhausted her, so many confidences, flattering though they were: and they looked as if they had exhausted him, too. He stood up, one foot sliding on the floor, cap in hands, eyes full of hope.

'Well,' he said, 'there's the good news, Miss Lark, and you'll be riding out the storm, I've no doubt.' He turned from her and left. Unlike his wife he looked neither right nor left as he drifted uncertainly down the aisle between the beds, head hung between hunched shoulders.

Brenda came often. Lark lost count of the times. She would frequently wake to find her friend sitting there, staring at Lark's nails rather than her face. Several times she re-painted the nails, apologising for her lack of skill, and she brought constant half-bottles of gin. One day, a clear time, Lark noticed Brenda looked tearful: eyes swollen, lashes damp.

'What's the matter?' she whispered. Definite tears came to Brenda's eyes. She remained silent for a long time. Then she said, 'Oh, Lark. It's my father. The good news, it's too much for me. He is an Admiral, you know. I always knew he was, didn't I? I saw his picture in the paper, shaking hands with the Duke of Edinburgh. I know it was him. No doubt.' Lark felt her own tears reflect Brenda's pleasure. She wanted to ask many questions, but could only muster strength for one.

'The paper?' she whispered.

Again Brenda paused. Then she said:

'The *Daily Telegraph.*'

Lark nodded. If the picture was in the *Telegraph* that somehow confirmed everything. That was the paper Lark liked to read on the days she felt like reading at all. That was the sort of paper that would be helpful at tracing the admiral in the photograph, and Brenda's joy would be complete. She had no energy left to say all these things, but reached for Brenda's hand, and grasped it. Then she indicated that they should share the gin in the glass by the bed: with so much good news she knew without saying that Brenda would understand it to be a celebration drink.

Evans came often, too. Each time he brought scarlet flowers – geraniums, poinsettias, carnations. He arranged them with great care on the small bedside locker, and when there was no more room he'd put some on the table that bridged the foot of her bed. They were always the first thing she saw on waking, a flurry of scarlet petals which made a confetti of pink shadows on the white blanket, reminding Lark of her own room. Evans spoke much of the progress of the house: it was nearly finished, now. They'd be moving in a few weeks and would combine their house-warming party with celebrating Lark's recovery. She better not drink too much gin that night, he said, because he didn't want anyone being sick over their new carpets. Lark at once pictured herself in her grey dress, fluttering among the guests. They'd be bound to ask her to sing. She looked forward to it.

One evening Evans arrived solemn-faced. Lark's mother, he said, was unable to visit her because her arthritis had taken a turn for the worse. She was in bed, unable to move, but sent Lark much love and would dictate a letter. It was nothing to worry about, Evans added: just a little extra discomfort brought about by the bad weather, bound to clear up in the spring. Lark had scarcely thought about her mother since she had been in hospital. With Evans's news she now imagined her – not with twisted joints lying in bed, but sitting on a shingle beach, dark hair blowing in a sea breeze, unwrapping egg sandwiches. Later they had held their skirts above their knees and paddled, and Lark had remembered it to be the nicest day of her childhood until, in the evening, eating ices on the pier, her mother had said that her Dad had gone off with a new lady and wouldn't be back any more. Now, she felt a small flicker of worry, but the worry slid about, eluding her concentration. But she knew Evans was right: arthritis was less bad in the spring, and when she was better she would go herself to Westgate-on-Sea. She hadn't been for months, and her mother never complained.

Lark felt more tired than usual that evening. She strummed her fingers on the sheet and Evans pulled up a chair to sit close beside her. He still clutched a new pot of poinsettias, burning red. Their colour reflected into his face, making Lark want to laugh.

'Lovely, thank you,' she said.

'Just adding to the collection.' Evans put them on the locker by her bed. 'Roses, tomorrow, if I can get them.' He lifted her hand, waggled it about as if it was a thing independent of her body. 'Not much flesh on this, then, is there?' he said. 'It's all that living off gin and eggs, you know. Not a healthy diet at all. We'll have to be fattening you up – and we don't want any complaints.' He was smiling and frowning at the same time. Lark could smell him: some kind of leathery after-shave, rather sweet. Familiar. His face so handsome, so gentle. The funny eye twitching. His big hand heavy on hers on the sheet. *Dear God, I love you Evans Evans*, she wanted to say: *you're the only one I've ever loved*. She opened her mouth, but no words came. Perhaps a good thing: misplaced love should be kept secret, for fear of encumbering. But, tonight, Evans so close and quiet, she wouldn't have minded risking . . . She opened her mouth again. It was quite dry.

'You remember that night . . .?' she whispered. The sound was like a scraping of leaves, far away. Evans nodded, blushing. His eyes were full of horror. 'Well, that night, Evans . . . That night was . . .' But she could not think what it was. She could not think what it was she had to tell him, except that she loved him, and he must be able to see that, this close.

The details of his face began to recede, then. She felt his arm behind her head, and she felt him holding the glass against her mouth. She swallowed a lot of gin: some of it ran down her chin and fell in cold spots on her chest.

'Reckon you needed a swig of that,' Evans was saying, and sat down again. He talked to her for a while, house news, and saying that she was the belle of the ward, mind she didn't let the doctors take any liberties or he'd be right jealous. Then he got up to go, promising to be back before work next morning. Lark would have liked him to bend over her and kiss her cheek: instead she watched him pick up her hands and kiss each scarlet nail, slowly, one by one.

When he had gone she reached for the glass of gin. It was empty. She picked up the half-bottle, surprisingly heavy, and drank directly from it. Soon, as she knew it would, her mind became beautifully silvered. Later that night she died.

Lark's mother requested that she should be buried near her friends. She herself, bedridden, was unable to attend the funeral.

It took place on a bitter day in early January. The sky was swollen with snow waiting to fall. The churchyard yews stood dense black shapes against it, and the elms quivered in an easterly wind. There were few mourners: Augusta Browne, Henry and Rosie, Brenda and Evans, and Lark's boss, a balding man with a permanent drip on the end of his nose. Now, he would have to offer his security elsewhere.

They stood by the grave listening to the monotonous threats of the vicar. Dust to dust, in his voice, lacked resonance. Everyone had sent scarlet flowers. They littered the coffin, and the ground near the grave, only brightness in the landscape. Augusta stroked her cheek with a bare hand. The cold hurt. Her skin was hard and icy as slate. She was thinking this sort of finality was in some ways easier to accept than the smaller deaths, the lesser endings, which life itself distributes. At least, after this kind of death, according to her own belief, there was no proven going on. In life, an era over, to continue with some measure of normality is the battle. To acquire optimism. To re-pursue. To believe in the possibility of further chances. When it came to such matters, and the time had come, Augusta was aware of her own helplessness. Her weakness. She shivered in a blast of wind, despising herself: here she was at Lark's funeral thinking about herself. Though perhaps that is the secret of most mourners. The death of another is the strongest reminder of one's own transience: one's own frailty: the body in the coffin narrowly thought of only in relation to oneself. Augusta tried to visualise Lark – not as she had last seen her, prematurely geriatric in hospital, but the night of the concert: enchanting the pensioners with her voice, drinking champagne by the fire, singing of Persian kings. But Lark's face had gone for the moment. Had it eluded them all so soon? How long did it take for buried flesh to relume itself in the memory? Augusta looked round.

Brenda could see Lark lying in the coffin clearly as if the wooden lid was transparent: white wax face, hands with scarlet nails crossed over her breasts, fluttery grey dress motionless now round her ankles. She had insisted Lark should be buried in that dress though she had refused to look at her, as Evans and Rosie had done, in the undertaker's chapel. Which, she wondered, would turn to dust first? The silvery materials, or Lark? At the thought of such decay Brenda let the tears run uncontrolled down her cheeks, to be dried by the wind. The bloody unfairness of it all. Lark so good, and dead. Ill for years and no one noticing. No one caring. Brenda blamed herself. She would never get over it. Never, never. She'd never be able to look at another geranium without thinking . . . and she hadn't even said to Lark, ever, how good she was. How much she loved her. Why didn't people take chances instead of spurning them for fear of looking foolish? Well, with Lark gone, there was one chance *she* wasn't going to lose, now: Evans. In the void caused by Lark's death his living presence had become desirable in a way Brenda had not experienced before. Not exciting, mind: just precious because it was alive, and firm, and steadfast. Worth clinging to, worth appreciating. Poor Lark: she had had a mean life, known nothing of the luxury of a man's fidelity. Just a few screws behind the filing cabinets. Remembering such indignities, given in generosity, Brenda sobbed more loudly, and got a look from the vicar. Silly old bugger. He ought to know people were entitled to cry at funerals. Evans pressed her arm.

He let his fingers twirl through the beaver fur of her coat, a clumsy but soft old thing she'd picked up at a jumble sale. Through its skin he could feel the warmth of her flesh: a strange sensation, out here: as if he was experiencing both the warmth of indoors and the harshness of the elements at the same time. There was comfort in the warmth beneath the cold. There was no comfort in the memory of Lark's bones, covered by a scant white sheen with little resemblance to flesh, that would haunt him always. He remembered with loathesome clarity the way that maddened night she had crumbled beneath him like paper, whimpering. He must have hurt her badly. Dear God, that she might have forgiven him. Poor little wretch: kind and lonely and uncomplaining, all her pleasures vicarious. Yellow kitchen walls, she'd said. Well, they'd have yellow kitchen walls all right, the last tribute he could pay her. When he had left her, that last time in hospital, she had tried to smile, dragging back her lips from teeth which had protruded more cruelly each day. He had meant to kiss her on the cheek, but had not the courage. Thinking only of his own horror and repulsion, his final gesture had been the formal kissing of her hands, a thing he had never done in his life before. He was sorry. Christ, when he heard she had died that night, how sorry he was. He hoped she had not thought too badly of him before death reached her. He hoped the gin had nicely silvered her mind (he remembered her description with a renewed pang) and brought her peace. On the coffin lay his huge bunch of scarlet roses, too late for her to enjoy, but symbol of his affection. Blasted by regret, his cold hand felt for Brenda's warm one. The vicar's intonations blurred in his ears with the wind as privately he thanked God, upon whom he rarely called, for the warmth of a girl he loved. Brenda, beaver-coated, breathing near him, who must not die for many years.

On his other side Rosie, in black mackintosh and velours hat and red scarf knitted by Lark, was beset by fatigue as well as sadness. She had been up much of the night before arranging flowers in the church in a way she thought Lark would have appreciated, and making a wreath of carnations from herself and Henry. The days preceding Lark's death had taken their toll: visits every day to the hospital, and Henry more difficult than ever at home – snappish one moment, morose the next. Almost constantly intoxicated. Scarcely eating, restless in bed every night. Rosie planned a secret meeting with the doctor, though the very idea of this caused a battle within her conscience. On the one hand she felt it would be disloyal, on the other she badly needed help and advice. Cheerfulness and tolerance, it seemed, were sometimes not enough. She still had not made up her mind what to do, and the problem battered her resistance.

Sudden tolling of the churchbells brought Rosie's attention back to the present. Poor dear Lark. Always such a scrap of a thing. Quite undeserving of so horrible an end. Of course, Rosie could have told anyone it wasn't indigestion Lark suffered from: but no one had asked her, and it wasn't her place to interfere. In the circumstances, it was a good thing Evans had chosen a healthy girl. She wouldn't wish any son of hers an instant widower: but she did wish Brenda would control her sobbing. The sound brought tears to Rosie's eyes as she remembered Lark's appreciation of her Christmas cake. In the end, *Henry* hadn't touched a slice. He didn't know how he hurt, Henry. Like this morning: it was only good sense to advise him to put on his overcoat for the funeral. Standing about in an east wind, Rosie had said, anyone could catch their death. But he had defied her, told her to mind her own bloody business. He could look after himself, didn't feel the cold. Afraid of the note in his voice, Rosie had said no more and had set about peeling the potatoes with inflamed hands that shook quite hard. She had silently prayed to God to make him change his mind, and put on the coat at the last minute. But God was evidently too busy welcoming Lark to heaven – where she was entitled to rest in peace, poor lass – to hear Rosie's prayer. And when they left the cottage for the church, Henry at her side, he was not only coatless, but undid the buttons of his jacket. Rosie had struggled hard and forced herself to say nothing. As the bell continued its melancholy tolling she glanced sideways and saw the wind bubbling under his shirt. She looked quickly back at the coffin. Lark, she knew, was safe. It was Henry she feared for now.

To catch his own death at Lark's funeral was precisely the idea that appealed to Henry very much, and once he had decided not to wear his overcoat nothing could alter his plan. He knew it would worry Rosie, but her concern was nothing to him. He also knew, should he actually catch pneumonia and die – pretty likely in his frail condition – he might risk missing the cruise and life with the Leopard. But cruising plans, since he had told them to Lark, had gone a little sour on him. The brochures had arrived in plain brown envelopes, and he had studied them many times in the lavatory at the Star. After several drinks, the white-shored, palmy islands tempted in their original fashion: but at other times, sober, they seemed very remote. Besides, where was the money to come from? Henry had reluctantly agreed to selling the car and Rosie had stored away the £75 in a secret place. To request it would mean her asking why. What convincing story could he tell? And anyhow, £75 wouldn't go far towards the kind of luxury cruise he planned.

While Henry's mind, at the graveside, was tormented by such problems, his body was happily wracked by the savage wind. He liked the feeling of it razoring through his bones, between his ribs, freezing his blood, numbing his face and hands. At this rate, it was almost certain he would become the next admittance to the graveyard. In the unlikely event of survival – ah, well, that surely would be an omen. That would mean that Fate endorsed his life with the Leopard, and he would re-encounter her quite soon.

Henry looked down to the coffin, encrusted with pillar-box-coloured flowers, vulgar as a hat, and longed for a drink. He couldn't say with any honesty he was that upset by Lark's death: she had been a nice enough little thing – pretty voice giving him a nasty turn that day in the woods – but he had not known her well. He would remember her, should he live, as the girl who had taken part of his secret to her grave. And due to the vicar's sense of self-importance, by God, she was taking a long time getting there. He must remember to tell Rosie he wished to be cremated, and none of this mumble-jumble over the scattering of the ashes. It required all his strength, now, not to protect his chest from the wind with his arms, but that would cause too much gladness in Rosie's heart. So he remained upright, frozen hands at his sides, and listened to the church clock strike four. Two hours till opening time. Jesus Christ. Bloody hell. He noticed all the others had their heads bowed, pinched faces, eyes shut. Could be they were coming up to the finale at last.

'Amen,' they all said, together.

Too late to join the chorus, Henry would not have liked it said of him he had failed to salute poor Lark. He looked up at the billowing sky and his heart ached for the rougher grave of a naval man. Burials at sea had always moved him to a tear: Lark's cage of earth left him without feeling.

'Amen,' he said, alone.

When the ceremony was over Augusta Browne invited everyone for a drink in Wroughton House. Henry was the only one to accept with reluctance, but decided it would be as good a way as any to pass the time till his visit to the Star.

They sat about, a disparate group, on odd chairs and upturned packing cases, in the hall. Rosie, always nervous on social occasions, immediately spilt sherry down her scarlet scarf, causing Henry unspeakable irritation. Mrs Browne filtered about in a long black coat and a black Stetson hat. She looked like a young widow, Henry thought, sad eyes bearing no relation to her kind smile as she poured large glasses of strong drinks. The heat of the fire and the strength of the alcohol induced the kind of post-burial conversation that is the final part of the mourners' duty. The sniffing boss took upon himself recollections the others could not dispute.

'Best little secretary of my experience. Not a natural one with figures, I will say that, but always humming away, always pleasant, always concerned I should have a nice selection of gâteaux with my afternoon tea.'

'Ah, God bless her soul,' said the vicar, who had never met Lark.

'Just a small one,' said his wife, to the offer of more sherry.

'You'll be leaving these curtains, will you, Mrs Browne, to the executives?' asked Rosie, who liked to think all businessmen were executives. 'I expect they'll be glad of them, such lovely stuff.'

Henry, too cold to speak, sat huddled by the fire. The decrees of convention seemed to him most unreasonable: why should people who had nothing in common except the death of a friend bother to gather uneasily together? In low spirits already, why tax themselves further? It all seemed daft to him. Only compensation was Mrs Browne's fine whisky. He drank three large glasses before leaving. She was a generous lady, ever alert to his empty glass, and he blessed her for that.

He accompanied Rosie down the drive and to the cottage, very steady, the depression of the day slightly lifted. He told

Rosie he would be back later for supper, and when she had gone upstairs to relieve herself of her gloomy hat, he quietly took down his overcoat. Melted by Mrs Browne's fire, he did not relish a second freezing.

Henry walked briskly to the pub. Though bitterly cold, it was a fine, clear evening, the sky full of stars. His footsteps, cracking like shots on the road, signalled the frost that would come later. Henry envisaged the warmth inside the Star: the lights and low voices, the small fire and thud of darts. There, at his corner table, – of late, he noticed, the others had given up trying to draw him into conversation – he could sit and think of the Leopard undisturbed. Drink his six or seven whiskies, and keep his eye on the door. An evening identical to countless others, only escape from the stifling life at home.

Soon as he went through the door into the lounge Henry smelt the gust of warm familiar smells: rubber flooring and hot pies and smoke, dearer to his senses than the more sophisticated scents of Mrs Browne's hall. He hung up his overcoat, rubbed his hands to scrape away the chill they had acquired on the journey, and looked round. A few of the regulars were already at their tables. A single figure, back to him, was on a high stool at the bar.

Henry blinked. He had only had three drinks with Mrs Browne. They had fractionally lifted his spirits, but that recognisable state of confusion, brought about by a heavy night's drinking, was far from him. He could see quite clearly. He could see quite clearly that the figure at the bar was a woman. She had blonde hair and wore a leopard skin coat. Beside her on the bar was a small glass of ruby-coloured liquid: snaking through it, among cubes of ice, a twist of lemon.

Henry experienced the timelessness of shock. He felt a spasm in his bowels and lethargy, rather than weakness, in his knees. Such ineluctable confusion, shrinking his skin as well as his reason, caused him to sway gently on his feet, as if already inebriated, and he noticed old Joe gave him a funny look. Then his head cleared, though the pounding of his heart had sent the blood to his face, and he felt himself to be as scarlet as Lark's horrible flowers. He moved slowly, thoughts trailing some paces behind his movements. In a way that sometimes happens in times of crisis, a plan came easily to him. He would go the bar, order his first drink, and take it to his table. He would consume it quickly, but give himself time enough to gather courage and gallantry. Then he would return to the bar and offer to buy the Leopard a drink, at last making real the moment he had imagined so many thousand times that the picture was part of the tissue of his mind.

The bar was suddenly before him, supportive. Bill was pouring his drink, muttering about the weather. The Leopard, his Leopard, was not two feet from him. He dared not look at her, but could smell her powerful scent. He was aware of her small movements: glances at her watch, the crossing and recrossing of her legs. Then, as he turned, drink in hand, to go to his table, the whole picture of her, three-dimensional, life-size, billowed into his vision. It filled in small blanks that had confounded his memory: her nose tipped upwards, delicate, in a way he had never recalled. Her hair fell in chunks, rather than curls, on her forehead. Her wrist, thicker than he remembered, was cut by the thin gold strap of her watch in a way that must have been painful. Pushed back from her poor wrist was the cuff of her fur coat. Its beautiful spots, which had patterned Henry's sleeping and waking hours for nine months, dazzled him now in reality. Incredible. Henry's eyes remained on the cuff. He could not drag them away. There was something about it he had not expected, a thinness of quality. As he stared harder, he realised the edge of the cuff was worn to a thread of baldness, and he bit his lip to stifle an amazed cry. For here, under the cruel lights of the bar, the fabric of the coat was exposed, the illusion broken. *Nylon*. Henry said the ghastly word to himself several times, weak with disbelief. But he knew his eyes were not mistaken. No one, then, had hunted a wild animal in the jungles and had its skins fashioned for his Leopard. She was but the possessor of a cheap nylon coat, the kind of thing thousands of women, of lesser breed than her, fancy will upgrade them in the esteem of men. How could she have deceived him so?

'Good evening,' she said, head turning to him, eyes wide, shadows from clotted eyelashes fluttering on her cheeks. A low voice, she had, and plum-coloured lips that shone as if with grease. One of her front teeth protruded a little, and rested on the cushion of her lower lip. It was a dark, inky colour Henry had not remembered.

'Evening.' His face burned. Should he apologise for having stared at her? Even as he contemplated the question Henry felt himself moving away towards the safety of his table. He sat down with relief and took a long gulp of whisky, determined to look no more in the direction of the Leopard until it was time to put his plan into action. Only two things crowded his mind: the thought that the Leopard's smile and greeting had been an invitation – she was making it easy for him. And, less good, that she had tricked him with her coat. However, he could forgive her for that. Christ, it wasn't even a case of forgiveness: simply a matter of overcoming his own foolish shock. He would love her whatever she chose to wear, whatever illusions she chose to employ. It was a woman's prerogative, after all, to attract by any means: the fact that the Leopard had turned out to be as weak as any other woman was suddenly more endearing than Henry could bear. Dizzy with love for her, he finished his whisky with shaking hand and wondered at the scorching sensation that scoured his body. Was he feverish? Had his death plan worked too well? Was he already struck by pneumonia? At the thought of such irony tears grazed Henry's eyes, and he had to dry them with his handkerchief.

In that moment when they were shut painfully behind a blur of cotton, smelling of Rosie's horrible lavender bags, Henry missed the entrance of a man into the lounge. By the time the handkerchief was back in his pocket, eyes and cheeks still burning, but dry, a new scene was taking place at the bar. A scene Henry could not resist observing (indeed, none of the regulars made any pretence of ignoring what was going on). The Leopard was laughing, *laughing* up at the great swarthy brute of a man beside her. He was unkempt, unshaven, cocksure – Henry could see that just from the mould of his back. One of his hands was over the Leopard's wrist on the bar, digging into the flesh in so familiar a manner that Henry felt a sour flame of nausea in his throat. The man, who then Henry recognised to be that vile brute Wilberforce (crooked bastard, shady past), was tugging at the Leopard's hair with his other hand, making her laugh more loudly: a sharp, frosty laugh, whereas Henry had always supposed it would have been musical as sleigh bells (at least, how he imagined sleigh bells would sound). As he tugged at her hair Wilberforce parted it and thus exposed areas of dark root. From where Henry sat, some yards away, he could see them quite clearly. It was perhaps a trick of those confounded bar lights. Was the Leopard's hair not pure gold, as he had remembered? But Henry had little time to contemplate such matters: stunned, he concentrated on the actions at the bar. Wilberforce was giving a handful of silver to Bill. Then, with the same hand that he had groped through the Leopard's hair, he wiped his glossy mouth, but failed to clean it of a long string of beer froth that ran down to his chin. The Leopard, with a spring of impatience, left her high stool, and stood beside him. She put her hand through his arm. Henry noticed the extraordinary smallness of her waist, gripped in its leather belt, and a spray of dried mud on one of her legs. He saw her smile at Wilberforce, and knew she was going for ever. He stood up, raised his arm, noticed the pattern of pulsing veins on the back of his hand: all he had to do was to stretch out to her, and take her, and protect her, and save her.

'My Leopard!' he cried, and no one heard. But she looked at him, eyes still for a fraction of a second, and for the same amount of time Henry saw himself as he appeared in her vision: a drunken old man, swaying by his table, indeterminate hand raised to indicate some kind of muddled idea that he could not hope to articulate.

Then she and Wilberforce were gone, together. They swooshed through the lounge, arms linked, exuding that peculiar heat and energy that a man and woman, sexually or emotionally enflamed, have no interest in hiding.

Henry lowered his hand very slowly. The pulsing veins reminded him of a dying animal. He picked up his empty glass and took it to the bar. Bill grinned at him.

'There's a pair that'll come to no good,' he said, but Henry did not answer. He stood at the bar, drank several more whiskies – he did not count how many. His left hand rested on the leather seat of the Leopard's stool. At first it still retained her warmth, but soon cooled. Her scent was strong in the air. Her sharp laugh, her bald cuff, and her puffy wrist cut by the gold watch strap – the visions ebbed and flowed in Henry's mind, flotsam against the nobler memories, unstable, giddying. Only the bar stool was firm beneath his hand.

When he left the Star Bill warned him to take care. He even offered to go with him. But Henry shook his head. He needed no help. There was a full moon: he was quite capable of navigation. He steered himself along the sharp roads, pausing only at a hedge to be sick. There, in the bitter retching, he rid himself of every living organism in his body, and with them he spewed out the illusions that had bred and festered within him for so long. So when he stood up again, pushing a hand into a mass of brambles for support, he could feel no pain, for there were no nerve ends left with which to feel.

Much later he arrived at the cottage and knocked at his own front door. He listened to the twittering of the elms, and watched the cracked image of the moon in the kitchen window. Then the door was opened, cautiously. Rosie's face, ridiculous with concern, but it no longer irritated him.

'I'm a dead man,' he said.

Rosie's mouth, feeble, shaking, fell open.

'Oh, dear, there you are, Henry,' she said. 'What on earth do you think you're doing, knocking like that? Come on in.' She dragged the door wider open. Henry staggered into the husky lights and shapes of a room he recognised to be his own kitchen.

'I'm a dead man,' he said again, and fell into his chair.

Rosie smiled, controlling her mouth.

'There, there, my love,' she said, bustling, somewhere. 'You're so cold, too. Chilled to the bone.' She stoked the fire. 'The kettle's on. We'll soon have you warm, won't we? Lark's death, it's given all of us a bit of a turn, hasn't it?'

'Lark?' said Henry. He had forgotten she was dead, too. Rosie handed him a mug of tea.

'Here, drink that up,' she said, still smiling.

'Dead,' said Henry.

'Buried this afternoon.'

'Was I?'

'Now, come *along*, love. You're all confused. Your tea.'

Henry let a dribble of the strong liquid spread over his tongue, dulling the bitter after-taste of vomit. He had never been less confused in his life, but the clarity of his new state could not be explained to Rosie, or to anyone on earth.

Augusta did not sleep the night before the move, but she felt no tiredness in the morning. She was glad, at dawn, to see the sky still gravid with unfallen snow. Winter sun would have been unkind.

She lit the fire in the hall, trying to pretend it was a normal day. She made coffee, and cupped the mug in both hands, hoping for warmth. There was a chill within her, there now for many days, that the brightest fire had not been able to melt. Since Christmas she had given up taking pills of any sort, tranquillisers or pain killers, thus leaving her senses exposed to each raw hour of every day. This, the last day, she was light-headed from lack of sleep, and still cold, but for the moment sensations more difficult to cope with had left her, a thin tide on the horizon, ready to encroach at some later hour.

The removal men arrived early. She recognised some of them from the day they had moved in. They were strong, elderly men in starched white coats. Their handling of the furniture was systematic and careful. When it came to the grand piano they acted with particular reverence, swathing its various pieces in blankets, and carrying it to the van in more respectful fashion than the coffin bearers had borne Lark on her journey through the graveyard.

Rosie and Brenda arrived later. They packed china and glass into packing cases in the kitchen and the dining-room. They carried piles of bright towels from the linen cupboard. They drank many cups of tea. Rosie's face was drawn and tired. She worked with a nervous energy, making two journeys where one would have been necessary. Brenda was in a dreamy state, hands moving slowly, pausing to comment on each thing as she wrapped it. She seemed sated in some private way, mind elsewhere. Augusta herself made an effort to be useful, but no sooner than she began to clear a shelf of books or china, she felt it imperative to leave the room she was in to observe the emptying of another one.

By half-past two the last van had gone. The house was quite cleared. Augusta, Rosie and Brenda stood in the kitchen, drinking yet more tea, in cups thoughtfully provided by Rosie. Crumpled newspapers made a choppy sea of the floor. Devoid of the bright colours made by pots and china, the empty room was unrecognisable.

'Henry's badly got down by Lark's passing,' Rosie was saying. 'He keeps speaking of dying.' Augusta noticed that her hands, clumsy on her cup, were mottled as snakeskin, an unhealthy mole colour.

'He'll get over it,' said Brenda, blowing her tea. 'We'll all get over it, I daresay, one day.'

Rosie found it difficult ever to agree with Brenda.

'Hasn't been a good beginning to the year, if you ask me,' she said. 'Lark going one way, Mrs Browne the other. Won't you have a biscuit, Mrs Browne? You're thin as a rake. You need the strength.'

Augusta shook her head. Evans arrived a few moments later. He and Brenda kissed, clinging to each other as if they had been parted for a long time. Arms linked round each other's waists, they leaned against the sink, warm and awkward in their protection of each other against the elements they had been subjected to of late: anger, jealousy, and finally death.

There was no further reason for any of them to stay, but to leave was not easy. Rosie kissed Augusta on both cheeks, sniffing back tears, and said the village would miss her. Augusta doubted this, but acknowledged the compliment with a smile. She shook hands with Brenda and Evans, who thanked her for the use of the attic room. It had made all the difference to their lives, they said. They wished her well in London, and left holding hands. Rosie had to be on her way, too, she said. She had an appointment with the doctor to see if he could give her anything new for her hands. Once they had cleared up, why, she'd feel a different woman, up to anything.

When they had gone Augusta made a final pilgrimage round the garden. It was dank and gloomy, quiet but for the dripping leaves of evergreens. She picked a small bunch of winter jasmine from the wall outside her study, brief reminder of sun, and put it in her car. Then she toured the house, room by room, banishing the unfamiliar shapes of emptiness from her mind even as she observed them: carpets dented by the feet of parted furniture, walls patterned with dark shapes left by pictures, bare shelves. She would never remember it like this. The rooms would remain in her memory furnished as they had always been.

When the church clock struck five she lay on the floor of her study, where the telephone now stood, and rang Hugh.

'I'm ringing you from Wroughton for the last time,' she said, knowing she should have forced herself not to have rung at all.

'Did it all go well?'
'Oh, yes. There's no news, really.'
'No, I don't suppose there is.'
'Sorry . . . to disturb you,' she said.
There was a pause.
'That's all right,' Hugh answered, more gently than in the past months. 'Drive carefully when you leave. There's fog on the motorway.'

They said goodbye. Augusta went to the hall. It was already almost dark. She put more logs on the fire, giving in to final weakness – carrying out her plan which was to wait until the fire went out before she left. She sat down on the flagstones beside it.

Some hours later, coming downstairs for the last time, she paused to listen to the comfortable crackle of the fire. Shutting her eyes, she imagined it was an ordinary night of a few years ago: one of the many times she had descended the stairs to the warmth of the hall. The sounds of shifting logs were the same – the dim, summery smell of apple boughs, preserved out of season in this winter house, unchanged. The polished wood of the banister beneath her hand, its familiar hump arching in her palm, the creak of a stair beneath her feet – if all was still tangibly the same, which it was, then the destruction that had taken place today was surely no more than a nightmare?

The illusion lasted only while Augusta kept shut her eyes. When she opened them, and returned to the bare hall, she smiled at her own absurdity. The emptiness of reality was all about her, intumulating that sudden, last, pathetic hope with a force that flayed the strength she had relied upon all day. She sat down by the fire again, to keep watch over the flames for a few more hours.

Much later that night Henry walked slowly home, agreeably surprised by occasional flakes of snow that melted against his face. Coming up the road to the cottage, he noticed a dim glow from the hall windows of Wroughton

House. Firelight rather than lamplight, he thought, and without determining upon any plan found himself approaching the house.

Reaching the front door, he saw the empty hall through its glass panes, and remembered today was the day Mrs Browne was leaving. Then he saw her sitting on the floor by the fire, which was little more than a frill of small flames among red ash. Her knees were drawn up, her head upon them, the whole structure bound together by her arms. She seemed becalmed. For a moment Henry thought of going to her, then decided against it. There is unwitting mockery in consolation. There are areas of despair no outsider should intrude upon, lest they are rekindled by well-intentioned kindness. Henry turned away. He was shocked at having witnessed another's private anguish, and at the same time consoled.

As he made his way back down the drive the snow began to fall more thickly, sticking to his clothes. He did not feel drunk tonight, though he knew by rights he should be. As far as he could tell, he walked quite steadily.

At home, Rosie was knitting.

'Mrs Browne's dead,' he said. 'I've just seen her. I looked through the window and saw her by the fire.'

A look of horror flared in Rosie's face, quickly replaced by one of understanding.

'Don't be silly, love,' she said. 'I was with Mrs Browne most of the day, helping her pack up. I expect she's just upset. She loves the house.'

'She's dead, I tell you.' Henry sat heavily in his chair. 'You may not know it, Rosie, but there are a lot of dead people walking about. You run into them everywhere.'

'Yes, yes, love,' Rosie replied in her patient cooing voice. He could see her gather her most welcoming smile, which she turned upon him, striking him as it always did with profound irritation. The uncomprehending busybodying old cow. Not that her welcomes mattered, really, any more. He could pass through their smothering as a ghost pierces solid substance. So she could carry on her smiling, much as she liked – he would have no care. One day, perhaps, she would learn that welcomes are nothing to the dead.

Brenda and Evans were married a few days after Augusta Browne had gone. Happily confused by the blurring of snow and confetti in their eyes, they left for a honeymoon in Brighton.

When they returned they found that Wroughton House was already being transferred into offices, and the elms were cut down. But they weren't very interested. They had their own home, now, and much to do to complete it. Often the convenience of the chickens – free-range birds at the bottom of the garden – seemed to come first. Bloody chickens, as Evans still thought of them, privately. They took up so much of Brenda's time and thoughts.

Gradually they acquired furniture and curtains and potted plants all of which, Evans liked to think, Lark would have approved. Augusta Browne had given them the brass bed as a wedding present, which reminded them occasionally of their attic nights, and sometimes they wondered what had become of her. But, their long wait over, its frustrations were almost forgotten. The room at Wroughton House had been merely a part of that time of waiting, and was banished now from their minds by the present interests of their new life.

Nowhere Girl

For Various People

Chapter One

My first husband, Richard Storm, was buried on a hot August day in the suburbs of London. When the funeral was over, a dozen of us, relations and friends, drove away in a procession of big black cars. Their seats had been built to force passengers into upright positions of respect. We sat uncomfortably and no-one spoke a word.

Richard's parents lived in a dark flat near Hyde Park. At their invitation we joined them there to re-form the funeral group we had made round the coffin, only this time it was round a table laid with fishpaste sandwiches. We drank sweet sherry and talked in cheerless tones appropriate to the occasion.

I left at four, the first to leave, and walked into the park. It was very hot, oppressively hot. The trees were quite still, like trees under snow. People walked slowly, or slept on the grass, careless of their appearance, legs apart, hands straggling over faces, like people on a beach. The sherry still tasted horrible in my mouth, and the skirt of my black dress clung damply to my legs.

There was no hurry. There was nothing to hurry for, and it was too thundery to hurry.

I sat on a bench. It was already half-occupied by two old women. They sat alert, on the very edge of the bench, as if they were about to move, but were waiting for some signal. In a way, they resembled some of the old people who had been at the funeral, except they were poorer. The one farthest from me was shrivelled into a bow shape, scraggy and grey. Grey skin, grey eyes, black coat faded almost to grey. She stared straight ahead and let the ugly knots of her hands lie dead in her lap.

The one nearest to me looked healthier, altogether sprightlier. She too had a black coat, but a poppy left over from some long past Poppy Day stuck in the brim of her hat.

She turned to me and said:

'You can hear the buses from here, can't you? That's nice.'

I listened. I could hear the rumble of buses.

'So you can,' I said.

'That's what I like about it here. You can sit down and listen to the noise, and yet you're in a nice bit of green.' She looked at the prickly hedge opposite our bench, the rim of scorched grass by the path, the litter-bin, and a motionless tree. 'Oh no,' she went on, 'I've nothing to grumble about now, have I? I never liked the quietness of the old days, you know. What I like is a supermarket on a Saturday morning. Or those demonstrations in Trafalgar Square. As a matter of fact, I was at one of those not long ago. I'm not quite sure what it was all about, to be honest, but there I was shouting away with the rest of them, and one of those policemen nearly took me away in a van. "Not on your life, officer," I said to him. "There's no law against innocent shouting. Besides, I'm enjoying myself." And his hands just fell away from me.'

She smiled. Her voice was quiet, but not so quiet as Mrs Storm's had been. Mrs Storm was Richard's mother. My presence at his funeral had embarrassed her. She had nodded to me in the church, and looked confused. Later, in the hot brown room, sickly with the smell of nervous sweat, she shook my hand and said:

'Oh, Clare, how nice to have the chance to see you again.' Then she coughed, and blushed a deep yellow-pink, realising that was not what she had meant.

She wore a musquash coat. All the women seemed to be in musquash coats, in spite of the heat. A mournful fur. They held their sherry in damp hands that left fingerprints on their glasses. They were hungry for the fishpaste sandwiches which Mrs Storm handed round. A gathering of mustard and cress had caught up in the short grey hairs on her top lip. She must have been conscious of them, because when I went to say good-bye her small mauve tongue darted to the corners of her mouth, and she bumped nervously against her husband like a pigeon on a high ledge.

The old woman on the bench was talking again.

'My sister, now,' she was saying, 'my sister is quite different from me. She doesn't agree with me at all.' She nudged the other old woman who turned reluctantly towards me. An empty face. A portrait whose oil paint has been scraped from it, leaving nothing but a faint drawing beneath. She blinked, so slowly that when her lids lowered I had a feeling that they wouldn't rise again.

'My sister always was the quiet one. Her name's Edith. Edith Smith. She never married, you see.' With her right hand Edith Smith's sister rubbed at the rings on the third and fourth fingers of her left hand. Next to her wedding ring she wore a small, dark ruby ring set in silver. On her third finger, a round, pearly blue star-sapphire. The fine rays of its star glinted in the sun. 'And my name is Ethel Fox. Mrs Henry Fox, though Henry died fourteen years ago.' Edith Smith blinked slowly again, in confirmation of all this.

'It's one of Edith's days in London,' Mrs Fox went on.

'She lives in the Gulliver Old People's Home in Herne Bay, and she's allowed up twice a year. Usually, we have a good time. But it's been rather heavy to-day, and Edith's feet are aching.' One of Edith's shiny black walking shoes twitched almost imperceptibly. 'Still, we had a nice lunch in Lyons, then bought some embroidery silks in Barkers. – Edith's good with her hands,' she added.

We sat in silence for a while. The air was still and lifeless, like it sometimes is before an August storm. The sky was piling up with sour green clouds. Mrs Fox was looking at them.

'It's rather far to go back to my flat,' she said, 'all the way to Earl's Court. And anyway, what can two people like us do just sitting in a room?' At that moment two large drops of rain broke on the path by our feet. Mrs Fox brightened.

'It's coming on to rain,' she said. 'Edith, it's coming on to rain. For myself, I don't mind being caught in a shower because I never catch colds. But it's Edith we must think of. Edith, come along.'

The two old women stood up. Mrs Fox took her sister's arm.

'Where do you think we should go?' she asked. Standing, she held herself very straight. Beside her, Edith Smith sagged, a crumpled piece of indeterminate grey, and yet she lacked that quality of inconspicuousness that makes some people stand out in a crowd.

'You could come back with me,' I said.

'That's the answer,' said Mrs Fox. 'We'll come back with you.'

We hurried along, the three of us, our heels rattling out-of-step on the pavements, past the Albert Hall, down the Exhibition Road. The rain thumped down slowly but spitefully. We concentrated on speed. At the funeral, the coffin bearers had concentrated on careful slowness. They were very good at it, and didn't joggle the coffin on their shoulders. Their lips were sucked in with concentration so that their mouths were thin pencil lines. At the church they all took off their top hats with one gesture, like chorus men in a variety show.

We reached the house – small, trim, pretty, in a narrow cobbled mews. Geraniums in the window boxes flared scarlet against the white paint. The gilt door-knocker and knob were of matching intricate design.

'I've always wondered what sort of people lived in these sort of houses,' said Mrs Fox, as I opened the door.

In the sitting-room Edith Smith at once fell back on to the sofa, tired. Her weight barely made an impact on the fat cushions. Mrs Fox stared curiously at a picture of Richard above the fireplace. A crayon drawing he had done in Salisbury as a present for our first wedding anniversary. He was dressed in naval uniform, sharp, antiseptic – attractive, I had thought, at seventeen. A mild but distant face. Certainly he didn't look the sort of man who would marry a girl twenty years younger than himself, treat her like a spoilt child for a couple of years, then desert her for a middle-aged woman called Matilda he met one leave in Barcelona. Our divorce had been very easy. Plain desertion. And Richard had remained friendly. He sent me cards on my birthday and at Christmas, and encouraged Matilda to send me boxes of liqueur-filled chocolates.

'That your husband?' Mrs Fox asked.

'It was, but he died. That's my husband now.' I pointed to a photograph of Jonathan in a silver frame. A kind but weak face, a little fleshy under the re-touched eyes, the mouth too full and high for its width.

'Oh, I see.' She fingered the frame. 'Is he musical?'

'Not particularly. He likes Strauss.'

'I thought he might be. He's got a musical face. But then Henry looked musical, and he couldn't tell Haydn from Mozart. So you never can tell.' She walked over to the record player. 'Could we put something on?'

'Strauss?'

'Oh no, not in this rain. Have you anything by the Beatles?'

I put on a record.

'"Lucy in the Sky,"' said Mrs Fox. 'I'd like Edith to hear that.' She turned up the volume herself and smiled. Edith Smith shut her eyes. I went to get the tea.

The time the sisters took to eat seemed to go very slowly. Mrs Fox and I nodded and smiled to one another as the biscuits were passed to and fro. Edith appeared as ex-communicated as ever. She toyed with a ginger biscuit, licking small bits round the edges to make it soft before she trusted it to her small, white, unsteady teeth. I wondered if she was deaf, or dumb, or both.

'There's nothing the matter with Edith, is there, Edith?' Mrs Fox shouted at me, suddenly, above the music. 'She just gets overawed by London, you know. Well, I mean, wouldn't you if you'd been in the Gulliver nine years?'

I nodded. She picked up a slice of supermarket chocolate cake, held it close to her face to approve it, and spoke more quietly.

'And I was wondering why you are wearing so much black, at your age?'

I wore the black cotton dress I had quickly bought that morning, and a black wool beret with a pom-pom on top that Jonathan had bought me in Switzerland for snowballing. I took it off, shook out my hair, and explained I'd been to a funeral.

She asked who had died. I knew the name would mean nothing to her, but she seemed to anticipate a truthful answer. I told her Richard Storm.

'Oh.' She was disappointed. 'I don't know why, but I thought it might have been one of Henry's friends. They're dying all over the place, these days, I hear. Was this a much younger man, then?'

'Forty two. He died of a heart attack.'

'Any relation?'

'My first husband.'

'You mean the one up there?' She looked towards the picture. 'Oh lord, your first husband. Well, I suppose that meant you had a hand in the service. Did you give him a good march?' I had had no part in the funeral arrangements, I explained. I had even forgotten who had composed the funeral march played at the service. Mrs Fox clucked with disapproval.

'When Henry died, now,' she said, 'I gave him the best funeral you can imagine. People came from miles round to hear it, didn't they, Edith?' Edith moved her head, perhaps remembering. 'I got the Salvation Army to top up the organ, you know, so that when we went outside with the coffin they could come with us. They played Chopin's funeral march, but, of course, we reached the grave long before they'd finished. So we stood for quite five minutes, wasn't it, Edith? – beside the grave, just marking time. At least, that's what I was doing, just like the Guards. Oh, it was lovely, I can tell you.' She put her cup to her lips but put it down again, smiling, without drinking.

'People said they'd never heard a funeral like it. The vicar, he said it was all against regulations. I had a little trouble with him, but in the end he let me have it my way. – Mind you, he did quite well out of it. I sent him a record – what was it called, Edith? Anyhow, massed brass bands playing folk tunes at the Albert Hall.' She picked up her cup again and drank this time with swift, silent sips like a bird.

'Funnily enough, just as the band stopped we had a lo of aircraft overhead. All screaming, those very big planes – I like the noise they make, high up. As a matter of a fact, I had quite a job to hear the vicar. I was following in my prayer book, but he'd finished *dust to dust* before I got there. I remember thinking how Henry would have laughed.'

The record had come to an end and we could hear the rain. It was five o'clock.

'Come along, Edith,' she cried. 'The bus to Victoria. We're going. No dawdling, now. Your feet have had a good rest.' She pulled on a pair of transparent nylon gloves, then took one of them off again to check with a naked hand the Poppy Day poppy in the brim of her velour hat. Edith Smith rose and made for the door, head down, preserving her silence to the end. At the door, she offered me a clenched hand, tightly packed into an old wool glove. But when I tried to take it, she quickly withdrew it, as if she thought it would repel me, but politeness had forced her to make the gesture.

'Come again,' I said to Mrs Fox.

'Well, I don't know your name, but I might.'

'Lyall. Clare Lyall. How about Tuesday?'

'Mrs Lyall, Tuesday.' She gave a little skip after her sister. 'Tuesday tea. Well, Mrs Lyall, I'm not sure, but I think I could fit in tea on Tuesday.'

'Make it about four thirty,' I said.

'Four thirty, Tuesday. I'll be here, then. Come along, Edith, or you'll miss your coach.'

I opened the front door and Edith shuffled past us out into the rain. She was huddled up like someone on a very cold day, reluctantly independent.

'She never likes going back,' said Mrs Fox. 'You can tell.'

*

When they had gone I went back to the sitting-room, meaning to take the tea tray out to the kitchen. But instead I sat in an arm-chair and looked again at the picture of Richard Storm. On a table beside me was a box of chocolates, liqueur-filled. I chose a heart-shaped one. Rum. My favourite.

It was the last box Matilda had sent me before Richard died. She can't have had any idea, then, when she posted them to me, that he was going to die. I wondered how she had felt, arranging to have his body sent home, by request of his parents, to be cremated in Golders Green. She seemed to have organised everything very efficiently. She had even strapped a large wreath of white wax roses to the coffin with Sellotape, so that they shouldn't fall off during the flight. Mr and Mrs Storm could not, with any decency, have started scraping away at the Sellotape when they received the coffin. So they had had to bear a wreath from his mistress stuck to their son's coffin. It had probably caused them as much anguish as Richard's death.

To me, it no longer mattered that he had died. But I did wish they had pushed him overboard, which he would have liked, instead of decorating his coffin to look like something from a *smörgåsbord*, and treating him to the absurdity of this afternoon's performance.

At six o'clock, by the clock whose soft tick was loud in the silence, I went to the kitchen. I grilled a small, unappetising chop. Ate it with a packet of heated-up potato crisps. Drank milk straight from a tri-cornered container. I sat on the kitchen table and ate the food off my lap, not because it was comfortable, but because now Jonathan had gone there was no need to go on laying those self-conscious places with linen table mats and Provençal china that he had insisted on our using. There was nothing I could do about changing the kitchen itself, though. It was a horror of grape-green Formica tops, and the tendrils of fiddly green plants curled about the shelves of the dresser. Jonathan called it an 'interpretation' of a kitchen we had seen in a magazine. In fact, it was an exact copy. I had always hated it, just as I had always hated his study, which had a contrived air of shabbiness about it, which Jonathan thought a suitable background for a writer.

I washed up my one plate, simply running it under the hot tap. Then I took a pile of recipe books from a shelf and began to read them, page after page, like a novel. Steak Bordelaise, Moroccon Chicken. Sickening thoughts. Veal in cream with mushrooms. Worse still. We had had that for our first dinner party. Jonathan's idea, of course. He said his mother did it very well and it was an ideal dinner party dish. I had cooked nervously, leaving him to sniff round the guests' glasses with a bottle of champagne. But he couldn't resist breaking off his hospitality, for a moment, to see how things were doing in the kitchen. Creeping up behind me, he sloshed half a bottle of sherry over my shoulder into the frying pan of bubbling cream, bleary with mushrooms. He said if we were going to entertain, we might as well do it properly. When all the guests had gone, he went on about how perfect it had been, and how you could tell how much they had all enjoyed it. Later that night I was sick: all mushrooms, sherry, cream and veal.

*

At a quarter to nine by the green kitchen clock the telephone rang. David Roberts, a friend of Jonathan's.

'Hello, old thing. I just happened to be somewhere in your direction and wondered if I could take a drink off you?' David was in Public Relations. He made it his business always to be in the right direction at the right time. Reluctantly, I said he could come.

'Splendid, splendid. Long time no see, and all that. Besides, I've got an idea. Be with you in half an hour.'

I didn't like David. He was one of those fringe people Jonathan had picked up somewhere. He was on the fringe of the advertising world, the art world, the cinema. Jonathan had trailed in his wake for a couple of years, lured on by David's promises to help him to success.

'You've got talent, old boy,' David used to say. 'Let me deal with it. I'm having lunch with someone who could help you a lot. Why don't you come along and let me slip him one of your plays?' He had shown one of Jonathan's two plays to numerous people for whom, David believed, they would be just the thing. But each time the project failed. Each time David blamed the failure on himself and promised to think of something else. What he never saw was that Jonathan simply was not good enough. His faith in Jonathan was unshakable, and Jonathan responded eagerly enough to this faith, the expense account lunches, and the whole fringe business of trying to make a break.

David arrived punctually at nine fifteen.

'My old thing.' He pulled back the hair from my forehead and kissed me on the nose. 'Sorry I haven't been round before, but you know how it is. Anyway. You look marvellous, don't you?' He went to the drink tray and poured himself a brandy. He was used to doing this in our house. Jonathan never offered a drink to anyone he thought of as a working friend.

David was a heavy man, Scottish, reddish. The backs of his hands and the back of his neck were furry as mohair. Large pores splattered down his nose. I had often tried counting them while he and Jonathan sat for hours making plans for future success. To-night he wore a well-cut, dark-grey suit, but his solid thighs rounded out the knife creases in the trousers even when he was standing, and his thick ankles bulged over his suede shoes.

He lowered himself on to the sofa, squashing flat the cushion Edith Smith had hardly managed to indent.

'Well, well, well. A lot of water's passed, what, Clare?' I remembered he once told Jonathan that the best way to put people at their ease was to ramble on in clichés for a while. This gave the uncomfortable person the chance to associate himself with you, the comforter, he explained. 'Yes,' he went on, swilling his brandy round in his glass, 'it's tragic when things like this happen. Especially to one's friends. It puts everyone in such a confusion. Whose side should one take? Or shouldn't one take sides? Should one just go on seeing both parties normally and never tell one you've seen the other? I don't know.' He looked distressed. I asked him if he had seen Jonathan.

'Well, yes, as a matter of fact I have.' Plainly he was relieved to be able to come to the point so soon. 'I ran into him the other day. He was just off abroad.'

'Oh?'

'He didn't tell me where to. I forgot to ask him, actually. I was in rather a hurry. We didn't have much chance to talk.' He squeezed a finger between his stiff collar and pulpy neck in some pain. 'This damn boil came up last week. It's still pretty tender. Anyway, Jonathan. The thing is, Clare, he looked pretty awful, I can tell you. Not at all his usual self. He's obviously lost weight and he looked pretty unhealthy. Bloody miserable he was, in fact.'

'Did he tell you everything?'

'No, not all of it. But, well, you know how it is. We're old friends. He can trust me. – I heard his side of the story.'

'Naturally,' I said. There was another pause while he sloshed his brandy about again. Then he finished it in one sudden gulp and stood up.

'Now don't be *difficult,*' he said. 'You know I'm only trying to help.' His hands stirred shiftily in his trouser pockets. 'I quite understand you don't want to talk about it, but I don't think you realise just how upset Jonathan is. Can't you think it over, or write to him, or something? I'd hate to have a suicide on my hands.'

I laughed. 'You're being over-dramatic. And anyway you ought to know Jonathan well enough to know that he's much too disorganised ever to commit suicide. – No, I couldn't write to him. We agreed to have no form of communication for six months, and I'm not going to break the agreement.'

David fingered his boil with clumsy care. 'Oh well, that

seems to be that, then. I won't interfere. But you must see I was just trying to help Jonathan.'

'Quite,' I said.

He shrugged his thick shoulders. 'I'd better go,' he said. 'I promised to look in at a party. A client. I'm trying to think up a campaign for his fruit-flavoured custard powders. Why don't you come?'

I don't know why, but I said I would.

Chapter Two

In the taxi David told me his client had made a fortune out of children's rabbit-fur slippers made in the shape of baby rabbits. With some of this money he had bought a huge, ugly house in Putney whose garden sloped down to the Thames.

It was a warm night and the rain had cleared the air of the heaviness of the afternoon. We walked down the front path between shining laurel bushes. The knocker on the high-waisted front door was a brass rabbit's head. Above it, short-sighted pebble glass panes glinted with light ırom a full moon. David was still having trouble with his boil. He kept running his finger round the inside of his collar and making the kind of peevish complaints that don't inspire sympathy. Dark crescents of sweat, big as slices of melon, stained the sleeves of his coat.

In the house a woman with an excess of teeth rushed at us with an unintelligible welcome. Client's wife. She led us to a large room that had the slightly incongruous look of a much lived in place that has suddenly been stripped of its furniture.

'Here they all are,' she said, 'I'm sure you know everyonc.'

I knew no-one. David's eyes shifted expertly through the crowd and he flicked a few confident smiles of recognition. It seemed that most of the chairs had been stacked away, and guests fought with the singlemindedness of people on a holiday train for those that were left. Those who stood pressed themselves against the walls for others to pass. Through the roar of voices no individual fragment of conversation could be heard. – People communicated with signs and grimaces so that, individually, each one looked innocent of contributing to the noise.

'Splendid party,' said David, automatically. He took my elbow and pushed me towards french windows that opened onto the garden. Our progress was stopped by a stringy young man smoking a Gauloise with the arrogant gestures of people who smoke French cigarettes. David introduced him as Roddy. Roddy put a sinewy arm round my waist.

'Roddy'll take care of you,' said David, relieved.

'Try the cauliflower dip,' said Roddy.

We joined a group of lean young men all nibbling bits of raw cauliflower dipped in pink mayonnaise, and flicking ash from wherever it fell on their bodies as if they were performing some private ash-flicking ceremony. Somebody fetched me a drink. One of Roddy's friends said something I couldn't hear and they all laughed. I left them.

In the garden people flickered round a barbecue. Sophisticated hands, flaring with jewellery, stuck out in primitive gestures towards the fire, holding sausages and chops. A fat woman in a Spanish shawl, clutching a piece of raw meat, swayed towards the barbecue. When its heat touched her she crumpled slowly to the ground, dropping the meat and a black glass which broke up like soot on the crazy paving. Red wine flowed among the splinters and reached the bloody piece of steak. Nobody bothered with the fat woman. I looked round for help. 'Leave her,' someone said, and suddenly I didn't care.

I went back to the house. I found a room where people

helped themselves to food from a long trestle table. I wasn't hungry. Should I go home? I sat down next to a girl with flat yellow hair. She was eating *paella* with sullen composure. She looked at me, unsmiling. I realised that by sitting next to her – there was no chair on her other side – I might be decreasing her chances of falling in with a passing man. But I had no energy to move.

In the old days, I had always longed for independence at parties. Jonathan, absurdly proud of me in a crowd, stuck by me all evening. He always found me the most comfortable place in the room to sit, and chose for me what he considered the best things to eat. He fetched me constant drinks. – The only time I could be on my own was while he scrabbled his way to the bar on my behalf. When I stood, he said: let's dance. We always danced round the edges of the room. Jonathan didn't like to be bumped. With him, I had no chance at parties. With Richard, there had been no parties. Except for one magnificent Naval Ball in Southampton before we were married. The tickets had cost three guineas each. I wore blue tulle. The whalebone bodice, puckered with more tulle, was moulded into two inhuman points that made no compromise with my breasts. We waltzed to Strauss most of the night, and Richard smiled cigar breath at me.

'Food?' asked yellow hair. 'I'm Rose. Rose Maclaine. *Paella*'s good.' I helped myself, for something to do, and sat down beside her again. 'I'm waiting for this guy David Roberts. He said he'd meet me here. He said he could help me. He knows a lot of influential people, he says. – I'm an actress, you know, in case you were wondering.' American.

'David Roberts is over there,' I said. He was shuffling towards us with an untidiness of bearing familiar to me from the days when he and Jonathan spent long drinking evenings together. His thick lips climbed slipperily about his teeth and his eyes sprawled greedily over Rose Maclaine. They greeted each other with the sort of enthusiasm peculiar to two people who know they can benefit from one another, and fell into a private form of monosyllabic communication until another friend appeared to interrupt. A tall pale man with black curly hair and black glasses.

'Not an affectation,' said the man, 'a misunderstanding.' He pulled off the glasses. One eye was closed, swollen and blue.

'Joshua Heron, Clare Lyall.' David introduced us, dragging his attention reluctantly from Rose Maclaine. 'I expect you've heard of him.' I hadn't. David was drunker than I had imagined. 'If you don't mind being left with a man with a black eye,' he slurred, 'I'm going to take Rosie off for a dance.'

Joshua Heron and I were left together. I went on eating, spanning out the last few grains of rice on the plate. He sat down beside me and lit a cigarette. The rice came to an end. I had to look at him. He put my empty plate on the floor. I could see my reflection in his black glasses, a pinhead in a halo of pin-prick lights.

'Strawberries?' he asked.

'No thanks.' His right thumb was stained a deep nicotine, like the fingers of a heavy smoker, and the skin was charred and flaky. We remained in unawkward silence, like two people on a bus, while he smoked till there was only an inch of cigarette left. Then he crushed the burning end onto his burnt thumb. At once the tobacco split through the thin paper, dead.

'Why did you do that?'

'The first time you burn your thumb,' he said, 'it hurts. It hurts quite a lot and you get a blister. I was fourteen when I did it originally, for a dare, at school. They quite often dared me to do things they wouldn't do themselves. This great bully called Buzzard, I remember, said he'd report me for smuggling cigarettes in if I didn't do it.' He smiled briefly. 'It was pretty lousy of him, considering he was the one who smoked most of the cigarettes I smuggled.'

'Why do you still do it?'

'Because the blister cleared up and I tried again, privately, and it didn't hurt so much. Then I tried again and again until it became almost painless. In the end I put every cigarette out that way and showed the trick quite casually to Buzzard and his friends. For a short time I was quite a hero.'

David and Rose were fumbling back towards us.

'Let's go,' said Joshua quickly. He led me to the room where the music thumped loudly. We danced. Joshua's body was hot and firm and jerked rhymically as an electric toy. Faces jumped about us at different heights as if sent up by a juggler from the floor. The throb of people dimmed and blurred. Music, rhythm, jogging bodies all flared into one sensation.

'My head's cracking.' Joshua was speaking from a long way off. 'Sorry. Must be something to do with this eye. Let's get some air.' In the garden the warm night was cool after the dancing-room. We came upon the heap of a woman I recognised as the one who had fallen by the barbecue. She sat slumped at the top of a flight of steps, a little apart from everyone else.

'It's Sally,' said Joshua. 'It usually happens later. We'd better see if she wants any help.' We climbed the steps. He bent over her, gently shook her shoulders, and urged her to get up. Her head was in her hands, her hands were supported by her outspread knees. Joshua sat beside her on the step and signalled to me to sit the other side. Together we heaved at her shoulders and slowly she lifted her head. She appeared not to notice either of us, but stared ahead. Her eyes were clear green in a face that was red and swollen as that of a newly drowned woman washed up on a shore.

'It's all over,' she muttered. 'It's all over.' She spoke with deliberate precision. 'Give me a moment to recover. Stay with me. It must not look as if I'm alone.' Her head slumped back into her hands.

'We'll stay,' said Joshua. Sally had trapped one of my hands in hers, and one of Joshua's, so that our fingers met squashed beneath her chin.

'It won't take long.' Joshua turned his black glasses to me. 'She gets like this, but she comes round quickly.' Her neck was exposed between us, dark with stiff private hairs that needed re-shaving. Beyond us, on the river, two swans dipped and recovered their heads from the flat black surface of the water without breaking it.

'What did you do to-day?' said Joshua.

'Went to my first husband's funeral.'

'Oh?' From the opposite bank of the river a mist crept down towards a couple of still, fat boats. I had pins and needles in my fingers. 'She's asleep.' He moved his hand slightly. I could feel the flaky skin of his thumb. 'Cremation?'

'No.'

'Wailing nuns?' He seemed to be smiling.

'He wasn't Catholic.' One of Sally's open sandals slipped off a babyish foot and fell down the steps.

'Have you ever been to a funeral on the Continent?'

'No.'

'They're quite impressive. The nearest foreigners get to any sort of controlled pageantry. The fiestas and parades are pretty vulgar, but the funerals are good. Dignified. I had a landlady once in Rome who was the only genuine funeral fan I've ever met. It was nothing to do with morbid curiosity. She just had this talent for hearing about forthcoming funerals, and off she would go, follow the procession the whole way and come back crying.'

Sally gave a great sigh and her whole body shuddered. Joshua suggested we should try to get her back to the house. We heaved and struggled with her. Finally, with a solid assurance for one so drunk, she stood up. We supported her to a chair on the terrace and left her.

Back in the house people were at half mast, sawn down from their original height. The music was slow and sleazy. Three or four couples were dancing almost without moving, swaying like statues loosely soldered to their base. We danced, clutching at each other with the sadness of two people who are very tired.

Then the client's wife, noisy in taffeta and with lipstick on her teeth, switched on the lights. She said, what about another drink? The other couples took no notice and someone switched the light off again. Through the semi-darkness Joshua and I followed her. We sat on gold chairs, the three of us, round a table. It was suddenly cold. A chewed leg of turkey lay in the ashtray and red wine stained the table cloth. Through the windows the night sky was thinning out, leaving a white mist below. A waiter with a busy face uncorked a bottle of champagne. We drank.

'Here's to,' said the client's wife.

It was funny, that Sellotape on the coffin.

It was funny, David thinking Jonathan would commit suicide.

By now Jonathan would have bought a new typewriter. He might even have found a suitable Roman attic. How funny. Everything was funny. I began to laugh.

'Joke?' asked Joshua, but I didn't answer.

We must have sat there a long time. I ate salted nuts from a cut-glass bowl. I wiped my fingers on the table-cloth when the client's wife wasn't looking. She said Putney was a good neighbourhood to live in. You got the people and the river, she said.

It was daylight when we left. The windscreen of Joshua's car was misted up. I played noughts and crosses on it while he unlocked the door. The engine made a dreadful noise in the quiet early morning. We couldn't speak. Joshua dropped me at the door.

'Your hair's a better colour in daylight,' he said.

In the kitchen the sun was pale on the green Formica surfaces, the fiddly plants and the Provençal china. I started to make breakfast.

Chapter Three

Later that morning I began to look for Joshua. I looked for him in the telephone book and in an old diary of David's that he had left behind a year ago. I looked for him for three days. I bought bundles of newspapers and magazines and scanned them all, in case he was a writer. I read bill-boards outside every theatre, in case he was an actor. I looked for him in the summer crowds at the Serpentine and the Albert Memorial: I wandered by rows of meters looking for his car. But I did not find him.

On the fourth day I went to two cinemas, abandoning the search. When I left the second film, it was evening. A stifling heat rose from the crowded screeching streets: I was stiff from sitting, but full of energy. I walked through Green Park, a bank of deadened noise beside the gush and roar of Piccadilly, and through Hyde Park, trembling with old, stale heat and dust. My eyes were sore from straining to look at every man I passed. As I turned the corner to my own street, still full of energy, I began to run – in case the telephone was ringing, in case there was a letter.

There was a postcard. It lay picture up on the front door-mat – the Changing of the Guard in colour. I snatched it up and ran to the green light of the kitchen to read it. The writing was thin, unfamiliar, and the message sloped sharply upwards.

I came to tea but you were not there, it said. *I will come again. Yours sincerely, Ethel Fox.* (*Mrs Henry Fox.*)

The telephone began to ring. I let it ring two, three, four times while slowly I walked to the sitting-room.

'Hello?'

'Clare? It's David. I just thought I'd call you up. I spent the weekend in Rome – with, you can guess who.'

'No?'

'Rose Maclaine.'

'Oh.'

'Guess who I ran into in Harry's Bar?'

'I can't.'

'Jonathan.'

'Oh.'

'He's got himself set up very nicely in Rome. He took me to his flat near the Piazza di Spagna. It's got a marvellous view. And he's got a huge new electric typewriter.'

'Good.'

'He asked after you and I said you were all right. You are, aren't you?' He paused. 'He was looking much better, actually. He's put on some of the weight he lost.' I said I was glad. 'I introduced him to Rose. Do you know what he said to her? He said: "If I wasn't married, you'd be a marvellous girl." How's that for loyalty?' It was easiest to agree with him, so I laughed.

When he had finished talking I picked up Mrs Fox's postcard again and looked for an address. But there was none, so I stuck it up on the desk, Guards facing me. *Christopher Robin went down to the Palace. . . .* I made myself a scotch and soda and went to the kitchen for ice. I ran the tray under hot water and flung three cubes into the glass. Last Christmas Jonathan had bought me a plastic pineapple ice-bowl. He knew I wouldn't want it, but it pleased him. 'All we need now,' I had said, sitting at the foot of his parents' Christmas tree, 'is a pair of ice tongs.'

'I'll get you some for our anniversary, darling,' he had said, seriously, and he and his mother had talked about hygiene while it snowed outside.

I threw the tray of ice into the sink, where it clattered and slid about.

'Don't be so *violent*, Clare,' Jonathan used to say.

I carried my drink up the steep, narrow staircase, carpeted with thick, expensive Wilton. I wandered round our bedroom and counted the chintz roses along the pelmet. Seventeen. I knew them by heart. I ran my finger along the fireplace, in and out of the pottery mugs Jonathan had bought in Greece. Dustless. I looked at myself in the old freckled mirror we had bought in an antique shop. Hooded my eyelids, ruffled my hair. I sang a verse of 'Where have all the flowers gone?'. I ran from the bedroom, an invisible wind machine fluttering at the edges of my invisible chiffon skirts. . . . *Long time passing*. The room we had never furnished had two pink walls and two white ones. Shapes of furniture and packing boxes were covered with dustsheets. There was a smell of cheap *pot pourri*. This was to have been the nursery. When I had suggested to Jonathan that it would be nice to have a baby, he had gone out and bought tins of pink paint, and every morning, instead of writing, he painted the walls. He would not believe that I had not conceived, only made the suggestion. When at last he grasped the situation, and no conception took place, he gave up his painting, leaving it half-finished. Instead he bought a huge pink bear – it took a whole morning to choose in Hamleys. 'Just to encourage the idea,' he had said, very pleased with himself. I had thrown it at him in a fury, so he had taken it up to the half-painted room, apologising for his tactlessness. The bear sat now in the undulating countryside of the gingham dustsheets spread over the hillocks of furniture. It had a black wool grin and a red felt tongue and pink velvet paws. I picked it up, clutched it to me, and swept round the room in a wild dance. Round and round the island of covered furniture, singing and swirling, faster and faster . . . . Then, tripping over a concealed lump, I crashed to the ground and lay panting on the pink carpet. The bear lay within inches from me, still grinning. I thrust it under a dustsheet and got up.

The front-door bell rang, short, sharp, impatient jabs. I ran downstairs and flung it open. The evening sun punctured my eyes. At first, I didn't recognise the tall figure.

'What have you been doing? You've got dust or something all over your face.'

I stepped back and Joshua walked in, passed me, and made for the kitchen. He carried a tall brown paper bag fat with things from a supermarket.

'I've brought enough for three,' he said. 'Cold chicken in jelly, asparagus tips, mock caviar, cottage cheese, ice cream and peppermint lumps. My Calor gas has run out.'

'Enough for three?' I stood beside him while he spread the stuff over the kitchen table.

'Somebody told me you were married.'

'But my husband's away for six months.'

'Then we can be greedy. Where are the glasses?' He rattled through drawers looking for a corkscrew for a bottle of red wine he had also brought. He no longer wore his dark glasses, but huge ordinary ones with heavy black frames that dominated his face. Through them the taut, pale skin of his face sheared away over his cheek bones.

His eyes were wide set, grey and speckled, as if sawdust had been flung into the irises. One eye was still puffy and swollen.

'What happened?' I asked, 'To your eye, I mean.'

'A collision,' he said briefly. 'I've had a bad time since the party, that's why I didn't call you. I had to get a script finished by to-day, and then they cut off my telephone because I had forgotten to pay the bill, and the American producer I am working for kept me up late every night suggesting to me a lot of ideas that I'd already given him every morning.'

'What are you working on?'

'A documentary on rural British life to be shown in Mexico. You may not believe it, but life in British villages still thrives. We've already overrun our schedule by two weeks.'

We ate. Joshua chose his food at random. A peppermint lump, a wing of chicken, cheese, another peppermint lump, caviar on bread. There was no pattern to his eating and in between mouthfuls he snatched at his wine or his cigarette with sharp defensive movements. He concentrated wholly on what he was doing, and seemed to be lost in the kind of trance that comes over people at pompous dinners when the guests beside them are impossible to talk to, and the only thing to do is to become absorbed in the food.

'I don't like this kitchen,' he said, when he had finished. 'Too glossy. How did you get that dirt on your face?'

'I fell over upstairs.' I fingered my face.

'You must have dusty rooms.'

'We do.' I plaited together bits of soft greasy paper off the peppermint lumps.

'What's your husband doing?'

'He's just away, I don't know where. We've separated for six months.'

'Isn't there somewhere more comfortable we could go?'

I led him to the sitting-room. It smelt unused and a little dank.

'There's this.'

'One of you has very chintzy taste.'

'Jonathan.'

'What's he like?' He sat on one of the chintz sofas. I had always disliked them. Now I blushed at owning them, and the warmth of the wine fired through me.

'Once he was furious with me because there wasn't a pile of funny books in the lavatory,' I said. 'He's hopeless. Nothing ever, ever works for him. Something marvellous is always going to happen and it never does. He's crazy about success but he will never be successful because he isn't prepared to work for it. Anyhow, he isn't good enough. What's important to him is to decorate his study to look like what he thinks a writer's study ought to be. Taking authors and editors and agents out to lunch. Changing his typewriter for a newer model. He only actually *writes* for about two hours a week.'

'I get the picture, I think,' Joshua said. 'Why did you marry him?'

'He wasn't like that two years ago. He was always weak. But in the beginning he was kind and undemanding. I really believe I loved him when I married him. But what I don't understand is how one day you can be quite happy loving someone, and the next day things that you never minded before drive you into a screaming frenzy of unreason. I began to loathe things he couldn't help. The shape of the back of his head, the way he wheezed in the morning because of his asthma. When I finally said either he or I had to go, he crept away without putting up any sort of fight. He was so reasonable I could have killed him, suggesting this six-month plan and making financial arrangements in a quivery voice. Then he packed a couple of suitcases and gave me an address to send on some shirts when they came back from the laundry. He kissed me good-bye and he was crying – can you imagine?' Joshua nodded but didn't answer. 'He was very kind,' I repeated, 'and stiflingly thoughtful.'

'I've heard it's often something like that, being married.' He lifted his hand to my head and tweaked at my hair. 'Those are funny colours you've had put in your hair,' he said. 'Like old straw and greenish hay.' He ran his finger down my forehead and down my nose, and stopped it between my lips.

'Shall I bite you?' I asked, without opening my mouth.

'No. Come here and kiss me. I like doing things very slowly.' He pulled me towards him with a sharp tug and I felt the fat chintz cushions crackle and flatten beneath me. Then the front-door bell rang.

Joshua snapped off kissing me and went to answer it. I could hear him talking to someone but couldn't make out who it was. He came back to say it was an old woman who said she was a friend of mine. At that moment Mrs Fox pushed her way impatiently past him.

'Mrs Lyall,' she cried, 'you know what happened to me? I knew somehow I'd find you here. I was on my way back from Leicester Square in the bus – I'd been to see the new Cliff Richard film, it's lovely – when suddenly I thought: why don't I buy some food and go to Mrs Lyall and we'll have a bit of a party? So I jumped off at Hyde Park Corner and bought a couple of sausage rolls at that all-night stall' – she patted a crumpled paper bag – 'and

I had some Kit Kat over from the cinema and, anyway, I thought we could heat up some cocoa . . .' She hesitated, looking at Joshua. 'Or whatever you drink,' she added.

She was wearing the same black coat and hat as before, but this time the Alexandra Rose Day rose replaced the poppy in the crown. She scratched at it with her free hand and waited for my answer. I introduced her to Joshua.

'I'm not an aunt or anything,' she said, screwing up her kid-gloved hand into a tight knot and offering it to him, 'so you needn't worry about that. I met Mrs Lyall on a bench. Now, the problem is, I only have two rolls. What is the best idea for dividing them into three?' She glared nicely up at Joshua.

'Why don't you eat them both yourself?' he suggested quickly. 'We had dinner not so long ago, but we could join you in a drink.'

Mrs Fox approved the idea. We fussed round her arranging a plate, a glass and a place on the sofa. I beat up the cushions which had the squashed look of a finished love scene, but Mrs Fox did not seem to notice. I apologised for having no cocoa in the house. She replied with relief that she would make do with a pink gin. We persuaded her to take off her coat, but her hat had a settled look about it which she evidently had no intention of disturbing. The dress beneath her coat was black crêpe and shapeless, but pinned well down her left bosom was a copper brooch of abstract design. She noticed my looking at it.

'Like it?' she asked. 'I only bought it yesterday. Before, I had so many of these cameo brooches. Henry used to give them to me, one every birthday. Well, I didn't like to tell him, then, but I don't like cameo brooches. They're ageing. Besides, they're gloomy. All those yellow ivory heads. – Anyway, as he's been dead many years now, I thought a decent amount of time had gone by and I could sell them. So I took them to a jeweller who gave me five pounds for the lot. Five pounds for thirteen cameo brooches! So then I went to one of those nice modern shops that has music coming through a grill in the wall, and tables covered with sackcloth instead of counters, and bread baskets and lumps of stone lying about – you know the sort of place I mean. And I found this. The girl there, she was wearing one very like it, and she said to me: "It suits you very well." She said these brooches suit all types. – So I've sent two pounds to Edith and the rest I'll spend on cinemas.'

She bit into a roll and the flaky pastry chipped on to her chin. Joshua crushed the end of his cigarette into his thumb and threw it into the fireplace. Mrs Fox watched him without surprise.

'Henry had his mannerisms, too,' she said. 'He used to make murmury noises in his throat just before he spoke. And if no-one was listening, why, he'd go on rumbling away until they paid attention.' She smiled at the memory and nodded towards the gramophone. 'Couldn't we turn it up?'

Joshua at once increased the volume and the familiar look of content began to unfold over Mrs Fox's face. It became difficult for her to concentrate on talking to us. So we all sat back and listened to the music. When it came to an end she gave a little jump, as if coming back to the present, and forced her attention upon us.

'What I really came here for,' she said, 'was to tell you about Edith.' She paused for a long time, hating to go on. Joshua asked what the matter was.

'She's ill. It's her heart.' She scratched the Alexandra Rose. 'I had a letter from the matron of the Gulliver yesterday morning, the old *bitch*!' She took a crumpled piece of writing-paper from her bag and read: '"*Dear Miss Fox*" – trust her to get it wrong – "*the doctor advises us to let you know that your sister's heart condition gives rise to anxiety and she must stay in bed. As we do not undertake to look after clients in a serious condition, I write to let you know that we shall have to send her to hospital as soon as there is an available bed. In the meantime I assure you we are doing everything in our power to make her comfortable*" – huh, I know what their power is – "*and I will let you know of any further developments. P.S.*" ' – Mrs Fox spat the letters – ' "*your sister does not complain and seems reasonably happy*".'

'Of course Edith doesn't complain,' she expostulated, 'Edith never speaks to any of them down there.' Now that she had finished reading the letter she sank back into the sofa deflated. 'What shall I do? Edith would die if they put her in a hospital. – That's one thing she's never been able to stand, the smell of disinfectant.'

'Why don't you go down and see the matron and see just how bad your sister is?' said Joshua.

An almost imperceptible reluctance crept over Mrs Fox. 'It's so still there,' she said with distaste. 'They all look at you, those old things, over your knitting. They all look at you all the time and you feel you can't shake their eyes off. – But I will go,' she added, 'if I don't hear in the next few days that she's better. She'll probably recover. She's had these attacks before.' Joshua said that in the circumstances she would probably recover again, before they sent her to hospital. His optimistic view cheered Mrs Fox considerably. She rose to leave, and attacked the government with something of her old vehemence.

'They ought to do something about Old People's Homes,' she cried, 'they're a disgrace to the country.

There ought at least to be some official standard of hygiene, stricter inspections – I don't know. But these so-called private homes are a farce. You must come down to the Gulliver and see for yourselves one day.' She skipped to the door and turned to Joshua with her most winning smile. 'That big noisy-looking car outside,' she said, 'is it yours? Because I'd very much like to go home in it.'

'I'll give you a lift, then,' smiled Joshua, helping her on with her coat. They pranced out together and Mrs Fox smartly lowered herself into the seat making no reference to her agility. Joshua revved up the engine with a roar, and before they moved away I saw that Mrs Fox was swaying to and fro, clapping her hands and laughing with excitement.

Chapter Four

I waited till two in the morning for Joshua to come back. But he didn't appear.

At midday Mrs Fox rang me from a call box. She wanted some geranium seeds for her window box, she said. Could I bring her a packet that afternoon, and stay to tea?

On the bus on the way there I sat behind a man whose head was shaped almost identically to Jonathan's. The same long sandy hair grew in clumps down his neck. Jonathan always wet his hair in the bath, it was so long. He was irritatingly slow in the bath. He would lie back, balancing his cigarette on the rack, and watching the ash grow to obscene lengths and then fall into the soapy water. Later, at breakfast in the green kitchen, he would drop marmalade over the newspapers because he swore he could eat without looking. And then he would stand up with a great performance of sighs and say he had to get down to work. He would drum his fingers inside his trouser pockets so that the knobs of his knuckles bubbled under the cloth like boiling water, and he would say he was thinking.

Oh Jonathan, I hated you sometimes. I hated the way you walked bouncingly on the balls of your feet, exuding a maddening enthusiasm. I hated the habit you had of pulling down your sock and scratching your ankle so that the dry skin flaked on to the carpet and people noticed with disgust. The way you always insisted on tongs for the ice.

'Pick the bloody ice up in your fingers,' I'd scream, and, 'Christ,' you'd say, 'does it really matter?' Did it matter?

I got off the bus clumsy with anger. There was a warm, muggy wind. I was too hot in my mackintosh. I walked slowly.

Mrs Fox lived in a tall Victorian house the colour of tarpaulin. The front door was answered by a fat slack woman with skin the same consistency as sweetbreads. When I asked for Mrs Fox she heaved her low-slung breasts together under one arm, then reinforced the support with the other.

'You might tell her from me to turn that bleeding row off,' she said through toothless gums, jerking her head from the cushion of her shoulders so that for a moment she appeared to have a neck. 'On all day, full blast. Top floor on the left.'

I followed her into the hallway and heard at once the music from Mrs Fox's flat. A Japanese mobile hung from a naked bulb in the ceiling, pivoting like something in a ghost tunnel, throwing spikey reflections onto the blotched yellow walls. I climbed the stone stairs, each one worn down in the middle, and read the names on the varnished doors on each floor: Noble, Eustace, Gray, Hall. Finally, Fox.

I rang the bell and Mrs Fox came to the door. She hadn't turned the wireless down so we didn't speak, but mouthed our greetings silently. She led me to a large room. It was furnished with a huge brass bedstead, an arm-chair, a tapestry stool and a round polished table, all large and solid pieces. In the bookshelves Ian Fleming thrillers were stacked neatly against medical reference books, but these volumes were the only evidence of Mrs Fox's past. There was no frantic clustering together of remaining possessions. On the table stood a jam jar filled with a collection of charitable poppies, flags and roses. A newspaper cutting of Cliff Richard shaking hands with the Queen at a first night was propped up against the dim mirror above the fireplace. The photograph had been carefully stuck onto a piece of cardboard. A reproduction Jackson Pollock hanging over the bed was the only picture in the room, but an empty birdcage hung from a piece of flex near the window, a sprig of dead grounsel wedged between two of its bars.

'I bought the bird,' said Mrs Fox, turning down the wireless, 'but it wouldn't sing. So I let it out. But Mrs Morris – she's the landlady you will have seen downstairs – reported me to the R.S.P.C.A. Well, they sent along an inspector to see me, and the funny thing was he turned out to be a very nice man. We got on like anything. He quite saw the point about my letting a useless bird out – he said he would have done the same, off duty. Canaries are for singing, I said to him, and he agreed. – To cut a long story short, we're now great friends and he comes to see me every now and then. In the spring I'm going to spend a weekend with his family at Epsom.'

She laughed to herself and skipped to the window. 'Are you cold?' The warm wind from outside was filtering into the room and hesitantly she pulled the window a little farther shut. 'The thing is, I like plenty of fresh air in one-room flats because you have no idea how they can smell. Especially old people's. I had to go and see a friend of Ethel's last weekend, down in Highgate, and I had to keep my handkerchief to my nose most of the afternoon. I came away feeling quite sick. I don't know what it is about us, old flesh or something. But then most of my generation have this morbid pride in musty old clothes and rotten treasures, pin cushions made in 1900 and all that sort of thing. Pah! Nostalgia is bad enough in itself, but it's even worse when they have to go and surround themselves with dreadful *in memorium* mementoes. No wonder they smell!' Defiantly she sprayed a tin of air freshener round the room. 'That will do for the moment. Now, sit down somewhere. I'll plant the seeds then we'll have tea.' She pulled a plastic box from under her bed, filled with neat fresh earth and set it on her knee. She dug a hole in the earth with her finger, very gently, and dropped in the first seed.

I sat on the tapestry stool by the unlit gas fire and watched her. The room flickered with grey shadows, like firelight shadows, from the moving treetops outside. The music on the wireless changed from the wail of a Venetian waltz to an old Benny Goodman record. Mrs Fox was looking down at the hole she was filling in, her web-like eyelids trembling slightly in their downcast position. Her feet tapped in time with the music.

'That was a very nice man, that Joshua,' she said. 'I liked meeting him.' Briefly she glanced up at me, then swooped to her earth again. 'We had a good time. He took me for a lovely drive. He revved up the engine in the tunnel at Hyde Park Corner and hooted his horn. You should have heard the echoes. Then he came right up with me, here. I showed him the bathroom and everything, and he seemed to like it all. Oh yes, he had very good manners,' she went on, 'and he was very interesting about his achievements.'

'What achievements?'

'He didn't say they were achievements, of course. But I could tell. He's made several very successful documentary films, you know. He's been all over the world making them,' she said, expansively vague, 'and they've been shown on television in many different countries. – I had to drag it all out of him. He wasn't very forthcoming. But I understand that when he's made enough money he wants to retire to Finland and write historical biographies in the forest. I said I thought that was a funny thing to want to do, and he said sometimes he thought so, too.'

She went to a small stove in the corner of the room and put on a kettle. We ate small pink biscuits iced with white crowns. Later she said:

'There was a marvellous riot outside the Russian Embassy last Sunday. Did you miss it? Pity. But next Saturday there's a good wedding at St. Martins-in-the-Fields, I hear. I shall enjoy that. You can hear the music right out in Trafalgar Square when it gets going. Once the bride has come out, you know, it's easy enough to slip into a seat and listen to the end of the playing. After a wedding, nobody notices one person going into a church when everyone else is coming out.'

'Did you find out any more about Joshua?' I tried to sound disinterested.

'He lives in Notting Hill Gate. He gave me his address – I have it on a piece of paper somewhere.' She scrabbled about in a drawer. 'Here you are. Take it – go on, keep it.' I put the piece of paper into my bag without looking at it. She filled my cup with tea and unconsciously turned up the wireless again. 'I hear you are parted from your husband for a while,' she shouted merrily above the music. 'Well, if you ask me, you should take a lover while the way is clear. I never had one myself, because if Henry had found out he would have insisted on a duelling match. He was very old-fashioned that way. So I went off to my concerts and parades and things instead. And look what its done to me now.' Automatically, she turned the volume up even louder. 'No, it's better to have a lover when you're young than a neurosis when you're old. Because if you do have lovers when you're young, when you're old, all people will say is that you had a lot of men. They'd probably be envious, but anyone can put up with envy. But if you make do with a substitute, then when you're old people will say: "She's mad, poor thing. She's mad. Dotty about chicken breeding," or whatever it is you take to. So it's better to have lovers when you're young, than pity when you're old.'

Her voice trailed away into the music. I could not think what to shout back. But suddenly she turned to me and snapped:

'They sent round one of those social workers here last week. Pah! She suggested I should join an Old People's Club. She couldn't believe that I could entertain myself. She couldn't believe I wasn't lonely. Interfering old thing. What did I eat? What did I read? She had one of those saintly voices that make me sick. She had *compassion* in her piggy little eyes, too. So I sent her packing, and I don't think she will be back for a long time.' She was laughing again, and making more tea.

I stayed till six. When I left she came with me to the door and the music burst on to the dusky staircase. She leant over the banisters as I walked down the stone stairs. 'Notting Hill Gate,' she called over the banisters, then slammed her door.

Outside the hot muggy wind was gathering force. I began to walk very fast, then to run. Buildings, traffic and people fled past my eyes like ribbons. Familiar shops jigged up and down, almost unrecognisable, as if I was seeing them from the whirl of a roundabout. I wasn't going fast enough. I shouted 'Taxi', so loud that people turned round and looked at me. I gave the taximan the address on the piece of paper and flung myself lengthwise on the leather-smelling seat. In order as not to look at our progress through the slow streets I read an advertisement for a night club in Fulham, nailed to the upturned seat in front of me, over and over again. I wiped the sweat off my forehead with the back of my hand.

We stopped at a tall block of flats. The taxi driver took a long, long time to give me the change. I ran through thick glass doors into a hall silenced with a thick, patterned carpet. There were pink tinted mirrors on the walls and I caught a brief sight of myself: red face, hair askew. The lift swooshed slowly up to floor fourteen. I ran down another carpet-silent passage to an anonymous brown door. I rang a shrill bell, waited. I rang again and the door opened. Joshua stood there, his shirt sleeves rolled up, a cigarette between his finger and thumb.

'Oh, it's you.' He didn't seem surprised.

'Mrs Fox gave me your address,' I said.

'I would have rung you if you'd waited. I've been in Essex all day, filming. You'd better come in.' I followed him into a square white room sparsely furnished with a couple of low Scandinavian sofas: in contrast, the sofas themselves were cluttered with scarlet, orange and purple cushions. Magazines, typescripts and three penknives littered the floor. 'Why are you wearing a mackintosh?'

'I thought it was going to rain.'

'How funny,' he said, 'I looked out of the window this morning and I remember quite distinctly thinking: It's not going to rain to-day.'

'You were right, then.' I took it off. I felt flat, regretful.

'Come and see my view.' We went to the large windows. London spread to meet the low grey sky. The buildings, a multitude of grubby bulbs, sprouted from indeterminate earth.

'It would be better if they were trees. I don't know why they don't build skyscrapers in the middle of forests. Think what it would be like when the wind blew. Do you want some vodka? It's all I have.' He poured me a drink and fetched ice from the kitchen. I was still sweating. I held the cold glass to my cheeks. They still burned. I told him about my afternoon with Mrs Fox.

'She was extraordinary the night I took her home,' he said. 'She made me drive her through the Hyde Park Tunnel three times, hooting. She laughed like a child.'

'Do you think she can find us here? She gave me the piece of paper with your address.'

Joshua laughed. 'She wrote both my address and telephone number down on the fly leaf of her Bible by her bed, so I wouldn't be surprised if she arrived at any moment.' He sat beside me on one of the low leather sofas. 'Pretty,' he said quietly. 'Rather nice, your untidiness. And you shine.'

'Sweat,' I said, dabbing at my forehead again.

'I was planning to take you out to dinner anyway, so it's funny you turned up. But now you're here, could you cook something while I finish some work? There's a tin of Italian tomatoes, frozen scampi and a Camembert in the kitchen. Could you do something with them? I'll go and buy some wine.'

He worked at a low table and I cooked. Later he pushed the papers from the table and we ate there, me kneeling on the floor. When it became too dark to see we stuck candles on saucers and put them on the table. Joshua said the lighting in the room was bad. The still-hot wind flickered through the open window and almost flattened the flames.

'What does your husband look like? I've been trying to agine.'

'Medium.'

'Height? You mean medium height?'

'Yes.'

'A nice, safe height, medium.'

'Sandy hair.'

'A good colour, sandy. Goes with everything.'

'Green eyes, rather bulgy.'

'Green eyes often bulge.'

'He smokes Olivier cigarettes and wears Old Spice after shave.'

'I would have guessed both those things.' We were rather drunk. 'What big eyes you have, Grannie.' He leant his head over the table near mine. 'And what tempestuous hair when you rattle it about like that.'

'What beautiful eyes *you* have, now the bruises have gone.' I wasn't talking very clearly. He pulled me to join him on the sofa.

'Marriages shouldn't come unfastened as easily as yours,' he said.

'I know,' I said.

'I don't think I shall ever marry. I'm too bad at sharing things. Besides, I like keeping whole areas of my life entirely private – just innocent things, meetings and ideas and so on. But I don't like being questioned and asked to share them.'

'That should be possible, unless you're married to someone abnormally possessive. Jonathan always told me everything, every movement of his day. There was nothing I didn't know about him. It was so tiring, and rather dull. And at the same time he wanted to know just as much about me. He interviewed me when I came back from being out for half an hour.' Joshua's hand was running down my thigh, feeling the muscles. I talked faster. 'He hated me to make any arrangements without asking him. He hated me to spend a party talking to one person in a corner. It was so claustrophobic that sometimes I would go and shut myself up with the suitcases in the attic – the only place he never thought of looking for me – and write terrible things about him on scraps of paper, then burn them, just for relief. Just for the pleasure of knowing he could never know what I had written. Privacy to him was totally meaningless. Inessential.'

'When I was about nine,' said Joshua, 'I built myself a house in a tree in a wood near where we lived.' He took his hand from my leg to describe the tree. 'It was the most private place I have ever known. No-one could see it from the ground. In fact no-one knew which tree it was built in. I'd go there most days and just sit, loving the fact that no-one knew where I was. Sometimes I'd take my collection of penknives there and carve weird shapes out of pieces of wood. Once, in the winter, I spent the night there. I wrapped myself up in a lot of rugs and went to sleep almost immediately – it wasn't a bit frightening. Then in the morning I looked out and it had been snowing. I climbed down the tree and spent a long time running round and round, still wrapped in my rugs, so that my footsteps would be too confusing for anyone who tried to track down my tree.'

'The odd thing about privacy is that although it's desirable it isn't quite so valuable unless other people know that you have something private going on.' I said.

'Quite,' said Joshua. 'I mean, no-one knew where my tree was, that was my secret. But the fact that people knew that I had moments going off, somewhere, made the secret even more important. It wouldn't have been the same, had nobody missed me.'

I thought of Jonathan's compulsive keenness to get at the post before me every morning. He would shuffle through the letters and arrange mine neatly on the breakfast table. He was curious about everything but bills.

'I suppose it's very difficult for people who believe, literally, like Jonathan did, that married people are one, to respect the need for privacy.'

'Exactly. Common sense should help, but on the whole it doesn't, with most people. But you don't have any of those sort of worries if you don't marry.'

The candles guttered low into the saucers. Joshua pulled my head down on to his shoulders. He kissed my forehead and eyes and curved his hand over my breast. 'How would you like,' he said, 'to take my car home, pack a suitcase of things, and come back? Pack quite a big suitcase, then you could stay for some time.'

'That would be practical,' I said. Jonathan had first proposed bed to me on a wet night in Berkeley Square while we waited for a taxi. 'Why don't you come back and have some Horlicks?' he had asked. We had drunk it sitting up in bed like married pensioners.

Joshua jumped up, helped me into my mackintosh, and thrust the car keys into my hand, all very quickly.

'Hurry up,' he said, 'it's already past midnight.'

I drove the car badly, never having driven one like it before. In the house the telephone was ringing. I hurried through the dark to the receiver. Maybe Joshua had changed his mind. It was David Robertson.

'Why are you ringing so late?' I asked.

'Just to tell you, darling, that I'm very happy. Rosie here and I are very happy. We wondered if you would like us to come round and have a drink?' His words were thick and slurred.

'I'm just going out.'

'Just going out at midnight? Oh, I see. I see. We'll come another time then. Did I tell you I saw Jonathan in Rome the other day?'

'Yes, you did.'

'Oh, all right then. Bye.' I slammed the receiver down angrily. Jonathan was gone but David was spying for him. I ran upstairs to our bedroom and switched on the lights, the ugly concealed lights over the bed that Jonathan had insisted upon. On the fireplace, rising from the pottery mugs, stood a sickly blue vase, tall and thin, that Jonathan had bought for me in Greece. It was a very ugly blue in this light. When he bought it Jonathan said to the shopkeeper: 'Very phallic, don't you think?', and laughed. The shopkeeper, who only spoke Greek, didn't understand. So Jonathan repeated his joke in very loud English, confusing the shopkeeper even more. I walked away in embarrassment. Later he accused me of being rude.

Now, I picked up the vase, wrapped it in a paper handkerchief, and put it in the waste-paper basket.

I packed quickly, choosing clothes and make-up indiscriminately. The case was so full it was difficult to shut. My hands were trembling.

I went and sat at my dressing-table and looked at myself in the ugly light in the mirror. Once, when we were first married, Jonathan crept up behind me when I was brushing my hair at this dressing-table and said,

'Darling, you look so pretty. I'll always be faithful to

you.' He must have seen some such moment in a film.

'So will I to you,' I remember answering, ignorantly. Richard Storm, on the other hand, warned me from the first week of our honeymoon that he was full of human weakness, and it wouldn't always be like it was then. I had believed myself and both of them.

I left the room, turned out the lights, and double-locked the front door. This time the car was easier and I drove back fast and noisily to Notting Hill Gate.

I let myself into the front door with Joshua's keys. The sitting-room had been cleared of papers and dinner, and all the lights were on. The uncurtained windows shone blackly, reflecting the harshness of the lights. The room had changed from a soft, seductive setting to one that was cold and mass-produced. I opened the white wooden door into the bedroom. Joshua was sitting up in bed, in an old wool dressing-gown, reading *Newsweek*.

'That was quite quick,' he said, barely looking up. 'There's an empty drawer over there for your things and the bathroom is through that door.' I went back to the sitting-room to turn off the lights. Rain streaked silently down the black windows. Then I went to the kitchen and poured myself a glass of vodka from the fridge, taking a long time.

When I returned to the bedroom Joshua still didn't look up. I unpacked, slowly, stuffing everything in a haphazard way into the small drawer. Then I took my cotton nightdress and tooth things into the bathroom, and shut the door.

It was a small, green-tiled bathroom with a cloudy paned window. Two black towels hung on the rail and a chipped cork bathmat was propped up against the bath.

I undressed, folding my things into small bundles and balancing them on a three-legged stool. On the shelf above the basin lay an electric razor, a tortoiseshell comb and a yellow rubber sponge. I opened the mirrored door of the cupboard on the wall: aspirin, pills in a white box, Optrex and a box of Smarties. I shut it again and stared at my own reflection. A moment later I ran the hot tap so that steam floated up to cloud my vision.

It was warm and very safe in the bathroom. I stood on the cork mat and washed my face in cold water, leaving it to run down my neck and shoulders in small tickling streams. Then I squeezed red and white striped toothpaste onto my brush. It spilled over and fell squashily into the bowl of the basin, a pretty, abstract, pattern. I added more toothpaste to the pattern. Then, with the brush, I lifted up peaks of the paste, testing it like beaten egg-white. The edge of the basin was hard against my hipbone, but I didn't move. I decorated the rest of the bowl with toothpaste flowers: they spread out in a fan-shape from the first, central splodge. Each flower was perfectly formed and took a long time to achieve. For six hours I had done everything fast. Now, time didn't matter.

The basin hurt my hipbone; the toothpaste tube was almost flat. A great dazzling heat sprang into my eyes and the petals of the toothpaste flowers blurred, and merged into one large scarlet and white pattern.

'Can't you squeeze the tube from the bottom?' Jonathan asked every morning. Roman-attic Jonathan with toothpaste nicely squeezed.

'What are you doing?' I quickly turned. Joshua was standing at the door, naked. Behind him the bedroom was in darkness. He looked into the basin, and then at the brush and empty tube in my hand.

'Why are you crying?'

'I'm not,' I said.

'All right then, you're not.' He stepped towards me, took the things from my hands and laid them on the edge of the basin. Then he picked me up in his arms like a child and carried me towards the darkness he had come from.

Chapter Five

The rain was no longer black and silent as it had been the night before. It scratched and pattered against the window panes and a diffused grey light pressed through the unlined curtains. Joshua was still asleep, his back to me. On the table his side of the bed a metal, schoolboy alarm clock and a thin gold watch both said ten to eight. Leaning over to see them I woke him.

'What's the matter? It's too early.' He turned to me and ran an unsleepy hand through my hair and down over my body. I curved towards him. The telephone rang. Joshua swore and flung his other arm out of bed to answer it. I could just hear a high, fast voice on the line.

'Oh Christ,' he said, when the voice at last stopped. 'Well, as a matter of fact she's here. Yes, it does make it easier. . . . I tell you what,' – he was pinching my thigh – 'I have to be on location to-day, but Clare could have my car and take you down there. No, I'm sure she wouldn't mind. Well, if you're up and dressed already, why not come round here and she will meet you downstairs in twenty minutes' time?' He put down the receiver. 'Fuck Mrs Fox.'

'What's happened?'

'Her sister's had a heart attack and she wants to go down there straight away.'

'Why couldn't she go by train?'

'She thought it would be quicker by car.'

'So I've got to take her? In twenty minutes?'

'I'm afraid so, you poor love.' He kissed me. 'I may go back to sleep.' He turned over and immediately slept.

I got up and dresssed, tense with the alert, empty feeling that comes after a sleepless night. The toothpaste flowers in the basin were hard and cracked. I washed them away. Through the kitchen window the sky was a hood of unbroken grey. Rain fell regularly down. The buildings far below were hardly visible. I drank black coffee.

Downstairs Mrs Fox was standing outside the glass doors under her umbrella. The rain dripped and spiralled round her. She wore the same coat and hat as usual, but two goose feathers replaced the poppies and flags. When she saw me she ran down the steps to the car, which was parked some way down the road. I hurried after her and unlocked the door. Inside, I turned on the wipers and pulled out the choke. The car smelt of dank, airless leather, and the rain beat noisily against the windscreen and the soft roof.

'I got this telegram very early this morning,' said Mrs Fox, as we pulled out into the street. 'I knew you wouldn't mind taking me in an emergency.'

'Did they say how she was?'

'No. You know how cruel telegrams are. I think she's bad.'

We sloshed and skidded down the early London streets, through the persistent greyness and the warm rain. The windows of the car steamed up and the de-mister didn't work, so our progress was slow.

'Please hurry,' said Mrs Fox, at a red traffic light. A little later her hand reached for the knobs of the radio. I turned it on for her, loud, and a moment or so later the skin of her face unclasped its tight hold over her bones.

I concentrated on driving. The faulty exhaust, the

engine, and the thumping music on the wireless made too much noise for us to speak. We arrived at Herne Bay sometime mid-morning. Reluctantly, Mrs Fox turned down the wireless a little to direct me.

It still rained hard. In the wet, the buildings of the town were the ugly red of sodden chickens. Despondent black streets ran through rows of cheerless stucco houses. Their owners seemed to have given up the battle against ugliness, and painted the window frames and doors in compromising shades of gloomy greys, browns and greens.

'It's nice here earlier in the summer,' Mrs. Fox said. 'Sometimes they used to wheel Edith down to the front. She liked that.'

The Gulliver was a grey-black house of hideous proportions standing in a row of others identical to it in all but the merest detail. It was approached by a red tile path cut between two patches of scurvy lawn. On one was a large wooden notice which announced in elaborate lettering: *The Gulliver Home for the Aged. All Comforts. For terms please apply to the Matron*. Round the word *Comforts* the sign painter had put four primitive daisies, and their gold paint had run down to *Matron.*

Mrs Fox pranced up the wet path, tapping it distastefully with her umbrella, and rang a rusty handbell. It was answered by a small dark-haired maid with unshaven legs.

'I'm Mrs Fox. My sister, Edith Smith. . .'

'Oh yes, one moment.' The girl hurried away and left us standing in the porch. In front of us was a hall papered with a dim, nubbly paper reminiscent of cheap brocade. The only furniture was a large polished hat-stand and a gilt-framed message that said *Love Your Neighbour* in a whirl of maroon peonies.

'Judging by this hall you might think the place was clean,' said Mrs Fox, prodding the multicoloured tile floor with her umbrella, and spattering it with drops of rain. 'That's why they receive visitors here and don't like them to go any farther.'

A door off the hall opened and a thin, hunch-shouldered woman came towards us. She had rimless glasses and a hairy face. She wore a dress of mauve cròtcheted wool, and under this small lumps of breasts, knotted straps and suspenders stood out obscenely.

'Miss Fox,' she said, 'good of you to come. It wasn't worth getting her to hospital, she won't live the day.'

'I'm Mrs Fox. – This is Matron.'

'A relation?' The Matron smiled up at me, stretching her thin bloodless lips over a crowd of ill-formed teeth. 'Would you like to come and see Miss Smith too?' I said no, I was not a relation and I would wait in the hall. But Mrs Fox plucked quickly at my arm.

'Do come,' she whispered. 'Edith would like to see you again.'

The Matron led us down a brown linoleum-covered passage which bulged out at the end into a shapeless inner hall or room.

'The lounge,' she said brightly. With a little clipped movement of her skinny hand she gestured towards a huddle of old people in arm-chairs round a gas fire. Seven pairs of faded eyes moved listlessly towards us. 'They're waiting for their dinner. I always say they're just like farm animals, you know. Up at the gate before the farmer gets there with his basket.' She laughed at her joke and clattered up a flight of narrow wooden stairs. On the landing at the top stood a pile of slop pails, wet rags and chipped enamel bowls. There was a smell of disinfectant.

'Didn't you move her room?' asked Mrs Fox, nodding towards a white door. 'You said you would, last time I was here. You knew she never liked the one she's in.'

'My dear Miss Fox,' the Matron replied, 'if I succumbed to even a fraction of the whims of the people in this place I'd be running round on my hands and knees twenty-four hours a day. You ought to be grateful we didn't send her to hospital.'

'My name is *Mrs* Fox.'

The Matron scratched at the white door and opened it curtly. She beckoned us to follow her in.

The blinds of the narrow room were drawn, so that when we first left the beige light of the corridor it was difficult to distinguish anything more than a few weak shapes.

'Hello, Miss Smith. Feeling better?' The Matron's voice vibrated through the semi-darkness. 'How is she, Lillian?' A young girl in nurse's uniform came into focus by the low, narrow bed.

'Not so bad.'

'We might as well let the light in, in spite of the rain, yes?' With the stealthy speed of a cat who knows its way in the dark the Matron moved to the window and snapped up the blind. The square of wet grey light rang through the room with a suddenness that almost shocked. The nurse looked up at us, as we stood cautiously by the bed, and smiled. She had large teeth that squatted on a plump vermilion lower lip. In the dim room the redness of her mouth was dazzling.

'Edith . . .' Mrs Fox put out a gloved hand and poked at the wan lumps under the blanket. Her fingers trailed up the sharp ridge of a leg, stopped at a peak of knee bone. Then, slowly, she made her eyes climb up over the undulations of the shrunken body till they reached the head, propped up on pillows.

'Edith, I'm here.' Edith gave no flicker of recognition. Her milky eyes hovered and trembled under the half-shut lids. The skin of her burned-out face raged under a mauve flush.

'Perhaps we had better leave them together,' suggested the Matron, cheerfully. She clacked her fingernails against the clutter of gauze-covered enamel bowls on the bedside table.

'Yes, you go,' said Mrs Fox to me. With an effort, she moved nearer to her sister. Edith's hand was lying on the blanket, a small bundle of bones tied up in a rag of spotted skin. Mrs Fox picked up this hand and shook it at me.

'Malnutrition,' she said, and let it fall back on to the blanket. Edith blinked very slowly.

The Matron tugged at my sleeve and we left the room.

'They get such funny ideas,' she whispered, spitting, as we went downstairs. 'Sometimes, the relations turn out to be as daft as the inmates.'

In the lounge, the seven old people were seated at a table now, eating some kind of stew out of soup plates. The table was covered with a squashy checked oil cloth, made soft by a blanket beneath. There was a napkin ring in front of each plate; seven plastic glasses, and plastic salt and pepper pots shaped like mushrooms. The room was very quiet, except for the hiss of the gas fire and the slopping noise of gravy being sucked out of spoons.

'Perhaps you would like to wait here for a while,' said the Matron, 'while Mrs Fox makes up her mind what she's going to do.' She indicated a flowered arm-chair. I thanked her, sat down, and picked up a copy of the *Radio Times* from the floor. She went away.

As soon as she had left, with one accord the old people edged round in their chairs to look at me.

'Is Edith gone?' asked one old woman, finally. She wore an apple green cardigan worn smooth as felt from washing. Her chin rested on her bowl of soup.

'No, her sister is with her.'

'If you ask me, she'll hang on for weeks,' said an old man. 'You might think you've come down here for the day, but you might have to stay weeks, or months.' He chuckled to himself. A streak of brown gravy ran down his pitted chin.

'Did she speak to you?' asked the first old woman.

'No, she didn't say a word.'

'She hasn't addressed anyone with a word, let alone a civil one, ever since she's been here. I would have liked to have met someone who had heard her utter.' The old man clawed at the elbow of the green cardigan, shaking with laughter.

'Don't carry on like that, George. Edith was very fond of her sister.'

'I never said she wasn't,' replied George, crumbling into another laugh. 'Anyhow, how could you tell who she was fond of, if she didn't speak?'

'You just could,' said the old woman, dabbing at her eye with her napkin.

The maid came in with a Pyrex dish of prunes and a sauceboat of custard. An old woman nearest to me looked up sharply. She had a pointed head, like a turnip, and a thin clump of white hair crowned the point – the kind of hair that can be snapped off a vegetable with one small gesture before boiling. She wore mittens on her hands. All the time the maid changed the plates and doled out helpings of prunes and custard this old woman followed her with hatred in her spiky eyes. When at last the maid left the room, she banged on the oil cloth with a clenched fist. The noise was no more than a muffled thud.

'In my day,' she said, 'we would rather have gone out to the kitchens and helped ourselves than be waited upon by foreigners.'

'Shut up, Avis,' said George, at once. Avis crooked her finger and picked up her spoon. Opposite her, another white-haired old woman whose skinny neck was pricked by a hundred ropes of sharp black beads, and who looked permanently indignant, chipped into the fight.

'You with your *folly de grander*,' she said, shaking a custardy spoon towards Avis. Then she gave Avis a huge, toothless grin. She had long gums the whitish colour of condensation in a polythene bag.

'How can I expect you to understand?' asked Avis benignly. 'To begin with, you've never had any education. You've never been waited upon in the style my husband and I were accustomed to. Why, we had the finest china and silver and glass in all of Hastings. And Firebird, the butler, used to clean the silver with his thumb, you know. . . .'

'I said lay off, Avis,' snapped George. 'If your china and that had been that bloody marvellous, why didn't you sell it? Then you could have retired to a Majestic Hotel somewhere, instead of here, and surrounded yourself with other fine-china ladies who would have appreciated you.' He chuckled again and several of the others joined in.

'You're always sniping,' replied Avis, with a little shudder, as if she was cold.

They left the table and moved slowly back to the faded chairs. The three old men pulled tins of tobacco from the sagging pockets of their cardigans, and lit pipes. Three of the women picked up sewing or knitting. Avis pulled a small plastic sponge bag from down the side of her chair, took from it a silver-backed looking-glass, and dabbed at her white clump of hair. I read the *Radio Times*.

Some time later Mrs Fox reappeared, stiffly upright and walking with a conscious quiet. She ignored the curious glances she attracted and came straight over to my chair.

'I wouldn't want you to wait for me here any longer,' she said, in a voice not too low for all the listeners to hear, 'I'll direct you to the Golden Sands. You can make arrangements from there, and have tea. They have the television on nearly all the time,' she added.

She came with me to the front door and I promised to wait for her at the hotel. 'It will only be a few hours,' she said.

The Golden Sands was clumsily built of black and greasy stone. It overlooked a long sweep of grey beach and a lustreless sea. Inside, the walls were the colour of old teeth and a sports programme on the television blared through the soggy atmosphere.

I went to the reception desk and asked to use the telephone. The receptionist, dressed like a stage parlourmaid, directed me to behind a Japanese screen in the hall. When I explained I wanted to get through to London, she did not hold much promise for my call. She was right. The line wheezed and spluttered, and the girl on the exchange could barely hear me. Finally Joshua's number rang, distantly, fifteen times. No reply.

I went to the lounge. As there was no one else there, I turned off the television. I sat in a brown damask chair and lit a cigarette. The receptionist brought me a tray with a plate of rock cakes and a china teapot painted to look like miniature bricks.

'I'm everything here,' she said, banging the tray on to the table. It was ten to four.

Several years ago Richard Storm and I had stayed in a hotel similar to the Golden Sands in Portsmouth. The smell of old furnishings was familiar. We moved there after a bleak, cold honeymoon in a Dorset cottage.

'It will be more convenient,' Richard had said, 'than a flat. The flats aren't very nice in Portsmouth, and you won't have to cook.'

He had taken the best suite, a faded blue room with narrow twin beds and a noisy cupboard, and a pink bathroom where long brown stains ate into the deep bath.

'A lovely view of the harbour,' Richard had said.

Every morning his alarm woke us at seven thirty and he sprang out of bed with a guilty fright that never decreased as the mornings continued. He had a bath, and dressed, as far as his shirt, in the bathroom. Then he returned to put on his naval uniform in front of me. He would ruffle my hair and say he was just off for a bite of breakfast, and take great strides towards the door that made the floor creak. Later he would return, smelling of egg or sausages on alternate days, kiss me on the forehead and wish me a good day. He left *The Guardian* on the bed.

Nine o'clock until ten went by easily enough. I would read the paper and have a long bath; dress slowly and look at the harbour. Then I would go for a walk and buy a paperback, and not let myself look at a clock until I imagined that an hour or so had passed. Sometimes Richard would surprise me by coming back for lunch. He would jaunt into the lounge, where I was waiting-for the dining-room to open at twelve thirty, and kiss me on the forehead again. He would take my arm and guide me to the bar. People would look up at us from their drinks and I would feel rather proud. We sat on tall stools and drank a glass of medium dry sherry, and ate a plate of crisps, and the bar took on a small air of excitement which I never could recapture when he wasn't there. He and the barman talked about the sea and winds and knots, and I gazed at Richard's profile through the reflections of bottles and glasses in the mirror behind the bar. Then we would lunch in the stiff, white dining-room – Spaghetti Bolognese served on toast, with sprouts, – and I would listen to a story about a night he spent in a Tahitian brothel. At the end of those sort of stories Richard always laughed guiltily, and said he shouldn't be telling his child wife such things.

In the afternoons I would go to a cinema, or feed the seagulls or have my hair done. Three evenings a week we would drive the yellow Ford Anglia to some local country pub for dinner. Sometimes, I would find a cottage near Portsmouth for Richard to contemplate. The hotel would make us up a box of fishpaste sandwiches and Penguin biscuits, and we would take a picnic to see it on a Sunday. But Richard was never tempted. The isolation or the unruly garden or the lack of heating depressed him. He preferred our hotel life.

When we came back to the hotel in the evenings, never later than ten thirty, it was always asleep. We would talk softly along the passages, and keep our voices low in our room. One night, after Richard had climbed back into his own bed again, he turned on the bedside light. The clock said midnight.

'I want to talk to you,' he said.

'What about?' I was sleepy, and unused to our routine being disturbed.

He leant on his elbow and did his pyjama jacket up to the neck. His ruffled hair stood straight up on his head, grey and stiff.

'I can never forget you're twenty years younger than me, little one, and there's a whole – gap of experience between us.' I thought of myself as a small rowing boat and him as an ocean liner. The rowing boat bounced hopelessly behind the liner, divided from it by a mile of churning sea. I giggled.

'No, seriously,' he said. 'That's what I think. And the thing is,' he paused, 'the thing is, an old sea dog like me isn't likely to change his ways. There's something I've been meaning to tell you ever since we were married. – I'm very ashamed of myself, but I must get it off my chest for once and for all.' He undid his top pyjama button and did it up again. 'Just before I came back from Barcelona to marry you, I was unfaithful to you. I had promised myself never to see Matilda again – but I did.'

I lay back on my pillow and he craned higher up on his elbow to see my face.

'Oh,' I said, 'you mean the girl whose photograph is in your wallet?'

'Now, don't cry and get upset, darling,' he said, extending a huge hand, with fingers outspread, towards me. 'You must understand. I had to tell you.'

I asked about Matilda, and with relief he turned out the light.

'You don't mind, do you?' he asked, and told me about her. She was thirty and divorced. Her skin was permanently suntanned and she smelt of tubor roses. She had black hair and kind eyes and three tom cats, and they had met in a night-club. She had a head like a rock, she cooked like a dream, and she wore tight silk trousers. We talked about her most of the night.

Every day for a week, after that night, Richard returned to lunch with me. We never mentioned Matilda. Instead, we made plans for some future day when we would have a house on the Solent, and three or four children. On the Sunday, Richard complained to the head waiter about the overcooked roast beef. He was not naturally a complainer, and seemed nervous.

On the eighth day he bought me twelve red roses wrapped in cellophane paper, and a box of liqueur chocolates. That evening I drove him down to the ship and waved good-bye. Duty forced him to return to Barcelona.

*

At five to eight Mrs Fox walked quietly into the room. In the subdued light, the dust of rain on her black coat made it glow like moleskin. Her hands were clenched at her side, gloveless.

'Edith is dead,' she said. 'She died fourteen minutes ago.'

I stood up and she sat down.

'Shall I get you some – tea, or brandy or anything?'

'No, no. I'll think about that later.' She stared at the blank television set. I asked if I could help in any way.

'No. You must go back to London. Joshua will be waiting for you. You have already done enough. I must stay here for a few days and arrange things.' She spoke very quietly, with pauses in between each sentence. At a sign from her I turned on the television and we watched a commercial for Quick Brew tea. 'I was thinking,' she went on, 'there might be a band down here, somewhere, who would care to play. . . . What do you think?'

'There might be,' I said, and she smiled. She stood up, came across to me and offered a clenched hand.

'Now please go,' she said, 'and no arguing. I will be all right.' She led me to the door, her hand taut but unquivering. As I left I heard her asking the receptionist for a room from which she could hear the sea.

*

Through the dark the lights crash on to the windscreen. Rosettes of blinding lights that split, multiply, divide and bloom again. The rain splinters the lights into a million petals that stay whole for a moment, then join into mean little channels and sneak down the glass. On another night like this Jonathan, driving in his fur-lined gloves, once said:

'Darling, I must get one of those cloth covers for the steering wheel. . . .' Why should I remember that?

The noise of the engine, the wet black margin of night round the brilliant windscreen. Among the fractured headlights swim the dying Edith's eyes, not quite burnt out. Was she frightened, or was she too tired to be frightened? Did the girl with the vermilion lips close the lids over her eyes when she died? Or was that the Matron's prerogative?

I turn on the wireless. Bud Flanagan is crooning 'Underneath the Arches', and I smile to myself because if I did not smile I would almost cry. But at the end of this journey Joshua would be there with aspirin for the pain in my head, and a drink with ice in it which he would get quickly with no fuss, like a good actor does on the stage.

I could have a bath and talk to him about his day, while he sat on the edge. Then he could take over the driving of the noisy car and we would go to a warm dark restaurant where candles and steaks and wine would crowd out Herne Bay and the ultra-black night. I accelerate. Doubly fast the lights crash on to the windscreen.

*

But Joshua was not in the flat. It was dark. The curtains were undrawn and the bed unmade. I threw myself on to the cold, rumpled bedclothes and shut my eyes. I had no energy to get up again.

It can only have been a few moments later, but it felt like several hours, that he came back. I could hear him in the next room, snapping on lights and flicking shut curtains. I didn't call and he came in.

'Are you asleep?'

'No.' I sat up. He put on the light.

'You look exhausted. Was it awful?'

'It was long.'

'I've had a terrible day, too.' He sat beside me on the bed and took off his glasses. 'In the cutting-room. Most of the good bits are on the floor.'

'I'm very hungry,' I said. 'Is there any food?'

'Not a thing. There's a coffee bar place where we could get an omelette downstairs. We'd better hurry, before it shuts.'

We drank neat vodka. Warmth began to ease out the empty tiredness and the room became as fluid as an underwater scene. In the lift Joshua held my hand. In return I leant against him, half for support.

The coffee bar was almost empty. We sat in a corner by the window at a Formica-topped table and I focused on the island of salt, pepper and tomato sauce in its middle. A waitress with a squint approached us.

'There's only omelettes left, you can have,' she said, with some triumph.

'We only want omelettes – they are the only thing in the world we want,' said Joshua, 'if you could give us the choice of everything, if you could set a banquet before us, all us would ask for is an omelette. Think of what you could tempt us with: whole sucking pigs turning on a spit – '

'Sucking what?' said the waitress, making a note on her pad.

'Sucking pigs. And wild boar and linnets' tongues, gulls' eggs and *boeuf en croute* and caviar; *fraises de bois* soaked in champagne and *tagliatelle verde*; and crumpets and waffles with maple syrup and steak tartare and *marrons glacés*. . .'

'That'll be omelettes for two, then,' said the waitress, and almost ran away. We laughed weakly and pushed the salt and pepper and tomato sauce away to hold hands again, and the grainy pattern of the Formica blurred like rain.

'Do you invite lots of girls back to your flat – to stay?' I asked.

'Hundreds of thousands,' said Joshua.

'Why have you asked me to stay? How long can I stay for?'

'I don't know. The thing about you – ' He shrugged. 'The thing with you, when you're not there I don't have to think about you very much. When you're there, it's so strong. I mean to-day, working, I didn't think about you at all. Not till I was coming home. Then I remembered, and it was something nice to look forward to.'

'Well, I thought about you,' I said.

'What did you think?'

'It was while I was waiting in the hotel Mrs Fox sent me to while she waited for her sister to die. I just wanted you to be there very much. I tried to telephone you, but you weren't there. It was a very dingy hotel with flowered calendars on the wall – '

'It's absolutely no use telling me,' he said, 'there's never any use in telling someone how you felt about them when they weren't there. Reported feelings don't carry. They become embarrassing when you try to recount them. The emphasis gets all wrong. Maybe I'm just biased – ' he smiled, 'but once I left someone at a station. – Stations are awful for making one feel: I must remember to tell her how I felt when she left. Anyhow, once the train was on its way I wrote her a long letter describing the gloom that came over me as she disappeared out of sight. I was only twenty and I posted it, I remember, at the first stop – Didcot. Of course, this girl completely misunderstood me. She wrote back and said she hadn't realised the extent of my feelings, and she presumed that if I felt like *that* about her, I wanted to marry her. Silly idiot. I didn't feel like that about her in general. I just felt like that about her when the train left. – That's what I mean.'

'There are whole areas about people you should never get to know about,' I said, 'however involved you are with them. Once I went out with a very sophisticated sort of man, something to do with films, who took me to the Caprice all the time and ordered Lobster Newburg for me without asking if I wanted it. He was very steely and rather frightening, and I would have done anything for him. Then one day he asked me, at the Caprice, if I knew of any good launderettes in the Cromwell Road. I said why, and he said because since he'd lost his housekeeper his dirty linen had been piling up and he didn't know what to do about it. The thought of this glossy, important man wandering about the Cromwell Road with his bag of dirty socks, hopelessly looking for a launderette, was completely disillusioning. So disappointing that I never went out with him again. He shouldn't have told me.'

'It's all the same sort of thing,' said Joshua. The waitress brought our omelettes. She put two white, frothy coffees down on the table as well.

'You didn't mention them in the banquet,' she said, her humour recovered, 'but I thought I'd better get them before the machine man goes home.' We laughed with her and ate hurriedly.

It was very late when we got back. We made the bed.

'It seems as if I've been here ten years, not twenty-four hours,' I said.

'You must forget to-day quickly. It can't have been much fun for you.'

'In a way, it's made it much better, getting back.'

When we went to bed, we curved into each other and slept at once.

Chapter Six

Joshua liked treacle and cream on his cereal for breakfast. He would pace round the room in his dressing-gown, holding the bowl, and stop to look out of the windows as he ate. In contrast to all the sweetness of the cereal, the other half of his breakfast was a large tin mug of sugarless black coffee. He would leave this on the low table and drink it when all the steam had gone and it was nearly cold.

It was a morning three or four weeks after Edith Smith's death. I was lying on the floor at breakfast time selecting stories from the papers to read to him. He was wandering round me, as usual, making no comment. It was October now, and the early sky, as if it had absorbed something from the grey shimmer of London below it, was a sombre blue. Joshua stopped at the window and looked down.

'The flower woman,' he exclaimed. 'She hasn't been by for a month.' He ran from the flat, still in his dressing-gown, no pyjamas beneath. I called after him but he didn't reply. I looked out of the window but couldn't see the flower woman he had seen.

He came back ten minutes later carrying a wooden box filled with pots of chrysanthemums. They were pink, gold, and deep wine red.

'Look! I almost bought her out.' He was ridiculously pleased. 'Do you like them? Do you like chrysanthemums? Where shall I put them? – Wait, stay there. Stay on the floor.' He knelt down, put the box on the floor, and began to take the pots of plants from it one by one. With them he made a barrier round me and the papers.

'Child,' I said.

'Don't you like them?'

'Of course I do.'

'Which colour best?'

'Gold.'

'So do I. Look, now you're in a fortress. I can't get you.'

'If I put my head on the floor you couldn't even see me unless you knelt up and peered over. They're so tall.'

'I could crush down the barrier.'

'Don't spoil the flowers – '

'To hell with the flowers – '. He parted several plants with the quick gesture of someone pulling back curtains and they scattered on the floor. They fell on their sides. Thin green stalks snapped, leaves bent, and crumbs of earth trickled from the cheap plastic pots.

'Joshua!' The papers crackled beneath us.

'Darling.' It was the first time he had ever said that. We lay in the middle of the ruined fortress of flowers. The plants that still stood were tall as trees, their petals bright balloons against the white walls of the room.

'Say that again,' I said.

'Darling, darling, darling. There you are.'

'Why haven't you ever said it before?'

'You always ask silly questions.'

'Joshua? – '

'Be quiet.' I was, for a moment.

'Joshua. You know what? I haven't thought about Jonathan, or being married, for about two weeks now. What must that mean?'

'That something has made you think about him now. What?'

'I don't know. I suppose just that we never used to have breakfast like this. He liked everything neatly laid on the dining-room table. Boneless kippers were his favourite food. Typical. He thought acts like boning fish were a waste of his time.'

Joshua pulled himself up on one elbow and took the cup of cold coffee from the low table.

'Did you ever make love after breakfast?'

'Not if he was already dressed. Sometimes he thought about it – I could tell the evening before, and he went about with a funny sort of smile so I knew that he was planning it all elaborately. He would come down to breakfast in his dressing-gown, and his pyjama tops undone so that I could see the St Christopher on his chest. The only thing was, he had shaved, so the uncalculated look was rather spoiled. When he got to about the toast and marmalade he would suggest that we went back to bed to *sleep* for an hour. He could never just say: let's go and make love. And if I hadn't realised about his plan, and had dressed, myself, he wouldn't say a thing – He could never bear to ask me to undress.'

Joshua lay back on the papers again.

'You know something nice?' he said quietly, shutting his eyes 'The film is nearly finished. And I thought when it was quite finished I might take you away somewhere for a few days.' He pulled my head on to his chest. His dressing-gown smelt of damp corn.

'Where would we go? France? No, I hate France. Please not there. Italy would be lovely. I could show you Florence or Rome. I know all those hills near Florence - I know farmhouses where you can just drop in and they fry you plates of bacon – Or we could try Spain, perhaps, or Corfu. Corfu's like Gloucestershire in the summer.'

'None of those places, baby,' he said.

'Where, then?'

'Norfolk.'

'Norfolk?'

'It's marvellous.'

'I don't know it.'

'You will. You'll like it.'

'But the weather?'

'It'll be rather dank, and quite cold in the evenings. I have a small boat up there. We'll take her out to the island and have picnic lunches. You could build a fire, even.' I could see him smiling to himself, his eyes still shut.

'A fire? Me? Won't it be too cold for outdoor cooking? How will we go? In the car?'

'My darling.' He sat up now and dragged me with him. 'You have an ad-type mind. I can see you imagining us in the red car, open, hair streaming in the wind . . . petrol people. The car is going to be repaired.'

I hit him and squealed. He flung me back on to the floor again.

'We're going by train,' he said, and the last of the flowers fell over.

We did go by train, a few days later. At the station Joshua did things quite differently from Jonathan. Jonathan always made a great show of organising the luggage, even if it was only two cases. He told the porter the time of the train two or three times. He told him which cases to put on which part of the luggage rack, then rubbed the coins noisily together before tipping the man with an air of great benevolence. Joshua's way was to carry all four cases himself and to discourage any helpful-looking porter with a scowl.

We found a carriage to ourselves.

'Are you glad we're going to Norfolk?' Joshua seemed distant, irritable.

'I wouldn't mind where we were going.' Witless answer, I thought. But he kissed me. The map on the wall of Southern England and the B.R.'s embroidered on the antimacassars spun about.

It was a clear, hard day. The fields we rattled through were mistless, the trees and hedges turning brown and gold. People on the platforms of small stations stamped their feet and rolled their hands about in their pockets. Joshua read the law reports in *The Times*. Jonathan's enthusiasm for train journeys was too devouring to allow him to read. Not one acre of the country we passed through could escape some boring observation.

'Darling, look at that spire – Norman, I should say.' 'The last time I passed through Cambridge Timothy was telling me about his electronics business . . .' 'Look! There's a '28 Sunbeam Talbot just like the one my father had . . . darling, do you ever listen to me?'

If by chance he was not sitting by the window the steward and the ticket collector would become his prey. As the steward approached the carriage Jonathan would tap a coin on the door and signal to him to stop.

'Let us know in plenty of time when the second lunch is ready, will you?' he would ask.

'That is my job, sir,' the steward would reply – He had been snubbed by many stewards on many trains, but it made no difference – Joshua was quite quiet all the way to Norfolk.

At the station an old taxi, whose seats were worn into deep shabby troughs, waited for us. The driver greeted Joshua with enthusiasm and reminded him of past holidays. The hotel was a rambling, pebble-dash building hidden from the main road by a high wall. A short gravel drive edged with trim grass led up to it. Chrysanthemums the colour of vintage marmalade were clumped in neat borders at each side of the heavy front door. Inside, the hall smelt of wet mackintoshes. The receptionist welcomed Joshua with no less pleasure than the taxi driver.

'I'll get Rita to show you to your room,' she said. She rang a small brass bell shaped like a labrador's head, and a young, plump girl wearing a short black skirt and a bad op-art shirt appeared. She had dark curly hair, slanting brown eyes and dimples even before she smiled.

'Hello, Mr Heron,' she dimpled. 'I heard you were coming so I persuaded them to put you in your usual room. I know you like it best.' She giggled, and glanced at me without interest.

'That was very thoughtful,' Joshua said. We followed Rita along husky passages whose floors, like the taxi seats, were worn into troughs, but shallower. Rita waggled her fat behind and trailed her pudgy fingers provocatively up the oak banister.

'There.' She opened the door and walked ahead of us. 'You'll find it just the same. Nothing about *the room* has changed.' She giggled again.

'Thank you,' said Joshua briefly, and for a moment held her glance.

'If there's anything you want, you know where to find me.' She closed the door behind her slowly.

The room was furnished very simply: two scrubbed pine chairs, a painted chest of drawers, a desk, two single beds which sank in the middle. Their covers were white damask, like unstarched table cloths. The air wasn't positively damp, but the carpets, the beds, even the walls gave the impression that if you touched them they would feel softer than you would expect.

I went to the window. A lawn sloped down to the creek. The tide was out. Small boats lay on their sides in the mud and a couple of seagulls rose and fell across the grey sky as if perched on an invisible wave.

'How many girls have you brought here?' I asked, crossly.

'Will you do something for me?' Joshua came up behind me, his voice patient. 'Will you, while we are here, stop imagining my past? Can't you stop being jealous of my past?'

'I'm not jealous.'

'What difference would it make if I had brought a hundred different girls to this very room? It wouldn't take away from how it will be here for you and me.'

'But that girl, Rita – '

'If you're silly enough to be upset by anything she says, I'm surprised. Come on, don't be silly.' He took my hand and dragged me from the window, smiling. 'Do you know what I like best about this place? It's the only hotel I know where they provide free sealing-wax. Look here.' I laughed, forgetting Rita.

We went to the desk. Two sticks of red sealing-wax and a small, half-gutted candle in a china holder lay on the blotter. Joshua sat on the chair at the desk and lit the candle.

'I used to play a game with sealing-wax when I was a child. I wonder if I can do it now?' He opened a pad of soggy writing-paper, cheaply stamped with the name of the hotel, and held a stick of wax over the flame. It softened, curved, and dripped into a large blob on the paper. A string of white smoke rose up to us, with the crisp mystical smell peculiar to hot sealing-wax. Quickly Joshua picked up a sharp pencil, also provided free, and wrote on the wax *I am Josh* . . . it hardened. Another letter was impossible.

'I used to be able to write my whole name,' he said. 'You try.' I sat on his knee and he made a new pool of wax for me. But I only managed as far as *I am Cl* . . . Then he wrote *We are* . . . in a third blob.

'I can't think what,' he said, watching the wax harden while he thought. I took the pencil from him and on yet another pool of wax wrote *We are us*.

'What silly things people do,' Joshua said. I slipped on to the floor and sat there with my head on his knee. A thin shadow of smoke still hung in the air, and the candle spluttered out. We stayed there, without speaking, till darkness filled the room. Then we had to stumble about, tripping over things, looking for the lights.

After dinner we went into the lounge. It was not conducive to a gay evening. In one corner a middle-aged woman vigorously attacked a piece of tapestry, as if she were mending a sail. In the other corner her husband's thick-set tweed legs and a beam of pipe smoke stuck out at different angles from behind a sporting paper. Joshua suggested we should go down to the quay.

The night was cold, almost frosty. A full moon lit our way down the narrow village street, and then down the cobbled way to the quay. No-one else was about. Joshua wore rubber-soled shoes and walked quite silently. My shoes made an irritating clatter.

Several large fishing boats were drawn up on to the quay: they sheltered round a huge Tarmaced barge. It was turned upside down, and looked like a prefabricated hut. In the water, the collection of small boats which had been cast on their sides in the mud had now regained their dignity. From time to time they twitched a little, when the water moved beneath them, then fell back into stillness.

Suddenly Joshua, who had been holding my arm, let go and ran away. I spun round to see what had happened.

I called him. No answer. I was faced by more empty boats, standing like high empty husks, and a confusion of thick black shadows. I looked up to the sky. For a moment the full moon balanced on a mast, a saucer on a juggler's stick. Then a black cloud straggled across its face, hiding all but the barest outlines of the place. I called again. This time there was a weird, high pitched wail for an answer:

'Here I a – m.' It was impossible to tell where the voice was coming from. I felt my way over to the upturned barge, stumbling through the smaller boats, bumping their sides.

'*Where?*'

'*Here.*' The voice was behind me now, not near the barge after all. I turned. The clouds cleared the moon again. The boats were empty. Then a figure leapt from the bottom of one of them, screaming with laughter, a ragged silhouette against the sky. It flopped back and the laughter stopped. I jumped with fright, knowing at once the stupidity of my fear. I put out a hand, groping for something to hold on to, and hit the hard belly of the barge. It was lumpy and damp. I shivered and tried to laugh.

'Please come out now. You gave me an awful fright. . . . Joshua?' No answer, and new clouds increased their speed towards the moon. Clumsily I ran to the boat he had jumped from. He was not hiding in the bottom. Nothing there but a long thin pool of water shining flatly as old glass.

'I didn't see you get out,' I called, and repeated myself

louder. 'Come on, let's go back. Don't let's play this game any longer. I'm cold. Please. . . .'

'*Please come out now.*' A high treble voice mocked mine. Once more it seemed to come from behind the barge. But the moon was re-blotted out, and the darkness more intense after the spell of brightness. All sense of direction left me. I clung to the boat I stood by, shivering with cold.

'You can go on playing your silly game by yourself. I'm going back . . .' I shouted, and didn't move. Long, slow moments passed. Then an ice-cold hand touched my cheek. I screamed. Joshua laughed.

'Don't you like playing hide-and-seek?' he asked, in his normal voice. I flung myself against him, angry and relieved.

'No, not in a place like this. Not in a place I don't know. And anyhow I can't see in the dark, and I hate boats out of water.'

'Did I really give you a fright? I'm sorry. It was just a game.' He was incredulous. He kissed my forehead and eyes.

'You do unsettling things.' For the third or fourth time, I had lost count, the moon reappeared. I could look up and see the reassuring hulk of Joshua's shoulders and jaw. Relief that the game was over was almost as unbearable as the former silly fear.

'You could have come down here on your own,' I heard myself saying, 'if you'd wanted to be alone.' Joshua laughed.

'That wouldn't have been any fun,' he said. 'The fun was running away from you.' He took my arm. 'Come on, laugh. I'm back, aren't I?' I laughed. 'I'll bet you anything you like,' he went on, 'I can guess what Jonathan's game is. – Golf.'

'Right,' I said.

'And what's more, if Jonathan changed from golf to hide-and-seek, he wouldn't be very good at it, because he's not a very sprightly man, is he?'

I laughed again, and in response Joshua speeded up his fantasy.

'He'd have a handicap, wouldn't he? – His running.' He broke away from me and ran a few paces ahead, the fat waddling run of a man clumsy on his feet. 'Like this?'

'Quite like that.' I was laughing hard now. 'Cruel, you are.' He wobbled back to me.

'And I have no doubt,' he said, 'that in the end you will go back to a man who runs like that, won't you?'

'Nonsense,' I said. Pausc. 'What makes you think that?'

He didn't answer. We were almost back at the hotel now. It was flushed by orange floodlights: tame, secure, warm.

In our room the coral bar of electric fire was no more than a faint reproach against the cold. Our single beds were intolerably narrow. We pulled all the blankets from one bed on to the other and arranged ourselves to spend an uncomfortable night.

For the time being, we spoke no more of Jonathan.

Chapter Seven

For several days it rained. We went for long walks in the rain, through wide cabbage fields. The huge cold cabbage leaves, some almost plum purple, clacked and clattered against our gum-boots. Joshua said he felt about cabbages like vegetarians feel about meat. He picked a large leaf and shook it, holding it like a bowl. A thousand balls of rain skidded about among the hillocky surface, looking for their holes, like the plastic balls in those children's games in crackers. He could not eat cabbages, Joshua said.

We walked over the sodden marshes smoked up with mist and slimy underfoot. Joshua was mellow, benign, almost expansive. He made me laugh. He held a piece of tarpaulin from a haystack over my head while I wiped his steamed-up glasses on my shirt. We went to the graveyard of a Norman church where he climbed the slippery black trunk of an old yew tree. When he reached the top he battered the coarse branches, so that for a moment part of the tree was shaken out of its lethargy and a few rain drops leaked through its great hood on to the soft, dry earth beneath.

Then at last there was a clear morning. The sky, drained of its cloud and rain, was pale and weak. We went to the beach. There, the high, wind-breaking dunes ran into the sand, and the sand ran into the sea indeterminately as the meeting of water colours. It was still cold, and Joshua began to run. I kept up with him for a while, then he began to outpace me. The wet sand made the going heavy. I slowed down, walked. The distance between us quickly increased. Soon he was no more than a small moving figure.

I turned my back to the sea and walked towards the dunes. Sudden desolation cut through me, like wire through cheese. They were scrawny dunes here, with bald patches of grey white sand between clumps of tough, skinny grass. Twenty years ago, as a melancholy child, a group of children cast me out from their ball game in dunes like these. I had run from them, tears cutting down my cheeks, into the fir woods behind the dunes. I had stamped on the earth and flung myself on the ground, stupidly enraged. Then I found primroses. It began to rain, and I picked them. A long time later I went back to the dunes. The children had gone and the tide was out. I found half a biscuit in my pocket and ate it, and lay on the sand uncaring about time, looking at the flat wet landscape. And then the melancholy rolled away and I was left ashamed.

I looked at the sea now. It didn't work like that any more.

'Joshua!' I shouted out loud. The voice lay flat on the wind, somebody else's voice.

Lumps of drying sand flaked off my boots. I could taste salt on my lips. Where was he? Why clouds again?

It hadn't been like this with Richard Storm. We had been fond of each other. Fond of each other like elderly relations who are accustomed to one another's ways. I was in awe of his age, obedient to him. When he had written to say he was staying in Barcelona with Matilda I had been surprised, but not hurt. He wasn't breaking up a great life between us.

It hadn't been like that with Jonathan. His consistent attention, often claustrophobic, was a contrast to desertion. He was always there, a habit, secure, harmless. The November afternoon we married in Caxton Hall was no more elating than many other afternoons we had spent together. We went to the Savoy for dinner and he insisted I ate *à la carte*, although I wanted the *plat du jour*. Within three days of living with him it was obvious he had preconceived ideas about what should be done on what occasions. The *plat du jour* on the honeymoon night was only the start. But marriage with him was just as I imagined it would be, for two years. It was only lately that its emptiness and its irritations, impossible to imagine, had become apparent and then intolerable.

And now Joshua. Why had he run away again? Why did he always tease? I lay down, my face against the chill sand, and the wind scattered my hair over my eyes so that it tickled. Then a hand pulled it away with a tug. I rolled over. Joshua was squatting.

'I've been looking for you everywhere,' he said. 'There weren't any ice creams.' I sat up.

'I didn't want an ice cream. I didn't ask for one. Why did you go? I couldn't keep up.'

'You might have liked one if I'd got one. But they told me the man packed up his stall last week. The season's over.' He lay beside me. 'I must have run a mile.' He smiled, he was pleased. 'I haven't had any exercise like that for ages. I feel marvellous.'

'You're lucky.'

'Why, don't you? What's the matter?'

'You keep running away.'

'Not very seriously. And anyhow I haven't run away for four days – not since the first evening.'

'I don't know what's the matter, really. I'm being inarticulate.'

'You funny, pretty thing. You look nice in the wind.' He brushed sand off my shoulders and pulled me down to join him. 'Nobody ever comes here at this time of year. We'd never be caught.'

'Are you sure?'

'Absolutely sure.'

The tough spiky grass bent all round us and the sand, which was dry in the dunes, swept about us.

*

It was at lunch that Joshua had his idea.

'Why don't we ask Mrs Fox to join us? She must be feeling low.' I had almost forgotten Mrs Fox. Lunch was Irish stew and apple crumble. Rita poured Joshua a glass of lager without asking if he wanted it.

'I don't think she'd want to come. There's not enough noise in Norfolk.'

'I think she'd like it. We could entertain her.'

'We're quite happy entertaining ourselves, aren't we?' I was drinking cider and my head was fuzzy. Rita was polishing spoons very slowly at the sideboard, putting them down silently so that she could hear what we were saying.

'Why don't you want her to come?'

'I'm happy as we are.'

'I thought you weren't.'

'I am.'

'Oh.' I fiddled with the salt, making little mounds with the spoon, then squashing them flat again. 'I'd like to ask her just for a few days,' Joshua said. 'Think how pleased she'd be.' I sighed.

'Mrs Fox's great message is that she never wants to be a nuisance to anybody. You can ask her, but I don't think she'll come. Do what you like, though. But I think it's silly, asking a dotty old woman like her to Norfolk in the autumn. Why don't you ask your mother?' I heard the sarcasm in my voice.

'My mother died when I was seventeen,' said Joshua, 'and I never did anything for her.' Rita started on a pile of knives.

'Oh, I see. You think that making benevolent gestures towards one old woman will compensate for doing nothing for another.'

'I hadn't thought of that. But, no, I don't think that. I'm not a do-gooder, and that's their line of thinking. Charity suddenly comes upon them like religious mania, and they cram in a few years of the gooseberry jam stuff to make up for all the years the idea hadn't occurred to them. – No, the thing is, about Mrs Fox, I like her. She doesn't make me feel guilty if I don't do anything about her. And she doesn't make me feel heroic if I do. You can't say anything more than that about any old person, can you?' I nodded. 'Can I ask her, then?' I said yes.

'Do you mind if I clear?' Rita was bored. We went to the empty, tea-smelling lounge.

'Have you ever thought about the worst thing between the young and the old?' Joshua went on. 'I don't mean all the obvious things, like lack of communication, lack of imagination to understand each other's era. I mean the way they fundamentally drain each other. A daughter looks after her old mother, say, or grandparent. It takes time and energy. The old grandparent feels the uncomfortable disadvantage of having to be looked after. And they are both so confused with duties and responsibilities, that any reserves of spontaneity between them are dried up. Then the motive behind any idea or action between the generations is suspect, for all that the people involved pretend that it isn't. It's so exhausting – it makes so many martyrs. In China, there's a much better system. In the compounds there, it's the natural duty of the young to look after and entertain the old. The responsibility doesn't have a ruinous effect, any more than here the responsibility of a mother towards her child is damaging.'

'But you're being too objective,' I said. 'The young don't look after the old purely out of duty. Love comes into it. A daughter, say, who is fond of her old parents or grand-parents, wants to help them. She isn't wholly a martyr.'

'She may not be to begin with. But in cases where love and responsibility are equally balanced, and responsibility means the daily grind of ministering to someone physically, then love is rarely the element that tips the scales.'

'What would you do in that sort of case?' I asked.

'I don't know exactly, as my parents died before the question arose. But I think that I'd have been dutiful to them if I had liked them, and done nothing for them if we'd never got on. I don't believe in loyalty between relations if they don't like each other. To me, that's one of the worst forms of domestic hypocrisy. A great breeding ground for martyrdom. I think the whole pattern of tribal feeling, of families sticking to each other just because they are related, is misconceived. Of course, if they *like* each other as well as being related, that's a different matter. But how many of them do? Do you?'

I thought of my mother, padded in maroon velvet, crocodile shoes and bag to match; her manic Conservatism, her crazy love of pets and sunshine cruises. My father: wispy, blurred, his conscience pulling him from Lords cricket matches back to his fat salaried job in industry; the signed copy of *The Just So Stories* by his bed. I didn't love them, I didn't like them, I didn't see them.

'No,' I said. 'But Jonathan is a perfect example, though, of someone who is embarrassed by his parents because they aren't as pseudo intellectual as he is, and at the same time inextricably bound to them by duty. I don't think he loves them, or has ever thought of loving them. They are just an area in his life that has to be visited. They have to be cared for, like his teeth. – You know how the newspapers always give people good marks for visiting their parents? When they write about a poor undergraduate who has become famous on television, say, they never stop repeating . . . *and he goes to see his parents in Beccles every weekend*. . . . When Jonathan reads one of those sort of reports he's almost overcome with smug pleasure at the thought of doing the same thing himself. And down we go to Somerset again for another look round Major Lyall's pig farm, and Jonathan lectures us all about Nabakov. None of us can argue with him, of course, so he has a clear field. But that's irrelevant.'

'That's the sort of pointless mesh hundreds of thousands of people have got themselves into and endure,' Joshua said.

He went to telegram Mrs Fox.

She arrived the next afternoon. We fetched her from the station in the taxi with the trough seats. She did not appear surprised to have been asked, but she conveyed her pleasure by delighting in everything. A Sailor's Day flag in her usual black hat was her only concession to her new environment.

We had tea in the lounge and she sat opposite us and acted as host, pouring the tea and passing us sandwiches. Any sadness about her sister was concealed. She looked at us with merriment.

'Henry and I nearly went away like you two, once,' she said, 'only in the end we didn't. We just had to imagine it. In those days, our respective families would have been very shocked. But it wasn't the shock that stopped us. It was the lack of opportunity. Never a chance we had! Edith and my mother guarded over me – they would hardly leave me to a private thought, let alone a weekend by the sea with Henry. As for him, he was always so busy, and all his life he put his duty – his patients – before me. So in the end, of course, when we had given up ever hoping for an opportunity, there was only one thing left to do, and we married.'

'How does that work as a reason?' asked Joshua.

'It worked very well in our case. Of course, it would be a very old-fashioned reason to get married to-day, wouldn't it? It seems to me not many modern couples suffer from lack of opportunity!' She looked round curiously to the other people having tea – middle-aged, outdoor people, in wind-smoothed tweeds. People who seemed too big for the small flowered arm-chairs.

'How do they take it – you?' she asked. 'Do they disapprove?'

'I don't think they know, or if they do, I don't think they care,' said Joshua. Then he put his hand on my knee, and kissed me lightly on the cheek. It was one of the few gestures of affection in public he ever made to me.

'Edith, now, she had quite an experience,' went on Mrs Fox. 'In 1919 a solicitor asked her to go to York with him for the weekend. She said no, but she didn't make herself firm enough. – She never was much of a one with words. Anyhow they went, by train, all the way to York. On the way there the solicitor schooled her to tell the hotel receptionist that her name was Edith Freeman, *Mrs* Edith Freeman, and not Miss Edith Smith. Edith promised. But she was a most honest character, and when the time came she couldn't go through with it. She signed Edith Smith in the book and the solicitor gave her such a dig in the ribs that she had a bruise for weeks after. He was mad with rage, and she cried and said she wanted to go home. So he put her on the next train back and he never saw her again. After that, Edith said she'd rather stay a virgin. And she did, till the day she died.' Mrs Fox laughed at her own story.

'I was never very good on the classics,' she continued, 'music was more my line, but there is one author I'm well acquainted with, and that's Jane Austen. Henry loved her. He would read her to me almost every day, every book, time and again. In the end I knew great chunks by heart. And do you know what Jane Austen said about – you?' She waved towards us with a slight movement of her hand, and straightened herself in her chair like a child about to recite a poem. 'She said: "While the imaginations of other people will carry them away to form wrong judgements of our conduct, and to decide on it by slight appearances, one's happiness must in some measure be always at the mercy of chance." '

Three or four of the big tweedy people glanced towards Mrs Fox with some amazement, then returned their eyes to their tea. But Mrs Fox was oblivious to them. 'I have never forgotten that. Why, if Henry had read me that particular bit *before* we were married, I really believe I should have insisted on an opportunity: it would have been justified for me. Oh well . . . perhaps it turned out for the best. But I wouldn't like it,' she bent close to us, 'if your happiness was at the mercy of *these* people.'

'Really, they don't bother us, we don't bother them,' Joshua told her, quietly.

After Mrs Fox's arrival, our lives in Norfolk changed. Joshua was protective towards her, and extended the protection to me. He was more approachable than I had ever known him before. He relaxed. He was mellow, and happy. I felt the same.

Mrs Fox was a perfect third party. Both of us were aware of an increasing affection for her, which we indulged in but never mentioned. It tied us, in a peculiar way, more deeply than living alone together had succeeded in doing.

The days were almost uneventful. We walked, we sailed coldly in Joshua's small boat, we ate large amounts of filling English food. In the evenings Joshua and Mrs Fox played chess or backgammon while I read a book. Mrs Fox wrote innumerable coloured postcards, very slowly, to her friends and her enemies. Really, she explained, it was sitting at the large desk in the lounge that appealed to her: the free writing-paper, and new blotting paper, the pen chained to the ink stand. Every morning she wrote there for an hour or so, newly delighted.

One evening she insisted that we took her to the local pub. She drank three pink gins and ate half a pound of Cashew nuts.

'They're free, aren't they? Henry always said it was immoral to take advantage of free food in pubs and writing-paper in hotels, but I never could agree with him.'

'When I was travelling round the States on very little money,' said Joshua, 'I once lived for a whole week on the free Saltines, ketchup, chutney and water that you get in drug stores. If I hadn't taken advantage, I'd have almost starved.' This cheered Mrs Fox. She began on the Onion Flavoured Crisps.

Joshua and I drank three or four whiskies. Joshua talked to the local squire about his days in the Air Force. We all became warmly drunk, expansive.

'Look here,' said the squire, towards closing time, 'let's not pack in the party now. There's a fair down the road with only a few nights till it closes for the winter. It may not be Battersea, you know, but why don't we see what's cooking down there?'

Mrs Fox gave a high pitched giggle of pleasure and slipped off her high stool.

'A *fair*? Squire, there's nothing in the world I would like more.' The squire, with somewhat unsteady gallantry, took her arm and led us out to his shooting brake.

It was a scraggy little fair, a chipped-paint fair with only half its coloured bulbs working. Music from the merry-go-round screeched into the cold air and bulbs of steam rose from newly made toffee apples. In between the stalls, the earth was crusts of semi-hard mud; the grass worn away. Few people were about. A few half-hearted couples stood with hands in pockets, chins in scarves, looking. Not all the quick-worded cajoling and shouted promises of prizes could persuade them to roll a ball or shoot a tin tiger.

Mrs Fox gave life to the fair. She was what the disheartened stall holders had been waiting for all evening. She pranced from one to another, accurate in her aim, lucky in her guessing, collecting handfuls of small prizes which she stuffed into the squire's pockets. Finally she persuaded him to escort her to the merry-go-round. There she mounted a billowing wooden horse, he took one beside her, the scratchy gramophone blasted pop music, and they galloped away.

Joshua and I went on the swings. They were large, shabby boats with curly manes of wood, bow and stern, their paint pale and cracked. They weren't very high off the ground, but by some trick of light, we balanced midway between the curve of stars in the sky and the lumpy threads of fairground lights. Here, the music was softer. We hummed, and could hear ourselves humming. Joshua, standing looking down at me, worked the swings violently.

'You're beautiful,' he said, suddenly, and I began to laugh. 'No, you're not really. But you look it in this light.' He sat beside me. The swing rocked almost to a standstill by itself, and we laughed and laughed for no particular reason.

We climbed down. The ground was unsteady. I clung to Joshua.

'What's happened to us?'

'We're rather drunk, my beautiful,' he said.

'But I didn't feel like this before we went on the swings.'

'Nor did I. It was the rush of air.' He turned to me, three faces. 'Think,' he said slowly, 'of Jonathan typing in his Roman attic.' The thought shook him with more laughter.

'Sick joke,' I said, and laughed too.

Then suddenly we were quite sober. The lights, the stalls, the red-faced men and the stacks of cheap prizes no longer swung crazily about. They just trembled slightly, like pacified leaves after a storm. But still we clung to one another in a dazed way, unspeaking.

Mrs Fox and the squire came round a corner arm in arm.

'That was the best time I have had in years,' said Mrs Fox, her hat askew, her voice familiarly high. 'We rode for twenty five minutes without stopping, and I could have gone on, but the squire couldn't.'

'I had to rescue you from falling off your horse from dizziness,' the squire confessed.

They argued happily. At midnight the squire drove us back to the hotel. He was in no condition to make the sharp turn into the drive.

The flood lighting had been turned off and we made our way up the gravel drive by the murky light of a half moon. Now it was all over, Mrs Fox seemed a little deflated.

'When's your birthday?' she asked Joshua.

'Two weeks to-day,' he told her, after a pause to work it out. 'Why?'

'Then I can give you a party,' she said. 'That will be nice, something to look forward to. It's lucky it's so soon. A lucky chance. I always like to have something to look forward to.' She straightened her back and quickened her pace.

*

We were wakeful. We talked and half-slept for a few hours. At four, Joshua got out of bed.

'I'm going for a walk,' he said. 'Coming?'

Automatically, I asked if I should wake Mrs Fox. She had been everywhere with us since her arrival.

'No, stupid. You're an idiot, sometimes.' He was irritable, unapproachable again, his mood of a few hours ago quite dead.

'Where I'm stupid, I suppose,' I said, 'is ever expecting you to be consistent. You change more quickly than anybody I've ever met. You never remember what you say, or how you've felt. Or if you do, it never makes any difference to you a few hours later.' I was pulling on thick stockings, boots, a duffle coat, by the frail grey light in the window. 'You can't bear the idea of surrendering yourself completely. You get halfway there, and you enjoy it, I know you do. And then you retract.'

'Quite right. But I'm not going to change.'

'It makes you difficult to be with, sometimes.'

He did up my scarf, frowning.

'Shut up,' he said.

We took the narrow wet lane to the marshes. It was very cold. Clumps of mist moved about us. On the horizon, above the thin line of sea, flaming streaks curled back into the sky like edges of burning paper, leaving an opalescent sheen beneath.

Joshua walked very fast so that I had to jog to keep up with him. I complained of a stitch.

'Grumpy,' he said, turning round but not slowing down, 'on such a morning.'

Perversely, he stopped a few yards later and waited for me to catch up with him. He indicated the sky, the view, with a gesture of mock pleasure, as if to kill any intent I may have had to take the beauty seriously. Then his hand swooped to rest on my shoulder.

'They stood there, looking at each other,' he began, in a voice that trembled with mock seriousness, 'there was nothing to say. It was bigger than both of them.'

'Stop sending me up.' I laughed. He smiled.

'You look so hopeful, sometimes,' he said. 'It's enough to put fear into any man's heart.'

'Hopeful? Me? What of?'

In answer he cupped my face in his cold hands, observed it seriously, then spoke once more in his spoof voice.

'Mrs Lyall – you know something about yourself? At this time of day, you have the most extraordinarily funny face.'

The mists were rising. He took my arm, and with exaggerated slowness we began to walk back for breakfast.

Chapter Eight

'Clare! Can I come round?' David Roberts, at eight-thirty in the morning. He'd never rung Joshua's flat before.

'Not really. We're hardly up. What's the matter?' Long pause.

'I'm back from Rome.' Joshua was working a small circle of the carpet into fluff with his big toe. 'I got back last night.'

'Was it nice?' I played for time till he was ready to break his news.

'Perfect weather. I saw Jonathan several times. We did a bit of drinking together.' There was something melancholy about his voice.

'How was he?'

'Your coffee's getting cold,' Joshua interrupted.

'Hang on,' I said to David. I put my hand over the speaker.

'Get rid of him,' Joshua said.

'Fine,' said David. 'Very nicely set up indeed.' He paused again. Then: 'Well, it's a pity I can't come round. Perhaps later on.'

'What *is* the matter?'

'Nothing much, really. It's just that I was wrong about Rosie Maclaine.'

'How?'

'Well, Jonathan was right about her, really. He said she was more sexy than trustworthy.'

'What's she done?'

'Stayed in Italy.'

'In Rome?'

'She wouldn't say where. I don't think so.'

Joshua got up off the floor and slammed out of the door. Irritable.

'I'm sorry,' I said to David.

'What was that noise? Don't say *you're* rowing already?'

'Of course not.'

'Well, that's all I had to tell you. I'll call you some time.'

I put down the telephone and looked round the untidy room. There was ash on the carpet, coffee stains on the cushions, books and magazines overlapping everywhere. Alison, who came twice a week, said we didn't give her a chance. We didn't care. Joshua was used to it, didn't notice it. I liked it after the prim tidiness of the mews house.

It was cold, in my dressing-gown. Dank November air. I shut the window and Joshua came back into the room. Dressed, now.

'What does that boring man mean by ringing up at this hour?'

'It's not that early. Rosie Maclaine has apparently left him.'

'What girl in her right mind wouldn't leave him? You needn't have prolonged the conversation.'

'You're hung over,' I said. We'd drunk two bottles of good wine the night before.

'Not at all. I just wanted to get at my own telephone.' He slumped dramatically on to the sofa and dialled a number.

His film was ready for distribution and he was out of work. It didn't suit him. He hated the forced idleness of the days, the fact that there was nowhere he had to be by ten o'clock. A company was negotiating tentatively about a documentary in Mexico, but the negotiations required no more than a couple of telephone calls a week. So Joshua fretted, chain-smoked, read quantities of magazines but never a book. The only time he was at peace was when he carved. In the last week he had made a set of wooden chessmen.

The number he dialled didn't answer. He banged back the receiver, exasperated.

'It's a loathsome day,' he said. Last night, only slightly drunk, we had danced together after dinner, and had fallen back on to the sofa where he sat now, laughing at nothing in particular.

'Why?' He didn't answer. I sat beside him and put my hand on his thigh.

'Leave me alone,' he said. I didn't move my hand so he picked it up, like an impatient housewife who has found some object in the wrong place, and thrust it back at me 'I said leave me alone.'

'What's the matter?' I felt myself irritating him.

'Nothing. Nothing's the matter. I must go.' He got up. I stood too.

'Where?'

'To see people. I must hurry things.' He looked at me distractedly, and rubbed his fist down my nose. 'Sorry. I'm hopeless when I'm not working.' He left quickly, banging the front door behind him. After he'd gone I remembered that to-day was the day of Mrs Fox's party for him. But as I didn't know where he would be, there was no way of reminding him.

*

I was last to arrive at Mrs Fox's party. She met me

eagerly at the door, expecting Joshua to be with me.

'I was just telling the others,' she said, when she saw that he wasn't, 'that I couldn't for the life of me remember how old he was.'

The others sat in a semi-circle of peculiarly assorted chairs. They looked as if they'd been sitting for some time, waiting for something to happen.

I was introduced. First, Cedric Plummer. Huge, kind face, and R.S.P.C.A. badge pinned to his plum satin-type tie. His wife, Nancy, had obviously had her hair in rollers all the morning. It rippled all over her head in curls still dented by kirby-grips.

'We've come up from Epsom,' she said. Beside her sat an enormous old woman, Mrs Plummer senior, who was vigorously enjoying the awesome introductions. She stood up, shook my hand with amazing ferocity, said: 'Don't mind me, dear,' and sat down again with the supreme confidence of an experienced party-goer. In contrast, Mrs Bell, from Highgate, cowered at the introduction, sniffling well back into the arms of her chair.

'Handkerchief,' Mrs Fox whispered to me, smiling. I remembered her story about her sister's friend whose flat smelt. Mrs Bell it was, I suppose.

The mixing of the generations at the party was provided by Philip Cox and his girl-friend Liz. Philip was the talented young baker who had made and elaborately iced the pink and white birthday cake that stood among crêpe paper flowers on the centre table. Mrs Fox was proud of Philip. He, like Mrs Plummer senior, seemed to be at ease with party situations.

'Seeing as I've rustled up that little cake for your old man,' he said, 'I think the least you should do is come and tell me whether I was right to take a risk on marzipan.'

He had beautifully greased hair whipped into waves neat and matching as the iced scallops on the cake. His girl-friend, Liz, watched him continually with harshly made-up eyes, her mouth smiling at everything he said.

The room itself was transformed into a premature Christmas room. Scarlet balloons hung from the empty canary cage, paper chains looped round the brass bed-head, and countless well preserved Alexandra Rose Day roses and Poppy Day poppies were Sellotaped to the walls, the curtains, and the table cloth. There were plates of fatly stuffed bridge-rolls, and intricate things that smacked of Philip's art: pastry tarts spiralling with cream, choco-late eclairs studded with silver balls and a wild choice of brightly iced buns. Two rows of neat cups painted with dragons stood waiting for tea. Orange paper napkins matched the orange of the dragons' tongues. It was ten to five by the clock on the mantelpiece.

I joined the semi-circle, sitting between Mrs Plummer senior and Mrs Bell.

'It's a pity more people don't do birthdays so well any more these days,' said Mrs Plummer, looking hungrily at the cakes. 'When I was young, birthdays were real birth-days.' Opposite us, Philip and Liz twirled little fingers. She nodded towards them. 'These days, birthdays don't mean anything to people like those. There's no respect left for sentiment in the world.'

'But Philip made that magnificent cake,' I said. He heard, and winked at me. Liz scowled.

'Ah, yes, but that's his profession,' said Mrs Plummer. 'Quite different.' Her son leant forward and smiled peacefully.

'Mother has her own views, don't you, Mother?' he said.

'I'll say,' said Nancy.

'Like there was the little matter of Mrs Fox's canary, wasn't there?' went on Cedric.

'*Ced*, don't get on to that again,' said Nancy.

'There was,' said Mrs Plummer senior, 'indeed.'

Cedric pulled himself up to his full sitting height, fingered his R.S.P.C.A. badge, and lowered his mouth.

'I won't go into all that again,' he said. 'Not here. It's not the time or the place. But I would just like to say this. If a canary owner wants to let his, or for that matter her, canary go – then what I say is: he or she should do what he or she feels. Now in the case of our friend Mrs Fox, here, she felt that her particular canary wasn't suited to cage life. She observed that it was pining. So what did she do? Quite simple. Let it out. Gave it its head. Gave it its chance for freedom.'

'Wicked,' snapped his mother. 'Sheer murder, letting it out to be pecked to death by the wild birds of London.'

'Wicked,' agreed Mrs Bell, suddenly lively.

'*Mother*,' snapped Nancy, 'what did you promise us about keeping your views to yourself at a party?'

Mrs Plummer slumped at her daughter-in-law's tone, suddenly deflated.

'And my son an inspector of a wonderful society,' she sighed, almost to herself. 'You wouldn't believe it.' She nudged me to come closer to her. 'The thing is,' she whispered, stretching her hand across her huge stomach, 'once you've had your operation, there's nothing to fall back on.'

Liz, bored, somehow managed to hear the confidence and laughed nastily. She glanced at the clock. Ten past five.

'Your old man's certainly waiting to make his entrance,' she said.

Mrs Fox came in from the kitchen, her hands clenched at her sides as they had been the day Edith died. She caused silence. Everybody looked at her, waiting for some decision.

'I've just put the kettle on,' she said. 'I expect Joshua will be here by the time it's ready. He's probably been held up at work.' She looked to me for confirmation.

'I expect so.' I sounded unconvincing.

'I could do with a cup of tea,' said Liz. 'I'm parched.' She managed to make everything she said sound accusing.

'Yes, that would be very nice,' agreed Mrs Plummer senior, trying again.

'Lovely,' said Mrs Bell.

'Just what we all wanted you to say, Mrs Fox.' Cedric rubbed his hands together, natural master of ceremonies.

Mrs Fox went away. I went with her. In the tiny kitchen her hands trembled on the dragon teapot, milk jug and sugar bowl.

'I expect he's been held up,' she said again.

'I'm very sorry. He's always vague about time.'

'Never mind, we'll start without him and just leave cutting the cake till he comes.'

We went back to the room with the tea. The silence of the waiting people oppressed Mrs Fox immediately. She suggested music, and put on the gramophone. A Strauss waltz blared through the room. Philip and Liz made faces. But protected by the music, there was no need for Mrs Fox to make any announcement. She gestured to everyone to come and help themselves. With the exception of Cedric, who was determined to show his enjoyment in spite of the music, they lumbered to the table uncooperatively. They stacked their small dragon plates high with food and returned to the chairs they had come from. Mrs Fox and I poured the tea.

'Lazy lot,' she whispered. 'You can never rely on people to have a sense of occasion.'

Mrs Fox, eating and drinking nothing herself, looked after her guests with great thought. She stirred Mrs Bell's tea because her hand shook too much to do it herself. She saved the last pink iced bun for Nancy because Nancy was fond of pink. She found a packet of cigarettes for Liz, a chain-smoker, who had none. The music gave them the excuse for no conversation and they ate very quickly. Soon all the food was finished and a second pot of tea made. Then the record came to an end.

'Well,' said Cedric, in charge again now that he could be heard, 'that only leaves the cake.'

Twenty to six on the clock. Still no Joshua. No sound of steps on the stairs.

'So it does.' Mrs Fox feigned some sort of amazement and gave a small laugh. She looked at her audience while they waited for her again to make a decision. 'Perhaps we should have just one more record . . .' Mrs Plummer senior put her huge hands on her huge parted knees.

'Mrs Fox, I don't want to speak out of turn, but speaking for myself I should say that our guest of honour isn't going to honour us after all and we should cut the cake.'

Liz applauded ostentatiously and laughed her nasty laugh. The others joined in the laughter without much reluctance, even Cedric.

'A splendid idea,' he said. 'How about me doing the cutting? Seeing as I'm the man nearest to the age of the absent guest of honour.'

But Mrs Fox was terse with indignation.

'Certainly not,' she snapped. 'If Joshua's not here, the poor man, because of hard work, then Clare shall cut the cake.'

She thrust a long knife at me. The handle was ivory, carved with a lion's head.

'The sort of thing Henry's patients left him in their wills,' she whispered.

I tapped at the icing with the long pointed blade. Suddenly, it was a familiar sensation. With a long pointed blade I had tapped at rock-hard white icing on a cake high with monstrous tiers. Richard Storm's hand, cold and bony, had been on top of mine, guiding. As the knife weighed down, splitting first the icing then slicing faster down through the marzipan and cheap, eggless substance packed with currants, tidy velvet people with feather hats cheered and murmured, and naval men grunted. A new batch of tears slid down my mother's mauve cheeks. I felt my nose prick with sweat, and I felt the burn of indigestion from two glasses of cut-price champagne – my father had always believed in the economics of bulk buying, even for his daughter's wedding.

'Ah!' Richard was saying over and over again, through my veil. 'Ah! What now? What now?' I suggested that we should get away quickly. But he said no, he was enjoying the party: it wasn't every day a man got married.

Hours later, we left, through squawking crowds who threw paper petals in our faces. In the taxi that drove us to the station Richard's hand crept over the seat towards my red tweed thigh.

'We're married now, you know,' I said, trying to smile, 'there's no need to be so cautious.' My voice was high and thin and far away. I covered my hand with his and immediately his fingers wriggled free and scrabbled for protection somewhere up my cuff.

'Slowly does it, my love,' he said, and coughed.

I looked at his translucent face, a map of blue broken veins on the high cheeks, the eyes dim and weak, the handsome pointed nose, the pale lips always lined with an inner rim of saliva – the face of a complete stranger. I heard myself give a great sob. His fingers climbed down my cuff again and clutched my wristwatch instead.

'What's the matter?'

'I don't know. I expect I'm tired. It's been a long day, hasn't it?' He frowned and I sobbed again. 'And you've only kissed me twice since we've been engaged.' That was nothing to do with the matter, but I couldn't think of anything else.

'Is *that* what's worrying you, little one? But we've all the time in the world. We'll make up for it, now. All you have to do is love, honour and obey me in bed, and it'll be quite easy, you'll see.' He laughed at his own joke and gave me a stiff white handkerchief for my eyes.

In the two raining weeks in a Dorset cottage that was our honeymoon, we did make up for my nineteen years of virginity. Every night, among sheets that remained damp even when they were warm, in the dark. Crudely, inadequately. There was no pleasure. It hurt. His wet mouth kissed my temples, never my mouth. He rubbed his long cold feet up and down my legs to warm them. He rocked with horrible noises, holding my ears as if they were handles. Sometimes, I sang to myself till he had finished. Sometimes I tried to remember all the people who had been at the wedding, or all the books I had read that year. When it was over, he snapped the light on again, sat up, and took a thin piece of string from the bedside table.

Then he would tie knots until he felt sleepy – minute reef knots, Granny knots, sheetbend knots. He could tie smaller, neater knots faster than anyone he knew, he said. He had learnt the art as a boy, and never tired of it.

*

I cut easily through the pink and white icing and Mrs Fox took over, chopping the cake into hunks that would keep even her guests going for some time. She put on another record. The eaters couldn't complain because their mouths were so stuffed with cake, which they scooped up with spoons.

*

My second wedding cake was eaten with spoons, too. At one hack with the knife the fragile chocolate icing parted and the innards gushed out.

'It's practically neat rum,' Jonathan had roared. He was rather drunk and pink. He had been drinking since before lunch and now it was six o'clock. Everybody laughed at everything he said. Everybody was very happy. He held my hand all the time, kneading the flesh over my knuckles with hot fingers, and led me round the room introducing me to all his neat friends, most of whom I didn't know. They all said how happy they knew we'd be. It always worked better the second time round, they said. When we got to the door I wrenched myself free of Jonathan and ran to the hotel lavatory. I shut myself in and leant up against the cool pink tiles. A marvellous smell of disinfectant. Then I was very sick – more of my father's even further-cut champagne.

Cold and dizzy, I walked back to the lobby. I looked about, unable to remember the way to the private room of the wedding reception. So I went to the Cocktail Bar and sat on the only free stool at the bar. I asked the barman for a peppermint. My mouth tasted sour.

'Peppermint what, madam?' He was quite friendly.

'Something strong to suck.'

'You're joking, madam. There aren't any slot machines in a place like this. What about a *creme de menthe frappé*?' I agreed. 'Not feeling well? You look a bit shaken.' I agreed again. He pressed crushed ice down into the glass with a spoon. 'There's a hell of a wedding party going on down the corridor,' he chatted on. 'They're drinking dreadful stuff, I hear. Poison anyone.' He looked at me carefully. 'You're not one of them, are you?'

'I'm the bride,' I said.

'No, no,' he said. 'You're joking again, of course. You wouldn't look like that if you were the bride.'

When I got back to the reception, half an hour later, Jonathan was in a state of great agitation. He thought I'd gone already. He thought I'd left him. More jokes were made, and he recovered. That night we ate *sole bonne femme* at a severely white tableclothed table and tried to think of things to say about the Thames looking so glamorous with all the lights. Then with the coffee Jonathan appealed to me never to leave his side again.

'In fact,' he said, digging a hole in a cigar I had hoped he wouldn't smoke, 'I'll see to it you never leave me again. Not so long as we're married.'

And so the claustrophobia set in.

*

Joshua's birthday cake was finished except for the slice that Mrs Fox had wrapped in greaseproof paper, with the one fat candle, for me to take home. Mrs Plummer senior was pulling on her angora beret, and Cedric was beginning to pace about. He was the first one to say good-bye, and thank you, Mrs Fox. It had been a lovely party, he said. The others were swift to copy him, and they all left in a rush.

'They're pleased to be gone, if you ask me,' said Mrs Fox, when she shut the door. 'You can never trust people to make a go of things, can you?'

'I'm sorry,' I said, 'about Joshua. Dreadfully sorry. I can't imagine what happened. The trouble was, I didn't know where he was going, so I couldn't contact him.'

'Now don't think about it, or let him think about it either. People forget to go to parties. What does that matter? What's a party?' She began to clear the things away. I helped her wash up, then we unstuck all the roses and poppies from their places of decoration.

'Shall we listen to a little music? You never did hear my favourite brass band.' 'Land of Hope and Glory' by mass brass bands filled the room. We sat each side of the fire-place. 'What's a party?' she asked, during a quiet phase. 'I ask myself, what's a party?'

When the record came to an end, I left her. At the door she stretched her arms up as if to hug me, then decided against the gesture and let them fall to her side again. I tried to apologise further, but she interrupted quite crossly.

'Off you go, he'll need you to do his supper,' she said. 'And don't get at him. It's of no importance. I mean that.'

Halfway down the stairs I heard the brass bands start up again. Phrases of intense anger filled my mind – anger against Joshua.

It was after eight when I arrived back at the flat, which was empty and dark. As soon as I opened the front door

I could smell strange cigarette smoke. I switched on the light in the sitting-room. It was more than usually untidy. Three ashtrays were filled with the white tips of French cigarettes. All printed with pale brown lipstick marks.

I stood there without moving. Through the blackness of the windows I could see my reflection, quite still. Then I began to walk about the room in swerving patterns. My walk felt very heavy, as if I pushed against a strong current in the sea. I touched things with a floppy hand – the backs of the sofas, the window sill, the picture frames. In the other hand I felt myself crushing the slice of cake in its greaseproof paper.

I stood still again. I began to blink very slowly, to see how heavy I could make my eyelids feel on my eyes. I blinked like a slow mechanical doll. Forty-one times, I counted. Then I went into the bedroom. No-one had been there. No cigarette ends in the ashtrays.

Back in the sitting-room I put the slice of cake on top of a cushion. It balanced for a moment, then fell on to the sofa. So I sat on the sofa and put it on top of the cushion again. The same thing happened. I began to repeat this sliding game faster and faster. Then I heard the key in the lock. Joshua came in.

I stood up. He stopped as soon as he saw me. His eyes bore into mine and held them there, unflinching.

'What?' he said at last.

'Who?' I said. He shrugged.

'It's been a difficult enough day,' he said, carelessly. Then his face turned into three faces, his eyes into two black holes that covered all three faces. I grabbed the still-wrapped slice of cake and threw it at the heads with all my force.

'A bad enough day! So it has. You lousy, stinking,

thoughtless idiot. Mrs Fox goes and does this whole party for you, and you just don't turn up. You just don't turn up!' My shriek filled the room, raw, ugly. 'She goes to all this trouble. All her best friends, a huge cake, everything decorated . . . and then you just don't turn up.' He was shaking me now.

'Stop that noise. Shut up, Clare. Shut up – .'

'I won't shut up!' Children's playground chants in my ears. 'I won't shut up, I won't shut up! It's the worst thing you've ever done to anybody.'

He slapped me hard on the cheek. It stung; it shocked. But I shut up.

'I'm sorry about Mrs Fox's party,' he said quietly. 'I quite forgot about that. I'll do something about it.' I backed away from him. Tears from the pain seemed to have blurred my eyes.

'I'm sure you will. You'll send her flowers – very expensive flowers, I expect, and imagine that will make up for everything.' His face was one face again now, taut and cruel.

'Of course they won't make up for anything, you idiot. I've said I'm sorry.' He took a step towards me, but I backed farther away. 'Do you want me to explain?'

'There's no need. It's quite clear. *Who was she?*' A scream again.

'Please don't shout any more.' His voice was a monotone.

'I said: who was she?' Control, this time.

'She was once my secretary. Annabel Hammond.'

'What was she doing here?'

'We had lunch, then we came back here and talked.'

'Talked?'

'Yes, talked.' The sting in my cheek was dying away,

comfortably, but there was a constriction in my throat. It spread across my chest.

'Have you and Annabel Hammond always just – talked?'

'No, we haven't always just talked.' I undid the bottom button of my mackintosh then did it up again. Two, three times.

'I see,' I said at last.

'So what do you want to do about it?'

'What could I want to do about it – her? There's nothing I can do.'

'I'm sorry if you minded, but there was nothing to mind about.' A feeling of great weakness swelled through my body. I dropped on to the sofa.

'Why did you want to have lunch with her?' I asked. Joshua sighed, trying to be patient.

'I don't know. I really don't. The idea suddenly came to me. I just wanted to see her. She was the person I rang this morning, in front of you, but there was no reply. So I didn't mean it to be a secret. If I had, I would have cleared up the ashtrays, wouldn't I?'

'I suppose so.' The warmth of relief.

'She makes me laugh. I wanted to be laughed out of my mood this morning.'

'Did she succeed?'

'In a way. But how can I keep it up, if you go on like this?'

'I'm sorry.' He sat beside me.

'For heaven's sake. You must meet her some time. You'd like her. She's a great girl.'

'She'd got it all ready for you,' I said. 'So much effort.'

'What do you mean?'

'Mrs Fox.'

'Oh, we're back on Mrs Fox. I'll go and see her later on this evening, I promise.' He took my hand. I marvelled at his picking it up, it was so heavy. 'Does this mean you want to leave me, just because I had lunch with Annabel? – It's difficult to talk to someone with their eyes shut.' I kept them shut.

'Don't you realise?' I asked. 'Don't you realise at all?' Under the lids, complete darkness.

'I'm hungry,' he said. 'Is there anything to eat?' The darkness behind my eyelids broke into flares of scarlet. A plummet swung about the ragged patterns, then fell deeper.

'Mrs Fox sent you a slice of your cake,' I said.

I heard him look about the sofa, then stretch down to the floor to where the package had fallen. I heard him snap off the elastic band, unwrap the greaseproof paper and screw it into a ball. Then I heard him cursing the crumbs and currants that fell into his lap as he ate his piece of birthday cake.

Chapter Nine

Jonathan was dressed up as a pantomime fairy. He wore a wig of long blond ringlets, a white net ballet dress that sparkled, and goose-feather wings. On his feet, pink satin pumps whose laces criss-crossed up his legs to the knees, cutting into the flaky flesh. Over his arm he carried a huge basket covered with a white cloth.

He stood in the centre of a circle of very old men and women, all dressed in pinafores, mortar-boards and tap-shoes. They applauded him and he began to sing:

'I've got gooseberry jam for you,
Jam for you,
Jam for you.
I've got gooseberry jam for you
On a cold and frosty morning.'

He began to skip round the circle, stopping briefly at each old person and handing out a tiny pot of jam, like the pots of jam on trains, from the basket.

'Here I come with my gooseberry jam,
My gooseberry jam,
My gooseberry jam.
Here I come with my gooseberry jam
On a cold and frosty morning.'

They applauded him again, and began to shuffle their feet with quiet metallic taps. Then they joined in the chorus, their voices croaky and out of tune.

'Here he comes with his gooseberry jam,
His gooseberry jam,
His gooseberry jam.
Here he comes with his gooseberry jam
On a cold and frosty morning.'

I woke up with a headache, a sore throat, and aching everywhere. Last time I had had flu, Jonathan had given up any pretence of writing for a whole week, with the excuse of nursing me. He had done it very well. Flowers. Books. A portable television at the end of my bed. He never left the house, except briefly to buy food. He did the cooking himself: steamed soles and baked custards neatly laid on trays with tray cloths. He remembered what medicines I had to take when, and read to me out loud. The fact that he felt he was positively helping someone else seemed to suit him. He became more vivacious than usual. We had no arguments; we were content.

'I feel awful,' I said to Joshua, who stirred.

'Need a doctor?'

'No, but I don't feel much like getting up.'

'You'd better stay in bed, then.' He frowned. 'I won't be able to be with you much. I've a meeting at ten and viewings most of the day. But I'll leave my number wherever I go.'

'Don't worry. I'll be all right.'

When he was dressed Joshua brought me a cup of tea.

'Are you sure you're all right?'

'Absolutely.'

'Take care of yourself. I'll – ring Mrs Fox and tell her to come round and see you.' He kissed me on the forehead. 'Don't want to catch anything. 'Bye.'

When he had gone I went back to sleep, but the fairy Jonathan danced no more.

*

Mrs Fox arrived later in the morning. She pulled up a chair by my bed and kept her hat and coat on.

'It's very Decembery out,' she said. 'Frost in the air. All the shops are filled with Christmas things.' She patted a crumpled paper bag. 'I don't suppose you feel like eating much, but I've bought a few little bits that might tempt you.' She pulled from the bag a honeycomb, six tangerines and a jar of gooseberry jam.

'How funny,' I said. 'Gooseberry jam.'

'It was always Henry's favourite. I used to make it for him myself, in a good gooseberry year. But then he was most particular about what he liked and what he didn't like. He never could stand liver or spinach. My sister Edith was the same about raw onions. She didn't like scarecrows, either. You couldn't get Edith into a field with a scarecrow, not for anything. Not even walking right round the edges.' She patted the Poppy Day poppy in her hat. 'But then there's no accounting for other people's tastes, and there's never any hope of changing them, is there? I never could get Edith or Henry to like music – not in the same way that I do. Edith did try, mind. They both tried, to please me. But they could never get the hang of it. I suppose I got it from my father, myself. He was what you'd call an artist, in his way. He did beautiful little silhouettes of people's profiles – he could have sold them for a fortune, but he never asked for money. He said you couldn't take money for a hobby. He was good on the violin, too. He used to practise in the front room on a Sunday afternoon, all in his best clothes.

He was a very upright figure of a man, my father. Dignified, you'd call him. It was after he died that Edith went so quiet.'

She was quiet herself for a while, fussing kindly about me, shaking the pillows and fetching me a drink.

'I'm no Florence Nightingale,' she smiled. 'I should be, I know, after all those years married to Henry. But to tell the truth, I never got used to illness. It always affected me. I'm ashamed to admit it, but each time a patient of his was near to dying, I was afraid. I'm a religious person, but imagining an after-life is past me. Where are Henry and Edith now, I ask myself? What are they doing? Do they know we're thinking of them? You can drive yourself mad with such questions.'

'So what did you do when Henry died?' She seemed to stiffen, remembering.

'It was all very quick, in the night. A heart attack, it was and' – she snapped her fingers – 'out like a light, before his partner could get to him. Then all his patients began coming in. I don't know what made them come, or how they heard. But they came, and they took over. They arranged everything except for the music. I don't think it was disloyal, really, letting them do it. I mean, he was dead, so what did it matter? Though I often wonder, even now. But I don't think he would have minded. He loved his patients.' She lowered her eyes to her hands. They lay in an unconscious position of prayer on her lap.

'What you must do when people die,' she said, 'is to treat it like an ordinary day. The funeral, too. It must be an ordinary day. You must have the same things for breakfast, and the same things as usual for supper at night. The weather was very ordinary the day Henry was buried. I can't even remember what the sky was like.

The Salvation Army – he'd always supported them – played quieter than I would have liked out in the graveyard – their form of respect, I suppose, but it was nice. They were completely silent, though, when his coffin was lowered into the grave. They must have misunderstood me. I had said music *all* the time. Anyway. They gave me this handful of earth to throw, and I threw it, and I just said "thank you." I think it must have been out loud, because people looked at me. But that's what I was thinking, so that's what I felt like saying.' She sighed. 'It was a very ordinary funeral, and a very ordinary death, Henry's. I realise that.'

It was still only midday when Mrs Fox left. I wondered when Joshua would ring. I had his number, but didn't want to disturb him. I would give him till three o'clock.

I wanted him to be here.

The room had become familiar so quickly. The morning after he had carried me in from the bathroom, leaving behind my toothpaste flowers, it was already familiar. Square, white, unadorned. A few shelves of books, a pine rocking chair, a Spanish rug, a carved wooden tree on the chest of drawers – something Joshua had done last week before his work had started up at this pace again. An immemorable room, but I would never forget it. Now, it was the roses on the pelmets in the bedroom in the mews house that were unclear in my mind; the exact placing of the ornaments that were never moved on the fireplace. And I had slept there six years.

The telephone rang. I felt myself smiling.

'Clare? It's David.'

'I'm ill,' I said, making my voice sound worse than it was. 'I can't really talk.'

'Oh, I'm sorry. Anything serious?' He sounded concerned. It was something he and Jonathan had always had in common. Instant concern.

'No, no. Just 'flu.'

'Is there anything you need?'

'No thanks. Just sleep.'

'I won't keep you talking then. Ring me when you feel better.'

I slammed down the receiver. I wanted Joshua to be here.

I had never become used to waiting. When Richard first went to sea I was very bad at it. I would space the days out between the arrival of postcards – he seldom wrote me a letter – and the rare events of a long distance call. There was nothing to do with the days in Portsmouth. It was almost unbearably boring and I disliked the hotel life. I hated eating dinner by myself in the dining-room at seven every evening, barely protected by my book from the fresh young headwaiter. I was intolerant of the young wives who tried to be friendly with their offers of coffee mornings and organised outings to a historical place – to keep their minds alive, as they explained. My lack of enthusiasm soon stopped their offers, and on many days I spoke to no-one but hotel staff.

I wrote to Richard every day. I liked writing letters, and believed he would be interested in my dull news if I could make a good story of the non-events. I told him about how I drove about the countryside in our Anglia, and how petrol had gone up, and how I was trying to teach myself Spanish from one of those do-it-yourself books, and how I'd like a baby, next time he came back. I told him I missed him, but I understood about his career.

Sometimes, though, when I tried to remember him, I

became confused. I had no photographs, and at one time the picture of his face completely eluded me. I panicked. I lay awake night after night willing myself to remember. His backview was clear: the high, bony shoulders, the upright back, the neat line of hair beneath his cap. I made him turn round, slowly, in my mind, but he had no face.

I went down to the harbour one afternoon to re-enact his last departure. There was a ship close by, much like his. I walked to the gangway and stood there, holding the ropes. We had both stood at an identical gangway two months ago, holding a small case between us. He had lowered his head close to mine.

'Good-bye, little one,' he'd said. 'Take care of yourself. I'll send you some chocolates.' Those were always his parting words. He kissed my cheek just below one eye, so lightly that the inner wet part of his lips did not touch me. Then he drew back and looked down at me from his skinny height.

I looked up now, to the width of dappled sky. Funnels, in the distance. Cranes. Two seagulls croaking, humped in slow motion on an invisible wind. Then, at last, the slow recollection of eyes, nose, mouth, the shape of a head with its gold banded cap.

It had worked. I ran back to the town. I ran into a tea shop and ordered home-made brown bread, doughnuts and coffee. I felt myself smiling idiotically at the other customers in their wheelback chairs. I didn't care. I had remembered Richard's face, and there were only three weeks till he came back again.

*

Lunchtime came and went. I sipped very bright orange juice. Still Joshua didn't ring, but the door bell did. A boy handed me a huge bunch of pink roses, prim and cultivated, arrow-pointed buds. Jonathan's mother had spectacular roses in her garden in Dorset – great shabby things with dappled petals that darkened towards their centres. It was in her rose garden, in fact, that he had proposed to me, one June evening, as we walked one behind the other, because of the narrowness of the paths, between the beds of Queen Elizabeth and the Golden Glory. He had obviously laid his plans for the proposal most carefully: he had resisted my attempts to take secateurs and a basket to the garden, and I had had no suspicions. When I said yes, all right, I would, he had pulled at a fat scarlet bloom, trying to pluck it for me in some appropriate symbolic gesture: but he tore the stem and the petals fell to the ground.

'Never mind,' he said, 'what matters is that now we're going to be together, together, *together* for the rest of our lives.' He hitched up his trousers, gave a little skip, and an instant tear ran from one eye.

*

Joshua had never sent me roses before. I ripped at the cellophane and slit the envelope to get the small card. Unmistakably, it was written in a florist's hand. *Clare – cheer up! Get better soon. Love, David.*

I rammed the roses into the kitchen sink, uncaring, because there was no vase deep enough to hold their long, anæmic stems, and no scissors to cut them with. Then I went back to bed and watched the hands of the clock till three.

Joshua wasn't at the number he had given me. They hadn't seen him and didn't know when to expect him. How to get through the long afternoon?

Find a flat, or a house, that was it. Do something useful. I wouldn't ring agencies, in case Joshua tried to ring me, and he never tried again if a number was engaged. But I could go through the papers. – In one glance, there were an amazing amount of suitable places for us. It would be easy when the time came. The small Georgian terrace house in Kennington, for instance. Joshua liked that side of the river. It would be quiet, and quite convenient. Probably not too good for shopping, but there would be plenty of time to go elsewhere. It would be an unhurried life. Time to read, to learn to cook, to find bargains in junk shops for the house. Even to have a child, perhaps, one day. I would go abroad with Joshua on his filming trips, and we would come back to find a pine grandfather clock still ticking in the hall, and expensive frozen things in the ice box because we could afford to spend a lot of money on food. The house had a small back-garden, it said, with two apple trees. Eating apples, perhaps. We could have windows on to the garden leading from one of those kitchen-dining rooms. It would always be untidy, with an old sofa and telephone books and strings of onions. I would cook breakfast there, go into the garden and pick an apple, and shine it on my *apron*. But perhaps Joshua would like better this studio flat near Ladbroke Grove with a spiral staircase to the bedroom? I marked the paper with huge crosses. My head began to thump.

It was very hot in the room, now. The sky darkened across the window, although it was only four o'clock. Sweat. Damp, scrumpled sheets. Aching throat.

In a studio flat we could begin to collect contemporary pictures. Great bursts of colour on the studio walls. We would change them about. Pictures should be moved. In Jonathan's parents' house the pictures stayed in the same place for so many years that when they were taken down for their annual cleaning, they left black rims on the walls.

Why was there no fresh lemonade with ice? Jonathan made the stuff by the pint. Joshua could only mix Bloody Marys.

My hair was sticking wetly to my head.

Perhaps Joshua could carve something *big* for the studio. He'd never done anything really big.

Where was he?

Hell, I wanted clean sheets, cool pillows, a voice telling me not to make such a fuss. Smooth hands, like Jonathan's, on my head; the reassurance that he wouldn't go away.

Where was Jonathan, now? In his Roman attic, still, with his electric typewriter? Why wasn't he here, comforting?

And then this face grinned at me again, friendly, helpful. He didn't speak, but he carried the basket covered with the white cloth, still, filled with things to make me better.

*

I was being shaken. Jonathan was here at last, rougher than usual, but with lemonade, perhaps, in our big blue jug.

'Jonathan. . . .?'

'It's not Jonathan. It's me.' Joshua was crouched on the floor by my bed, his head close to mine. 'You're still half asleep. Having bad dreams?' He smiled. 'How are you?' He touched my cheek with his flaky thumb. 'You're burning.' He pushed the hair back from my forehead. 'Speak to me.'

'I've found some nice places to live,' I said. Very slowly, his face tightened into a frown.

'What do you mean?'

'Well, we can't stay here for ever, can we? It's too small.' It hurt to talk.

'I suppose it is,' he said, then he got up. 'Guess what I've brought you? Fresh limes. I thought we could squeeze them. And a bag of hot chestnuts for my supper. You won't be able to eat those, will you? – your throat.' He was funny, somehow. I laughed. Later he came back with a glass of pale green, sweet lime juice, filled with ice. He put it on the table, sank on to the bed, and lay heavily across me, taking my face in his hands.

'I'm sorry,' he said. 'I'm sorry, I'm sorry, I'm sorry.' His mouth closed over my dry lips, his hands began to pull back the bedclothes so that I was suddenly cold.

'Together, together, together . . .' went on a voice. But it was Jonathan who had said that. Joshua was still kissing me.

Chapter Ten

Mrs Fox complained that Joshua, like the friends who had come to her party, had no sense of occasion. She spent Christmas Day with us, her festive spirit battling with his unseasonal one. We ate fried joints of supermarket turkey so that there would be no cold carcass to finish up. We ate frozen peas and baked potatoes and tinned Christmas pudding with brandy butter made by Mrs Fox. In comparison with everything else that, at least, was a triumph.

A pink nylon tree stood on the table, glowing with silver balls spaced mathematically by the manufacturer. Joshua had bought it because, he said, it was the most anti-Christmas symbol he could find. He hated Christmas, but liked not to ignore it. He was good at his discontent, funny. To make up for his apathy he bought us extravagant presents. Mrs Fox had a fur muff and velvet cushions for her bed. For me, Indian jewellery and a set of Victorian prints in beautiful frames.

After lunch we ate the box of crystallised gooseberries Mrs Fox had brought.

'Henry's favourites,' she explained. 'The only ones that didn't get in his teeth.' She was wearing, over her customary black dress, a cardigan made entirely of sequins. They winked and fluttered in the dull electric light. A bunch of goose feathers, dipped in silver paint and dried into hard spikes, was stuck in the band of her hat.

'What are we going to do now?' she asked. 'Christmas

afternoon is always such a problem. I remember, it always was. Edith always came to us for the day, of course, because she never had many social invitations, all her life. Edith never came immediately to people's minds when they planned a party, if you know what I mean. So Henry and I always had her over. We'd have a nice lunch, then Henry'd always be off, in his black coat and carrying his bag, just as if it were a normal day. He wouldn't wait for a call – just go off to a few of his patients who lived on their own, and take them a small present. Some of these, usually, for those who could digest them.' She held up another gooseberry. 'They loved him, Henry's patients, and no wonder.' She looked at us, sitting near her together on the floor, and sighed, smiling.

'So Edith and I were faced with this long afternoon. Well, she wasn't much of a walker, so we couldn't go out. She didn't play cards, or chess, or backgammon or any game. She didn't do tapestry, or sew, or knit. So occupation-wise, if you see what I mean, we had a small problem. Then one year – what, thirty years ago, I suppose? – I hit on this idea. You see Edith always gave me the same present every year – a black fountain pen with a gold nib and a gold rim round the middle. She was funny like that: she always gave people presents that she would have liked to have herself. One of her peculiarities, you could call it. Anyway, she always gave me this beautiful pen – it was much too good ever to wear out in a year, of course, but I couldn't tell her that could I? – and I *knew* what handling a new pen would mean to Edith. So one year I thought to myself, I thought: I'll give Edith writing-paper, and she can spend the afternoon writing her thank-you letters with *my pen*. I found a beautiful box – I'll never forget it, the box I found that first year. It was covered with violets, raised up sort of violets, on the lid, and inside the paper was the palest violet colour you could ever imagine. It even smelt of violets. I don't mean those rubbishy synthetic smells they douse paper with these days. I mean just a trace of woodland violets. Each sheet of paper was stamped with a flower in the corner, and the envelopes were lined with purple tissue paper. Edith was quite taken aback. "Oh my," she said. And I said to her, "Why don't you use it now, Edith? We've got a long afternoon. I could help you with your thank-you letters." "But I don't have my pen with me, Eth," she said. "Ha ha," I said, "perhaps we can find a solution to that." '

Mrs Fox paused in her story and with one hand rubbed over the lumps of ruby and star-sapphire rings on her fingers of the other, as if to warm them.

'So I went over to the big roll-top desk by the fire and cleared a space among the cards on the blotter. Edith laid out the first page and smoothed it very slowly with her hand. She sat down, and I knew she was ready. I picked up my pen and handed it to her. Well, you should have seen her face. "But Eth, it's the pen I've just given you," she said. "Are you sure?" "Of course I am, silly," I said. "I've even got you ink to match." And I took out a bottle of lovely deep purple ink that I'd hidden in a drawer. Edith dipped the clean nib right into the ink, and filled it, and I remember she was trembling. And then the funny thing was, she held it over the paper, and she turned to me and said: "What can I write, Eth?" Well, of course, that was the start of it all. From then on, every year, I dictated her letters on Christmas afternoon while Henry was out. Not that she had many to write. But Miss Turner from the post office always sent her handkerchiefs, and her butcher once sent her a nice crown of lamb, and the woman next door always made her a woolly robin – rubbish, really – in a kind of arrangement which had to be thrown out when the holly died.'

She stopped again, briefly, for breath. Then went on: 'The funny thing about those afternoons was that as soon as we had fallen into this letter-writing habit they never seemed long again. In a jiffy, it felt, Henry would be back out of the snow, laughing at us and asking for tea. I would always put on the kettle, because Edith would be busy sealing up the envelopes. But somehow, after Henry died, we didn't get so many letters written. For one thing, Miss Turner died too, and I couldn't find the quality of writing-paper to give Edith any more.'

She had kept still for the whole story. Now she swivelled round in her chair to look out of the window. Her sequin cardigan flashed and flared again, kingfisher colours. She tapped at the waxy cardboard of the empty gooseberry box with her quick fingers.

'So what are we going to do?' she asked. 'We should go out.'

'We're going,' said Joshua. 'To the country.'

'What do you mean? Where?' He hadn't told me of any plans.

'Annabel Hammond's coming round. She's invited us all to tea with her mother.' He got up, his back to me. 'Near Windsor.'

'Very nice too,' said Mrs Fox. 'Anything but Kent.' Joshua turned to face me and grinned. He picked up one of Mrs Fox's new velvet cushions and flung it at my head.

'It's all right,' he said, 'she's coming with her friend Bruce. So don't look like that.' He turned to Mrs Fox. 'The trouble with Clare is that she's wracked with jealousy. If I tell her I spent a nice day on Brighton Pier with my mother when I was a child, a green flush spreads from her ankles upwards.'

'Stupid,' I said, half smiling.

'If you've never had reason to be jealous, you've never had reason to love,' said Mrs Fox.

'Well, anyway, it'll all be all right this afternoon.' Joshua was pacing the room now, tweaking at things, the balls on the Christmas tree, the dying poinsettias, as he passed them. 'We'll all be together, and Annabel loves Bruce. – At least, he loves her. And we'll have a terrific tea with Mrs Hammond. She's the best cook I know. She'll make Bruce a lovely mother-in-law.'

'As I said,' repeated Mrs Fox, 'Christmas afternoon can be such a problem.'

Annabel and Bruce arrived punctually at three o'clock. Annabel was tall and thin with smooth blonde hair strained back into a bow. She wore a leather coat with silver studs, pale knubbly stockings and fragile walking shoes made of suède. Perfect for Windsor tea.

'I've heard so much about you – hello.' She held out her hand. I took it. It was bony and compact, taut as a frightened bird's wing. 'This is Bruce Winham. Brucey, where are you?' Without releasing me from her look, she folded her arm behind her back and tugged at a huge cable-knit sweater. A small man with hungry sunken eyes twitched eagerly forward. He had a neat black beard that was forced by the height of his polo-neck collar to stick out at right angles, and he wore gym shoes. He grinned at me, his mouth wide with merrily distorted teeth. A friendly, hopeful face. Joshua introduced Mrs Fox. She stood up smartly. Only Bruce shook her hand.

'Why don't we go straight away?' asked Annabel. 'We can take my car. It would be better than yours, if I remember it rightly, wouldn't it, Josh?' She gave him a narrow, knowing smile.

'It's changed since your day,' he said, 'but it's just as uncomfortable. We'll go in yours.'

Annabel swung her efficient look towards Mrs Fox.

'Can we drop your – aunt anywhere on the way?' she asked me. 'Or does she want to come too?' Her tone was uninviting.

'Mrs Fox is a friend,' I said.

'Of course she's coming too,' said Joshua.

'Very well, let's go then.' Annabel clacked her long silver nails against the silver studs of her belt.

Her car was a white Fiat coupé 124. Joshua, Mrs Fox and I sat in the back, Bruce hunched beside Annabel in front. He began rhythmically to tickle the nape of her neck with a prematurely old finger.

'Stop that, Brucey,' she snapped, 'how can I concentrate on driving?' Obediently he stopped. Joshua held my hand.

We sped to Windsor in almost complete silence. There was ragged snow in the fields and barely a car on the road. It was curiously peaceful. Joshua had been truthful about Annabel. For the moment she was no threat.

Mrs Hammond lived up a long laurel hedged drive. Icy puddles spat under the wheels of the car as Annabel screeched round the gentle corners. For a moment Mrs Fox clutched at Joshua's knee. He covered her hand with his, and we jerked to a halt in front of the Tudor house.

It looked warm and comfortable. A garland of holly and scarlet ribbon on the front door. Mullioned windows back-lit by fires and shaded lights indoors. Inside, it was full of labradors, real ones and china ones.

'Typical sort of place,' Mrs Fox whispered to me. 'Henry had patients from these sort of houses. Smart lot.'

Mrs Hammond stood in front of a large open fire waiting to greet us. She was a smaller version of Annabel, equally thin and neat. Her hair, jersey, skirt and shoes were all of a matching blue-grey.

'Darlings!' She welcomed Joshua by curving clinically against his body, and reaching up with her skinny hand to touch, briefly, his face and hair with her diamond-ring fingers. 'You haven't been to see me for so long, my love? Why haven't you been?' Her voice was a whine.

She all but ignored me, but was warm to Mrs Fox. Instantly benevolent, confident in her skill at dealing with other people's odd relations, as she apparently supposed. At the other end of the room Bruce gave a little skip, light on his feet in his gym shoes.

'Lovely thick carpets,' he remarked happily.

'What was that, darling?' Mrs Hammond's whine rose.

'I said: lovely thick carpets.' He skipped over to her. She disapproved of him, but could hardly resist him.

'They are rather nice, aren't they, on a parquet floor?'

Annabel switched in with her organising voice again.

'Why don't we all go out before it's dark? I feel like some exercise. Anyone else? Brucey? Josh?'

'We'll all come,' said Joshua.

Except Mrs Hammond, we all went. Annabel, in spotless gum-boots now, led the way through the misty garden. We followed her through a small gate into a ploughed field. Here, the hard black earth split through the old snow, leaving it to lie in frozen white snakes between the ridges. We began to walk single file round the edges of the field. The hedges, wet with cobwebs, scratched at our sides.

Suddenly Joshua, who was in front of me, stopped. He bent down and scooped up a handful of the icy snow. Then he jumped at me and rubbed it quickly over my cheeks. It stung.

'You dare!'

'Catch me, then.' I flung out my arms, but he had gone. Leaping over the plough.

'I will.' I sprang after him. I was aware of the other three, behind me, stopping and turning to watch. I chased him to the middle of the field, half-running, half-jumping from furrow to furrow. It was heavy going. The solid wet earth clung to my feet.

'You'll never get me!' He stopped for a moment, panting, his face alight and excited.

'I will.' With mock ferocity I now made a snowball, picking up lumps of earth with the snow, in my haste, and threw it hard at him. He ducked, and it missed. He laughed.

'Bad luck, Funny Face. It's the aim that counts, you see. Look, like this.' Quickly he made another snowball and leapt up, stretching his whole body, to fling it at me with all his apparent force. This time I turned my head to duck and dodge it, imitating his speed. I took a step backwards at the same time, tripped over a hard ridge of earth, and fell. I fell in the middle of a furrow, knees apart, hands askew beneath me. Icy bits of snow stung through my tights, and I felt the black earth push up behind my nails. Joshua was still laughing.

'Are you all right?' He came over to me, unconcerned.

'I think so.' He helped me up and brushed snow and earth from my coat.

'You're not much good, are you? Here, you've got mud on your face, too. How did that happen?' He scraped it away with hard cold fingers. 'Now you look marvellous.'

'Don't be funny,' I said.

'No, really, I mean it. Your cheeks are bright pink, for once, and your eyes are shining quite ridiculously.'

'And I suppose you'd rather have me with mud on my coat and an undignified mess than the immaculate Annabel?' I asked, tightly.

'Yes,' he said. He held my hand. It was cold, but warmer than mine.

We began to walk heavily back over the plough to the hedge. The others, equally spaced, stood where we had left them, watching our progress in silence. Mrs Fox stood to attention, her new fur muff hanging from a black satin ribbon round her neck, her hands clenched at her sides. Beneath the black sleeves of her coat hung small sparkling rims of cardigan, flashing silver and white now as the sequins reflected the scattered snow. She looked very serious.

Annabel spoke first, as soon as we were in earshot.

'That was very amusing,' she said. 'You always were so energetic, Josh.'

'I think we better go back to the house,' said Joshua, coldly. 'Clare should get cleaned up.'

'Oh heavens. Is it that serious? Surely no-one minds a bit of mud. I mean, we've only just started.' Annabel stamped her foot. Her nostrils flared.

'She's pretty wet,' said Joshua.

'For myself,' said Mrs Fox, 'I'm going back to the garden. I want to take a look in the greenhouse we passed. If that's all right with you, of course, Miss Hammond?'

'Of course,' said Annabel. Having made her successful interruption, Mrs Fox thrust both her hands disapprovingly into her muff, and turned to plod back down the field towards the garden gate. The rest of us watched her go without speaking. Eventually her small, upright figure disappeared through the gate.

'I'll go back to the house on my own,' I said. 'You all go on.'

'That's the solution,' said Annabel, 'if you don't mind.' Joshua looked from her to me.

'Shall we do that?' He seemed not to mind which way the problem was settled.

'Sure.' I turned to go. Annabel suddenly smiled, her lips two thin slithers of silvery grease.

'We won't be long, anyway,' she said. 'Mother will show you round in the house.'

Then, spontaneously, Bruce took my arm.

'I tell you what, *I'll* go with Clare. Come on, Clare. Don't let's dither any more. I'm getting cold.' He was shivering. Joshua and Annabel turned the other way. We parted.

Almost at once Bruce was forced to walk behind me because of the narrowness of the path.

'Bloody damp,' he said, after a while. 'I loathe the bloody country.'

The sky was full of deepening shades now, grey and pink, turtle-dove colours. Against it, winter trees stood with tousled heads of hair on skinny necks, and pigeons flew towards the same wood that Joshua and Annabel were heading for.

By the time we reached the garden gate the daylight had closed down almost to darkness. In the silence, cinder paths between navy-blue hedges scrunched under our muddy feet.

'Let's join Mrs Fox in the greenhouse,' Bruce said, bouncing amiably to my side again. 'I can't face too long with Mrs Hammond without Annabel's protection.'

We made our way to the greenhouse, but Mrs Fox had left. Bruce turned the rusty key and we went in. It was warm and damp and neat. Shelves of poinsettias, cyclamens and azaleas, searing red and mushy pink in the feeble electric light. Bruce ran his hand along a rusty pipe bound up with rusty rags.

'She sells them, as you can imagine,' he said, indicating the flowers. 'She's the sort of woman who would put six tame chickens into a battery unit if she thought she could make a profit out of them that way.' I laughed, feeling warmer at last. He sat on the pipe, now, testing it carefully first, and looked up at me. 'So now it's you and Joshua?'

'How do you mean?'

'Annabel told me he was nuts about someone.'

'I don't think he is.'

'It still hurts her, you know. She pretends it doesn't, but I know bloody well it does. She was crazy about him for three years. Nervous breakdowns, the lot.'

I turned from him to prod the warm, feathery earth in a small pot of cacti.

'What are you?' I asked.

'Film industry. What else? Totally unsuccessful, of course, and with little potential. Just striving, hoping, as they say. But I'm quite a pleasant fellow to have around on any set, so I get the jobs, and who cares about the prestige?'

'How long have you known Joshua?'

'Oh, years. I can't remember when I first met him. I've always admired him and, to be honest, I suppose I've tried to model myself on him. But I've always been the utility model. What I can never achieve is his – distance, shall I call it? There I am, grinning away, showing exactly what's going on in my mind, while he switches into this beautiful – distance.' He grinned. 'You can never tell what Joshua's thinking. That's what I admire. The enigma. The apparent lack of concern – then all of a sudden he surprises you. Like, when I was in hospital once for a long time, he didn't make any promises to come and see me, like everyone else. But unlike everyone else he just came, every day. Bloody miles out of London it was, too. And I don't mean that much to him.

'Funny thing is, I've done a lot of the same things as Joshua – only some years later. Including Annabel, of course.' He laughed, amused at himself. 'Naturally, I'm nothing like Joshua was to her. But at least I offer her security, which is more than he ever did. Her mother can hardly abide me, as you can imagine, what with my lack of what she calls "background", and that. But still, probably she won't marry me in the end, so Mrs Hammond will be no problem.'

I wondered how Joshua had treated Annabel.

'Like a bastard,' replied Bruce crossly. 'Really dreadful. Always letting her down, getting at her, threatening her. He had the upper hand completely. Of course,' he sighed, 'he was right. That's what she responds to best, and that's what I just can't do. I *can't* treat her like that, not loving her like this. In fact there's only one way I know I really can please her, and that won't last for ever, will it?'

He stood up. We were exactly the same height.

'So now you're going through it all? I wonder how you're making out?'

'Who can tell?' I asked. 'I can't.'

'Well, as long as Joshua can't tell what effect he's having on you, you'll keep him. That's where Annabel went wrong. He was bored stiff as soon as she began declaring her love. He's a terrible child like that. Win the chase, and the game is over for him, no matter how good the prize.'

We left the greenhouse and he locked the door again.

'If you ask me, you're doing pretty well,' he said. 'You've got him in pretty good shape.'

'I hope so,' I said. It was quite dark in the garden now. The lights from the house flickered through a tangle of silhouette bushes. Bruce took my arm and led me to the path.

'If ever I can help,' he said.

*

Back in the drawing-room Mrs Hammond and Mrs Fox sat in opposite arm-chairs by the fire. Mrs Fox had a pile of magazines dumped on her knee. Mrs Hammond had probably put them there, saying 'Something to read,' like a doctor's receptionist, not caring how unsuitable they were as long as they kept Mrs Fox quiet. Mrs Hammond herself dabbed expertly at a piece of *petit point*. Her spiky diamond fingers made small rhythmic jumping movements that flashed with flames from the fire. A table with a white cloth and fragile plates covered with silver lids was laid by the sofa.

'Oh, there you are,' said Mrs Hammond, raising her blue eyes to us above her pale blue sewing glasses. 'I was beginning to wonder what had happened to you.'

'Clare fell over and we had to get her clean,' said Bruce. 'The trouble is, there are so many bathrooms in this house it took quite a time deciding which one to use.'

'*Bruce*, your bitter little jokes,' said Mrs Hammond. 'It's Christmas Day, don't forget. Well, shall we start without them?'

Mrs Fox thankfully removed the pile of magazines from her lap to the floor.

'I could do with a nice piece of Christmas cake,' she said. 'That's one thing we always did away with, Christmas cake. Edith couldn't manage the icing, what with her teeth, and Henry was allergic to marzipan.'

'What's that?' asked Mrs Hammond.

At that moment Joshua and Annabel came through the door. Joshua rubbing his hands, Annabel with noticeably shining hair that looked as if it had been brushed extra hard to disguise previous dishevelment.

'Sorry we're late,' she said, 'you should have started. God, what you missed, though. It was so beautiful in the woods, you can't imagine.' She looked at me, elated. I felt my face red from the fire. 'You should have come, in spite of the mud.'

'What was so beautiful?' asked Mrs Fox.

'What?' Annabel ran her hand impatiently through her hair.

'I said: what was so beautiful in the woods?' repeated Mrs Fox.

'How do you mean?' said Annabel.

'I mean exactly what I say,' said Mrs Fox.

For a moment there was puzzled silence in the room. No-one cared to help. I glanced at the loud ticking clock. Ten past five. We could leave at six. Annabel drew a chair up to the table and sat down. She motioned to Joshua to sit beside her.

'For heaven's sake! Am I being that inarticulate? Perhaps you're not a country lover. Perhaps you only like towns in winter . . .' Her voice was feeble. She was put out.

'Not at all,' said Mrs Fox, and gave me a small, private smile.

The rest of us joined Annabel at the table. Mrs Hammond, with a flicker of new respect, poured Mrs Fox the first cup of tea. We ate crumpets and banana sandwiches. The huge Christmas cake was decorated with icing-sugar hills. Small plaster figures ski-ed down the slopes and nylon fir trees were dotted in the valleys. Mrs Fox laughed with delight.

'Have you ever seen anything like it?' she asked Bruce.

'Never,' he said, 'dreadfully vulgar, isn't it?' Annabel and Joshua both laughed at the same time. 'When I was a child my mother would buy a slab of Dundee cake at Christmas time and spread on a thin bit of icing herself. We thought *that* was lovely.'

'Really, Bruce, you're always trying to shock me,' said Mrs Hammond.

'We must all *play* something after tea,' said Annabel. 'Wouldn't that be a good idea?'

'I think we really ought to be getting back,' I said.

'What on earth *for*? You can't be that engaged on Christmas night. You're either *doing* something *positive*, or you're not.' I looked at Joshua.

'I'm in no particular hurry,' he said. 'What about you, Mrs Fox?' Mrs Fox was trying to unstick a fir tree from her huge slice of cake.

'Can I keep it?' she asked, as it broke away, a heavy chunk of icing clinging to its roots.

'Of course,' said Mrs Hammond, 'and if you all agree to stay to dinner we'll have my special soufflé that comes in on fire.' She smiled conspiratorially at her daughter.

'In that case we should stay, shouldn't we?' Mrs Fox asked Joshua. 'We couldn't miss that. In my day,' she explained to Mrs Hammond, 'I was quite a gourmet. It was all because Henry's patients would come to me to try out their little experiments.' The fir tree and the thought of a fiery pudding had won over Mrs Fox. Her noble stand against the Hammonds was weakened, and she had them in her control now. Annabel, triumphant, encouraged her to tell stories. Mrs Fox took her cue, performed, and was well received.

'*Such* a beautiful cardigan, that, Mrs Fox,' said Annabel at one moment. In the firelight its icy coloured sequins sparkled with gold; fulgid, alive, reflecting dancing patterns on her face.

'You exaggerate,' said Mrs Fox, 'it's just an old thing I got at a jumble sale.' Bruce turned wickedly to Annabel.

'What do you mean by beautiful?' he asked.

'For heaven's sake!' She screeched with laughter.

'You'll learn to laugh *with* people one day, you patronising bitch,' he said quietly, so that Mrs Fox shouldn't hear.

After tea he and I played Scrabble while the other four played bridge.

'I'm sorry you weren't able to get away,' he said. 'Dinner will doubtless be the kind of merry occasion you wouldn't have minded missing. Mrs Hammond likes her champagne.'

A white-coated Spanish butler appeared with the first bottle at six-thirty. Mrs Hammond broke up the game of bridge to take a glass with her to the kitchen. Annabel went up for a bath.

'I can't lend you anything for dinner, I suppose?' she said, before she left. 'We're not exactly the same size, are we?'

'She's a great one for always making her point,' said Bruce, when she had left.

'She hasn't changed,' said Joshua. He came and sat

down on the low fire stool. 'You seem to be casting a certain gloom.'

'I'm not feeling my gayest.'

'There's nothing to worry about, idiot.' It was then, in the light of the fire, that I saw a miniscule speck of silver grease glinting on his chin. I took my handkerchief and wiped it off.

'Silver shines,' I said. I paused, fighting not to say it. I lost. 'It *must* have been beautiful in the woods.' For a moment Joshua stiffened, then he smiled. Bruce watched him carefully.

'She pounced on me like a tiger,' he said.

'The bitch. Christ, the bitch.' Bruce winced. 'It was only after lunch, just before we came round to meet you. . . .'

'I'm sorry Bruce. But anyway, she didn't succeed.' Joshua put his hand on my knee. Bruce untied the laces of one of his gym shoes then re-tied it, more tightly, with a fierce tug.

'My trouble is, I love the girl,' he said. 'I love her with a ludicrous passion that doesn't get either of us anywhere. I know my role. Unfortunately, I can't seem to stop playing it.'

Annabel reappeared an hour later. She wore a magnificent gold trouser suit whose top was unzipped to just below her breasts. Plainly she wore no bra beneath.

'Wow,' said Bruce, sadly.

'Fantastic,' said Joshua. They both rose to fill her glass. She laughed at their attention.

'Isn't this fun?' she asked me.

'Great fun,' I said. My cardigan felt enormous and hot. My feet blazed in my thick boots. My head ached from the heat and champagne.

At eight o'clock a gong was rung. Dinner was served. We filed in like two badly matched teams; Mrs Hammond, Annabel and Mrs Fox dressed for the occasion; Bruce, Joshua and I decidedly out of place in the claustrophobic, red dining-room. The mahogany table was laid with a clutter of candles and crackers, dazzling silver and glass, and a dreadful winter-scene centrepiece with a mirror lake, cotton-wool snow and more nylon fir trees. Jonathan would have loved it.

Soup, first. Mulberry coloured stuff thick with *croutons*.

'What an amusing little soup,' said Bruce, to break the warm silence.

'*Bruce*, I never know whether to take you seriously or not,' said Mrs Hammond. Her cheeks were flushed to the same colour as the soup. 'The funny thing about me is, I never know whether someone is complimenting me or insulting me.'

'That is a happy confusion in which you should always remain,' replied Bruce.

'What a lovely centrepiece!' Mrs Fox left her soup to prod the cotton-wool snow with a finger. 'Did you make it, Mrs Hammond?'

'Of course. Everything in this house is home-made that can be home-made. I've always been very good with my hands.'

'And does Annabel take after you?' The old sharpness had returned to Mrs Fox's voice. Bruce answered her.

'She's marvellous with her hands,' he said. Joshua spluttered into his soup. Annabel glanced at him through half-shut fake lashes.

'What do you say to that, Josh?' Joshua looked from Bruce to her.

'Oh, marvellous,' he said lightly. 'Anything you undertake to do, you do well.' Everyone but me laughed. Mrs Hammond joined in the spirit of the joke.

'I don't know what Joshua and Bruce can know about it,' she said, 'I swear they've never caught her knitting, or arranging flowers or anything. How can you judge?'

'We can judge,' said Joshua.

I pushed my soup away, sickened. Annabel noticed immediately.

'Anything the matter, Clare?'

'No.'

'You must be dreadfully hot in that cardigan.'

'I am, rather.'

'Poor you. We can't open the window, either. There's something wrong with the sash.' I felt a hot icicle of sweat trickle down my spine. The candle flames wavered and fattened before my eyes. I removed my hand from where it had lain slumped on the table. Five misted-up fingermarks remained on the shining surface. 'It's ghastly, suffering from heat,' Annabel went on. 'I feel so sorry for people who do. I love it, myself. Crazy about the sun, aren't I Josh? Do you remember? St Tropez? I'm quite happy just to *lie*. Just to lie in the sun for hours, doing nothing but getting brown. I suppose it's awfully *boring*, really, for anyone who's with me. Wasn't it, Josh?'

'Fairly,' said Joshua. They smiled at each other, acknowledging the lie. Something grated behind my eyes. On Christmas night last year, Jonathan, in his shiny old dinner jacket, had said I was beautiful. His mother's dining-room had been uncomfortably hot, too. But he had noticed my unease halfway through the smoked salmon. Without saying anything he had opened the door and make a chink in the heavy curtains. He had cared.

Joshua was warming to Annabel's reminiscences. He

sat with his fork suspended over his plate of left-over turkey disguised in a spicy sauce, his face hard-cut shadows and planes in the candlelight, his eyes restless behind the massive frames of his glasses, his mouth up-turned on one side only as he smiled – beautiful.

Joshua – get up from the table now, come over to me, take my hand, and tell everybody we are leaving. . . .

'Annabel is such a sophisticated traveller,' Joshua was saying. 'Wherever you go she knows about the most interesting church, the best local wine, the cheapest good restaurant, don't you? And then she's always changing, aren't you? Three or four times a day as far as I could make out. She manages to produce endless clothes and yet a very small amount of luggage. I could never understand it.'

'Quite,' snapped Bruce.

Let's go right now, please Joshua. Out into the night, quickly to the airport. Let's catch a plane to anywhere, anywhere as long as it's away from these people. And let's tell them why we're leaving.

The promised soufflé came, swaying pale and high above its dish, blue brandy flames lapping up its sides. Mrs Fox clapped her hands.

You could buy two of those miniature bottles of brandy, and we could ask the air-hostess for a rug. . . .

I looked at Joshua, but his eyes flicked away, back to Annabel. She was flushed now, not an ugly red flush with hard edges, as I felt my own to be, but the natural colour of her cheeks was intensified just enough to make her hard eyes bluer. She was excited, beautiful, prepared to make her next move, any move, so long as Joshua kept reacting.

'But my darling Josh,' she said, '*you* are such a child on

holiday. Remember? Remember how you always used to be running away from me in foreign towns, playing childish games. I could never speak the *language*, that was my problem, so I could never ask if anyone'd seen you.' Joshua paused in the middle of helping himself to the soufflé.

'You exaggerate,' he said, no longer smiling. On my own plate the flames fizzled out round a fiery mound of fluff. I held on to the solid mahogany underbelly of the table.

'I exaggerate? Absolute nonsense.' So concerned was she with her own pace, that Annabel was unaware now that Joshua had fallen behind her. 'Don't say you've forgotten that time – where was it? God knows, England somewhere, I think – that time you ran off for *hours* leaving me on some God-forsaken beach. And when at last you came back you didn't care a damn that I was *perished*. You were very pleased with yourself, in fact, because you'd managed to get us *ice creams*, two bloody choc bars if I remember – '

'Shut up, Annabel!' My scream ripped into her. She stopped. In silence, everyone looked at me. I trembled, I burned. 'You reminiscing bitch. What are you trying to do?'

'What have I done?' Her voice cool, concealing a smile. Her head tipped up towards me now, innocently. Then all the heads tipped up, so that shadowy cheeks suddenly flared with gold light from the candles. I was standing. I looked at Joshua and the others faded.

'Come on,' I said. 'Come on, let's go.' Pause. No answer. He still held my eyes. 'Quickly. Please. It's time for us to go.' He got up, came to my chair and pulled it away, freeing me from the trap between it and the table.

Then he went to the door, opened it for me, and gestured to me to go through. He didn't follow. I turned round to wait for him. He was shutting the door.

'That was a pretty scene,' he said, so quietly I could hardly hear, and the door closed.

I began to run through corridors – close-carpeted, hunting scenes on the walls, dimpled light from chandeliers. I chose a door with an ornate brass handle. An unused room, cold. Very high leather chairs. Grey walls, guns, a stuffed labrador in a glass cage, a steel-framed photograph of a man with Annabel's eyes, one of them was widened behind a monocle. Leather arm-chair very cold behind my knees, very cold arms under my hands. Directly opposite my chair the labrador, its flinty pink tongue painless on icicle teeth, smiled its dead smile.

*

About half an hour later there was a tap on the door. I didn't answer. Mrs Fox came in.

'Heavens, child, you'll catch your death in here,' she said, going to the small electric fire that stood dwarfed at the foot of the huge fireplace. She switched on its two thin bars. 'Typical meanness of these sort of people. Henry was always having to go to people who'd caught pneumonia by economising on the central heating when they needn't have. They'd cut out a radiator here, a radiator there, just to prove to themselves they weren't extravagant. But then the rich have some funny illusions about cutting down, don't they?' She went over to the dog and tapped at the glass case, her back to me. 'What an awful creature! Joshua said I should tell you we will be leaving shortly. I wouldn't have liked to have a dog like that alive, let alone dead.'

She turned to me. In this room her sequined cardigan glittered deep violet, navy, and dull silver, subdued. She still wore her black hat with its silver painted goose feathers and, as usual, one hand rubbed at the lumpy rings on the other.

'They put on Stravinsky in the drawing-room when we went through,' she said. 'Well, I thought, if you start listening to *that*, you'll never leave. So I thought I'd come and find you. Joshua saw me going and gave me the message.'

'Mrs Fox,' I said.

'That's all right,' she said. She went now to the huge desk in the corner. It had a carved roll-top which she fingered gently. 'Very like ours,' she said, 'very like ours. I mean, like the one I was telling you about where Edith used to write her Christmas letters. Do you think anyone would mind – ?' Gently she pushed up the lid. Underneath, polished brass handles shone on a pattern of small drawers. There were no papers, no pens, no ink. Mrs Fox was disappointed. 'It's all deserted,' she said, pulling back the lid. 'I've never liked an empty desk.'

Through the door came the distant sound of Joshua calling us. I didn't move.

'Come along now, up off that chair.' Mrs Fox spoke with the same voice she had used to Edith on the park bench. 'We must go, and about time too.' Still I didn't move. Mrs Fox moved slowly towards me. She seemed to sag a little. 'Come along, please.' She put out her hand, the one with the rings, so that they flashed like a morse code back at her sequined sleeve. 'Take my arm, if you would. You'd never believe it, but I'm a little tired.' It didn't matter whether or not she spoke the truth. I got up, and took her arm. The sequins felt splintery under my hand. We walked past the smiling dog and out into the passage.

'I didn't turn the fire off on purpose, of course,' said Mrs Fox, 'it just might make that little difference to Mrs Hammond's bill, mightn't it?'

We turned the corner. At the far end of the passage, in the brightly lit hall, the Hammonds, Joshua and Bruce, unaware of us, were talking and laughing round the Christmas tree, pulling on coats, kissing Mrs Hammond, saying they'd love to come again; saying, yes, really, it had been a lovely time, a lovely Christmas Day.

Chapter Eleven

'There's something about your quietness,' said Richard Storm, 'that never bores me.' We were driving along country lanes looking for another cottage which Richard didn't want to see, but had agreed to for my sake. It was a Saturday morning. Spring. Primroses on the steep banks of the lanes. A hotel picnic, or 'wrapped lunch' as they called it, in a basket on the back seat. A day full of anticipation, full of promise. But weighing against it, a familiar heaviness of limb: a solidity of heart where there should have been lightness. But never mind. Excitement, when we found the cottage, was just round the corner.

'No, I can never understand it. It never ceases to puzzle me.' Richard was talking quietly, almost to himself. He steered our light Anglia with heavy solemnity, as if he guided a huge ship. 'When I'm away at sea, I picture you sometimes – '

'Oh, you think of me?' I smiled at him. He looked back seriously.

'Of course. What do you imagine? You're my wife, aren't you? Sailors think of their wives when they're away at sea.'

'I wasn't being very serious.' He was never a receptive person to joke with.

'Well, I was. I think of you often. I think of you as my child wife, far away from me, waiting for me, and it makes me sad.' He paused.

'What does?'

'Mostly, that we're wasting time. Not just wasting time by being apart, but that I'm wasting time when I could be – educating you.'

'When you could be what?' He coughed, and steered elaborately round a gentle corner.

'Perhaps I haven't chosen the right word. But you know what I mean. You know what I said I'd always do – I'd make my child bride grow up. As I've always said' – now it was his turn to joke, his small mouth cracked appropriately – 'you're good potential material.' A long pause.

'How am I coming on?' I asked. He didn't seem to notice anything about my voice.

'You've come on a lot, in just a year, but the hard way, I'm afraid. Waiting about in hotel rooms for your elderly husband has inevitably matured you, but we've a long way to go, haven't we?' He patted my knee. 'Now don't look offended. You want me to tell you my fantasies, don't you? You've never minded before.'

'I don't mind now. What fantasies?'

'Well, you know, my ridiculous dreams. My old man's dreams, if you like.'

'You're not *that* old. What are these dreams?' A few dots of sweat had gathered on his aquiline nose, and he licked his lips. Under the thin grey flannel of his sporting trousers I could see the muscles of his scraggy thighs gather and tighten.

'Oh, what do they matter on a lovely morning like this? I'll tell you some other time. We've only about a mile to go.'

The cottage, once pretty, now dirty and decaying, stood in an acre of garden over-run with briar roses and apple trees. There was a rotting chicken house at one end of a small orchard, and mushrooms in the grass.

'It's lovely,' I said to Richard. His eyes narrowed as if to scan a far off horizon, although he stood only a few yards from the cottage.

'Hardly lovely,' he said. 'Totally impractical. Miles from anywhere. It would need a fortune spending on it.'

'We haven't looked, yet.'

'A fortune, I can tell you.'

'It might not. Anyway, it's good potential material.' He didn't smile.

'You're childishly stubborn when you want something.' He looked at his watch. 'It's two, already. Let's eat first, then look. Not that looking will take long. It can't be more than two up and two down, whatever the agents say.'

I fetched the basket from the car.

'Let's eat in the garden,' I suggested.

'It's much too chilly, and there's nowhere to sit.'

'On top of the chicken house?'

'And I wouldn't be surprised to find a wind getting up. It's only April, after all.'

'I know you know about winds,' I said, 'but I think it's lovely and warm, the sun.' He didn't hear me, but walked impatiently towards the tattered front door. I followed him.

Inside, bulging walls were streaked with damp, and a pool of water from some old shower had leaked through the window onto the red tiled floor. A smell of rotten apples.

'Marvellous,' said Richard, crossly. 'So much you could do with it for ten thousand pounds.'

'I like it,' I said, 'and I'm the one who would have to be here most.'

'Perhaps,' he said, 'soon I will arrange not to be away so much.'

'Good,' I said. 'Really?'

After one egg sandwich he had rejected a fishpaste sandwich, a chocolate biscuit and a Swiss roll, and now he hungrily ate an apple. We sat on the only piece of furniture, an old chest, mildewed at the sides, with the food spread between us on a paper napkin.

'It could be so nice,' I said. 'Imagine: I would be cooking your breakfast at this window. Birds on the lawn outside. Roses – .'

'I can't imagine,' he said. With every bite of the apple his own Adam's apple jerked up and down, in and out of the slot made by the crisp white collar of his open shirt, which in turn fitted into the V neck of his blue jersey, all the pieces fitting into each other like a puzzle. His thin, neat hair shone, still dented by the cap which for once he wasn't wearing. In mufti Richard looked naked, ill at ease. 'There's one thing,' he said, looking at the damp, 'my child bride will never be able to provide me with, no matter what I do.' The sweat had returned to his forehead.

'What's that?' He turned to me and ran a finger from my shoulder down to my waist.

'I've always liked big breasts.'

'I'm sorry about that.' I laughed. He got up and went to the corner of the room. Tested the wall with the flat of his hand.

'Mushy. Come here. Feel.'

I went over to him and put my hand near his. He took me in his arms and crushed his mouth down on to mine. Peppermint and apple breath. Briefly I struggled.

'What are you doing?'

'What do you think, little one? You're my wife, aren't you?' His bony thighs jiggled against mine. His hand ran up my jersey. 'Will you ever have big breasts for me? Will you?' His voice was breathless.

'Of course not.' I pulled back my head to look at him. There were white spots like cuckoo spit at each corner of his mouth. He grabbed at my waist, screwing my jersey in his hand as it if were loose wool.

'But you could – pull in your waist a little, couldn't you? Wear clothes that show you off more. Eat more and put a little weight on your bottom, couldn't you? Couldn't you?' He panted slightly. One of his claw hands circled round and round my back. 'You could wear more on your face. Your eyes. I like lipstick – .'

'What's the *matter* with you, Richard?' I heard my voice from a long way off, trying to be gay.

'What's the matter, little one? Nothing's the matter except that I want you. And do you know what? I'll want you even more in a few years time, when you're riper, fuller. . . .' His face crushed down on to mine again. His hand hurt in my back. I began to cry. Immediately he let go of me and stepped back. 'Now what's up?' Impatient rather than concerned.

'Nothing. I mean, you frightened me.'

He sighed. So tall, so neat, so pale. His white collar hadn't moved even in the scuffle. A man with sea charts in his head and horizons in his eyes. My stranger husband.

'I'm sorry,' he said, 'but I suddenly wanted you very much. Don't you want me?' A long pause.

'No, not just now,' I said.

'Very well, then, we'll go.' His hands moved almost imperceptibly at his sides, just scuffing his trousers. I put my hand on his arm and felt it stiffen.

'I'm sorry,' I said. 'I don't seem to be what you want. You seem to be stimulated by the thought of older women. Is that what you think of when you're making love to me?'

'Of course,' he said. Then he touched my hair quite gently. 'Men have their passions, little one, and a woman's job is to welcome them. But you have a lot to learn.' He began to pick up the picnic things, humming to himself, 'Lady of Spain'.

With me, that was the nearest Richard Storm ever came to passion, and it was the last cottage we ever saw.

*

'You realise it's January, I suppose? Time's nearly up.' David Roberts on the telephone again. 'Have you decided anything? What you're going to do?'

'No.'

'Hadn't you better be making up your mind?'

'There's time,' I said. It was only eight thirty, still dark outside, but Joshua had left at six this morning. Hadn't said why. He was out so much now. Working very hard sorting things out before going to Mexico next month. Mexico.

'I suppose I'd sound like a sentimental old fool if I said I can't help imagining a lovely homecoming,' he said.

'Yes,' I said.

'You're pessimistic about the chances of a happy ending, then?'

'Not pessimistic. Not anything.'

'At the risk of interfering, I think you ought to *think*, soon. Make a positive decision one way or another.'

'There's *time*,' I repeated.

'Not much.' David coughed. 'Anyway, old thing, as an

old friend, I think there's something I ought to tell you – you ought to know.' He paused, coughed again. 'He'll never marry you.'

'What do you mean?'

'Joshua.'

'Why do you assume I want to marry him?'

'In the end, like most other women, you'll want to settle for that sort of security.'

'You might think,' I said, 'that after two marriages I might not feel inclined to that sort of security any more.'

'You might, but I don't. – But anyway. Don't take any notice of me. Who am I to advise? I just don't want you to say I didn't warn you. Joshua does not marry people, I'm telling you. Usually, he doesn't love them, either.'

'Thank you for the warning,' I said.

He forced a laugh.

'By Christ, is there anything more touchy than a separated woman? I don't know why I bother to go on ringing you. I'm only trying to help, you know.'

'I know, I know.'

'So perhaps it would help to tell you that I have in fact spoken to Jonathan lately?'

'Oh.'

'And he sounded much more cheerful. Resigned to the situation, at last, you might say. Very friendly about you. He asked how you were, what you were doing and so on. I told him you were getting on fine, without giving anything away.'

'That was nice of you.'

'He sounded – maybe I got this wrong, we only spoke on the telephone – but he sounded as if he was *looking forward* to February. That's what gave me hope. That's what got the old imagination going, if you know what I mean.'

'Quite.'

'So that's all the news, really. I just wondered how you are, and if you had made the big decision. And I thought you'd be pleased to hear about Jonathan's change of heart, as I know you couldn't want him to be positively unhappy, could you? I mean, hell, he may have his faults. But he's the heck of a *loving* man, isn't he? Which is more than you can say for Joshua. . . .'

*

'Oh, I'm happy, happy, happy,' said Jonathan, 'aren't you, Suki Soo?' This was his name for me at moments of supreme happiness.

We lunched at the hotel, restricted by our *demi-pension* terms, at the balcony restaurant under a striped awning. Jonathan was grateful for the shade. In his determination to stay by my side he had refused, that morning on the beach, to allow himself the protection of the parasol. Instead, he had spent an agonising couple of hours on the glaring white sand. The sun shrank and burned his pale skin, and frizzled up the many oils he dabbed himself with continually. Now, sweat bubbled over his scarlet face and his hair hung in damp peaks under his small straw hat. He looked down on to the beach below us, crowded with browning sunbathers.

'There's something about the Italians, isn't there?' he said. 'I don't know why, but I've always felt something very special towards the I-ties.' He helped himself to a couple of strips of green pepper from the plate of *hors-d'oeuvres*. As he leant forward, his cotton shirt strained over his chest and a button flew off. He didn't notice. 'I wonder what it is? So many Englishmen – creative Englishmen, that is – seem to have it in common. I suppose I'm smitten with the same bug as Keats and Shelley and Lord Byron. I have whatever they had – in that respect.' He bent down to scratch, under the table, the dry skin of one of his legs.

Lunch over, we went to our air-conditioned room because Jonathan, like Shelley, felt he was capable of some of his best work in Italy. His typewriter and papers were spread over the dressing-table. In a week he had typed a couple of pages, the 'outline' for some new play.

I drew the shutters, so that slits of sun and shadow patterned the tiled floor, and lay on the bed. I shut my eyes. I could hear Jonathan sit down at the dressing-table, light a cigarette, search about for an ashtray, shuffle a few papers. Silence for a moment, followed by seven slow thumps on the keyboard. Then the squeal of his chair being pushed back over the tiles.

'Darling? Could you help me a moment? I need your advice. I want to try out something on you.' I opened my eyes. He sat towards me now, legs apart, shorts riding high up his thighs, the curly black hair thickening towards his crutch. His tinted spectacles had slipped down over his nose which even in this light was a sore pink. He re-arranged the few papers in his hands, as if the new arrangement was enormously complicated.

'The thing is, about this kind of outline, it brings the whole thing to life if you throw in a few lines of dialogue to show them the sort of thing they can expect in the final script. Well, how about this for the start of Scene Two?' He cleared his throat.

' "*Scene: the kitchen of a large, comfortable farm house.*" ' He looked up and smiled. 'I hope you note, darling, that I'm not writing a drawing-room comedy. Far from it. Anyway, as I say, the large, comfortable kitchen of a farm house – or the other way round, as I think I said before. What does it matter? ' "*A middle-aged couple and a young couple are sitting at a table eating soup. There is silence, except for the supping*" – good word, that for soup, isn't it? – "*except for the supping of the soup, then suddenly the oldest man, Thomas, stands up.*

THOMAS: *My God, Marcia! My God! Say something, can't you? How can you carry on eating your soup like that?*" '

'Jonathan scraped his chair a few inches nearer to the bed and raised his eyebrows in preparation for Marcia's high voice.

' "MARCIA: *Sit down and get on with your soup, Horace. It's lovely soup. It'll get cold if you don't get on with it.*

THOMAS: *How can you all think about soup at a moment like this?*

MARCIA: *Come on, Horace, it's your favourite, isn't it? Carrot and onion. I did it specially for you* – " '

Jonathan turned, slammed the papers back on the dressing-table, then swivelled back to me again.

'You see the kind of thing I'm trying to do? Here's this fat, insensitive man, Horace, in a rage, and the only reaction he can get from his wife Marcia is comments on the soup. The strumming of emotion against lack of understanding, if you like. Non-communication of the highest form. Of course, it should have been read with a lot of Pinteresque silences, really to get it across, but I don't pretend to be an actor.' He began to undo the buttons of his shirt. 'What do you think? Do you think it'll give them an idea of the sort of thing I have in mind?'

'Oh yes,' I said. 'It'll do that very well.' A mean pause

in which he looked uncomfortable. So I went on: 'But it's difficult to be much of a judge not knowing anything about the characters. What happened in Scene One?'

He stood up, startled.

'Scene One? I haven't thought about that yet. This was just – a fragment, a particle of the play I thought worth getting down on to paper while the words leaped through my head.' He threw his shirt on the floor and undid the belt, and flies of his shorts. 'Hell, it's far too hot to go on working. We'll take a cottage on Lake Como in the autumn, perhaps. I could work very well, there, in the cool.' His shorts dropped to the floor and he stretched his arms high about his head. 'Let's sleep for a couple of hours, then go for a swim, then go out to dinner at that place you like along the coast, and dance. Would you like that?'

'Lovely.'

He padded towards the bed.

'You've still got your hat on,' I said. He threw that, too, onto the floor and lay beside me.

He lay beside me, naked, on top of the bedclothes, holding my hand.

'You're beautiful, Suki Soo,' he said, with his eyes shut. 'There's never been a luckier man.'

'Nonsense.'

'It's true. Beautiful, brown, warm, gay, loving. What more could a man want?' He hoisted himself up on one elbow and looked down at me. Arms, legs and face an incongruous red against the flat whiteness of the rest of him. 'I feel so loving towards you I don't know what to do with myself. How can I ever tell you how much I love you?' He flung himself on top of me, his hands parting my bathing robe, his tongue swooping into my mouth. His body was hot and heavy. He was hard against my thigh, breathing fast, shuddering.

'What's the matter?' He rolled off me again. 'Do I smell of garlic, or something?'

'Not much,' I said.

'Don't you want me?' I didn't answer. 'Don't you like it in the afternoon? Is it too soon after lunch? We'll wait a while.' He lay back on his pillow but still held my hand.

'I think I'm nearly asleep,' I said. We lay in silence for a while, looking at the ceiling. Then:

'Don't you ever feel anything violent?' he asked.

'How do you mean?'

'Well, I think it could be said I *express* my love for you. I want you all the time, and show it, wouldn't you say?'

'Yes.'

'But you have a funny way of expressing your love for me. You don't do anything. In fact, you crudely resist me sometimes.' He watched one of his feet as he bent each toe slowly in turn, as if he played a five-toe exercise. 'I mean, sometimes, when we're walking down a street or going to a theatre together, say, and I want to take your arm or hold your hand, you don't do anything or say anything, but you just make it very clear you don't want me to touch you. Don't you?'

'I admit I'm not by nature demonstrative. But then you're very calculated.'

'Nonsense, darling. What utter nonsense you talk. If there was ever a spontaneous lover, it's me. Think of the mornings – working mornings at that – we've had breakfast and I've said: "Let's go back to bed." '

'They've hardly been spontaneous,' I said.

'You silly old Suki Soo,' he said, rolling over towards

me, 'you've got on that funny hard voice that means you're a thousand miles away from me. Come on, cheer up. Smile. We're on holiday, remember? We're having a lovely time.'

I smiled. Encouraged, he let two fingers walk up to my breast like a child pretending to be a spider.

'I love you,' he said. 'Do you know how much I love you? I love you, I love you, I love you.' The fingers walked over to the other breast. 'Do you love me?'

'Yes.'

'How much?'

'I don't know. How can I measure?'

'Do you need me?'

'I expect so.'

'Do you want me?'

'I expect so.'

Sudden heat, a blackness in the shade of his heavy face. His tongue, enormous in my mouth, loiters at the roots of one tooth, then shambles on to another. Three more days till the aeroplane home. Sing things, sing things. *Te voglio bene tanto tanto, bene tanto tanto*. . . . how did it go then? Count things. How many people at the table next to us at lunch? Three. Remember things. The fat woman wore a red dress. Very good. And the others? Now my nose squashed flat under his, spreading across my face, setting like fungi. His hand, confoundedly gentle and nosy, prying over my stomach, and up and down and up and down –

'Jonathan! Stop it! Stop it!' He rolls off me, a freak tide ebbing in fright.

'What on earth's the matter? What have I done now?'

I stand, pulling at the belt of the bathing robe. The floor tiles warm from the sun under my feet. I look at him, quickly crumpling, hurt.

'You must have overdone the sun,' he says at once, covering his anger. 'I told you you would.'

I sit on the bed again, thankful.

'That must be it, I'm sorry.' Silence. To calm, or to attack? I wonder which he will choose.

'Go to sleep, darling. You'll feel better when you wake up. As I said, the sun, and all that lunch. . . .' His voice full of care. I sleep.

When I woke up, some hours later, he had opened the shutters. A dusky mauve sky, a strip of mercury sea through the balcony railings. On the table a bottle of champagne stood in a primitive bucket of ice. I could hear Jonathan moving about in the bathroom. He came in, tying a blue-flowered tie that matched his blue flowered shirt and blue Terylene trousers. He indicated the champagne.

'Non-vintage, I'm afraid, but it's the best they could do. I thought it'd be nice to wake up to.'

'Lovely. Thank you.'

'At least it's cold.' He fingered the bottle, opened it easily and filled the glasses. 'After this you must have a slow bath, and put on those beautiful lilac trousers, and then we'll take one of those awful tourist carriage that you're always on about and go to the *Prima Trattoria*. I've booked a table.'

I tried the champagne. It was warm and sweet. Jonathan knew I had never liked it, but this was no reason to stop him ordering it for special occasions.

'Do you really need to book a table at the one restaurant in a small village two miles from anywhere?'

'I suppose not. But I like booking tables, don't I? You must let me book my tables in peace.' He smiled. 'Anyway. It's booked. Feeling better?'

'I'm fine.'

'It was only the sun – '

' – and all that lunch.'

'And all that lunch, yes, as I said.'

'Yes, yes.'

Jonathan refilled his glass and took my hand.

'You're not cross with me, darling?'

'No, why should I be?'

'I just thought you might be.' He cleared his throat. 'I was thinking, while you were asleep. I was thinking, we mustn't let this sort of thing get us down.'

'What sort of thing?'

'The sort of thing that happened this afternoon. It's not important.'

'What isn't important?'

'Well, we mustn't make a fuss about it, worry ourselves about it. The thing is, my love, in the long run sex doesn't matter. You know that, I know that.' I sat up and he gave me his arm to help me off the low bed. He smelt of lemoney after-shave. 'Well, when I say that, you know what I mean. I simply mean it shouldn't become too important, should it? There are lots of other things besides, aren't there, that are so much more important? And anyway, everyone has their off moments, don't they? – '

'I'm going for my bath,' I said. 'I absolutely agree.' He followed me into the bathroom and turned on the taps.

'So we won't make a fuss, we'll forget all about it,' he said, 'and I'm sorry if I was – a bore.'

'Of course you weren't,' I said. 'I don't know what came over me. I'm sorry too.'

He sat on the edge of the bath while I washed, playing

with a sponge. Filling it with water and squeezing it, filling it with water and squeezing it.

'So what we'll do is, we'll have a lovely dinner and lots of drink, and dance a bit, and talk to that nice man at the bar. Then we'll come back here, and it'll be nice and cool. And then, if you can bear it, if you're feeling like it, that is, we'll try again.'

As David Roberts said, Jonathan was indeed a loving man.

*

'Funny,' said Mrs Fox, 'this is the very bench we met on.'

It was eleven o'clock in the morning of a mild January day. Mrs Fox and I had been walking through the park feeding the birds. We were going to have lunch in a cottagy restaurant she knew in Kensington where they sold home-made pies and cakes. But it was too early yet, and warm enough to sit.

'Oh yes,' she went on, 'I shan't be likely to forget that day. Edith's last outing, that was. And you all in black, looking very down. But then you'd been to that funeral, hadn't you? One of your husbands. – It doesn't seem like five months ago all that happened, Edith dying, does it? – Lovely yellow, that.' She pointed towards some early yellow crocuses nearby. 'Yellow was Henry's favourite colour. We always had yellow crocuses, just like those, in a bowl in the front room, every spring. But of course what Henry really liked was daffodils. You've never seen a man like him for daffodils. They were the first flowers he ever gave me. Bunches and bunches of them. He must have bought up a whole flower stall, I think, honestly, and he was only a student at the time – what it must of cost him. As a matter of a fact I wanted daffodils, for that very reason, for his coffin. But it was the wrong time of year. I went to all the flower shops I knew for miles, and I said I must have daffodils. Forced, I said, if need be, as long as they were daffodils. Oh madam, there are limits to forcing, they told me. They said I couldn't have any, no matter what I paid. I don't think they cared, really. Not by the way they spoke to me. Forced daffodils! I might have been asking for an extinct plant, the reception they gave me.'

She took a handful of crumbs from a small paper bag and threw them to some starlings.

'I forgot to tell you,' she said, 'I've got two tickets for a pop concert at the Albert Hall to-morrow night. I was wondering if you would like to come? I'm not sure of the name of the group, but it's their farewell concert, I heard people saying in the queue. They're bound to have lots of those amplifier things – they almost burst the Hall with noise. I've heard that sort of thing there before. It should be good.'

'That would be lovely,' I said. To-morrow night Joshua was working very late, he said. Two starlings came right up to Mrs Fox's feet.

'February,' she said. 'My, it's almost February. Your decision's coming up then, isn't it?'

'Yes,' I said.

'What's it going to be?'

'I don't know.'

'Well, it's better to admit you don't know than to pretend you do, as Henry always used to say. He was the quickest doctor to admit he didn't know I ever met. More like him would save patients a lot of time.' Her bag of crumbs empty, she touched the Poppy Day poppy in her hat.

'That reminds me,' she said, 'I never told you what they did that day.' She rubbed the rings on her bare hand and gave a small kick towards the starlings, as if their greedy pecking, now that the crumbs were finished, suddenly annoyed her. 'As soon as she died, that is. As soon as she died, before they'd even closed her eyes, they pulled the bedclothes back. Her nightgown had all wormed its way up round her, if you know what I mean, and her body, it was like a skeleton. Imagine it! There was never a more modest woman all her life, and yet the minute she dies they expose her. I pulled the sheets up again because her nightgown was all under her. I couldn't have moved that without moving her. But that bossy matron – trust her to nose her way in at the dramatic moment – was on to me in no time. "What do you think you're doing?" she says. "She'll be cold," I says. – Stupid, I know, but I felt she would be cold. The matron laughed at me. "Cold?" she says. "She'll be cold in a jiffy on this earth, no matter how many blankets, and if she's been a good woman she'll be warm in Heaven." I'll always remember how she said that. Then she told me to go away, unless I wanted to watch the preparations.

'The funny thing is, ever since then, and this is what's troubling me, I've never been able to think of Edith with her clothes on again. I lie awake for hours in the night, sometimes, trying to imagine her in her brown wool dress, or her navy floral summer one, or her best dress, the greeny crêpe. I knew them all well, all those dresses, but for the life of me I can't imagine them on her any more. What I do is, I lay a dress out on a chair in one corner of my mind, then she walks in from the other side, like in a film. She puts on the dress, slowly, like she used to dress, and stands with her back to me zipping it up. When she turns round again I can see her face, clear as anything, but the dress isn't there. She's naked. All I can see is her poor thin body, like it was the day she died. And I hadn't seen it bare for fifty years, remember. "Edith," I says to her in my mind, "get dressed Edith. You mustn't stand about like that or you'll get cold. . ." But she just looks at me, silent like she often was, silent and bare and getting cold. . . .'

Without warning it began to rain, gentle rain from the mild sky. Mrs Fox stood up. As she rose she gave a small gasp. I gave her my arm but she ignored it.

'For heaven's sake, child, I'm not having a heart attack, you know. It's just indigestion. I tried frozen hamburgers last night, all laid out with the rest of the meal in a tinfoil tray. All I had to do was warm them up. They must have done it. That's the trouble with instant food.' We began to walk towards Kensington.

'Lots of funny things, this morning, if you think about it,' she said. 'That other time, you remember? That other time it began to rain upon us too.'

*

Somewhere in a place full of light further lights explode. Way out beyond the petty rim of the globe there is a soaring and a swooping and an ultimate meeting as flesh dissolves flesh, bones are liquid, blood flames. On the way back there is a lesser light, a more ordinary light, shaped like a window. And the blare of inaudible music is scraped to nothing but the tick of an ordinary clock.

Joshua is kissing me, my eyes, my hair. He is slung all over me, his arms and legs heavy as fallen boughs.

'Funny Face?'

'Joshua?'

'I was only just awake, too.'

'I know.' I hold him. He is soft. He is warm.

'Funny Face?'

'Yes? What?'

'Nothing, really.' He falls to my side now, his head on my breast. 'You're very *small.*' My smile moves his hair.

'You're huge.'

'Like that?'

'Um.' I wriggle. 'You know what?' I say. 'It's Sunday.'

'Sunday?'

'Sunday.'

'Imagine. Sunday. I didn't know that.' He moves higher on the pillow now, so that he can look down at me.

'We can spend all day in bed.' I rub his scratchy chin. 'I've got kippers for very late breakfast.' He twists a strand of my hair in his fingers, pulling it quite hard.

'You funny old planner. You must have worked it all out yesterday.'

'So? Normally, you say I'm not efficient.'

'I wouldn't like you to be any efficienter. What did Jonathan think?'

'He made up for anything I lacked in efficiency. He stocked up the whole store cupboard, one week. Things I would never have thought about. Only the best brands of everything. He was a terrible snob about marmalade. Nothing but Elsenham.'

'You speak of him with great affection.'

'It was rather endearing, his brand-snobbism. That's all.'

Joshua reached for a cigarette. Our legs stayed in a confused knot.

'You realise it's the end of January?' he asked.

'Everybody's been reminding me,' I said.

'I have to leave for Mexico in three weeks. And you have to make your decision.' He smoked almost to the end of his cigarette in silence. 'Are you going back to Jonathan?'

I sighed.

'I don't *know*,' I said. 'There's time.'

'Not a lot.' He crushed the cigarette out on his thumb. 'And sadly, I'll have to miss the kippers, unless you'd keep them for to-night.'

'Why?'

'Work.'

'But it's Sunday.'

'So you say. I'm sorry, Face, really I am. But I've got to get this thing finished before we leave. When I say work, I mean work, you idiot. I'm not off with a blonde.'

'With Annabel.'

'I'm not off with Annabel.'

'I believe you, but you're always *going*.'

'Cheer up. I'm always having to cheer you up. I'll be back about five, I expect. You can have a whole day to think in.'

He sat up, so I sat up.

'I don't need a whole day,' I said. 'I've made up my mind. I'm not going back to Jonathan.'

Joshua smiled disbelievingly.

'How odd. If I'd had to put a bet on it, I would have sworn you would have decided the other way. So what will you do instead?'

'Stay with you, of course.'

'That might be difficult, fixing for you to come to Mexico. But you could wait for me to come back.'

We looked at each other for a long time.

'All right,' I said.

'I haven't been very nice to you, really, when you think about it. I can't think why you want to stay.'

'Don't you want me to?'

He laughed.

'Face, you must know me by now. As I never know what I want in the abstract, I'm usually fairly satisfied with whatever I have in reality.'

'That doesn't sound as if you would be exactly desperate without me.'

He took my chin in his hand and lifted my face towards him.

'You funny thing,' he said. 'You funny, small thing.'

Very soon after he left the flat forgetting, as he sometimes did, to say good-bye.

Chapter Twelve

The first time I discovered I was pregnant was in Portsmouth, ten days after Richard had sailed for Barcelona. I had felt sick for several mornings, and skipped those hushed breakfasts alone in the dining-room. Finally, I went to a doctor. 'Two months gone,' he said.

It was news for my next letter to Richard. '*Won't that be lovely?*' I wrote, '*I'll be having it in April.*' I sent the letter express. The baby would be a girl, I decided. Called Ophelia.

That night a searing pain strangled my stomach and I began to bleed. I rushed from the bathroom, a bath towel between my legs, and picked up the old, heavy telephone beside the bed. The receptionist, who had taken the job because it fitted in with her insomnia, took her usual three minutes to answer.

'What is it, dear? It's getting on for midnight.'

'I need a doctor.'

'A doctor?'

'Yes. Quickly, please.' The blood was beginning to soak the towel.

'Is there anything the matter?'

'*Yes*. I need a doctor.'

'Is there anything I can do? I took a course in nursing, once, you know, myself – .'

'Please,' I said. She seemed immune to the urgency in my voice. 'Please just get me a doctor.'

'Well, Dr Harris, I know he's on to-night. But then you

know he hasn't been well, himself, lately. I wouldn't like to call him out unless it was really urgent.'

'It is,' I screamed.

Dr Harris arrived an hour later. The receptionist let him into my room.

'Ooh dear,' she said, when she saw me, 'you did need a doctor.' Dr Harris sent her to ring for an ambulance and immeasurable time later I groaned and cursed on the stiff white sheets of a hospital bed. By the next morning it was all over.

My mother came down to Portsmouth to drive me back to the hotel. She had gold chains on her crocodile shoes to match the handles of her crocodile bag. She was dismayed by the fact that I had been treated the same as everyone else.

'Good heavens, darling, why on earth didn't they get you into a private room?' She wrapped a rug round me in the car and said I looked pale. 'You're such a *worry*, Clare. Are you sure you don't want to come home for a few days? You know you can come whenever you like.' I thanked her, but declined. She was used to my declining most of her invitations.

Back at the hotel she filled my hot water bottle and put a vast basket of fruit on the table beside my bed. It was wrapped in cellophane paper and topped with a cellophane bow.

'There are figs, somewhere,' she said, brightly, with the confidence that figs would cheer my day, 'I know you've always loved figs.'

She paced about my room uncertain what to do, picking up then putting down her precious handbag. We listened to the rattle of the central heating and the croak of gulls, clear against the traffic noise, outside the window.

Finally she picked up a photograph of Richard from the dressing-table, stiff and alert in his uniform.

'What a good looking man Richard is, darling, isn't he? So mature, I've always thought. Do you suppose he'll fly back?'

'Not for a moment,' I said. 'Anyhow, there's no point.'

'I suppose not.' She picked up her bag again. 'I must be off, I suppose. Are you sure there's nothing else you want? Just let me know if there is. Ring me any time, won't you?' She bent down to kiss me. She smelt sickeningly of the oily gardenia scent she always wore. 'I hope you don't mind my going, but you know what it is. It's such a busy time of year, one way and another. – No, no. It hasn't *been* a trouble, coming all the way down here. You mustn't think that.'

Three days later came the reply to my first letter to Richard. '*How lovely, little one, as you say. I'm sure it'll be a boy. We can call it either Richard or Clive – both family names. You choose. I don't mind as long as it's one of those. I will, of course, expect him to follow in the naval tradition of our family. Anything else would be unthinkable. Take care of yourself and I'll be home long before April. . .*'

That night he rang me from Barcelona.

'So sorry to hear, little one.' He sounded quite sad. 'Still, these things happen. Don't take it too badly. We'll try again next time I'm back.'

'Of course,' I said. I felt no enthusiasm about starting again. My stomach ached and my room was a huge, vacant gap all around me. 'I wish,' I said, 'I could join you in Spain. I'd like to be with you.' There was a long pause.

'Little one,' he said, at last. 'I don't think you should. For your own sake. You'd do much better to recover where you are, quietly. I'm out most of the day, and you know what the food's like over here.'

'None of that would matter,' I said.

'I don't think you should,' he repeated. I felt cold. My hand began to sweat on the receiver of the telephone.

'I could spend most of my time lying on the beach,' I said.

'The beach isn't very nice.'

'Well, I could drive about.'

'You don't speak Spanish.'

'I could get by.'

'I don't think you should.' He sighed. I sighed.

'All right,' I said. 'I'll stay here.'

'Oh, little one.' His relief was infinite. 'I think you'll find I'm right. I'll call you again soon. Or you ring me, any time, if you want anything, won't you?'

I got up the next day and went back to normal life. The days went slowly as they had done before. Richard didn't ring again. Three weeks went by. Then a letter:

'*Little one,*

How can I ever explain? You know I once told you about a woman called Matilda? Well, in a word, I love her. I have fought it, she has fought it, but there is no denying it. We are in love with one another. We live together and want to get married one day. None of that is to say I don't love you. In a strange way I still do, and perhaps always will. I will always think of you as my Little One. Please, please don't take it too badly. These things happen. Perhaps we should never have married. Your mother always said I was baby snatching. But still, I believed in it, in us, at the time. Oh dear, I never have been very good at letters. I'm putting it all very badly. You can cite Matilda, of course. Your father will know a good solicitor. I think of you often. I wish this needn't have happened just after the miscarriage, but love attaches little importance to timing, does it, and I felt it would be wrong to keep it from you any longer.

Please forgive me if you can, and don't think badly of the many good times we've had together.

Love, Richard.'

*

The second time, with only two weeks to go before Joshua went to Mexico, I felt sick in the evenings. I had kept it from him for a couple of weeks, but decided to tell him when he came home that Sunday from work.

'Two bits of news in one day,' I said. 'Not only am I not going back to Jonathan – '

' – but you're pregant too, I suppose.' He was flipping his vodka backwards and forwards in the glass.

'Exactly. How did you know?'

'You look pregnant,' he said. 'You've looked very – careful for the last two weeks.' I laughed.

'Aren't you pleased?'

'Of course I am.' He paused. 'Did you mean to?'

'No, honestly.'

'I believe you.' He smiled, quite kindly. 'The only thing is, don't forget, I haven't said anything about marriage.'

'Nor have I,' I said.

'So what are you going to do about it?'

'Do about it?'

'Are you going to *have* it?'

'*Have* it? – '

'Are you going to have it, I said?'

I paused to think, pushing the ice cubes round my glass with a numb finger. At last I said:

'Of course I'm going to have it.'

'I see.' He got up and went over to the table for a packet of cigarettes, not looking at me. 'If you changed your mind, I know a particularly good doctor, even though it's all legal now.'

'But I'm not going to change my mind. Don't you see? I *want* it.' Joshua sighed and went back to another seat, farther from me.

'In that case,' he said, 'you'd better find us somewhere to live. Quickly. We couldn't stay here with a child.'

'Of course not.' Potential houses. Prams. Joshua lifting it up to look at it when he came home. Warm milk, small fingers. I began to drown in a heavy calm. Mrs Fox would knit things. 'And there's just one other thing,' I said.

'I know what that is, too.' Joshua shifted about on the sofa, unusually restless. 'As you're pregnant, it would be quicker and easier and generally more convenient if Jonathan cited me in the divorce. Yes, I accept that too. Is there anything else, while we're about it?' He was frowning. I got up and went over to him.

'What's the matter?' I asked.

'Go and sit down or you'll feel sick.' I stood my ground. 'Go on. You must take care.' He seemed briefly concerned. I went back to the sofa.

'About the divorce – ' I said.

'There's no more to be said.' He stubbed his cigarette out with his thumb. 'I've agreed happily to being cited. You go ahead and do whatever it is you have to do, as fast as possible, for the sake of the baby. I won't make any kind of fuss, I promise, and the whole pattern will fall into place. We will all play our parts, Jonathan and I, I've no doubt, just as you imagined. It will all be very neat and easy and tidy. No fuss. First husband dies, second husband is divorced, lover agrees to support both you and his child. What more could you want? – Oh, and probably, if you play your cards right, which no doubt being you you will, one day I might even offer you marriage as well. So there's a lovely future for you, all planned out. All lovely – '

' – Joshua!' I rose in a daze of nausea and tears.

'Sit *down*. You'll feel sick. Stop stomping about.'

'I *do* feel sick.'

'Sit down, then.' I sat. There was a long silence. Neither of us could think of anything to say. Then:

'I won't have it if you really don't want it,' I said. 'I could have an abortion.'

'No, no. You wouldn't want that.'

'Would you?'

'Probably not, when it came to it. I'm sorry, Face. As usual, I went too far.' He smiled. 'But you've sprung a lot on me in one day.' I smiled back.

'Oughtn't we do something?' I asked.

'You have an infallibly awful sense of occasion,' he said, 'but as there's no food in the place, I suppose we ought. If you're not feeling too sick, we'd better go out to dinner.'

*

The morning Jonathan brought home the pink toy bear for our unconceived baby he also brought pink roses and the inevitable bottle of champagne.

'This is nothing,' he said, 'nothing compared with what I shall bring when the real time comes. You won't believe it. I shall have bells rung, guns fired, jewellery delivered. . . . You wait.' He was in one of his gayest moods, happy to be away from his study and the blank sheet of paper.

He scooped my hair up behind my ears and held it high in an untidy bun. 'My darling Suki Soo, if you could ever for one moment believe how much I loved you – ', he stooped to kiss the neck he had made naked, ' – well, you couldn't ever believe it. Now. Let's open the bottle.'

Jonathan toasted our future child. We sat there, side by side on the chintz sofa, hand in hand – his hands were always warm and very soft – Jonathan cooing about what he and his son would do together when the time came. He kissed me on the cheeks, the eyelids, the temples, his lips wet and bubbly with the champagne. He had taken off his coat. He sat in his braces, his shirt very white in the morning sun which slanted through the room and lit up the pot plants in their vases, still tied up in bows.

I drank till I felt weak and dizzy. I laughed and giggled and kissed Jonathan back, on the nose, on the puffy jaws that tasted of after-shave, and at last I was able to say, with all conviction, that I agreed with him. It would be nice to have his baby.

*

Joshua woke in the middle of the night. He put his hand on my stomach.

'The awful thing is, Face,' he said, 'that it looks as if I will probably have to be in Mexico for at least three months. Will you be all right?'

*

Some nights later I was wakened by sharp, familiar pains in my back and stomach. It was three o'clock. I woke Joshua.

'There's something wrong.'

'Oh God.' He put on the light. 'Same as before?' I

nodded. He smoothed his hand gently over my stomach and down between my legs. Then he drew it back to the light. It was covered in blood.

'So the plans have gone wrong after all,' I said.

'Shut up,' he said. 'Maybe we can save it.'

Everything happened very quickly. I heard him telephoning people, making arrangements in short snappy sentences. I heard my own moans as he lifted me from the bed, wrapped me in a blanket and carried me to the car. The leather of the car seat was very cold. As the engine shuddered to a start I bent double, trying to shut out the pain.

'Hold on, Face,' I think Joshua said. 'The doctor said it would be better if we got you in. I thought I could make it quicker than an ambulance.'

The car screamed through empty streets, the blood rushed warm down my legs.

'The floor of your car,' I kept saying. 'I'm sorry about the floor of your car.'

Someone met us with a stretcher. Grey corridors blistered with neon lights waved like streamers past my eyes. Then there was a white room that smelt of disinfectant. Badly drawn dog-roses on the beige curtains. A nurse bent over me. Three blackheads shaped like a clover leaf were stamped on the side of her nose, sharp points in her starchy skin. She gave me something bitter to drink. A doctor came in and patted me on the flanks like a friendly farmer.

'How is she feeling, then?' he asked Joshua, as if I wasn't there. He flicked down the sheets, lifted my nightgown and pulled the reading lamp, on its metal arm, towards him. Joshua held my hand.

Hours later the doctor came back again. His face was

stripped into a thousand coiling pieces as if it had been through a mincer.

'Good heavens, what a thing, you're biting the sheet, sheet, sheet, sheet. . . .' he said, his voice echoing away. I felt Joshua fold up both my hands like a ball of wool and hold them in both his. Then the doctor's voice came again.

'I'm afraid that's that,' he said. 'That's that, that's that, that's that. . .' I could hear watery noises on the lino floor, someone with a mop, the crackling of paper, nurses' quick feet going tap-tap, tap-tap, the dry rub of the doctor's hands. But when I opened my eyes they had all gone. All but Joshua.

'Oh, Face,' he said. 'Are you awake?' He bent his head down over mine. 'I didn't want that to happen, either.' Then he got up brusquely and strode over to another part of the room, so that without moving my head I couldn't see him any more.

'I'll leave you to sleep,' he said. 'I must go. It's getting on for eleven. The doctor said it would be a good idea for you to stay here for a few days. You're a bit torn about.' He returned to my bed and stood looking down at me.

'You must go,' I said, 'you'll be late.'

'Poor old Face,' he said.

*

Mrs Fox, of course, was my first visitor. She arrived with daffodils and a honeycomb later that afternoon.

'There was a helicopter going over towards Battersea Bridge,' she said. 'I saw it from the bus so I got out at the next stop and watched it go by. That's what made me late. The noise! Then there wasn't another bus for twenty minutes.' She dumped her parcels at the end of my bed and drew up an upright chair. This morning she had two poppies in her hat and the silver painted goose feathers, left over from Christmas Day, pinned to the lapel of her coat. She looked me up and down and pulled her chair nearer.

'Shall I tell you something? Last night I went to this Bach Society evening. Well, it was very interesting. We all sang for a couple of hours, then we went into the Meeting Room for coffee and sandwiches. The members, that is. It was a 'members only' night. The cream of the Bach followers they think they are, too. I wouldn't have joined them if I'd known what snobs they were.

'Anyhow. Roger Nevern, the young American conductor, you know, had agreed to come and meet us. He was half an hour late, which got some of them very worried. The coffee was finished. And when he did come, my! You could hear the gasps going up. All because his hair was long and he was wearing a lovely flowered shirt and tie. I suppose they expected white tie and tails. They could hardly sustain their titters, I can tell you. The rudeness of it, and he was being so polite, taking an interest in each one of us and repeating our names when he was introduced. When he'd gone they all huddled together, these old things, and the rumour was he'd been seen at another do in a pale blue fur coat almost down to his ankles. What a crime! I said. I felt I had to speak out. What a crime! I said, a blue fur coat. Well, they must have heard the note of sarcasm in my voice, because they all turned on me, you know, all their heads spun round simultaneously and they began to go at *me*, as if I was wearing blue fur.

'Well, they got as good as they gave, I can tell you. I told them what a bunch of hypocrites they were. Stupid old fools. If Shakespeare himself came back from the dead they'd expect him to be dressed by Moss Bros. Poor dears, they have no notion of genius. They are so confined by their own mistaken little priorities.' She smiled to herself and began to wander round the room. 'This is a nice place you're in,' she said, 'will you be out soon?'

'In a few days,' I said.

'When you're out we will all go to Brighton for some sea air. You need a bit of sea air. We'll go for the day. I'll ask Joshua to take us. We'll go and look for the house Edith and I were brought up in. I hear it's a bed and breakfast place now, but never mind. You need the sea air.'

When she had gone a young nurse with red hair came in with pills.

'What a night,' she said, brightly, 'we had the same thing happen next door. A very young couple. They'd only been married three months, too. We had a terrible time with the husband. I think he was rather the hysterical type, mind, but we had to give him sedatives. Your husband gone? Back to work, I suppose.'

It was easier not even to pause.

'Yes. He's very busy.'

'He'll be back,' she said, 'and you'll feel quite different in a few days, I can tell you.'

That afternoon was one of those slow, white afternoons that often happen in late winter, when shadowless light from the sky stretches taut across a window, flatter than the light of spring and more melancholy. On the table that made a bridge over the foot of my bed twelve daffodils, cruelly yellow against the white walls, squashed rigidly together in a tall, thin hospital vase. A thermometer stood in a glass of pink liquid, above the basin, and in a room so drained of colour the yellow of the flowers and the pink of the liquid jarred my eyes. My stomach ached. It was a scooped out hole. I could feel the shape of the hollow among my guts. I waited for it to wither, to close back into place, and the beat of the ache throbbed in my head like a chant.

The bed was uncomforting, narrow and hard. I stretched my feet down and felt the hardness of the iron bed-end. I turned away from the glare of light in the window, and shut my eyes.

*

I kept my eyes shut for several moments after the matron brusqued in on Sunday mornings, shouting at us with a vicious gaiety to get out of bed *quickly*, or else. She would clatter down the linoleum aisle between the two rows of beds, tweak back the thin curtains with a petulant snap, and stand triumphant as the daylight gushed in on us. I opened my eyes to watch her return journey. Barely raised the lids, for fear of catching her glance and having no energy to reject it. Through a blur of lashes I saw the familiar, low-slung calves that bulged just a few inches above the well-polished heels of her flat brown sensible walking shoes. A confident walk. Miss Peel was full of confidence and authority. She had an amazing head for name-tapes, too. She could recall the precise condition of scores of pairs of bras, vests and knickers, and whether or not they were adequately marked. Her anecdotes, which invariably appealed to her rather more than they did to her audience, were all about underwear. There was one old girl, famous in Miss Peel's memory, who went through four pairs of gym knickers in one term. In her own mind, Miss Peel felt her sense of humour to be a little *risqué*, and among the juniors she managed to curb her conversation to shoes, socks and overwear; but her heart was not in it.

Her usual Sunday call echoed down the dormitory.

'Nylons for those going out with parents, lisle for everybody else, of course, and no powder for *any* noses, or there'll be trouble.'

Sunday at school was an icy, lumbering day that bore no relation to the rest of the week. A gap to be endured until the bustle and normality of Monday: a day when the passing of time was unusually slow and the strictures of confinement almost intolerable. We were forced to observe the Lord's day of rest with stalwart exactitude, and smarten ourselves up to a standard that would delight Christ Himself should He care suddenly to descend. Scratchy overcoats. Straight seamed, lumpy stockings thick as gloves; pathetically drab brown dresses which, in an attempt to liven up, we scrunched in at the waists with huge elastic belts – the most desirable accessories of the early fifties.

On Sundays we wrote uncomplaining letters to our parents and walked in crocodile to church. We were allowed to listen to classical music and read good books, and there were hundreds-and-thousands on whatever the pudding at lunch. But it was the evenings, the fragile evenings full of the sad thundering church bells from the priory church, that filled us with the wild folly of anticipation and the tremulous ache of longing to be free. We would sit on the summer lawn, rugs spread over pine needles from the vast trees, eyes cast down over our pieces of sewing. The headmistress with her tired Rosetti face, curved eyebrows and wispy hair was the only one to sit on a chair. A bible lay on her lap. She would glance, as she glanced a thousand times a day, up to the hills; two dramatic great purple swellings in the sky now, nothing like the scurvy lumps they were to walk over, diseased with sweet-papers and council notices. The headmistress believed in her range of hills. She took strength from them. 'I will lift up mine eyes,' as she so often said.

On Sunday evenings she would talk to her seniors about going out into the world, as the time approached – the great unprotective world beyond the school gate. Her voice was always full of promise.

'Always remember, girls, to kick against the pricks, as St Paul said.' All would be fine if we kicked against them. She lulled us in to security. 'And remember, too, that if God be for you, who can be against you?' She spoke often of the love of God, never of the love of man. We wondered if she had ever been loved herself, by man as well as God. She was so confident of the happy outcome of loving God. She looked happy on it. And the school magazine was full of the news of old girls who, having learnt like us to love Him, had on the way found husbands too, and were leading lives of pleasurable security, as the child-bearing wives of Midland farmers, solicitors, humble aristocrats and industrial tycoons.

On those Sunday evenings on the shadowy rugs, there wasn't one of us who didn't believe that it would all fall into place for us, too. We felt a blinding, overpowering resolve to make our own future work; to kick against the pricks, to stick to what we promised, to go on believing. Trembling with good intention, tears scalded our eyes.

So we left school with all the privilege of having been warned. We left believing in God, in Wordsworth, in our role in life as good wives and mothers. For several years, in fact, some of us still remembered, from time to time, how these old beliefs felt.

*

'Soo,' said Jonathan, once, 'however much I fail you, will you go on forgiving me?' We were having breakfast in a hard, high and narrow bed somewhere, and he had egg on his chin.

*

Joshua came back in the evening.

'Feeling better?' he asked. I raised myself on the pillows and he kissed my forehead. He looked round the bare room. 'There were such awful flowers on the barrow downstairs that I knew you'd know they had come from there, so I didn't get any. I'm sorry.'

'That's all right.' The hole in my stomach felt smaller. Joshua grinned.

'You don't look your best, Face.'

'I don't feel my best.'

'But well enough to come home to-morrow? It'd be nice to have you there for the last few days. I leave on Monday. It's all finally fixed.' To-day was Thursday.

'Of course I'll come,' I said.

'Good.' He sat on the chair close to my bed and took my hand. His heel began to tap on the floor. 'Face, Face,' he said quietly.

'What is it?'

'I don't know. All this muddle. There doesn't seem much point now, does there?'

'Not much point in what?'

'You know. In going ahead. Breaking up your marriage. Living together.' For a moment or two I thought of moving my hand from under his. But I had no energy to make the gesture.

'Oh,' I said. 'I see what you've been thinking.'

'If we'd had the baby, then of course – '

' – of course it would have been different.'

'Of course.' Silence. Then I said:

'What a pity I'm not better at having children. I didn't realise, when the miscarriage began, two things were at stake.'

Joshua thumped the bed and stopped tapping his heel at last.

'For God's sake don't say things like that. You make me sound more of a shit then even I thought I was.'

'Sorry.'

He bent very near to me, holding up his hands expressively, like a man trying to sell something.

'Listen, Face. Listen to me. You've got to go back to Jonathan. You've known that, I've known that, really, all along. You can't leave someone, just like that, just because your heart doesn't leap about any more every time he comes into the room, and he annoys you the way he eats his kippers. That's not what marriage is about, if it's worth anything at all. Besides, you've told me hundreds of times you love him, in a way, haven't you? Perhaps that way is good enough. And hundreds of times you've missed him, I know. Even though you haven't said anything. But I know, because I've watched you. Sometimes, when I've been particularly cruel or thoughtless, I've seen your face. I know what you've thought. You've thought: maybe Jonathan isn't particularly clever or witty or interesting, but at least he's kind, and he's always loving and reasonable. You've thought that, haven't you? Am I wrong?'

'Go on,' I said.

'My trouble,' he said, 'my trouble is that I'm not *present* in all that I do. Baldwin once pointed out that one should be present in order to be sensual. I'm cruel because I'm thoughtless, and I'm thoughtless about one thing because I'm thinking about another, and so often I get my priorities wrong. And when it comes to you – I have thought about it so much, honestly I have – I don't think I'm prepared to give up enough for you. I'm too unreliable, too unwittingly unkind. I would only make you unhappy. Perhaps I don't care enough – and there you are, you see, that's cruel.' He began to play with my fingers, hot stony fingers at the end of a weightless arm. Then he smiled at me, quite cheerfully. 'At least you could rely on Jonathan's constant loving. It's a great virtue, consistency. Besides, think how he must miss you, how much he must want you back. Anybody who had been loved by you, and has lost you, would want you back.'

I shut my eyes. Images shifted as in a gently shaken kaleidoscope. The flaring colours of butterflies, a great arc of Norfolk sky, the spray of sand in windy dunes, omelettes on Formica tables, the shimmer of blue sequins.

'How do you know we'd survive, Face?' Joshua was saying. 'Please open your eyes.'

I did. His pale face, now so near, was a fall of imperfect skin – pitted, lined, shadowy. His dark eyes were far back out of reach, sealed behind reflecting lenses.

'Perhaps we wouldn't,' I said.

He sat back. A confusion of expressions crossed his face – surprise, relief, disappointment, perhaps.

'So what will you do?' he asked.

'Go back,' I said, 'of course.'

After a long time of silence he fell upon me, kissing me, touching my hair, my ears, my breasts.

'You're right, you're right, you're right,' he kept saying. 'We're both right, aren't we? But oh Christ, Face.' He sat up again, still holding both my hands. 'It'll be funny, after six months.'

'It's been a pretty good time,' I said. I heard myself laughing, a sort of small, quiet snort. 'Joshua Heron', I said.

'Mrs Lyall?'

'Joshua Heron, now it's all over, now everything is over, I feel terribly, terribly tired.' He smiled back.

'Don't go to sleep just yet. I've got something for you.' He felt in his pocket. 'I didn't know what to get, really, so I went to Mrs Fox for advice. I'm no good at presents.'

I opened a small box. On a bed of cotton-wool lay her star-sapphire ring, the colour of milky forget-me-nots. When I moved it, even in the fading evening light, the spikes of a star, dazzling razor lines, split the stone.

'She gave it to me,' Joshua was saying. 'She said I could do what I liked with it. What else could I do?'

At that moment, I think it was, when he put it on my finger and held my hand up to the light, I began to cry. Weakly, hopelessly.

'Shut up,' he said. 'Shut up or I'll think you don't like it. It looks marvellous. Much better than on her old hands.'

'I'm thinking of how she'll miss it. She must have been rubbing it with her other hand for years.' I was also wondering what Joshua would do that evening. I didn't want him to be unfaithful now, not before Monday, when our term officially ended. It was a wasted evening, being in bed.

'I know what you're thinking,' he said. 'But you needn't worry. I'm taking Mrs Fox to the Festival Hall. Verdi.'

I stopped crying. Calm, calm, calm.

'But you hate that sort of music,' I said.

'It'll be different with Mrs Fox. She'll explain it all to me.'

'I wish I was coming too.'

'You don't like Verdi either.'

'No.'

'I wish you were, though. But still, we'll go to Brighton on Sunday, by special request of Mrs Fox. Would you like that?'

'Oh yes. I'd like that.'

'We'll do that, then.' He paused, bent down, took my face in his hands and kissed my eyes, forcing them to shut.

'It's very odd,' I said, half-asleep, 'how the most difficult decisions to make are the easiest ones to change.'

'I daresay,' said Joshua, 'I'll think of you. I daresay I'll think of you all through the Verdi.'

Chapter Thirteen

Almost as soon as I arrived back at the flat David Roberts rang.

'Your friendly adviser here again,' he said. 'Your time is up, old thing.'

'I know, I know.'

'If it will fit in with your plans, Jonathan would like to meet you at six o'clock on Tuesday evening.'

'Why then, particularly?'

'Because that is exactly and precisely when the six months will be up.' He coughed. 'As a matter of fact, though don't say you know this, Jonathan is already back in London. I saw him last night. He looked very fit. Remarkably well, considering.'

'Good.'

'Might I be so bold as to ask what is going to happen? I mean, after all, I'm the one who's been keeping the two of you in touch, as it were.' He laughed to himself.

'I'm sorry,' I said, 'but I can't very well tell you before I tell Jonathan. Ring on Tuesday evening.'

'Ah well, I won't press you. Anyhow, you know me – the eternal optimist. I'll be thinking of you both.'

'Thank you.'

'Shall I tell him that will be all right, then? Six o'clock, Tuesday?'

'Yes please. Tell him I'll be there. And thank you for all your trouble.'

'That's all right, old thing. Any time.'

*

Sunday we went to Brighton, the three of us. Mrs Fox wore an old musquash coat dyed blue. The dyeing had not been wholly successful. Streaks of dull brown rippled through the dull blue.

'I was reading about those fun furs,' she explained. 'That's what gave me the idea.' On her hat an Alexandra Rose Day rose and a Poppy Day poppy were intertwined with a shining cherry I had not seen before. She rubbed uneasily at the finger on which she used to wear the star-sapphire ring. Now it was replaced by a dim moonstone, whose feel was still strange to her.

It was a cold, bright day. We parked the car in one of the crescents and walked to a small restaurant for lunch. Inside, the dark patterned carpets felt peculiarly soft after the sting of the pavements, and our breath jerked into the air in silver globes.

We climbed a winding staircase to an upstairs room. It was half-filled with people who talked in quiet Sunday voices. On the unoccupied tables stiff white napkins stood on empty plates like solitary flames, and a shaft of winter sun lit up a trolley of puddings. We chose a corner table with comfortable bench seats. Mrs Fox and I sat together with Joshua opposite. He chose things for us from the long menu. The last lunch this, perhaps, with Joshua, for ever. And yet, no feeling of frustration, no warning of sentimental tears. Instead, a surprising sensation of peace, like the unique luxury of stretching between sleep and wakefulness.

Mrs Fox took off her coat. Her long strings of bead necklaces clacked against her plate as she leant over it. As she chattered I only half-listened to her, leaving Joshua to reply. I studied him with intense concentration, trying to imprint every small movement on my mind. The way he cut his roll – he cut the top off like other people slice the top off a boiled egg, then, without looking, pulled out the doughy inside with finger and thumb, rolling the bits into hard pellets and dropping them under the table-cloth. The way he looked right into his glass when he took a sip of wine: the way he caught his bottom lip under his top teeth to trap a smile while he listened to Mrs Fox. And when the story came to an end, the way he laughed with his mouth wide open, so that the polo-neck of his jersey was tipped over by his chin. I pushed the plate of butter towards him and briefly he held my hand.

'You're beautiful to-day, Face,' he said. Quietly, so that Mrs Fox shouldn't hear.

When lunch was over we walked along the front. Joshua between Mrs Fox and me. We each took an arm.

'In the old days,' Mrs Fox was saying, 'the bands in the tea-houses along the front were something remarkable. During the season, Edith and I spent most of our afternoons drinking tea in one or other of the places, just listening. There was one place we especially liked, I remember. Rusco's, I think it was called. They did a very good chocolate cake. It was so full of rum you had to eat it with a spoon. Well, at Rusco's, the leader of the band took a fancy to Edith. I could tell. He would always give a special bow in her direction at the end of every piece. He always wore a carnation in his buttonhole, this man, and he had the shiniest black hair I ever saw, right flat on his head, almost like another skin. – Edith was pretty in those days, mind. She had curls all round her face. Well, one day the waiter brought us over a little note from the bandleader. *Ladies*, it said, *is there any request you would like us to play for you?* But Edith, being so shy, just turned her head away and blushed. After that, she wouldn't go to Rusco's any more. I often think of the chance she might have missed.'

It was quite warm, walking fast, in the sun, although a sharp wind was blowing from the sea. The grey waves dipped and swooped restlessly, and above them a few gulls imitated their movements in the air.

'It's funny about Brighton,' said Mrs Fox, 'it's where all the best things have happened to me. It was on the train from Victoria to Brighton that I met Henry. In truth, I was going to Hove. But we got on so nicely on the train that some instinct made me get out at Brighton, too. We lived close by the station, then, so he walked me home. The next day he came round in the afternoon and asked my mother if he could take me out for tea. Well, my mother, of course – she was very old fashioned – was very shocked. Someone I'd picked up on the train, she called him, and sent him packing. But he was on holiday down here, staying with his aunt, and he had nothing to do, so he came every day with the same request, but each time my mother sent him away. I was afraid he would give up. But then, luckily, my mother found out that his aunt was a very respectable old lady reputed to be worth a fortune. So at last she said yes, just for tea. Well, we didn't bother with tea, of course. We just walked for miles and miles, in the rain, all over Brighton. Then we walked all along the beach and got quite soaked, and it began to thunder. We sheltered under the pier for a while, and do you know what he said? He said: "Ethel Smith, I'm a penniless medical student and there's nothing I can give you, but I love you." Then it came on to rain even harder, and we decided we'd better make a dash for it. So we ran home. And then, of course, my mother scolded us, and what with all the flurry of drying our clothes and making hot drinks I never had a chance to tell him that I loved him too.'

Mrs Fox came to a standstill, and pointed towards the town.

'Funnily enough, although it's all changed now with all these new blocks of flats, I believe we could still take the short cut to my mother's house that Henry and I took that day. Shall we try?'

On the way there she told us she had heard the house had been a bed and breakfast place now for many years. But she would like to see the outside again.

It was a small, redbrick house between two creamy stone Regency houses. The only things it had in common with them was a bow window on the first floor, and a bed and breakfast sign on the front door. Joshua was enthusiastic to see inside, but Mrs Fox tried to restrain him.

'You know how unsympathetic landladies can be,' she protested. But he disentangled himself from her arm and rang the front-door bell. It was answered by a middle-aged woman with a bunch of dazzling blonde curls perched precariously on her head, stage make-up and a stained apron.

'I have a friend here,' said Joshua, dragging the reluctant Mrs Fox towards him, 'who lived in this house till just after the First World War. We've heard so much about it from her, we wondered if we could just glance at the inside?'

'Well, I don't mind if you do. There's no-one staying at the moment. Come on in.' She gave us a welcoming landlady smile and we followed her.

The room stretched from one end of the house to the other, a window at each end. Three different wallpapers covered the walls: one flowered, one geometrical and one covered with storks flying through pink clouds. Mrs Fox gasped, and dabbed at the flowers and cherry in her hat. She turned slowly round, taking in the lurex glitter of the curtains, the television on its spindly legs, the flight of paper angels left over from Christmas, above the modern brick fireplace with its electric fire, the leatherette three-piece-suite and the jumbo ashtray from Torquay.

'I bought it thirty years ago,' said blonde curls, 'and spent every penny I had doing the place up. It was a right shambles. Then only last year I did it right through again. Cost me a fortune, but it's worth it. I'm fully booked years ahead.'

Mrs Fox didn't seem to hear her. Suddenly, she smiled.

'You've certainly improved the place,' she said. 'I never could have imagined it so lovely and bright.' She struggled to take off her fur coat. I helped her. Its warm satin lining smelt faintly of her violet scent. 'It was always chilly, too, in spite of the coal fire. You've got it lovely and warm, haven't you?' Again she looked in some amazement round the sparkling room. 'When we lived here, this was two poky little rooms. Here, in this part, the front room, my father would play his violin on a Sunday afternoon. We weren't allowed near him. It was very dark, I remember, and filled with huge mahogany furniture which seemed to suck up all the light, and it always smelt musty. It seemed so much smaller.'

The landlady looked at her kindly and invited us to join her in a cup of tea. When she had gone out to the kitchen, Mrs Fox snapped back to the present.

'But still,' she said, thinking out loud, 'you should never go back. It's a silly thing to do. A silly thing to do.'

She sat down on one of the leatherette arm-chairs. It squeaked, and the embroidered antimacassar skidded sideways behind her head. Joshua and I stood in front of the electric fire, close but not touching. Mrs Fox looked up at us.

'We've had some good times,' she said. Joshua laughed. 'You'll have to meet Clare's husband,' he said. Mrs Fox sniffed.

'I'm not looking forward to that. It isn't that I'm not pleased that it's all worked out so well. It's just that I'm used to you two. We're all used to each other, aren't we?' She was unusually subdued. But then the landlady came back with a tray of tea, and switched on the lights. Mrs Fox slid forward on her chair.

'Edith would never have believed her eyes,' she smiled, and for some reason the rest of us laughed.

When we left the landlady Mrs Fox had one more request before we turned to London. She wanted to take a short walk on the beach.

The wind was colder now and the afternoon light had almost faded. Street lamps made pale holes in the sky, and the pier stuck out into the sea like a huge, dusky barn on stilts. As we walked along the front an old, shadowy man came towards us, distorted into strange shapes by the instruments that hung about him.

'You'd never believe it!' Mrs Fox cried out in delight, 'who would have expected such luck? A one-man band. I wonder if he would play for us?' She skipped up to him like a child and put a hand on his arm. She asked him to play.

'I'm on my way home, aren't I, lady?' he replied, nicely.

Mrs Fox pleaded with him further. Eventually, they struck up some kind of a bargain. Then while the musician tuned up – weird squeaks and thumps flew from his various instruments – Mrs Fox led Joshua and me down a flight of steps to the beach.

'He'll be some time,' she explained. 'Those things go out of tune as soon as you finish playing them.'

The tide was high. There was only a narrow strip of shingle along which we could walk. Mrs Fox pranced along the stones making them clatter and crunch in a kind of harmony with the small crashes from the breaking waves. She stopped, stooped down, and picked up a smooth white pebble. Fast and skilfully she curved back her arm, lunged forward and threw it with all her force. It made a brief white arc in the sky, then plummeted down into the dark sea.

'Did you see that? Did you see where it went? Not bad for my age, in a fur coat, is it? So out of practice, too.' She picked up another pebble. 'Henry and I would compete for hours. He was a marvellous pebble thrower, Henry.' She broke off to throw again. This time the pebble didn't go so far. 'Not such a good one. You have to choose your pebble carefully. You can blame a poor shot quite a bit on the pebble, you know.'

Joshua chose himself a flat white stone, and with less grace than Mrs Fox, hurled it into the water.

'Not bad! Not bad at all. But just you see, I can beat you.' She bent down again to look for another stone.

At that moment the musician on the pavement high above us stepped forward. A street lamp behind him threw his huge shadow down on to the beach, a bulging monster shape. With a nice sense of the dramatic, he raised his arms for a second, like a conductor, so that his shadow became a bird shape. Then the wings dropped and he began to play.

'When I'm Sixty-Four' thumped down upon us. *Bang clonk oink doom, clonk*... Mrs Fox paused mid-throw to laugh.

'Cheeky!' she said. 'I'll show him I'm not in need of any looking after, am I?' and she thrust another pebble into the sea.

Joshua and I began to compete with her. Faster and faster we chose our stones and threw them with diminishing skill. The musician's shadow lapped over us, shrinking a little and swelling a little according to which instruments he played together. Joshua took my hand and whirled me round in a mad dance. Mrs Fox joined us. We skipped round in a circle, singing. The shingle slipped and scraped beneath our feet. On every fourth beat we paused, bent down, picked large stones and threw them, with one gesture, into the black chips of the waves. The wind, no longer cold, smelt of seaweed. A solitary gull cawed steeply up into the thick sky. We were confused with laughter.

When the tune came to an end, the dance came to an end. We clapped, but the noise was barely audible above the sea. Mrs Fox panted a little, and held her side. Joshua took her arm, suddenly concerned. She looked up at him, her face pale but excited.

'With a little more practice I wouldn't be surprised if you couldn't take on Henry one day,' she said. 'But I'm definitely not as good as I used to be. Give me a few days here, though, and I'd soon be up to my old standard.'

'I think we've done enough for one day, don't you?' Joshua let go of her arm. The musician began to play the march from *The Bridge on the River Kwai*.

'Just one more throw,' said Mrs Fox, 'to see if I can't beat you.'

Still panting, she stooped to choose another stone.

'This is a beauty. You couldn't find a better one on the whole beach.' It was flat, white, and almost perfectly round. She curved her arm again, tightened her mouth into a determined line, and threw. But this time it was feeble. The stone sank a few yards into the water. Mrs Fox sagged with disappointment.

'It's no good. Like Henry says, you should know when to stop.' Her hands fell to her sides. Her fingers plucked at bits of blue fur which straggled from her long sleeves. 'Well, perhaps we had better go.'

Joshua took her arm again and led her back towards the dark flight of steps. In slow motion they climbed the steps, in time with the music. On the pavement of the front again, now brilliant with lights, the wind seemed colder and fiercer. With a bare hand, her rings sparkling, Mrs Fox rammed her hat farther down on to her head.

'We must thank the man for his kindness,' she said. 'We must thank him for his splendid playing.'

Then, quite upright again, dignified and full of purpose, she marched towards him.

*

'D'you think I've remembered everything?'

'I think so.'

'All those new shirts?'

'Yes.'

'Plenty of socks?'

'Yes.'

'Pentels?'

'Yes.'

'You don't look after me badly, do you?'

Joshua was in the bath. Lying back, in the steam, not washing. I was on the three-legged cork stool.

'That was good, that chicken thing for dinner, wasn't it? We should have tried that place before.'

'Yes,' I said, 'we should.'

'We always meant to. You should have reminded me.' Pause. 'What are you thinking?'

'Nothing much.'

He offered me a soapy hand.

'Did you remember to get my sun lotion stuff?'

'Yes.'

'And a spare typewritter ribbon?'

'Yes.'

He grinned. Began to rub soap under one arm.

'You're marvellous, Face.'

'Oh, shut up.'

He grinned again and began under the other arm.

'Are you sure you're feeling all right now? I mean, your stomach and everything?'

'Yes, thank you. Fine.'

'You'll take care for a while, though, won't you? Thing like that takes a bit of getting over. Make Jonathan treat you carefully. Say you haven't been too well. Or are you going to tell him?'

'No.'

'What are you going to tell him about the last six months?'

'Nothing very much. I think it was part of our contract that we shouldn't make each other confess about whatever we'd been doing.'

'What do you think he's been up to?'

'I can't imagine. I expect he's been lonely. He's not

very good at being alone. Perhaps he really has been writing in his Roman attic.'

'Perhaps he's just about to have an epic novel published.'

'Perhaps.'

'So you'll be rich and famous.'

'Perhaps.'

'Will you ever want to see me again?'

'If you want. – Would you want to?'

'Not really. Small talk with Mr Lyall. "And perhaps you'd sign my copy for me, Jonathan old boy." You can imagine.'

'I suppose so.'

'Still, we might run into each other sometime, somewhere.'

'We might.'

'Not that we know many of the same people.'

'Well, just in the street.'

'Well, yes, we might, in the street.'

Joshua sat up, lifted a foot from the soap-misted water, and with intricate care began to wash each toe.

'Mrs Fox seemed tired this evening.'

'I think she overdid it.'

'Will you go on seeing her?'

'Of course. I'll probably go round to-morrow afternoon.'

'I'll send her lots of postcards. I wonder how she'll take to Jonathan?'

'Oh, she'll be won over by him in the end, I expect. He's got great charm.'

'So you've always said. But what else will you do?'

'When?'

'To-morrow.'

'Oh, to-morrow. To-morrow I'll finish packing up and tidying up here, then I'll go home and begin to get things ready for Tuesday.'

'For when Jonathan comes home?'

'Yes.'

Joshua dropped his first foot back in the water and picked up the other one.

'Well, you know my address in Mexico.'

'What do you mean?'

'You could send on anything I've forgotten.'

'Of course.'

'But I don't think I *have* forgotten anything, do you?'

'I don't think so.'

'All my new shirts?'

'We've been through all that.'

'So we have.'

He turned on the hot tap so that for a while we could not go on speaking. When the bath was full he lay back again, knees bent, hands tracing patterns under the water, an occasional finger surfacing to break a floating bubble of soap.

'D'you think it'll work?' he asked.

'Absolutely. I know it will.'

'Good. I always wanted you to go back, you know, all along.'

'Why?'

'Nothing to do with your not being the right person for me. Just because I always knew you believed implicitly in marriage, and that really you wanted it to work.'

'That's true,' I said. 'But that's not to say. . . .' Pause. This was my last chance to find out what I still didn't know. I would risk his anger. 'Was I ever all right for you?' I asked.

Joshua lifted a dripping arm and touched my chin with two fingers.

'Oh, Face,' he said, 'don't be silly.'

He stood up, then, and began to dry himself with a small black towel. I squeezed striped toothpaste for him on to his toothbrush.

'Do you remember?' Gaily I said it.

'For God's sake don't start remembering.' He rubbed the towel viciously over his face, then his hair.

'In fact, when I've gone, don't remember anything except that you once met a man called Joshua Heron, and by some measure of chance you and he were happy for a while. Will you do that for me, Face?'

'I will.'

'Good.' He opened the door so that the cold air from our bedroom blew upon us. He brushed his teeth, rinsed out the basin, turned out the light, got into bed and stretched out a hand for his schoolboy clock. With some difficulty, he set the alarm.

*

The next morning two members of the film crew picked him up early in a hired car. He didn't want me to go with them to the airport. He kissed me quickly and left in a rush. When he had gone, I searched the flat. For once, it seemed, he had remembered everything.

Chapter Fourteen

First, I opened the windows. The house smelt of polished furniture that has not been aired. Unlived-in. The woman who came twice a week had covered the sofa and arm-chairs in the sitting-room with dust sheets. She had arranged two piles of letters, one Jonathan's, one mine, on the desk. She had left me a note on the kitchen table. *I have taken the liberty of throwing away the piece of Stilton, it had gone mouldy.* Dated two months ago. It was the first time I had been in the house for three months, and that was only to collect more clothes. There was nothing in the fridge. Only two tins of soup in the larder.

Next, I had a bath. It was a pale blue bath. The wall-paper had matching pale blue roses. Jonathan liked blue. All his pyjamas were blue, with white initials on the pockets. He kept his pyjama tops on while he shaved in the mornings, while I was in the bath, but he took great care never to wet the collar. He hummed while he shaved. He was rather good at humming. Never out of tune. One Christmas I had found some blue after-shave lotion for his stocking. There was still a little at the bottom of the bottle on the shelf above the basin. I would get a new bottle, later to-day.

I dried in a huge navy towel, then walked naked into the bedroom. I sat on the kidney-shaped chintz stool in front of my dressing-table. The chintz seat felt cold for a moment. Half a dozen snapshots were stuck under the glass of the dressing-table. I studied them, tracing my finger on the cold glass round their frames: there was Jonathan with his arm round me in some Swiss mountain restaurant, a ski-ing holiday, our faces made harshly black and white by the flash bulb. We had drunk a lot of *gluwein* that night, and danced, and laughed. Enjoyed ourselves. There was Jonathan in his mother's rose garden, hands on hips, face screwed up against the sun; Jonathan sailing a small boat in Devon, slightly out of focus because of the choppy sea; Jonathan aged twelve, with smarmed-down choirboy hair, receiving a huge silver cup for swimming from a distinguished old woman in a velvet hat. There was one of me alone that Jonathan had taken with his Polaroid camera, a little faded. I sat on a rug in an indeterminate garden. I wore a cotton dress with a billowing skirt, and a cardigan. My hair was short and curled, and I smiled widely. It must have been a week or so after I first met Jonathan – perhaps the first weekend at his mother's house. I remember laughing at something he was saying while he took the photograph. He hadn't asked me to smile.

I looked at myself in the looking-glass. My face was much thinner, now. My hair much longer, straighter, straggly. It needed new highlights. There would be time, to-morrow. To-morrow in the morning. To-day I would shop, dust, clean, arrange roses. They would be expensive at this time of the year, but still. They were Jonathan's favourite flowers. He would hate to come back and find the house dusty, untidy and without flowers. It would have been so much easier if we could have met somewhere, caught a plane and flown away. Anywhere. Anywhere so long as it avoided all these preparations. But Jonathan expected preparations.

He would expect me to be ready for him, neat, in his favourite dress, the ice out – the ice tongs. I mustn't forget the ice tongs. Where were they? He would expect us to welcome each other home, and to forgive one another, and to make it all up over one gin and tonic. Or, knowing him, champagne. Well, we would. We would go on from there. I would heat up the veal escalopes cooked, as he had taught me, in cream sauce with brandy and mushrooms, and we would eat in the unused dining-room. Drink special wine. Candles. I must remember to get candles. By the end of dinner we would probably find ourselves laughing. In the past, it had always been easy to laugh together, in the end. If we could start laughing, if we could find something to laugh about, it would be all right. But which was his favourite dress?

I went to the cupboard. Everything hung limply. Thin, dim dresses they all seemed. Lifeless. They needed starch and ironing and air. They needed to be worn again. I took out a green dress covered with blue cornflowers. He liked that. I put it on. It was too long, drab. Side view, my bottom stuck out. My breasts sloped down and did something ugly to the front. I looked terrible. But perhaps with shoes, and a bra, and my hair done, to-morrow night, it wouldn't be so bad.

I took off the dress and hung it outside the cupboard to remind myself it needed ironing. I put on a pair of jeans and a shirt, and went downstairs, barefoot. Sat at the neat desk, found a piece of paper, and began to make a shopping list. *2 grapefruit pt. double cream roses veal sugar tonic water frozen peas coffee matches* – I could write with mechanical ease. I didn't have to think. The words appeared on the paper by themselves. *Hair lotion apricots soap candles I love you Jonathan Lyall I am your wife Clare Serena Lyall and this time it will be for ever more sempre toujours tomatoes salted peanuts and all the usual things like butter.*

All afternoon I shopped.

By the time I arrived home again it was too late to go and see Mrs Fox. I would go on Wednesday, perhaps even take Jonathan. She would be missing Joshua, I thought.

I dumped my shopping bags on the kitchen table and began to put things away. Very slowly, very methodically. Then I re-arranged the shelf of cookery books so that they were in order of height. The kitchen seemed to be paler green.

When there was nothing left to do in the kitchen I went back to the sitting-room. There, I re-arranged two more shelves of books. Five other shelves were filled with leather-bound volumes all the same height. I began to replace them so that the titles were in alphabetical order. But half-way through it seemed pointless, and I stopped.

I lit a cigarette, sat at the desk. Pulled open one of the drawers. It was neat with bundles of letters. Jonathan's writing, spidery and black. I pulled out one of the letters. It was written four years ago, from Manchester. He was up there seeing a man who had liked one of his plays.

My own darling, I read, *It's nice to be feeling as happy and as optimistic as I do at the moment about Screwball, but why does genius have to take one to God-forsaken places like Manchester? I miss you so much I can't tell you. I think of you all day and wonder what you're doing and I'm writing this because there's still another two hours until I can decently telephone you again. If the play is put on you will come up all the time, even for rehearsals, won't you? Just to say I love you, I love you, I love you, your silly old husband J.*

In those days he rang me every few hours if ever we

were forced to be apart, and wrote every day. I found the letter that told of Screwball's fate.

After all that waiting about, wasted days away from you, the beastly Mr Lewis said I was on the right lines but he saw no hope of actually putting the thing on. I could have cried. I needed you to be there to love and comfort me. Oh my darling, do you mind my constant failures? You say you don't, but I only half-believe you. I will stay till Monday when he says he will see me again – it just might be worthwhile. I do want to surprise you one day. Wait for me. The only thing I feel I'm good at is loving you. God knows what I'd do without you. Please don't ever leave me, darling. All love as ever your adoring husband J. P.S. I've bought an electric mixer in a cut-price shop.

I wound up both clocks. Checked the telephone to see it was working. Smoked several more cigarettes. Put the roses, expensive scentless buds, into a bucket of water.

Upstairs, I began to unpack my case. Slowly, again. I came to the box with the star-sapphire ring. Tried it on. Not strong enough light to force the star. I put it in a drawer under a pile of scarves. Then I found two notes from Joshua – the only notes he had ever written me.

Joshua Heron crept out because he didn't want to wake Funny Face. He doesn't apologise for not washing up his coffee cup and will be back at six to take various people to a theatre if they would like that.

The second one was written on the back of a restaurant bill, three months old.

Joshua Heron came back hopefully at lunchtime but found no-one. Would F.F. please ring J.H. as soon as she gets back to make up his mind about buying a corduroy jacket the colour of best quality hay?

I tore them up, into very small pieces, and threw them away. After that, I couldn't unpack any more. I left the rest of my clothes half in the case, half strewn about the floor. Then I went to bed. I had forgotten what a comfortable bed it was. At eight-thirty I turned out the light.

*

Four drum-majorettes skated across a huge rink towards me, holding up a striped canopy. Under the canopy, dressed in a dinner jacket, Jonathan skated in time with them. They stopped at the edge of the rink, in front of my seat. I rose, and moved the few paces towards them. As I did so, the huge audience, massed round the rink, began to applaud. Under the canopy I smiled at Jonathan and he gave me his hand. His fingers crackled and stung with ice. We began to skate away, looking for the exit to the wings. But it had disappeared. We skated round and round and the applause became louder. We kept passing Richard Storm, Mrs Fox and Joshua, sitting together in the front row. They had their arms intertwined, like people about to sing 'Auld Lang Syne'. They were laughing and laughing.

*

I woke at nine-thirty. I drew back the curtains and a cold grey light revealed the extent of the confusion on the floor: books, clothes, a pair of gum-boots still muddy from Norfolk. I would clear it all up, slowly, later. There were nine and a half hours to go.

I lay in the bath for a long time. After a while I thought I heard the creak of footsteps on the stairs. I listened again. Silence. Then a soft knock on the half-open door.

'May I come in?'

Ridiculously, I answered: 'Yes – who is it?'

Jonathan opened the door.

I stood up so fast the water swayed over the edge of the

bath and onto the floor. It streamed down my stomach and thighs, and I felt myself crossing my arms over my breasts.

'Darling! Wait a minute. Here's a towel.' He held it in front of himself like a shield, and came towards me. We kissed, lightly, the towel still between us. Then I put my wet arms round his neck.

'Jonathan,' I said.

'Hurry up and get dry.' He seemed to stiffen a little, and moved away from me. I took the towel from him and stretched up to flip it over my shoulders. In the few seconds that I was naked to him his eyes flashed up and down my body. 'Heaven's, you're thin,' he said.

'So are you.' His hair, as well as his face, seemed thinner. I climbed out of the bath, sat on the edge, and began to dry. 'I thought you weren't coming till to-night,' I said. 'I'm afraid nothing's ready. It would have been, by to-night.'

'Well, there didn't seem much point in hanging around for another day, doing nothing, knowing you were back.' He sat on the lavatory, hitching up both legs of his trousers as he did so. It was a new suit, trim grey flannel. He fiddled with his navy silk tie. 'Do you mind?'

'Of course not. I'm just sorry I haven't got the house organised.'

'That doesn't seem very important.'

I raised my eyebrows.

'You look very brown,' I said, 'very well.'

'I am. I've had so much sun that I actually turned from lobster to brown. I bet you never imagined the day when that would happen.' He laughed and I smiled. He had a nice face.

'No,' I said. He folded his arms, leant back against the cistern and looked at me.

'How are you, darling?'

'I'm all right, too.'

'It's been a funny old six months.'

'Yes.' I was dry. 'I'm just going to put on some clothes. I won't be a moment.' He followed me into the bedroom.

'I'll go down and put on some coffee.'

'That's a good idea.' When he had gone I quickly made the bed. He might not want to wait until to-night.

By the time I went downstairs Jonathan was in the sitting-room, a tray of coffee set on the low table in front of the sofa. He had found the best cups, the ones I used when his mother came to tea. Suddenly I realised I was hungry and thirsty.

'How lovely,' I said. I sat beside him on the sofa. The chintz cushion crackled beneath me. 'Where's your luggage?'

'Still in the car.' He smelt of unfamiliar after-shave. Too sweet. He poured the coffee and hot milk, put in the sugar and stirred mine as well as his own.

'Well, well,' he said. 'Six months to the day. I heard from David you were well and happy.'

'I heard the same about you.'

'I think he quite enjoyed his self-appointed role of keeping us in touch. He doesn't change, David.'

'No, he doesn't.'

'He doesn't change.' He sat hunched up on the edge of the sofa, his knees wide apart, his hands clasped between them. 'Well, it's strange to be back.' He looked down at my hands. 'Where did you get that ring?'

'It belonged to Mrs Fox.'

'Who's she?'

I paused for a moment.

'Mrs Fox is an old woman I met. A friend. You must meet her.' I fingered the ring, imitating her gestures, the gestures I knew so well. Then: 'It's nice to have you back,' I said.

He turned to me, smiling.

'Look darling, you don't have to pretend. After these six months, we might as well be honest with one another.'

'What do you mean?'

'You know perfectly well what I mean.' He put a soft hand on my knee. 'Let me tell you something, Soo. Let me try to tell you something. That is: it's all right. You needn't worry any more. You needn't feel guilty any more, you know. I know what your decision is, and I want you to understand and believe me. *I don't mind.* I really don't, this time. No pretending. So long as you are happy, I'm happy for you. I mean that.'

'But darling, you've got it all wrong.' I put my hand on his. 'About my decision, I mean. What on earth made you think I wouldn't want you back? Why did you think I wouldn't want to come back to you?'

'I just assumed, from your behaviour before we parted. I hoped for a while you might change your mind. Then I heard you were happy with Joshua Heron. So I gave up hoping.' A long silence. Then:

'In that case, I've got a surprise for you,' I said.

'Oh?'

'It's all over with Joshua. There wasn't really any question of – anything permanent. He's gone to Mexico. I told him I was going back to you, and he was pleased.'

'You mean? – You want us to stay married? Is that what you mean?'

'Of course.' A look of something like fear crossed his face. He patted at his soft, sandy hair with a hand that shook a little, then bent his head and pressed his eyes into his palms.

'Oh Christ, my love,' he said quietly. 'Oh Christ, what a mess. What a bloody awful mess.'

'Why?'

'Why? Because it was true what I said earlier. Absolutely true. About my not minding about your not wanting me any more. You see, the thing is, I'm fixed up elsewhere, as it were.'

'You mean – ?'

'I've found somebody else.' He sat up then and took both my hands. Lowered his eyes. His eyelashes had gone very blond in the sun. 'I'm sorry, Soo.'

'Somebody else?' I said.

'Somebody else.'

'I see.' I tried to draw my hands away but he held them firmly.

'Don't run away from me.' I flopped back in the sofa. He let go of one hand to stroke my hair. 'I thought you'd be so pleased. I thought you'd be delighted when I told you I had booked an appointment with my solicitor this afternoon, and we would get divorced as soon as possible, and you could go back to Joshua. But what an irony of timing. What a cruel irony.'

'You want to marry her, then?' I asked.

'That's the plan.'

'Is she Italian?'

'No. She just lives in Rome. I think you met her once, actually. She says she remembers you, at a party you apparently went to with David. She's called Rose Maclaine.'

'The American? But I thought she and David – ?'

'They did. A rather one-sided little affair. David was

dotty about her. But she never pretended the feeling was mutual.'

'Then he introduced her to you?'

'Then he introduced her to me. And that was that. Very awkward for David and me, being such old friends, as you can imagine.'

'I imagine.'

'Still, it seems to be all right now. He's forgiven me. I took him out to dinner last night and he drank our health and said he hoped we would be happy.'

I smiled.

'Last week he rang me to say he hoped *we* would be happy.'

'He changes.' Pause. 'Oh Christ, Soo. What a mess. What are we going to do?'

'What do you want to do?'

'Don't sound like that. Here, let me kiss you. You're shaking.'

I let him kiss me. He kissed me on the eyes and the cheeks. Then he ran the hard point of his tongue round my closed lips, trying to make me smile. A trick he hadn't practised since before we married. But I didn't smile and he soon gave up.

'I can't very well fall out of love with Rosie and come back to you just because – '

'Of course not.'

'So what shall we do?'

'You had better go ahead with your plans.'

'How would you feel about that? I thought you were in love with Joshua, anyway? So it wouldn't matter to you very much, would it? I'm sure he'd have you back.'

'Don't worry about me.'

'Don't be silly, Soo. I do worry about you. I still care

about you, you fool. It's just that living with Rosie did the trick. It made me see all the things that were missing in our marriage. It made me realise that I was looking for something in you that didn't exist, and making do with all the things *you* thought I minded about. And it also dawned on me that I was absolutely the wrong man for you. I drove you mad, remember? I don't wonder, really, when I think back on it.'

'You've got it all nicely worked out.'

'Oh, my love. Forgive me.'

'There's nothing to forgive. Does Rosie make you happy?'

'Very. She's a marvellous girl. So – organised.' He looked suddenly hopeful. 'Do you think we could all be friends?'

'I expect we probably could.'

'Are you going to make a fight for me? Try to get me back?'

'I don't see any point, if you want to go.'

'Quite.' He smiled again. 'The trouble with you, darling, is that you're so bloody reasonable you'd drive any man to despair. Let me give you one bit of advice. If ever you fall in love with anyone again, be unreasonable.' He stood up and hitched up his trousers. 'You've taken so much trouble. Those lovely roses, and I saw there was veal in the fridge. It could have been a marvellous homecoming.'

'Don't put off your solicitor,' I said. 'And you might recommend one to me.'

'Are you sure? I'm sorry, darling.' He paused. 'As a matter of a fact, what I had planned to do was to fly back to Rome to-night and settle a few things over there, then come back again next week. But I could go later.'

'No. Go to-night. You might as well.' I stood up and picked up the tray. He took it from me. 'How's the writing?' I asked.

'Going rather well, actually. I'm working on a little play called Back to Front. Rosie's keen to play the lead, so we're going to try to organise that. I showed part of it to David, and he's really enthusiastic. He says he knows a new young manager who might like it.' He smiled wryly. 'So nothing's changed.'

'No,' I said. 'I hope it gets put on.'

We went into the kitchen. A light rain sprayed against the window.

'Bloody English weather,' said Jonathan. 'It looks nice in here, though, darling. I always thought this kitchen was my *pièce de résistance*, didn't I?'

'Yes.'

'You can keep the house if you like. I mean, I don't want any of my money back.'

'You're very generous. Thank you.'

'And you can cite Rosie, of course.'

'All right, if that's easiest.'

'But we could talk about all those sort of arrangements when I get back next week. I don't really feel much like going into them now. I mean, I'm bloody happy and all that, I really am. But it's always nasty, having to make the actual break.'

'Quite.' He came and stood very near me. There was a long thin scratch on his chin where he had cut himself shaving. It was covered by a delicate scab of barely dried blood.

'You must think I'm a terrible shit,' he said.

'Oh no. It was my fault just as much as yours. More, probably.'

'But I don't think, feeling like I do about Rosie, and you feeling like I suppose you do about Joshua, that there's any point in our trying to make a go of it any more, do you?'

'Absolutely not.'

'Besides, six months apart kills a lot of things.' He kissed me on the cheek again. 'Oh darling. What a confounded mess. I think I'm going to cry.'

'Don't do that.'

'Well, there's not much point in my hanging around any more, is there? It'll only upset both of us. I'll call you next week.'

'I'll be here.'

'Will you be all right?'

'Of course.'

'I don't think you really mind.' He took the clean white handkerchief from his breast pocket and blew his nose very loudly. 'What fools we are.' We went to the front door. 'You must put on some weight,' he said. 'You're too thin.'

Outside, his old blue Vauxhall was covered with a million drops of rain that weren't heavy enough to run down. A leopard printed scarf lay on the back seat.

'Bloody English weather,' Jonathan said again. 'Always the same in this country.' He squeezed my hand. 'Well, darling, I'll be off, then.'

'See you next week.' We kissed each other on the cheek once more.

'I was so convinced you wouldn't want me. Funny how wrong you can be, even about someone you've been married to for six years.'

'Go on,' I said, 'I'm getting wet.'

He got into the car and started the engine. Its muffled rumble was horribly familiar. Jonathan's thumbs met at the top of the steering wheel. He had often said he thought it was the most comfortable way to drive. He raised one hand to wave. I waved back. The car drew slowly away. Puddles spluttered beneath the wheels for a moment, then were still again. I shut the front door.

*

It was definitely cold in the sitting-room now. I sat on the sofa again and wondered how to get warm. I had forgotten to ask Jonathan to turn on the central heating.

I blew on my hands. The crayon drawing of Richard Storm smiled down at me. Later, I would take it down. Jonathan smiled from a silver frame, too. It was his favourite picture of himself, taken when he was in the Coldstream Guards by a Bond Street photographer who had touched up his pale eyebrows. I would take that down as well.

I thought how I had felt quite proud when Jonathan had walked into the bathroom this morning. He had looked so agreeable. I was pleased he was back.

I wondered what to do with the veal and the roses.

I listened to the clocks ticking, sometimes together, sometimes one just a little ahead of the other.

I don't know how long I sat there.

But after a while I went to the kitchen and turned on the cold tap. The water pattered on to the zinc bottom of the sink, louder as I turned the tap faster. I held my hands so that the fingers drooped under the cascade of water. It was so cold, they soon felt quite numb. I turned the tap off with the palm of my hand.

A walk, I thought. If I walked fast I would get warm.

I put on my mackintosh and left the house, slamming the door behind me.

It was raining harder now. I walked carelessly, not bothering to avoid the puddles, so that water splashed up my legs. Soon my hair was soaked and drips kept on running into my eyes.

It took about half an hour to get to Mrs Fox. Surprisingly, the downstairs front door was ajar. I pushed it open and went in. The landlady was coming downstairs, her huge slack breasts rolling about under a pink jersey.

'Oh, it's you,' she said. 'Another of her friends.' She slapped the banisters with a fat hand and heaved herself down the last few steps.

'Is she in?' I asked.

'No dear, she's out. Out for good. Didn't you know?'

'Know what?'

'Oh, I see. You didn't know.' She lowered her voice. 'Mrs Fox passed away Sunday night, they reckon.'

'She's dead?' I said. The landlady's eyes hardened with power.

'Dead as a doornail, dear. Heart attack. She might have been there for days if yours truly hadn't noticed her milk still outside her door yesterday dinner time. She always took her milk in, regular. So I thought, I thought to myself: my, something funny's up. I banged on the door, noisy as you like, but not a cheep. So I phoned the police. They come up, of course, and break the lock. They found her on the bed. Hat still on and all.'

I leant against the wall. A bit of plaster crumbled behind my shoulder and fell to the stone floor. The landlady's face erupted into a huge sun of crumbling white flesh that sprouted from the grey stone stairs rising behind her.

'Where is she?' I asked.

'They took her away, ambulance men, not long after. They asked me if I knew any of her relations. Course, I couldn't help them.'

'Where did they take her to?'

'Blow me if I didn't ask. Fulham, I should imagine. The hospital.' More plaster broke and fell away from the wall behind my shoulder. 'Careful,' she said, 'that wall's coming down.'

'So it is,' I said. The landlady opened the front door. She looked at the rain, diminished to a drizzle now.

'Ooh, it isn't half coming down cats and dogs, isn't it? Well, I must be getting back to work. See that other man shuts the door behind him when he leaves, will you? You know what men are.'

'What man?'

'There's another of her friends upstairs. Don't know for the life of me what he expects to find, poking about up there. The door's locked, but he asked me to leave him on his own – I don't know.'

She went out, shutting the front door. I went to the well of the staircase, held on to the banisters and looked up at the regular flights of stairs. Quietly, a man was coming down from the top, his footfall clacking gently on the stone. As he came nearer I saw that it was Cedric Plummer. The man from the R.S.P.C.A.

'Hello,' he said, as he saw me.

'Hello.'

He came down the last flight, leaning heavily on the banisters. He wasn't wearing his uniform, but the dark suit and plum tie he had worn at Mrs Fox's party.

When he reached the bottom he stopped beside me. We stood looking at each other in the dim light of the drab hallway. There were rims of yellow crust at the roots of his eyelashes. The eyelids themselves were red and puffy.

'The landlady told me she was dead,' I said.

Mr Plummer shrugged his shoulders, unclenched his hands, and held them up like two heavy white flags.

'Who could conceive such sadness?' he replied. 'Who could conceive such sadness?' He moved away from me, towards the front door. 'I'd just come up to take her home to us for the day. She had always wanted to see Epsom. Nancy had baked her special sponge cake, and we had the place all looking spick and span.' He paused. 'She always said she wanted to see Epsom, Mrs Fox did, you know.' He paused again. 'To think, she never saw it.'

He turned his face quickly from me, pulled the door open, and went down the steps.

Alone in the hall I listened to the silence. For the first time, no music came from the top floor. The Japanese mobile that hung from the naked light bulb swung a little in the draught, faintly patterning the dingy walls.

It was cold and damp. Rain from my wet hair ran down the inside of my mackintosh collar.

I went on holding the clammy banisters, until a moment of dizziness passed, and then I followed Mr Plummer through the front door.

Outside, the rain had almost stopped. The sky was brightening. I began to run in the direction of Fulham. Somehow, I had to find a brass band.

Wanting

For James

1

On the morning of the girls' departure, Alfred Baxter woke two hours earlier than usual and dressed himself hurriedly. In the quiet hours of the night, when he had lain fretfully imagining the emptiness of the house without them, he had decided that only his best clothes would befit the occasion of their leaving. And so now he brushed at the jacket of his navy serge suit with a hand which, he noticed, seemed to be trembling, and blew at the thin ridge of dust and scurf that had gathered round the collar. He then chose a grey tie, its solemnity scarcely broken by the small crest of his old cricketing club, and he gave his lace-up shoes a quick polish on the eiderdown.

In the kitchen, it occurred to Mr Baxter that to stick to his normal routine, at least in part, might quell the pain in his heart and the tightness in his chest that made it difficult to breathe. His customary cup of tea would perhaps melt the incredulity that sat like a lump of stone on his head, and give him the strength to put on a cheerful face. He lit the gas ring under the kettle and took down the tea caddy, with its four portraits of George V, from its place on the shelf.

It was early summer. Dawn was beginning to lighten the curtains – Eileen's last curtains – and fill the kitchen with grey. This was all as Mr Baxter had planned. To say goodbye to the girls in broad daylight, he had felt, would be too harsh. Sunlight would seize upon tears, making them sparkle shamefully on his cheek. Like this, they could leave unnoticed.

Mr Baxter sat stirring his tea, his eyes imprinted with the familiar pattern of cornflowers on Eileen's last curtains drawn across the window above the sink. He remembered, as he did every day at breakfast, how in her final ailing months Eileen had taken those curtains with her everywhere, as if knowing her time to finish them was limited. Even on picnics on the beach – Mr Baxter always fearing for her warmth and comfort – she had insisted on hemming them with her arthritic hands. The process of their completion was a slow one, for her stiff and clumsy fingers could scarcely hold a needle. By autumn she was still at them, painfully concentrating as she sat by the evening fire, right up to a few days before she died. She sewed into them the last of her energy, but she had never seen them hung. Mr Baxter had taken that job upon himself as soon as the funeral guests had left – half-eaten bridge rolls and cups of tea all over the place – as the only alternative to the horrible task of clearing up.

As soon as the cornflower curtains were in place, Mr Baxter remembered, he had felt much happier. It was as if Eileen's spirit was fluttering in the room again, reminding him to be cheerful. And indeed, until the sad winding up of the business, he had been cheerful.

He was glad she had not lived to see the demise of the drapery shop. That would have broken her heart. It had been their lives, after all. Fifty-three years. Mr Baxter had started the shop, in this his father's house, in a very modest way: silks and threads, and nice sharp scissors, bone and ivory and tortoiseshell buttons. Business was as good as could be expected in a small village. Then Mr Baxter discovered a recipe for considerable success: any item that a customer required, should it not be already in stock, he would endeavour to supply as soon as possible. Thus the shop expanded far beyond the bounds of mere drapery and haberdashery, and carried such disparate items as canary seed, bundles of kindling, linen dishcloths and blackcurrant throat pastilles. Baxter's became a shop to rely upon, its reputation spread up and down the coast. Soon Mr Baxter realized he could no longer manage entirely on his own, and advertised for help.

Eileen was the first to apply. She came for her interview, one bright afternoon in 1920, tripping through the door with a measure of confidence and expectancy that Mr Baxter recognized immediately. She did not, however, display any traces of boldness or cheekiness – things that would have quickly deterred Mr Baxter. She was very young: not long eighteen, with a bonny face and brown curls that bobbed about her face. Her figure was neat and slim and Mr Baxter noticed with pleasure her highly polished brown shoes, with their

Louis heels and small twin straps, a pattern of holes punched over the toes. Within a few minutes' conversation it was apparent Eileen was full of enthusiasm – a quality Mr Baxter much admired – and he took her on at once.

Eileen filled the shop with a warmth and flurry which made Mr Baxter realize what the place had previously been missing. Along with her enthusiasm, she came bursting with suggestions. Within days she had taken it upon herself to order things appertaining to the more delicate feminine areas in which Mr Baxter admitted he had neither experience nor taste: satin hair ribbons, shell brooches and cards of spare suspenders. From there she took over the buying of the materials. Shelves that had once been stacked with dull worsteds, calicoes and coarse linens now rippled with flowered cottons and handsome lace that Eileen found in local markets. Mr Baxter came to depend on her tastes, her instincts, her constant cheerful presence and when, one afternoon – as she polished the old oak counter – Eileen suggested that life would be much easier if they married, Mr Baxter found himself flared with enthusiasm identical to her own. Soon after their tenth wedding anniversary, celebrated in the rain at Lowestoft, they finally accepted the doctor's word they would have to remain childless, and Eileen suggested the girls.

Mr Baxter finished his tea, rinsed his cup, and told himself he could not afford to postpone the moment any longer. He took the key of the shop from its place under the clock, and opened the door that led from the kitchen.

The girls were as he had left them last night, grouped in a conversation piece in the window. Lily, the oldest, but of eternal youth, stood facing him, her fluid china arm stretched, as it had always stretched over the years, in welcome. Lily's creator had bestowed her with a Mona Lisa smile which Mr Baxter had never fathomed. He had been unable to work out what went on in her mind, though sometimes – and he had never dared mention his suspicions to Eileen, who had always loved Lily best – he felt it might be a tangle of disparaging thoughts, despite the superficial kindness in her pale eyes.

To Lily's right stood Winnie – dear, stupid Winnie, disaster-prone but good-humoured in face of all trouble. Her waxen cheek was burnished with a perpetual blush. In her heyday in the early thirties this had given her a coquettish look which Mr Baxter, and many others, found attractive. But for the past thirty years she had merely looked permanently ashamed, and evoked sympathy. Lily and Winnie were the only ones who still retained their original, flat-waved hair. (From real nuns, Eileen had said.) Joyce, on Lily's right, a product of the unglamorous early forties, had been refurbished by Eileen, some twenty years ago: her original wig had been replaced by one of back-combed chestnut hair. She had taken to it gallantly, but it had never suited her, and Mr Baxter often regretted the old sausage curls that had fitted neatly into the back of her chilly neck.

Joyce's special friend, Maud, stood close to her. Maud was smaller, more brittle-boned than the others. In the mid-fifties she badly chipped her heel which had never quite recovered. Mr Baxter and Eileen had laid her carefully on blankets on the counter and done their best to re-fashion a smooth curve with plaster and glue, but the operation was not wholly successful. Maud had never regained her old uprightness: no matter what the Baxters did she remained fractionally lop-sided to the knowing eye, and Mr Baxter observed a distinct downward curve on her cherry lips that had not been there before the accident.

Deborah was the newest arrival – November 1959, to be precise – and secretly Mr Baxter had never fancied her much, though he believed Eileen when she said Deborah brought a touch of real glamour to the group. Deborah had a mass of stiff blond nylon curls and blood-red nails that had often spiked a customer who brushed too close, causing her to totter perilously for a moment or so, until the customer re-established Deborah's balance on her long, thin legs. And while the other four had closed mouths, in varying degrees of smiling red, Deborah's lips were cheekily half-open, as if in permanent expectation, and revealing two small plastic upper teeth, which lodged on the full lower lip. On the first of every month, before the shop opened, it had been Eileen's habit to clean Deborah's teeth with a soft, dry brush, relieving them of the skin of dust that had formed. But that was one job Mr Baxter had never relished, and he had not been able to bring himself to attend to them more than once since Eileen's death. In the intervening years of neglect, a positive frizz of dust had formed in Deborah's mouth, serving her right for all her sexiness. And yet the sight of it always filled Mr Baxter with a terrible guilt, and sometimes he prayed to his dead wife to forgive him.

'Oh, my girls,' said Mr Baxter.

It had been in his calculations to allow himself just a few silent moments alone with them before transporting them to his van. He laid his hands flat on the familiar surface of the oak counter – still shining as deeply as ever, for it had been his private memorial to Eileen to keep the counter in its accustomed pristine condition – and dragged his eyes from the girls on a weary journey round the shop.

The shelves to the ceiling – also solid oak, built by his father – were empty now: the closed drawers empty, too. Cleared of its baskets of assorted wools, its piles of woven rugs and boxes of white candles (no salesman had ever managed to persuade Mr Baxter to experiment in a line of those silly fancy candles that cost a fortune and gave no better flame), the floor space seemed much bigger. Mr Baxter fancied for a moment the girls had been dancing there all night, but then he remembered they would have been in no mood for dancing. His eyes were drawn back to the group of them, all in their summer best, dresses that were quite out of fashion now but which Mr Baxter had recovered from the attic last night: dresses that had been Eileen's favourites. Lily herself wore Eileen's honeymoon dress, a navy silk which hung slackly over the hips. Mr Baxter could not help recalling the rustle that dress made when Eileen walked and how, in different lights, its skirt flickered with a dozen blues and silvers. On Lily it was a dead dress, but a reminder.

How pretty the girls looked, Mr Baxter thought, in the dim morning light of his dying shop. A group of fashionable ladies conversing, perhaps, at the races. He found it hard to blame them for their share of responsibility in the collapse of the business. But it was so. After Eileen's death they lost much of their sparkle. Besides which, try as he did, Mr Baxter did not have Eileen's taste. The lemon twinsets and the mournful skirts which he chose the girls to model did not appeal to the customers. Sometimes they remained unsold for months, even years. The storeroom and the shop itself became cluttered with dead stock, and after a while Mr Baxter was obliged to give up altogether the clothing side of the business. And other strong lines dwindled. The fault of this was not Mr Baxter's, but the manufacturers'. Mother-of-pearl buttons were replaced by plastic copies; satin ribbons were only available at a wicked price, and Mr Baxter's old customers spurned the nylon replacements. It was the decline of quality goods he regretted, and deplored the shoddy substitutes. Thinking they would bring down his high standards, in the last year or so Mr Baxter had bought less and less, allowing stocks to run down. New generations of customers found nothing to lure them to his shop, and eventually Mr Baxter had been forced to admit to himself it was time to close down. It was, after all, the age of the decline of the small business. Its future, the country over, was black. Mr Baxter accepted these facts without bitterness. It was only the parting from his girls that caused him any active pain, and there was no way round such a measure. He could not take them with him. There would be no room for them in the small flat he had bought in the nearby town.

'Girls,' said Mr Baxter, 'it's time for your hats.'

Bending over, he took from the shelf under the counter a pile of Eileen's favourites – summer hats to go with the dresses. He carried them over to the group and gently placed one on each unmoving head – fancy concoctions of straw, feathers, ribbons and cherries.

'There,' he said. 'You look splendid. Eileen would have been proud of you.'

He stood back, admiringly, waiting for their replies, which normally jingled in his head. But this morning there was silence. They had nothing to say to Mr Baxter and he did not blame them. What is there to say at the moment of betrayal?

Behind them, the shop window was now silvered with early morning sky, a colour which, as Mr Baxter had learnt from years of such early May mornings, hinted at a fine summer ahead. Well, if it *was* a fine summer, the visitors to the village would be rewarded by the Gift Shop that this place was to become. Within weeks the old oak fittings would have been ripped out and replaced with those silly hessian wall coverings that fade and fray within a year. There would be spotlights,

God forbid, piercing the comfortable darkness of the corners. And as for the goods: useless little notebooks with stupid messages on their covers, tins – poor imitations of the real Victorian things – of sweets, of a price that would have made Eileen weak with disbelief, lotions and potions – all packaging, no quality – and egg cups with *legs*. Pha! The decline in standards . . . Mr Baxter passed a hand over his forehead, not liking to think.

'We must go, girls,' he said. 'It's time.'

In his mind, in all his weeks of planning this departure, Mr Baxter had imagined the girls following him in single file to the yard. He was puzzled for a moment when they did not move. Then he allowed himself a smile. Of course. They would have to be carried, one by one. For a moment Mr Baxter resented this dependence of the girls upon him. It would have been so much more dignified if they had left the shop for the last time swinging their dresses, tossing their heads, as they did in his mind's eye. It was an outrage, a terrible liberty for a man to have to lift a girl. But time was running out. Mr Baxter put his arms round Maud's waist. She was very light, a quarter of Eileen's weight. Her sad mouth bruised Mr Baxter's temple and her beautiful hat of organza roses fell over one eye.

'Easy does it,' said Mr Baxter and turned, Maud very awkward in his arms, for the door. Behind him he felt the silent fury – or was it bewilderment or distress? he couldn't be sure – in the eyes of the other four. He forced his clumsy feet to hurry, much put out by this turn of events so different from his imaginings.

A quarter of an hour later the five girls stood in the back of Mr Baxter's small van. They were wedged into secure positions by crates of homemade wine – the last of Eileen's elderberry – at their feet. Mr Baxter had intended they should have nothing but the best at the end, and he had no desire to drink dozens of bottles on his own.

It was by now light enough to see the girls quite clearly. They looked so pretty, no longer worried or afraid. They stared at the *For Sale* sign outside the shop, slashed with its scarlet *Sold* banner: how cruel were estate agents in their boastful dealings. But the girls were smiling. Perhaps they knew their old friend to be right, given no alternative. Perhaps they were looking forward to their final party.

Mr Baxter turned from admiring them, got into the driving seat. There was no one about. He started the engine, quietly. He moved out into the road very gently, not wanting to dislodge his passengers. But once through the village, in a lane unlikely to be troubled by witnesses, he gave a small burst of speed, knowing that the breeze would make the girls' dresses flutter with the life he remembered, and the streamers and feathers on their hats, too, would be dancing.

The cloakroom of the old rectory, a few miles down the coast, was disproportionately large in a house of solid, square rooms with no pretensions of grandeur. But had it not existed, its contents, which represented the outdoor pursuits of its deceased owners, would have been forced to flow into other passages and rooms. As it was, there was plenty of space for Colonel Windrush's fishing rods – a huge collection, by any standard, gathered over the years – to loll in the corners against the stone walls, their spindle necks bent in downward glance at their more squat companions – leather cases of Purdy guns, canvas bags of golf clubs.

The wooden draining board of the old sink was still a-clutter with Mrs Windrush's wicker baskets, in which, in the two inconsolable years of her widowhood, she had gathered flowers with a trembling hand of manic speed. When the cut flowers outnumbered the vases she pushed them into jam jars, saucepans and old chamber pots from the attic, and fed them so little water that a premature death made it necessary for her to start culling all over again. In her husband's lifetime Mrs Windrush had no interest in gardens, and would never deign to pick any of the garish blooms that a young boy from the village chose lovingly from a catalogue, producing a border of colours so vulgar that Mrs Windrush dared not complain lest she should become too offensive in her opinion. No: all she cared about in the days of Bill was that the lawn should be permanently trim, a pleasure to bare feet under the tea table, and the yew hedge should be kept low enough to reveal the marshes beyond it, and the sea.

It was only after her husband's death that Magda Windrush

fled to her shambles of a garden, with the thought in mind that since she could never bring herself to shoot, fish or play golf, gardening would be a token gesture to the outdoor life he loved so much. The very day of the funeral she bought herself a pile of gardening books, and set about their study with a concentration that surprised even herself. Garden tools – which the wretched boy had been requesting for years – were ordered in abundance: implements with shining stainless steel blades and prongs, and smooth wooden handles comforting to the hand. Mrs Windrush dug, hoed, weeded, pruned, planted: the bleakest weather could not keep her from her labours. But she was not rewarded by speed of result, and this caused her much distress. Impatient by nature, she daily inspected plants put in some months back, and cursed them for their slow progress. Indeed, 'blast the hollyhocks' were her dying words when Viola told her, in all truth, they were still only three feet high. She died long before her garden would reach its prime and left behind, in the shape of piles of opened catalogues and books, reminders of what was still to be done.

When Viola opened the cloakroom door, early on the morning of her departure from England, she was at once assaulted by guilt at the sight of these books piled among the baskets on the draining board. For all her good intentions she had done nothing more than prune the Albertines on the south wall: although she did faithfully polish the silver from time to time, which her mother had cared about very much before her father died and affections were switched to things outdoors.

Viola looked about her, as if to seal the imprint of the place on her mind before she left. In the early light the stone flags of the floor were almost colourless, like mushrooms, and crowded with boots and shoes of many sizes. A gathering of bodyless people, Viola thought, and remembered how some of the bodies had been. Above the old black waders rose her father's long legs in mackintosh trousers: his ancient tweed coat and fishing hat with its bluish feather fly stuck in the band. Above his green gumboots, their toes a mosaic of mud from his last stroll over the marshes, she saw his thick plus-fours, and his bright eyes screwed up beneath the shaggy white brows as he scanned the sky for flighting duck. Pitifully small beside her father's gumboots was her mother's favourite gardening wear: fur-lined ankle boots whose zips made a savage scar up their entire body. Their sides still bulged from Mrs Windrush's swollen feet: but there were reminders of more elegant days, too – three small pairs of pale summer sandals, worn for many years before the onslaught of arthritis.

The original owner of the vicarage, Viola often thought, must have been an exceptionally tall man, for the rows of brass hooks round the walls were so high that she had never been able to reach for her coat without tiptoeing. When she was a child her brother Gideon had let her stand on his shoulders to hang things. But since she had been grown up the acquiring of clothes from the hooks had always been a struggle, resulting in many a heap of garments being dropped to the floor.

But the coats, mackintoshes, blazers and anoraks were all in place now, and had not been touched for months. Hanging from tabs at their necks, the garments all drooped in shapes of dead poultry in a fishmonger: dullish things, their previous air of protection or warmth or even smartness – in the case of Mrs Windrush's mulberry tweed – quite gone. Only the Colonel's shooting mac seemed not to have slumped. Its wide shoulders were still hunched in memory of its owner's stoop: its cracked waterproof stuff ready defensively to crackle if touched.

Above these ranks of outdoor garments hung an assortment of hats: and it was the dead hats that kept smiling, Viola thought. Gideon's topper, unworn since his schooldays, was misty with cobwebs: her father's sou'westers gleamed as they always had, while the various golfing and shooting caps were discs of pleasing muted tweed. But it was the straw hats that retained most of their spirit: the Solar Topee that the Colonel brought back from India – where he had read the entire works of Kipling in a week – her mother's lacy sunhats of wheat-coloured straw. She would wear one of them every summer afternoon, no matter what the weather, often forgetting to take it off indoors for dinner. Viola's earliest memories of her mother's beautiful face were framed by a straw brim which threw a cobweb shadow across her pale skin. The favourite of these hats had a garland of imitation cornflowers round the brim. Their blue had not faded. Viola, looking at the hat now, remembered it so well: on how many occasions had her mother sat upright at the tea table, covered with its white cloth of drawn thread, in a cornflower blue silk shirt to match the hat's flowers, her thin arms pricked with gooseflesh, for she scorned the covering of a cardigan no matter how cool the breeze. Mrs Windrush was always bluer, brighter than the sky, which in this part of England absorbed so much grey from the sea that even on the brightest day the grey outshone the striving blue.

Viola shivered. It was quite cold. It was always cool in the house, even in the hottest summer. The flagstone floors and thick walls were impenetrable by the fiercest sun. Coming in on a very hot day, the house could be relied on to give relief. But there were always warm patches, if you knew where to find them. On spring mornings in the library the sun would fall through the windows making a fretwork on the rug that stretched as far as the Colonel's desk. As a child, Viola remembered, she would run barefoot through the patchwork of warmth, feeling it very briefly on her legs, then dash into the complete cool of the shaded part of the room by the fireplace. It was like swimming in and out of warm patches of sea: sometimes she would pretend she was in fact swimming, and make movements with her arms. But this private game was quite silent. She did not disturb her father, who kept his head bent over his desk as, unwillingly, he went through his papers.

For a moment Viola contemplated going to the library to see if the sun was on the carpet. But she knew it was several hours too early. Besides, the library distressed her, now that her father's desk was so empty and tidy that for the first time in her life she could see the Moroccan leather blotter – his wedding present from his wife. The trouble was, there were still hours to go until the taxi arrived to take her to the station, and there was nothing left to do. Her cases were packed, her sheets folded and in the laundry box at the back door, the food – except for a single egg for her breakfast – all eaten. Having got up far too early after a sleepless night, she was in no mood to read, or to wander through the empty house only to be nagged at by memories. So she had decided to go out.

With a gesture of great determination Viola reached up for her father's old mackintosh. She had been meaning to do this for ages, knowing that the longer her parents' things were left untouched the harder it would eventually be to get rid of them.

As she lifted it down, it creaked in her hands and smelt sourly of salt dried on plastic. Such distaste overcame her that she was tempted to put it back, postponing once again the disagreeable moment. But she fought her own battle, and won. She put on the mackintosh and, avoiding the sight of herself in the speckled mirror, jumped up to reach for her father's favourite fishing hat. It smelt of distant hair grease. Viola rammed it on her head. Then she looked at the floor to make her selection of footwear. She could not bear her mother's zipped boots that aped, so cruelly, the latterly deformed feet. She turned from them, and settled for a pair of Gideon's old gymshoes.

Thus dressed, Viola left the cloakroom and hurried across the lawn – over whose long grass her mother would have despaired – to the gate in the hedge that led to the marshes. There, she felt happier as the familiar squelch beneath her feet broke the silence and a single bird – a lark, was it? – was swooping and singing above her. It was light now, flat whitish sky showing an economy of cloud on the horizon, behind which the sun was rising. The tide was far out, leaving the beach vast and empty. But if Viola cocked her head, leaving her ear free of the noisy plastic collar, she could hear the merest whimper from the sea.

On this walk, she determined, she would go through once again in her mind the long list of reasons for not selling the house, which she would put to her brother in New York. It had been a democratic gesture, on her father's part, to leave the place jointly between them, and while Mrs Windrush was still alive there were no disputes. Now, it was different. Gideon had been in New York for a year, doing very well in Wall Street, and had no intention of returning to England for some time. When he did come home, he would be living in London, not Norfolk. To Gideon, the solution was obvious: sell the house and they would share the money. Viola, at almost thirty, could buy somewhere of her own. The alternative was helplessly to watch it fall into disrepair, unable to afford new slates for the roof or anything else that needed expensive attention. Viola saw the sense of these arguments, and agreed she herself could not hope to earn a living based in so faraway a place. Besides which, a house once so full of noisy, happy people, now empty, would be conducive to melancholy. So Gideon was right. And yet . . . Viola was going to argue against him.

But try as she did the list of good reasons for keeping the place evaded her this morning. As she walked on the firm wet beach the entire compass of her eyes was filled with the soft translucent light. Feeling the ribs of sand beneath her feet she remembered that as a child she had imagined they were the imprints of the bodies of underwater monsters who liked to lie on the sea-bed when the tide was high, unseen. She had often wondered if she might one day see the monsters, woken from their sleep by the pull of an outgoing tide, scurrying after it in fright. But her father, who was so often up early duck-shooting, had never mentioned any such sight, and she had not liked to ask.

Viola made her way towards the wreck, whose jagged black outlines were the only harsh thing in view. It was a large ship, destroyed in the last war. Viola had remained uncurious about the details of the event, and had never discovered what exactly had happened. She had heard all the passengers were saved, but no one had bothered to claim it for salvage. Although at high tide only small prongs of the ship were visible, like a broken fence, when the sea was out it made a huge and ugly hulk on a ridge of slightly raised sand. Viola had never been very near it and had never felt the slightest desire to examine it closely. Gideon, as a child, had swum out to it numberless times and enjoyed diving through its glassless portholes with his friends: the competition was to see who could get through the smallest porthole. And when his gang wanted to get away from girls, it was to the wreck they went at low tide, to smoke their illicit cigarettes, quite sure Viola and her friends would never follow.

Viola knew her fear of the wreck to be childish: she knew that barnacles and slimy planks and even skeletons – should there be any of those left at the Captain's table – were all harmless, but nonetheless a nameless distaste, a real horror, seized her whenever she made a private attempt to go near to the old ship. But this morning, now surprisingly at ease in her father's mackintosh and shooting hat, fear was a distant thing, and she thought it worth trying once again for her private satisfaction.

Thus resolved, she stopped for a moment, and turned back to look at the distance she had come. It was quite a way. The familiar line of the village roofs and chimneys was indistinct in a thin mist that trailed across them, echoed vertically in two thin spires of smoke. Viola could just make out their own roof: from this distance the illusion was that it almost touched the church tower. She could see the smudged shapes of the copper beech and the horse chestnut in the garden, then came the swirls of marsh divided from the beach by a barricade of reeds. It was a water colourist's view: everything fluid, barely defined, insubstantial. Lowering her eyes to the sand, Viola then saw the tyre marks – parallel to the path she had been walking and aiming for the sea. She looked about her, puzzled. There was no sign of either man or vehicle on the beach.

She turned once more to the wreck. She reckoned it was not more than half a mile away: the nearest, she calculated, she had ever been. With firm step she continued on her way. She looked for more tyre tracks but could see none, and felt relieved.

Some moments later Viola stopped again. She had discovered the best way to keep herself going was to concentrate on her feet. To see the wreck looming larger with every step would have intimidated, made the journey harder. But now, instinctively, she stopped and looked up with a great effort of will. She was surprised by her proximity to the ship. She could see, which she had never seen before, ragged fringes of seaweed flapping from its sides. She could see the blackness of its gaping portholes, eyeless sockets, staring. Her heart began to race uncomfortably, and she clenched her hands in her father's pockets. It was quite a while before she could bring herself to move again, and when she did it was sideways rather than forward.

She was now not far from the sea and could hear its snarling more clearly, although the sound scarcely interrupted the huge silence. But suddenly there was a piercing squawk, and two seagulls rose from an invisible part of the wreck. The fright they gave Viola made her smile to herself, aware of her own foolishness. But all the same, her heart still beat very fast.

Stopped by the gulls, she once again willed herself to go on. Icy sweat needled down her spine, and her knees were shaking.

But inwardly she laughed herself to scorn, determined now, having got this far, to get into the *shadow* of the monster . . . even to stretch out a hand and touch its vile bark.

Viola took three uneasy paces, then clamped a wild hand over her mouth to stifle a scream. Unless she was mad, she could see, half hidden by the bows, a *naked bent arm.* When she dared to look again, a little higher, she saw half the back of a straw hat, almost identical to the hats in the cloakroom at home, from which fluttered two pink ribbon streamers.

As she felt her eyes flatten against their sockets in disbelief, Viola hoped the whirling wheel of her brain would stop at some solution. There were *people* at the wreck. They were not dead sailors, were not ghosts. They were solid figures. Who were they?

When she had recovered herself enough to step cautiously sideways once again, all was then revealed. Simply: a picnic was taking place. An early morning picnic. She was the intruder. Before turning away, hoping not to be seen, she regarded the picnickers curiously for a moment, still afraid.

It seemed a strange time of the morning for a girls' outing – which it seemed to be, for Viola could discern no men. She counted five women in summery dresses that flapped in the breeze, and all but one wore pretty hats. The bare-headed lady – her hat had flown to rest some yards away – was propped up in an uncomfortable sitting position, leaning against the dark bows of the ship. Her companion seemed to be lying down, her skirts raised over her knees. The arm Viola had first seen belonged to the tallest lady, who had her back to Viola: the other two stood opposite each other, their heels strangely dug into the sand, so that they leaned slightly backwards. There was a rug on the ground, and an open hamper. Several bottles of wine and glasses were placed on the rug between the lady who sat and the lady who lay. There was something very intense about their attitude: a silent kind of enjoyment, and there was no sound of laughter or of voices.

Viola never knew how long it was she took to realize that this was no ordinary picnic. It was only when she grew conscious of the fact that the sitting-down lady, who wore a dark gleaming dress, was staring at her, completely unmoving, that she knew she had entered upon something more horrible than she could ever have envisaged. They were dead sailors' wives she was looking at, come together for some motionless celebration, or memorial. Their limbs, their heads, remained quite, quite still. Only their skirts and floppy hats were rustled by the breeze. They stared, and behind them the tide was coming in very fast.

Viola screamed. She thought later it might have been a warning. At the time it was the only way to release her terror. Then she turned from the grotesque sight and began to run back across the miles of empty beach, throwing off her father's mackintosh as she went so that she could run faster. As she flung it across the sand the thought of its being swept away by the next tide brought tears stinging to her eyes, but she knew there was no possibility of going back.

2

Harry Antlers, pressed daily into an early rising by an abundance of nervous energy, stood in the hotel bathroom shaving. He hated this forced examination of his reflection every morning. Neither his individual features nor the overall impression of his head gave any encouragement in the hopes that he could be considered even slightly handsome. Harry was cursed by outstanding ugliness. As a child, he had thought this state was a phase that would pass. He lived in hope, scrutinizing daily the unkind assembly of features, searching for improvement. But he was never rewarded. The only changes were for the worse. And unfortunately for Harry, the unfair moulding of his countenance was not made up for by a fine and manly body. Harry was not a large man, nor finely made. He was narrow shouldered, a little stooping: a womanly back view. The legs were badly bred, bandy from the thighs down and flaring into thick, square ankles. Well cut trousers could have gone some way to disguising this ungainly shape, but Harry was a man of no taste in clothes, and remained unconscious of the fact that his ill-fitting nylon garments enhanced the unattractiveness of his body.

But for all that he had against him physically, except at shaving time Harry was not unduly depressed by his appearance. He had learned that women's tastes in men were perverse. They were completely indiscriminate – judging from his many conquests – in the matter of physical appearance. Apparently almost any man was better than no man. And provided the male specimen was just a little famous, could provide money, an air (at least) of power and some show of romantic treatment, then girls, even beautiful ones, were his for the asking. Only last night, he had proved this once again. At a cocktail party in the Plaza he had met a fluttery young thing called Susie. She had dyed blonde hair and huge eyes whose lids trembled with well-rehearsed interest in others. On hearing that Harry was in the theatre she declared that her life's ambition was to act: she would get there one day, but meantime was working for an airline.

'You're a very lovely lady,' Harry said. 'Why don't I buy you dinner and we can discuss your career?'

By his reminder that the pleasure of dinner had to be paid for, Harry left Susie in no doubt of her obligations. They ate seafood in Greenwich Village, having held hands all the way there in the taxi, and within half an hour Harry was so profoundly bored by this lovely lady's attempts at communication that he could scarcely bring himself to describe his reasons for being in New York. She was predictably impressed: her half exposed bosom quickened its anticipatory rising and falling.

'You're a very, very special man, Harry, you know that?' she said, as he paid the bill.

But the attraction was not mutual, and Harry had to be up early. He saw her home, refused to come in, but promised to call. He knew he would do no such thing. Susie, like all the rest, was not what he was looking for.

Harry carefully wiped the last of the shaving cream from his cheeks. He rinsed them with a cold wet flannel. The slapping noise echoed sullenly in his head, as it always did, reminding him of the constant thwacks of his childhood, the vicious noises that leaked through the thin walls of the bungalow telling of his father's daily anger with his mother, and the beatings she endured. One day he would meet a girl who would listen to stories of his childhood, and soothe away the memories. In the meantime, the screams, the thumps, the brutal silences and joyless meals lodged darkly in his mind, stirred – much less frequently these days – only by the dabbing of his own cheeks each morning.

He patted them dry, now, leaving the skin dull and colourless, dark shadows under the eyes. Then he brushed his hair: that, at least, was something to be proud of. It always gleamed, Harry Antlers' hair. He could not remember how many girls had run admiring fingers through it, exclaiming at its fineness. The other thing they admired was his name, and there Harry was bound to agree with them. It had a resounding clash. It evoked images of noble beasts, fighting. It was a distinguished name, a name that people remembered. *Antlers*. It was the only thing for which he could be the slightest bit grateful to his father.

Harry swung into the bedroom, impatient to be getting on with the day. He dropped on to the unmade bed and picked up the telephone all in one movement. Irritation pricked his skin, making him physically uncomfortable.

'Where's my breakfast, for Christ's sake? I ordered it half an hour ago.'

'Sorry, sir. I'll put you through – '

'Don't put me through anywhere. Just tell them to hurry up. And where's my post?'

'Post?'

'*Mail.* You know I like it sent up as soon as it arrives. I've told you a hundred times I like it – '

'One moment, sir.' Pause. 'There's no mail for you this morning, Mr Antlers.'

'*Nothing*?' Harry heard his voice turn into a whimper of incredulity. It was always a bad day, the day that started with no letters, albeit of the dullest kind. Wherever he was in the world Harry arranged that letters would follow him. They gave him a sense of being planted rather than temporarily placed. Also, a sense of importance. Without constant correspondents seeking to be in touch with him, Harry was a more easily angered man. He slammed down the telephone receiver, switched on the radio. He was always anxious to catch at least four news bulletins a day: not so much because he had an avid interest in world affairs, but because they gave a rhythm to the day. He lay back, briefly relaxed, listening to the droning American voice, and sensed a sudden nostalgia for the Britishness of the BBC's eight o'clock news. He wondered when he would be returning home.

An hour later, Harry walked down Sixth Avenue, script beneath his arm. He liked New York. He liked its speed, its punch, its lottery of fame and failure, its glinting soaring buildings of menacing glass. But the gentle sun of an early summer morning, the soft air as yet unpolluted by the day, were lost on him. He was not a man who noticed the benefits of nature, or cared for them. His chosen earth was covered with pavements, he cared not a damn for trees or unpeopled landscapes. The restlessness of cities reflected the restlessness of his own blood and spurred him, occasionally, to something near contentment. And within cities his preferred places were indoors: underground theatres, small dark rooms, stuffy offices lit with neon – places that daylight could not penetrate. Sometimes he reflected that he would like all seasons but winter to be abandoned. If the sky had to show itself, it should be a dour grey sky. Only a moonlike sun, less cruel to the ugly, should be allowed. Spring, with all its vulgar promotion of newborn things, should be abolished. For many years Harry had planned his life so that he should avoid the headache-making greens of April and May. It was with gratitude, now, that the screaming yellow metal of taxi-cabs streamed past his eyes. Manmade colours held no horrors for him. Concrete soothed his nerves.

Harry stopped at a drugstore. Whenever possible, he was a two-breakfast man. His over-active adrenalin glands caused him constant hunger, and here in America his appetites were wonderfully satisfied by a diet of waffles, maple syrup and ice cream sodas.

He looked through the window, wondering whether there was time for griddle cakes and bacon. One hand on his paunch, he glanced idly at the breakfasters on their high stools – people in a hurry, eating with one hand, reading the paper with another. Office folk, there for sustenance rather than pleasure. Harry, if there was time, would eat for pleasure rather than sustenance.

About to enter the drugstore – to hell with being overweight – Harry caught sight of a girl at the far end of the counter. She, like most of the other eaters, was reading. But not for her a newspaper or magazine. The book she held, Harry could see from the cover, was Jane Austen's *Emma*. As Jane Austen was hardly a best-selling author among commuting breakfasters on Sixth Avenue, this seemed to be an unusual sight. Harry found himself looking more closely at the reader. He could not see much of her face, for a mass of corn-coloured hair fell over it. She wore a navy sweater, and jeans. Nothing in the least remarkable. And yet there was something very attractive – touching, almost – about her air of concentration. She was apparently oblivious of the noise and surroundings, totally immersed in a very different world. To escape? Harry wondered, and found himself betting his last dollar she was English. Had there been time, he would have gone and sat on the empty stool next to her and asked a few questions. He was often successful in such approaches. But there was no time. He was late already. Harry walked on, thinking suddenly of Mr Knightley. Of all fictional heroes he had always considered Mr Knightley the finest, the one with whom he would most like to be confused.

A couple of hours later Harry sat in the third row of the stalls of a small and dingy off-Broadway theatre. On the seat beside him were three empty cups of coffee and a couple of half-eaten doughnuts, which had in some part made up for the missed second breakfast. So far, he had seen eight girls: eight girls desperate for the part of Laurie, heroine of *Begone*, the play he was directing by way of a personal favour for an old producer friend, a long-time admirer of Harry's work. Laurie was a good part. The girl was on stage throughout the play. Whoever got it, should the play have any success – and Harry had no doubts about that – would make her name. No wonder they were all so nervous. But had there been any real talent, Harry would have seen it at once beneath the nerves. As it was, the right girl had not yet come forward. As the next candidate came on to the empty stage, Harry sighed. His belt was too tight, his legs ached from being in the same position so long. Miss Haley Bead, the name on the list, a short and stocky girl with a definite moustache, was not going to be any good. He could tell that at a glance. But she had to be given a chance.

Harry stood up. His benign mood of an hour ago, induced by the doughnuts, was beginning to wear off. Haley Bead came to the front of the stage, frowning against the two spotlights.

'Haley Bead, Mr Antlers,' she said.

'Hello, Haley Bead.' Harry tried to sound gentle. But judging from the way the girl winced, there must have been something gruff or unwelcoming in his voice. He tapped the open script he held in his hand. 'Now as you know, Haley Bead, this is the scene where Laurie tells her mother she's going off to live in Ohio with a truck driver.'

'Yes, Mr Antlers.'

'Good. I'm glad you understand that.'

'Oh, I do.'

'Excellent. Now, the mother is sitting there, on that chair.' He pointed to the only prop on the stage. 'See? The mother's a tiresome old cow but she loves her daughter. Laurie has a lot of good reasons for going . . .'

It was the ninth time Harry had said all this and he felt the tediousness of repetition drag in his stomach. 'Right. Let's see what you can do.'

Harry sat down. He regretted not sending Chris Heep, his assistant, out for another doughnut to keep him going through Ms. Haley Bead's performance. Chris Heep was at this moment retying his gym shoes, an act which occupied a large amount of each day, slumped in a seat two away from Harry. The familiar sight was enraging.

'For Christ's sake, Christopher Heep, concentrate,' snapped Harry.

The girl on the stage looked startled. She took a moment or two to recover herself, clenching her hefty fists, and taking a deep, audible sigh. She turned to the empty chair on which sat her invisible mother. She stared ferociously into the space as if confronting Banquo's ghost rather than a middle-aged woman from Brooklyn. Swallowing, she braced herself for the announcement. The familiar words grated in silence of the small theatre.

> Laurie: I'm going, mother. I am, you know. I'm really going this time. I've had it up to here.

Haley Bead's large hand swiped across her neck in a gesture of self-execution. Her eyes never moved.

> Laurie: It's no use you looking like that, mother. You don't understand. You've never understood. You've caged me all my life, telling me what to be, how to be, and now I've a chance to go and find out for myself who I really am, and you throw a *fit*.

To emphasize the word, Haley Bead, who had less talent than all the others put together, bent one knee. Harry, who had always found something faintly uneasy-making about these words, thought them particularly embarrassing as spoken by the present candidate. He tapped Chris on the knee, signed that she should be cut off.

'Better let her go on down to the end of the page,' whispered the languorous Chris, whose sense of fairness was the only thing keener than Harry's.

Harry leaned back, thumbs lodged in his belt, and shut his eyes. He had envisaged Laurie as a frail blonde, steeliness beneath her frailty, and all he had seen this morning were butch, liberated girls who equated independence with aggressive unattractiveness. And Haley Bead's rendering of Laurie's anguish was the greatest mockery yet. The girl had so little observation she would not get a job picking up rubbish in Central Park. Aggrieved, Harry let her drone on to the end of the page. Then he jumped up, punching the air, cutting her off.

'Enough, enough. Thanks. I see what you're getting at.' He tried to be decent. 'Very interesting.'

The girl blinked, extricating herself from the misinterpreted skin of Laurie. She was confused by the rude shock.

'You don't want me to finish, Mr Antlers? I was just – '

'No thanks. I don't need to see any more. You'll be hearing from us.' He tried to smile. 'And now, it's goodbye Haley Bead.'

'Very well.' Crushed, the girl left the stage. Harry turned to Chris.

'And now, *we* break for lunch.'

At the most annoying times, Chris Heep could be quite firm. He flipped one of his long legs over the seat in front of him.

'No, we don't. It's only twelve-thirty. We can fit in one more. Otherwise we'll be here all night.'

'Shit,' said Harry, sitting down again.

'Next,' Chris called.

The girl with the corn-coloured hair, the reader of *Emma*, walked on to the stage. Harry looked at his list. Viola Windrush. A note said she had had a couple of small parts in plays for BBC Television, and a summer season at the Salisbury Playhouse. So he was right about her nationality.

When Harry looked up again Viola Windrush was sitting on the empty chair.

'That's the mother's chair, not Laurie's,' he roared. Viola turned to him.

'I was merely waiting for instructions,' she said.

Harry scratched his ear. It was the first English voice he had heard for weeks, and a very sweet one. Totally useless for playing Laurie from Brooklyn.

'What the hell are they doing sending you to audition for this part? They might have known a nice English girl like you would be the last thing I want.'

'God knows,' said Viola, with a small smile. 'I made the same point myself. But they said I might as well try.' She remained on the chair, hands folded in her lap, unmoving.

'Well, I suppose you might as well, now you're here.'

A small rise of Viola's shoulders indicated a stifled sigh.

'If you like,' she said, looking at him, 'I could save your time by not going through with it. To be honest, I should hate to get the part, even if I was suitable. I think it's a terrible play.'

Viola, who was by nature a placid creature not inclined to provoking scenes, was amazed by her own forthrightness. She had heard of Harry Antlers, of course. In the theatre he was known as a brilliant bully. Working with him was reputed to be exciting in some respects, but full of hazards due to his irrational responses. If an actor was able to stand up to the Antlers' form of treacherous behaviour, then an exceptional performance was sometimes achieved. He had his loyal followers and fans: there were those who claimed there was a kind and touching side to him. But for the most part, actors and producers who had worked for him once would never deign to do so again. He was taken on by new people confident they could handle him – only to join the ranks of those who could not. Actors who did not know him met him with a mixture of dread and hope: fear that he would use his usual bullying tactics in front of the whole company, but hope that he might use his rare magic to inspire a great performance. Viola, for her part, had felt a natural apprehension about the audition, but as she positively did not want the part of Laurie she knew she risked nothing by being honest. What mattered greatly to her was that she should not become yet another of Harry Antler's crushed victims.

Her impudence – Harry did not give himself time to think of her gesture as one of consideration – immediately angered Harry.

'Right,' he shouted, standing again. 'Right, right, right. Thank you very much for your opinion, Miss Windrush. Very grateful for it. Delighted you're not going to waste my time.'

Under the spotlights Viola was frowning, unnerved by his anger. She wished she had not been so foolish as to agree to come for the audition. Chris heaved himself to his feet, confident some sort of scene was about to take place which he had no desire to witness, or to be called upon later to give evidence.

'I'm off to a movie, back at two,' he said, and hurried away. His heart was not in the theatre, but in Hollywood. Even working, reluctantly, for Harry Antlers, he managed to see three or four films a day.

Harry and Viola remained alone in the theatre. Viola stayed in her place, unmoving on the chair. Her stillness, her calm in face of his fury, enraged Harry further.

'Well, come on down from the stage. Or are you going to stay there thinking things over all through the lunch hour?'

Harry's tone, despite himself, was less harsh. Viola stood up, moved to the steps that led down into the small auditorium. She stopped a few paces away from him. She was much shorter than Harry.

'No,' she said, 'I'm going.' Away from the spotlights, her hair was dimmer, an unburnished mass that foamed about her pale face. She had very dark eyes, but Harry could see that they were not brown. They seemed to be navy. The first navy eyes he could remember seeing.

'Right,' he said again, and felt an annoying pulse begin to beat in his temple. 'But if you change your mind I daresay we could still fit you in somehow this afternoon. It'll only be *mildly* inconvenient.'

'I'm not changing my mind, thank you.'

'Would you like something to eat?' This was not a premeditated question. It came without thought, surprising Harry himself. Viola shrugged.

'All right. If you like.'

Harry looked at his watch. An hour and ten minutes till he had to be back for the afternoon session. He had intended to go across the road to an excellent hamburger bar where he could seek comfort in a couple of jumbo burgers and a thick malted milk shake. But with this sudden turn of events his appetite suddenly fled. He could not bear the thought of such food eaten in upright discomfort, and quickly calculated how long it would take a taxi to get to his favourite restaurant on Third Avenue.

'We'll have to hurry,' he said. 'There'll be just time for you to give me a few of your interesting opinions on the play.'

Outside, the sun was aggressively bright. Warm. Sweat dampened Harry's armpits in instant reaction. In the blessed shade of the cab he was aware that he smelled quite pungently. Viola screwed up her nose, turning her head away, looking at the cross-town shops. Neither spoke.

In the crowded Italian restaurant, they had to wait ten minutes for a table. Harry sweated harder. He would have liked to have walked out to express his indignation at the outrageousness of keeping so regular a customer waiting. But there was no time to go elsewhere. He pouted, frowned, tapped his paunch with impatient fingers. Viola kept on looking away, as if she had nothing to do with him.

At last they were seated in a small corner table. Harry ordered himself a fillet steak with French fries, without looking at the menu.

'I always have the same,' he said. It sounded like a boast. He then suggested a whole list of American cocktails Viola might like: she politely rejected them all and asked for mineral water with her plain grilled fish. Her skin was the colour of moonstones.

'So what have you got against the play?'

'Almost everything.'

'And what makes you think you're any kind of judge?'

Viola shrugged. 'I don't ask anyone to consider my opinion. But I read a lot of plays, for pleasure, and because I'd like to write one myself one day. Reading so much, it gets easier to detect a false note, a hollow core, or just plain bad writing.'

'Ha ha! So we have here a budding writer,' Harry sneered. 'A budding writer as well as a budding actress. A multi-talented lady, indeed.'

Viola smiled slightly, ignoring his sarcasm.

'Oh, I'm not really a budding actress. I used to think I'd like to be one and I was lucky enough through *devious* means' – she smiled again – 'to get one or two parts in England. But I didn't enjoy it. And I wasn't much good. So I've returned to the original desire of writing – one day.'

'Connections,' Harry snapped, his mind still on the earlier part of her explanation, which infuriated him. 'If there's one thing I really hate, it's people who not only *have* connections, but use them.'

Viola took a sip of water. When she put it down a thin line of silvery bubbles made a jewelled moustache on her curly top lip. She blushed, her pale cheeks briefly colouring.

'Do you?' she said. 'That must cause you a lot of discomfort much of the time.'

Having prepared himself for an invigorating argument, Harry found himself mellowed by the first mouthfuls of steak and chips. He saw no point in pursuing this particular course and asked why she was in New York. He was rewarded with no more than a cursory explanation: her agent had arranged the audition, but the real reason was to talk to her brother about the future of a house they jointly owned. The very idea of such a problem annoyed Harry. He could feel irritation, a physical thing, spiking up through the cushion of food that lay heavily in his stomach.

'Ah,' he exclaimed. 'You're obviously from the privileged classes.' His voice was bright with resentment. Viola flinched. 'Well, I have no such fortune – or misfortune, whichever you like to call it. I come from a very ordinary background.'

'Ordinary backgrounds are such good excuses, aren't they?' said Viola, quietly. Harry chose to ignore this remark.

'Believe it or not, until three years ago I had never seen an avocado pear.'

Viola sighed. She tried to contain a smile. To take such chips on the shoulder seriously would be insulting to their owner.

'If that sort of revelation is designed to make me feel uncomfortable,' she said quietly, 'I'm afraid it hasn't succeeded.'

Harry said nothing. They only had five minutes for coffee, and so far things had not gone well. He had failed to intimidate this cool, arrogant young English girl, and he was unused to such failures. He ordered coffee, made a great effort to quell the turbulence of feelings that clashed within him.

'Why don't you give me your address and telephone number?' he said at length.

'Whatever for? Why would you want to get hold of me? Besides, I shall be going home in a few days.'

Harry thought quickly.

'You're not entirely wrong about the play,' he said. 'I have to believe in it if I'm directing it. But there are some weaknesses, I have to admit. Perhaps you could . . . give a hand with a bit of rewriting.' He knew he had played skilfully upon Viola's vanity, and was rewarded with an encouraging smile.

'I could try,' she said, and gave Harry the address of her brother' apartment.

In the taxi he said:

'Are you going anywhere special? Because if you're not doing anything I'd be very grateful if you'd sit in on the rest of the auditions this afternoon. I'd like your opinion.'

Viola's eyebrows rose under her hair.

'Very well. But I'm no judge of an actress, really. It'd be interesting, though.'

'Thanks,' said Harry, with his most charming smile.

Back in the theatre, stuffy and airless in the afternoon heat, Viola refused to sit with Harry next to Chris in the front row. Instead she took a place at the back, a little guilty at having agreed to this privilege. She enjoyed watching the actresses do their best with Laurie's clumsy speech, and wondered why Harry made so little effort to put each one of them at her ease. Mid-afternoon, a girl from California appeared on the stage. She seemed without doubt to be the best. Viola wondered if Harry would agree. She wrote the actress's name on the back of her cheque book, and began to think how she could improve Laurie's part by some rewriting. It would be exciting to be given the chance. A modest beginning, but a beginning. At five o'clock – the hours had passed uncommonly fast – Viola remembered she had promised her brother she would be back early for an uninterrupted talk before his girlfriend came home. She left the theatre unnoticed.

Harry, too, was surprised by the enjoyment of the afternoon. The fact that Viola sat silently ten rows behind him caused a peculiar sense of well-being he had no time to define. Without articulating the idea very clearly to himself, he imagined discussing the afternoon's candidates with her over a drink . . . perhaps dinner. In the girl from California he reckoned he had found as near a perfect Laurie as he could get, and wondered whether Viola would agree. At six, when the last girl had gone, he turned to the back of the auditorium, full of pleasurable anticipation. At first, seeing Viola had gone, he was unable to believe his eyes. He stood quite still, fingers rubbing against the bristly stuff of the seat in front of him, rage piling within. Like everyone else he had the misfortune to meet, she was a traitor. She had betrayed him – accepted his proposal happily enough, only to betray him.

'*The bitch*!' he shouted out loud, startling the sleepy Chris. 'She'll pay for this.'

He marched up the aisle to the door, to the dreaded gold light of early evening, his head flaming with plans for revenge. Outside, he hailed a cab and ordered it to drive to the nearest McDonalds. He needed several hamburgers and a thickly malted milkshake before he would be in any condition to fight for calm and give himself a chance to think.

An hour later Harry entered the dusky lobby of his hotel a placid man. The rage and disappointment of so short a time ago had ebbed away, to be replaced by an irrational optimism, a quiet acceptance of some kind of unclear but possible happiness. Such feelings in Harry were rare, and to be made the most of: he smiled extravagantly at the man behind the reception desk, who handed him a letter. A girl's writing, and sent round by hand. Thinking it could only be an instant apology from Viola for her untimely disappearance – hell, the girl needn't have apologized, he had judged her too harshly – he handed the man two dollars, murmuring 'Get yourself a huge drink, George.' (It was one of his habits to call members of the hotel staff by their Christian names, to show he was at one with them, on their side, understood their ordinary lives.) George, whose actual name was Jack, smiled gratefully.

In the dusk of his room – Harry liked shutters always to be closed – he slit open the letter with shaking fingers. At a glance, the handwriting was not that of an educated English girl.

He read:

Dear Harry, this is to thank you for a truly wonderful evening last night. I find it hard to put into words what I felt when I woke up this morning. It was that something really good, and unusual, had gone on between us, and I wondered if you felt like that, dearest Harry, too? It isn't often that one meets a real soulmate and such chances shouldn't be missed. I know you're a very popular man and probably have hundreds of girls at your beck and call, and perhaps only think of me as yet another blonde. But I am a blonde who really cares for you – yes, even in so short a time. I know I would like to do all sorts of things for you, like cook your breakfast and clean your windows and mend your socks. You make me feel wonderfully unliberated, which is a great relief these days. I have thought of you all day and am keeping my fingers crossed you will call me tonight and we can go on from where we left off. With great affection, and with love, Harry – Susie.

Harry owned a suitcase in which he kept all such letters and photographs of their writers. It privately entertained and comforted him to think he had so valuable a store of evidence of the love and admiration he inspired in a multitude of heterogeneous women. Sometimes he ruffled through the letters, picking them up and letting them fall over his head like overgrown confetti. Sometimes he re-read them, laughing out loud at their incompetent phrasing, the clichés they employed to try to express the passion they felt. None of them had ever been rewarded with an answer that indicated requited feelings. Harry did not write love letters. He did not love. He had never loved, though sometimes he had imagined it was a state, like a tropical storm, that might blast him one day.

Susie's letter, had Harry been in a less impatient frame of mind, would have been filed to take back to England and added to the store. As it was, he screwed it up and threw it across the room into the wastepaper basket. Clean his windows, indeed. What made her suppose he owned any windows to clean? And why *hadn't* Viola sent an apology?

Harry was uncertain what to do with his evening. He had tickets for a Broadway musical. Chris had invited him to see a film. Neither idea appealed. For some weeks, after his arrival in New York, which had been noted in a small paragraph in a gossip column, he had received many invitations from hospitable Americans. His name was still well-known, even outside theatrical circles: fame had come upon him in his early twenties with a play called *Host of Lies*. Harry had met the author, an undergraduate, in a pub. Secretly sympathetic to the subject, and recognizing an original talent in the writer, he had agreed to direct the play. It was put on at the Edinburgh Festival, where overnight it became the star show of the Fringe. Later, transferred to London, it received ecstatic reviews and ran for two years. To Harry's further amazement it then went to New York, where it had a short but successful run off-Broadway. Thus Harry's reputation was made on both sides of the Atlantic.

And the two years of the play's life had been happy ones. Harry enjoyed the fame, the recognition, the being in demand both professionally and by ambitious girls. He enjoyed the sudden money, too, though he spent little on himself. It did not occur to him to leave his unsalubrious flat, or get himself a powerful car. His pleasure was to buy a larger bungalow for his parents and realize his sister's ambition by setting her up in a shoe shop in Dibden Purlieu. The rest he spent on food, travel and flowers for the extraordinary number of beautiful girls to whom he had suddenly become desirable.

But those heydays were many years ago. Since then he had been in fairly constant demand – diminishing, of late – to direct both for the stage and minor feature films. But there had been no success similar to that first play. Harry was still known as the man who had discovered and directed *Lies*, a reputation which no longer gave him any joy – only reminded him just how long ago that single triumph had been.

'Harry Antlers, director of the controversial *Host of Lies* in the seventies, is back with a new play,' the story had run. But the novelty of English visitors of fading fame wears off quickly. A stay of more than a few weeks ensures a decline in popularity and Harry had been here for two months. Invitations were no longer forthcoming. He was reduced to engendering his own fun, or spending his evenings alone. This evening, if he could not be with Viola, Harry wished to be alone. But he was plagued by restlessness, and had no desire to sit in his airless room watching television. And so when he was sure the sun had gone down behind the skyscrapers, leaving the streets in merciful shadow, he left the hotel, heading for Third Avenue. He walked slowly at first, enjoying a small breeze that had cleared the heat of the day. Then, from nowhere, an idea came to him. Spurred by the excitement of this idea, he doubled his pace, twisting skilfully in and out of the people who, unfired by love, moved more slowly on the crowded pavements.

On the few occasions in her life that Viola had been forced to spend Friday nights in a city, she had felt strangely depressed. As one brought up in the country, comforted by the rhythm of the seasons so apparent on the quiet coast where she lived with her family, she had always had a horror of Saturday mornings, and particularly Sunday afternoons, spent in parks or streets, neon-lit places, flats where time was of no consequence and Sunday lunch drifted into unnerving Sunday evening. To her, city weekends were wasted days. Even when, on leaving home, she had been forced to live in London during the week, she had always made the long journey back on Friday nights for the pleasure of two calm days on the earth, uncovered by concrete, that she loved. Given this strange quirk in her nature – which she did not bother to fight very hard – it was not surprising that here in New York, on a fine evening in May, Viola found herself dejected.

The airlessness of the theatre had given her a headache. Her limbs felt heavy, a sense of claustrophobia constrained her chest. In the mirrorless, stale lift that soughed up to her brother's apartment, she longed for the wide emptiness of the beach at home. Shutting her eyes, she imagined it. She would be there, thank God, this time next week. She had had enough of New York.

Viola let herself into Hannah Bagle's front door. Her brother Gideon had been living with Hannah since his arrival in New York, and having experienced just a week of Hannah's company, Viola hoped Gideon was not contemplating marriage. Gideon and she had always respected each other's private lives, and asked no questions. But in the case of Hannah Bagle, chief buyer in the nightwear department of a Fifth Avenue store, Viola felt apprehension on her brother's behalf. He had been changed by his liberated lady in ways which Viola could not admire, and even at the risk of angering him, she felt she should give him some warning. She had been awaiting the right time: perhaps it would be this evening when, at last, they would have a few hours alone.

In the stark white box of a kitchen – lifeless and tidy as a show kitchen in a shop window – Viola poured herself a drink of iced orange juice. She took it into the bleached living-room – glass, carpet and furniture all white, flowerless pot plants and a few shelves of books the only apologetic colours. Hannah Bagle, as she often said, hated colour, and she had drained it not only from the place in which she lived and from her own wardrobe, but also from Gideon. He had worn a cream tie and, worse, cream socks, every day. Viola had laughed at the change in his once colourful appearance, remembering his purple socks and rainbow jerseys at Oxford. He had merely replied that Viola was, as usual, too critical.

Viola sat on the white linen sofa, put her glass of orange on the low perspex table beside her. It glowed unnaturally, a single flame in the pallor of the room. In the stifling silence she recalled the events of the day, which had been no more satisfactory than any of the other days in New York.

It had been a relief not to have had to go through the audition, which she would have failed without a doubt, and she would not have enjoyed being humiliated by Harry Antlers as the others had been. He had lived up to his reputation of being a man of exceptional rudeness: boorish, chippy, charmless – except for a few moments. And ugly. Quite outstandingly ugly. On reflection, Viola could not imagine why she had accepted his invitation to lunch, except that she had been hungry and did not like eating alone in drugstores. His flattering suggestion that she should do some rewrites on the play was a very silly one. She had no experience, merely what a single producer, some years ago, had assured her was a natural ear for dialogue. If Mr Antlers was serious, of course, then she would be prepared to try. But no. She would not. It would mean staying longer in New York and associating further with the disagreeable Harry. While all she wanted was to return home very quickly.

Oppressed by the white room, Viola was relieved to hear the

key in the door. Gideon hurried in, strangely dressed in a caramel-coloured suit, white shirt and white tie. He was a tall, untidy man, clumsy and vague in some respects, infinitely skilful in others. There was a friendly clattering of ice as he poured himself a martini of American proportions. He flung himself upon a white chair, disturbing its etiolated cushions. His presence livened the room.

He smiled – what Viola used to call his front smile. While his face moved in adequate imitation of a grin, she said, the back of his mind, elsewhere, played no part in the gesture.

'Had a good day?'

'You've picked up so many American expressions.'

Gideon briefly shut his eyes, the smile gone. He had a fine, intelligent face: the temples and long nose identical to those of his father. A curved and sensuous mouth from his mother. When he was a child, and conversations bored him, he would shut his eyes for quite long spells. The habit would enrage his father. 'I'm practising in case I go blind,' Gideon would always say, shoving sausages skilfully into his mouth as his eyes screwed up with added defiance.

'Well, did you? What happened at the audition?'

'I didn't even bother to go through with it. The director saw at once I was completely unsuitable for the part, and I told him I wasn't interested anyway.'

'After all the trouble your agent took. Won't he be disappointed?'

'I don't think he cares very much.'

Gideon pushed off his shoes and wiggled his white-socked feet in the long white wool of the carpet.

'So there's nothing much to keep you in New York?'

'No. I'll be going home on Monday.'

'We'll miss you.'

'I think Hannah probably finds three rather too much in this flat, doesn't she?'

'Oh, I don't know. She's quite easy.'

Viola judged this not to be the time to disagree. They sat in silence for a while, Gideon sipping at his martini.

'I suppose we'd better talk about the house,' he said at last.

'That's the idea.'

'How on earth do you suppose you can keep it going on

your own?' His eyes, an opaque grey that he had inherited from no one, were suddenly tired and troubled.

'It'll be difficult, but I'll manage.' Even as she spoke Viola knew it would be impossible. The small amount of capital left by her father brought in an income that scarcely covered a frugal life of her own, but would not begin to cover the expenses of running a large and ailing house. Already she was in debt, although there were still a few hundred pounds left by her mother which would go towards outstanding bills.

Gideon sighed.

'You won't, you know.' He lit a cigarette and smiled a proper smile. 'It's hard to know what to do. You're the young sister and all that, but it's difficult to take care of you –'

'I'm quite all right, you know –'

'Well, keep an eye on you, whatever. It's hard with three thousand miles between us. And the parents would have considered it very unbrotherly to take no interest whatever, wouldn't they?'

Viola smiled in reply.

'And so, my Violetta, I've been thinking.' Viola sensed a thin thread of excitement in her spine. Whenever, in their childhood, Gideon announced he had been thinking, it was usually because the time had come to announce a good idea. 'I've been thinking, and I've changed my mind. About selling. Just yet, I mean. I don't know at all what your life is, or what you want to do, or how long you will really want to hang about by yourself with all those ghosts: but I understand you not wanting to let it go. With the present state of the economy, it can't be unwise to hang on to it for a while.' He paused, taking in his sister's face. 'And, no, you won't have to worry about the money. I'm making a ridiculous amount over here. I can take care of all that.'

'*Gideon*.'

'So you can organize getting the roof done as soon as you get back.'

'Oh heavens. Thank you, Gid.'

'Well, I'm not being entirely altruistic.'

'You mean, one day, you might . . . ?'

Gideon nodded. He held up his empty glass.

'I shouldn't be drinking this stuff for a start. Milk is

doctor's orders. I've got an ulcer. One gets ulcers, making so much money.'

Viola laughed.

'Would you come back soon? And Hannah?'

'A year or two, perhaps.' He paused. 'Hannah wouldn't be keen on a change of environment.'

'No.'

Gideon was mellow now for the first time during her stay in New York. As he curled his long legs under him on the sofa, indicating in some unspoken way that the comfortable position would not have been permitted in Hannah's presence, for fear of the white socks blemishing the white covers, Viola was reminded of the long night hours he spent thus on the library sofa at home. In vacations from Oxford he would bring two or three friends to stay, and they would hardly appear by daylight, but come out at night with bottles of port to sustain their endless philosophical discussions. Viola, only understanding half they said, would listen but not join in. Now, recognizing the same mellowness of those evenings, she ventured an old joke.

'Maisie's still waiting in Docking,' she said.

'Ah, Maisie! Is she still the same shape?'

'She's thinner, I've heard, in memory of you.'

'Dear fat obliging Maisie. Maybe I shall be bound to look her up one day. But you, Violetta, what about you? You never write real news. Any plans? Isn't it about time you settled down? Babies and all that. Who's been in your life of late?'

'Brief visitations. No more.'

'You'd be quite hard to love, I suppose.'

'Thank you!'

'By that I mean merely that it would take a lot of perseverance to see the point of you. Once somebody had, of course, they'd never let you go.'

They both laughed. The whiteness of the room was less alien now. Outside Viola could see pink clouds with underskirts of silver. They cast blue shadows on the floor.

Gideon stood up, stretching, huge.

'Hannah rang me to say she was going to be so late we should get ourselves some food. Shall we go down to the Village and eat raw fish in a Japanese restaurant? Hannah hates it.

But that would be nice, Letta, wouldn't it?'
'Wonderful,' said Viola, gulping her forgotten orange juice. She knew that for the first time in New York she would enjoy her evening.

3

Viola was walking on the beach, familiar in all but colour: it had been blanched white. Above her was a white cloudless sky and in the distance, on shining wet sand, the wreck. She could see the picnickers, their dresses blowing in the breeze. She could see them beckoning to her. But fast though she walked she came no nearer to them. Then she heard a scream, her name.

Viola woke. The scream again. She opened her eyes to the dazzling whiteness of her small room, and saw the anguished face of Hannah Bagle, baring white teeth that had been chiselled to an unnerving uniformity in California.

'Viola! For heaven's sake! Look what's come for you.'

She threw on to the bed a huge cellophane package. Struggling against drowsiness, Viola saw it contained a bunch of dark red roses.

'And that's just the beginning,' Hannah shouted. 'The porter's gone down to get the rest. There are *dozens* more, apparently. What the hell are we going to do with them? You'd better come.'

Dazed, Viola got out of bed. Following Hannah to the small doorway, she tried to think clearly. Who was the sender of the roses? The porter stood at the open front door, arms spread wide to hold another five packages of flowers.

'And this isn't all,' he snarled. 'What, someone died in here, something?'

Hannah relieved him of the two top packages. Viola took the other three. They crackled in her arms, the red of the flowers flaming through the transparent paper. Together they went to the sitting-room and without saying anything lay the packages in a neat line on the bleached floor, like a row of corpses.

'For heaven's sake,' Hannah said again. She stood back surveying them, arms folded in her white towelling robe, stiff with disapproval. 'If there's one thing I really can't abide it's roses. Especially red.'

'I'm sorry,' said Viola.

'What dumb idiot sent them?' She smiled briefly. 'You must have captured some New York heart, I'll say that.'

'Can't think who it can be,' said Viola, honestly.

'Better set about finding a card, then.' Hannah bent down and tore at the window of cellophane paper on one of the packages. Her hand was long and pale, fretted with blue veins, older than the rest of her. The paper tore easily. Hannah pulled out a rose, sniffed. 'Doesn't even smell.'

She threw it to the floor with distaste. For a moment Viola could see the flower through Hannah's eyes: a globe of searing red that bloodied the carpet and violated the careful whiteness of the room. Hannah began to scrabble at other packages, randomly. Soon floor and sofas were gashed by dozens of roses. Viola stood helplessly by, scrunching up the paper, pressing crackling balls of it to her chest. She apologized many times, eyes on Hannah's tight mouth.

'We'll have to put them in the bathtub for the moment,' said Hannah, 'then take the goddam lot of them round to a hospital. We can't have them here.'

By now in an icy rage, her hands snooped through the flowers in search of a card. A thorn tore her finger. She watched impatiently for the bead of blood to rise, then sucked at the finger, moaning. At that moment, Gideon, in pyjamas, appeared at the door holding three more packages of flowers. Incredulous, he looked down at his sister and girlfriend huddled in their red sea, and laughed.

Hannah snapped the wounded finger from her mouth and glared up at him.

'So glad you think it's funny. Have you ever seen such a mess? Well, she's your sister. The two of you can deal with it. But I'll tell you one thing: if these flowers aren't gone by tonight, there'll be real trouble.'

'Now, Hannah, really.' Gideon was good-humoured. He threw his packages on to one of the sofas. They slithered about like enclosed shoals of bright fish, landed on the floor by Viola. Hannah stood, tightening the sash of her robe as she did so, thereby increasing the size of her breasts. She paused briefly in front of Gideon, both angry and provocative, then made much of tiptoeing her barefoot way among the flowers to the kitchen door. It slammed behind her. Gideon shrugged.

'Well, well,' he said. 'Suppose she's never been bunched on quite this scale. Who the hell are they from?'

'I honestly can't imagine.'

Viola unpinned a small white envelope from the last of the packages. She took out the card and read the message: *One hundred red roses for Viola Windrush from Harry Antlers, in admiration.* The handwriting was pleasingly firm, masculine. Viola handed the card to Gideon.

'The director I had lunch with yesterday.'

'What on earth did you do to him?'

'Nothing.'

'Rubbish. He's either fallen dottily in love, or is the master of the flashy gesture.'

'He must be mad. I didn't like him, and I made it quite plain.'

'The feeling can't have been reciprocal. He'll have succeeded in making himself remembered, if only for all this.'

Gideon looked round in some despair at the galaxies of roses, reflecting on just how much trouble they would cause. But when Hannah then entered, carrying a tray of orange juice and coffee, her previous bad humour seemed to have gone. Clearing a space between the flowers, she put the tray on the low white table, and made herself a place between the roses on the sofa.

'Well, I guess this is all a hell of a nuisance,' she said, quite nicely, 'but seeing it's happened and we're flooded out with the things, I've been thinking we perhaps ought to make some use of them. Why don't we ask some people over, Gideon? Tonight? We could have a farewell party for Viola.'

This was forgiveness. Viola smiled gratefully. She did not care what happened, now that the house was secured and in two days she would be going home.

'You could ask the suitor,' said Hannah. 'I'd sure like to meet the suitor.'

'I don't know where to find him.' Viola knew she would have to locate Harry Antlers in order to send a polite note of thanks, but she had no desire for a reunion.

'Easy,' said Gideon. 'Get a message to him through your agent.'

Viola realized she would have to do this. She agreed reluctantly, and also agreed to spend the day arranging the hundred red roses in places least likely to annoy Hannah. A bright sun came through the window then, burnishing the flowers so brightly that Viola feared for Hannah's peace of mind. But Hannah, engrossed in plans for the sudden party, was now unaffected by the colour that splattered the savagely guarded white of her room. She stroked a clutch of scentless petals on her knee, her gentle touch indicating surrender, even if temporary. Viola did not miss Gideon's loving look, and imagined her brother's break from this strange, uneasy girl would not be imminent.

When Harry Antlers received an invitation to the party, later that day, he was attacked by such a weakness of relief and joy that his dash to the nearest drugstore for a celebratory milkshake was achieved on very wobbly legs. He had trembled all day in nervous anticipation of no word of response from Viola – although surely none but a real bitch would accept such roses unacclaimed. Now he trembled more violently. His hand shook on the tall icy glass of frosted pink froth that was his balming drink. When he wiped away the moustache of pink bubbles that it made on his upper lip with his other hand, he could feel the vibrations of his wrist. Somewhere among the manifestations of extreme elation struck a cold and nagging thought: he was ill. He had been struck with some fever, or unmentionable disease. Typical of his luck, at what might be the most important turning point of his life.

But with the downing of the milkshake – sweet, soothing strawberry, gentle on the stomach, the horror of such a thought evaporated. He was not ill. Definitely not ill. He was never ill. There was a simple solution which for some absurd reason had taken twenty-four hours to become clear to him. But now it was abundantly, wonderfully, gloriously clear: there was no more doubt. He had been claimed by a force which he had always suspected might exist, and here was the proof that it did. There was no more doubt. There would never be doubt again. Harry, swallowing the last threads of pink froth, acknowledged himself a man possessed. Yes, thank God, he was at last a man possessed. He ordered another strawberry milkshake.

In the ghost train of his mind Harry had journeyed his whole life in fearful anticipation. Things had sprung out at him from the darkness – bright things which faded even as he passed them by. Things had goaded him, prodding him in incomprehensible directions, urging him on, he knew not where. Sometimes he imagined he saw the faintest light at the end of the haunted tunnel, and would hurry faster, crushing anything that blocked his path. But the light was as evasive as every horizon. He came no closer to it. With despairing regularity it faded altogether, leaving him to thrash about in total, angry darkness.

But within Harry's turbulent heart there was a calm always trying to escape. He thought of this calm (for surely it must exist) as his Sleeping Prince. One day, if there was any truth in legends, some Princess would come to awake the calm: to unlock the prison and set him free. Spooning the creamy depths of his second milkshake, Harry remembered the old metaphor and smiled to himself. Well, here he was at last, awake. The Princess approached. Now all he had to do was to possess her, for life, with the promise of undying love. In considering the gifts he had to offer, it did not occur to Harry that the girl of his choice (or, rather, the more skilful choice of Fate) would deign to refuse them. He stood, rubbing at his contented stomach, happy in his innocence, his limbs throbbing with a tiger energy that made it hard not to yell and shake himself in ecstatic pleasure. With great effort he walked quietly from the drugstore.

At 7.25 precisely that evening, Harry entered the uptown apartment block wherein he would find the girl who was now the point of his life. To celebrate the occasion he had bought a new jacket of seersucker stripes in varying shades of blue. It was not a comfortable jacket, as he had learned within minutes of leaving the hotel. Its sharp cuffs stung his wrists, its hard collar rubbed the back of his neck. But it was a jacket of distinction. In a room full of beautiful New York people, who Harry had no doubt of finding at the party, eyes might veer from his face but they would not be able to ignore his jacket.

In the hours that had chafed between the arrival of the invitation and the journey to the party itself, Harry had contemplated the purchase of a further hundred roses. But on reflection the excess of this idea troubled him. He did not want to arrive ridiculously laden with cellophane packages, and it was possible Viola's brother's girlfriend was not the owner of enough vases to contain two hundred roses. Instead, Harry settled for the acceptable gesture of just one further flower. He chose it with infinite care, thrusting his nose among dozens of proffered petals, dizzying himself with all the scents, before at last declaring a deep blackish-red rose to be the one he required. At his request it was laid in a transparent box and tied with spotted ribbon. But it looked naked there, a corpse in an unadorned coffin. Patiently, the shop assistant undid the bow and bedded the box with crumpled tinfoil. On this small silver sea, the rose appeared to Harry's satisfaction, and he complimented the girl on her imagination and good taste. Her attentions cost him five dollars.

Harry rang the apartment bell, holding the box to his chest. He felt no sense of foolishness. As a man setting off for a journey might check his wallet, his passport and his ticket, so, in that last moment of aloneness behind the closed door, Harry checked his heart, his desire, his determination. They were all there, ready, waiting.

The door was opened by a tall blonde of some thirty years. She wore silk: the palest silk Harry ever saw, and yet not so drained of colour as to be called pure white. It looped in a complicated fashion across her breasts, leaving much of them efflorescently exposed. Impressed, Harry met her eyes: the whites unskeined as those of a child, while the density of black mascara signalled their maturity. Had his heart not been entirely captured so recently, it might have occurred to him that here was a woman upon whose numinous bosom he would like to comfort his raging head for a while. As it was he looked at her so sternly, to indicate her attractions moved him not one bit, that she clutched the door quite nervously.

'Why, you must be Harry Antlers,' she said at last.

'Yes.'

'I'm Hannah Bagle. Come on in, won't you? Heavens above, you've brought another rose.'

She laughed a tinkling laugh that was like sun on ice, disguising the essential chill. Harry followed her into a white room lit by tall windows filled with green sky. It was crowded with people, the kind of faces he had expected. No sign of Viola. His red roses were on every shelf and table, rows of them in jugs and vases and buckets and empty beer cans, their heads stiff and lustreless, disappointing in their masses.

'Here's our hero,' Hannah Bagle was saying. Her hand rested lightly on his arm. 'This is the rose man, Harry Antlers, Viola's friend. Now Harry, what can I get you to drink? Martini?' Harry nodded. Hannah went away, leaving Harry with Gideon. They shook hands, which meant Harry had to change the transparent box from his right hand to his left. Gideon smiled, glancing at the lying-in-state rose. His mouth was a coarser version of Viola's.

'I'm Gideon Windrush. Really, we're giving this party in honour of your roses. It was brave of you to bring one more.' He watched Harry's impassive face. 'I've never sent a girl so much as a bunch of daisies myself.'

'Really.'

'Your gesture was quite something.'

'I make gestures, sometimes,' said Harry, curtly. 'Where's your sister?'

Gideon nodded towards the window. Harry saw Viola. She must have moved there when he was talking to Gideon, his back to her. She was listening to a tall young man with a beard. He held a glass of wine to his cheek as if seeking its coolness. Viola's profile, against the darkening green sky, was very simple in its perfection. She wore a dress of lavender, or grey, which hung straight from a gathered yoke, an ageless dress that made no concessions to current fashion. Her companion, who was tall, stooped to emphasize some point. Viola nodded, oblivious of anyone else. Harry clutched his box, feeling its sides bend. Hannah returned with his drink. He moved away from Gideon, led by her, and was introduced to a professor at Columbia.

The news had somehow travelled that Harry was the provider of the roses. It soon became apparent that he was the hero of the party, and he found himself greeted everywhere with exclamations of wonder and admiration.

'*One hundred* roses?'

'One hundred roses,' Harry conceded.

'Gee. You must be in love.'

Harry allowed this observation to go unchallenged. After three quick martinis his head felt as if it were choreographed by Busby Berkeley: a dazzling silver globe in which girls high-kicked their legs and jostled with feathered fans, causing him to sway a little. Somewhere beyond this fluttering vision, real ladies, stout and eager, plucked at his successful jacket.

'Harry! Really. You're terrific.'

'Thanks.'

'No, I mean it.'

'Thanks.'

'Are you over long?'

'A while.'

'You must come and visit with us, mustn't he, Ed? Mustn't Harry come and visit with us?'

'Sure.'

'Thanks.'

'No, I mean it.'

'Yes, yes.'

'We'd like to have you over. Ed, my husband, he's away a lot on business, aren't you, Ed? But that wouldn't matter. Now this, Harry, is my friend Martha.'

A tall approaching girl opened her huge mouth as if to swallow the entire chorus line within his head.

'Martha, this is Harry of the roses. He *sent* all these roses. Imagine.'

'For heaven's sake.' Pure green voice of jealousy.

'Now, Harry, why don't we all sit down?'

'Really – '

'No, I mean it.'

Propelled between the two women to a small white corner of three empty chairs, it occurred to Harry he was probably the most attractive man in New York. Roses were a passport to anywhere, it seemed. But where was Viola?

His bodyguard of keen ladies were plunging forks into risotto. They had not managed to persuade him to eat, even though the one who meant everything she said assured him that brown rice was an aphrodisiac. Harry's icy glass stung his fingertips, their voices volleyed back and forth across him. Eventually they accepted his silence as being part of his attraction, and talked about him as if he was not there, as visitors do across the bed of a very ill patient.

'He's quite a guy, Martha. Harry here is quite something.'

'He sure is.'

'He's enjoying himself, anyway.'

'He is, too.'

'He's promised to visit with us.'

'Has he?'

'Maybe he'd even send me some roses, then. What d'you say, Harry? Daresay he sends roses all over town.'

Hyena laughter. Through its hideous waves Viola walked towards Harry, alone. Her glass had gone, her hands were at her sides. Harry stood. The music-hall in his head vanished instantly. He was firm on his feet, quite clear. If the women behind him kept up their chatter, he did not hear them.

'Thank you,' said Viola. 'I've never had such flowers. They were . . . overwhelming.'

'Listen,' Harry said, 'when all this business is over, will you have dinner with me? It's important.'

The question seemed to shock. Viola took a step back.

'I'm sorry,' she said, 'but I can't possibly. This is my farewell party. I must stay and help clear up.'

'Farewell?'

'I leave Monday morning.'

'*Leave?*'

Viola shrugged. She could have no notion of the powerful dagger she had thrust into Harry Antlers' heart.

'I must get home.'

'What for?'

'Things to settle. Besides, I've had enough of New York.'

'But you agreed to help me on the rewrites of the play. *You agreed.*'

Viola frowned, puzzled.

'Agreed? I don't remember doing that. I said I could try, but I wasn't being very serious. Besides, I wouldn't have a clue.' She noted Harry's look of confused fury. 'I'm sorry,' she added. Harry went on staring at her.

'You agreed,' he said again.

'*I didn't.*' Viola raised her voice slightly, annoyed by the false accusation. 'Look, I'm terribly grateful for all these lovely roses' – she glanced round the room – 'and it was very sweet and generous of you – '

'I'm a "sweet and generous" person,' Harry mimicked.

'. . . and I'm flattered. But I'm going home on Monday, that's definite, and I can't help you with the play.'

She met his eye. Her corn-coloured hair, full of green shadows from the sky, clouded the contours of her innocent face. Harry rapidly sifted through the next lines that came to him: *You are the most beautiful girl I've ever met, Viola Windrush, and I love you entirely. Come away with me now, for ever. Please just have dinner with me.*

'Bitch,' he said.

The word hit Viola between the eyes, a well-aimed bullet. The next moment she was aware of Harry Antlers crashing through the room towards the door. People turned, aware of some impending drama. He was a man who could impress his own feelings tangibly into a room. Viola followed him. In the hall she found Hannah was with him. Confused by his sudden insistence on leaving, Hannah seemed to be urging him to stay.

'Please, Harry. What's happened?'

Harry saw Viola.

'That bitch your lover's sister has betrayed me, that's all,' he said, and turned to Viola. She stood bewildered in the doorway. 'Bitch, bitch, bitch,' he said again. Then he turned back to Hannah, took her face formally into his hands, and kissed her on the cheek. 'Thank you for your party,' he said. 'You're lovely.'

He was gone.

'Christ, he's a nutter.' Hannah wiped her cheek with the back of her hand. 'What happened?'

'God knows,' said Viola.

Following Hannah back into the crowded room, she hardly cared. Harry Antlers' extreme gesture of the roses was merely the one event she could laugh about in her week in New York. And yet, as she concentrated her attentions on a group of people who were still congratulating her on being the receiver of such flowers, a small feeling of guilt began a persistent ticking, which is the nature of guilt, somewhere within her. She was unused to upsetting people, on purpose or inadvertently, and if she did so it troubled her greatly. She would like to have apologized for the misunderstanding over the so-called agreement. But where was Harry Antlers now?

As the party guests clustered round her in all their friendly amazement at her good fortune, Viola began to feel claustrophobic. She wanted desperately to leave the small white crowded room, the interested inquiries about her plans, her flight, her life in England. She wanted, inexplicably, to follow Harry, to smooth things over before she left New York, to be left with a clear conscience. Though *why* he should have stirred such guilt, she knew not.

'Here Violetta, have a proper drink.'

Gideon, perhaps understanding her dilemma, was handing her a bourbon on the rocks. Gratefully she sipped it, knowing he would not mind if she left for a short while. She would simply drop in at Harry's hotel, and if she found him there, would apologize and leave. Hannah was suddenly at her side.

'Seems Harry left you this,' she said, and handed Viola the transparent box holding the last single rose, forlorn on its silver foil sea.

Viola thanked her and took the box with distaste. In the privacy of her bedroom she dropped it, unopened, into the waste paper basket. She collected her coat, bag and enough money for the journey downtown, and slipped away unnoticed.

Half an hour later, Viola rang Harry Antlers' bell. After a long moment he let her into his hotel room. It was lit only by a dim light on the desk. There were papers everywhere, as if several scripts had just been flung into the air and let fall at random. Harry backed into the room, sat in the only armchair. He was pale, sweat glistened on his brow.

'So you've come,' he said in a monotone.

'Just to apologize.'

'You shouldn't have bothered.'

'I didn't like the thought of a misunderstanding.'

'There wasn't a misunderstanding. You simply betrayed me.'

Viola sighed, not prepared to argue. She sat on the bed.

'You could take off your coat,' said Harry.

'I'm only staying a moment.'

'As you like.'

They sat in silence for a while. Harry's hands were crossed in his lap. There was something both pathetic and repellent about his state of abjection.

'Well,' said Viola, eventually, wishing she had not come, 'I'm sorry if I've offended you.'

'Offended me!' Harry snorted, an obscene, rumbling noise. 'If you had merely offended me, that would be quite bearable. As it is, you shone a torch in the blackness of my life and now, immediately, before any chance of warmth for us both in its light, you're determined to extinguish it. I hope you know what that means.'

Viola looked at him carefully. She wondered if he was mad. She also felt some impatience with his elaborate accusation.

'I'm sorry,' she said again. 'To me, you were simply someone I met by chance, and had you not sent me the roses I should probably never have thought of you again.'

'I'm glad you're able to feel like that.' Harry gave a small, sneering smile. 'That's very fortunate for you.'

It was then he began to tremble violently, alarmingly. Viola leaned over, put a hand on his bare forearm. The skin felt waxy, icy cold.

'Are you ill?' she asked.

'Probably. You could call it an illness.'

'Can I get anything for you? Should we call a doctor?'

'No.'

His arm was trembling harder under Viola's hand. She withdrew it, stood up.

'I think I should go back now.'

'I think you should. To your important friends.'

Viola went to the door.

'Order yourself some hot soup,' she said, hopelessly. Harry gave her a look of utter loathing.

'Hot . . . soup,' he repeated, mimicking. 'Remember this, Viola Windrush, on your escapist plane back to England: I, Harry Antlers, have entered your life now in a way that's far too profound to be shaken off by apologies, and suggestions of *hot soup*.' He spat out the words, gripping his trembling arms to his chest. 'So as you go about your petty little life, you should bear in mind that here's a man who, for reasons of his own, won't give you up, come what may.'

Harry's look was changed momentarily to one of hope. But Viola laughed and the look was dashed to pieces.

'God, you're melodramatic,' she said. 'No wonder you choose bad plays. You've an incredible penchant for bad lines.'

She left, then, slamming the door behind her. He had angered her, irritated her, embarrassed her. He had also, ridiculously, frightened her. Viola realized this in the stuffy warmth of the taxi as it sped her back to safety. Beneath her scorn were intimations of the fear of having become a victim, a terrible feeling that she might be hunted and not manage to escape.

But, back at the party, Viola's fears soon evaporated, and the idea of the Atlantic coming between her and Harry Antlers was reassuring. It was with great relief and pleasure that she left New York on Monday morning. On the aeroplane, drinking champagne in celebration, she gave no thought to his preposterous warnings, but concentrated instead on plans for her future. Somewhere on the journey the idea came to her that she should find a caretaker for the house, to keep it from disintegrating, and also so that she would not be entirely alone. This small domestic plan filled her with unaccountable happiness, and she ordered more champagne in further celebration.

4

Alfred Baxter, settled physically in his small bright flat overlooking the promenade of a seaside town along the coast from the old shop, was, as he put it to himself, out of sorts.

To begin with, all had been well. There had been so much to organize: moving, unpacking, painting the two small rooms, putting up Eileen's curtains and finding a place for all the clutter he could not bear to throw away, that his mind and time had been kept fully occupied. But at the end of six weeks there was nothing further to do. The place was in as much order as it ever would be: the pictures up, the old wedding photographs in their oval frames arranged along the fireplace, the bars of soap and tins of dried milk to last his lifetime (left over from the shop) stored away, suits all cleaned and checked for loose buttons before being squashed into the small bedroom cupboard. Now, time hung heavy about him.

The hours were hard to fill, the days surprisingly sluggish. In the past, a busy morning behind the counter would pass with amazing speed, and no sooner had he finished his lunch than Eileen's delicious high tea was upon him, the hours between having flown by while he checked stock, sharpened his cutting scissors and polished the mahogany drawers between serving customers. But in the last few idle days in his seaside flat, Alfred had learned the sharp lesson of the hours that all those who live alone must become acquainted with. For the first time in his life he was aware of the precise difference between ten o'clock – a chilly time when the whole morning lies bleakly ahead – and eleven o'clock, which brings with it a little more warmth if only because preparation of lunch, a sparse midday meal, is not far away. He learned about the pangs of mid-afternoon, the zero hour of three o'clock when all those fortunate enough to be employed are about their business, and all those with no well-defined occupation are drained of ideas as to how to pass the afternoon before the merciful relief of early evening television. He learned how approaching night can loom like a great black mountain, to be climbed alone. When Eileen was alive, bedtime was always a happy ritual: the damping down of the small wood fire, the checking of the back door while Eileen made two mugs of cocoa, the climb of the steep stairs to their small bedroom under the eaves, skilfully balancing the mugs on a tin tray. And finally, the quiet pleasure of a hot drink, propped comfortably against their pillows, before Eileen read a few verses from the Bible and put out the light. Tired out by their busy day, they both slept instantly. They took sleep for granted.

It was only now that Alfred Baxter realized how fortunate he had been all those years. A considerable worry on his mind was the fact that Eileen's Bible had disappeared in the move. For it was the nightly verses, he began to believe, that had induced their good sleep. He searched for the Bible everywhere, and eventually, despairing, gave up. Buying a new one was an idea soon discarded; it would not be the same. He was forced to face the truth to himself: should he not find the Bible, easy sleep would never come again.

In the days of his marriage to Eileen, on the rare occasions there was time to imagine their retirement (which naturally Alfred had never envisaged would be spent on his own), they had painted for themselves some pretty pictures. They would spend much time cultivating a small garden, both vegetables and flowers, and while Eileen made herself useful in whatever way she could in the village, Alfred would at last take up his old ambition of becoming a bowls player. For years he had dreamed of treading the emerald turf of the green, smooth and shining ball in hand, white flannels scarcely creasing as he bent to cast his accurate eye on the target . . . Then the splatter of applause, that muted English sound of spectators on a summer's day – he had heard it so many times in his mind's ear. Retired, he would also listen to the music of brass bands on a fine new record player, and buy himself a bumper book of crossword puzzles, and perhaps invest in a couple of Khaki Campbell ducks. In spring and summer he and Eileen would travel to some of the places they had always meant to see: not to anywhere fancy, abroad, but short trips in their immaculate Austin 30 to the cathedral cities of England and unexplored beaches on their own east coast. Thus they would fill their years before death most agreeably. And each was convinced that as soon as one died the other would follow very quickly.

In reality, such pictures were smashed beyond all repair. For a start, despite the adequate radiators and a cheerful sun that shone through the south-facing windows, Alfred felt permanently chilly. He never remembered feeling cold when Eileen was alive and this particular, unreasonable chill – which often caused him to tremble quite violently, and would not disappear even after a hot bath – depressed him. It seemed to drain him of energy. Purpose, he realized, is warming, and he had no real purpose now. But he did try. He established some kind of routine to divide up the days – walk to the newsagent after breakfast, walk to the pub for a single pint at one o'clock, walk along the Front after tea. He even went to the Bowls Club, but then lacked the impetus to apply for membership. Without Eileen there to watch, there would be little point in his becoming a champion. He managed a crossword puzzle a day, and he acquired a taste for Afternoon Theatre on the radio, but still there were many hours in between. He received several letters from friends left behind in the village, urging him to come and visit them. But the car had been sold – Alfred had no desire for cathedrals without Eileen – and a dull apathy, caused by the permanent gooseflesh on his skin, meant the journey on rural buses was quite beyond his declining ability.

On a fine morning in late May he sat in his armchair at the window reading the local paper, which he had fetched at seven, having been awake since five. There was a warm smell of burnt toast and fried egg in the room. He had not had the heart to wash the breakfast things: procrastination, he noticed, was beginning to afflict him. Something he would have to fight.

Now, after a bad night, Alfred was feeling pleasantly sleepy. (Heavens above, what a time to feel sleepy, he thought. Mornings are for hard work. Have been all my life.) His eyes were closing over reports of local fêtes and council meetings. Then a headline caught his attention. *Models Washed up on Shore*, it said. At once Alfred was quite awake. His heart began to thump violently. The chill on his skin fled, to be replaced by an uncomfortable sense of burning on cheeks and chest.

'Oh no,' he moaned out loud. 'God, let my girls rest in peace.'

He read the paragraph several times. It seemed that earlier this week five 'corpses' had been sighted washed up on a nearby beach. The man who had seen them through his field glasses, fearing a major disaster, had alerted coast guard, police and ambulance before approaching them. Accompanied by two policemen and six ambulancemen bearing stretchers, the man had walked over the sands to the pathetic huddle of beached ladies. It was not until they were a few yards away from them they discovered the corpses were 'models', as the reporter called them. 'One of them was wearing a straw hat trimmed with cherries,' he wrote. (Trust the vain little minx Deborah to keep her hat on in a crisis, thought Alfred.) 'Police and ambulancemen put on a show of very good humour in face of loss of precious time.'

There the story ended. No mention of what happened to the girls. Had they been callously flung back into the sea? Buried deep beneath the sand? Or flung on to a municipal tip?

The thought of an ignominious end, after all his efforts to speed them on their way with dignity, brought tears to Alfred's eyes. In all his plans for their final picnic it had not occurred to him what might happen when the tide came in. He had not liked to picture a scene of floating bodies, pretty dresses adrift in the sea. Now he came to think of it he had had some unclear notion that a boat of merry sailors would pass by, join the girls in their revelries, and carry them off to a South Seas island to live happily ever after. But on reflection Alfred knew this piece of fanciful thinking was only to disguise the thought of the reality: and it had always been hard to put his finger on reality in the case of the girls.

He sat with the paper folded on his knee, mild sun fiery on flushed cheeks fretted with hot tears, feeling the weight of anguish roll from the edges of his body to some painful depth in its centre. He had let the girls down, after all. He had drowned them. Would to God in heaven that he had kept them with him, here, to share his retirement. Life might have been much better, then.

The day was a terrible struggle for Alfred. Every hour was haunted by visions of how the girls might have met their final end. Perhaps they had been *chopped up*, or *melted down*, their wigs donated as spare parts, their beautiful clothes washed and ironed for a jumble sale. As the ghastly imaginings crowded his mind, Alfred felt the burning of his skin die away and the old chill return. He sat by his window all day. He could not eat. In the evening he forced himself out for his stroll along the Front, but there the sight of the sea that had been so cruel to the girls filled him with further despair. Once he stopped at a telephone booth, determined to ring the newspaper and inquire what had happened to the 'models'. (He could scarcely bring himself to mouth the word in his mind.) But it occurred to him his inquiries might lead to further publicity. They might even send a reporter round to write a mocking little story: that, he could not have tolerated.

Some time after midnight he went to bed, dreading the sleepless hours ahead, hungry, but still with no desire to eat. He could not face the darkness, so decided to read every single small advertisement in the paper. Perhaps that would do the trick, dull the turmoil of his wretched mind.

An hour later – Alfred was not a fast reader – he discovered he had read one particular advertisement several times over. 'Take a grip on yourself, Mr Baxter,' he said out loud, in imitation of Eileen on the rare occasions she was slightly cross with him, 'and read it again.'

Wanted, it said, *friendly competent caretaker/odd job man to live in wing of old rectory. Suitable someone who would find overgrown garden a challenge and who would like to help look after a much loved house that was once full of people.*

A different ring, that advertisement has, thought Alfred to himself. A decidedly different ring. He lay back, closing his eyes, saying the words over to himself, letting their message seep into the chill of his body. If anyone in the world was suitable for such a job, surely it was he. To be able, so soon, to abandon this nasty little flat, to live in a village again, and above all to have something to do, to care for once more, would be a chance he would never have dared to imagine.

He did not like to think of the possibility too hard. But, cast in hope, the mind runs happy riot, and as dawn pressed through his window in his imagination Alfred found himself firmly established as caretaker of the rectory. Full of such bright new thoughts, his worries about the girls rested for the time being.

Three days later Alfred boarded a bus bound for the village of the old rectory. He wore his navy serge suit and his grey tie. He had had a haircut and polished his shoes. There was a clean white handkerchief in his breast pocket and a dab of Old Spice behind his left ear. Eileen would have been proud of him.

Since making the date for this interview – which Alfred had arranged early in the morning after his sleepless night – he had been blessed with a revival of energy, so that he found himself doing quite unnecessary things like ironing his underpants and sewing up the small tear in the lining of his jacket. He felt both anticipation and apprehension. Never before had he experienced an interview, having been a self-employed man all his life. But he knew quite well what a prospective employer found impressive in a prospective employee, and he spent many hours in his chair by the window working out what to say that would best convince Miss Windrush of his suitability for the job. He also wondered whether Miss Windrush might be any relation to a good customer of the same name who came to the shop years ago, sometimes with two small children.

Walking up the drive to the rectory – a fine old house, he immediately thought, but needs a bit of work on it – Alfred could hear the beating of his own heart. His nervousness amused him. At my age, he reflected. Ridiculous. But fear was reasonable enough. If he failed to get the job, then he would be forced back to the new life he hated. He did not like to dwell on such a prospect. God be with me, he said to himself, and rang the bell.

The door was answered by a young lady with a pale face and untidy hair. She wore a fisherman's jersey that was far too large for her and cradled her arms under her breasts as if, for all the fineness of the morning, she was cold.

'Miss Windrush?'

'Mr Baxter! Come in.'

They shook hands. She smiled. The smile seemed vaguely familiar. He followed her along a darkish passage to the kitchen. It was a high-ceilinged old room that rambled at large towards its thick walls. Plainly it had received little attention for many years, and yet it had the air of being loved. There were faded patchwork cushions on the chairs, rows of pickled fruits and vegetables on the dresser, a crowd of potted sweet geraniums on the window ledge. The table, it seemed to Alfred, had been built for a giant. It could surely seat twenty, made from enormous slabs of solid pine. The high-backed chairs all round it spread their arms widely. The whole scene reminded Alfred of *Jack and the Beanstalk*, his first pantomime, in Lowestoft, when he was a child. The giant's kitchen had impressed him with its enormous proportions – ten cups the size of teapots, a table a small man could walk under without bending his head. And here it was again, in real life. The image was further heightened when Miss Windrush sat in the huge chair at one end of the table. Curled up, legs beneath her, within it she looked tiny. Alfred chose the chair next to her. Viola dragged towards her a giant tea pot made of brown tin, and two enormous pottery cups. She poured. It was then Alfred remembered.

'You're not by any chance – excuse my asking . . . But could you be the daughter of a Mrs William Windrush? I had a very good customer in Mrs Windrush, years ago. We were Baxter's, you see. Baxter's, the drapers, though of course we ended up with many other lines.'

The light of recognition filled Viola's face. She smiled again, delighted.

'Mr Baxter of *Baxter's*? Of course I remember you! I used to come in with my mother quite often. She used to buy all my dress materials from you, and all her sewing things. You were the only shop for a hundred miles, she said, that kept a supply of bone thimbles.'

'We did, too.'

'How extraordinary.'

Alfred smiled, touched his head.

'My memory . . . but of course, I remember you as a child. I remember Eileen saying Miss Windrush had very definite opinions for one so young, when it came to ribbons and that.'

He smiled. Viola remembered him as a lean and upright man, always in a starched brown overall.

'And your wife . . . Eileen?'

'Eileen. She passed on some time ago. So I was forced to sell up and go into retirement. But I don't like being retired. I've got a good few years of usefulness in me yet. Silly to waste them.'

Viola passed him his tea. They both drank, thinking of their meetings in the past, and of the changes in their appearances.

'Both my parents are dead, too,' said Viola at last. 'And my brother Gideon – he used to come into the shop sometimes, remember? – he lives in America now. So it's a struggle to keep the house on. But I don't want to sell it if I can help it.'

'A very natural feeling, Miss Windrush. No one in their right mind would want to sell a place like this.'

Viola's hot strong tea had warmed Alfred right through, he was warm as he had not been for weeks. And extraordinarily at home. It was as though he had sat in this room for years. Already the ticking clock, the faded curtains, the framed engravings of snipe and teal on the copper-coloured walls were wonderfully familiar. He had not had such a happy morning since Eileen died.

'Your mother, Mrs Windrush, was an exceptional lady,' he said. 'Such style, Eileen used to say. You could tell she was a great English lady before she ever opened her mouth. She was one of our most treasured customers.'

Alfred hoped this would not sound like flattery. For it was the truth. Mrs Windrush had had a *presence*, as Eileen called it, that was unforgettable. A calm and dignified presence although she always maintained her distance. Alfred respected that. He could not abide a gushing woman, but admired friendly reticence. A great English quality, he often thought.

Viola and Alfred reminisced for a while, listening to each other as one memory sparked off another. They mused over the coincidence of this meeting. They drank several pots of tea.

An hour went by and still Viola made no mention of the job. It occurred to Alfred, at last, that perhaps she would find broaching the subject difficult. So he decided to take matters into his own hands. Give her an idea of the sort of thing he would be willing and able to do for her.

Viola sat back gratefully listening while he outlined his

plans. Alfred volunteered to be in charge of the garden, the fires, the rough work and polishing in the house ('Nothing I like better than to kindle a polish on an old piece of furniture'). He would care for the place when she was away: see that the larder was well stocked when she came back. He would patch the roof, clean the gutters, stoke the boiler, do any decorating that needed to be done. Would that be the sort of thing she had in mind? And, in return, all he would require was the pleasure of occupying his wing, and a little pocket money, whatever she felt she could afford. He was not interested in money: he had enough put by for his needs, and his needs were minimal. If Miss Windrush would allow him to take the liberty, he would like to try raising a few bantams, and some Khaki Campbell ducks: something he had always wanted to do, and of course she would be welcome to unlimited eggs.

As he spoke, a look of relief began visibly to gleam in Viola's face. A shaft of sunlight backlit her hair. There was a quality of goldness about her. Alfred Baxter found himself touched by her appearance of vulnerability. She seemed a somewhat helpless young thing – Alfred tried but failed to guess her age – although there was strength beneath her fragile appearance. With great passion, Alfred found himself wishing to help her: end his days in this house. Even as he spoke of the birds and the eggs he prayed to God that Viola would offer him the job. He did not often call upon his maker's aid, though he had always intended to spend much of his retirement thanking Him for the blessings of his life, kneeling beside Eileen beneath the soaring roof of an English cathedral. But Eileen's death and the sale of the car had forced him to abandon that form of thanks, and now Alfred felt acutely neglectful, and speedily prayed for forgiveness as well as for help.

He was rewarded. As Viola sat, hand on her chin, thoughtful, Alfred could see she had made up her mind.

'Well,' she said at last. 'There doesn't seem to be much doubt about it, does there? You are obviously the right man.'

Alfred made no effort to control his delight. He stood up, shook her hand, assured her of his undying service.

'Unexpected blessings, Miss Windrush,' he said, 'are what can save a man.'

Viola saw his eyes were sparkling with tears. She hastily

began to discuss practical matters concerning his instalment the following week. Then she showed him the wing, joined to the main house by a door from the kitchen. It consisted of two good rooms, a bathroom and small kitchen. They smelled of damp, and had not been painted for many years. But Alfred immediately saw their potential, and delighted in the thought of refurnishing them. Eileen's cornflower curtains, he fancied, would fit the kitchen windows to perfection.

It was not until well past midday Alfred eventually braced himself to leave. At the front door he shook Viola warmly by the hand again, not trusting himself to speak of the pleasure of his anticipation. Viola, whose feelings were very similar, gave him a smile that was so like that of her poor dear mother that Alfred, ungrounded by looking both at the past and the future simultaneously, found himself weaving down the drive with the unsteady gait of a man incredulous of his good fortune.

It was almost fifteen years ago that Gideon had brought home Richard Almond from Oxford for the weekend. Viola, aged sixteen, was eating scones at the kitchen table and studying *King Lear*. Her concentration having been interrupted by the arrival of her brother and his friend, she pushed away both book and food and turned her attention upon them. In Gideon's friends, though she barely admitted it to herself, she was constantly on the look-out for potential lovers, or at least loves, and in Richard Almond she at once recognized a possible candidate.

He was a tall, thin Irishman with fierce green eyes and wild black hair: a restless traveller, a compulsive reader, a man beset by small misadventures which he turned into hilarious anecdotes. He was reading Classics at Oxford, intending to go on to read medicine and ultimately become a neurosurgeon. Viola, noticing his immensely long and tapering fingers, judged they would be calm and skilful with a scalpel, in contrast to the sometimes irritable movements of the rest of his body.

In his first weekend at the house Richard Almond charmed the Windrush family, not least Viola. Unlike many other of Gideon's friends, who regarded her merely as a younger sister, he helped her with *The Wife of Bath*, he took her sailing on Sunday morning while Gideon remained in bed with a hangover. By the time he left on Sunday evening, Viola was in love. *I aspire to him*, she wrote in her diary that night. *If this is my first real love, and comes to nothing, then I shall wait until this quality of feeling strikes again before I commit myself to any other man.*

Viola lived in exhilaration with her secret. She worked with new energy for her exams: there was now someone she felt a vital need to impress with her results. In between his frequent visits – Gideon seemed particularly attached to Richard and brought him often – she lived in a kaleidoscope of memories of his last visit: small, rewarding moments such as his smile to her at breakfast, his listening seriously to her views, his remembering to bring her a copy of *Isis* in which he had written an article. And when he was gone, beyond the brightness within of all such memories, the solid things of every day took on an ethereal quality that made them unrecognizable. The scintillant that is the magic product of first love scattered Viola's small quiet world, and she feared that the glitter of her exhilaration would be visible for all to see.

But she made a great effort to contain herself, and if Richard or the others guessed at her feelings they kept their thoughts to themselves. Richard, for all his friendliness, never made the slightest gesture that Viola could interpret as requited love. But she was happy enough, for the time being, that he should be her friend, and flattered that he should treat her as a contemporary rather than Gideon's schoolgirl sister.

One summer weekend in June, by which time Richard had been a frequent visitor for six months, there was to be a dance to celebrate the twenty-first birthday of Maisie Fanshawe, who lived nearby, and who had loved Gideon fiercely since childhood. Viola had not been invited, Maisie considering her too young. But at lunch on the Saturday of the party Richard suddenly declared that it was unfair that Viola should be left behind, and he would refuse to go unless she came with them.

Viola's parents quietly argued the matter. Mrs Windrush thought the idea delightful, especially as her daughter would be so responsibly chaperoned. But Colonel Windrush foresaw many a danger to his young daughter once exposed to 'wild young blood' in a Norfolk marquee. He abandoned his favourite rice pudding to make his points against young girls being thrust into the lascivious world too soon, but was mellowed by several glasses of port pressed upon him by Richard and Gideon. They made promises to protect her from all conceivable dangers, and Mrs Windrush wondered, with a sweet smile, at her husband's lack of trust in Viola. The argument was won. The Colonel conceded with dignity and went to find solace in an afternoon on the golf course.

There then arose the problem of what Viola should wear. Her own wardrobe contained nothing suitable for a dance. The only possibility was to sift through the mothball cupboards of Mrs Windrush's old clothes. This prospect all but crushed Viola's excitement: it was with many misgivings she followed her mother – all enthusiasm and optimism – into her bedroom whose window overlooked the sea.

They spent the afternoon untying plastic bags, so old that they had turned a dull opalescence, through which flaming silks and satins shone grey as shadows. As they untied bows of tape the bags crackled quietly, brittle in their age – the only sound in the quiet room. Mrs Windrush pulled out dozens of dresses – she never threw old clothes away – and for all Viola's worry as to whether they would find anything suitable for her, she enjoyed seeing them for the first time, each one a piercing memory of her mother's past.

Beautiful they were indeed: the sheerest, flimsiest fabrics, hand-embroidered and hand-made: sprigged cottons Mrs Windrush had bought in her youth in India, striped taffetas, sequined chiffons and bruised glowing velvets, soft as feathers. But none seemed right on Viola. They fitted her, for she had inherited her mother's slimness, but she looked as if she was dressed up – as indeed she was – from a store of clothes kept nowadays for charades. In dress after dress she surveyed herself in the long looking-glass: the sky had become overcast and a light rain speckled the windows, throwing a grey despairing light into the room. Mrs Windrush sat on the end of the bed in gumboots and fisherman's jersey, her arms filled with a bright writhing snake of multi-coloured dresses, her voice sing-songing with pleasure as each one of them brought back to her another event of her youth.

'And this one, the peacock blue, was for a ball at the Savoy. But perhaps this watered silk would suit you better – *livelier*, don't you think, darling? That was for a dance at Skindles, the banks of the Thames lit by candles for miles and miles . . .'

'It won't do, Mama. I'm sorry. I won't be able to go after all.'

Finally, there was only one dress left. Mrs Windrush pulled it reluctantly from the bag. It was very simple. White satin, sleeveless. Thin silver shoulder straps to hold up the camisole bodice. The hem was embroidered with lilies, delicate trumpet heads, picked out in silver thread.

Mrs Windrush stood up. She held the dress in front of herself, dark jerseyed arms sticking incongruously out at its sides, gumboots peeping beneath the twinkling hem. Viola made room for her at the mirror. Mrs Windrush smiled at her reflection.

'I was wearing this when I first met your father,' she said. She turned to her daughter. The silvery light of the bodice reflected kindly up into her face, bleaching out the lines, burnishing the fine bones and magnificent eyes. Viola could see exactly how beautiful she must have looked.

'Then I can't possibly wear it,' she said.

'No, I suppose not.' Mrs Windrush, rocking the skirt of the dress from side to side, was dreamily transported to a private world of long ago. Then she said:

'Though I don't see why not, really. In fact, I think you probably should. After all, it's the best one there is. It would suit you.'

She handed the dress to Viola, instantly transformed once more, in her old clothes, to her real age. The summer rain jittered more darkly against the window, and in the strange light of that late afternoon Viola agreed: they had found the perfect dress.

To the sophisticated eyes of Richard and Gideon the party was not a very imaginative affair: salmon pink gladioli propped stiffly as guns in their bowls, the sides of the marquee bunched fatly with yellow net, personifying the essence of debutantes themselves, the aged orchestra fatigued and slow. But to Viola, watching the dancing strangers, listening to the ho-ho-ho of the privileged laughter and feeling the ice of a champagne glass in her hand, it was a wondrous occasion. She feared only that Richard would leave her side and she would be humiliatingly alone. But he seemed to have no intention of doing that. Taking her elbow, he guided her through the silken crowds to the dance floor.

'I'm terrified, Richard,' she whispered, feeling the spring of the temporary parquet floor beneath her feet.

'No need to be. You look, eh, how can I put this? All right.'

He gave her what she knew in her heart was an avuncular twinkle, but tried to believe was more than that. She was grateful to him and enjoyed their dance, his hand firm on her back, their legs entwined, spinning with no mistakes.

Later, moments or hours, Viola had no idea which, they walked in the garden, keeping their distance. The rain had stopped now. It had left the grass glittering like melted frost under a clouded moon. The briny air was warm but damp. There was a smell of roses and tobacco plants.

'Only the nightingale missing,' observed Richard, with a quality of laughter in his voice which did not reflect the seriousness of Viola's thoughts. 'In fifty years' time, you know, there's a good chance he'll be quite extinct. Imagine that.'

Viola was more inclined to imagine Richard's motives for coming into the garden at all. Had it been in his mind to declare the undying love for her that she felt for him? Followed up, of course, with sensible suggestions about patience in the face of youth, but promises of some kind of permanence in the future? In all her sixteen years Viola had never known such steeliness of conviction in her veins: she had been blessed very early with the kind of love that lasts a lifetime, and knew better than to endanger it with silly games of inaccessibility.

'When I eventually retire from neurology,' Richard was saying, 'I shall have a garden like this.'

Too soon their path was returning them to the house. The sleepy music was loud again. Chance was fleeing. Despite herself, Viola stopped. Richard, a pace or two ahead of her, sensed her reluctance to return indoors. He turned, looked at her for a long time in silence, compassionate. She was silver, serious, sad in the moonlight.

'Look what the wet grass has done to the hem of your dress! I'm so sorry. Those beautiful lilies. Come on, you'll get cold.' He gave her his arm. 'I shall never forget that dress, you know. Never, never.'

They were walking with a swift sense of purpose up a gravel path, now chequered with lights from windows of the house. Viola felt herself being swept reluctantly along, not daring to hesitate again. Richard was being *nannyish*, she thought, and it was only a surge of all-forgiving love that squashed her disappointment. Then suddenly there was a girl before them, a huge great looming girl in swathes of ill-fitting green stuff whose folds did not disguise its essential limpness.

'Oh, Richard,' she said heartily, 'I've been looking for you everywhere.'

She had long black hair, middle parted. She pushed it back from her face with both hands, lodging it behind sticking out ears, and grinned. There was a wide gap between her middle teeth. She did not look at Viola, but her ignoring intimidated.

'We were on our way back,' he said, more friendly than he need have been, thought Viola; but she loved him for his lack of explanation as to why they had been out at all. She hoped the giant would imagine they had been making love in the orchard.

'This is Viola Windrush,' he was saying. 'Viola, Sonia Heel. We meet in Oxford.'

A vast hand was reaching out for Viola's: clasped it without interest. Had Richard only said *met*, not *meet*, with all its horrible implications of regularity, Viola would have been happier. And now they were moving along together, all three of them in step, Richard in the middle, his arm withdrawn from Viola. She knew with each eternal second she was the one whose turn it was to be dropped. The keen bounce in Richard's new stride – surely not her imagination – conveyed a desire which in truth had been lacking in his reaction towards herself. It was, of course, all a matter of age. The disadvantage at the moment was in being Gideon's younger sister. Untouchable, inaccessible. But how unenlightened of him not to foresee the growing . . . The giant was laughing about something, tossing her awful hair. The marquee, now just a yard or so away, bulging with its light and music, looked down on Viola like a firing squad. Her time was up: she wondered how the slaughter would take place.

Richard, helped by the immediate sight of Gideon at the bar, managed everything with a skill that suggested in the matter of shuffling ladies he was not unpractised, and to cause them the least pain in the process of repositing was his utmost desire. Viola could never precisely remember the words with which Richard suggested Viola should have a drink with her brother while he took a whirl with the giant. Perhaps she chose not to hear. Certainly she did not respond to the gap-toothed smile of triumph as the massive green hulk strode away, hand possessively on Richard's shoulder. Viola, deliberately turning her back to the dance floor, watched her brother's eyes follow the couple. 'Sonia Heel,' he said, 'is not just in love with Richard. She's unhealthily obsessed by him.'

Viola managed a smile. 'Will she get him?'

'I doubt it. Being the object of somebody's obsession is dreadfully tedious.'

Encouraged, Viola turned to look. But the sight of Richard and the giant dancing did not encourage her hopes: he seemed to be willingly imprisoned in a clumsy embrace, head buried (easily, for he was a couple of inches shorter) in the dark cavernous places beneath the swilling hair, while one rapturous hand idled about the vast green landscape of her back. Viola, craving to die, felt an unsteadiness in her legs that warned of impending death. Gideon noted her stricken face and thumped down his glass.

'Well, this isn't much of a party, is it?' he said. 'Three *Rock Around the Clocks* with Maisie and a scintillating waltz with her aunt. The band's almost asleep, I'd say, and I wouldn't mind going to bed. How about you?' Viola nodded. 'Sonia will no doubt drop Richard home in her nasty little car, and he'll be very sorry in the morning he didn't come with us.'

Viola approved the tone of her brother's disapprobation. It was the only consolation. She followed him from the marquee, head held high and face set into a rigid smile lest Richard should glance up from his nesting place and see her. On the way home in the car Gideon patted her on the knee and said:

'Don't worry, Violetta. It's only a passing lust.'

Later, very awake in bed, dawn bleaching the windows, she

realized the wisdom of Gideon's observation. It was sex, of course: all sex. How could it be anything else in the case of a plain giant such as Sonia Heel? Her advantage was that she was twenty or more, and was available. She would sleep with Richard. Well, Viola would patiently wait until Richard's appetite, surfeited, would sicken and so die. Then he would return to her, for love. Sonia would be relegated to the category of a woman of no importance in his life. The surety of such notions consoled. Eventually Viola slept.

In more positive form comfort came next day, too. Richard described the party to Mrs Windrush as 'a bit of a disaster, though Viola and I had a lovely dance', then did not refer to it again. Nor did he mention Sonia Heel, and Viola asked no questions. She trusted her expression did not convey her feelings, and judging by Richard's behaviour had reason to believe she had succeeded in her efforts. He was warm and friendly as ever to her, courteous and attentive. Before leaving, he invited her to his farewell party in Oxford and said he would be very disappointed if she did not come.

Viola spent eight weeks imagining all the possible horrors of another party haunted by the permissive giant. When the time came, she made a great effort to look her best and did not much enjoy herself. This was because, apart from her brother and Richard, she knew no one, and the hundred strange undergraduates showed little interest or even politeness to someone outside their world. But one cheering fact made up for the disappointment of the occasion: Sonia Heel was not present. Viola spent much of her time surreptitiously scanning the room, but her rival was quite definitely not there. Viola did not like to interpret this sign too hopefully, but found it hard not to imagine that perhaps Sonia, already, had outlived her welcome.

Three months later her speculations were to be ruthlessly dashed. Gideon gently broke the news that Richard and Sonia were to be married. Sonia was pregnant.

'Then he's an honourable man,' Viola managed to say.

'Honourable, my foot!' shouted Gideon, extraordinarily upset. 'He's an honourable fool! He doesn't love her, he never has. She was out to catch him and now she'll ruin his life. I've done my best to dissuade him but he won't change his mind. Perhaps you could –'

'Me? Don't be ridiculous. He wouldn't listen to me.'

'He might,' said Gideon, curiously.

But Viola, after much reflection, could not bring herself to write to Richard either in congratulation or condemnation. His marriage was none of her business. To try to persuade him against his course might mean losing his friendship and reveal the feelings which now more than ever she was anxious to conceal. With reluctant composure she went to the wedding, a small affair of little ceremony, and returned with double concentration to her studies. She had little faith in the idea of time as a healer, but was left with no choice other than to give it a chance.

Richard and his pregnant bride moved into a small cottage a few miles up the coast. They planned to leave for London, where Richard would begin his medical studies after the birth of the baby. Gideon visited them occasionally and once Richard came to the rectory, without his wife, wearing an expression which did not wholly convey newly-married bliss. It was impossible not to hear news of them, although Viola never allowed herself to ask questions.

The baby was born three months prematurely, and died almost immediately. Some weeks later the Windrushes heard Sonia had had a nervous breakdown and had been sent to a psychiatric home. Gideon reported that Richard was much distressed but when Sonia 'recovered', some months later, and came home, difficulties multiplied. Eventually she was re-admitted, and had now spent some twelve years in various homes. She did not recover again nor, apparently, regress: but lived in a dark and stagnant world that veered regularly between apathy and violent paranoia. Richard visited her dutifully, though over the years he admitted his visits were less frequent. Once it was established his wife would not be coming home he returned to his old habit of seeing the Windrushes frequently. He never spoke of Sonia: merely explained, that in order to be near her, he had given up his plans to study to be a neurologist. His ambition in that direction seemed to have withered. Instead, his medical training over, he became a general practitioner, continuing to live in his cottage near the Windrushes.

Viola let the rest of the morning drift by, sitting in her

kitchen chair, when Alfred Baxter had departed. She wondered if Richard, as he always seemed to, would hear of her return from America, and come and see her. She hoped he would. She was always pleased to see him. If too many months went by without a visit from him she felt a curious sense of loss, a wintry bleakness of the soul that did not decrease with the years.

5

The day that Viola left New York for England Hannah Bagle was surprised and delighted to receive her own flowers from Harry Antlers. In comparison with Viola's roses it was but a modest bunch of two dozen orchids, representing an expensive amount of care in their choosing. They were delivered to Hannah's office (in her flurry of pleasure she had no time to wonder how Harry had managed to discover where she worked) with a note of apology for his sudden departure from the party. An hour after their arrival, Harry telephoned Hannah with an invitation to lunch next day.

'My lady's left me, as you no doubt know,' said Harry. 'I'm a desperate man. I must talk. Please come. I want very much to see you.'

Hannah agreed. She put aside the fact that Harry's reasons for wanting to lunch with her were not wholly flattering, and concentrated on the pleasurable idea of his choosing her bosom to cry upon. To watch strong men crumble beneath her sympathy, so that she could then concentrate on a magnificent job of restoration, was her speciality. She knew from secret reverberations in the depths of her promiscuous flesh that she fancied Harry, and if it was his choice to begin things with a moan about a faraway English girl, well, that was fine with her.

Swinging round on her leather chair, Hannah looked at the afternoon sky, toothy with skyscrapers, and wondered how Gideon would react to Harry's invitation. It then occurred to her that this was one of those occasions about which it would be wiser to say nothing. Gideon rarely talked about his sister, but Hannah was aware of his loyalty to her – a loyalty Hannah herself had never experienced towards any member of her own family. He might not understand. Silence rather than an issue, therefore, she thought. Besides, it would be by way of a *business* lunch really – Viola being their business. This justification for intended silence pleased Hannah greatly. She swept a self-approving hand through her blonde hair, and buzzed her secretary to make an appointment with the hairdresser. The afternoon trembled with anticipation.

Knowing the restaurant Harry had chosen was a dark and ill-lit place, Hannah decided to appear her most bleached: white silk shirt, under which bra-less breasts would glow with the gold of a carefully maintained tan; cream skirt, silver nails, ashy hair. In the midday dusk she would palely shine, demure, soft, irresistibly sympathetic. She arrived early, for unlike most beautiful women she did not consider unpunctuality either forgivable or an aphrodisiac. Indeed, to be there settled and waiting, so that an instant apology was required, had often meant the scoring of the first point.

She shimmied into her place at the reserved table, sat facing the room. She felt no need to hide non-existent awkwardness in the pretence of studying a menu. Her lighting of a cigarette was only so that she should appear almost ghostly in her tranquility behind the blue smoke. Hannah had often thought of herself as a wood nymph, whatever that was.

Harry arrived ten minutes later. He strode across the room, ignoring all waiters on seeing her, a fat and anxious man. His plump and womanly hands clasped both of Hannah's including the cigarette, while his eyes roved tragically from her face to her breasts, where the tragedy turned to appreciation. Hannah suggested he needed a daiquiri very fast. She could see his tired body slump with gratitude at her instant sensitivity to his condition.

'My God, you're a lovely woman, Hannah Bagle,' he said with a charming smile, so that the ugliness of his face disappeared for a moment. 'I'm overwhelmed by your loveliness.'

Hannah, unused to such coarse compliments – Gideon, in his rare observations, would never stoop to the vulgarity of the word 'lovely' – was for a moment caught off her guard. But with a sip of the fierce cold drink she re-established her equilibrium and softened her face into a smile that reflected Harry's own.

'I thought,' she said, 'it was Viola you were overwhelmed by.'

'Oh. *That*. Her. That is an entirely different matter. That's a matter of total, passionate, eternal love, such as not many men are blessed with. Or cursed, perhaps.'

'I don't know her very well. She was only with us a week. She seemed a nice enough girl. Quiet. Very English.'

'Then you missed getting to know one of the most remarkable ladies of our time.'

Hannah, determined not to be irritated by such hyperbole, stubbed out her cigarette so that Harry should now have an unclouded view of her sympathetic eyes.

'I'm sorry about that.'

'Does your lover Gideon talk about her a lot?'

'I'd rather you didn't refer to Gideon as my lover.'

'I thought that's what he was.'

'The acquisition of a label indicates a fixed position. I don't like fixed positions.'

'Oh.' Harry gave the merest smile. 'Anyway, what do you know about my lady? Through Gideon or otherwise?'

'Very little. Could we order? I'm ravenous.'

'Ah! I'm sorry. You can see at every turn I'm not a gentleman.'

Harry summoned the waiter and the business of ordering was accomplished fast, without interest.

'You must know something,' Harry persisted.

'Honestly. I don't.' Hannah shrugged. 'Apparently she tried her hand at acting – wasn't bad. But since the death of her parents she likes sticking around in some old family house miles from anywhere on a cold bleak coast. That's all Gideon said.'

'If my only rival is a house, then I've a good chance. Hasn't she got any lovers?'

'Not that I know of.'

Harry sighed. Hannah's lack of help exacerbated the frenzy in his stomach. He signalled to a waiter to hurry with the steak.

'I shouldn't worry so,' said Hannah. 'You'll get her.' She did not believe what she said, but it was time for the subject of Viola to be abandoned in favour of the subject of themselves. But Harry persisted.

'How?' he asked. 'There are three thousand miles between us. That doesn't make for a good start.'

'Precisely,' cooed Hannah in her most soothing tones,

wonderfully disguising the irritation she felt. 'The Atlantic Ocean is quite a little impediment to courting. You'll have to go over.'

'I have to stay another month till the play's safely on its feet.'

'I daresay you'll survive.' Hannah gave an encouraging smile.

'I doubt it,' said Harry, shoving large quantities of mashed potatoes into his mouth. 'The very fact it's impossible to see the girl is tearing my heart out.'

'Then I'll have to lend a comforting shoulder,' answered Hannah, eyes down, and giving a small shudder so that she could feel the silk of her shirt tremble against her breasts.

'Thanks. You're terrific.' Harry paused. 'Have you never felt like this? Blasted, *totally blasted* by love?'

Hannah looked up, cool. 'No.'

'Ah. Then I must be speaking a foreign language to you.'

'You are.'

'You've missed a lot.'

'I'm not sure I'd want the discomfort you seem to be suffering.'

'I like to think it's only temporary. It'll all be worth it, fantastic in the end.'

'I hope so.'

At last Harry paid her some attention. She enjoyed the way his eyes seemed to penetrate the superficial gloss of her appearance. She suspected his understanding of her was accurate, without having to ask any questions. He did ask some questions, though, with flattering interest, probably knowing the answers in advance.

'Aren't you waiting to be totally consumed by some wonderful man? To give yourself completely?'

'Good Lord, no.' Hannah looked quite shocked. 'I should hate that. That would be the end. I'm a dilettante, so far as affections are concerned.'

'I'm not, unfortunately,' said Harry, downcast again. 'I always knew it in my bones, and meeting Viola confirmed it for ever.'

'Very bad luck,' murmured Hannah.

The food tranquillized Harry. By the time he was halfway

through a vast concoction of chestnut and cream, he felt quite mellow. He sensed a certain weakness of the flesh come upon him: they had drunk many glasses of wine.

'If it wasn't for the fact that my heart is so utterly cast in other directions,' he said, with an apologetic laugh, 'then I'd probably find myself suggesting you and I – '

' – and I might agree at once,' said Hannah quickly. They joined in sudden laughter.

'Ridiculous.' Harry shrugged. 'As it is, maybe I will take up your offer to cry on your shoulder sometimes.'

'With pleasure.'

Harry took her hand. They were locked together in that hopeless gaze that binds millions of lunching companions bent on flirtation: they felt the sexual thrill that comes with the coffee – doomed not to be consummated because of work in the afternoon – turn to the cold flat shiver of postponement.

'There's one thing, perhaps, you could do for me.' One of Harry's soft hands still held one of Hannah's.

'Anything. I'll do anything I can.' In a swift calculation Hannah juggled her afternoon appointments, prepared to accept.

'You could find me Viola's address in the country.' He noticed Hannah's sigh: tightened his grip on her hand. 'I'd do almost anything in return.' He gave a smile that was as near to charming as the ugly set of his mouth could achieve.

'Thanks,' said Hannah, pulling away her hand, drawing herself up and back. She was irritated with herself for not having handled the lunch better. Normally, she would have some definite – albeit unspoken – plan agreed upon by now. Harry Antlers, for all his probing feelers, had proved elusive. Something of a challenge.

They parted quickly in the street, neither satisfied. Hannah promised to contact him as soon as she had the information he wanted. Harry pecked her without interest on the cheek (wondering if he had imagined the desirous feeling of only half an hour ago) and strode a little dizzily down the street. He was not accustomed to wine at lunch.

The prospect of the afternoon's rehearsals held no cheer for him. There was an ache all through his body, powerful and solid, making his legs difficult to manipulate with any firmness of step. In his mind's eye Viola twisted herself from man to man in an obscene orgy: he could not slay the men because in his horrible vision they had no heads. That jealousy spurred by fantasy, that is near to madness, tore at Harry with its lacerating nails: with wild heart and sweating brow, he stumbled into a drug store, collapsed on to a high stool at the counter, and in a scarcely audible voice ordered a double strawberry malt milkshake.

At the same time, back in her office, Hannah Bagle said to herself: Harry Antlers, you'll pay for using me this way, you'll see.

By the time Alfred Baxter returned to his flat after his interview with Viola Windrush, the afternoon was completely topsy-turvy. He knew that both good news and bad news played havoc with habitual timings, and could even change the look of a room or a place that you were used to seeing on an ordinary day. Full of his good fortune, therefore, Alfred found it no surprise that the afternoon had turned into an unrecognizable mess, so that he felt as if he were walking on air, a sensation he remembered the day he took off work many years ago to attend the wedding of Eileen's niece.

He enjoyed the feeling. As one who was punctilious about mealtimes, he now found himself cooking fish fingers and a tin of carrots at five past three, and looking forward to them with pleasure. Perhaps, having eaten so little over the last few weeks, he had been hungry all along but had not realized it, and his happy morning had released the pangs. Or perhaps this sudden flexibility in his ways was all part of the unexpected bonuses of the day.

When he had eaten his hot food on a plate at the kitchen table, Mr Baxter took a plastic carton of Caramel Dessert from the fridge, and a teaspoon from the drawer. With not a flicker of guilt he then made for his armchair at the window of the sitting-room, tore the foil lid from the carton, and with great relish proceeded to peck the spoon into the golden top of the dessert, and feed himself minute helpings, throwing back his head to savour the taste of each one, reminding himself of a blue-tit stealing cream from a milk bottle.

In her lifetime, Eileen would not have abided such behaviour, any more than Alfred would have considered acting thus. But, he thought now, from her place in heaven she would be looking down on him with compassion and understanding, and probably that funny smile of hers that she gave him when occasional moments of disapproval fought with the great love in her heart for her husband. She would understand. He had need to celebrate. Small, private celebrations were essential to the well-being of those who live alone. Eileen would not begrudge him his enjoyment of the Caramel Dessert on his knee.

When the last small spoonful was licked clean, Alfred lay back with a contented sigh and contemplated the view he had never liked and soon would never have to see again. He began to plan in his mind all the things that would have to be done: possessions to be packed up, transport of the few pieces of furniture to be arranged, the flat to be let. The prospect of days ahead busily engaged in such activities was very pleasing. 'I must thank the good Lord, Eileen, for falling on my feet,' he said.

Alfred often spoke to Eileen, still: sometimes out loud, sometimes what seemed to be out loud but was really a voice in his head. He knew this because his lips did not move, although the voice was as clear as if he had spoken. On such occasions he always imagined Eileen. He could see her, luminous in his mind, almost tangible, sitting or standing before him, usually with a piece of sewing in her hand. He supposed that this was what was meant by death not being that much of a divider from life, the force of the spirit living on, especially in the case of a loved one. Certainly, for all her bodily absence, since Eileen's death Alfred had never felt she was far from him. He had never had trouble in conjuring her vision before him.

But this afternoon the trick, the magic – whatever it was – didn't work. The picture did not come. He spoke to Eileen but could not see her. At first Alfred thought it was a trick of the light, confusing his mind. There was a bright afternoon sun in the sky: its dazzling rays might have bleached out the picture of her. Alfred turned his head from the window and closed his eyes. Now there was blackness beneath his lids, but still no sign of Eileen. Alfred concentrated very hard. He felt his fingers gripping his knees as he willed a sight of her. After a while, to his relief, she began to unfurl, something in the manner of those Japanese flowers that you put in water and they bloom before your eyes. (A very successful line at Baxter's one Christmas.) Eileen materialized feet first: her small brown shoes with the delicately punched holes and the double straps, that she had preserved for twenty years or so: her blue skirt with the daisies embroidered on the hem, her yellow blouse with the mother-of-pearl buttons acquired in the days when buttons *were* buttons – and her lacy blue cardigan, painfully knitted not long before she died. But then Eileen stopped. At her shoulders. There was no neck, no head, no more of her. Alfred concentrated again, afraid, but there was no blooming of her dear face. And for all his efforts, Alfred could not remember anything about that face: the face he knew best in the world, stamped so deeply within him it was surely indelible.

He opened his eyes, heart thumping, and looked about the room. On the fireplace stood their wedding picture in its curly silver frame, a little tarnished, for Alfred had not felt like polishing in the last few weeks. There was Eileen's face as it had been that overcast morning in Lowestoft, as a shower of rain caught them as they came out of the church, and Alfred wondering if the effect of powdered diamonds on her nose would come out in the photographs. (The fact that it did not was always a regret.) Nevertheless, there was a radiance about her, the hallmark of happy brides, that shone through the photographer's static pose and brought a pricking dryness to Alfred's eyes that he would have liked to have relieved with tears. As he stared at the photograph the years fell over backwards, catapulting him back to that day: the memory of Eileen's warm and trembling hand in his so vivid that Alfred released the grip of his own knee for fear of hurting her. Time plays funny tricks on ageing men, he thought. With unblinking sore eyes, staring at the photograph, he remembered, he remembered – how he remembered that day.

But although the picture of Eileen gave back to Alfred the sight of her face as it was then, a picture of her more recent face still would not re-blossom. Eventually, exhausted by his efforts of hopeless recall, Alfred stirred himself and decided he would further confuse the afternoon by having his tea an hour early.

As he stood, rubbing with one hand at a painful shoulder, he had the strange impression that he was not alone, but that the presence near him was not Eileen. Then he heard – he could swear it was not a jest of his imagination – a soft, familiar laugh: Winnie's. Dear, stupid, disaster-prone Winnie. Shutting up the shop, winter evenings, while Eileen was out in the kitchen cooking the tea, Alfred had often heard Winnie laugh at his meticulous ways, straightening things on the counter so all would be shipshape for the morning, checking every bolt on the shutters twice. Alfred enjoyed her amusement. She kept him in touch with his own absurdities, reminding him that even in our striving for perfection we stand accused of foibles.

And now here was Winnie laughing at him again, although she was, in reality, on a South Seas island, eloped with a sailor, picnicking for the rest of her life. Further confused, Alfred rubbed his eyes, and then his ears, and listened to the accustomed silence that proved he was alone.

Suddenly businesslike, and rubbing his hands in the manner that often encouraged his customers to remember the very thing they had forgotten, Alfred hurried to the stove and toasted himself two tea cakes. He also opened a tin of whisky fruit cake and, for the first time since Eileen's death, took out the large teapot. He ate and drank slowly, at the kitchen table, enjoying the food, feeling strength return to him. He looked forward to the evening: he would pack a tea-chest full of books and papers, polish the old pair of boots that would do him nicely for work in Miss Windrush's garden. He would see to it that everything was efficiently organized by the time of the move next week: efficiency was his second nature.

As he washed the tea things, Alfred gave little thought to his recent unnerving experience. Being a man of good common sense he put it down to fatigue, worry, simple hunger (which affects the mind). These last few weeks had not been easy and now, today, with his change in fortune, there was naturally a feeling of considerable excitement. All these elements might well contribute to hallucinations. They were nothing to worry about.

Thus satisfied with his own explanation, Alfred set happily about his tasks. He fell asleep at once that night and dreamed of Eileen. Her face returned, clear as always, smiling at him.

In her chair in the kitchen, the real world obliterated by her memories, Viola was unaware of the rapid passing of the hours. It was only when she noticed the brightness of the afternoon had faded and the shadows of things on the window-sill had changed, that she stirred herself. She stretched her stiff legs and looked round the room.

Her eyes drifted first to the huge dresser which soared high as the ceiling, dominating the kitchen, and which was laden with plates, mugs, dishes, glasses, straw baskets, postcards, jars of herbs and spaghetti and beans, balls of string – all the things that people dump down in kitchens and, becoming used to them, have no desire to move or put away more tidily. An old shopping list hung from a hook. Viola saw that it was in her mother's writing and the paper had turned to pale gold, indicating its age. Next she observed with some shock that the two yellow candles, always the colour of sunlight, had faded to a dull cream, and their copper holders were tarnished. Things had slipped a little, thought Viola, since the death of her mother: and that would have made Mrs Windrush sad. But for the moment she could not summon the will to change anything, though perhaps with Alfred Baxter's help the house would gleam again. For the moment, the preservation of things just as they were was a comfort.

When she was away from home, the kitchen was the place Viola remembered most often. In her mind its every detail was so clear that, when she returned, she had the strange sensation that reality was merely a transparency which slipped over the imaginative picture, confirming it. Places she loved were ingrained within her more strongly than people. It was to them she turned, in solitude, or despair, and found tranquillity.

The door bell rang. Its old-fashioned clanging, reverberating along the passages, interrupted her reveries and forced her to make the effort of getting up from her chair. She went slowly to the hall – the bell rang impatiently again – expecting no visitors and resenting the intrusion of an unexpected caller.

A florist's van stood in the driveway. Its driver, at the door, was scratching his head, his face awry with indignation.

'Windrush the name? Roses for you. Bloody van full. They'll take a bit of carrying.'

He went to the van, flung open the double doors. Viola followed him. She saw the entire interior was filled with cellophane packages of red roses.

'Oh, no,' she said.

'One hundred, apparently,' said the man. 'Better get them shifted.' He lifted up a package, but Viola called out, restraining him.

'Please don't. I don't want them. I don't want a single one.'

'*Don't want them?*'

'I'd be very grateful if you could deliver the whole lot to the hospital on your way back.'

'That would be very irregular. But then an order like this isn't exactly regular, is it?' He threw the roses back into the van and slammed shut the doors. 'Still, if that's what you want. Here, you better have the card.' He handed her a small envelope. 'Look, I'll have to cover myself in this matter, you understand. Would you mind signing something to say I've delivered the roses to the hospital on your orders?'

Smiling, Viola obliged him with a note to that effect, written on a bill from the florist. Then she watched gratefully as the van drove away with its unwelcome cargo.

Back in the kitchen, Viola opened the envelope and reluctantly took out the card. *From your ardent admirer, Harry Antlers, with love*, it said, in florist's biro writing. With sudden anger she tore it into small pieces and threw it into the fireplace. The idea of Harry Antlers discovering where she lived filled her with unaccountable fury. She had not thought about him since leaving New York, and did not care to think of him again. His second ridiculous gesture, absurd in its extravagance, did not strike her as flattering. She did not think of it as a measure of passion or love, but merely as an intrusion into her private world. Enraged, she made herself a new pot of tea and switched on her portable radio. She determined not to acknowledge these flowers: all she desired was no further contact with the flamboyant Mr Antlers.

A Brahms symphony filled the room. Viola returned to her

chair. After a while, calmer, and the tea finished, she got up and went to the larder. She was hungry, but there was little to eat. She stood looking at the almost empty stone shelves, smelling the familiar scents of cold stone and slabs of strong cheese and apples: smells which had clustered so thickly in the small space over the years that they had permeated the air for ever, even though the food itself had gone. Viola sighed. In her mother's time the shelves were always crowded with home-made jams and bottled fruits, cold pies and hollowed Stiltons. Now, there were six eggs, some tins of fruit and a jar of pickled onions. Viola picked up two of the eggs, and the door bell rang again.

In an instant she decided not to answer it, knowing it must be the return of the man from the florist. The hospital, too, had rejected the roses. Nobody wanted Harry Antlers' wretched flowers. As the bell clanged impatiently again, Viola shut the larder door. Silence. Then she heard footsteps outside. The window was too high to see through, but Viola could tell it was the heavy tread of a man.

Remembering the back door was open, she prayed whoever it was would not come in. Unmoving, she listened. Someone was tapping on the window. Then there was a voice calling her name.

Viola dashed back into the kitchen at the same moment as Richard Almond came through the back door. They fell into each other's arms, hugging, laughing. Viola drew back first.

'I was hiding in the larder. I didn't want any visitors.'

'Not even me?'

'I wasn't expecting you. Of course I want you.'

'I heard you were back.'

'You hear things very quickly.'

'Thought I'd come to dinner.'

'*Dinner*? Is it dinner time?'

'It's five past eight precisely.'

'But I've only six eggs and a jar of pickled onions . . .'

'I took precautions. There's a whole basketful of stuff in the car. I'll get it.'

When he had gone Viola stood, dazed, by the table. She made vague movements, trying to clear a space, to remove the tea mugs and teapot and newspapers. What had unnerved her was not just Richard's unexpected arrival, but the sudden age in his face. She knew that after the age of thirty, if you do not see someone for several months the rapid change comes as a shock; new lines, a puckering of skin not observed before, a gathering of wisdom in the eye. Richard, for the first time, had prominent grey hairs at his temples. His unclouded young face, forever in her mind, was now the face of a middle-aged man. The reality and the mental image did not fit, and it was disturbing.

But such thoughts evaporated on Richard's return with the basket. The fact that he was here, his familiar presence filling the kitchen just as it used to, so that all the solid things trembled as if seen through a heat haze, was all that mattered. Filled with the sudden luxurious sense of being looked after, Viola watched while he unpacked the food and laid it on the table. He put two bottles of cold, greeny-yellow wine in the fridge, fetched knives and forks and spoons from their places, remembering where everything was. Weakly, Viola's only contribution was to take the two faded candles from the dresser, put them on the table and light them. Outside, gold clouds curled about the setting sun like honeysuckle. Opening the window, Viola could smell the sea of a high tide, and the paler smell of her mother's early roses.

They ate hungrily the delicious things Richard had brought: mackerel smoked locally, bread (which he warmed in the oven), tomatoes from his greenhouse, and home-made ice cream from his mother's deep freeze. Although food had never been of particular importance in Viola's life, she was conscious of enjoying this unexpected meal more than any eating she had done for many weeks. The food filled her with a new sense of optimism, though what there was to be optimistic about did not concern her for the moment. In high spirits she found herself telling Richard about New York, the saving of the house (about which he rejoiced) and the finding of Alfred Baxter. Finally, she described the puzzling antics of Harry Antlers. The return of the second lot of roses caused Richard much amusement.

'You've always been a one for inspiring such extravagant gestures,' he said. 'Orchids from Hong Kong, remember? God knows how many smoked salmon from Scotland arriving at Kings Lynn. That diamond heart from Cartier, a return first-class ticket to Bermuda . . . I remember them all.' He smiled. Viola wondered whether it was the wine that made her think there was wistfulness in his smile.

'I returned the airline tickets, don't forget.'

'So you did. I mustn't malign you. But you were always so wickedly funny about your suitors. I sometimes wondered if any of them were aware of the scrutiny you subjected them to. Poor wretches: they lost you through such innocent things. Do you remember that one upon whom you turned your scorn because he pulled a muscle blackberrying?'

'Oh, *him*. The essence of feebleness.' Viola laughed.

'Perhaps this Mr Antlers, then, with all his strength of passion, will be the one to win you.'

'Mr Antlers doesn't stand a chance.'

They had finished eating. A full but pale moon shone through the window. The sky was deepening, but far from dark, as if it found the brightness of the day hard to absorb in its shades. Richard opened the second bottle of wine.

'Don't let's move from here,' said Viola. 'The sitting-room's very unlived in, these days. And I still don't really like to go into Father's study.'

'No. We'll stay here.' Richard sat down at the table again. Her own news over, Viola waited for Richard to begin. He gave a small, reflective smile which, Viola knew of old, was prelude to some piece of self-criticism.

'I must have been the only one not to make you grand gestures,' he said.

Viola laughed. 'For a start, you were never my suitor, but my brother's friend, very kind to the younger sister. Secondly, over the years, you gave me the entire works of Dostoevsky, remember?'

'In paperback. Yes.'

'Which have given me much more pleasure than a diamond brooch.'

'Good, good. You've always been appreciative of small things.'

He was silent for a long time. They listened to the ticking of the clock on the wall. As a child, Viola had thought a minute man lived in its works. His duty as caretaker meant he paced round and round it, checking all was well, and the ticking was the sound of his regular footsteps. They never faltered, and the clock never went wrong. Now, suddenly remembering her image of the clock-keeper, Viola tried to recall how she had imagined him able to stick to the vertical face of the clock: but she could not remember. Eventually, she said to Richard:

'How's your life?'

'Busy. There's been a flu epidemic.' It was Richard's way to be both honest but brusque when asked such questions. Viola let a few more silent moments pass.

'And Sonia?'

Richard briefly closed his eyes. The deep lids, the colour of violet bruises, trembled very slightly, disturbing a fan of small lines at the corner of each eye that Viola had not observed before. She thought she had never seen him look so old or so tired. But when he looked at her again he was quite cheerful, and sipped his wine.

'I saw her yesterday, as a matter of fact. She's been quite ill. Flu turned into bronchial pneumonia. But she's better now.'

'But how . . . in general?'

'Much the same, I suppose. No great developments for the worse of late. Terribly depressed and pretty confused. Yesterday she thought I was a doctor, but had no idea I was her husband. Usually, she refers to me as "husband" all the time. I sometimes think she doesn't any longer know my name.'

His unusually detailed revelations gave Viola reason to think it would be in order, for once, to risk a further question.

'Perhaps, I shouldn't ask you this . . . the wine. But do you ever think of leaving her?'

Again Richard was cheerful, making the forbidden subject easier than it had ever been.

'Oh yes. Heavens, yes. Of course I think about ending it all, divorce, whatever. I think about it every day of my life.' He sat back, hands in pockets. 'But I made her those promises, you see. I may have made them for foolish reasons – and looking back I see I was certainly more foolish than honourable – but nonetheless I made them. How can I go back on my word?' He sighed. 'There's just a chance, one day, she may recover, and be returned to a normal life. If that happened, she would need someone to be there waiting for her. She wouldn't survive on her own.'

'You wouldn't survive with her.'

'I'd have to try.'

'You're too noble, sometimes, for your own good.'

'I believe in constancy.' Viola smiled in silent agreement. 'Some of us, I suppose, are just born constant, and there's nothing much we can do about it.'

'But what are the chances of her recovery? Of her coming out? You ought to be practical.' Viola was aware that her voice had risen.

'Very small, I must admit. No, it'll all end in its own time.'

'You mean, she'll stay in that place her whole life and die of old age?'

'I very much doubt *that*. No, one day she'll kill herself.'

Richard watched the surprise in Viola's face. He knew that of all the solutions she had contemplated as an end to his predicament, that particular one had never occurred to her.

'She had anorexia as a teenager and first felt death "looming", as she called it, then. I've never known her threaten to kill herself, exactly, but she's got this awful Keatsian phrase she keeps on producing out of the blue. "Now more than ever it seems ripe to die," she says, quite conversationally, while we're having a cup of tea or something. Very menacing. In her maddest moments she screams it out loud over and over again.'

'I'm sorry,' said Viola, after a while. 'I didn't really mean to ask about Sonia.'

'I don't mind *your* asking,' Richard said, quietly. 'I'm loath to bring up the subject myself, simply because it's a subject without news one way of the other. It's just there. The odd small changes, but basically it's the same. Sonia exists, mad. I have a mad wife who exists. I await her in case one day she needs me. What else is there to be said?'

'Nothing,' said Viola.

Richard got up and went to the sink, poured himself a glass of water. When he turned back to Viola she saw a look of such old, resigned sadness in his eyes that she did not trust herself to speak.

'But you,' he said, jolting himself from whatever the private reverie, 'what about you, Violetta? Any plans? What are you going to do?'

'I'm trying to decide.'

'You can't just sit here, stagnating.'

'No. I suppose I'll go to London, find some kind of job. But I'll be here for a while, settling Mr Baxter in and organizing the roof.'

'So I'll be able to call on you.'

'Whenever you like. Of course.'

'We could do some sailing. Picnics. Do you remember Gideon's loathing of picnics?' He smiled, looked at the clock. It was almost midnight. 'I must be off.'

Viola went on sitting at the table, unmoving, watching him approach her. She relived the old longing felt all those years ago in the garden at Maisie Fanshawe's dance. She wanted him to enclose her in his arms, ravish her, take her away for ever. But of course nowadays she allowed no such desires to show. Richard's view of her was of an impassive young woman whose stern pale face was only mellowed by the light of the candles.

'Thank you for coming,' she said, standing.

In the shadowy light he looked quite young again, green Irish eyes fired with things Viola could only guess at – regret, possibly, and the strain of his self-admitted constancy. He was within a few inches of her now. Viola, rigid to disguise her trembling, waited for the repeat bear hug of their greeting. Instead, Richard drew the back of his hand over one of her cheeks, feeling the bone, almost as if searching for an ache or a pain in his professional capacity. He bent his head, as if to kiss her, then changed his mind, and drew himself upright.

'I'll be back,' he said.

When he had gone, Viola went straight to bed, leaving the mess in the kitchen. She slept fitfully, dreaming of Richard, a kaleidoscope of events in their past: sailing, walking, reading, arguing at the kitchen table. The only thing that bore no resemblance to reality was that at each event Richard was accompanied by a large mongrel dog on a lead. The dog had centrally parted shaggy hair and the mad face of Sonia.

6

Viola was woken by the telephone. (The only change she had made in the house since her parents' death was to move a telephone into her room.) Dawn showed bleakly through the windows. Her instant thought was that Richard was in trouble. She was at once wide awake. But it was not his voice.

'Viola?'

'Yes?'

'This is your friend Harry Antlers.'

'Oh God, Harry.'

'I'm calling you from New York.'

'How did you get my number?'

'That's no business of yours. I'm through to you, that's the main thing. Were you asleep?'

'Yes.'

'Sorry. I couldn't wait any longer. Did some flowers arrive?'

'Yes. Thank you.'

Her bare shoulders chilled by the early air, Viola had not the heart to tell him of the flowers' fate. She lay back under the bedclothes, shivering: partly cold, partly the fear of the hunted.

'Look,' she said, as gently as she could, 'you're very kind, all these flowers. But please don't send me any more. Two hundred roses is enough to last anyone a lifetime.'

'Nonsense. By the end of your life you'll have had two hundred thousand roses from me.' A terrible threat, in the early light. 'You'll see.'

Viola laughed falsely. 'Please, Harry. Don't be silly. There are plenty of flowers here in the garden.'

'Plenty of flowers here in the garden,' he mimicked. 'I'm sure there are. Some people are born into very privileged gardens, full of flowers. But is that the point, my love?'

Only great self-control stopped Viola shouting her protest

at being referred to as Harry Antlers' love: she was nothing of the kind. How dare he presume to refer to her as such? A jangle of answers clamoured through her head, but rejecting them all as impolite on a transatlantic phone call, she said nothing. There was a long pause. Then Harry repeated:

'That isn't the point, you idiot woman.'

He sounded so despairing that for a moment Viola was guilty of feeling unsympathetic towards so gloomy and pathetic a character. But at the same time a menacing quality in his voice clouded all clear thought and sensible answers. He had a strange capacity to make her feel in the wrong, and afraid, for all the distance between them. Hopelessly, she said:

'This call must be costing you a fortune.'

'Who cares about money?'

Viola sighed. 'How's the play going?'

'Badly. But what do I care about the play?'

'A lot, I should hope.'

'I care for nothing that keeps me on the other side of the Atlantic from you.'

'For heaven's sake, Harry . . .' Viola's irritation boiled over. 'You're suffering from a terrible fantasy about me. Quite honestly, the sooner you get over it the better it will be for us both.'

'I'm glad that's what you like to think. But I don't believe you. You're not a girl who would not recognize truth when she saw it.'

There was a long pause. Viola's mind whirled. What was he talking about? The sun was rising through her window. She wanted to slam down the receiver: his call was a loathsome intrusion into her uncontaminated room.

'I've been hearing about you,' he was saying. 'I had lunch with a mutual friend of ours. She told me a lot about you. Very interesting it was, too.'

Despite herself, Viola's curiosity was aroused.

'Who was it?'

'That doesn't matter. The point is, I learned a lot about you. About all your lovers.' There was a note of triumph in his voice.

'Lovers? What are you talking about? I don't know anyone in New York except for Gideon and Hannah, and Hannah doesn't know anything about me.'

'Ah.'

'So I don't know what you mean.'

'It's a possibility a friend of yours was over from London and I ran into her. New York's a very small place. And you must remember not to trust your friends.'

As Viola's mind reeled through friends who might have gone to New York, met Harry Antlers and told tales of her private life, a painful pressure of bone began to constrict her head. She felt physically sick at the thought of such betrayal. Shivering beneath the warm bedclothes, in her pain and confusion it never occurred to her Harry was so devious as to shoot poisoned arrows in order to get some reaction.

'Everyone betrays everyone,' he was saying. 'You'll learn that.'

'Look, there's not much point in continuing this conversation,' said Viola weakly.

'No. I can see it disturbs you. Must be disturbing, being reminded of old lovers so early in the morning. Are you with one of them now?'

'I'm quite alone, but it's nothing to do with you.' Viola's voice was shaking.

'I'm sorry, my love, I seem to be upsetting you. That's the last thing in the world I want to do. I'm just terribly lonely here in New York. I'll be back with you as soon as I can.'

'Please. I shan't be here.'

'Where will you be?'

'I don't know. I'm leaving here soon. I have to get a job.'

'Worry not, little one. I'll find you. I love you with my entire being. You realize that? I can't let you escape now, can I? After a life's search. I'd be mad. And don't forget I know a lot more about you than you think I know. I *love* you, woman, do you hear me? Is sending roses across the Atlantic the act of a man who doesn't – '

Viola slammed down the receiver. She buried herself beneath the bedclothes into a cocoon of complete darkness, as she used to as a child. She tried to control the shivering, to clear her mind. Much later, she heard the telephone ring again, but did not answer it. She did not get up till midday, the sun high in a summer sky, but blighted. Without warmth. Years later, looking back, she realized this had been the morning the bullying had started, and the horror of dealing with an irrational man had begun.

In New York, Harry Antlers kept himself from the daylight as much as possible. When he was forced to make brief excursions into the streets the sun bored painfully through his head, adding to the many other discomforts he suffered in mind and body. He ate hamburgers and milkshakes obsessively, but their tranquillizing effects were diminishing. He was aware of putting on weight. His clothes felt tight and uncomfortable. Sleep, which had never been elusive before, was now tormented. In the noisy, muggy nights, Viola's nasty little voice, so cold on the telephone, played an endless tape in his head. By day, in the stuffy theatre, rehearsals went badly. Harry could not speak to his cast without shouting. Normally so articulate, so arrogantly fluent in his ideas, he found himself struggling to convey what he wanted. And everybody, a talentless lot, did everything wrong. Chris tied and retied his shoelaces more frequently and more sullenly. All about him people looked at Harry as if there was something the matter with him, while visions of Viola exploded endlessly in his head, obscene visions which goaded with relentless agony. It was time for revenge.

Revenge? When the idea came to Harry's mind for the first time, he was shocked. In truth, it was the last thing he wanted: he knew its dangers. But if you loved a woman who did not realize she loved you, you must fight for her, breaking all rules if necessary. In the past his only fights had been to rid himself of the many girls who – once he had become successful – crowded him with their desperate love. (Before that, there had been years of shyness on his part, rejection on theirs.) Their attentions had flattered him, given him confidence. He had used them, but not loved them in return. Now, for the first time, he was bedevilled by total passion, and this lady seemed to have no care for the havoc she was causing him. If only he could show her a glimpse of his private vision – a somewhat hazy picture of domestic peace, a state Harry had never witnessed in reality – but it included thick carpets, bowls of flowers, a chuckling baby, and the constant Viola with open arms to welcome him home each evening, dinner waiting on the table. Oh, how he would love her! Overwhelm her. That was the way to keep things going . . . overwhelming: presents, proclamations, everything. His own childhood had proved to him there was nothing to be said for emotional parsimony. There had never been a word of love uttered in his parents' house. Starved always of affection, friendship, understanding, here he was, now, a man locked in his own inadequacies – full of strange love which he could not handle. And so although the idea of revenge came unwanted from his well-meaning heart, there might be no alternative.

The play opened and was unanimously scorned by the critics. Harry did not care. He sat in his dim hotel bedroom, eating a vast breakfast as he read the papers, silently scoffing back at his detractors for not understanding the essence of the work. But their cruel jibes had no power to hurt. Nothing hurt but the absence of Viola.

The telephone rang. (It had been ominously silent for many days.) He pounced eagerly upon it, hoping against hope it would be Viola. But it was Hannah Bagle, condoling.

Harry was in no mood for sympathy, and had not given Hannah further thought since the day she rang him with Viola's English telephone number. Now, hearing her gentle voice, an idea came to him: she could help in his revenge. He asked her round that afternoon. She accepted at once.

'I have some information that might interest you, Harry,' she said. This excited him. The five long hours till she was due passed in a state of barely controlled frenzy.

When Hannah arrived, punctually at five, she saw a desperate man. Slouched in the room's one armchair, he looked pale, ill. His smile of greeting was also one of gratitude – something Gideon infrequently gave – and Hannah found his fat, ugly, pathetic state infinitely desirable. She sat on the end of the bed. Harry returned to his chair.

'I'll order drinks. What would you like? Thank God you've come.'

'Nothing for the moment. Later, thanks.'

Hannah crossed her provocative legs and fiddled with gold chains at her neck. For his part, Harry observed she was his for the taking, and was glad there would be no struggle to involve her in his plans. But for the moment he was impatient for the news of Viola.

'What have you heard? Tell me, quickly. Your interesting information.' He gave the small, friendly laugh of a conspirator.

Hannah shrugged, maddeningly unhurried. 'Oh, nothing *much*. I'm sorry if I gave you the impression it was very exciting. Only that Gideon let it drop the other night – I have to be very careful how I question him for fear of arousing his suspicions – that years ago Viola'd been in love with his best friend at Oxford. But nothing came of it. The friend married someone else, who's mentally disturbed, and that was that, really. Although he and Viola remain friends.'

Harry sighed, disappointed. He had expected more useful ammunition, although there were ways of utilizing even such a paltry scrap.

'Do you know his name?'

'I didn't ask.'

'Do they still meet?'

'I believe so.'

'Anything else about the man? What he does? Does she still love him?'

'He's a doctor. That's all I know.'

Harry sighed again, dissatisfied.

'Look here, Harry,' said Hannah, 'if my only use to you is one of spy, or detective, then I think I'd better go.'

'Don't be ridiculous.' He smiled so warmly Hannah's small flare of indignation was quelled. 'Look, I'm sorry. You know my feelings about Viola, even if you can't understand them. As you can imagine, I'm passionate to talk about her, to get to know more about her. But on the other hand, she's miles away, there's nothing I can do about her at the moment. And you're here, just a few feet away from me, for heaven's sake.' Pause. 'A lovely woman, Hannah Bagle . . .'

Hannah smiled, eyes down, flushed. She thought how Gideon, master in the school of British understatement, would scorn such dialogue. And she did not care. If Gideon had need of her, then he did not show it. While this strange, ugly man before her could be comforted. She could make use of her superior strength. She looked down to see he was unbuttoning her shirt.

'Is this . . . forbidden?' asked Harry, so gently that, had

Hannah been that sort of woman, tears would have come to her eyes.

'No.' She trembled.

Then her breasts were exposed, Harry's hands were upon them. He was kneeling on the ground, his head plunged between the breasts so that his hair tickled her chin, and she was cradling him like the child she would never contemplate having for fear of destroying her career. Harry was weeping. In all her various experiences, Hannah had never known a man cry in her arms before, and found it curiously stimulating. She brushed away his tears with fingers that she hoped were tender rather than nurse-like, and, surreptitiously glancing at her watch, wondered how long she would have to wait before Harry had spent his tears and would begin thinking of her pleasure. She whispered comforting words, flattered that the beauty of her body should have so devastating an effect upon a man, never guessing that his damp moaning was for himself and for the absence of Viola. The woman upon whose breasts he lay his self-pitying head for comfort was of no more significance to Harry than a hot-water bottle.

When he had finished with her, he was instantly overcome by the disagreeable state of having glutted his desire on something he had not really wanted. He lay back on the bed, listening to her having a hurried bath, watching her dress, without interest. She was flustered, late, and Harry cared not a jot for her anxiety. He did not even bother to raise himself from the bed as she prepared to leave. She knelt beside him, suffused with that temporary softness that overcomes the hardest woman after she has been seduced.

'Goodbye, Harry.'

'Forgive me for not coming down with you. They'll get you a cab. As I've told you before, I'm not a gentleman.'

'Will I see you again soon?'

'Of course.'

'I'd like to see you often, often.'

'You will. You will, you will.'

'Take care of yourself, Harry.'

She kissed him lightly on the eyes, tasting the salt of still damp lashes. He was a man who could sure worm his way into her heart, should he like to try . . .

When Hannah had gone, Harry breathed deeply with relief, exhausted. He dozed for a while, then woke in a calmer, happier state. The ammunition he had acquired through Hannah's cooperation was invaluable. Tricking Viola's brother meant that, in a confused way, Harry held a strong card. With a grim smile he picked up the telephone, got through to the airline and booked himself on a flight back to England the next day.

There is a rhythm to the solitary life, as Viola had discovered long ago. Many empty days go by, then comes a cluster of unexpected events. Some of these may change the whole direction of life, some may shift it just the slightest degree from the normal routine. On her return from America Viola had anticipated habitual quiet, and had already been surprised by three things: the good fortune in finding Alfred Baxter, Richard's visit, and Harry Antlers' telephone call from New York. A few days after that third, and disagreeable happening, came the fourth surprise, in the shape of a letter from her Uncle David.

Uncle David, her father's brother, was a millionaire anthropologist: an elderly and eccentric man who spent most of his time in the jungles of Brazil. On the rare occasions he was in England he had always shown a particular concern for Viola, and indeed several generous cheques since her parents' death had saved her from financial difficulties on many occasions. He now had a typically benevolent proposal to make to her.

The sitting tenant in the top-floor flat of his house in Holland Park had died, and it required complete renovation. Knowing Viola enjoyed that sort of thing, he wrote, he wondered if she would care to undertake the task for him, for which he would provide a handsome budget. In return, she could treat the flat as her own, rent free, until such time as he sold the whole house. He was returning to South America in a week's time, and would be obliged if Viola could let him know her decision before he left, so that they could arrange finances and keys. Until the flat was ready for habitation, he would be delighted if she lived in his part of the house, where she had stayed many times before. 'You may run into a quiet, scholarly fellow,' he wrote, 'son of a friend of mine, one Edwin Hardley. He's writing a book on moths – been writing it for about twelve years, and seems to prefer working in my library to his own flat or the British Museum. He's a silent sort of chap, wouldn't do a thing to hurt you. In fact, I call him Hardley There: his presence is so transparent, somehow, you're scarcely aware of him even when he's in the room. Do hope the whole plan might appeal.'

This was a cheering and unexpected solution to the menacing worries that were beginning to accumulate in Viola's mind. Amazed by such well-timed luck, her morning was suddenly sparked by plans. Once Alfred Baxter and the mending of the roof here were settled, she would go to London to convert the flat and find herself a job. The adrenalin of ideas began to flow, uncontainable. She immediately sat down to write her uncle a letter of grateful acceptance and then, still restless, jotted down the beginnings of a poem which came to her in a blinding strike of light. She had always been ashamed of her attempts at poetry, shown them to no one and hidden them away. She had no doubt they were of little merit, but she was unable to resist writing them when the Muse, or whatever, was upon her. By the end of the day she felt something was accomplished: a poem, and a letter confirming plans for a change in life. With a new peace of mind she lit the fire and sat listening to a concert on the radio. When the telephone rang she knew instinctively it was Harry Antlers, not Richard, and did not answer it. It continued to ring many times during the night. Viola ignored it with great satisfaction, and when at last she slept she dreamed of walking for miles along the empty beach with Richard. She remembered, in her dream, to tell him about the picnic she had observed at the wreck: the stillness of the ghost ladies in the fluttering dresses. But Richard's only reaction was to turn to her and say:

'Oh, Viola, *you* must be mad, too.' He looked distressed, gazing at the far-off wreck where there were no picknickers to be seen. And in her dream Viola understood his distress: he did not want two mad women in his life.

By the time Harry's plane landed at Heathrow he was in a

state of such frenzied impatience that regulations had become barriers designed for his annoyance alone. Passport control, waiting for the baggage, Customs . . . Harry stomped about gleefully noticing the effect he had upon calmer passengers. Alarmed by his audible snorts and furious face, they backed away from him, nudging, whispering, fearing attack from the apparent madman among them. Their unease further spurred Harry's mania. Free with his suitcase at last, he ran clumsily to the taxi rank. There he shouted at the driver to speed as if it were a matter of life or death.

But such disorderly emotion spends itself quickly. In the journey to London, heavy rain making the taxi a watery cage, the strength went from Harry. It left him cold and weak. He craved hot food, dreaded the silent dampness which he knew awaited him in his bleak bedsitting-room.

Heavy with self-pity, he dragged himself up the narrow staircase of the semi-detached house which had been his unambitious home for the past ten years. A dark passage beside the stairs led to the steamy quarters of his spinster landlady. It was her preoccupation with washing clothes – rather, boiling them in preserving pans on the stove – that Harry believed sent dampness billowing into his own quarters. Beside the clothes the landlady boiled daily quantities of vegetables and stew. The combined smells of hot soap and murky food was vile in the air. They greeted Harry with sickening familiarity. He determined to complain once more when he was next in a strong mood, loth though he was ever to enter the landlady's kitchen. But for the moment there were more urgent matters to be considered.

An hour later, from the shallows of an ugly tweed chair, Harry surveyed his aloneness. Temporary numbness of feeling had come from a packet of stale biscuits and a bowl of powdered mushroom soup. Rain continued to pour with slatey sound against the windows. The gas fire hissed, unwarming. A large pile of opened letters lay scattered on the floor. Harry recognized the false calm before another outbreak of maddened desire, and picked up the telephone.

He dialled Viola's number – a number by now indelible in his mind. It rang for a long time, the rhythmic buzz soothing, simply because it manifested some connection with the one he loved. Eventually he replaced the receiver, dispirited but not deterred. Looking at his watch, he saw that it was almost five. He calculated that by the time he had had several hamburgers at his local Wimpy, he could be in Norfolk by 8.30.

Standing, he took from his pocket a small jeweller's box and opened it. There lay a round black stone veined with white. He did not know its name but, in New York, trembling as he chose it, had thought it beautiful. The shopkeeper had said it was a most unusual brooch, and it had cost Harry far more than he could afford. But here, in this gloomy room, sodden plane leaves slapping at the windows, its magic had quite gone. Gloucester's eye, it was, now: plucked, solidified, turned to stone. The thought made Harry shiver. He hurried back down the damp stairs, slammed the warped front door and hurled the brooch far into the gutter. (One day it would be replaced with diamonds.) There was urgency upon him again. Head down, smeared glasses impeding the view, Harry charged the rain.

Richard's surprise visit had alerted Viola to more surprises. She anticipated that, in the short time she was to remain at home before going to London, he might appear several times. She determined to be more ready for him when he came again. And so each evening she tidied the kitchen a little, saw that there was enough food and wine for supper, and put his favourite Schubert on the record player.

The fact that Richard did not come for several nights left her undismayed. She was strong with the certainty of his return at some time, felt curious pleasure in exercising patience. But patience is capricious, deserts its captor without warning to leave the nerves exposed and shivering once again. On the third night of waiting Viola felt the warmth of certainty stripped from her. Such doubts and fears assailed her that despite a lighted fire she felt quite cold.

And so on this particular evening she paid especial attention to her preparations. She took the chill of her flesh to be a warning, a premonition. Tonight Richard would appear and she had no intention of letting him catch her unawares. All traces of the anguish she felt would be wholly disguised. A bath first, for warmth. Then she dressed, choosing clothes with care: an old silk shirt so large it must once have belonged to Gideon, but whose soft sleeves, rolled up, gave protection: a wide belt of frayed silver leather, punched with silver studs, that emphasized the Edwardian smallness of her waist, and which Richard had often admired. Quite pleased with her appearance, and at the same time scorning her own vanity, she returned to the kitchen and lit the fire. She turned on Elgar's cello concerto, a piece she had always considered of such dignified sadness that it should be used as a remedy by anyone venturing towards the shades of self-pity. She polished apples on her skirt, studied her mother's old shopping lists hanging from the dresser. *Mince for cottage pie*, she read, and wished she could remember the forgotten day on which her family, all alive, had eaten that pie. The Colonel and his love of Worcestershire sauce . . .

There is madness in waiting, thought Viola.

At ten past nine she went to the window. It had been raining heavily all day, had now stopped. But the sky glowered over the garden ready to burst again. Viola stayed at the window, eyes searching the clouds, waiting for the first drop on the glass. But it did not come, and the music and the shuffling of the fire behind her were but rags of sound thrown over the fundamental silence. Then the front door bell rang.

Viola stirred. It rang again, and again. Viola merely went to the fire, stood so that its heat flared up her back, instantly warming the silk of her shirt. She surveyed the kitchen, defiant. For some reason, perverse even to herself, she did not wish to go to the door and open it. Rather, she would wait for Richard to come round here, as he had before.

There were footsteps in the passage outside. A pause. The kitchen door opened. Harry Antlers stood there.

'Hello, my love,' he said.

Viola felt the flames scorch her back. Her shirt pounded. She took a deep breath in the hope that it would steady her voice.

'What are you doing here?' she asked.

'Oh, I can see what kind of a greeting I am going to get. I should have imagined it, the rapturous greeting.'

Harry stepped further into the room, slamming the door behind him. Despite herself, Viola jumped. Harry's eyes scoured her nervousness. Then he cupped a hand over them as if to secure the vision of her in his mind. Viola's fingers played among the studs on her belt. When eventually he took away his hand, he smiled, as if with a great effort of self-control.

'I'm sorry if I've interrupted your evening. I'm sorry if my presence is inconvenient. Were you waiting for someone?'

'No,' answered Viola, after a long pause.

'Perhaps, then, you'd grant me the decency of the minimum of hospitality. I've come a long way to see you. I left New York this morning, only stopped in London long enough to get my car. I've been circling round your bloody Norfolk lanes for hours. I'm wet and hungry. God, I'm hungry. Would it be too much to ask for a simple piece of cheese? A glass of wine? Or milk? Anything.'

Pulling off his jacket, Harry Antlers strode to the fire. He flung the jacket on the back of a chair, turned it to the flames. Viola moved to the fridge. After some searching she took from it a saucer holding a small wedge of Brie.

'Cheese,' she said.

Harry, from his position by the fire, sneered down at it.

'I meant real cheese,' he said. 'The sort of thing people from my background call cheese. You know, or perhaps you don't, being such a grand lady. Cheddar.'

'I'm sorry . . . It's all I have.'

Even as she heard her own words, Viola cursed herself. It was ludicrous to find herself apologizing for having no Cheddar for this unwanted and unwelcome visitor. She returned the Brie to the fridge.

'There's a cold sausage,' she said.

'A cold sausage? That should keep me going for a while,' Harry scoffed.

Viola went to him, holding out a plate. Harry took the sausage. There was a long silence while he admired it intently. Viola, heart fearfully pounding as she looked upon the disagreeable mass of this ugly, bitter man, felt irrational guilt again. The sausage was undercooked.

'Very appropriate,' said Harry at last. 'Thanks. And could you, perhaps, run to a slice of bread and marge to accompany this very wonderful sausage?'

'Of course. And there's some wine . . .'

'*Wine*? You amaze me. Your hospitality.'

While Viola clumsily buttered a crust of stale bread – all that remained in the bin – and poured a glass of wine, Harry observed his surroundings. They did nothing to mellow his unease. Spurred by acute hunger now, he felt his old rage kindle within him. He loathed the untidy arrogance of the room: the high ceiling, the faded prints hung low on the walls, rush matting split and frayed on the stone floor – the feel and smell of a room that has housed a happy family for many years. Suddenly he stood, unable to contain himself any longer, full of the fury of one threatened by a past he has not shared. Viola handed him the bread. He snatched it from her, banged it down on the table.

'Privileged bitch,' he said quietly. 'Typical of your kind.'

He swung round to the sink, grabbed an empty milk bottle and, turning back to Viola, smashed it against the edge of a chair. The neck broke, fell to the floor with a small chink. Harry waved the rest of the bottle triumphantly, pointing the end of jagged glass at Viola. She screamed. Harry laughed.

'I come all the way from New York to see the only woman I've ever loved and I'm given a *cold sausage*!'

'Get out! Or I'll call the police!' Viola's voice was faint. She wondered how she was going to get to the telephone.

'Ah, the melodramatic little lady – '

' – and put that bottle down.'

Viola lunged unthinkingly at Harry, locked the thick wrist that held the bottle in both her hands, nails digging into his flesh. Strangely, he did not fight back. At the touch of her, all strength seemed to ebb from him. He sagged, put the bottle gently back on the table, slumped down into the chair by the fire. 'Oh, my God, my love, I'm sorry.' Sweat on his brow, tears in his eyes. 'You'll never believe me, I'm a total bastard – but I'm sorry. I don't know what came over me. Please forgive me if you can.'

Viola, shaking, handed him the bread which he ate wolf-like in one mouthful, butter smearing and glistening at the corners of his mouth. Then he drank the glass of wine. The fire spat and crackled. Viola looked at the jagged glass teeth of the broken milk bottle.

'Please,' she said. 'Just go. If you leave now, with no fuss, I won't call the police.'

Harry smiled. 'That's good of you.' He put out a hand towards her. She backed out of his reach. 'You're trembling. Don't tremble. No need. Here, come nearer to the fire. Let me hold your hand.'

Viola looked down on him. She could feel no sympathy in her heart, only a strong revulsion such as she had never known before. It froze and numbed her limbs. She did not move. Harry, wiping his mouth with a grubby handkerchief, made a soft, whimpering noise like a chained dog under a full moon.

'I don't think you can begin to conceive what I feel – the agony I've been through.'

'No.'

'And you probably don't care.'

'No.'

'But I'm not going to give up.' He smiled, almost twinkling. 'When a man has found his ultimate prize he doesn't let it go that easily. All my life, till meeting you, I've been stumbling along in the darkness. Don't you see?'

'I'm not interested. Please understand that. I'm sorry if I've caused you so much despair, but I don't want to know or hear of your feelings any more. I don't want any more to do with you, please. And I don't want you in this house. I don't want you ever to come back . . .' Her voice rose. Harry stood. 'Oh, this is ridiculous. This isn't ordinary behaviour.'

'Quite.' Full of calm sympathy now the rage was exorcized, Harry was able to laugh. 'Well, there'll be no more such behaviour, I promise, if you give up fighting. Just submit to what you know in your heart you want – '

'You're *mad*, Harry Antlers. The only thing in the world I want from you is that you should go, and never attempt to see me again.'

'Calm down, little one. I'm off. I'm looking forward to another long drive through the rain, *driven out* . . . No, don't worry: I am going. But I must eat something first. I can't drive another mile on an empty stomach. I don't believe there isn't *something* in a great house like this . . .'

He began to move about the kitchen, touching things, opening biscuit tins, tapping glass jars of rice and sultanas. It was then a new fear flared in Viola: he would find the larder and the cold chicken pie – the pastry had taken up most of her morning – which she had made in case Richard came. Even as this terror gripped her, Harry opened the larder door. Viola screamed.

'Come out of there!'

Very calm, Harry turned back into the kitchen holding the chicken pie.

'Look what I've found. Isn't this wonderful? A pie.'

'Get out, please. Go.'

Viola tried to snatch the pie from Harry, but he held it out of reach above her head.

'No fighting, now. I'll eat as fast as I can then leave you as I promised. For the moment,' he added, ominously. He sat down at the far side of the table, picked up a nearby fork and dug into the pastry.

In the silence, now that the music had stopped, the sound of Harry's eating struck every nerve in Viola's body. Unable to bear the sight of him, creamy sauce and flakes of pastry askew on his chin, she went over to the sink, folded her arms to give herself support, and stared out at the night sky. A small part of her mind could observe the absurdity of the situation: woman helpless in her own kitchen while unwanted man ravishes chicken pie made with love for another. But the humorous element was not strong enough to overcome the horror and the fear.

It was one of those summer nights when there is no denseness to the dark, when small clouds shimmy about the moon, restless in their duty of casting shade over the land till dawn. The rain had stopped, leaving a faint glitter on the leaves. The tide must have been out, for there was no whisper of the sea.

Viola heard a footstep on the path, a cautious scrunch of gravel. She tightened. Not wishing to indicate by movement that she had heard anything, she strained her eyes. She saw the shape of Richard. He seemed to stare at her, then past her. She was about to shout for his help when he backed away, over the lawn: a lithe, surprised motion. He quickly disappeared through the gate that led to the marsh.

Viola took a deep breath to help control. She turned to face Harry. He had pushed the pie away from him, entirely eaten but for a few bits of pastry that clung to the sides of the dish. He wiped his mouth with the back of his hand.

'Your lover, I suppose,' he said. 'Yes, I saw him.' Viola opened her mouth. Harry put up his hand. 'Don't bother to deny it: I know all about your lovers, past and present. Well, I'm sorry if I disturbed an assignation. I'm sorry if I've eaten the bastard's dinner, too. But it was very good, and my need was greater than his.' He stood, benign from the food, and smiling. 'I'm going now, but I warn you. I shan't be far away. Hope the thought won't disturb your screwing.'

At this word, in connection with Richard so obscene and so far from the truth, a searing rage and indignation flared in Viola so that her whole body trembled. But she managed to speak quietly.

'Harry Antlers,' she said, 'you need medical help.'

Harry smiled charmingly. 'How touching you are in your concern! But I don't need a doctor, thank you. I'm merely struck by an illness for which there's only one remedy, and that remedy will soon be mine.'

He moved clumsily to the door, flung a final look of scorn about the room. Then he turned to Viola, menacing.

'But there's one thing you must know, and never forget. When a man loves in the way that I do, there's no holding him. He's filled with a demon energy that knows no bounds. He will go to any length to get what he wants, any means. And strangely – you must believe this – it's remarkably easy to find out all one wants to know. This man, this doctor in your life – there's little I don't know about him, for instance. Loved him for years, haven't you? Perhaps you know how it feels, then: wanting. Perhaps even a beautiful girl like you knows the despair of wanting. I hope so.'

He was gone, the door banged behind him. Viola heard the muffled revving of his car. Then merciful silence, but for small shifts among the dying logs in the fire.

Viola screamed out loud, a wordless spewing forth of all the things held back since seeing Richard in the garden. Then she ran to the window, banged it with shaking hands, her fingers scrabbling among the moving clouds, calling his name, calling his name. From the window she ran to the dresser, picked up the telephone and dialled his number. It rang for a long time, but there was no answer. Shaking, she ran again, footsteps frantic on the flagstones, to both doors, making fast the old bolts and turning the huge keys in their solid locks. Turning, the sight of the empty pie dish on the table, parsley sauce solidifying on the prongs of the fork, renewed the horror. The solid comforting things of this womb kitchen, protection for a lifetime, had tonight been cracked beyond recognition, ravaged by Harry Antlers' loathsome presence. His threats savaging through her, Viola went to the fire, crouched down before it, hands stretched out to the last of the flames. Victim now of a terrible fear, the violation of her peace causing an unearthly chill to her flesh, she clutched painfully at her own arms in all her wretchedness. Escape was her only thought.

7

By late afternoon of the next day, Alfred Baxter was installed in the wing of Viola's house. He had always prided himself on his efficiency in practical matters, and the day of moving had passed with an ease which filled Alfred with retrospective content, although at the time of humping his possessions through the door there had been moments of anxiety. Would, for instance, Eileen's cornflower curtains fit the sitting-room windows? His first act, once the removal van had gone, was to try them, and he was well pleased with the result. The fact that they did not quite meet in the middle, and fell short of the window sill by some inches, was of no significance to Alfred. They were good enough to secure him from a dark night, and what they lacked in measurement they made up for by reasons of sentiment and loyalty. Eileen's last curtains would never be abandoned by Alfred in his lifetime.

He stood, now, surveying his efforts in the sitting-room, sun livening the old familiar furniture and sparkling on the brass ornaments. He had made a good beginning, but there was still much to be done: more carpet to be found – his rugs covered only small parts of the floor – and the walls to be repapered, one day. There was no hurry. It would be a pleasure to do things slowly, to take time choosing, gradually to get the place up to scratch, of an evening. But already the room had a solid, welcoming air: already it felt far more like home than the flat on the seafront had ever done. Alfred knew in his bones he would be happy here, and thanked the Lord for his good fortune.

As he stood looking about him, Alfred's thoughts naturally turned to Eileen. What would she have made of the place? Would she approve his positioning of armchairs, sofa, table? Where would she consider the best placing of their painting of Ely Cathedral? Eileen had always had such a sure touch in such matters. Arranging things – rooms, flowers, biscuits on a plate, had never been any bother to her. She placed them instinctively, to best advantage. She could, for instance, have been a top window-dresser in a large store, had she been so inclined – Alfred had often told her. But she had always said she was not interested in that kind of job. Her ambitions had never extended beyond their own shop which, with her talent for bringing life to a place, she had made as delightful as any shop you could find on the east coast. Ah, Eileen.

Hungry from his work, Alfred went to the small kitchen. This was still in considerable disorder, but it was the room Alfred cared about least. There was much to be done here: cleaning, scouring the sink, new tiles on the floor, a good gloss paint to cheer the walls. But all in good time, as he used to say to Eileen when on some occasions she would chide him for being so slow to set about things. He rummaged about in a box of food and found a tin of baked beans. He ate them with a slice of bread, untoasted as the grill would not work, and drank a mug of strong tea. Once he was settled, in a few days, he would revert to a more orderly timetable: high-tea at six, back to the old disciplined ways. He was not quite sure how he had fallen into the unsatisfactory habit, of late, of eating at odd hours, causing himself severe bouts of indigestion.

His tea over, Alfred returned to the sitting-room and the armchair that faced the window. He lay back, stretching out his legs, arms folded over his stomach, and began to accustom himself to the new view. This was, of course, made easier by Eileen's curtains which made a familiar frame: and the trees outside, thought Alfred, would soon become friends. They were good mature limes, a lovely yellow-green in all weathers, their leaves very light in the air. Pity there was no sight of the sea from this side of the house, but you couldn't have everything, and he was a very lucky man.

The next thing Alfred knew he was struggling to wake himself: through mists of sleepiness he saw Miss Windrush standing in the doorway, two glasses and a bottle of whisky in her hands.

'So sorry to disturb you,' she said, moving towards the kitchen to fill the glasses, 'but I thought you'd probably need a drink by now.'

Alfred rose in confusion. What had come over him, falling

asleep in the middle of the afternoon? He looked at his watch: half-past six. He must have been too busy to notice his weariness, which had sprung upon him as soon as he sat down.

The whisky was most welcome, restoring his spirits very quickly. Miss Windrush sat on the sofa, chatting about plans for the roof and garden, very concerned that he was comfortable and content, and begging him to let her know if there was anything he should need. She was, Alfred noticed, even in this fading light, very pale – as she had been when he arrived this morning. For all her kindness and interest in his wellbeing, Alfred felt she was distracted, there was something on her mind. Well, he could imagine: responsibility for a house like this, on young shoulders like hers, must take its toll. He hoped his presence would ease her burden.

Miss Windrush stayed half an hour, leaving Alfred with the rest of the bottle of whisky. He protested, but she insisted: a small present of welcome, she said it was. On leaving, she urged Alfred to make sure all the doors were locked last thing at night.

'We never used to do any such thing in my father's day,' she explained with a wry smile, 'but there have been cases of vandalism nearby, of late.'

'There are those who aren't respecters of other people's property,' agreed Alfred. 'I shall see to that every night, never you worry.'

'Not that locked doors are any deterrent to someone who is really set on getting in,' said Miss Windrush, 'but we might as well make it harder for them, don't you think?'

She asked the question a little nervously, Alfred thought, but things would quickly change, now. With him around to protect her and the house, she would have no more cause to be afraid.

When Miss Windrush was gone, Alfred busied himself with more unpacking for the rest of the evening. Not until it was quite dark did he draw Eileen's curtains and return to his favourite armchair. He looked slowly round the room, wondering whether his late wife would have approved his positioning of the lamps. He decided she would, and felt pleased with himself. 'Well, Eileen,' he said out loud. 'I'm nicely settled here and thank the Lord for that.'

He tried then to imagine Eileen sitting opposite him, as they had sat for so many evenings of their life together, each side of the fire. He tried in his mind's eye to see her bent head, nodding in agreement, her sweet smile with its funny way of starting one side of her mouth and slowly uncurling. But the conjuring did not work. Once again, as that bad time some weeks ago, he was able to envisage her body – clothes and shoes down to the last detail – but the picture stopped at the neck. She was a headless vision, and her going from him again made Alfred sit up in fright. It must have been the whisky, he thought. He was unaccustomed to the stuff, had never really liked it, certainly wouldn't be finishing the rest of Miss Windrush's bottle if this was the effect it had. He stood up and took the wedding photograph from the mantelpiece – he had placed it there early in the afternoon with a sense of grave priority. Eileen's face came back to him then, of course: staring at him. But only her young face as it had been on that day. The older Eileen, the one he knew better, had grown to love more, would not return.

'Dammit,' he said, putting back the photograph. 'Tricks of the mind. Cruel tricks of the mind.'

With a great effort of will he decided to stop thinking about Eileen and calm himself with a crossword puzzle. He found a book of puzzles in the kitchen. Disinclined to return to the sitting-room, he sat down at the small table in the window and took up his pencil.

For an hour or so Alfred gave himself up to the pleasure of tracking down clues and filling the blank squares with his neat answers. He had always had a good head for puzzles, Alfred, he had to admit. In the old days he had won several competitions and gathered quite a number of prize book-tokens. Eileen never knew how he did it. It was a knack, Alfred explained patiently, many times. But still she never understood, could never get the easiest clue herself. In the end, she ceased to wonder at Alfred's skill, and he stopped trying to explain. The pleasure of the occupation was something he kept to himself. He silently whipped through a puzzle most evenings while Eileen did her sewing. Enclosed in his small world of blanks and spaces and words, he was able to cast off the worries of the day before going to bed.

This old familiar feeling of relaxation was just beginning to seep through Alfred, reminding him it would soon be time to venture into his new bedroom, when he was disturbed by voices. At first he thought Miss Windrush must have visitors in the kitchen. But she had said she was going to bed when she left him, wanting an early night. Perhaps she had changed her mind. Alfred listened hard.

He heard a laugh. It was a thin, high, familiar laugh. No. It couldn't be. But it was. Definitely was. *Lily*'s laugh . . . Laughing at him like she used to those evenings he bolted up the shop with such care. How could it be? Lily was picnicking . . .

When she laughed again, Alfred stood up, heart beating uncommonly fast, clutching at his book of puzzles. Then he heard her voice, coming from the other room.

'Alfred! Alfred, really. You can't go on like this. Boring old memorials. Eileen's curtains again! They don't even fit. You must see they don't fit. Tear them down and throw them away. Why not? They're not the prettiest curtains, after all.'

Mocking, she sounded. She'd always had a nasty side to her, Lily. Jealous, really. He'd always thought that, privately. Alfred scratched his head.

'Come on, Alfred. Come on, love,' the voice went on, more sweetly. 'You can let your hair down a bit now, can't you? After all those sewn-up years . . . You can let your mind wander, now, can't you? Let your mind take its fancy. Be kind to yourself, love. Let yourself remember me . . .'

The voice faded away. Alfred sat down again. He sat for a while like a man stunned, his hands heavy on his knees, mouth open, eyes glazed. Then he remembered Lily.

From the start she had been a tantalizing enigma, pale and brittle-boned, her Mona Lisa smile confounding Alfred with its mystery every new day. She was beautifully dressed in those early days, Eileen saw to that – silks and satins and vague scarves round her neck that fluttered when the shop door opened. Sometimes she wore a small hat on the back of her head. Alfred recalled a damson velvet pillbox with a trailing ostrich feather that curled under Lily's beautiful chin. She had been wearing it on a particular evening, God knows how many years ago . . .

Alfred bowed his head, shutting his eyes. He asked forgiveness as he remembered.

On that particular evening, November it was, he heard a wind blowing up as he bolted the doors. He shut the windows and closed the shutters against a smell of snow in the air. He turned off the lights, leaving himself in almost complete darkness but for a shaft of light coming from the open door that led to the kitchen. He stood for a while in the middle of the shop, sniffing at the familiar smells of material and *pot pourri* and polished beeswax on the oak – all the scents enhanced by the darkness, he thought. And then he looked over at Lily, upright and alone in her corner, feathers tickling her chin but smile unbroken, and a strange sensation seized Alfred's heart. He felt great weakness at being so close to such beauty, for in this semi-darkness Lily was quite perfect. And he felt an almost overwhelming yearning to acknowledge this beauty – how, he did not know. A picture flashed through his mind of himself in the unlikely position of sitting next to a girl like Lily in a café in Paris, sipping at green drinks in long glasses. The very thought made him smile at his own absurdity: he must have seen a film with some such scene. But the smile did nothing to lessen the pain. He stretched out his hand and whispered goodnight to Lily, guiltily left the room with her eyes upon his back.

In the warm, bright kitchen, where Eileen was beating at a lump of dough on the table, the yearning did not cease. But it became more comprehensible. Alfred realized that for all their friendliness he and Eileen were quite distant in some ways, and after much abstinence he wanted to take her in his arms, dough included, if necessary, and hug her.

But Eileen's face – maybe she read his mind – deterred him from any such rash gesture. She had never shown much enthusiasm for what she called the other side of life, and anything that had to take place should be strictly confined to the bedroom. For Alfred to take her in his arms, in her apron in the kitchen, would be nothing short of an affront. It would widen their particular distance, and Alfred had no wish to risk that. So he kept his patience through their beef stew and dumplings, and refrained from offering her a glass of cider lest he should arouse her suspicions.

Later that night in bed, the Bible reading over, the light off, the bony wind rattling at their window, Alfred moved close to his wife. He pushed up the sleeve of her wool nightdress, put a hand on her arm. But the flesh which had looked so warm and soft in the kitchen felt strangely hard, cold as china. He moved his hand to her breast, Lily quite forgotten, only wanting Eileen. He felt her small hand slide over his. It lay still for a moment. Then very gently pushed him away.

'Oh, Alfred, love,' was all Eileen said.

The chill in her voice was enough. Alfred scrambled back to his side of the bed, telling her to sleep well, as always. Then, in the dark, Lily's lips smiled at him, and he ached to split that smile and crush her tantalizing little mouth and his desire twisted agonizingly through him. But he lay absolutely still for fear of waking Eileen. Thus she knew nothing of his night and made no comment on his pale face next morning.

Alfred raised his head, remembering, ashamed.

The night of Harry Antlers' visit Viola slept little. Her greatest fear was of the thing Harry had warned her, the demon energy that knows no bounds. She believed he had the cunning to gouge out things most private in her life, and the thought made her feel physically sick. How had he discovered about Richard? How? How? How? Her mind twirled, a Chinese ball of ivory rats, the useless speculations skidding round and round each other, getting nowhere. Eventually, towards dawn, she slept with the help of pills, only to wake an hour later, sweating and shaking from a nightmare.

At least there were no telephone calls the next day, and by the time she had had her drink with Alfred Baxter, Viola felt calmer. But again she worried her way through the night, wondering at what point she could go to the police and complain of harassment, and if she should elicit Gideon's aid. But what could he do? Richard would be better help, but Richard had enough concerns of his own. Besides, the thing that most shocked her, the knowledge that Harry Antlers had discovered her love of the doctor, she could never divulge to Richard.

This morning, woken from fretful sleep by bright sun, she went to the window. She surveyed the marsh, beach, thin distant line of sea, huge dome of cloudless sky, their various boundaries running into each other, translucent as water colours. In the garden Alfred Baxter was pushing a wheelbarrow towards the neglected herbaceous border. Viola could hear him whistling. She supposed it must be quite late, and did not care. The events of the last two days seemed mercifully to have receded, leaving her etiolated but composed. She returned to bed, picked up her book.

There was a knock on the door.

Immediately Viola's heart leapt like a wild thing and she cowered down under the bedclothes, saying nothing. The door opened. Richard walked into the room, carrying a breakfast tray.

'Hey, Violetta! I can't be that frightening. What's the matter?'

He put the tray on the end of the bed, took her hand and pulled her into a sitting position.

Viola managed a smile.

'I wasn't expecting – '

'Of course you weren't. I'm sorry.' He pulled a chair to the bedside, sat down. 'I should have warned you. But the idea only came to me very early this morning. Naturally I didn't want to wake you.'

'You mean you woke up this morning and thought: I must take Viola breakfast in bed?' Viola laughed, incredulous. The violent pumping of her heart was no longer caused by fear.

'To be honest, I thought, *as a doctor*, Viola could do with a morning in bed. I'm sure I was right. You look pretty worn out. Here. Look what I've brought you.'

Richard placed the tray on Viola's knee. There was a boiled egg, brown toast, homemade marmalade, coffee, a single *Rosa Mundi* in a jam jar. Richard picked up the rose and held it under Viola's nose.

'Have to admit I'm not responsible for this. Alfred insisted on the rose. Dashed off into the garden and spent a long time choosing. In fact he was so long I had to boil a second egg as the first one grew cold.'

Again Viola smiled, still unbelieving.

'Did Alfred let you in?'

'He did. Very pleased, we were, to see each other again. I

hadn't seen him since just before his wife died. He seems in much better spirits now, delighted to be here. I'm glad all that's worked out. Very good plan all round. Now, come on: the egg.'

Viola chipped at the shell with a small silver spoon. Richard peered at the rich yellow of the yolk.

'From one of my two free-range hens, I'll have you know,' he said. 'Three and a half minutes.'

'Perfect.'

'Toast all right?'

'Wonderful.'

'I'm not bad at breakfasts. But you know what I've forgotten?'

'Can't imagine – '

'*The Times*. No decent woman should ever breakfast in bed without *The Times*.'

Viola laughed again. Her hand shook as she held the coffee cup.

'Aren't you meant to be on your rounds?'

'Unusual morning, luckily. No surgery as I have an appointment at the hospital in half an hour. So I'll have to be off in a moment or two.'

But he had an unhurried look, hands clasped round a crossed knee. He observed Viola carefully, in silence as she ate. He saw her struggling.

'Don't eat any more, just to please me,' he said.

'All right. But it was lovely. Thank you.'

Gratefully Viola handed him the tray which he put down on the floor. She shifted her legs, making an uncalculated space on the bed. Richard moved to sit there.

'The other night,' he said, 'I came round to see you but there seemed to be a fraught little scene going on. It was difficult to work out whether or not I would have been welcome. Perhaps I did wrong, leaving. But I didn't want to intrude.'

'I saw you. I wanted desperately to call you to help. But then I thought there was no point in your getting involved.'

'Presumably it was your wild suitor?' Viola nodded. 'Is there anything I can do?'

Viola thought. 'Not really.'

‘Promise to call upon me any time.’

‘Promise.’

‘I think you should leave here as soon as possible. There’s no chance of his finding you in London. He’ll soon give up. With nothing to go on, obsessives soon burn themselves out and turn their focus to something else.’

‘Hope so.’ Viola sighed. ‘But don’t let’s talk about all that if you’re about to go.’

‘No.’ Richard took her hand, smiled. ‘If you were a real patient, I’d say you were a case for listening to the heart.’ He glanced down. ‘As it is, I can see it.’

Viola’s look followed Richard’s to her breast, visibly heaving beneath the thin cotton of her nightdress. Without giving herself time to think she dragged Richard’s hand – curiously light and willing – to her heart, held it there for a moment or two, then flung it back on the bed.

‘It’s all been rather unnerving,’ she said. ‘But you’re right. I must go very soon.’

‘Shall I give you some tranquillizers?’

‘Certainly not.’

‘Then take care of yourself, Violetta. Eat. Sleep.’ He stood. ‘I’ll be in touch.’

Viola held out her arms. Richard bent over her, briefly kissing her hair. She could almost have sworn, too, that for a lightning moment he stroked the back of her neck with his finger. But in a giddy state of joy mixed with hopelessness, nothing was quite certain. With a supreme effort of will she released him from her arms as soon as he began to pull away. Impeded by her own state, she could not be sure whether a fleeting look on his face was one of confusion. A moment later he seemed to be quite normal, looking down at her with affectionate eyes.

‘I almost forgot,’ he said. ‘I ran into Maisie Fanshawe last week, happened to mention you were home. She seemed anxious to see you but said she didn’t like to call after so long. I said I’d put it to you. I was sure you’d be pleased.’

Viola smiled. ‘How’s Maisie?’

‘Definitely older.’

‘Happy?’

‘Who knows? She pretends to be.’

'Anyone in her life?'
'Not as far as I know.'
'Poor old Maisie.'
'Will you ring her?'
'Of course.'
'I'll take down the tray – '
'Please – '
'Must hurry. Bye, Violetta.'

Morning bedroom huge with sun, now. Alfred Baxter stooping over the weeds in a bright garden. Tide coming in. Richard gone. But Richard having been.

Everything was new about Maisie except her anticipation, and even this she managed to burnish quite convincingly so that people might suppose her hope of better things was not undimmed. Her frequent wearing of new clothes was her unspoken sign: she was ready, should the chance arise.

On the afternoon of her reunion with Viola she wore a new cotton dress covered in Picasso-like squiggles and new navy shoes, though their shape was one she had first been attracted to twenty years ago. She was very thin with long, shapeless legs flaring slightly at the ankle. Gaunt-faced, her eyes seemed to have been pressed under a heavy brow by the thumb of a careless sculptor – their outline indefinite, they sagged downwards at the sides. Crimson lipstick was painted meticulously on to her indeterminate mouth, which in her youth had been baggy and faintly sexy. But there was no disguising of the greying hair. Age had trammelled Maisie very fast in the last few years, thought Viola. Even her neck had not escaped its ravages. Once her best feature, exceptionally long and pale, slack skin now danced in the V of the ugly dress. Gideon had admired Maisie's neck quite genuinely. 'It's unfair that so fine a neck should support so disappointing a face,' he used to say. He would be shocked, now. Maisie's only physical attraction quite gone, she was definitely older, as Richard had said.

With little else to do, Viola had taken considerable trouble with tea for Maisie. She had laid a small table in the garden with a linen cloth and the old teatime china wild with green dragons. She cut honey sandwiches and found a packet of ginger biscuits, made China tea in a silver pot. Fearing the encounter would at best be stilted – she and Maisie had nothing in common except for their various loves for Gideon – she felt that at least if she constructed an occasion similar to bygone days it would enable them to talk about the past.

They sat, now, in attitudes of women much older than themselves, smelling the warmth of the garden and the faint salt of the sea. A breeze tugged at the lace hem of the tablecloth and blew Maisie's frizzled grey hair across her eyes. She drew her new mackintosh about her shoulders, always nervous of sea breezes. As Viola had predicted, the setting gave her the opportunity eagerly to remember.

'So many afternoons like this,' she said. 'Your mother in those wonderful hats.'

Viola smiled. If they could glide along on such trains of thought it would be quite easy.

'Things have slipped a bit, since then.'

'Oh, I don't know. It all looks very trim to me. The grass a little longer, perhaps. But that's all.'

Viola nodded in the direction of Alfred. He was tying hollyhocks to stakes at the end of the garden.

'Now Alfred Baxter's come, I'm hoping to get everything back as it was. Do you remember Baxter's, the haberdashery shop?'

'Of course I do!' Eager for small and happy memories, Maisie listed some of the good things the Baxters used to stock and which were unobtainable now, elsewhere. 'But I could never understand,' she whispered, nodding towards the distant Alfred, 'how he could stand that bossy wife.'

'Bossy? I always thought her timid.'

'That's how she liked to appear.'

Surprised by the force of her own conviction, Maisie fell into guilty silence. It was not her way to be uncharitable about people, especially the dead. A purple flush appeared on her grey cheeks. She took a long sip of tea, stamping the cup with a curve of red lipstick.

'*Lu*pins,' she said, embarrassed now and glancing across the lawn. 'I've always so loved your lupins.'

Viola tried to help.

'In her dotty gardening days,' she said, 'after my father died, my mother had a tremendous thing about delphiniums.

But in fact she wasn't much good at them. While lupins, which she hated, seemed to spring up all round her.'

Maisie smiled. Silence again. Then she said, 'Richard told me you'd been over to New York.'

'Yes.' Viola paused, judging it unkind not to give Maisie the information she craved. Her smudged eyes were desperate for news. 'I stayed with Gideon for three weeks.'

'Oh? And did you have a good time?' She sounded very old, like a great-aunt.

'I don't much like New York.'

'How does Gideon find it?'

'He enjoys making a lot of money, working long, hard hours. I think it suits his temperament.'

'Well, he's always been a hard worker.'

Viola noticed that Maisie's hand trembled on a sandwich.

'But he won't stay for ever. I think he plans to come back. He might even live here one day.'

'*Really*?' Maisie dropped the sandwich, clumsily picked it up again.

'I mean, in five or six years' time, perhaps.'

'Well, quite.'

Viola recognized the look of contrived nonchalance, as if five or six years would make no difference to Maisie.

'There was a terrible moment,' Viola went on, to give Maisie time to compose herself, 'when we thought it would be impossible to keep the house. Luckily, that crisis passed.'

'Oh, I am glad of that.' Maisie turned to Viola with a real smile. 'I mean, it's been in the family so many years, hasn't it? I always imagined that one day Gideon would want to return. Bring up his own family here,' she added.

'Yes, well, I expect he'll do that.'

Maisie bit her bottom lip, shuffling words in her mind.

'I imagine he's . . . set up with someone in New York, is he? I hate to ask, but it's very hard, not knowing.'

Viola paused, thinking about her answer. 'As you can imagine,' she said at last, 'a bachelor like Gideon is much sought after in New York. He goes to a lot of parties, gets pursued by a lot of girls. But as far as I know his heart remains untouched. He doesn't seem to have any plans for marriage, or anything like that.' She was pleased to be able to be quite truthful.

'I see,' said Maisie quietly. Fearing further questioning on this delicate ground, Viola changed the subject. She asked Maisie how she spent her time, now. Maisie drew herself up, dignified, a little defensive.

'I run a small bindery,' she said. 'We're lucky enough to have more work than we can cope with. And then, I'm pretty occupied looking after my father. He's virtually senile now. So I'm very busy. I have plenty of interests.'

She suddenly slipped her arms into the sleeves of her stiff new mackintosh and did up the belt. Viola enquired if she was cold and would like to go in. But Maisie shook her head.

'It's just that I can't afford to catch a cold, or anything like that, because I'm all my father has. He depends on me totally.'

She gave a small laugh. Her eyes swerved beyond the garden to the sea. The eyes were quite hard, as if they had become accustomed to masking despair. She looked back to Viola.

'If ever you and Gideon and Richard think of me at all, and I don't suppose you ever do, but *if* you ever do . . . I expect you must wonder why I'm still here, unmarried – ' She laughed again. 'Five years off forty and nothing much changed. Well, believe it or not, I was propositioned many times by an old boy, a widower, who lives near here. He even promised he'd take out a large life insurance, assuring me I'd benefit from it quite soon. I think he just wanted me as a nurse, though his offer of marriage was quite convincing. But of course I couldn't contemplate any such thing, could I? Though my father kept urging me, a bird in the hand and so on. There were one or two other minor interests. But it was so hard, after Gideon, you see. He set such an impossible standard. I can't imagine any other man coming anywhere near it. So here I am, still, poor old Maisie of Docking, as I believe you all used to call me.' She stood up.

'Oh, Maisie . . .'

'No, no. For heaven's sake, don't feel sorry for me. I have no pity for myself, I promise you that.' She sat down again, surprising herself by the bump on the seat, brushing away the hair from her eyes once more. 'In fact, I often feel detached enough to see the whole thing in all its absurdity: first love binding one to a standard from which one is never set free. Well, I waited quite hopefully at first. It took me ages to realize Gideon scarcely acknowledged my existence, let alone had any designs upon me. So then I slipped into waiting without hope, and the years have gone by. It's hopeless waiting that takes the toll. Look at my hair!' She pulled at a wild bit of fringe. 'Quite grey! Oh, I've aged wickedly young. I know it. I see it in people's faces. I saw it in Richard the other day. I saw it in you when we met. I see it every morning in my own mirror – '

'But you look very – '

'Don't deny it,' snapped Maisie, 'please.'

She stopped and looked out to sea again. Then she turned to Viola with a melancholy smile that must have enchanted the old boy with the plans for life insurance.

'Do you remember my dance?'

'Of course I remember your dance.'

'My parents were so worried about the rain. I didn't think it mattered at all.'

'No. It didn't at all.'

'I hated you that evening,' went on Maisie with a new smile. 'You spoiled my whole evening because Gideon took you home early.'

'I'm very sorry,' said Viola.

'He only danced with me once then he said he had to go and take care of his sister. I could have killed you. Still, I daresay if he'd stayed, and hadn't danced with me again, that would have been worse.'

'Had I known, I would never have – '

'You could never have known. I don't blame you,' interrupted Maisie. 'The young never have an inkling what their contemporaries really feel. Particularly the plain ones. They're too busy fending for themselves.'

'Quite,' said Viola. 'The young can be very cruel.'

Maisie stood up again, this time with a more determined appearance of going. She dabbed at her forehead under the tiresome hair with a transparent hand of blanched bones.

'Oh dear, one of my headaches. Brought about by all the remembering, no doubt.' She smiled wryly.

'The past can be exhausting,' agreed Viola.

'Well, goodbye dear Viola. Violetta, they used to call you, Richard and Gideon, didn't they? I'm glad you're here. Come and see me one day. And thank you for the tea. I must have a word with Mr Baxter before he goes. He'll remember me, don't you think? I'll tell him to take care of those lupins, shall I?'

She was on her way towards Alfred Baxter's newly weeded border, voice petering out, grey hair tossing bravely, horribly thin beneath the bulges of her spotless mackintosh, mere ghost of the fat girl in pink tulle whose dance was spoiled by Gideon's kindness to his sister so many years ago.

In Maisie, Viola saw herself very soon, should she not take hurried steps to change things. She decided to leave tomorrow.

Alfred Baxter much enjoyed his mornings weeding in the garden, sun on his back, back soon aching but nothing serious. He had enjoyed, too, seeing Dr Almond again: fine young doctor, though he looked a mite older these days. He had been good to the Baxters through Eileen's last months: kind-hearted man, pity about his troubles. Everyone knew his fondness for children. He deserved to have some himself. Life without them was not –

– *Hollyhocks*. Hollyhocks, Alfred told himself over his lunch of bread and cheese, were what he should be thinking about. He would stake them all afternoon to give his back a rest. They were almost his favourite flower, hollyhocks. At least, a close second to lilies of the valley. Eileen it was who had introduced them to their garden – yellow, pink, a lovely deep red, huge great spires that the Lord had so cleverly designed with the flowers getting smaller towards the top. Eileen went on and on about her hollyhocks, and the importance of giving them support. Once, in a summer gale, they'd all been smashed to the ground as a result of his careless staking. She hadn't half been angry, didn't get over it for days. Sometimes, Alfred tried to bring her round to other tall flowers – the sunflower, for instance, with its cheerful beaming face. But Eileen said she couldn't abide sunflowers. Only hollyhocks.

The afternoon was spent no less pleasurably than the morning, tying and restaking. It was among Miss Windrush's hollyhocks that Alfred came to the definite conclusion it had been her whisky which had given him such trouble the other night. For here in the bright sunlight there was no trouble whatsoever in recalling Eileen's face. Not that he was trying to, mind: in fact, he hadn't, for once, given her so much as a thought, and there she was grinning at him through the petals, all over the place, images of her scattered high and low, all angles, skin redder than he remembered, mouth smaller – quite confusing. She came and went all afternoon, but was no hindrance, really. He carried on with the job. He thanked his lucky stars . . . And then he saw Miss Windrush laying up tea on the terrace by the house. The sight of everything so neat gladdened his heart and Eileen disappeared. Every now and then he turned for a surreptitious glance at the two young ladies sitting there – Miss Fanshawe, he believed the other one must be, though she had changed quite a bit – pouring tea from a silver pot. Again and again he was glad. He had the definite impression life was going on here, in Miss Windrush's house. Visitors. Plans. Memories. Things he had not been able to witness, let alone share, for a good while too long. Thank the Lord, then, and now to empty the wheelbarrow. But there was a voice behind him. Calling his name. He gave a small start. Lily again? He turned and saw his own stupidity. It was Miss Fanshawe, striding towards him, a painfully thin version of her former self, but smiling and waving and coming to speak to him.

Oh yes, life was going on, here.

8

While Viola and Maisie partook of their silvery tea in Norfolk, Harry Antlers searched a London gutter. It was his belief that the fault lay in his stupid gesture of throwing away the brooch. That's where it had all gone wrong. If only – he now saw – he had arrived armed with a jewel in its smart New York box, Viola would have welcomed him. She could not possibly have refused the beautiful thing, knowing what it must have cost Harry in money and in love. And so it had to be found, for the next attempt.

He had been looking most of the afternoon, but with no luck – kicking his way up and down the seedy pavement, peering through other people's box hedges, poking at old leaves with a stick. As the hours passed his original patience turned to fury, and his fury to despair. By evening, there was nothing for it but to give up. The brooch was utterly lost. He returned to his bedsitter to console himself with a packet of chocolate biscuits.

Since his return home Harry had received one offer of work: to make a documentary film about prostitutes in Sweden. Although he had had some success making short films in the past, he regarded himself as a stage director, and the offer an insult. But an insult that should, perhaps, be given some consideration, for his finances, since the failure of the play in New York, were not in a comfortable state. The film company had suggested a very large sum for his services, and he would only need to be in Sweden for a week.

By the last chocolate biscuit Harry had come to a decision. He would do the film. It would not be shown in England and no one whose opinion he cared for would ever know. As for the money – the money would be spent more wisely this time. It would be invested in a new life.

His first purchase, of course, would be diamonds to replace the Gloucester's eye brooch. No girl could refuse diamonds.

Harry had in mind a small star, nothing too flash to begin with, which Viola could either pin on her bosom or hang round her neck. His girl in his diamonds. The thought of it . . .

On another scale altogether, he would begin to look for somewhere more salubrious to live. For it occurred to Harry, looking round his meagre room with new eyes, this would be no place to attract a girl like Viola. What she would want, as indeed would he, would be a penthouse flat in Notting Hill Gate, huge windows on to the view of London, black leather and steel chairs, television and stereo behind sliding mahogany doors, all that sort of thing. It was funny to think he had spent his grown-up life quite happily in this room with its stretch covers on the chairs, the Boots' prints and plastic mugs – and now, having met Viola, there was a great need for something better.

After the flat, the car. He would buy a great snarling lion of a car, gold or silver, two seats only, and roar about with Viola beside him. In the meantime, he would not ring her for a day or so: give her time to forget her anger and forgive him. He knew he had done wrong, very wrong, but everything had been against him – fatigue, anxiety, fear of the great arrogant house in which she seemed to be so secure. Sometimes Harry worried about his unaccountable violence. He knew that within him a loving soul struggled to be seen. But it was as if the birth channel through which it had to pass to enter the world was contaminated. Thus, the feelings that had been sown so gently, emerged full of hurt fury, forcing Harry into outrageous gestures of dismay. He knew he should never have threatened Viola with a milk bottle, but something about her haughty little face, refusing to acknowledge all his love for her, had made his hands fly up like two wild birds over which he had no control. And then the vile lover appearing in the garden, ready to pounce on her as soon as Harry turned his back – the thought of Viola being ravished by other hands had caused Harry such physical anguish on the way back to London that he had had to stop at a transport café and eat three eggs on toast.

Fired with the warmth of his plans, Harry grew impatient for morning when he could begin to put them into action. He began to pace his room, thinking of some way to release his impatience. A particularly vigorous waft of Brussels sprouts and boiling clothes drifted up through the floorboards and thin carpet. That was it: now was the time.

Harry crashed down the stairs, and entered his landlady's kitchen without knocking. Marjorie Whittle, sixty-year-old spinster of scant joy, stood like a pantomime dame at her pre-war stove stirring at a pan of bubbling dishcloths. Beside it simmered a pot of rabbit stew and sprouts, while on the table a plate of lights and other innards glared up like a giant bloody eye. A scrawny cat, about to enjoy this supper, leapt in terror from the table when Harry came in.

Rage swelled in Harry. A roar thundered from him, snapping tendons all over his body.

'Marjorie fucking Whittle,' he shouted. 'This has got to stop! How many times have I told you? I pay you a bloody great rent and what do I get in return? Stench! Excruciating stench. Clouds of your filthy smells working their way up to my flat to gas me out. This can't go on, do you hear?'

He banged the kitchen table with his fist. The plate of lights quivered, glassy red. Harry charged to the stove, pushing Marjorie Whittle to one side. He crashed lids down upon the bubbling pots, damming the steam, and switched off the gas flames. The cat squawked piteously. Miss Whittle whimpered, yellow tears gathering in her eyes. Their fear spurred Harry to one final act. He picked up the bloody mess of lights from the plate, paused a moment before throwing it at his landlady's face, as if it had been funny pantomime shaving soap, and laughed at the terror in her eyes. But some minute particle of pity, rarely felt through the obscurity of his rages, overcame him. With all his force he threw the mess, instead, to the floor. where it spilt and slobbered over the cracked linoleum with a dull thwack.

'That's what I think of you, you hideous old cow,' he bellowed with some effort, for the adrenalin was draining away now, 'and I'll do a great deal worse if it happens again.'

'I'm going to fetch the police this time, Mr Antlers,' mewed Miss Whittle.

'You go and fetch the police,' smiled Harry, and left the room.

From upstairs he heard her sobs, and then the banging of

the front door. Through the window he saw her hurrying out, cat under arm, bowed. She turned out of the gate in the wrong direction for the police station – she would never report him. There had been many such scenes in the past and Miss Whittle always failed to carry out her threat. She would be going to her senile old sister down the road, and to buy more lights for the repulsive cat.

Having nicely upset his landlady's tranquil cooking, Harry felt much better. He went to his own kitchen and heated up three tins of spaghetti rings. He ate them on his knee, sluiced in brown sauce, listening to the Brahms piano quintet, temporarily at peace.

The next morning Harry gave himself a rare smile in his early shaving mirror, his mind concentrated on the important matters of his active day.

'Oh, my lovely Viola,' he said out loud. 'I have such plans for us.'

But even as he said the words, a picture of Hannah Bagle came to him. He had not given her a thought since she had left him that night in New York, and now here she was, surprising so early in the morning, golden skin palpitating beneath the silk . . . Something chafed within Harry. He needed breakfast.

A large bowl of porridge and brown sugar followed by three Chelsea buns quelled his puzzling feelings of desire for one he did not love, and before dismissing her entirely from his mind he decided it would be judicious to call her occasionally. Keep her alert. He might, after all, have need of her for vital information in the future.

Harry rang his bank. He requested that his entire savings, some two hundred pounds, should be transferred to his current account. He was saddened it could not have been two thousand, but that would come later. Next, he rang the producer of the film company and they agreed to have lunch. Then he took a taxi to a jeweller's shop.

By the end of the morning Harry had found his diamond star. It was very small, with a pearl centre, and very expensive – double his savings. But an overdraft was of no concern in such important matters. Harry paid without quibbling – the first of a whole collection of jewels for Viola, he told himself, and with a feeling of extraordinary wellbeing, set off for the Ritz to meet the film producer.

Late that afternoon, contract agreed upon, stomach stretched with quantities of food and wine, Harry's unusual sensation of peace with the world still brushed over him like fur, and he fėlt inclined to make some gesture to reflect his content. At the flower stall at the underground station he bought the entire stock of peonies, some half dozen bunches. Smiling to himself, he unlocked the cracked maroon front door quite eagerly. He stood in the hall calling Miss Whittle's name. No answer.

Harry went quietly into the kitchen, not wanting to frighten the old girl any further. But there was no sign of her. The pots were still on the stove, untouched since he had left them. The meat was still on the floor. The smells were horrible, though damper and less pungent than before. His benevolence thwarted, Harry felt impatience rising. He threw the bunches of peonies into the sink, called Miss Whittle once again. Still no answer: he would have woken her had she been asleep. It occurred to him, then, he had not heard her usual morning noises, shooing the cat in the garden and hoovering her carpets. Perhaps she had stayed overnight with her dotty sister. Well, it was no concern of his. Her fault if the bloody peonies died.

Harry returned upstairs. His lunch having subsided, he cooked himself a huge tea. Then he took the diamond star from its box and studied it for a long time. It was the first possession he had ever cared for in his life. There was something strangely encouraging in its small sparkle, giving him hope. Happily, he set about making his plans.

Gideon Windrush was suffering from the heat of the New York summer, and as his suffering increased so did Hannah's irritation. The sympathy she used to feel for his grumbles about her native city, and his boring views on the superiority of London summers, seemed to have evaporated entirely. Besides, she had other things on her mind.

Hannah's concept of fidelity – a thing about which she knew Gideon cared greatly – was not in strict accordance with the general meaning of the word. To her, it was loyalty of mind, while short excursions of the body were of no importance. Indeed, they were of so little significance that it was not worth recounting them, particularly to such a sensitive man as Gideon, who might find in them reasons for anger or outrage. Quite happy with her own working out of things, Hannah conducted her double life with tact and skill. Nothing would alter her admiration for Gideon's mind, and mostly she enjoyed his company. But he was a busy man, tired by evening, not always up to her demands. It was, therefore, quite reasonable to satisfy hereself elsewhere, which she often did.

In fairness to Gideon, she never allowed herself to think about her short-time lovers as anything other than means of gratifying the flesh. She refused all dates with them after the initial encounter, and, lust satisfied, they were abandoned.

It was much against her will, therefore, that Hannah realized, some days after Harry's return to England, she was thinking about him quite frequently. There had been something so unsatisfactory about their three meetings that she could not put them from her mind. Besides, the fact that he had made it clear he had wanted her for nothing but quick relief was most unusual, this position being her normal privilege. She tried to put him from her mind, but to no avail. His ugly, angry face kept returning. Increasing her range of infidelity, she thought of him while making love to Gideon, and for the time being spurned other lovers. She lost considerable weight. Tension between her and Gideon grew daily.

It was Gideon who produced the appealing idea of easing things by going to England for a week. He would like to check up on his sister in Norfolk, he said: see all was well and make financial arrangements. Besides, he would like to show Hannah the house of his childhood – the beaches, the old sailing boat. They could go for a picnic on the Point. Hannah smiled sympathetically.

'Darling, it's all a wonderful idea, England. Fabulous idea. But I couldn't take the beaches bit. I mean, you know me. I'm a city girl. I'd be mooning about on beaches, now, wouldn't I?'

'Maybe.' Gideon hoped to conceal a sense of private relief at her reaction.

'So what I think is this: you go off to Viola and your

wonderful old house, I'll stay in London. Hell, I haven't been there in years. I'll have a ball looking round the shops, looking up old friends. Besides, darling, we could do with a break from each other, couldn't we? I'd say that's just what we need. Then we'll fly back together. Restored.' She cooed charmingly.

'I take your point,' said Gideon.

He poured her a large Martini on the rocks and immersed himself in pleasurable thoughts of a week at home. Hannah, for her part, was more agreeable than she had been for some time. While her mind raced with nefarious plans, she coolly made chicken salad with great care, changed into a silk kimono with nothing on beneath, and made sure it fell apart long before official bed-time.

The following day, having deliberated for hours on her plan during the night, Hannah called Harry from the office. He sounded surprised, not particularly pleased, to hear her voice.

'Well, I thought we might as well keep in touch,' she said. 'Did you have a good day?'

'Yes, yes.'

'I have news for you, Harry.'

'Oh?'

'May not be of interest to you, but I'll try it out.' She paused. 'Are you still crazy about your wonderful Viola?'

'Of course.'

'Seen her?'

'Naturally.'

'Then maybe you know what I'm going to tell you. I presume you know she's moving to London?'

Harry's turn to pause. 'Er, yes. She said something about it.'

'Did she tell you where she was going?'

'Not exactly.'

'That's where I can help. Save you any difficulty finding out.'

'What do you know, for heaven's sake?'

Taking a long drag on her cigarette, Hannah let Harry wait again. She detected an edge of anxiety in his voice.

'Oh, nothing much. Nothing important. Just her London

address and telephone number. She should be there in a few days.'

'For God's sake, woman, did you ask her brother for all this?'

'Don't be such a damn fool, Harry. So happens she wrote him a letter. He didn't say a thing. By chance, I read the letter. You know, letters lie about.'

'Quite. Well. Thanks.'

Hannah slowly dictated Viola's telephone number and address. Considering all her trouble, he sounded ungrateful.

'This is all a bit unnecessary,' he said. 'She was going to get in touch with me when she got there.'

Hannah smiled to herself. 'Well, like this, you know what you can do? You can have a whole lot of roses waiting for her when she arrives.' She laughed.

Harry did not join her laughter. It was not easy to gauge another's mood on a transatlantic call. Hannah was disappointed at Harry's apparent lack of enthusiasm. But, business over, she decided to change her tack and her voice. She could afford to be more alluring, now.

'Say, Harry. Don't go, darling. I've more news for you.' Pause. 'Gideon and I are coming over in the next couple of weeks.'

'Ah.'

'Small vacation. Gideon's going on down to Norfolk to see Viola. I'm staying in London to visit with a few friends, go round the stores, have myself some fun.'

'Re-ally?'

The minute break in the question indicated to Hannah she was doing better. She purred on an even lower note.

'So I thought, Harry, maybe you and I could get together? Just a drink or something?'

Harry was silent for a very long time. Then he, too, spoke in a lower key.

'Perhaps we could. Ring me when you get here, will you? I might be in Sweden making a film, but leave a message on the machine.'

Hannah was impressed. She squirmed in her expensive leather chair. A strange warmth, like liquid wax, seemed to be surging through her limbs.

'Oh Christ, Harry. You know something? I can't wait. I dunno what's got into me. I'm a tough old bird, normally. None of this sentimental stuff. But our night at the Algonquin keeps running through my mind . . .'

'You're a beautiful lady,' said Harry. 'You're a very beautiful lady. If I was with you I could show you how I felt.'

Although this last remark was roughly in the region of what she wanted to hear, Hannah found it faintly distasteful. But still, it was all the things Harry did wrong that she found so endearing. The other telephone rang, breaking her mood.

'I'll call you then, hon,' she said.

'I'll look forward to that,' said Harry. 'We'll have a drink. Or something.'

Viola went to London. At the top of her uncle's house she found the flat of four rooms in considerable disrepair, but full of sun. She saw great potential. In her practical way she set about their renovation, intending to finish the job as soon as possible. Feeling safe from Harry Antlers, and with the prospect of Gideon's visit to look forward to, she was happy. She immersed herself in the task of choosing, measuring, ordering, and thought of little else.

As her uncle had suggested, while the flat was being transformed, she stayed in the main part of the house – a house of tall, austere rooms with grand furniture and gloomy Turkish rugs. It was friendly but intimidating. Viola found herself creeping up and down the stairs and shutting the huge doors of silky wood with a strange shyness. On the fourth day of her stay, on her way up to the flat, she heard a mild cough. It came from the library, not visited since her arrival.

Viola paused, remembering, then, something about a scholar called Edwin. It would only be friendly, she thought, to make herself known to him. She walked down the dark passage. Opening the library door, she came upon the standing figure of a giant, tall as Michelangelo's David, it seemed. His head was bent, a sculptured hand at rest on the open pages of a leather-bound book.

'I am sorry,' said Viola. 'I didn't – '

The man looked up. 'Ah. That's all right. Don't go away.'

It took Viola several moments to assimilate the facts. The

speaker, at first a silhouette against the light, was no giant, no statue. The first impression melted to be replaced by a man in undistinguished clothes standing at the top of a library ladder. He snapped the book shut and returned it to its shelf. Viola noticed the bright shine on the seat of his low-crutched trousers: a spindly ankle beneath the turn-ups. She watched him feel for the step beneath him with a cautious and unpolished shoe.

'I didn't mean to disturb you,' she said.

'Oh, goodness me, you aren't disturbing me. At least, I suppose technically you are. But I love disturbances – anything to take me from my reference books. I haven't had such a good reason for *wrenching* myself from a page for weeks.'

Viola smiled. 'I'm David's niece,' she said.

'I suspected that. He told me all about his pretty niece.'

Even standing on the floor he was much taller than Viola. He wore a yellow jersey beneath his jacket which reflected on to his chin like buttercups in a child's game. His pale eyes were set far apart, divided by a wide, blubbery nose. He ran a hand through a lock of greasy hair.

'I'm Edwin Hardley,' he said.

Smiling, friendly puckers rippled through his cheeks. He must be quite old, Viola thought. At least, he had the air of one who had never been quite young.

'How do you do.' They shook hands formally, but with all the concealed pleasure of two British strangers meeting in a desert.

'Getting on all right, up there, are you?' asked Edwin.

'There's a lot to do, but it won't take long.'

Edwin sighed in admiration. He seemed fatigued for so early in the morning, perhaps by his excursion up the ladder.

'I mustn't keep you,' said Viola, making for the door.

'Oh, don't feel that.' With a surprising surge of energy, Edwin leapt ahead of her to the huge door, opened it. 'The mornings I like best are the mornings I manage to escape.' He gave a mysterious chuckle. 'If there's anything I can do to help – not that I'm much of a one with paint.'

'You must come up and see it when it's all finished.'

'That would be very nice. Meanwhile, I daresay our paths might cross on the stairs.'

'Possibly,' smiled Viola, and turned back into the dark passage.

Edwin paid his first visit to Viola that evening. He found her standing in her bare sitting-room trying out strips of different red paint on the walls. Anxious not to disturb her, he came cautiously into the room. He stood by the window, presence at once indeterminate, troubled shadows watery on his face. The lock of greasy hair fell over one eye.

'Ooh, I am sorry. Hope I'm not – '

'Course not,' said Viola, grateful for the interruption. 'Light's going, anyway.' She replaced her brush in a tin of turpentine, waved at a bare wall. 'That's going to be all bookshelves and cupboards and drinks. But I'm afraid there isn't a thing in the place to offer you at the moment.'

'How *mar*vellous,' said Edwin, 'to be able to imagine a completely bare room like this when it's furnished. I could never do that. Oh, I don't want a drink, if that's what you mean.'

'Well, I do. Let's have some gin, downstairs. I know Uncle David wouldn't mind. He said I was to help myself.'

'That would be nice.' Edwin laughed gently. 'But what I *thought*, what I *had been thinking*, this afternoon, was that perhaps it would be a good idea if we had dinner. I mean . . .'

'Well, I am hungry, I have to admit.' Viola nodded acceptance.

'Just a modest . . . I mean, I haven't a tie or anything here. Just round the corner, if that's all right.'

'Fine. Tell you what, you go and have a drink in the drawing room. I'll have a bath and put on something less covered in paint.'

Viola enjoyed her own mild bossiness to this transparent stranger. He took it well, smiling consent.

She lay in the huge Victorian bath filled with bluebell-scented bubbles, a crystal glass of gin and tonic on the rack, small sips deliciously silvering the mind, the gaunt walls of the old-fashioned bathroom beginning to sparkle behind the steam. Anticipation, out of all proportion to the forthcoming modest dinner round the corner with a scholar of moths, seized her in its wild dance . . . For all the pleasures of her solitary life, unexpected invitations were a treat. She was excited. She took unusual care with her appearance, brushing her hair until it shone, and choosing a cotton dress of pink and cream stripes in which she felt particularly comfortable.

'Oh, you do look . . .' said Edwin, standing duskily in a corner of the huge dim drawing-room, as if in fear of exposure on the wide carpet. 'I'm afraid I'm . . . Shall we go?' He tugged vaguely at his dreadful shirt.

They walked the short way to the restaurant through the tangible warmth of a London summer evening, scarcely talking. The restaurant was a dark place of green felt and well-worn hessian, Elizabethan dishes on the menu.

'Terribly pre*ten*tious, I daresay,' said Edwin, 'but rather good food.'

Studying him across the small table, Viola was of the impression that life's practicalities wafted round Edwin like underwater plants, and it was a matter of luck if he could secure anything firmly in his hands. She watched him looking about as if tangible objects and human beings were the stuff of dreams, and any negotiation with real life was a struggle. The waiters, for instance, seemed not to see his beckoning signs. His own ineffectualness was evidently a constant source of frustration: he grew quite pink waving arms and a menu. When the waiter did at last notice him, he was in a dither about ordering. The Elizabethan dishes they had chosen slid confusingly from his mind. When all was at last in hand, wine poured and tried, he sighed with relief at the end of the trauma.

'Oh dear,' he said. 'Dear me, I find the disapproval of waiters terribly unnerving, don't you?'

Edwin made so many gentle enquiries about Viola's life (to which he received well-edited replies) that it was not until the coffee that she was able to extract information about his. He admitted moths were his passionate interest and most hours of his day were spent in their study. He had begun a six-volume work on his subject some twelve years ago, and there were still five and a half volumes to go.

'But, well, time does get a little *dissipated*, doesn't it? I mean, I suppose I'm Chairman of the Moth Society of Great Britain, and that takes up far too much time. Endless meetings. A very bitchy lot, the moth people, you know. Hopelessly vague, too. *Flitting* from one thing to another, never making up their minds. It's dreadful, being Chairman. And you may think, quite reasonably, due to all that silly palaver with the waiter, that I'm not chairman calibre.' He smiled disarmingly. 'But believe it or not, I'm a *very fierce* chairman. I bark and bang my fist and almost always get my way.'

Viola laughed.

'What's very nice,' he went on, 'is being able to work in your uncle's house. It's such a *refuge*. So safe. Nobody knows where I am, there. No one has my telephone number. Nobody can *get* me.'

'What sort of people are after you?'

'Well, you know what London is.' He smiled. '*Girls*, I suppose. Oh, girls. They're so tiring in their pursuits. You'll find the same with men, I daresay.'

'I don't suppose so. I don't know many men in London.'

Edwin looked a little wistful.

'You soon will. With a face like that, there's not much chance of your remaining undiscovered. Still, as the other occupant of your uncle's house, I shall consider it my prerogative occasionally to trap you into dinner.'

'Of course!'

'But no lunches, I warn you. I can't abide lunches any more. I've had a surfeit of lunches. Good heavens, if you give a girl lunch in London she wants *the whole afternoon* as well. Imagine that. Afternoons are for working, I'd always been taught. But girls don't seem to be of the same opinion. They seem to think three o'clock to five in bed' – he blushed at the word – 'is quite in order. Well, it exhausted me, I can tell you. I could scarcely summon the energy for dinner with the next girl. Luckily, your uncle's house has put a stop to all that. Oh, I'm grateful to your uncle. Marvellous library, too.'

Edwin insisted on walking back to the house with Viola, though his own flat was in the opposite direction. He took her arm, gentle fingers playing lightly on her wrist. When they came to the tall flight of steps leading to the front door, he sighed, surveying them with the dread of an exhausted climber facing the last steep slope of a mountain.

'Don't bother to come up,' said Viola, aware of his fatigue.

'Of course I'm coming up. I'd like to see you safely through the door.'

Viola smiled. They mounted the steps, clutching each other in the manner of an elderly couple. Viola unlocked the heavy studded door, pushed it open.

'Thank you so much,' she said.

'*Through* the door,' said Edwin. He went ahead of her, shutting the door behind him. For one so seemingly tired a moment earlier, he was quite firm. They were close in the darkness of the hall. Viola put out her hand, searching for a light switch. Edwin caught her hand. He pulled her tentatively towards him. She could feel him kissing her hair.

'Oh dear, you're a *dangerous* girl, I'm sure of that,' he said, and snapped on the light. 'I daresay we shall run into each other tomorrow or the next day on the stairs.'

His attempt at brusqueness made him blush: he was eager to be away. Viola did nothing to detain him. He bid her good-night and left with the speed of the guilty.

Viola sat for a while in the brown shades of the drawing-room, reflecting on the evening. She was able now fully to understand her uncle's nickname for Edwin Hardley: Hardley There was an apt description. A most peculiar fellow, she thought: funny, particularly about himself, gentle, kind, oddly endearing. And yet not of this age, and in spirit too old for his years. She wondered if he had ever been young, or was one of those people born old. She wondered, too, why he should be the victim of such tiresome pursuit by women. They felt he needed mothering, perhaps. Or maybe his elusiveness acted as an aphrodisiac: for in the flesh he was far from the average idea of a robust sexual partner.

Unable quite to understand why, Viola felt disappointment. In her sparkling bath, possibly unconsciously, she had hoped that a strong man might march from the frail frame and devour her. But there was no hint of devouring in Hardley There. Nibbling, she thought, was more in his line. Still, he would be a friend; the quality of friendship shone about him. Viola liked the idea of his daily presence in the house. His quiet reading in the library would provide a comfortable under-current to the prevailing silence. And, as he said, they could meet occasionally.

When the door bell rang, soon after H.T.'s departure, Viola leapt up in sudden, renewed hope. She imagined that in his vague way he had forgotten something. She also supposed, gratefully, that he rang the bell, rather than used his key, so as not to frighten her coming upstairs. Pressing the buzzer on the entryphone, Viola shouted to him to join her in the drawing-room. She heard the front door open and close.

Returning to her old place on the huge velvet sofa, Viola wished she had a drink to occupy her hands. The excitement of earlier in the evening came back to her. She sat very still, listening to the creaks as Edwin climbed the stairs: she wondered at her state of puzzling joy as she waited.

9

Harry Antlers kept watch for several days. He parked his car some way up the street from Viola's front door and settled himself behind many a newspaper, too alert to do any real reading. His many hours of patience were rewarded by several sightings. Once he saw Viola enter the house carrying large carrier bags and tins of paint. Another time she was accompanied by a scruffy-looking man in white overalls, provoking in Harry acute agitation. It took him several moments to recover when he realized the man was a builder or painter. On a third occasion, an evening, just as Harry had started his engine to leave, Viola came running out of the house in a great hurry and hailed a passing taxi. Distant though his view of her was, Harry could see that she always looked as beautiful as he remembered, and his desire to run after her and throw himself at her feet was only quelled by the hurried swallowing of a packet of fruit drops he found in the glove compartment.

Harry had worked out that the longer he left Viola alone, the easier his next attempt to woo her would be. Surely she would at least give him a grateful smile; even that would be rewarding. And then he would be so gentle and loving to her, no matter how violent the emotions that seared him, that she would see a new man in him, and, surely, be intrigued at last.

He planned his next foray on the evening before he left for Sweden. This Harry thought a subtle piece of strategy. For if, as he supposed, this time Viola was conquered, and then started to behave like all the other girls in his life – well, telephoning him, she would find out from his answering machine he was away. Not that he wanted to play games with Viola: his love for her was much too serious for that. But in Harry's experience, a little rough treatment, a touch of unavailability every now and then, did wonders for increasing ardour. On the other hand, were she still to remain stubborn and resistant, silly bitch, then he could glut his fury on some of the nubile Swedish ladies who were to appear in his film. That, at least, would be some antidote to the physical pangs, if not to those of the heart.

Harry put great effort, all day, in preparing himself for the meeting. He had decided against asking Viola out to dinner: a girl can escape quite easily from a restaurant. By the time the bill was paid, she could have made such a good start it was impossible to catch up. He decided, instead, to approach the vast house in which she apparently lived alone, at about ten at night. Ten had always been a propitious hour for him: time when intimations of weariness in a lady can magically be transformed.

But it was a long day and evening to wait. To rid himself of excess adrenalin, Harry tried walking through Hyde Park, a way of passing the time he found particularly obnoxious. The sun beat down on his head, the bright light dazzled him, he kept tripping over lovers in the grass. In exasperation he ate a huge lunch, then a huge tea, followed by high-tea at six. In the hours between seven and ten, spent back in his room, he finally anchored himself into a peaceful state with the help of baked beans and bacon. Strangely, no more smells came from his landlady's kitchen. He had not seen her about since their little scene, and assumed she was on holiday.

By the time Harry set off in his car, in best suit and imitation silk tie, he felt unusually calm, patient and optimistic. The curtains of Viola's house were not drawn. There was a dim light on the first floor. Harry slowly mounted the stone steps to the front door. He fingered the small jeweller's box in his pocket.

To his dismay, he found there was an entryphone: should Viola recognize his voice she might not let him in. He rang, and the Gods were on his side. Amazingly, he heard her voice cheerfully asking him to come up to the drawing-room.

Harry managed to control his instant scorn at the idea of a drawing-room being 'up' in any house, and pushed open the door. He stood for a moment accustoming his eyes to the huge, lightless hall, and made his way to the grandest staircase he had ever seen. His heart continued its furious pounding, outraged that any one person should live in a house of this scale. But calmly he put his hand on the polished banister –

it gave a solid, comforting support – and felt with his foot for the first stair. The carpet, as far as he could tell, was either thick velvet or pure mink. *Bloody mad . . .* But, with admirable control, he began to climb.

When Harry Antlers entered the drawing-room he felt he had walked into a cavernous place full of shadows. There was only one lamp lit, on a low table beside a sofa. Viola sat in the corner of that sofa, a look of wonderful expectancy on her face. But even as he looked, silently, the radiance fled from her and she covered her face with her hands.

Harry strode across the room till he was as far from her as he could be. He turned and contemplated Viola, still hidden behind her hands, shoulders hunched. She appeared to be sobbing. Harry felt a moment's distress. But this was soon replaced by a stronger feeling of discomfort, prickling over his entire skin, that came from the scale of the room, the huge pictures, the ornate looking-glass over the marble fireplace. He said nothing, waiting.

'How could you have found me this time?' Viola cried. She looked at him through cracks in her fingers.

'I'm sorry if I've caught you at a bad time. Once again. I've come to apologize for my untoward behaviour in Norfolk.' Harry smiled.

Viola let her hands drop from her face. Her eyes were narrowed. There were no visible tears.

'I don't want an apology, or anything else from you,' she said. 'I'd just like you to go. Please. I was quite happy until you came.'

'Then I'm sorry about that. Perhaps I could try to restore your happiness before I go?'

Viola watched him take a few steps forward, pat the chestnut velvet seat of a sofa opposite her own.

'Would it be permissible,' Harry asked, 'for a humble man like me to sit on this wonderful sofa?' He did not smile.

'Of course,' snapped Viola, irritated by such absurd but serious humility. 'Sit where you like.'

That fact that she did not give him a second order to leave gave Harry courage. He sat down, made so bold as to lean back among the alien cushions, ill-shapen legs stretched out before him. He felt the small box in his pocket. It had been his intention to sit near Viola, make her shut her eyes as in a childish game, and press it into her hands. But now he saw any such move would be unwise. Her resistance seemed to be melting a little, perhaps in response to his soft voice, though her expression was not inviting. He pulled the box from the pocket and threw it across the room to Viola, surprising himself by his unpremeditated action. It landed beside her. She ducked in fear. Then she picked it up.

'What's this?'

'Just a beginning.'

Viola opened the box. She took out the diamond star.

'Very pretty,' she said. 'I love Victorian jewellery.'

'It's yours,' said Harry.

'It most certainly isn't,' Viola retorted. 'You must have a very wrong impression of me if you think I'm the kind of girl who would accept jewellery from men.' She knew she sounded pompous.

'From one who loves you. Surely that's different,' said Harry.

'Not at all.' Viola was brusque. She returned the star to its box. 'It was a kind thought, but I don't want it. I wouldn't dream of accepting it. Please take it away.'

She placed the box some distance from her. Harry did not move, watching her. They listened to the tick of the gilded clock above the fireplace.

At last Harry shifted. He sat up, arms resting on knees, hands clasped as if in prayer. He was further encouraged by Viola not having thrown the box back at him. For the first time, with her, he felt in control. Instinctively he longed to make some extravagant gesture, throw himself on the floor at her feet, babble all the things that had been pent up in him so long concerning his love. But he knew any such action would be fatal, undoing all the good achieved so far this evening. What he would do, he thought, the resolution grim in his heart, would be to go very soon, as she requested. Show how reasonable he could be. But first he must put to her just one or two things.

'What you must understand, my beautiful lady, is that I'm a bit of a nutter, but I respond well when I'm treated well, as you can see. I'm not tearing up the carpets tonight, am I? I'm not throwing things about. I can be quite civilized, you know.' He smiled the charming smile that had endeared him to Hannah Bagle. 'I'm sorry, as I said, for my tantrums the other night, for bullying you over the telephone. But my lovely Viola, you can't know what it's like, this passion I feel for you. It's almost killing me.' He gave a small, self-deprecating laugh. 'Your face is constantly in my mind, your voice in my ears. I can't think about anything else, don't care about anything else. You can't begin to conceive of the torment.'

'No,' said Viola.

Hard little bitch, thought Harry, clasping his hands more tightly, *but I'll keep on smiling*.

'Look, I'm only asking one thing of you – it's not much. But give me a break. Have a bit of sympathy. Try to understand. And I for my part will try to act more reasonably. I won't pester you further, I promise. But in return, just out of human kindness, I'd much appreciate it . . .' His voice seemed to be near to breaking. '. . . if you'd let me visit you from time to time. Just to talk to you for a few moments. Like that, I can take new pictures of you away with me in my mind.'

He smiled again, stood up. The sag of his shoulders, the swell of his stomach, the tugging at his belt with ugly hands all conveyed his wretchedness. He was aware of this, looked to Viola for some reaction. And, wondrously, he detected some very slight interest in her eyes. Things were going better than he could have hoped for. He waited, but still Viola said nothing.

'Well, I must be going,' he said. 'I won't be bothering you for some time as I shall be away in Sweden, working. So that will keep me occupied while you're in Norfolk –'

'How do you know I'm going to –'

Viola leapt up, fiery, beautiful, so close to Harry he felt quite weak. He put out a hand, indicating she should come no closer. 'Calm down, calm down. I haven't been spying, I promise you that. Just keeping in touch. Any word of you makes the agony a little more bearable, you must see that. And I warned you: passion is a great spur to discovery. But I shan't be pursuing you to Norfolk again, have no fear. I shall wait till you get back.'

For all his gentleness, it sounded like a threat. Viola fell back on to the sofa, uttered a cry of fury curdled with fear. Harry knew he must leave at once. He went quickly to the door.

'Take your brooch,' hissed Viola.

Not answering, Harry hurried from the room and down the thick stairs. Much had been achieved tonight. Perhaps he should not have mentioned Norfolk, but that was the only mistake he had made. One thing was quite definite: despite her shouts from upstairs about taking back the brooch, he had established himself as a new and intriguing man in Viola Windrush's mind. Of that he was quite sure. He banged the huge front door behind him, wishing it would shake the whole bloody palace of a house to its foundations. Pity he had forgotten to ask Viola how she felt about living in such a ridiculous place on her own, when ten homeless families could easily be housed there. But there was plenty of time. In his new position of strength, patience would surely come to him.

For all the success of the evening, by the time he reached his room Harry Antlers was shaking. He made himself a cup of tea to accompany a cheese sandwich, then took to his chair to review the evening, in film director's language, frame by frame. Viola's face, palpably beautiful, struck blindingly in his mind's eye, so that even though reason said she was a stupid, resistant, spoiled cow, he could not believe this. She was in fact as near perfect as you could find on this mean earth – and one day she would be his.

Lulled by the cheese, Harry had just turned his thoughts to the future penthouse for his loved one when the front door bell rang. He rose with some silly hope that Viola had followed him: her heart had turned, and here she was, offering herself to him in her entirety.

Harry opened the front door. A slight girl stood before him, blonde hair falling out of a scarf. Scarcely visible with her back to the glow of street lights, Harry's heart surged for a moment, believing his fantasy had come true. The illusion was broken as soon as she spoke.

'I'm Annie Light,' she said. 'Miss Whittle's great-niece. My mum sent me over with a message for you.'

Harry paused. Disappointment gathered in his stomach. He felt a sudden longing to talk to someone. Perhaps this stranger would do.

'Come in,' he said.

The girl followed him upstairs. Unasked, she took off her coat and scarf, laid them on a chair. She was as small as Viola, scared.

'Do sit down,' said Harry.

'I'm all right standing if you don't mind.'

'Shall I get you a cup of tea?'

'No thanks.'

'What's the message, then?'

Annie looked up at him, dull-eyed. She had too large a gap between her front teeth, but was quite pretty.

'It's my auntie – well, my great-aunt Marjorie,' she said, looking down. 'She's dead.'

'Oh?' said Harry.

'Yes. Dead. Few nights ago she arrives to see her sister, my grandmother, like, in a terrible state, with the cat. She didn't seem to be making any sense. Next thing: heart attack. They got her to hospital straight away. But she was dead on arrival. Just like that.'

'I am sorry,' said Harry. 'Very sudden.'

'Very sudden, yes,' said the girl. She paused for a moment, making some effort to remember. 'My mum said I had to tell you two things. She said great-aunt Marjorie's solicitor would be on to you soon about the rent and that, and selling up this place.'

'Quite,' said Harry.

'And then she said would I ask you if you knew if there was anything on my great-aunt's mind?'

'I'm afraid not. We very rarely spoke to each other. We had almost no communication.'

'Yes, well, she didn't speak to anyone much. She was that quiet. So it was unlike her to come round to me grandmother in such a dither. Something must have happened to upset her, that's what we thought. It's terrible, somehow, not knowing.'

'Well, I'm sorry I can't help,' said Harry.

'It, like, haunts us all,' said Annie.

Harry stared at the pitiful sight of her, forlorn shoulders

and scrunched-up hands. He cared not at all about the demise of his churlish landlady, and slammed down the small voice of conscience that accused him of possibly contributing to her death. But the sight of Annie served to inflame his feelings of self-pity: the unfairness of things in his life surged through him. He longed to weep on a shoulder – any shoulder. So when Annie then said, with a sniff:

'She was such a lonely thing, my old auntie, all her life,' Harry could contain himself no longer.

'We all are, we all are,' he whispered. 'We're all despairing, lonely creatures. What can we do?'

Annie, alarmed by the urgency in his voice, looked up.

'I don't know,' she said, sounding stupid.

'Comfort: comfort is all we ask of each other. And yet, where do we find it?'

Annie took a step back from him, by now much alarmed by the look in his eye.

'I must be going,' she said.

'Stay one moment.'

Before she knew what was happening, Annie was clutched in Harry's arms, crushed to his awkward body, listening to unintelligible murmurings as he nuzzled his mouth through her hair. He seemed to be strangely upset. But Annie, still frightened, felt a sudden pity for this stranger. The comfort he had spoken of seemed, magically, to be running through her.

For his part, Annie surprisingly in his arms, Harry sensed no relief: rather, her compliance only made it worse that she was not Viola. He kept his eyes shut, a picture of the girl who was not there in his mind. Fired by the beauty of this imaginative picture, he crushed the real girl more desperately, kissed her hard on the mouth, pushing back her head. He only had to start undoing her clothes, whisper a suggestion, and she would be his.

But, as suddenly as his desire had come, it left. Harry pushed Annie away from him, drained, disgusted. He saw that her mouth was red and bruised, and blood threatened a small cut on her lip. Her mascara had run, her dyed hair had fallen into dark partings. He wanted to be rid of her as fast as possible.

'I'm sorry,' he said. 'I'll see you downstairs.'

'That's all right.' The girl sniffed again, pulled on her coat. 'It's been a funny sort of day all round, matter of fact.'

Harry hurried her out of the house. She waved goodbye, friendly, saying that she'd drop by again one day to see how he was getting on. Harry considered this proposal nothing less than a threat. He must hurry to find new accommodation: he wanted no more Annies in his life, pestering him with stupid letters and declaring their unwanted love.

Viola had been so completely absorbed in the sudden thought of Edwin's return that when, in reality, he had been substituted by Harry Antlers, she had found it impossible to grasp the reality of the situation. Thus, while one half of her slipped into the old fear and anger that Harry always engendered, the other half was locked in contemplation of what might have been. As a result, she had no spare energy to chastise Harry and order him from the house. Anything to avoid a scene, she had acted in pathetically mild fashion, no doubt giving Harry reason to feel encouragement.

Most of the rest of the night was spent cursing herself for her own feeble reaction to Harry's violating her privacy once again. His sickening humility disgusted her as much as his violence, but she knew that if he now redoubled his efforts she had only herself to blame. She should have thrown the diamond brooch after him into the street. She should have . . . Wearily, Viola got up late next morning.

All the calm contentment of the last few days seemed to have disappeared. Those twin destroyers of a peaceful mind, rage and fear, agitated her limbs, making her restless. In no mood to continue painting, she could only think that a short talk to Hardley There, intimating, in the lightest way, some of her troubles, might be of comfort. She knew he would welcome an interruption from his moths.

But Edwin, Viola could see at once, when she met him on the stairs, was in no mood for other people's problems. Rather it was he who needed soothing. His blanched skin and unshaven jaw told of a night as sleepless as Viola's own.

'You'll never believe it,' he wailed, 'but I found one on the front steps when I got home.'

For a moment, with her slow morning reaction, Viola misunderstood him. 'A moth!' she asked.

'A *woman*. Imagine! Eleven at night. Waiting for me for hours, apparently. *Howling*.' He wrung his hands, moaning again. For the first time since she had woken, Viola felt like smiling. But she controlled herself.

'Did you invite her in?'

'Oh, well, yes. I had to, didn't I? She was making such a noise. Any minute the neighbours would have complained.' The thought of this possibility seemed to cause Edwin further distress. He sat on a stair, head in hands.

'What was her trouble?'

'Ah! Gracious me. She kept me up the best part of the night explaining. Apparently, I hadn't acknowledged some poetry she'd sent me. Well, I mean, obviously I wasn't encouraging her to send me poetry. God knows what *that* can lead to. Mind you, she's rather a good poet, I suppose. But as I keep on telling her, she shouldn't address the stuff to *me*. It's dangerous for married women to write poetry to bachelors. I keep *on* warning her. But she pays no heed. Reams of the stuff pours out, gets pushed through my front door. What can I do? She leaves copies all over her house, I gather. Very careless. It's only a matter of time till her husband finds out. Then what? I'll be unwillingly involved in some terrible scandal. Cited, or whatever. But how can I get rid of her? Every time I shut the door in her face her fixation only increases. Oh Lord, honestly . . .'

'But you must have done something to encourage her,' suggested Viola, intrigued. She sat on the stair above Edwin.

'Not really. We met at an AGM of the Hampstead Moth Society. We're in the same *world*, you see. Her husband writes for a scientific magazine – very well, as a matter of fact. Our paths cross officially. Too damn often for my liking. She said she had a lot of questions to ask me on some paper I'd written. I asked her out to lunch, thinking it would be a purely professional date. Not her intention at all, of course. Well, somehow, several more lunches happened.'

'Long lunches?'

'They did somehow stray into the afternoon, I'm bound to admit. But I made it quite clear that for my part there was no possibility of things developing. But she heeded not a word. And now she's gone completely off the rails, threatening to leave her husband and children, give up her entire life to me. I don't want *any part* of her life, let alone its entirety. Oh, dearie me, married women are terrible, terrible pests . . .'

Viola, feeling a little foolish, patted his shoulder.

'You *are* a kind girl,' Edwin went on. 'In fact, this house is my only refuge. I was wondering if staying here a few nights might not be the solution? Then she couldn't possibly trap me again. She's no idea of the address.'

'I'm sure my uncle wouldn't mind,' said Viola. 'Why don't you stay for a week? You could go in the dressing-room. I won't be in your way because I'm going home for a while to be with my brother who's coming over from America.'

'Oh?'

It was hard to tell whether Edwin was disappointed by the news of her departure. But by now his feelings for her were of little consequence to Viola. Last night had been a one-night flight of fantasy, dead this morning. Edwin Hardley was a friendly, rather pathetic creature, driven by a complex web of insecurities that Viola felt no desire to untangle.

He moved into the dressing-room that night, and was there for the two remaining nights before Viola left for Norfolk. But she scarcely saw him. There were no more suggestions of dinner. From what Viola could gather, from their brief meetings on the stairs, the unhappy poetess was not the only lady in pursuit of his reluctant love. He crept about with a hunted look, indicating, with the merest droop of his weary eye, that he suffered from being the most wanted man in London.

Alfred Baxter, alone in the house in Norfolk, established a routine of work as hard as it had been in the days before his retirement. His self-imposed hours were long: eight in the morning till eight at night, with only short breaks for lunch and an afternoon cup of tea. The rewards were the results. Within a week the lawns were all mown, the borders weeded, climbing roses pinned back against walls, gravel drive swept smooth. Up on the roof two builders – men he had known as boys – replaced slate tiles, and waved to him from their ladders. So he felt there was company, should he want it. But on the whole he was too preoccupied with his work to require anything more than the occasional greeting. He had never been a gregarious man, and was not lonely.

No: he was definitely not lonely. But strange sensations, which he could not account for when he forced himself to think about them, made him uneasy. It was something to do with getting himself settled – that was it. Not so much in a physical way: that was all taken care of nicely, his rooms all shipshape and tidy, only the kitchen to paint. It was more a matter of settling his mind.

In detached fashion, Alfred regarded his problem – if so unidentifiable a thing could be called a problem, that is – as very peculiar. Here he was, in the perfect job at last, lovely house and surroundings, part of the coast he had known all his life, time usefully occupied, great respect for his employer Miss Windrush – and yet at times he found himself shaking, physically shaking. It was fine during the day, outside. But the evenings Alfred dreaded. Forced to give up his gardening by the dark, he would reluctantly go into his kitchen, fiddle about getting himself a pork pie and a piece of cheese, and eventually go to his chair in the sitting-room. Very comfortable it was, too, at the end of a long day. Good support to aching limbs. Nothing to grumble about in the view out of the windows, either. The limes, their shapes by now familiar, scarcely moving in the still summer nights, moonlight on their leaves. Alfred would sit in the dark, so that insects would not fly in to the light and annoy him, and Eileen would start up her tricks.

Trouble was, once her face began bobbing about he couldn't get rid of it. It didn't obliterate his view, exactly, but behaved like a transparent yo-yo, up and down, up and down, the solid things of the room showing through. Sometimes Alfred would smack his brow, crying out loud in protest, and shut his eyes tightly. But that was no good. The face merely danced in blackness, alone, decapitated.

Even worse – the thing that caused Alfred to shake – was that although he knew the vision *was* Eileen, the face was not as he remembered it in life. It was a decidedly nasty face, pinched, mean, unfriendly. The real face, the good and smiling

Eileen he knew and loved, would not return.

Eileen did not haunt him on her own. Some nights, when he returned to the sitting-room particularly late, she was joined by the girls. He had no visions of them, but could hear voices, laughter – all of them laughing, not just Lily, now. One particular night, summer lightning playing in the sky outside, lighting up the limes so that they looked like giant silver birds with their feathers all a-ruffle, he heard them *singing*. A mocking sort of song, it sounded, though Alfred could not make out the words. Alarmed by the strength of the hallucinations, he stood up and went to the open window, just as the church clock boomed a melancholy midnight. Alfred could not bear the sound. He slammed the window shut and ran from the room. He went through the door to the kitchen of the main house, sat at the table and threw his arms across the massive planks of pine. He lay his head on the wood, smelt the beeswax polish. Here, thank the Lord, there was complete silence. Not a voice to be heard, his wife's face vanished.

In time, Alfred grew calm. He raised his head, reason prevailing again. He had had one of his funny turns, that was all. Well, he should be grateful that was all he suffered. Physically, he was sound as they come, full of strength and energy for his years. But old men, he remembered, do sometimes have funny turns. Nothing serious. And if he had another one, well, he'd know what to do next time. Come in here straight away. The peace of the Windrush kitchen was something very strong. It acted like magic. It took away his fears.

Quite recovered, Alfred switched on the lamp on the dresser and looked gratefully round the room which had soothed him. It was then he remembered that Miss Windrush and her brother were expected in two days' time: *two days*. Alfred's look turned from gratitude to severe criticism. Why, with all the work outdoors he had not even begun on the house.

He glanced at the clock: almost one o'clock. Well, no time like . . . Besides, he didn't really fancy returning to his own quarters, yet. Alfred eagerly took cloths and brushes from the cupboard. He gathered dusty china plates, untouched for months, from the shelves: he washed, replaced, swept, polished, scrubbed and tidied all through the visionless night. For once, the swift dark hours had been a happy time.

10

When Viola and her brother Gideon arrived from London, their immediate delight in everything Alfred had achieved gave him great satisfaction. Much of their first day was spent going from room to room noticing things Alfred had never supposed would be noticed. Then they turned to the garden. They made a long, slow tour with Alfred, listening to his plans, praising what he had done so far. The vegetable garden gave them particular delight: Alfred had managed to rescue globe artichokes and asparagus from the undergrowth. Viola declared in great excitement they would have friends to dinner the next evening, with fruit and vegetables from the garden. Their enthusiasm was most rewarding.

But, privately, Alfred felt some concern about his employers: Miss Windrush looked pale after two weeks in London, while Mr Windrush looked positively unhealthy. Thin, strained. Well, that was city life for you. Alfred and Eileen would never for a moment have entertained the thought of living anywhere but the coast. Cities were poisonous: they corroded a man's guts, they shut him off from the rhythms of the earth, they were no resting place for a peaceful soul. Back in the kitchen, Alfred put the kettle on the Aga, found biscuits and mugs. He was determined to restore the Windrushes to the lively health he remembered in their childhood. In the meantime, he could hear footsteps and real laughter upstairs. The house had come alive again.

Maisie Fanshawe tucked a tartan rug round her father's paralysed knees. Despite the warmth of the evening, he felt cold. His skin was always cold these days. She dabbed a handkerchief damp with eau de cologne round his neck, and placed a new biography of Milton, open at the right page, on his lap. His eyes, fixed somewhere in the middle distance, took a long time to lower their focus to the book. The telephone rang. Maisie's father did not seem to hear it.

As the telephone ringing in their house was a rare occurrence, it gave Maisie a small start of anticipation. She could not have said whom she hoped might be calling her, but almost any outside voice would be welcome in the long, stuffy evening. She went to her father's desk, sat in his leather chair, picked up the old-fashioned receiver, very heavy in her hand, and shyly gave the number. It was Richard Almond.

'Maisie,' he said, 'here's an order for you. I'm calling for you at seven tomorrow evening. Please be ready. We're going out to dinner.'

Stunned by disbelief, Maisie giggled. 'Dinner?' she repeated. 'Where? Why?'

'Just dinner. That's all I'm going to say.'

'But, I can't. Father – '

'You know perfectly well there are a dozen people who'd be willing to look after him for an evening. So don't worry about that.'

'I suppose – '

'Fine, then. See you tomorrow.'

Maisie put down the telephone. In flippant reaction to the extraordinary invitation, her mind leapt to the new Fair Isle jersey she had been knitting herself to occupy the evenings. She would sew it up this evening: must have something new. Then she wondered why, after all these years, Richard should suddenly issue her with a mystery invitation. He was lonely, she supposed. Had a rotten life, really, what with Sonia . . . Perhaps he wanted to talk about her at last. Perhaps he wanted to try out a new restaurant in King's Lynn: he was quite a gourmet, Richard, and she was last on his list of possible ladies to accompany him. Well, she didn't care, really. For whatever reason Richard wanted to take her out she would be happy. To be spared just one evening with her silent father would be an infinite treat. But heavens above, what a disloyal thought! Guilt sprang within Maisie's thin breast. She stood up, fetched her knitting, returned to her chair beside her father.

'Richard Almond has asked me to dine with him tomorrow night, Father,' she said. 'I hope you won't mind. I'll arrange for Mrs Ray to come in and look after you.'

Her father made no movement. It was impossible to tell

whether he understood, or cared. Maisie, excitement mingling with her guilt, patted his speckled hand. Then she lifted it, kissed it gently, and returned it to his lap.

'Dear Father,' she said.

Gideon and Viola spent the entire afternoon in preparation. Gideon, who enjoyed cooking more than his sister, concentrated on mint and lemon sauce for a poached chicken, while Viola slowly chopped chives and polished tomatoes the size of marbles from the garden. At peace in their work, they scarcely spoke except to remark on each other's progress. The sun shone fiercely outside. But the thick stone walls and the flagstone floors of the kitchen maintained coolness within.

Now, evening, everything done, they sat in the garden awaiting their guests. Viola had changed into a lavender cotton dress that threw shadows of the same colour on to her pale cheeks. She took a sip of Pimm's from a tall glass, smiled as a protruding fuzz of borage tickled her nose.

'I can hardly believe you're here,' she said.

Gideon was sprawled in a deckchair, long legs slung apart, etiolated New York clothes replaced by old corduroy trousers and dark shirt. In contrast to his expression on arrival here, he now had the look of a relaxed man. His fine eyes lowered almost sleepily.

'Must find out about the tides from Alfred,' he replied. 'I'd like to go for a sail.'

'What, tonight?'

'Should be a full moon.'

They sat looking out to sea, the smell of night-scented stocks sweet behind them, that veil of fragile warmth peculiar to English summers light upon them.

'I realize I must come back here for good, soon,' said Gideon after a while. 'I kid myself, week after week in New York, there's no point in returning home. But of course I'm wrong. I only have to be here five minutes to know how wrong I am.'

'What about Hannah?' asked Viola.

Gideon thought for some time in silence.

'She wouldn't like it,' he said at last. 'She's a real New Yorker, only really happy there. I couldn't ask her to come with me.'

'So?'

'So, things will resolve themselves, I daresay,' he said, and they listened to the church bell striking eight.

There were footsteps on the path. Richard and Maisie, arm in arm, appeared round the corner of the house. Gideon leapt to his feet, went first to Richard. There was much jovial hand-shaking, while behind the laughter each man's eyes scoured the other, assessing the changes. Their prolonged greeting, Viola saw, gave Maisie time to contain herself as best she could. Richard had said nothing about Gideon being here: the shock unsteadied her. She stood clutching at the hem of her dreadful Fair Isle jersey, salmon pink and lime and yellow, sour colours in the quiet light of the terrace, blushing. Viola quickly handed her a drink. She took a deep, grateful gulp.

'Oh God,' she whispered, 'I never expected *this*.' She avoided looking at Gideon, cast her eyes towards the beach, the hollyhocks, the sky – anywhere but the two men so close to her.

In her narrow life, Maisie had learned no wiles. Amazed to see the man she had loved for years, unrequited, the shock was too all-consuming to think of a ploy to disguise that amazement. And when eventually Gideon left Richard, came over to her, hugged her, declared his pleasure in seeing her, the blush vanished from her face to leave her pale and lost for words.

'Gideon, you're *here*,' was all she managed to say.

Richard, meanwhile, busying himself with drinks, ignored Viola. He, too, was overcome by the pleasure of seeing Gideon again. But then he turned to her. She sat upright in a wicker seat, the pattern of its high back a halo behind her head. He spoke before he could stop himself.

'Christ, you look . . .' He bent down and kissed her forehead. 'Violetta, Violetta, why so silent?'

'It's your turn for Gideon,' she said. 'I've had a whole day of him here. I've got him to myself for a week to come.'

It was Gideon's evening. He sat at the head of the vast kitchen table, in his father's old chair, telling stories of New York life, making them laugh, master of the scene. Maisie sat on his right, entranced. The candlelight muted her jersey, and despite the wild grey fringe she was suddenly years younger, smudgy eyes a-glitter, ungrounded by rare happiness. She did not trust herself to eat: picked at the delicious food, scarcely touched the champagne Gideon had brought, and dared but a few glances at him as he told his stories.

Seeing that the others were too preoccupied to be of practical help, Viola produced the food and cleared plates, aware that Richard's eyes were often upon her. Pouring the coffee, she noticed the laughter wane. Gideon's stories had come to an end. The four of them found themselves drifting into another key with the ease of friends who have known each other all their lives. Merry from the wine, delighted by the reunion, unanimously they seemed to pause, listen, feel: let the sensations break over them like music. At such times, thought Viola, the present is a positive thing, caught with both hands, grasped, felt, infinitely precious. So much of our lives we flail in anticipation or reminiscence. The *conscious* present is elusive, a rare thing, that strikes only in times of great crisis, or happiness. Here it was this evening, alive, trapped for an hour or so, luminous in reality as it would become in memory.

Viola looked about her, accumulating detail: three shadowy heads, two candle flames, firelight dimpling the walls, smell of strawberries and roses, hands round half-filled glasses, no one speaking, each of them resting with their private thoughts. And she knew that those moments, silently acknowledged by Gideon, Richard and the trembling Maisie, would be remembered by each one of them.

Gideon turned, at last, to Maisie.

'And you, Maisie,' he said. 'I've been hogging the conversation. I'm sorry. I want to hear about you. What have you been doing?'

Maisie looked straight at him, alarmed to be called upon. Then she glanced at Richard and Viola, hating the attention.

'I've been looking after Father,' she answered. 'He hasn't long to live now.'

Despite her protesting hand, Gideon filled her glass.

'I would like to see your father again,' he said. 'Could I come up tomorrow?'

At the thought of a further encounter with Gideon, Maisie blushed deeply.

'Oh yes. Of course. He'd love . . . I mean, he might not know you. It's hard to tell what he knows.'
'I'll be there for tea,' said Gideon, and Maisie's head trembled in disbelief.
Gideon then suggested, as the tide was out, a walk on the beach. So warm a night, he said, would otherwise be wasted. Richard declined. Viola kept her silence.
'I'll come,' volunteered Maisie, at last, her voice no disguise to her eagerness.
'Right, Maisie. You and I shall walk a mile up the beach. Come on, come on.'
Gideon was all impatience, up and off as if the kitchen suddenly oppressed him. The others hurried to follow.
'Violetta and I will come as far as the garden gate,' said Richard. Had it not been for all the years of small gestures that never added up to a fundamental change, Viola might have thought his assumption, that she would want to stay behind with him, bore some significance.
It was still warm outside. The violet sky was as deep a colour as ever it could turn on an English summer night fluttering with stars. They walked across the lawn, the four of them: Maisie and Viola ahead, the two men behind, in conversation about boats. Maisie's shoes were causing her anxiety.
'They'll be hopeless on the beach,' she said, trying to find something upon which to focus a more abstract worry.
'Then take them off,' suggested Viola gently, recognizing Maisie's condition.
Amazed by such an obviously good idea, all notions of practicality having deserted her tonight, Maisie slipped off her gloomy shoes at the gate leading to the marsh. She laid them neatly under the hedge. Her long, narrow feet gleamed like silver fish in the moonlight.
Gideon opened the gate, guided Maisie through it as if escorting an elderly aunt. Richard and Viola watched them for a while, as they made their way down the path, single file. When they reached the beach, Gideon took Maisie's arm again. Soon they became invisible in the distance.
Richard and Viola then turned away from the sea, looked in silence at the reassuring shape of the house, the massive

trees, the lawn chequered with squares of light from the various windows.

'That nightingale, whose extinction I predicted,' said Richard. 'I was wrong. Listen.'

Viola, listening to the birdsong cascade from some hidden place in the trees, remembered at once the conversation.

'You said fifty years. It's not even half that.'

'It seems a very long time.'

'Maisie told me the other day she hated that evening. She confessed she was furious with me because Gideon took me home early.'

'He took you home early because I failed in my duties.'

'You were whirled away by Sonia.'

'So I was.' They both smiled. 'Poor Maisie. I wonder if she's loved Gideon all these years?'

'Things of a certain quality don't fade,' said Viola. 'Hope can die, but a conviction that something would have been right, had it been given the chance, can exist for ever.'

'You're probably right,' Richard said.

They moved slowly over the lawn. Viola, straight-backed and head held high, looked sternly towards the house. She was aware that Richard, close beside her, walked at a slight angle, eyes upon her.

'I've a rotten memory,' he was saying, 'but there's another thing I remember about that night. Your dress. It was silver.'

'White,' corrected Viola.

'Well, silver by moonlight. Flowers embroidered on the hem. Daisies, I think.'

'Lilies.'

They laughed again. 'Silver lilies! That was it. Wet from the grass.'

'You showed some concern.'

'It was the prettiest dress I've ever seen.'

'My mother's.'

'And you looked . . . I have to confess, on our walk in the garden I had a considerable struggle with my conscience.'

'I don't believe you.'

'I swear it. I had a terrible desire to touch you.'

Viola stopped. '*Did* you?'

'I did. I promise.'

'Then you put up a very good show of being quite impervious to my lilies.'

'What else could I do? You were sixteen. My friend's younger sister. I was supposed to be looking after you.'

Viola gave a small sigh. She began to move again. 'The rules of a gentleman can cause wicked suffering,' she said, lightly.

'I'm sorry. Perhaps I should have given in to my instincts. But it would have been a terrible shock to you. I must have seemed so old. I thought you must have been very bored, lumbered with me all evening. That's why I released you by going off to dance with Sonia.'

By now they were back at the terrace. They sat on the iron bench, listening to the church clock striking twelve. Its chime seemed gentler than by day, the echo of each note shuffling furtively into the quietness of the night, fearful of disturbing. As Viola remembered the desolation of that moment Richard had left her for Sonia, she felt its pain.

'How much we miss through our disguises,' she said. She allowed herself a sideways glance at Richard. His expression was one of such bleakness that, with no thought of the consequences, she lay her head on his shoulder, to comfort.

'I've often wondered, Violetta,' said Richard, taking her hand, 'if I made a mistake that night. I've never liked to admit it to myself, because we both know, if I did, it's impossible to put right.'

'You still keep to the rules of a gentleman,' said Viola. She could feel him smiling, guessed it was the mocking smile he kept for use against himself.

'I do,' he said. 'But not quite always.'

Richard kissed Viola on the mouth. As they drew near that moment when a kiss takes flight, he pushed her gently from him, though still kept hold of her hand. They returned to the kitchen and began the job of clearing up. An hour later Gideon appeared, alone, having driven Maisie home.

'Maisie of Docking has changed,' was all he said. 'I wish we'd been able to have our sail.' Then he engaged Richard once again in talk about his boat. Viola left them, with a new bottle of wine, knowing they would talk long into the night.

The next day Hannah telephoned. From what Viola could hear of the conversation there was some dispute between her and Gideon. All that he reported was that she was complaining about London, boredom, lack of his presence: wanted him to return early and entertain her.

'But I'm not going to,' he said. 'I was adamant about that. I'm staying for the full week, as planned. There are masses of things for us to do. That includes Richard,' he added. 'God, it's good to see him again. And dear old Maisie.'

Harry Antlers, in Sweden, was full of disillusion. His stomach never satisfied by the ubiquitous *smorgasbord*, he was permanently irritable and melancholy. The activities he was bound by his contract to film he found distasteful: the amorous advances of various interchangeable blondes, far from satiating his vanity, only served to exacerbate the condition of his pining heart. He wrote Viola many letters describing in minute detail the hourly fluctuations of his misery and longing. Some of these he posted to her Norfolk address. Finally, in desperation, from the bleakness of his hotel bedroom, he rang his own answering machine. There were various messages from Hannah Bagle. She was in London as promised. Bored, lonely, longing to see him. Why wasn't he there? There were also three messages in a girl's voice that he did not recognize, and she did not leave a name. Harry could only understand that she wished to see him most urgently. In the hope that Hannah could temporarily deflect his wretched mind, he decided to return to London for the weekend. Somehow, he could always fiddle his expenses.

Richard took a much overdue holiday during the time of Gideon's visit, and joined him and Viola every day. Maisie was also included in their plans. Incredulous at her good fortune, she arranged a rota of people to care for her father in her absence, and wondered at her lack of guilt. But it was not often such happiness befell her, and she was determined not to miss a moment of the glorious week. It might, after all, be a memory she would have to live upon for many years to come.

The good weather continued. It was very hot, though a constant breeze from the sea diffused the burning of the sun. A daily picnic lunch was taken out on the boat: they swam, walked far along the beaches, dozed in the hollows of the dunes. Although all these expeditions began as a foursome, somehow the couples always divided for part of the day. Gideon, full of pent-up energy after so long in New York with no proper exercise, was always keen to walk. Maisie was eager to accompany him. She did not pretend otherwise, simply said she would like to come with him. Viola would stay silently guarding the sleeping figure of Richard, his cheeks quite sunburnt by now, the lines of fatigue cleared from under his eyes. She was happy merely to lie back beside him, head on a comfortable tussock, fingers weaving through the soft white sand, sun pouring through her, arc of cloudless blue filling her eyes, small rustle of the sea the only sound. Here I am with Richard, was all she thought. When he stirred, she said: 'First time for weeks, I feel quite safe.'

Richard sat up, yawning. 'That man still bothering you?'

'He's persistent.'

Viola had had two Express letters from Harry here in Norfolk – pages and pages of rampant passion, unnerving while she read them, reminding her of his constant menace. She had said nothing and burnt both letters. But they left a small flame of fear, somewhere in the depths of her, that would not quite die despite the distractions of the present.

'If he's a real nuisance you must promise to let me know. I'll deal with him.'

Richard patted Viola's bare knee, the first time he had touched her since the night he had kissed her. Viola smiled.

'How?'

'There are ways. Anyhow, promise me.'

'Promise.'

Richard removed his hand, turned and looked down at the beach. Viola followed his gaze. They could see two minute figures in the distance walking slowly through the shallows of the sea. Gideon's hand was on Maisie's shoulder.

'I wouldn't be at all surprised,' said Richard, 'if Gideon didn't find great relief in Maisie.'

'I'm sure he does. She's part of his old childhood pattern, like us. He doesn't have to make an effort. He's fed up with new faces. Part of this holiday is sticking to old ones. But poor Maisie. He's being nice to her years too late. God knows what she'll suffer when he goes.'

'Perhaps, in the end . . . Who knows?'

'I doubt it. Hannah's very demanding and very strong. It'll take him a long time to extricate himself from New York.'

'I'm sure he'll end up here.'

'Probably, but not for a long time.'

'And I'll take quite a large bet with you he'll end up with Maisie.'

'Nonsense!' Viola laughed. Gideon and Maisie: absurd thought.

But when they returned from their walk, Viola found herself observing them anew. There was a tranquillity about Maisie which obviously attracted Gideon. She was calm, responding to his gentle teasing with a quiet smile. Her supply of new clothes exhausted, in the last few days she had taken to wearing jeans and an old jersey. She looked years younger, despite the grey fringe. Her hands were beautiful, Viola noticed for the first time, and there was a sort of lonely dignity in her upright carriage. Often she and Gideon caught each other's eye, and just looked, a little surprised, as if surveying each other for the first time. Viola, who had been preoccupied by Richard's presence for five days, wondered that she had not noticed these things before. She let herself briefly imagine Gideon and Maisie settled in Norfolk, living in the house. Although that would mean moving herself, it was a pleasing thought. It would be good, then, if Richard's instinct proved right.

On their last evening, Gideon and Maisie went for a final sail. Richard and Viola stayed in their usual place on the terrace, flagstones warm beneath their feet. Alfred Baxter was clipping a hedge nearby. The snip of his shears pecked at the silence. In the evening light the patterns of finely mown lawn among the shadows was an intense green. Tomorrow's parting, not mentioned, weighed heavily.

'As a matter of fact,' said Richard, 'most unusually, I have to come to London next week. My old mother's birthday. I'm taking her out to lunch. She won't stir in the evenings.' He paused, looked at Viola. 'I wondered, if you weren't too busy, if you would come to the theatre with me in the evening?'

Viola, who had been dreading the return to London, and who had never received any such invitation from Richard in her life, accepted with alacrity.

'I shall look forward to that,' said Richard and, occupied with their own thoughts, they fell into silence for a while.

Viola, her eyes on the beach, suddenly remembered the dawn picnic she had encountered the day she left for New York. The memory made her shiver slightly, the luxurious shiver caused by recalling a fearful experience from the safety of a protected present. She heard herself telling the story to Richard.

'I'll never know the answer,' she ended. 'Some existentialist joke, perhaps. Some form of artistic happening. But whatever it was, it was chilling. I dreamed about those stiff ladies, their clothes blowing about them, for weeks.'

'Most peculiar,' said Richard. 'I hate unsolved mysteries.'

'Telling you, perhaps, will exorcize it.' Already the vision, now described, was less sharp in her mind.

'Hope so. No more bad dreams.'

'No more bad dreams.'

They could see Maisie and Gideon coming through the gate from the marsh.

'Has ever a week gone so fast?' said Richard, and stood to pour drinks for the approaching couple.

11

Harry Antlers, on his return to London for the weekend, found a letter from his late landlady's solicitor giving him notice to leave. The house was up for sale. This spurred Harry to ring several estate agents and urge them to find him a penthouse flat. There was also a note, in uneducated writing, that had been delivered by hand:

Dear Mr Antlers, I have rung several times and left messages. Please could you phone me when you come back? I feel very wretched and would like to talk to you again. Yours, Annie Light.

The mystery of the anonymous voice on his answering machine thus solved, Harry sat down, heavy with disappointment. Remembering the girl, dark roots to her divided greasy hair, cruelly unlike Viola after a superficial glance, he made a note of her telephone number and angrily screwed up her letter.

Harry was very hungry. There was no food in his kitchen, no energy to go to the shops. He contemplated driving to Norfolk and peering through the bushes at Viola, her brother, most probably her doctor lover. But he felt no enthusiasm for such a trip: were he caught, things might be awkward. Instead, he wrote Viola another letter. Then the telephone rang. Hannah Bagle.

'Harry? Hi. I've been calling constantly.' Her annoyance was plain.

'I'm only just back.'

'How are you?'

'Ravenous.'

Hannah laughed, misunderstanding him.

'We can easily take care of that. Why not come on over? I'm at a horribly loose end, you could say. I'll order you up a huge steak, French fries. Leave it to me.'

'I'll be with you in an hour,' said Harry, his stomach aching at the thought of the food.

In the damp silence of his room he had a feeble battle with his conscience, but it was a fight quickly resolved. Once Viola was his, he would never go elsewhere. Until then, if other beautiful ladies wanted him, if others would assuage his hunger, why should he deny them?

He drove quickly to Hannah's hotel. She opened the door of her suite to him wearing only a silk dressing-gown. His greeting was to tear the lapels apart, gaze upon her until his look shifted, even more hungrily, to the white-clothed table laid for two in the window.

'Food first, if you don't mind,' he said.

They remained in the hotel for the rest of the weekend.

Viola and Gideon parted in London. Gideon was to spend a couple of days with Hannah, then they would return together to New York. It was quite apparent the prospect of this return held little joy for Gideon.

'The week seems to have confirmed all my instincts,' he told Viola. 'Maybe it's been the lever. Perhaps I shall be back quite soon.'

'Wouldn't that mean a lot of extricating?'

'It would. But when I recognize the right time has come, I shall brace myself up for the severing.' He looked far from happy as they said goodbye.

For her part, Viola took care to conceal from Gideon her own low spirits on her return to London. Entering her uncle's house, the anguished figure of Edwin Hardley did nothing to cheer her.

'Oh, you've been *away*,' he groaned. 'It's been the longest week this summer.'

He carried her suitcase upstairs to the half-finished flat, made cups of coffee. Viola, in her melancholy, felt grateful to him.

'You seem sad,' said Edwin.

'Not really. I never like coming back to London.'

'It's time we had another dinner. I shall tell you funny stories about a gathering of moth men last week. How about this evening?'

Viola paused, thinking.

'Not tonight,' she said at last. 'I think I must . . . resettle myself. Besides, I'm terribly behind with all this.' Her eyes ran over the unpainted kitchen walls. 'But it's very kind of you. Perhaps next week.' Next week, once Richard had come and gone, there would be nothing further to look forward to.

'Very well.'

Edwin swilled out his cup under the tap, put it on a paint-spattered draining board. He glanced around for a dish cloth. Seeing none, he seemed struck with unease, unnerved by the fact that he was unable to accomplish his job.

'I shall wait to be summoned,' he said, with a courageous smile, and put out a hand to touch Viola's hair.

When he had gone, Viola reluctantly went to the bedroom. She knew the turmoil that awaited her: unpacked suitcases all over the floor, rolls of wallpaper waiting to be hung, stacks of pictures, unmade bed. She knew she should begin to establish some kind of order, but felt drained of energy. All she wanted was to shut her eyes and slowly, luxuriously, relive every moment of the week in Norfolk.

The room faced north. Despite the sun of the day, no warmth had reached it. In her thin dress Viola shivered. She sat on the cold, crumpled sheets of the bed and after a long time, listening to the absolute silence, feeling the weight of her body, she picked up the letter from Harry Antlers that had been waiting for her.

My beloved Viola, she read, *What are you doing to us? Can you really want to lacerate a man's heart so cruelly? Can you not understand the great love I have for you, and let me prove it to you? You resist, you scorn, you ignore : this surely must be out of innocence, because I cannot believe the creature I love would intentionally ruin a man's life. However, I have patience. I shall wait, for ever if necessary. Such love as I have is not concerned with time, but it cannot be scorned, or wasted. So know that I shall never give up. I am sorry you did not find that little diamond star acceptable : I shall relieve you of it soon. I am sorry they were not greater diamonds, but they will be one day. Hope you had a good time in Norfolk with your lover. Think of me. H.A.*

The old fear, almost quelled by the security of the week in Norfolk, shot back, dizzying. She felt a chill sweat, the stuff of her dress stuck icily to her back. She heard herself cry out loud, rending the silence of the darkening room. Such bleakness she had never known. She wondered where to turn.

Sated by quantities of good food at Hannah's hotel, and by her own generous provision, Harry was able to return to Sweden in reasonable calm. He was not a little intrigued by Hannah's apparent affection for him. Had Viola not existed, he reflected on several occasions, he might have been inclined to encourage her flattering desire. As it was, she was an agreeable vessel, and her infidelity would be useful ammunition some time in the future.

But the two lustful days with Hannah proved only a temporary antidote, inadequate balm to the real wounds of Harry's heart. Within a few hours of his return to Sweden, he had forgotten Hannah, was suffering again, more acutely than ever, from his love of Viola. His pain was further exacerbated by lack of filling food, and with no care for the standard of his work he hurried through the last days of filming. Sleepless nights were spent planning his next move. This was to be the taking back of the diamond star, as he had warned Viola in his last letter.

The week of agonizing in Sweden finally came to an end, and the evening Harry chose for his next visit to Viola he was in good spirits. In his absence the estate agents had found him a flat. It was not quite the exotic penthouse he had imagined, but at least it was at the top of a tower block in Notting Hill Gate, with large windows and a fine view. It was in good order, merely needing repainting. Harry had hopes that Viola would be tempted by such a place, would willingly leave the gloom of the great house in Holland Park. So, he felt, he would be bringing good news, which would mean an auspicious start. Also, she would be touched that he intended to take back the diamond star in response to her wish. This, surely she would feel, showed dignity and understanding.

Harry spent an unusually long time preparing himself, rejecting all his man-made fibre shirts for the only one of pure cotton. Then he set about his normal method of inducing some semblance of calm: a four-course dinner in an Italian restaurant. The fact that Viola might be out had not come into his calculations. Instinct told him he would find her. With great hope of a rewarding evening, at last, Harry set off for Holland Park, stomach bulging.

He climbed the aristocratic flight of steps. The front door opened before he reached the top. A man stood there, carrying a briefcase. Of indeterminate appearance – in a seizure of suspicious fury Harry tried to imprint the lover's features on his mind, but they slipped from him even as he looked – the man was grey-skinned and anxious looking. Harry reached the top step, heart pounding.

'Ah,' he said.

'Were you coming in?' asked the man, hand on the vast gold door knob, clutching it as if for support.

'I was,' said Harry. 'Were you going out?'

Edwin licked his dry, grey lips.

'I was,' he said eventually. 'But in fact I've forgotten a couple of books, so I'm returning to the library for a moment.'

'Ah,' said Harry again.

He followed the lover inside, noting the odious width of his shoulders, the salmon pink polyester of his shirt. Viola's love for this creep must be quite blind to accept *that*. Harry would remember it, should it be necessary, to taunt her.

The two men stood in the dim speckled light of the hall weighing their mutual antipathy. It was an occasion that called for politeness above all else, Edwin thought. The hideous chap beside him, plainly deprived of public school good manners, should be treated courteously for Viola's sake.

'Are you looking for Viola?' he offered.

'I am.'

'I believe you'll find her in her flat at the top of the house.'

So *that* was it. Viola already had a penthouse – in Harry's estimation any top-floor flat was a penthouse – Goddamn the spoilt little bitch. And where would that leave his plans?

'She's waiting for me,' he managed to say. 'I'll go on up.'

He took a clumsy leap up the first two stairs, with an air of one familiar with grand staircases. In fact he was obliged to clutch at the mahogany balustrade to prevent himself from falling. Recovered, he sped on up three flights, the thick-piled alien carpet a deterrent to his impatient feet. The familiar sensation of a million pins piercing his veins was almost intolerable. He felt Edwin's scornful little eyes upon him. Indeed, Edwin's scornful eyes did follow Harry till he was out of sight. Then he made his own slower way to the library.

When the stairs ended at last, Harry found an ordinary door – there seemed to be an economy of mahogany towards the top of the house – half open. He paused, breathing noisily. He found himself to be hot, sweating, smelling. His plans, together with his intentions to present a calm and loving front, jeered through his head in tatters. The confrontation with the lover – dreadful, prying face of a medical man, he had – had quite unnerved him. His whole being seethed with outrage and self-pity.

But somewhere in the maelstrom of his despair a small voice of reason could be heard. Now, more than ever, Harry knew, it was essential he should contain himself. He must diffuse the wildness within, dwell on the moment later. If he was to win the heart of his beloved Viola, he should appear a rational man. He must pause and strive.

Sitting on the top stair, plump thighs supporting arms and head, Harry made the effort of a lifetime. Eyes shut, he willed pictures of tranquillity to flower in the darkness: slow clouds in a dull sky, grey rocking sea, a tablecloth of muted checks he had loved as a child – he remembered the comfort of twisting its soft stuff between his fingers. Music would have helped. Harry summoned Beethoven's Seventh to his ears, but the imagined notes were no match for the real sound of his own breathing.

Gradually, the sweat on his body dried, though the smell remained pungent. Cold, now, he opened his eyes. He had no idea for how long he had fought his battle. Time had been immeasurable. Harry stood, calm. The effort had succeeded.

He tiptoed through the door. Within the flat, he found himself in a narrow passage of bare boards. At the end of the passage was an open door. Harry crept towards it.

Peering into the room he saw Viola, back to him, kneeling on the floor turning the pages of a leather-bound photograph album. There were others in a pile beside her, open. The wall to her left was entirely taken up with newly painted bookshelves, half filled with books, ornaments, glasses, and two bottles of wine. There was also a large photograph of a handsome elderly couple in sporting hats. They smiled from an expensive frame. Parents, no doubt. (Extraordinary idea, displaying a photograph of parents.) The room, like the passage, was uncarpeted. The wall opposite the bookshelves was painted the kind of arrogant scarlet that evoked Harry's instant hostility, but he fought to control this reaction. The other two walls were as yet unpainted, though pots of scarlet paint on the floor indicated the end of their naked plaster state was imminent. There was no furniture, just two tea chests of objects wrapped in newspaper. No curtains in the single wide window. The darkening sun flared through Viola's hair, making it translucent as the fluff of dandelions.

'Hello, beloved lady,' said Harry, at last.

Viola's body snapped round to face him. Her beautiful mouth split into a hideous scream. She clutched at her ears through her hair, swaying. Harry felt himself smiling, seeing her as if through a sheet of protective glass. He squatted on the floor beside her. As he did so, he heard the rip of material: the zip of his flies had broken. Glancing down, he saw a tuft of white shirt protruding.

When the horrible noise of Viola's scream had subsided, Harry eased himself into a more comfortable position on the floor. He was not shaped for sitting happily on floors, and in this position he was at a disadvantage. He moved to support himself against the bookshelves, thus freeing his hands to try to disguise the gaping of his trousers. As usual, everything had conspired against him, but for the moment, adrenalin pulsing happily through his veins, he was in command of the situation.

'Calm down, beautiful Viola,' he said. 'I'm sorry if I should have taken you by surprise. I came merely to relieve you of the diamond star, as you requested. I'm sorry if it's been a burden to you.'

He could see Viola's heart pounding beneath the gossamer cotton of her jersey. He gripped his hands more tightly to prevent himself crushing the fearful creature to him. That would ruin everything.

Viola reached up to the bookshelves, took the small box with a shaking hand. She handed it to Harry.

'Now will you go?' she asked quietly.

'Thank you.'

Harry put the box in the pocket of his jacket with one hand, leaving the other to guard the split in his trousers. But the small exertion, combined with the strain of taut stomach against waistband, was fatal: the single hook upon which the sole responsibility of keeping the trousers together now lay, snapped. Viola's eyes joined Harry's in falling to the general disarray of flesh and sprouting shirt. Viola had the grace to smile. Harry, relieved, gave a grim laugh, patting and tugging to no good effect.

'Just my luck,' he said.

He realized that in some peculiar way this inauspicious happening had brought Viola closer to him than he ever had been before. They were briefly joined in mirth. The joke dispelled the anger and the fear. Heavens, thought Harry, the gods act curiously: but they had given him an advantage he must surely take.

'I'll go,' he said. 'Of course I'll go. Who am I to stay, unwanted?'

'You're unreasonably persistent,' said Viola, lightly, 'considering you must know by now that pursuing me is hopeless.'

'Ah, but there you're wrong. It's not hopeless, and I've only just begun.' Harry, too, tried for lightness: he did not want to scare her with what might sound like threats. 'My aim, of course, you beautiful, beautiful creature, is to make you realize *your* love for me, which up to now you've been fighting against like a wild cat.' Viola gave a small laugh. 'That's so often how real love starts. A great fight against commitment, against acknowledgement. But you must know, in your heart of hearts, you're as inextricably bound to me as I am to you . . . That evening in Norfolk, before I went berserk and did everything wrong, you standing there by the fire in your bloody great kitchen – you wanted me as passionately as I wanted you. I could *feel* it. Why else do you suppose I persisted, was eventually driven to violence by your stubborn refusal to recognize . . .?'

He saw her eyes widen. He was going too fast, too far, but she was still gazing at him, curiously. He still had her sympathy – just.

'Dear God, my love. Here I am, desperately uncomfortable on this dreadful floor, trousers split, ridiculous . . . loving you with all my heart, asking you just to think a little of my plight. You try to be so heartless. But you aren't, you aren't.'

He put out a hand towards her. She shifted away. He returned it to its place on the trousers.

'I'm sorry,' Viola said, quite nicely, very practical. 'But you've got it all wrong. You misjudged everything. You believe something that's patently not true. I'm sorry if I've hurt you, tormented you, even, resisting you. But how can I make you see the truth? You're a prisoner of some sort of wild delusion. It'll go, it'll die. Honestly.'

Harry swallowed. Paused. 'It won't,' he said at last. 'And it's you who are mad, as you'll realize when all these absurd preliminaries are over and we're a happily married couple with four children. However, you must take your own time to understand yourself. I shall wait patiently, constantly, wishing you well with your pink-shirted doctor downstairs.' His first mistake. Viola's eyes hardened. 'Well, whoever he is. Perhaps the doctor is in Norfolk? I get muddled, so many lovers . . . But let's not speak of them. Let's concern ourselves with us.' He pronounced it *uz*.

Viola looked as if she had much to deny in response, but decided to resist. 'Please go now,' was all she answered. 'I can see nothing I can say will make any difference to you. But if you really love me as you say, then perhaps you'll be kind enough to leave me alone, as I want.'

Perhaps you'll be kind enough to leave me alone : the triteness of the phrase swatted at Harry's mind-shattering passion as if it was an annoying fly. Oh, she'd learn, the girl: she'd learn. Though if this kind of patience, the infinite gentleness of his manner this evening, achieved no response either, then perhaps he would have to rethink his strategy once again.

'Very well: I'm going,' Harry said.

The performance of rising to his feet Harry was not able to conduct with the dignity he would have liked. He had to try to keep his trousers together with one hand, while pushing himself up from the floor with the other. He found it intolerable that Viola, who had leapt up quickly in a single youthful movement, should be looking down on his struggle. Mocking, no doubt. Seeing him as a figure of ridicule. But as quickly as such thoughts about her came to him, they were dispelled by a firm hand holding his, pulling. With the politeness of her class, she was helping him, though the help meant no more than just that, of course. No one like the upper classes to help an enemy . . . And there he was, now, panting foolishly, but standing, very close to her, the sky almost dark behind her luminous hair, her huge eyes confronting him with the wary sightless look of the blind. The brief physical contact, Viola touching him for the first time, had further confused Harry Antlers. He felt the approach of sentimental tears, and in that weakened state took the risk of saying one thing further.

'Viola Windrush, if you are never to be mine, then there is little point in continuing my life. I ask you to remember that.'

'Rubbish,' he heard her say, gently. 'You should never make such foolish threats. Please.'

The sympathy in her voice – no mockery there, Harry could swear – was his undoing. He flung himself upon her, crashing his mouth down upon hers – a brief chink of teeth, he heard, before her screams. He felt her writhing, struggling, scratching, shouting for help, scotching instantly his loving desire. Rage slashed over him: he felt his hand squeezing Viola's cheek, its soft pulp flashing him a memory of summer peaches he had tortured as a child, to bring forth the trickle of sweet juice – except that the juice he could see was blood. Blood! Dear God, here he was near to killing . . . Could nothing make her understand the love that lived behind his rage? And why would his hands not obey him, signalling what he really felt? With a great effort he tried gently to wipe the tracks of blood from Viola's cheek, but he could tell by a flick of her head he was rough, hurting again.

Viola was trapped against the window. From Harry's arms, curved crab-like, she could not escape. Wanting to roar his love for her, some indistinguishable abuse spewed forth, alarming him. He hit her on the bleeding cheek, saw her sway, moaning, left, right, left, about to fall. Then she splayed her arms out behind her against the window to support herself, and was still. Also, silent. She looked at him from the eye that remained open. Blood dripped from the corner of the other one, making a scarlet gash down her cheek, falling to spot the white of her jersey.

Silence, silence. Room nearly dark. Viola an immobile

poster stuck to the window, spectral. The silence crashed in Harry Antlers' ears, increasing the darkness in his eyes. Wrenching up the trousers, which were fast sliding over his hips, he lumbered across the bare floor to the pots of paint, kicked them over each in turn. Fascinated, he watched scarlet snakes sprout across the floor. Then he barged back to the bookshelves, both hands deserting trousers while he picked up the photograph of the parents with their nice kind smiles. He threw it to the ground. There was a crash of glass, miniscule splinters flew across the dark floor boards, glow worms in brief flight. He heard an intake of breath from the unmoving Viola.

'Not that . . .' she whispered.

'I'll destroy you, and everything that's yours.' This was a thick cry Harry did not recognize as his own. By now his arms were full of books. He threw them about the room, watching them land like clumsy birds in the red paint, their pages sprawled pathetically.

Shouting obscenities, Harry threw books more wildly, with both hands. In his preoccupation, he did not notice that his trousers had slipped below his knees. He took a step. They slid to his ankles. They fell.

From the small stone pebble of her mind, whose one eye could see but hazily, Viola Windrush watched Harry Antlers grovelling on the floor. He was both weeping and moaning at the same time, tears and spittle joining in the deep runnels at the sides of his mouth. His words were slurred, barely understandable: something about begging and forgiveness and madness, and Viola's fault. He crawled backwards and forwards, an obscene monster baby, a caged and spent tiger, trousers twisted round his feet, flashes of appalling underpants beneath the drooping shirt.

Some infinitesimal part of Viola's mind registered that had she not been involved in this melodrama, she would be able to appreciate the black humour. Men in the depths of their wretchedness can be shockingly absurd. She was reminded – in halting thought that came in single words – of an amateur production of Shakespeare, in which a slain man had not been able to bring himself to die, rolling round and round the stage in an extravagance of last breaths. The audience had laughed. Viola stretched the tight line of her clenched mouth just a fraction, and tasted blood.

'Get up,' she managed to say. 'You're a horrible sight.'

She thought: why am I here? A sane woman, pinned to my own window, bleeding, silent, forced to watch so degrading a scene? And why do I feel nothing, nothing?

The weeping and crawling continued for another couple of lengths of the room. But then, like an actor whose part is over and who must gather himself for his bow, Harry Antlers stood up surprisingly fast, considering the state of his trousers. Viola shut her good eye against the sight of thuggish thigh and bandy calf. Harry held on to his trousers with one hand, blew his nose with the other.

'You can call the police, my love,' he said. 'It won't matter. This is the end.'

Viola, opening her eye as he spoke, and seeing his loathsome face greasy with tears, shut it again. Thus she only heard him shuffle from the room, down the passage, and bang the door behind him.

When he had gone, she lowered her arms from their place across the window, dead, bloodless things which felt huge as balloons. She made her way through the dark passage to the bathroom, switched on the light. In the small mirror above the basin she observed the damage to her face. She bathed her closed eye with a sponge of cold water, wiped away the blood. She told herself she must find the energy to go downstairs and telephone the police. But, leaving the bathroom, savage pain began to fill her head, and such deadly tiredness accosted her that it was a wonder she made it to the bedroom. There, she pulled off her clothes and fell on to the bed. Blackness absorbed her, instantly.

12

Two flights beneath Viola's flat, Edwin Hardley was suffering a perfectly horrible evening. He tried to convince himself that in his favourite chair with an article on the Prosperine hawk-moth in his hand, his thoughts could be deflected. But no such miracle occurred.

Three things were troubling him. The first – and this was the merest graze of anxiety on a skin thickened by available women – was that a nubile young painter was waiting for him in her flat for dinner, and she had no telephone. She would have to accept a note of apology next day.

Second, the man who Viola was apparently expecting, and of whom she had made no mention, had looked extremely undesirable. Well, the light in the hall had been very dim, fair enough – it would have been impossible to observe in detail. But Edwin had received a strong impression of squatness, ill-bred thickness, and unusual ugliness. Edwin himself, for instance, would not have been happy about meeting such a chap alone in an alleyway on a moonless night. An instinctive fear, on Viola's behalf, had fretted at his stomach. With no forethought he had told the lie about returning for a book. Now, on reflection, he knew he had made that decision with good reason.

The third worry was a nameless one. That is, pressed, Edwin *could* have put a name to it: but that would have been an ungentlemanly thought, an undignified confession even to himself. Especially, it seemed quite clear for the moment, as Viola and he were merely affectionate friends. All the same, fighting against the very *suggestion* that he could be . . . taken that way, made Edwin restless. He put down the dull book. Paced the room a while.

When the library clock struck eleven – which meant Viola's visitor had been with her an hour – and he had not been called upon for help or company, Edwin decided it was time to go.

This thought was quickly replaced by another one: that would be a most cowardly act. Villains struck at midnight – how could he ever forgive himself if he fled an hour before Viola needed him? No. He must stay, her protection.

The fearful novelty of the evening had put all thoughts of food from Edwin's mind. A drink, however, was another matter. As pictures of rape and violence upstairs multiplied in his mind, the thought of a drink became imperative. Edwin went quietly to the drawing room, fetched whisky and a glass, and returned to the comfort of his armchair. There, one ankle twirling, he drank three glasses of whisky with unnatural speed for so cautious and moderate a drinker. By the time the alcohol had reached the third or fourth stages of benign effect, and he was beginning to think there would be no harm in having a short nap, the library clock struck twelve.

At that very moment, as he had known he would, Edwin heard a muffled scream from upstairs. He leapt to his feet, ran a wild hand through his greasy hair. Courage, engendered by the whisky, so rampant within him only a moment before, now abandoned him with distressing speed. More screams, distinct this time. Edwin gave a small jump, muttering 'dearie me', clinging to the wing-back of the chair for support. His head was a bright haze. Then, merciful silence.

As Edwin looked about him, he perceived the library furniture and the hundreds of books in their shelves had taken on an unnerving life of their own. They floated hither and thither through Edwin's confused vision. He tried to anchor them back into their old positions with no success. They spun and danced about him, so that he was forced to hesitate a long time before taking a single step. But despite the disadvantages Edwin suffered, a firm and noble part of his mind deliberated with great determination: rescue Viola he must. Bold bodyguard, he. He thumped his own chest, a gesture he could not recall ever having made before in his life, and made himself smile.

After some time Edwin made his uncertain way to the door, bending and swaying to miss the objects that seemed to be hurling their way towards him. At last he reached the vast door, pulled it ajar, leaned heavily against it. Now he could hear, with sickening clarity, moans, screams, and the violent thuds of objects landing angrily. 'Dearie me,' Edwin whispered to himself once again, and recognized with extraordinary cool wisdom, considering the havoc of his head, the fact that he would never be able to leap upstairs and rescue poor Viola unless he allowed himself a short rest.

Somehow, he found his way back to the chair, sank into it. There, he urged himself to listen to the good reason which was pressing its way into his wretched head: a man should not interfere. That was definitely it. Interference could lead to terrible confusion and misunderstanding. After all, it was possible Viola was enjoying herself. Some girls, he had heard, liked a rowdy time, a bit of horseplay. Who was he to . . . ?

At which point the whisky obliterated the reason, and Edwin Hardley fell into a deep sleep.

The library clock woke him at four. Confused, stiff, with aching head and dry mouth, he looked at the empty bottle of whisky beside him. Then he fingered the empty glass, longing for water. After a while, the events of the night, and his own behaviour, came back to him. He moaned gently, protecting his eyes from the gash of grey in the sky, with a shaking hand. Remorse is powerful at dawn.

Edwin mustered all his strength. He stood, smoothing his rumpled hair and clothes, small tongues of anxiety lapping within him. Once more he went to the door – a less precarious journey this time – opened it, listened. Silence. He made his way to the kitchen, drank two glasses of water. Then, forcing back thoughts of what he might find, he crept upstairs to Viola's flat.

Its door was shut, but not locked. First, he went to the sitting-room. At the sight of the devastation – for a moment he thought the red paint to be blood – he gave an anguished cry and ran to Viola's bedroom. He found her, in a dressing-gown that seemed to have been pulled on carelessly, lying on the bed. Flinging himself down beside her, Edwin opened her folded arms and pressed his head to her heart. It was beating firmly. Weak with relief, he stared down at her pale profile – head on one side, the other side buried in the pillow. She seemed, thank God, not to be harmed. Gently, he made to return her arms to their former position. But they resisted, then rose up: Viola's hands were on his shoulders. Her visible eye opened.

'Hello,' she said. 'I'm sorry, I don't look too good, do I?' She spoke thickly, like one emerging from an anaesthetic.

'What nonsense you talk,' whispered Edwin. Suddenly he cared no more about the violent activities Viola and her lover had been engaged in. In the dim light she did not appear ravaged, but beautiful. And now she was alone, warm: it was his turn. After all, he needed her to assuage the terrible night she had caused him. He pulled up the blankets.

Viola, shifting through pain and sleep, recognized a pallid light in the window, the soft voice of Hardly There. Some time later she felt a new warmth, of blankets, limbs, flesh. She was dimly aware of a faint struggle with clothes, a soft hand on her hair, and on her brow, the friendly voice saying 'There, there,' over and over again. She was just conscious of a slight, surprising sensation, not altogether disagreeable: the merest hovering above her, it seemed, before the weight rolled away.

Then, never having been fully woken by the fluttering of Edwin Hardley, Viola returned to a dreamless sleep.

When Harry Antlers emerged from the house in Holland Park, the warmth of the night was gentle upon him, evaporating the last of the mingled sweat and tears on his face. He felt calm, sane, exhilarated. Despite the exertions of the last few hours he was full of energy, and knew that sleep would be impossible.

He drove to a telephone kiosk, found Annie Light's number in his diary. The process of telephoning her was an awkward one, conducted with one hand, while the other secured his trousers. She took a long time to answer. Then, her voice was confused with sleep.

'This is Harry Antlers. You know, Harry Antlers I'm coming round to see you.'

Annie gave a small squeak of gratitude and told him her address. She was in bed, she explained.

'Stay there,' ordered Harry. 'That's just where I want you.'

Ten minutes later, clutching his trousers with both hands, Harry barged up the scurvy path that led to an uncared for terraced house similar to the one which he was shortly to leave. He found the front door ajar, pushed it open. Annie was waiting behind it in her nightdress. There were no lights. The hall smelt of wet cat and boiled fish, familiar smells. Annie, a dim blade of whiteness in the dark, put a trembling hand on Harry's arm.

'Good thing me mum's working nights, this week,' she whispered. 'Dad won't hear a thing. He's out cold, as usual.'

Harry was in no mood for conversation. This was not the time for explanations, or the nicety of preliminaries.

'Upstairs,' he grunted.

Because Annie refused to put on the light, Harry was spared details of her room. The darkness also concealed the rumpus of his shirt and trousers, and sight of her greasy hair and ratty face. He was aware of a hard, narrow bed that smelt of cheap scent. Annie, in his arms, was rigid with some imbecile love for him, muttering how she'd thought of him day and night, idiotic declarations of passion straight from the pages of a romantic novel. Briefly amazed that he had had so powerful an effect in such a short meeting, Harry told her to shut up: he wanted to get on with it. She eagerly complied.

Harry crashed through Annie, thinking only of Viola, her shut and swollen eye, bemused face, scarlet blood on white jersey, arms outstretched against the London sky. Annie's stupid moans of ecstasy spurred him to put on his jacket very quickly once it was all over. (The sweaty shirt he had not bothered to remove.) Her pleas for him to remain a while were of no avail. His business finished, Harry's only thought was to leave as soon as possible. The activities of the night had made him ravenous.

'I'll be in touch, one day,' he snarled, and left the ravaged girl to make sense of things in the dark.

Harry's next stop was at an all-night cafe in Shepherds Bush. There, he ordered three eggs on toast, bacon, sausages, tomatoes, several cups of tea. The food acted as a quick restorative, filling aching caverns that had made a honeycomb of his body. By four o'clock, dawn sky silvering pearls of condensation on the cafe window, revenge was sweet within him. To celebrate his new idea, Harry ordered a fourth cup of tea and two currant buns.

Viola woke at midday. Getting up was a slow and painful business. Having confronted the horrible sight of her face in the bathroom mirror, and dabbed her bruises with witch hazel, she forced herself to assess the havoc of the sitting room. There, she knelt on the floor slashed with scarlet paint, fingering the contorted shapes of her books. She did not think of returning them to their shelves. Then she picked up the smashed picture of her parents. The glass was a web of cracks – she traced a finger over them – but the photograph itself was little damaged. She replaced it on the floor. Later, she would set about putting the room in order. For the moment, she had no energy.

Viola left the brightness of her flat for the duskier regions of her uncle's quarters. Grateful she had somewhere with no memories of the night to go, she made herself a cup of black coffee in his kitchen, took it to the soothing browns and greys of the drawing room. She ensconced herself in the depths of a velvet chair by the window, the telephone on a small table beside her. In a moment she would ring the police. In the meantime, she concentrated on the pattern of sycamore leaves outside the window, dull green against a dull sky. An hour or so went by. She ached against the cushions. She may have dozed.

Then Edwin Hardley was beside her: he must have crept so quietly over the carpets she had not heard him enter. His face was stricken, a look Viola recognized when he spoke of the ladies who hunted him. He was crouched on the floor beside her, clutching her hand. He seemed to be in a state of much anguish.

'What's the matter?' she asked.

'Matter?' he cried. 'Dear God, what's the matter with *you*?'

Viola fingered her closed eyes. She essayed a small smile.

'Slight disagreement with a hunter,' she said.

'But, last night – well, I suppose it was more like dawn this morning, I came up to you, found you asleep . . . Didn't you hear me?'

Viola frowned: dim memory of some vague visitation. Edwin, troubled, had blushed.

'You were on your side,' he went on. 'I can only have seen the unharmed side. Oh my God. Let me ring a doctor.'

It was then Viola remembered she would be seeing a doctor tonight: Richard was coming to take her out. She gave a small moan.

'I'm all right,' she said. 'No need for a doctor. It's only bruises and a headache. I'm filled with aspirin and I've bathed the eye. Sorry I look so awful. Perhaps you could buy me an eye patch when you next go out?'

'Oh Christ. This is unbelievable. Of course, an eye patch . . . I'll go in a moment, and get us something for lunch. But please let me call a doctor.'

'No.'

'The police, then.'

'I'll call the police this afternoon.'

In truth, Viola knew it was unlikely she would do so. The thought of being questioned, of involving the law, and the publicity of a traumatic court case were more than she could bear to think about.

'What happened?' Edwin was on the window seat now, legs crossed, an ankle twirling. Viola shrugged.

'It's quite hard to remember, at this moment, exactly what did happen. Some form of dispute got out of hand, obviously. But what gave you the idea of visiting me at dawn?'

'We-ll. I met this . . . *man* on the doorstep. He looked a bit menacing.'

'*That's* how he got in.'

'He said you were expecting him, so who was I to detain him?'

'Quite.'

'Anyhow, at the risk of interfering, I had some funny instinct I should stay. I didn't like the thought of you being alone in the house with him. So I returned to the library for the evening.'

'That was very kind.'

'Not of much use, in the event. Sleep, unfortunately, overtook me.'

Viola smiled. 'You didn't hear anything?'

'Well, I'm bound to say I did. A few thumps and cries. But then I thought perhaps . . . well, you know. You might have been enjoying yourselves. People have their different tastes, don't they?' Edwin had blushed again. 'I was about to go home when I heard the front door slam. So I crept up, just to make sure you were all right. I'm sorry if I . . . I had no idea. I mean, your bruises were turned away from me. It was scarcely light.' He paused. 'I'm sorry if I woke you.'

'You hardly did.'

They both smiled at the joke, looking at each other for a long time. Viola was struggling to remember. Then Edwin leapt up, patted her hair. In the grey summery light, muted further by the shadows of the room, he looked exhausted.

'Now, you just stay there,' he said. 'I'm off to buy lotions and potions and eye patches and lunch. We're going to have a picnic lunch, right here.' Again he patted her hair, kissed her very gently on the nose. 'And then you might find yourself doing a little explaining. I think there are probably some things that will have to be sorted out. We can't have any more such . . . carryings on, can we?'

'You're very kind,' Viola said again. She was grateful and tired, glad of Edwin's protection.

'I hope you'll forgive . . .' he added quietly.

'For what?' murmured Viola, fighting against sleep.

Later, Edwin woke her with a tray of lunch. They ate smoked trout and ice cream, and drank a bottle of iced white wine. Sitting on the floor, Edwin told funny stories about the gathering of moth men he had attended last week. Viola found herself laughing. Dear Edwin: spindly on the carpet, the mildest of gladiators, the most charming of companions when safe from pursuit by desperate women. She liked him. She was glad he was there.

Lulled by the wine, Viola dozed most of the afternoon in the warmth of the armchair. Her only struggle was to keep at bay pictures of the evening before. At five she was woken by the telephone. It was Gideon in New York.

'Violetta? You all right?'

Viola paused, decided a transatlantic telephone call was no place for explanations. Besides, he sounded exuberant.

'Fine,' she said.

'Good news. I'm coming home. The return here hasn't worked out too well. I've just got to wind up a few business things, then I'll be with you.'

'Will you be alone?'

'Absolutely. I'm afraid we reached a crisis point. I had to tell Hannah I no longer – '

'Good.'

'Quite. Hope you'll be able to spare a few days in Norfolk while I sort myself out?'

'Of course. In fact I'm going there for a few days next week, when the flat is finished,' said Viola, making up the plan as she went along. 'Catch a few more days of summer before I get a job.'

'You might look up Maisie,' said Gideon. 'She'd like to see you.'

'I will. I'll tell her the good news.'

Gideon's turn to pause. 'She already knows, matter of fact,' he said.

'Oh?'

Viola sat up in surprise. But there was no time for further questions. Elated by her brother's news – something to look forward to once Richard's visit was over – she returned to her flat, for once not regretting the lost day. She began to prepare herself as best she could for the evening.

Heavy from his enormous breakfast, still clutching at his trousers, Harry Antlers left the café at six in the morning. The ebullience of a few hours earlier had left him. A profound wretchedness seeped through the cushion of food in his stomach. He no longer cared, as he shuffled ungainly down the street to his car, how foolish he must look.

An early sun, sharp-edged, rose in the sky above the buildings of Shepherds Bush. Still the watery colour of a moon, it hurt Harry's eyes. He cursed summer, light mornings, the general brightness of the world. To add to his pains, city sparrows, perky little bastards, were tweaking about the place as if auditioning for a Disney film. Their ghastly cheerfulness and piercing squawks damaged Harry's ears. He longed for silence, dark, the oblivion of sleep. But sleep, he knew, even now, would not be forthcoming.

When eventually he opened his front door, he was greeted with a smell so vile that he was forced to bury his nose in his handkerchief. It occurred to him, on his melancholy way upstairs, the innards destined for the cat that he had cast upon the floor had never been removed. The smell had insinuated itself into his flat, too: quite definite, today, whereas yesterday it had been a mere hint of the stench to come. Unwelcoming though this homecoming was, therefore, the idea of clearing up putrefied lights after such a terrible night turned the lump of Harry's breakfast into an alarming swill. He felt tears returning, his trousers falling again. Locking himself into the bathroom, he lit the Ascot heater, whose whistling gas flame was the only friendly sound he had heard in the last twenty-four hours. Next, in something of a frenzy, he dabbed his bottle of Jungle Man Aftershave on every available soft surface: towel, bathmat, candlewick lavatory seat cover, and simulated silk dressing-gown that hung on the back of the door. He then relieved himself of the offending shirt and trousers, plummeted into the steaming bath. Rotten meat smell at last quite overpowered by Jungle Man, Harry was able to breathe deeply in relief. Gradually, the nausea subsided.

Some two hours later he was eating a second breakfast in an unsalubrious café off Oxford Street. He wondered if that vilest of bitches, his beloved Viola, was suffering due remorse. If she was tormented by imaginings of Harry hanging dead from his knotted socks, that was the least she deserved. More likely, in her accustomed and unfeeling way, she was sound asleep. Well, her luck was running out. Harry decided to reflect further upon those matters when his head was clearer: though God knows how he could be expected to get a good night's sleep among the smells of rotten meat and, he presumed, rotting peonies.

He spent the day with his film editor in a small, dark and airless room watching beautiful girls degrade themselves in indecent positions and he remembered, briefly, his skirmish with Annie Light. At least she loved him, poor wretch. Might be someone to fall back on, one day, if all else failed. As long as she never turned on the light he could probably keep fancying her in a purely salacious way.

Harry's unappealing film also reminded him of the money that had made it worthwhile: he decided to take a further look at his penthouse flat, later, and put in an offer. He could not bide his present quarters much longer. A sudden longing to be an admired man again came upon him. Fame had had its sweetness once: he longed for its return. He would work with his old energy, repeat his early success, earn a new fortune and give it all to Viola. The penthouse would be the first step towards his happy new life of riches and power. Soon, once more he would be a man so irresistible that even the obdurate Viola would be bound to succumb.

Harry was pleased by the second viewing of the flat. It seemed to have great potential.

'By the time I've painted the sitting room a fiery red,' he told the agent, 'every glossy magazine in the country will be clamouring to photograph it.'

'Why, I'm sure they will,' the agent agreed, impressed by so much confidence. With some excitement, Harry made his offer. By 5.30 it seemed reasonably sure the flat would be his.

That matter dealt with, next loomed the imminent problem of the long evening ahead. Very tired by now, Harry wanted only two things: a hamburger, and to be near Viola. He would like to catch a glimpse of her, make sure that her eye was not seriously damaged. He would like to ask her forgiveness once again: beg for one last chance.

Too weary to think with any clarity, Harry drove to Holland Park, stopped his car fifty yards from her house. He wrote her a short note, but the humble, loving tone he strove for was inexplicably lost in the writing. Having slipped it through the letter box, Harry decided he would sit in the car for a couple of hours, watching. Just in case. Just to be near her. Then, he would eat.

When Viola fell asleep after her second glass of wine, Edwin returned to the library. It was his intention to make up for the lack of morning's work, but he found himself beaten. Too many things conspired against him.

He sat at the round table, piled with books for comfort, and tried to take stock of the disparate matters jostling his weary brain. First – the only clear part – he was infinitely glad the assault upon Viola had not been more serious. Had she appeared worse, he would have insisted on sending for a doctor, whatever she said. As it was, her cuts and bruises were plainly superficial, though she would definitely have a black eye.

Next, the unknown assailant. The outrage Edwin felt about this mysterious man he had tried hard to disguise from Viola. It was not up to him to pass judgement on her friends and, strangely, Viola had conveyed no hard feelings against him. Perhaps she had been too shocked and tired. Edwin had tried to press her a little for some sort of explanation, but with no success. She had repeated she did not want to think about any of it for the moment, and naturally he had respected her wish. He had urged her, though, very strongly, to summon the police. You could not let such an assault go unreported, he said: for her future safety she must prosecute so dangerous a man. But again he had met resistance. In time, she had said, with a weariness of spirit he could well understand: in time.

It occurred to Edwin that he felt more fear on Viola's behalf than she felt for herself. The idea of the violent thug pursuing her further chilled his flesh. He himself lacked qualifications as a bodyguard. Besides, he could not spend night after night in this library, a sort of volunteer coastguard waiting for danger signals. When Viola was stronger, therefore, he would have to press her further to organize some sort of protection for herself and, indeed, for him.

The third worry was a great billowing mist that almost obscured all other thoughts, important though they were. It was a matter so delicate that Edwin strove not to put it into words. Yet, cruelly, the words pounded at him, tormenting.

Did Viola know, or not? Should he tell her? And if he did, how would she feel?

The unanswerable questions made him shake like a man beyond his years, while the stuffy, summer air of the library was cold on his hands. Worse, the particular questions led to more general ones, dragged from the darkest corners of his soul, a place he was never anxious to frequent. Could it be that, as the most conscientious and overworked lover in London, he might also be the most unremembered? Could it be that he was so much in demand simply because, due to his *lightness of touch*, as it were, girls, scarcely aware of his impact, asked him to return to make sure of his existence? Oh God, the thought. He cradled his head in his arms. The unfairness of the Creator: it was intolerable. For within him, he had always known, crouched the most robust of lovers. But this inner man was a most cowardly chap. Faced with reality, his inspiration would flee with cruel speed, leaving Edwin to his own feeble devices. These, he also knew, were no more than a kind of disappointed, disappointing hovering. Immemorable.

Always frightened of his own inadequacy, Edwin had begun his amorous pursuits at a late age. What he had lacked in quality of performance, he had made up for in quantity. Girls, girls, girls. Streaming through his life, shouting their love, so that many times he had almost convinced himself that he *was* that heroic inner man who had struggled to the surface. But he knew this was not true. He knew it would never be true, and that always he would have to go on searching, for ever finding disappointment. On this black afternoon, hating himself, the whole bleak state of the truth set before him, Edwin Hardley quietly wept.

He was disturbed at 6.30 by the front door bell. Instantly alert, he leapt up, scorning himself for the wasted afternoon. Viola had said nothing about an expected visitor this evening. She was upstairs, presumably asleep. Well, here was her bodyguard's chance. Tonight he would comport himself in more heroic manner: go down and deal swiftly with the violent maniac. For self-protection, he armed himself with a small brass poker.

On his way downstairs, Edwin was conscious of his thumping heart. He hurried, trying to ignore it. In the hall, he found a card on the doormat. Picking it up, he strained his eyes in the perennial dim light to read:

Beloved Viola, Forgive me if you can and think of me when I am no more. Ever yours. H.A.

That, thought Edwin, was the sort of melodramatic rubbish Viola was certainly not going to be allowed to see. He tore up the card, shoved it in his pocket. The bell rang again, making him jump. He clutched the poker, quite prepared to slug the brute across the face at the first glimmer of menace. Slowly, he opened the door.

A very agreeable looking man stood there, eager face,

slight smile, but worried lines round bright green eyes. Edwin let the poker drop by his side. The man, plainly well-mannered, pretended he had not observed Edwin's curious weapon.

'Am I at the right house for Viola Windrush?' he asked.

'Oh my goodness, you certainly are,' answered Edwin, very confused, and strangely nervous considering the gentleness of this new visitor. His mind snapped into a flashback of the evening before: the whole performance of the Entry of the Unknown Visitor once again, except that the nature of the visitor was very different.

'Do come in,' he heard himself saying. 'And go on up to the top floor. That's Viola's flat.'

'Thank you so much.'

When the stranger had climbed the first flight of stairs, Edwin, making a great effort, followed him, then made his way back to the library. It had been his intention to take out the young painter whom he had let down last night. But such weariness, such sickness of spirit came over him as he sank into an armchair, that he knew he would have to disappoint her once again. Strangely enfeebled, now that his intended valour had been thwarted, Edwin only wanted time in which to think. Viola would need no protection from this man, that was clear. But perhaps it would be wise to stay nearby, just for a while. He was puzzled she had said nothing about going out tonight, but then she was never one for revealing her plans. Unlike ninety per cent of the girls he knew, Viola was reticent in talking about herself. Dear, funny Viola. So pale . . .

Edwin himself felt considerably pale, too. He needed music to restore his tranquillity. He chose a record of a Schubert quartet, let the familiar sounds sponge over him, smoothing away all thought, leaving him a tired and empty husk, splayed out in the chair near his books. Thus began his second night of vigil.

Viola heard Richard running fast up the stairs. She met him in the passage, dark enough to conceal the shock of her face.

'Richard! Richard, listen. I warn you. I look a bit of a mess.'

Richard had kissed her on her unharmed cheek. His eyes had now grown accustomed to the dim light. He saw the eye patch, pushed Viola almost roughly from him, pulled it off.

'What on earth has been happening? What have you done? Quick: let's go to the light.'

They hurried to the sitting room, still strewn with collapsed books, upset tins of paint. At the window, severely professional, Richard observed the swollen eye. He touched it gently.

'Violetta . . .' Frowning, his eyes danced round the room. 'I'll be back in a minute. I'm going to get my things. That eye needs bathing. I've something in the car that'll help till we get to a chemist.'

He was gone. Viola touched her own face with cautious fingers. She thought about how this first evening in London with Richard should have been: herself waiting prettily for him, drinks ready, flat in some order if things had gone to plan, hours of pleasure ahead. As it was, she felt suddenly weak, shaky. She would have to muster all her strength to sit through *Hamlet* and dinner: a poor companion for the one for whom she most wanted to be otherwise.

Harry Antlers, from his concealed position, had seen a car with a doctor's sign draw up at Viola's house. He had watched the doctor, a well-dressed looking bastard, obviously one of those millionaires from Harley Street, ring the bell. There had been a long pause, and then another ring, before the door opened. Presumably Viola had taken some time coming downstairs. That meant, at least, she was not confined to bed. Harry had strained to see her as the door opened, but caught no glimpse. He decided to wait till the doctor left, in case he could catch sight of her then.

A short time after the doctor's entry, Harry observed him scurrying back down the steps very fast, leaving the front door open behind him. He had the look of a very worried man. It was also a fierce look, as far as Harry could tell from such a distance, as if the doctor had some cause to be angry as well as concerned. He snatched a medical bag from his car and hurried back up the front steps, slamming the door impatiently behind him.

It was then the truth came blindingly to Harry. Viola was

gravely ill. Although it was all her fault, he, Harry, was responsible.

He started the engine. There was no point in sitting here any longer. The only thing he could do now was to go back to his vile flat and carry out the idle threat he had written on the card. He had a large supply of sleeping pills. If he did not stop to think, it should not be too difficult a process.

Dreading the smell that would greet him more than the act he was almost determined to commit, Harry let himself into his deceased landlady's house once again. It took him some moments to take in the magical transformation that had taken place in his absence.

For a start, there was no more smell. Harry sniffed several times, to make quite sure. Rather, there *was* a smell, but a new one: disinfectant. Curious, incredulous, Harry went to Marjorie Wittle's kitchen, peeped in. It was in a state he had never seen it before: pristine, with shining surfaces and polished floor. No sign of meat or flowers.

Wonderfully confused, but also fearing that this was some mad hallucination brought on by lack of sleep, Harry made his way upstairs. He noticed the thick drifts of dust, lodged for so many months on the scrawny carpet, had disappeared. His bathroom and kitchen were both equally clean and tidy, though there was still a faint trace of Jungle Man in the air. Shaking with disbelief – this surely was some trick of the mind sent to punish him – Harry went finally to his sitting room. Again, a room transformed. And there, on the table in the window, was a plastic cup holding three wallflowers. Propped up beside it was a note. Harry snatched it up, read wildly.

Dear Harry, My mum gave me Aunt Marjorie's key and sent me round to tidy up a bit. She said the agents wouldn't like it all dusty. Was it in a mess! I did my best. I hope the smell has gone. I took the liberty of doing your rooms too. Hope you don't mind. Thank you for the most wonderful night of my life. Please let there be others. I love you. Annie Light.

Harry read the note several times. As he did so, the shadow of death seemed to evaporate. Some stubborn new hope descended upon him: this had been an act of God, physically carried out by a girl, showing him the way. After a large dinner and a good night's sleep in a sweet-smelling room, Harry would go forth with new heart. In the end – he knew not how, precisely, at this moment – he would win his Viola, and they would spend the rest of their days in peace. Meantime, he would choose himself an expensive French restaurant . . .

Harry let the pleasure of such plans for himself sink in for a while, then his thoughts turned perfunctorily to Annie Light. In a way, he supposed, it could be said she had saved his life. He had to be grateful for that. And there was no doubt she loved him. Poor lady: even if Viola had not existed, he could never return that love. A ratty girl with silly hopes. Still, he would not abandon her completely, just yet. Annie Light, he felt, might one day have her uses.

Richard bathed Viola's eye, insisted she swallow a pill. Viola did not enquire what it was. But on the way to the theatre she felt her limbs begin to relax, though her head still throbbed. After the play they had a simple, one-course dinner at the Savoy Grill. Feeling stronger, Viola found herself telling the whole story of Harry Antlers' pursuit, and the climax last night. She also told him of Gideon's plan to return home for good, of which Richard approved strongly. He judged it not the time to make any comment on her predicament. When her tale was over he talked lightly of their week in Norfolk, which already felt long past, and told amusing stories of one of his oldest patients who refused to die.

When they returned to the flat, well before midnight, Richard insisted Viola should go straight to bed. While she did so, he said, he would clear up her books, replace them in the shelves. Otherwise their spines would be damaged beyond repair.

Viola obeyed quite readily. Once in bed, propped up among the pillows, she felt much better. She called Richard. He appeared with a glass of whisky for himself, water for Viola. He gave her two more pills.

'They'll help you sleep,' he said. 'I'll leave some more, too, for the next few nights.'

'Thank you.'

Once again, Viola obeyed without protest, swallowing the pills with a gulp of water. She would have done anything in the world Richard wanted. She wondered if he had any notion of her compliancy.

Richard sat on the bed. His look was grave.

'It's now my duty, Violetta,' he said, 'to give you some professional advice. Something has got to be done about the activities of this maniac before he does any worse damage. What are your plans?'

'None, just at the moment. I did intend to ring the police this afternoon, but somehow I hadn't the energy . . . all it would involve.'

'Dear, silly girl, you should have rung them the moment he went last night. Having left it so late, they won't be much interested. They won't regard it as a very serious matter if you let so much time elapse before reporting it.'

'No, I suppose not.'

'You must get on to your solicitor in the morning, go and see him. You must get an injunction taken out against Mr Antlers. He must never be allowed near you again.'

'All right.'

'Are you taking in what I'm saying?'

'I think so.'

'Because it's very important. You must understand, you're the victim of a man's obsession: a man whose mind is severely disturbed. I've known several similar cases. In each one, the victim has always tried to be rational, relied on the aggressor's reason prevailing in the end. But you see, that's not how it works. Do you understand? Common sense, logic, rational dealings, are not the answer for one whose mind is disturbed. Heavens, I of all people ought to know, oughtn't I? No, they need help. And meanwhile, it's imperative you have some form of protection, Violetta. I don't like the idea of your being here all alone, vulnerable. A man obsessed overcomes all barriers. He could easily get in. I think you should come home for a while, till your eye has recovered. Besides, you're probably suffering from shock, you know. You need a few quiet days.' He paused. 'You need to feel utterly safe. Alfred would, of course, guard you well. If you liked, I could move in for a few days, too. Make sure you were all right.'

For the first time since her attack, Viola was near to tears. She felt her mouth twitching in her fight for control.

'Thank you,' she said. 'But let me think about it. My plan was to finish everything here – just a matter of a few days, despite the setback in the sitting-room – then I was going to go home and get things ready for Gideon, anyway.'

'Why don't you let me drive you back tomorrow?'

Viola shook her head. 'I can't, really. It's very sweet of you. But I'll come soon, I promise.'

'You're being dreadfully stubborn.'

'I'm sorry.'

'*Please* . . .'

'No. I refuse to allow him to interrupt my plans.'

'Then you must make me one promise.' Richard sighed. 'If this bastard ever threatens you again, in any way whatsoever, you must let me know *at once*. I shall come immediately, and deal with him myself.'

'I promise. Absolutely.'

'Wish I wasn't so far away.'

'Wish you weren't, too.'

There was a very long silence between them. Richard finished his drink. Then he took Viola's hand.

'Violetta, let me ask you one more thing, impertinent though it may be. Are you, in any way at all, attracted to this man?'

Viola's visible eye, beginning to droop with the sleepiness that was descending, widened in shock at the suggestion. She managed to smile.

'Are you mad? You should see him. He's totally abhorrent. He fills me with a deep revulsion I've never felt for anyone in my life before.'

'Has he no charm, no endearing ways, whatsoever?'

Viola thought hard.

'I suppose he might have for some. His bulldozing ways, his wild passion and energy. But not for me.'

'And you've never done anything to encourage him?'

'Not knowingly. In the very beginning, in New York, I agreed to help him with his play. I was flattered he should ask, I suppose, and foolishly agreed without really thinking. Later, I retracted my offer, of course. He considered that my first betrayal. Since then, I've done nothing, nothing, but beg him to leave me alone and try to convince him his feelings are totally unreciprocated. He seems to think it's only a matter of *time*, till I come round to realizing the *truth* – which is: did I but know it, I love him as much as he loves me. In that way,' Viola went on, 'he's very good at making me feel as if *I'm* the one who's mad. Last night, for instance, at one point I began to doubt my own sanity. Perhaps I was deluding myself, after all, I thought. Perhaps he knew something I didn't, and I was being very dim, not seeing it. But then, watching him slobbering about the floor on all fours, I thought, No: *he's* the one out of his mind. Surely. But it was an unnerving moment.'

'The great art of the expert bully is to make his victim feel guilty of madness,' said Richard. 'I've seen it often.'

'I have to admit,' went on Viola, feeling the relief of being able to tell Richard everything, and wanting to say just a little more before she fell asleep, 'I don't attack him back. I try to be calm, polite. Perhaps you could call that encouragement. I did scream in fear when he first turned up last night, but then I controlled myself. I've no doubt he's able to see how frightened he makes me. Perhaps that urges him on.'

'The coward's spur,' said Richard. He was still holding her hand.

'Well, he's caused me to live in daily fear. Isn't that silly? I never imagined a time would come when I would wake up every day dreading the hours ahead. Nothing can ever quite put that fear out of my mind, not even that lovely, protected week in Norfolk.'

'So I observed.'

'Did you? I imagined I looked very happy and cheerful.'

'You did, in a way.'

'Well, now, you know what? Now more than anything in the world I long for peace. I long to wake up in the morning unafraid of the day. Unthreatened peace would be the greatest luxury I can think of. I wouldn't even mind a boring life so long as I was unafraid.' She sniffed. 'Oh, heavens, Richard. I've gone on and on. I'm so sorry. And I can't say any more. I'm falling asleep.'

'Good. I'm going to leave you now. I'll ring you tomorrow evening, make sure you're all right.'

'Thank you. And for this evening. I'm sorry I wasn't . . .'
'Goodnight, my love.'

Richard kissed her good cheek. He stood up, looked down upon her until he was quite sure she slept. Then he left the room, closing the door, and began the long descent downstairs.

Edwin Hardley, strangely restless despite the hours of music, heard Viola and her friend returning. An hour later, he heard the friend depart. Relief, exhaustion.

Slumped in the armchair, the fact was Edwin had had a most exhausting evening. He had not even dared to revive himself with a drink, for fear of repeating last night's shameful performance. While he had managed to put the searing thoughts of the afternoon aside – other, more *local* speculations had come upon him in their droves.

Viola, it seemed, was their cause. Imagining her dining in some superior restaurant (by heavens, he would take her somewhere better next time) with her well-dressed friend, the question had suddenly struck him: do I love her? Or if I do not love, is this not an uncommon devotion, or affection, that might well be confused with love?

Love had been an elusive thing in Edwin's life, always one woman away. Never having experienced its sureties, he could not be quite sure how to gauge its tricks. There had been moments when he had liked to think *this* was it, here he was, feeling heady as millions of others. But no sooner than he had analysed any such delight, slippery as a worm the conviction slipped from him, leaving him alone with his broken vision. What's more, he had on occasions felt the faintest twinklings of unease – nothing greater than that – at the thought of others dallying with his girls: but last night was certainly the first time in his life he had felt . . . Even to himself he could not spell out the loathsome word. So maybe Viola had touched some part of his psyche previously undiscovered.

Edwin shuddered at the thought. For all about him those who pledged their hearts were forced to change their selfish single lives, and that was usually a disaster. Edwin tried hard to imagine changing his own life for Viola. Sharing a small flat with her, for instance. Having to move some of his books out of her way. Meeting her friends. Being forced to accompany her occasionally to forlorn parts of the countryside, that seemed to mean so much to her. Agree to children . . . God forbid. No: it was all a preposterous idea, brought about by lack of sleep. And yet, what was this unaccustomed restlessness, that even music and his beloved moths could not seem to calm?

When Edwin heard Viola's friend depart, he decided it was time for him, too, to go home, try to catch up on all the lost sleep. He was confused to find himself, therefore, creeping upstairs rather than down. Fascinated by the force within him in whose command he seemed to be, in detached manner he watched himself creep into Viola's flat, open the door of her bedroom, move to her bed.

By the light of the full moon he was able to look at her beautiful face lying back on the pillow, hair awry, poor swollen eye a blackish colour. She breathed deeply. Edwin's eyes went to the bottle of sleeping pills beside her bed. The idea came to him that he could slip in beside her without disturbing her. There, head on her breast, he could sleep for hours. Once again, she might never know.

But even as he reflected, the foolishness of his plan rasped through Edwin. He was a gentleman, after all. Gentlemen do not take such unfair advantages or unwise risks more than once. With regret, he would leave her sleeping. He left her room.

His secret visit, unfortunately, had done nothing to calm his blood. Sadly, by the light over the front door, Edwin found himself scanning his address book. There were girls all over London longing for nocturnal visits. The problem was merely one of choice. When considering the recipient of his tired state, he had to choose one who would be full of sympathy, and not likely to make too many demands.

His finger paused at an address not far from Holland Park. Edwin hailed a taxi, wondering at the fickleness of man, and continued on his way.

13

Though not for one moment did Alfred Baxter cease to appreciate his good fortune in working for Viola Windrush, the week after she and her brother left he found something of an anti-climax. The comings and goings engendered by their visit, the laughter, the carefully prepared meals, the frequent appreciation of all his work in the garden, had been a constant pleasure. Their apparent happiness, thought Alfred, had brushed off on to himself. Besides which, being kept so busy, there had been no time to dwell on the mystery of Eileen's elusive face, and the haunting voices of the girls were never heard again.

But alone once more, wife and girls returned in their strange forms. No matter how hard he worked in the garden, Eileen's face flew back and forth in Alfred's mind, a silent pendulum, taunting him with an expression he could have sworn he never knew when she was alive. This imagined face was pinched, mean, accusing. It did not smile. The eyes were unforgiving. It was filled with dislike.

Sometimes, Alfred thought it must be the heat that was affecting him. He would break off from his digging, sit on a bench in the shade of the limes, take off his cap and wipe his balding head with a large handkerchief. He would listen to the flutter of the leaves, and sniff the distant smell of sea. With some pride he would then let his eyes dally among the lovingly cared for herbaceous border, the massed white roses, the velvet-eyed pansies and starry pinks that edged the stone paths. He alone had rescued the garden, and the transformation gave him a satisfaction that could not be denied. But no matter how much he filled his eyes with flowers and leaves and sky, the unpleasant face of Eileen remained in his vision.

At the end of his day's work, she was replaced by the chatter of the girls. After his tea, once Alfred had retired to his chair in the sitting-room, hoping for a peaceful evening, they would begin their gossip. He could not make out exactly what they said, though sometimes odd sentences came to him so clearly that he would look round and be surprised to find himself still alone. It was the tone of the girls' talk that made him shiver: he had the distinct impression they were in some way against him, mocking – like Eileen, accusing. In fitful dreams, at night, they lined up in court and interrogated him. He could see they were shouting, but he could not hear the questions. When he was unable to answer, they laughed and jeered. Night after night Alfred woke up sweating and afraid. Dear God, he prayed, what did I do to them that they should punish me like this?

After a week of solitude, Alfred could bear evenings in his own sitting-room no longer. Instead, he took the liberty of passing the hours in the Windrushes' kitchen. There, he would drag up a chair to the fire, which he liked to light despite the warmth of the evenings, and read his paper or do his crossword puzzles. In peace. Merciful peace. No one followed him there, and by day Eileen's face was less persistent. Alfred felt the balance of his mind gradually returning.

One evening he came across a report in the local paper that Admiral Fanshawe, Maisie Fanshawe's father, had died. It gave the time and place of the funeral. Alfred, remembering the Fanshawes had been good customers in the old days, felt he would like to pay his last respects. He had not, by his own volition, taken a day off since he had been there, so he would feel no guilt in going to the funeral on Friday. He would like to say a word of condolence to Miss Maisie, who had been here recently. Yes, Admiral Fanshawe's funeral would make a pleasant outing.

On Friday morning Alfred went early into the garden and gathered a bunch of white roses. He was not much of a one with flowers once they were cut, but he managed to gather them into a reasonably tidy-looking spray. Eileen would have laughed at his effort, no doubt: but he was not ashamed, and the smell was wonderful. Alfred wrote a small card to accompany the flowers, and placed them in water while he dressed.

For the first time since the morning he left the shop, Alfred took out his navy serge suit and a plain cream shirt. He found the sad black tie that he had bought for Eileen's funeral, but nowhere could he lay hands on his old black bowler. This was a much-loved and well-worn hat, purchased when Alfred was made church warden forty years ago, brushed and used most Sundays since, until the sale of the shop. The hat had also accompanied Alfred on his many journeys with Eileen to cathedral cities. It had been respectfully taken off as they had entered some great portal, and put to rest on a chair beside him while Alfred prayed for strength to do his duty and love his neighbour. The fanfares of stone arches, flaring hundreds of feet above his head, always made Alfred feel strangely naked. He was glad when he could replace the hat once more, outside.

The loss of the bowler – in the move, Alfred supposed – was something of a shadow on the bright day. Luckily, inspiration came to him: in the many hats in the cloakroom, surely a suitable replacement could be found. In the circumstances, he felt, Colonel Windrush would have understood, and approved the loan. Alfred hurried off, found what he needed almost immediately – a most superior bowler, a size or so too big, perhaps, and in need of a good brush, but otherwise perfect.

With clean handkerchief sprightly in his pocket, white rose in his buttonhole and the Colonel's hat bobbing on his ears, Alfred set off in some excitement for the bus stop. He enjoyed the long wait in the sun, sniffing at his funeral spray, admiring the shine of his shoes, and the general feeling of wellbeing. He enjoyed the ride on the bus, the view of harvesters in wide fields, the grey line of sea becoming fainter and fainter. But by the time the bus arrived in Docking, the sun had disappeared in an overcast sky. Very appropriate, thought Alfred. Climbing down the steps, he felt the first drops of fine rain.

The village church was half full, mostly elderly people. Alfred was a little shocked to see many of them had not bothered with funeral clothes: some of them were in positively cheerful dresses and scarves, and some men wore no ties. But perhaps that's how it was these days: perhaps showing respect for the dead through sombre clothes was an old-fashioned idea.

Alfred found a seat with a good view of the altar and settled down to enjoy the music. There was a nice show of flowers, though he himself had never had a fondness for gladioli. But the lilies were magnificent: probably from the Fanshawes' own garden.

After a while a small group of Fanshawe relations were escorted up the aisle by the vicar, and shown to the front pew. Miss Maisie was the tallest, and very thin. Unlike the others, all in black, she wore a neat coat of grey flannel, cut on almost military lines, Alfred thought. She wore grey stockings, grey shoes and gloves, and a hat that was no more than a puff of dotted net, half concealing her eyes. It reminded Alfred of a bunch of *gypsophila*. Very pretty. He trusted the word was not out of place on such an occasion.

From where he sat, Alfred had a fine view of Maisie Fanshawe's profile and high shoulders, bony through the grey flannel. The coffin arrived, the service began: Alfred knelt, sang, listened, prayed with the congregation. But the conscious part of his mind he found entirely preoccupied by the sight of the Admiral's daughter. There was something about her, he could not for the life of him explain what it was, that held his complete attention. She was, in some way, like the Windrushes' garden, *transformed*. Alfred turned his mind back to the pictures he had of her, so recently, on her visits to the Windrushes: an awkward-looking lady, really, in clothes that never looked quite right, like Miss Windrush's, and grey hair that made her older than she really was. She had seemed cheerful enough, but had – how could he put it? – no *presence*. That was it. Nothing about her that made you look again. Rather pathetic, was his impression, really: the downcast air of an eternal spinster.

But now, so great was the change, here in the church, that Alfred found it hard to believe he was looking at the same person. Her pale bony cheeks, flecked with tiny shadows from the dotted net, were – well, not exactly beautiful, but arresting. The mouth, significant before for its definite downward curve and damson lipstick, was colourless, perhaps to disguise in its corners the hint of a smile. It occurred to Alfred that relief, obviously, was what had caused the change: that was it, sheer relief. After all, it had been well known the poor girl had had to look after her paralysed father for many years. His passing on, for all its sadness, must also afford her secret joy. But there again, it wasn't just her sense of freedom that seemed to burn through the slight grey figure: it seemed to be something more positive than that. She had about her the sort of calm exhilaration that you see on the faces of lovers when one is forced to catch an early train and the other, bidding him farewell, knows she will be following shortly.

The service over, the funeral procession moved out into the graveyard. Most of the villagers then dispersed. Only a small group of relations and friends made their way to the open grave. Alfred was undecided what to do: he would not like to offend the Fanshawes by intruding in a private occasion, but on the other hand he felt to leave now would be to cut his outing short. Settling for a compromise, he placed himself behind a tall gravestone some way from the coffin. Thus he could silently join in and observe, but cause no offence.

Alfred pulled the bowler well down over his ears, watched the almost invisible rain spread a gossamer sheen over his navy serge. The funeral group intoned their prayers, eyes cast down into the gaping earth. The severity of black yew trees, behind them, was dimmed with rain: the sky was a solid grey, church and gravestones were grey stone and, matching them in her grey flannel, Maisie Fanshawe shone like an ethereal being, a dove among crows. Once again, Alfred stared and stared, trying to put his finger on what it was he was seeing.

Once the ceremony was over, Maisie detached herself from the others as if she wanted to be alone for a few moments. Unknowingly, she approached the gravestone behind which Alfred stood, half concealed and at attention. He took his chance.

'Miss Fanshawe,' he said, stepping on to the path and raising the bowler. 'May I offer my condolences?'

'Oh, Mr Baxter. Thank you. It was good of you to come.'

She looked surprised to see him. They shook hands. Her eyes, smudged through the *gypsophila*, were not mourning eyes, but sparkling.

'Your father was a fine man, if you don't mind me saying,' added Alfred. 'And a very good customer.'

Maisie smiled. 'I'm glad his suffering is over,' she said. 'Now, it seems to be raining harder. Would you like to join us back at the house for a drink and something to eat?'

Alfred, taken aback by such unexpected kindness, hesitated

in his acceptance. But Maisie insisted. She tugged at his arm, laughing. 'Come along. You need something before your journey back.'

Then, amazingly, Alfred found himself in step with her along the path, some distance from the others. He felt her high spirits, dancing within her slight form. It was as if she had been untouched by the death, the rain, the grey.

'I suppose you're getting into order for the return,' she was saying. 'Isn't it a nice surprise?'

'What's that you're saying, Miss Fanshawe?' Alfred was confused.

'Didn't you know? Well, as a matter of fact I only heard myself last night. Gideon is coming back. For good. Isn't that lovely?'

'Good heavens,' said Alfred. 'I suppose Miss Windrush has been ringing me and I haven't been there. She may be trying even now!'

'No matter: she can ring again.'

'And when will he be coming, if I may enquire?'

'Some time in the next few weeks. He sounded as though he intended to stay in Norfolk quite a while, this time.'

'Just what the doctor ordered,' said Alfred, very pleased, observing Maisie's light grey shoes almost skipping on the gravel path.

'Exactly,' she agreed, and they reached the house.

Alfred spent a most agreeable hour in the company of some polite Fanshawes, partaking of thin pink meats and garden salads, and he found himself accepting several glasses of sherry and white wine. Maisie Fanshawe herself ate nothing, but saw to it her guests were as happy as could be expected in the circumstances. She rustled from one to another of them in a grey silk dress that put Alfred in mind of Eileen's honeymoon silk. A diamond dust of rain was on her nose – again, like Eileen's wedding day. Her dotted net was pushed back to reveal happy eyes and a private smile.

All the way back in the bus Alfred thought of Maisie Fanshawe, wondering what it was about her. Strange thing was, it seemed to be something he recognized: some look he had seen, been warmed by, many, many years ago. Funny he couldn't put a name to it. Perhaps it would come to him, like the answers in his crossword puzzles, sudden from nowhere, making sense of the clues.

Hannah Bagle quickly observed the change in Gideon on their return to New York. He was preoccupied, distant, restless. The things about her he used to appreciate – her efficiency, cooking, beautiful clothes, well-informed mind – he seemed not to notice any longer. It came as no surprise to her when he announced he was returning home for good, which meant farewell for the two of them.

Hannah took the news calmly, inwardly furious she had not taken her chance and been the one to do the breaking off. She was practised at leaving but did not care to be left, however unsatisfactory the arrangement had become. And she had to agree with Gideon the best of their relationship had passed. Some vital energy had gone astray, died, whatever, to be replaced by irritation and apathy. Ah well: their measure of time having come to an end was no great cause for regret in Hannah. Her weekend with Harry Antlers in London lingered excitingly in her mind: maybe she should now take her chance to visit him for longer, and persuade him to return with her to New York. But should that plan not materialize, there were always others. Plenty of others.

Thinking Harry might display some interest in the news – Hannah guessed his affair with Viola was not progressing as well as he claimed, she rang him from her office. She explained the situation. His voice was dull in response, tired.

'So,' said Hannah, 'Gideon will be back in a couple of weeks. I understand he's going to jolly old Norfolk for a while. Hope he has himself a ball. Your Viola, I understand, is going there next week.'

'Is she?' Harry's voice brightened with interest.

'Funny, the English way of loving some old seaside dump. Yeah, she's going on down there, she told Gideon. Doesn't like London in the summer. Didn't you know?'

'She may have told me. I probably didn't take it in.'

There was a long pause. Hannah took her chance.

'Which leaves the way open for you and me, honey. I've reason to be over myself, quite soon. We could get together again.'

'Maybe,' said Harry. 'I'm going to be busy moving. I've found my penthouse.'

'That's terrific. I could help. Viola all right?'

'Fine.'

'You sound tired.'

'Just overworked. Offers for films and plays have been streaming in, somehow. Difficult to know which to do.'

Harry glanced at the letter he held in his hand: a single offer to direct *Measure for Measure* for an autumn festival in southern Ireland.

'That's terrific,' said Hannah again. 'It's nice to know I'm in with a famous director.' Her words were strangely cheering.

Having finished editing his film with extraordinary speed, Harry occupied himself with the move to his new flat. This involved buying furniture, china, linen, everything: he owned almost nothing but books and records. Unaccustomed to choosing such things, his searches round the shops confused and irritated him. He found himself in a perpetual state of frustration and bad temper, breaking off more and more frequently to fill himself with soothing snacks. His only means of judging any piece of furniture or household object was by its price. If it was very expensive he thought it must be all right, and took it. Thus his film money dwindled in a matter of days. Sliding towards an impoverished state increased his general despondency. Completely desolate, one evening, he turned into a French restaurant he could not afford, with the intention of eating and drinking till his troubles receded.

He stood at the door, eyes refocusing in the gloom, waiting to be shown a table. It was then he saw, in a distant corner table, Viola and the scholarly-looking worm who had opened the front door to him. A waiter approached. Harry fled into the street.

This was the first time Harry had set eyes on Viola since the evening that had gone so wrong. Since then, he had sent her a series of letters, varying in tone and assurances (*I swear I have not laid a finger on anyone since the day we met, more than can be said for you and all your lovers*) but he had made no attempt to meet her. The unexpected sight of her, this bleak evening, was the final undoing of a desperate, ravenous man. The revenge which he had contemplated in Shepherds Bush at dawn, but rejected later, now screamed back into his heart. This was it: the time had come to hurt Viola as much as she had hurt him.

As Harry hurried along the street in search of another restaurant, rage and venom so contorting his features that people stepped away from him, the calculating part of his mind was coolly at work. Thanks to Hannah's recent invitation, a plan formed quickly in his mind. He would have to hurry, though: make sure he had moved into his flat, when the deed was done, so that no one could find him. Today was Friday. Viola would be going to Norfolk tomorrow, of that he could be certain. In private celebration, Harry ordered spaghetti, two steaks, baked potatoes and a whole bottle of good wine.

The brief sight of Harry destroyed the pleasure of dinner for Edwin and Viola. Viola's reaction was one of pounding heart and shaking hand: panic, fear, the desire to run away. They left halfway through their sorbets. Viola clung to Edwin's arm the whole way back to the house.

She had planned to go to Norfolk that afternoon. But Gideon had rung to say he had booked a plane on Sunday evening, a week earlier than he had expected. So Viola changed her mind, decided to wait for him over the weekend, and drive him to Norfolk on Monday. Edwin, hearing the changes of her plan, had invited her to dinner tonight. He had also come up with a whole list of agreeable suggestions as to how they should pass the weekend.

Back in the house, they fetched themselves large glasses of whisky, went to the library. They both preferred the comfortable clutter of books to the austere tidiness of the drawing room.

'I shall stay here in the dressing-room, tonight, and the whole weekend,' said Edwin. 'If that man's on the warpath again, you need someone to protect you.'

Viola smiled gratefully. Her face still ached when she moved it.

'Perhaps a little music would unwind us,' said Edwin.

He put on a record of a Brahms quartet. They lay further

back on the same sofa. Edwin took Viola's hand. She did not resist.

The inspiration of the music filled Edwin with a deep longing – for what, he could not precisely define. Comfort, perhaps. Peace, perhaps. Viola, almost certainly.

When the music was over, Edwin sat up, still holding her hand. Warmed by the whisky he felt bold and happy.

'Do you know what I think?' he asked.

'No,' said Viola.

A dozen declarations, in a hopeless tangle, knotted in his head. He sighed.

'Dearie me,' he said. 'Well, perhaps one day . . . In the meantime, I shall take it upon myself to guard over you when you're here. It's the least I can do in return for your Uncle David's kindness.' He went to refill their glasses, then picked up one of his books. 'I shall insist you go to bed in a few moments,' he went on, with mock fierceness, 'but I shall also insist you spare me just a minute to look at this. I've found the most wonderful seventeenth-century engraving of the *Smerinthus ocellata*, the Eyed Hawk Moth. Look at those fierce eyes painted on its wings! When it fears it's going to be attacked it raises the wings. They look like the face of an owl, or a cat, and the predator is scared away . . . Just what I need as your bodyguard.'

They both laughed. Edwin went on to tell Viola about the cautious nature of the Oak Processionary Moth, whose larvae have extraordinary habits.

'They're the hippies of the moth world,' he explained. 'They live in communal webs in the trees. During the day they travel to other trees to eat their leaves. They move, head to tail, in long processions – sometimes twelve metres long, spinning a silk thread to guide themselves home again. You'd be surprised by the infinite wisdom of the humble moth.'

Safe in Edwin's world of gentle creatures, Viola found herself enjoying the rest of the evening, her mind happily diverted from thoughts of Harry Antlers.

It was by now the ragged end of summer, late August. The long hot days were coming to an end. The sun, when it moodily appeared, gave off an irritable heat as if to spite the dregs of its own high season. There were frequent clammy showers in London. Storms of thin thunder by night, summer lightning.

On the Saturday marked for the execution of Harry Antlers' plan, rain fell heavily all day. But Harry's mind was not on the weather. He was busy trying to make some order of his own flat, in which he intended to spend that night. His new plan had made it essential that he never return again to his old address. This meant moving sooner than he had intended – a matter of loading his car with his few possessions, and unpacking the many things that had been delivered. Surprisingly, the activities of the day, which he had been dreading, gave him pleasure. He was proud of his view and his expensive furniture. A little disappointed, perhaps, that the place looked so small, once the stuff was arranged, but he would continue to call it a penthouse. A penthouse would be some compensation for the odious behaviour of his beloved lady. His own home at last, it was but a beginning of greater things . . . Full of energy, Harry ate quantities of fish and chips in his soulless kitchen, and felt rising within him the heady mixture of determination, resolution and revenge.

It was raining hard in Norfolk, too. Alfred Baxter, with only the weekend left to prepare the house before the arrival of the Windrushes on Monday night, set about his favourite job of cleaning the silver. He lit the fire in the kitchen, for it was quite cold, made a pot of tea, and hummed to himself, as was his habit, while he polished.

His mind was still on Maisie Fanshawe. Funny thing was, thinking about her so much since the day of the funeral, Eileen's nasty face had not been giving him so much bother. It was as if all Maisie's gentleness and goodness had blotted out the badness of Eileen, which Alfred still could not remember in real life, but which had haunted him so after her death. Thinking of Maisie gave Alfred the same shivery feeling as looking at a sunset, or walking through the door of Lincoln Cathedral: a sort of private communion with something that understood. He still could not be sure of the reason for her elation at the funeral – indeed, he sometimes thought it might have been his imagination, the impact of a rare outing. But he was no longer concerned about its cause: merely grateful for the warm effect it had had upon him. In his nightly prayers he now thanked the Lord for so strange a blessing in his old age. He also approached his Father on the delicate subject of timing. Dear God, he said, why was it not your will that I should have met someone like Miss Fanshawe when I was at an age to do something about it? Why should you have chosen to show me, too late, what I have missed all these years? He pondered these questions many times. As yet, the good Lord had not given him an answer.

At the end of the day, the silver completed and returned to its cupboard, Alfred went upstairs. With the rain still battering so hard, he wanted to check all the windows were firmly shut and there was no leaking since the new repairs to the roof. The thundery sky made it very dark upstairs. Alfred switched on several lights, checked every room. He had it in mind to put flowers in Miss Windrush's room before she arrived, by way of welcome. His funeral spray had given him confidence when it came to cut flowers. That was another thing: Maisie Fanshawe had written a very nice letter thanking him for the roses. A beautiful spray, she had said.

Downstairs again, Alfred went to his part of the house. With the Windrushes coming home so soon, he felt he should revert to spending his evenings in his own sitting-room. It was not inviting, there. Unlived in for several weeks, it was cold, damp and gloomy, though through the windows the lime trees were a searing yellow-green against the blackish sky. Alfred made himself a cheese sandwich. He boiled the kettle. As it began to whistle he heard the mocking laughter of the girls coming from the sitting-room. At least, he thought he heard it: he could not be quite sure, for when the noise of the kettle died down there was absolute silence. He may have been confused, but it was enough to cast aside all his good intentions about keeping to his own quarters. A stormy night was not the sort of night on which a man should be alone listening to the ghostly laughter of his former girlfriends. Alfred hurried back to the fire.

In the high-backed comfortable chair, crossword puzzle on his knee, a cup of tea beside him, Alfred soon put himself to rights. The flames from the apple wood were warm upon him. He had Monday, and all the delights of a lived-in house again to look forward to. Yes, he was a man of good fortune, thought Alfred, and may it please the Lord to let things thus continue.

He listened to the rain chipping at the window, and the grumbling of thunder. Maisie Fanshawe glowed in his mind, an indefinable colour like early dew. She smiled at him through her *gypsophila*, and he smiled back, with tears.

At seven that evening Harry Antlers opened his brand new formica kitchen drawer and studied the collection of brand new carving knives and kitchen implements. After much deliberation he chose a knife-sharpener, a long steel implement with a heavy handle of carved bone, which had made it very expensive. Harry tested it in his hand. He liked the feel of it.

When he had placed his chosen weapon in a plastic bag, he gathered up two apples, a packet of biscuits, a hunk of cheese and a bar of chocolate to be added to the bag. These were in case of urgent hunger on the journey, despite a three-course supper in an Indian restaurant. Harry had no intention of experiencing for a second time the pains he had suffered on his first journey to Norfolk.

He set out into the pouring rain. Just his luck, he thought, the heavens should be so against him whenever he wanted to visit Viola in her loathesome seaside house. But, with the curries filling his stomach, he was not really disconcerted. He rather liked the rhythm of the windscreen wipers slashing through the lemon pearls of water, the slooshing noise of the tyres as he drove fast through the London streets.

There was an extraordinarily clear picture in Harry's mind, so precise that he was convinced it had been sent to him by way of a message. It was a picture of Viola, happy in her monstrous kitchen. He knew, quite surely, she would be there. Less definite in Harry's mind was whether or not she would be alone. He guessed, judging by her general promiscuity, she would probably be entertaining her doctor lover. In which case the doctor would be dealt with by the brand new weapon. In fact, Harry hoped the lover would not be there: he did not contemplate murder but, unused to armed

attack, his plans might get out of hand. Besides whic
lover might well recover from his wounds, thus more cl
bonding him to Viola.

No: Harry's aim of attack was something he suppos
might hurt Viola more than a few blows to one of her mar
admirers. He had noticed through his tears, that dreadfu
night in London, the only thing that had seemed to pierce Viola's hard little heart – the smashing of the photograph of her parents. Harry had reflected on this fact, and suddenly it had all become clear to him. What she was, plainly, was a materialist of the worst order. What mattered to her were things, places. She knew nothing of love or charity: there was not an ounce of goodness in her. (God only knew why he loved her.) But she was moved by *things*. Things, therefore, were his target. Smash up a few things that meant most to her, and she would see what it felt like to have a broken heart.

Harry arrived at the Norfolk village as the church clock was striking ten. He spent some time driving round to find a concealed parking place away from the house. There was no one about on such a wet night: the elements were, after all, on his side.

He finally chose to park in what appeared to be a deserted track leading to the marsh. He finished off the food, then realized he had foolishly left nothing for the journey back when he would certainly be in need. Cursing his stupidity, he put the knife sharpener in his pocket and got out of the car.

In crime stories, Harry remembered grimly, the villain always makes one silly mistake: his was to have forgotten his mackintosh. The force of the rain surprised him. It soaked through his thin jacket in moments, while muddy puddles seeped through the synthetic leather of his shoes. Angered by these unexpected handicaps, Harry made his stumbling way towards the house. There was no moon, just darkness, all the more disagreeable for being warm.

He came at last to the drive of the house, saw two lights upstairs. They indicated Viola was preparing for bed. Good. That would leave Harry free to smash up the kitchen – he knew that trusting country idiots like her never locked doors – and get away easily. He went down the front drive, round to

.k door that led directly to the kitchen. There, to his .rnation, he found more lights. This must mean that gh Viola was probably upstairs, it must be her intention ome down again and switch them off. Harry swore.

For a long time, standing under the mulberry tree for shel- .r, he wondered what to do. His eyes were fixed on the lighted kitchen window, some twenty yards away. There was no sign of life. Perhaps Viola was in the bath. With the soaking sleeve of his jacket Harry wiped at the rain on his face. Curiously, his violent intentions had subsided a little. He thought perhaps he should wait until all the lights went out. But then a loud crack of thunder brought him to his senses. He jumped, enraged again: must get on with the business with no more thought.

A dripping figure, Harry moved slowly towards the window. Overhead, the thunder crackled and rumbled, and he thanked the heavens for their aid. Like this, his entry would never be heard.

A yard or so from the window, Harry stopped. He could now see the high-backed chair drawn up by the fire, turned away from him. He could also see a small part of a man's bent head, and his arm.

So that was it, the bitch. The lover waiting downstairs while she prepared herself for him. Well, she would get no fun from him tonight.

Harry crashed through the back door, half blinded by rain in his eyes and the light after darkness. Thunder filled the room. Harry felt himself hurtling towards the chair, catching his hip on the corner of the table as he went, causing a sharp pain. He heard his own roars climbing against the thunder, saw the startled flash of an old man's face, open mouth spewing forth a pitiful cry. The rough bone handle of his weapon gave courage to Harry's hand. He slashed at the cowering head, over which defensive hands fluttered feebly as fledgelings. The skin at the temples broke like egg shell. It was so easy. So easy. Serve the baby-snatching bastard right.

In the room of laughing thunder, Harry watched a thin claw of blood spout from the head fallen over the side of the chair. The blood gathered speed and density, began to drip on to the flagstone floor. Harry moved backwards, one hand on the table. The thunder stopped, quite suddenly. In the silence he thought he could hear the drip of blood, but it may have been rain from his own clothes. The quiet unnerved him. He gave a feeble slash with the knife sharpener at the only two things on the vast pine table: a bowl of white roses and a pot of home-made strawberry jam. (Naturally home-made, scoffed some part of Harry's mind.) They fell over, a small noise. Roses sprawled in spilt water. Jam oozed from broken glass. The old man did not move.

Harry Antlers ran.

An hour later, driving home from a late call, Richard Almond passed the house. He was surprised to see a lighted window upstairs. Viola had sent him a card to say she and Gideon were returning late on Monday night. Perhaps there had been some change of plan.

Richard drove past the house, thinking he would ring in the morning, when he found himself stopping the car. He had a strange feeling that he should just check everything was all right. He knew all too well the ruthless energy of those possessed. Harry Antlers would stop at nothing. If Viola had arrived early, pursued by the madman, she would need more than Alfred Baxter's protection.

Alarmed by his own thoughts, Richard skidded into the front drive. Viola's car was not there. He rang the front door bell, shouting his name through the clatter of rain. He did not want to alarm anyone by so late a call. He waited, ringing and shouting, for some moments. Then he went round to the back door. It was open. The kitchen lights were on.

Richard's appalled eyes leapt from the spilt jam to the spilt blood. In a moment he was pushing the unconscious figure of Alfred Baxter upright in the chair. It was at once apparent the old man was alive. Shallow breathing, profuse bleeding. With remarkably quick fingers Richard snatched a dishcloth and bound it round Alfred's head to quell the flow of blood for the few moments while he fetched his case from the car.

A short time later, having made his patient as comfortable as he was able and covered him with rugs from the cloakroom, Richard went to the telephone in the hall. First he rang for an ambulance. Then he called the police.

Harry Antlers drove slowly and calmly back to London through the rain. He stopped only once, on the outskirts of Newmarket, to throw his knife sharpener into a field. Hungry though he was, he judged it unwise to relieve his hunger at a transport café.

By three in the morning – having made sure no one observed his entry into the block of flats – he had bathed, put on dry clothes, and consumed an early breakfast of eggs and bacon. His only regret was that he had not had more time for wrecking the kitchen. Still, incapable though she was of loving, even the hard-hearted Viola might suffer some punishment on hearing of her elderly lover's attack.

A very small worry nagged beneath the fried eggs: the bloody old man had looked curiously dead. The blow, Harry was sure, had not been hard, nothing to a younger man. But he had not counted on Viola's taste for geriatrics. Some time, he would try to find out how serious the damage had been.

But for the most part Harry's mind was wonderfully clear of thought or conscience. He imagined he must be a true villain, feeling like this, and the reasons for his villainy – ugly face, dreadful childhood – were not his fault. Juries were very sympathetic to such cases these days. Not that the incident would ever get to court. For Harry was about to carry out the final part of his plan.

He rang Annie Light. Once again, sleepily, she urged him to come round. Having granted her the compliment, this time, of undressing completely, Harry insisted on a serious talk before they indulged in anything else. They clung to each other in the narrow bed.

'Now listen, Annie. If you love me as you say you do, and you must know by now the feeling is pretty mutual, I want to ask you to do something for me that might make a whole difference to my life.'

'Of course, Harry. Anything. *Anything*.' Annie wriggled, impatient.

'I don't want you to ask me any questions. What's been happening is no concern of yours, and never will be.'

'No.'

'But I want you to *extend* tonight in your mind. Should anyone ask you questions about what you were doing this

evening, I want you to say you spent the *whole* evenin[g with]
me. We went for a drive, came back here. You can adm[it we]
made love, if necessary.'

'What sort of people might question me?' asked Ann[ie.]
'Are you in trouble?'

'No, my love, I'm not in trouble. But I could be without
your help. It's all far too complicated to explain. Just trust
me: I need your help.'

'Of course,' said Annie.

'So if by any chance one day the police –'

'*The police?*' Harry felt her fear.

'I love you, Annie.'

'I'll do anything you like.'

'You swear you will keep to your story?'

'Of course. I'd do anything in the world for you. You
know I would.'

She had relaxed at last, silly little thing. Harry thought he
could count on her, though plainly she would need a little
encouragement from time to time.

'I was so touched, the way you cleared up my flat,' he
whispered. 'The flowers.'

'It was nothing.'

'You mustn't be frightened by the police. It's a very small
chance it'll ever come to that.'

'No. I'll do my best.'

'Swear I was with you all night?'

'Swear. Wish you had been.'

'You will be. Another time.' Harry braced himself to seal
her promise. 'I've always loved you, you must know that,'
he said.

Early on Saturday morning Viola and Edwin left the house to
visit the Tate Gallery. They were out for the rest of the day
and went to a film in the evening. Thus Richard, who had
been ringing continually, was not able to get hold of Viola till
very late that night. She at once rang Gideon in New York
with the news, and rose at dawn on Sunday to drive to
Norfolk. Her farewell to Edwin was very brief: she woke him
in the dressing room with a hurried explanation. She could
give him no idea of when she would return, she said. Perhaps

, to her uncle's house. Horrified by her various bits of ›, Edwin leapt from his bed with uncharacteristic speed. .h no conscious thought he ran to the library, snatched up e engraving of the Hawk-Eyed moth and thrust it into her .ands.

'Hurry,' he said, 'and take this.'

'But its your precious moth with the fierce eyes –'

'I'd like you to have it. Off you go, now.'

He put up a hand to pat her hair. But she was gone, shouting something about trying to remember the moth's name. Edwin, clutching at his pyjamas, ran after her.

'*Smerinthus ocellata*,' he called down the stairs. But .the front door had slammed. He doubted if she heard.

Richard met Viola at the house. Having told her all he knew, in greater detail than on the telephone, they drove to the hospital to see Alfred. He was recovering well and was expected home in a week or so.

'The police can't get much out of him,' said Richard, on the way there. 'He remembers very little about the whole thing. He keeps saying the man was very wet, as if he'd been in a river, and very fat. He remembers seeing the buttons of his shirt were undone. He had no clear picture of his face except that it was nasty. Nothing else has come back to him. The police are coming up this afternoon to see you,' he added. 'They wanted to know if you might have any ideas.'

'You told them nothing?'

'Nothing. I thought it was up to you.'

'It's quite plain. Harry Antlers was out to kill either me or my imaginary lover.'

'He's overstepped himself,' said Richard. 'It's a traditional end for those suffering from his particular affliction. You'll put them in touch with Mr Antlers, then?'

Viola paused only for a fraction of a second.

'Of course,' she said.

'I know, quite positively, I've made the right decision,' said Gideon. 'My life is here, not in America. It's a tremendous relief to be so sure.'

It was Monday night, late. Viola had waited up for him.

They sat by the fire with bread, cheese and wine.
full of the adrenalin of one who has made a long j
is not yet ready to sleep. They had talked at leng
assault on Alfred, the obvious fact that Harry Antlers
culprit. Viola had discussed her own attack, horrifyi
brother. Now, they turned to their plans.

'And what about you, Violetta? When the flat is finis
will you live there? I hope not. I don't want you anywhere o
your own till that maniac is put safely away.'

'I've been idle long enough,' said Viola. 'Getting a job is my first priority. But not in London. I don't want to be there any more. Ever.'

'No. You could be here.'

'Only for a while. There's no work, here. Perhaps I should go abroad.'

'It might help,' said Gideon, 'if I told you about an even more important decision than coming home.' He twirled his glass, spinning his wine. 'I'm going to marry Maisie of Docking.' He laughed, seeing Viola's face. 'That is, I can't be *quite* sure of that: but I'm going to ask her tomorrow.'

Viola, speechless, found delight in the idea slowly coming to her.

'I've thought about nothing else since I left here,' Gideon went on, 'and it seems to be the only decision in my entire life about which I've not had a single doubt. She's the one for me. The only puzzle is why I never realized, years ago . . .'

'She was different, then.'

'She was. Well, we've left it a bit late, but not too late. We'll get married in the next month or so, live here as much as we can. I'm sure she'd want that. Though I shall probably have to be in London a few days a week.' He studied his sister's face again. 'But you, Violetta – and I know Maisie will agree – you're not going to be turned out of your house. You can stay here for as long as you like.'

'That's very kind of you,' said Viola, 'but I would never do any such thing. Quite impossible for everybody. Really. But if you could perhaps buy me out, then I could find myself something else. I rather fancy the West Country.'

Gideon smiled down at her.

'Of course I'll buy you out if that's what you want. But

ɪat be a lonely life? The West Country would be rom us.' He paused. 'And Richard,' he added.

would,' said Viola. 'But you know me. I like my ess.'

deon got up.

Well, there's time to think about it all. Now, I must get a w hours sleep before the proposal. Do you think she'll ıave me?'

Viola laughed.

'Not a single doubt.'

'And you think it's a good idea?'

Viola rose, too, and embraced her brother.

'The best idea you've ever had,' she said.

Now that the pain in his head had almost gone, Alfred was rather enjoying himself in hospital. Everyone made a great fuss of him, changing the bandage over his eye very gently, propping up his pillows, constantly enquiring after his comfort. They intended to take out his stitches in a few days time, then he would be allowed home.

He had had visitors every day. The first time the police had questioned him he had still been quite drowsy, and remembered nothing of what they had asked him or what he had told them. Since then, they had been several times. But he was not able to give them much help, try as he might. The fact was the picture in his mind was very unclear. Trying to remember did nothing to help. One moment he had been imagining Maisie Fanshawe – he had omitted to furnish the police with this detail – the next, an ugly mug of a face had loomed above him, shouting. After that Alfred knew nothing till he woke up to find himself surrounded by the flowery curtains of a hospital cubicle. So, regretfully, he had not been able to be of much use to the police. He only hoped they caught the bugger. Shouldn't be at large, a maniac like that. It was a very good thing, though, and Alfred thanked the Lord for His blessing, that *he* had been the one to be attacked rather than Miss Viola.

She herself had been to see him every day, sometimes with the gallant Dr Almond. They brought roses from the garden, and books and jars of honey and jam. They were kindness itself. What a fortunate man he was.

Then, the day after his return, Mr Gideon
Fanshawe came. Alfred could hardly believe it w
them walking down the ward towards him.

'Well, I never,' he muttered to himself, str ighte
pyjama top.

Maisie Fanshawe sat by his bed and gazed at him with
vellous concern, so that he felt he was basking under a br
sun. Dressed in a lovely pink, this time, she still had that fun
radiance about her, so it hadn't been his imagination at th
funeral. When her eyes were not on himself, Alfred noticed them swinging constantly across the bed to Mr Gideon. Beautiful, she was, sort of, thought Alfred. But it was not an uneasy thought.

They asked all about the attack, and were evidently pleased to see him so well on the way to recovery. Not until a few minutes before the end-of-visit bell did they then tell him their own news: they were to be married very shortly. What's more, Norfolk was to be their home, and Alfred's job and flat were there for the rest of his life, should he want them.

Alfred gripped each one by the hand, unable to speak, overjoyed. Not in a million years would he ever have imagined Mr Gideon going for such a *quiet* lady, but how right he was. Alfred, had he been able, could have assured him how right he was.

When they had left, promising to return next day, Alfred lay back on his pillows. Although he was delighted by their news, and looked forward to serving them to the best of his ability for many years to come, they soon went from his mind. Lovely young couple though they were, they were replaced by the person who had been occupying most of Alfred's thoughts since he had regained consciousness: Eileen.

Yes, Eileen was with him again, laughing and smiling and sweet as ever, just as she had been in real life. He tried, just once, to remember the disagreeable face, the face which had gone wrong in his mind, somehow, in the last few months: but it would not return. And another thing: he had a dream one night about the girls. Turned out they had enjoyed their picnic so much they had been taken short by the incoming tide and drowned. Somehow, in his dream, he wasn't sorry.

…d they had gone. Awake, he never gave them …ought. He heard no more laughter.

… thing, really, thought Alfred, sniffing the white …old man gets a blow on the head, and it brings back his … Brings her back just as she always was, his dearest …en. So in a way, and Alfred would confide this to no one … the world but the smiling Eileen – he couldn't bring him-…elf to feel that hard about his attacker. Poor man. Perhaps he had never known a happy life, or what it was to love.

14

The first visitors to Harry Antlers' penthouse were two plain-clothes policemen. They were received with cool courtesy, and tea in the brand new Worcester cups. Harry conveyed no surprise at their visit. He merely wondered how they had tracked him down, considering he was ex-directory and had given his address to no one, but he supposed they had their ways.

The interview, he thought, went very well. Privately relieved to hear the old man was alive, he showed concern at the plight of Alfred Baxter who was, said the police, 'living in the house'. This news ignited fury in Harry's breast, for he had never supposed Viola's lover was actually *installed*. To quell his agitation he quickly ate several digestive biscuits and maintained his outer calm. No, he said, he had never met the Baxter man or heard of him. He himself had only visited the house on one occasion, and Viola Windrush had been on her own.

The police then questioned him, in most delicate fashion, about his own relationship with Viola. Was it true there had been some harassment?

'Ah, that,' said Harry, giving a pained smile. 'Well, you know what women are. They get these fancies in their heads . . . Make up incredible stories when they're spurned.' He sighed. 'I'm sure you know what I'm getting at.' He sounded so solemn, pained, and full of understanding, the two men exchanged a glance that might have been of sympathy. One of them wrote a very short sentence in his notebook.

Finally, he was asked in the nicest possible way if he could prove to them where he was and what he was doing on the night of the attack. Harry's eagerness to oblige, he later considered, might have been the only moment he went slightly over the top. He jumped up and fetched his diary, rummaged through the pages.

was probably somewhere Miss Windrush –' he
. a look – 'wouldn't like to hear about. I trust you'd
eet in this matter?' They nodded. Harry's finger
a page of the diary. 'Yes! Here we are. A.L. 7.30.'
hat, may I ask, sir, is A.L.?'

arry assumed his conspirator's face.

A.L., Inspector, is my girlfriend, Annie Light. To put it mply, it's a matter of mutual love. Not, as is the case with Miss Windrush, a case of your unrequited. On the night in question, we met at 7.30. We spent the evening together. Then, well – you know how evenings with the girlfriend are inclined to end?'

He thought one of the policemen allowed himself the faintest smile.

'Could you give us Miss Light's address, sir? We'd like to have a word with her, confirm all this.'

'Of course.'

Harry supplied her address and, also by heart, her telephone number which he had taken the precaution of learning that morning. He felt confident in Annie. Since their last night together, he had spoken to her several times, tutored her on what precisely to say. Only yesterday he had sent her a dozen yellow roses, with the promise that if she was interviewed, and all went well, he would take her out to what he called a champagne dinner, plus much else besides. So there were incentives for Annie. Harry was not afraid.

The policemen thanked Harry for his trouble and said they hoped they would not have to be in touch again. Harry urged them to come any time, often as they liked. Nice to see them.

Once they had gone, he felt it appropriate to congratulate himself on a brilliant performance. The brand new fridge being stuffed with delicacies from an expensive shop nearby, he was able to celebrate in his favourite manner.

A few days later he heard from Annie the interview had gone according to plan. The police believed her, definitely. To prove to himself there was some honour in his heart, Harry took the girl out to dinner and did indeed buy her half a bottle of inferior champagne. Promising there would be many more such occasions, he visited her narrow bed for the

last time. The next day he arranged for his teleph
to be changed – Annie did not know his address – a
more roses proclaiming his undying love. But Ar
was over. He never saw her again.

The next visitor to the penthouse was Hannah Bagle. Sh
flown over on an extended business trip, which meant
would be occupied by day, but have many a free night, shou
that be of interest to Harry.

She sat on his low, pale sofa – not unlike her own in New York – looking, thought Harry, just the sort of girl most men would give their eye teeth to have in a penthouse: dressed in a cream satin shirt slung with gold chains, long silky legs flowing over his new carpet. She was sinuous, alluring. Harry found himself opening his one bottle of good wine, boasting of its year.

'So tell me,' he said, 'what's been happening? You and your lover parted on good terms?'

Hannah looked down into her drink, modest.

'Not at all,' she said. 'Unfortunately not. I would have liked it that way, as you can imagine. But it wasn't to be.' She sighed. 'No, I'm afraid poor Gideon was pretty cut up about the whole thing. I didn't mean to hurt him, of course I didn't mean to. But the thing had come to its natural end, as far as I was concerned. It would have been pointless to go on. So I just had to take the bull by the horns and tell him goodbye.'

'Difficult,' said Harry.

'And now, you know what? Almost as soon as he got here he called me to say he was getting married. Next week. Can you imagine?' She laughed. 'The quickest case of rebound I've ever heard in my life. Some middle-aged spinster, I gather – though he didn't put it quite like that – who's never been out of Norfolk. Taking her last chance, poor old thing. Well, good luck to them.' Hannah raised her glass. 'I think it's all very funny.'

'Quite,' said Harry.

'Poor old Gideon. He was so British. I hope he's happy. Such odd things seem to please him. That week in Norfolk when we came over, remember? Apparently he and his sister spent most of their time in a boat. He said it was wonderful.

ave our different pleasures.' She fiddled with the
of her shirt, finally leaving it undone. 'And you,
w are you and the elusive Viola?'
in Norfolk for a while. Helping prepare for the
g, I dare say.'
ost probably.' Hannah gave a small laugh. Her pale
ks had turned to apricot. Harry had never seen her so
arable. 'Shall I tell you a cute idea that came to me? I
hought it might be quite amusing if you and I went to the
wedding.'

'*What?*'

'Sit down. Let me explain. Not officially, of course. Just take a peep, from a distance. I could feast my eyes on the country wife, you could get a glimpse of your beloved Viola.'

'It's a very mad plan,' said Harry, recognizing in this beautiful woman something of his own deviousness.

'Well, think about it. It might be entertaining.'

'It might indeed. And as you can imagine, I know the layout up there pretty well.'

Hannah stood up, slunk towards him.

'Well, then. Besides, I'd like to get a glimpse of this *Norfolk* that Gideon was always going on about.'

Harry took her hands.

'Norfolk stinks,' he said.

Many of those who had been at Admiral Fanshawe's funeral now came to see his daughter married. Alfred Baxter, an usher with no more than a bruised temple and a mending scar, had seen to it the church was billowing with flowers from the garden. Miss Windrush and he had arranged them the previous day, and now the smell of roses, pinks, lavender and honeysuckle had gathered like a whole summer into the cool grey stone of the church walls.

Richard Almond was best man, very handsome in his morning coat. Alfred liked seeing him and Miss Windrush coming down the aisle together, after the bride and groom. They made a fine couple. Would that things could have been different, but no doubt the Lord had His reasons.

Outside, a crowd of villagers had gathered at the gate. Some distance away, a short fat man and a tall blonde girl,

both wearing dark glasses, strove to be inconspicuc
a small group of elderly people.

'Seems he's married his grandmother,' Hannah ob

Harry agreed, though his eyes were not on the bric
was watching Viola, in a lavender dress much like the o
which he had first seen her, and a straw boater with danc
white ribbons. She went to a car with the best man. Admitte
ly, the best man gave no indication of being anything bu
polite to Viola, but the fineness of his tired face caused a
jealous shaking in Harry's legs.

'Come on,' he said. 'I know a good vantage point for the
next part.'

Hannah, thoroughly enjoying herself, followed her co-conspirator.

The small reception, as Harry had discovered from one of
the villagers, was to be held on the lawn of the Windrushes'
house. It was a warm September afternoon, gentle breeze
from the sea fluttering through flowers and skirts and ribbons.
Alfred was proud of the garden. He had put in a great deal of
overtime, since his return from hospital, and he thanked the
Lord he felt fit as a fiddle. The roses were clinging to their
prime: a week from now any breeze would shake their petals
to the ground. But this afternoon every rose head was firm,
scenting the soft air.

Alfred Baxter, while hurrying dutifully around with trays
of champagne, managed to spend much time admiring the
bride. In cream satin, which emphasized the delicacy of her
bones, to Alfred's delight she wore another dotted veil –
white this time, naturally – which was as near as you could
get to real *gypsophila*. She shimmied about the lawn among
her guests, holding her husband's hand, smiling, smiling.
Alfred recognized the look: a development of how she had
been – though properly sad to outward appearances, of
course – on the day of the funeral. So *that* had been her
secret: Mr Gideon. Well, she deserved him. She had had too
many years on her own. Nice to think, at last, she'd found
herself one of England's gentlemen.

In the course of his duties at the reception, Alfred was
urged to partake of several glasses of champagne himself, and
after a while his own wedding day merged happily with the

s Maisie Fanshawe glided about the garden with nd, he saw himself and Eileen in a state of similar nent all those years ago. The only difference was that Eileen had been less fortunate with the weather. It een raining. Eileen's pretty face, smiling at him here ng the guests, was sprayed with diamonds of rain, just he remembered. And then he came upon her with her old oman's face, the sweetness of it unclouded, still smiling at him. As Alfred raised his glass to toast the young couple, he knew quite certainly Eileen was near him now for ever, good as he had always known her to be, and he thanked the Lord.

Sometimes Viola drew away from the guests, looked back at the whole picture, securing it for the future. She recognized the day as the end of an era. She wanted to preserve its essence: the air, light with roses, the trembling trees dappling the lawn, the smiling faces and nostalgic hats, the solid protection of the house behind them. Once, she turned towards the marsh and sea, and for a mad instance thought she saw the face of Harry Antlers peering through the hedge. She knew it was a silly fantasy brought about by the champagne, but her heart began to pound in its accustomed way. She turned, to find Richard at her side.

'What's the matter?' he asked.

'For an awful moment I thought I saw Harry Antlers spying through the bushes.'

They both laughed. Richard looked about.

'Imagination, this time,' he said.

'I hope so.'

'When are you off?'

Viola took a small sip of champagne. Her eyes, huge over the rim of the glass, were violet against the pale sky.

'Very soon.'

She had found a cottage in the West Country, an isolated corner of the land sheltered by the Downs, which she would transform slowly over the years.

'You must let me know where you are,' said Richard.

'Of course.'

Richard sighed, looked out to sea.

'Weddings,' he said. 'Weddings.'

Viola looked at him. She had drunk enough to make he
bold.

'They make one think,' she said.

'They do. They sadly do.'

Gideon and Maisie were approaching, a shining galleon through the waves of friends.

'Come on,' said Richard, touching Viola's arm. 'I must go and do my duty: the toast. We must drink to the bride and groom.'

He lifted his own glass fractionally in the direction of Viola, then drank, emptying it, shutting his eyes.

'They don't seem to have many friends,' observed Hannah. She had a ragged view of the proceedings through a thick hedge. Her high heels were sunk in marshy earth. She was hot and uncomfortable.

Harry, from his superior position lower in the hedge, had recognized Alfred Baxter from his wounds, and was fascinated. He watched him hand a glass of champagne to Viola, watched him talking and laughing with all the ease of an old lover. How could Viola bring herself . . .?

'That,' he said, nudging Hannah, 'that small one there with the balding head, is another of Viola's admirers.'

'Don't be ridiculous,' she scoffed. 'That's some kind of servant. Look, he's taking the tray round to people.'

Harry plunged his face so far into the bush his cheeks were scratched by thorns. But no discomfort could interrupt his studies.

'By God,' he said at last, 'I do believe you're right.'

At that moment, Viola, who had disengaged herself from the crowd and moved alone towards the hedge, her eyes on the sea, looked straight at the small gap through which Harry was carelessly peering. In sudden terror, he dropped to his knees, pulling Hannah with him. Through the thickness of the bottom of the hedge, he could now see only Viola's shoes, suddenly joined by those of a man.

'Time we left,' he said.

On the way back to the hidden place where Harry had parked the car, Hannah suggested they paid a short visit to the beach. Harry was reluctant. Too many matters were essing to be turned over in his unhappy mind. He wanted get back to the safety of London as fast as possible. But Hannah was persistent.

'Come *on*, Harry, for heaven's sake. We've driven all this way. Now we're here, I want to see a bit more of this Norfolk. The wedding wasn't much of a show.'

Harry agreed to half an hour. They settled themselves, after an awkward walk in unsuitable shoes, in the curve of a dune.

'This isn't bad,' said Hannah, brushing sand from her silk trousers.

'The place is a dump,' said Harry. Somehow, sand had crept into his socks. He looked across the beach. The tide was far out. He could see the black ribs of an old wreck. Despite the warmth of the air, he shivered.

'Your Viola looked all right,' said Hannah.

'She's a lovely lady.'

'Gideon was putting on a cheerful face.'

'His class are very good at disguising,' agreed Harry. Then a wayward thought came to him. 'I wonder how he'd feel, your ex-lover, if you and I went off together?'

Hannah laughed. 'What an idea! But you're not a free man. There's Viola.'

'Quite,' said Harry. 'But supposing I were free?'

Hannah laughed again, a little puzzled.

'Why, that'd be salt in the wound all right. He'd go mad.'

Harry strove to find a more comfortable position in the sand. He was very hungry. He put his hand in his pocket, searching for the last of his fruit gums. Coming across a small box, he drew it out. Opened it. It was the diamond star.

'My, that's pretty,' said Hannah.

'It's for you,' he said, handing it to her. 'Here, take it.' A wonderful plan was beginning to form.

'You're kidding,' said Hannah.

'No. I mean it.'

'For me? Really?' Hannah pinned it to her silk breast. 'It's marvellous. Heavens, Harry, that's the kindest thing.'

'Well,' he said, 'it's just a small tribute to a very beautiful lady. There'll be others.'

'Listen, you're sounding serious!'

'I am serious. I'm dead serious. I wouldn't give a di
star to a lady unless she meant . . .' Harry's voice almost b
Cursing the lack of fruit gums, he controlled himself. 'H
nah, will you marry me?'

With great surprise, Harry watched her rolling about t
sand, bent knees caught in her hands, laughing in a way tha
was highly amused, though he failed to see the joke.

'*Marry* you, Harry? That's the greatest. Oh, that's quite something. For a moment, I almost took you seriously.'

She knelt, then, before him, gently touched his ugly face with a luminous hand. Behind them, the sun was falling.

'Did you?' he said.

'What's in store for you and me,' she answered, 'is one hell of a good time. Don't you think?'

At that precise moment, Harry recalled later, Hannah's silvery face almost touching his, his bottom uncomfortable in the sand, a kind of mist lifted in his brain. It was then that he knew the demon of Viola had gone from him: his love for her was dead. But rising from the gap she left was the most beautiful creature on earth. He wanted her more than life, and he would get her. He would try his utmost to set about it in a tranquil fashion: he had no doubt he would succeed. Then, together, they would go to southern Ireland while he made *Measure for Measure*. They would return to New York while he directed a hit on Broadway. In London they would buy a bigger penthouse. He would be the envy of all men, including her ex-lover Gideon. Viola herself would not be unmoved. The adrenalin of his new plans charging his veins, Harry heaved himself up.

'Come on, my love,' he said. 'Time to go.'

Hannah stood beside him. They looked at the darkening beach and sea.

'Oh, Harry,' Hannah said, 'I forgot to tell you. While you were showering, there was a call. The police, they said.'

Harry laughed. He had no worries now.

'The police?' he said, and touched her diamond star.